Leslie Charteris was born in ⟨...⟩
his mother and brother he mo⟨...⟩
Rossall School in Lancashir⟨...⟩
University. His studies there came to a halt when a publisher accepted
his first novel. His third book, entitled *Meet – the Tiger!*, was
written when he was twenty years old and published in 1928. It
introduced the world to Simon Templar a.k.a the Saint. He
continued to write about the Saint up until 1983, when the last
book *Salvage for the Saint* was published by Hodder & Stoughton.
The books, which have been translated into over twenty languages,
number nearly a hundred and have sold over 40 million copies
around the world. They've inspired, to date, fifteen feature films,
three TV series, ten radio series and a comic strip that was written
by Charteris and syndicated around the world for over a decade.
He enjoyed travelling but settled for long periods in Hollywood,
Florida and finally in Surrey, England. He was awarded the Cartier
Diamond Dagger by the Crime Writers' Association in 1992 in
recognition of a lifetime of achievement and died the following
year. To find out more about Leslie Charteris and his work visit
the website—

www.lesliecharteris.com

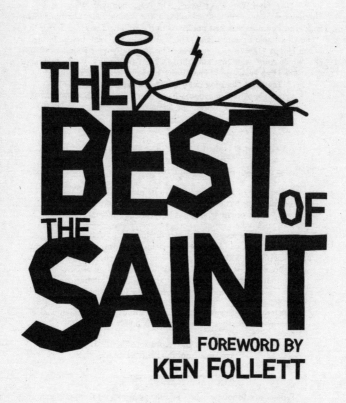

# THE BEST OF THE SAINT

FOREWORD BY
**KEN FOLLETT**

# LESLIE CHARTERIS

HODDER

This collection *The Best of the Saint Volume One* first published in Great
Britain in 2008 by Hodder & Stoughton
An Hachette Livre UK company

'The Man Who Was Clever', 'The Policeman with Wings' and
'The Lawless Lady' were first published in the volume *Enter the Saint* in 1930.
'The Inland Revenue' was first published in the volume *The Holy Terror* in 1932.
'The Charitable Countess' and 'The Star Producers' were first published in
*The Happy Highwayman* in 1939. 'The Simon Templar Foundation' and
'The Art of Alibi' were first published in *The Misfortunes of Mr Teal* in 1934.
'The High Fence' and 'The Elusive Ellshaw' were first published in
*The Saint Goes On* in 1934. 'The Miracle Tea Party' and
'The Affair of Hogsbotham' were first published in
*Follow the Saint* in 1939.

1

A CIP catalogue record for this title is
available from the British Library

ISBN 978 0 340 96362 3

Typeset in Monotype Sabon by Ellipsis Books Limited, Glasgow

Printed and bound by CPI Mackays, Chatham ME5 8TD

Hodder & Stoughton policy is to use papers that are natural,
renewable and recyclable products and made from wood grown
in sustainable forests. The logging and manufacturing processes
are expected to conform to the environmental regulations
of the country of origin.

Hodder & Stoughton Ltd
338 Euston Road
London NW1 3BH

www.hodder.co.uk

# CONTENTS

*Acknowledgements*                    vi

*Foreword by Ken Follett*             vii


The Man Who Was Clever               1

The Policeman with Wings             86

The Lawless Lady                     158

The Inland Revenue                   234

The Charitable Countess              301

The Star Producers                   326

The Art of Alibi                     350

The Simon Templar Foundation         425

The High Fence                       496

The Elusive Ellshaw                  573

The Miracle Tea Party                639

The Affair of Hogsbotham             710


*The Saint Club*                     785

# ACKNOWLEDGEMENTS

The publishers gratefully acknowledge the invaluable assistance given by Ian Dickerson in putting together *The Best of the Saint* and David Salter for the idea in the first place.

Thanks are also due to the Estate of Leslie Charteris for all their help and particularly for their permission to use the sign of the Saint.

# FOREWORD
## BY KEN FOLLETT

Near my grandparents' house in Cardiff there was a small stately home called Llandaff Court, set in an ornamental park. The place belonged to the city council and housed a branch library. This offered more popular literature than most public libraries—lots of science fiction, romance and thrillers, often paperbacks with reinforced covers. It was there that I discovered the Saint.

This was in the early sixties, so he was already old. He had first appeared in 1928, and most of the best stories came out in the thirties. I belonged to what must have been the third generation of fans. He was noticeably out of date by then, with his patent-leather hair and immaculately creased pearl-grey trousers; but it hardly mattered.

In fact the Saint belongs to a group of two-fisted crimefighters known as clubland heroes. The original is Richard Hannay, who first appeared in 1915 in John Buchan's *The Thirty-Nine Steps*. In the twenties and thirties, Hannay had as many pale imitations as Sherlock Holmes. Like Hannay, most of them belonged to gentlemen's clubs in Pall Mall and St James's.

Few of these survived until the sixties, but I was enthralled by those that did. (An exception was Bulldog Drummond, whom I disliked for his Fascism and his leaden banter: 'Verily I believe that we have impinged upon the goods,' he says, and much more as bad or worse.)

The Saint stood out, and indeed has survived to entertain another couple of generations since I found him in Llandaff Court Library. He did not belong to a Pall Mall club. Unlike Hannay or Drummond, he was delightfully anti-establishment. He scorned the government, despised the police, and never paid taxes. He was a criminal: 'He had run guns into China, whiskey into the United States and perfume into England,' according to the first novel, *Meet – the Tiger!*

His sexual morality was not made explicit, but implicitly it was clear he paid little regard to the conventions. Patricia Holm simply appeared at the breakfast table: no explanation of her presence was offered. In the Saint's world, it seemed perfectly natural for a beautiful single woman to be there to share a man's coffee first thing in the morning. Even more exciting, Pat looked on with an indulgent smile whenever the Saint flirted with a new heroine. This was heady stuff, even when I was twelve.

But what most distinguishes these books, lifting them far above most of the genre to which they belong, is the exuberant, captivating prose in which Leslie Charteris tells the story. I never tire of reading such descriptions as this, from *The Saint in New York,* as Simon takes off the disguise of a nun: 'She was revealed as a tall wide-shouldered man in a blue silk shirt and the trousers of a light fresco suit—a man with gay blue eyes in a brown piratical face, whose smile flashed a row of ivory teeth as he slapped his audience blithely on the back and sprawled into an armchair with a swing of lean athletic limbs.'

Pat is described in the same spirited style that manages to stay just this side of the ridiculous. From *The Simon Templar Foundation:* 'There was the grace of a pagan goddess in the way she stood, caught in surprise as she was by the sound of his voice, and the reward of all journeys in the quiver of her red lips.'

Charm and a dashing pace often carry the reader past what might otherwise be an awkward hole in the plot. When 'Pappy' Papulos glances in his rear-view mirror and sees the Saint in his back seat, in *The Saint in New York,* we are too caught up in the action to wonder how the Saint knew that Pappy would get into his car without looking, or that he would not be accompanied by two or three other hoodlums, much less how the Saint knew which car was Pappy's.

The Saint is nearly always flippant. 'Yes,' he says to a Customs officer in *The Simon Templar Foundation,* looking at the list of prohibited articles. 'I'm carrying large quantities of silk, perfume, wines, spirits, tobacco, cut flowers, watches, embroidery, eggs, typewriters and explosives. I also have some opium and a couple of howitzers—'

But in most of the books there is one moment of genuine moral passion, all the more effective for the contrast with his perennial facetiousness. From *The Simon Templar Foundation* again: 'Nassen and the other detective, staring at the Saint in sullen silence, felt as if an icy wind blew through the room and goose-fleshed their skin in spite of the warmth of the evening. The bantering buffoon who had goaded them to the verge of apoplexy had vanished as though he had never existed, and another man spoke with the same voice. ". . . All those amazing millions—the millions of which you and others like you were paid, Lord Iveldown—were the wages of death and destruction and wholesale murder. They were coined out of blood and dishonour and famine, and the agony of peaceful nations . . ."' The same extravagant style, with its hyperbole and alliteration—sullen silence, bantering buffoon, death and destruction—serves equally well for a passage of solemn emotion.

Like most good stories, the Saint's adventures are not, fundamentally, credible—far from it. The conspiracies, the hairsbreadth escapes, and the coincidence of one man's casually encountering so much crime and violence are as implausible as the number of murders that take place in Miss Marple's sleepy village of St Mary Mead. But, while we are reading, we doubt nothing, and are carried recklessly along by wit, charm, and the sheer skill of the writing. And that, in the end, is what popular literature is all about.

© Ken Follett 2008

# THE MAN WHO WAS CLEVER

I

Mr 'Snake' Ganning was neither a great criminal nor a pleasant character, but he is interesting because he was the first victim of the organisation led by the man known as the Saint, which was destined in the course of a few months to spread terror through the underworld of London—that ruthless association of reckless young men, brilliantly led, who worked on the side of the Law and who were yet outside the Law. There was to come a time when the mere mention of the Saint was sufficient to fill the most unimaginative malefactor with uneasy fears, when a man returning home late one night to find the sign of the Saint—a childish sketch of a little man with straight-line body and limbs, and an absurd halo over his round blank head—chalked upon his door, would be sent instinctively spinning round with his back to the nearest wall and his hand flying to his hip pocket, and an icy tingle of dread prickling up his spine; but at the date of the Ganning episode the Saint had only just commenced operations, and his name had not yet come to be surrounded with the aura of almost supernatural infallibility which it was to earn for itself later.

Mr Ganning was a tall, incredibly thin man, with sallow features and black hair that was invariably oiled and brushed to a shiny sleekness. His head was small and round, and he carried it thrust forward to the full stretch of his long neck. Taking into the combination of physical characteristics the sinuous carriage of his body, the glittering beadiness of his expressionless black eyes, and the silent litheness with which he moved, it was easy to appreciate the aptness of his nickname. He was the leader of a particularly tough racecourse gang generally known as 'The Snake's Boys', which subsisted in unmerited luxury on the proceeds of blackmailing bookmakers under threat of doing them grievous bodily harm; there were also a number of other unsavoury things about him which may be revealed in due course.

The actual motive for the interference of the Saint in the affairs of the Snake and his Boys was their treatment of Tommy Mitre on the occasion of his first venture into Turf finance. Tommy had always wanted to be a jockey, for horses were in his blood; but quite early in his apprenticeship he had been thrown and injured so severely that he had never been able to ride again, and he had had to content himself with the humble position of stable boy in a big training establishment. Then an uncle of Tommy's, who had been a publican, died, leaving his nephew the tremendous fortune of two hundred pounds, and Tommy decided to try his luck in the Silver Ring. He took out a licence, had a board painted ('Tommy Mitre—The Old Firm—Established 1822') and enlisted a clerk. One day he went down to Brighton with this paraphernalia and the remains of his two hundred pounds, and it was not long before the Snake's Boys spotted the stranger and made the usual demands. Tommy refused to pay. He ought to have known better, for the methods of the Snake had never been a secret in racing circles; but Tommy was like that—stubborn. He told the Snake exactly where he could go, and as a result Tommy Mitre was soundly beaten up by the Snake's Boys when he was leaving the course, and his capital and his day's profits were taken. And it so happened that Simon Templar had elected to enjoy a day's racing at Brighton, and had observed the beating-up from a distance.

Snake Ganning and a select committee of the Boys spent the evening in Brighton celebrating, and left for London by a late train. So also did Simon Templar.

Thus it came to pass that the said Simon Templar wandered up the platform a couple of minutes before the train left, espied the Snake and three of the Boys comfortably ensconced in a first-class carriage, and promptly joined them.

The Saint, it should be understood, was a vision that gave plenty of excuse for the glances of pleased anticipation which were exchanged by the Snake and his favourite Boys as soon as they had summed him up. In what he called his 'fighting kit'—which consisted of disreputable grey flannel bags and a tweed shooting-jacket of almost legendary age—the Saint had the unique gift of appearing so immaculate that the least absent-minded commissionaire might have been pardoned for mistaking him for a millionaire duke. It may be imagined what a radiant spectacle he was in what he called his 'gentleman disguise'.

His grey flannel suit fitted him with a staggering perfection, the whiteness of his shirt was dazzling, his tie shamed the rainbow. His soft felt hat appeared to be having its first outing since it left Bond Street. His chamois gloves were clearly being shown to the world for the first time. On his left wrist was a gold watch, and he carried a gold-mounted ebony walking-stick.

Everything, you understand, quietly but unmistakably of the very best, and worn with that unique air of careless elegance which others might attempt to emulate, but which only the Saint could achieve in all its glory. . . .

As for the man—well, the Snake's Boys had never had any occasion to doubt that their reputation for toughness was founded on more substantial demonstrations than displays of their skill at hunt-the-slipper at the YMCA on Saturday afternoons. The man was tall—about six feet two inches of him—but they didn't take much count of that. Their combined heights totted up for twenty-four feet three inches. And although he wasn't at all hefty, he was broad enough, and there was a certain solidity about his shoulders that would have made a cautious man think carefully before starting any unpleasantness—but that didn't bother the Snake and his Boys. Their combined widths summed up to a shade over six feet. And the Saint had a clear tanned skin and a very clear blue eye—but even that failed to worry them. They weren't running a beauty competition, anyway.

The important point was that the Saint had a gold cigarette-case and a large wad of bank-notes. In his innocent way, he counted over his pile before their very eyes, announced the total at two hundred and fifty pounds odd, and invited them to congratulate him on his luck. They congratulated him, politely. They remarked on the slowness of the train, and the Saint agreed that it was a boring journey. He said he wished there was some sort of entertainment provided by the railway company for the diversion of passengers on boring journeys. Somebody produced a pack of cards. . . .

It can be said for them that they gave him the credit for having been warned by his grandmother about the danger of trying to find the Lady. The game selected was poker. The Saint apologetically warned them that he had only played poker once before in his life, but they said kindly that that didn't matter a bit.

The fight started just five minutes before the train reached Victoria, and the porters who helped the Snake and his Boys out of the compartment were not thanked. They gave the Boys a bucket of water with which to revive the Snake himself, but they couldn't do anything about his two black eyes or his missing front teeth.

Inspector Teal, who was waiting on the platform in the hope of seeing a much-wanted con-man, saw the injured warrior and was not sympathetic.

'You've been fighting, Snake,' he said brightly.

Ganning's reply was unprintable, but Mr Teal was not easily shocked.

'But I can describe him to you,' said the Snake, becoming less profane. 'Robbery with violence, that's what it was. He set on us—'

'"Sat" is the past tense of "sit",' said Teal, shifting his gum to the other side of his mouth.

'He's got away with over three hundred quid that we made today—'

Teal was interested.

'Where d'you make it?' he enquired. 'Have you got a real printing-press, or do you make it by hand? I didn't know you were in the "slush" game, Snake.'

'Look here, Teal,' said Ganning, becoming more coherent. 'You

4

can say what you like about me, but I've got my rights, the same as anybody else. You've got to get after that man. Maybe you know things about him already. He's either on a lay, or he's just starting on one, you mark my words. See this!'

Mr Teal examined the envelope sleepily.

'What is it?' he asked. 'A letter of introduction to me?'

'He gave it to Ted when he got out. "That's my receipt," he said. Didn't he, Ted? You look inside, Teal!'

The envelope was not sealed. Teal turned it over, and remarked on the flap the crest of the hotel which had provided it. Then, in his lethargic way, he drew out the contents—a single sheet of paper.

'Portrait by Epstein,' he drawled. 'Quite a nice drawing, but it don't mean anything to me outside of that. You boys have been reading too many detective stories lately, that's the trouble with you.'

II

The Saint, being a man of decidedly luxurious tastes, was the tenant of a flat in Brook Street, Mayfair, which was so far beyond his means that he had long since given up worrying about the imminence of bankruptcy. One might as well be hung for a sheep, the Saint reflected, in his cheerfully reckless way, as for a foot-and-mouth-diseased lamb. He considered that the world owed him a good time, in return for services rendered and general presentability and good-fellowship, and, since the world hitherto had been closefistedly reluctant to recognise the obligation and meet it, the Saint had decided that the time had come for him to assert himself. His invasion of Brook Street had been one of the first moves in the campaign.

But the locality had one distinct advantage that had nothing to do with the prestige of its address; and this advantage was the fact that it possessed a mews, a very small and exclusive mews, situated at a distance of less than the throw of a small stone from the Saint's front door. In this mews were a number of very expensive

5

garages, large, small, and of Austin Seven size. And the Saint owned two of these large garages. In one he kept his own car; the other had been empty for a week, until he had begun smuggling an assortment of curious objects into it at dead of night—objects which only by the most frantic stretch of imagination could have been associated with cars.

If the Saint had been observed on any of these surreptitious trips, it is highly probable that his sanity would have been doubted. Not that he would have cared; for he had his own reasons for his apparent eccentricity. But as it was, no one noticed his goings-out or his comings-in, and there was no comment.

And even if he had been noticed, it is very doubtful if he would have been recognised. It was the immaculate Saint who left Brook Street and drove to Chelsea and garaged his car near Fulham Road. Then, by a very subtle change of carriage, it was a not-nearly-so-immaculate Saint who walked through a maze of dingy back streets to a house in which one, Bertie Marks, a bird of passage, had a stuffy and microscopical apartment. And it was a shabby, slouching, down-at-heel Bertie Marks who left the apartment and returned to the West End on the plebeian bus, laden with the packages that he had purchased on his way; and who shambled inconspicuously into the mews off Brook Street and into the garage which he held in his own name. The Saint did not believe in being unnecessarily careless about details.

And all these elaborate preparations—the taking of the second garage and the Chelsea apartment, and the creation of the character of Bertie Marks—had been made for one single purpose, which was put into execution on a certain day.

A few hours after dawn on that day (an unearthly hour for the Saint to be abroad) a small van bearing the name of Carter Paterson turned into the mews and stopped there. Bertie Marks climbed down from the driver's seat, wiping grimy hands on his corduroys, and fished out a key, with which he opened the door of his garage. Then he went back to his van, drove it into the garage, and closed the doors behind him.

He knew that his action must have excited the curiosity of the car-washing parade of chauffeurs congregated in the mews, but he wasn't bothering about that. With the consummation of his plan, the necessity for the continued existence of Bertie Marks was rapidly nearing its end.

'Let 'em wonder!' thought the Saint carelessly, as he peeled off his grubby jacket.

He switched on the light, and went and peeped out into the mews. The car-washing parade had resumed its labours, being for the moment too preoccupied to bother about the strange phenomenon of a Carter Paterson van being driven into a garage that had once housed a Rolls.

The Saint gently slid a bar across the door to shut out any inquisitive explorers, and got to work.

The van, on being opened, disclosed a number of large, wooden packing-cases which the Saint proceeded to unload on to the floor of the garage. This done, he fetched from a corner a mallet and chisel, and began to prise open the cases and extract their contents. In each case, packed in with wood shavings, were two dozen china jars.

As each case was emptied, the Saint carried the jars over to the light and inspected them minutely. He was not at all surprised to find that, whereas the majority of the jars were perfectly plain, all the jars in one case were marked with a tiny cross in the glazing. These jars the Saint set aside, for they were the only ones in which he was interested. They were exactly what he had expected to find, and they provided his entire motive for the temporary and occasional sinking of his own personality in the *alias* of Mr Marks. The other jars he replaced in their respective cases, and carefully closed and roped them to look as they had been before he tampered with them.

Then he opened the marked jars and poured out their contents into a bucket. In another corner of the garage was a pile of little tins, and in each jar the Saint placed one of these tins, padding the space that was left with cotton-wool to prevent rattling. The jars so treated were replaced one by one and the case in its turn was also nailed up again and roped as before—after the Saint, with a little smile plucking at the corners of his mouth, had carefully laid a souvenir of his intervention on the top of the last layer of wood shavings.

He had worked quickly. Only an hour and a half had elapsed from the time when he drove into the garage to the time when he lifted the last case back into the van; and when that had been done he unbarred the garage doors and opened them wide.

The remains of the car-washing parade looked up puzzledly as the van came backing out of the garage; it registered an even greater perplexity when the van proceeded to drive out of the mews and vanish in the direction of Bond Street. It yelled to the driver that he had forgotten to close his garage after him, but Mr Marks either did not hear or did not care. And when the parade perceived that Mr Marks had gone for good, it went and pried into the garage, and scratched its heads over the litter of wood shavings on the floor, the mallet and chisel and nails and hammer, and the two or three tins which the Saint had found no space for, and which he had accordingly left behind. But the bucket of white powder was gone, riding beside Mr Marks in the front of the van; and very few people ever saw Mr Marks again.

The van drove to an address in the West End, and there Mr Marks delivered the cases, secured a signature to a receipt, and departed, heading further west. On his way, he stopped at St George's Hospital, where he left his bucket. The man who took charge of it was puzzled, but Mr Marks was in a hurry and had neither time nor the inclination to enlighten him.

'Take great care of it, because it's worth more money than you'll ever have,' he directed. 'See that it gets to one of the doctors, and give him this note with it.'

And the Saint went back to the wheel of his van and drove away, feeling that he was nearing the end of an excellent day's work.

He drove to the Great West Road, and out of London towards

Maidenhead. Somewhere along that road he turned off into a side lane, and there he stopped for a few minutes out of sight of the main traffic. Inside the van was a large pot of paint, and the Saint used it energetically. He had never considered himself an artist, but he manhandled that van with the broad sweeping touch of a master. Under his vigorous wielding of the brush, the sign of Carter Paterson, which he had been at some pains to execute artistically the night before, vanished entirely; and the van became plain. Satisfied with the obliteration of the handiwork which only a few hours before he had admired so much, the Saint resumed the wheel and drove back to London. The paint he had used was guaranteed quick-drying, and it lived up to the word of its guarantee. It collected a good deal of dust on the return voyage, and duly dried with a somewhat soiled aspect which was a very fair imitation of the condition in which Mr Marks had received it.

He delivered it to its home garage at Shepherd's Bush and paid twenty-four hours' hire. Some time later Mr Marks returned to Chelsea. A little later still, the not-so-immaculate Simon Templar turned into another garage and collected his trim blue Furillac speedster, in which he drove to his club in Dover Street. And the Simon Templar who sauntered through to the bar and called for a pint of beer must have been one of the most impeccably immaculate young men that that haunt of impeccably immaculate young men had ever sheltered.

'We don't often see you as early as this, sir,' remarked the barman.

'May it be as many years before you see me as early as this again, son,' answered the Saint piously. 'But this morning I felt I just had to get up and go for a drive. It was such a beautiful morning.'

III

Mr Edgar Hayn was a man of many interests. He was the proud proprietor of 'Danny's', a night club in a squalid street off

Shaftesbury Avenue, and he also controlled the destinies of the firm of Laserre, which was a small but expensive shop in Regent Street that retailed perfumes, powders, rouges, creams, and all the other preparations essential to modern feminine face-repair. These two establishments were Mr Hayn's especial pets, and from them he derived the greater part of his substantial income. Yet it might be mentioned that the profits of 'Danny's' were not entirely earned by the sale of champagne, and the adornment of fashionable beauty was not the principal source of the prosperity of the house of Laserre. Mr Hayn was a clever organiser, and what he did not know about the art of covering his tracks wouldn't have been missed from one of the microscopical two-guinea alabaster jars in which he sold the celebrated Crême Laserre.

He was a big, heavy-featured man, clean-shaven, pink complexioned, and faintly bald. His name had not always been Hayn, but a process of naturalisation followed by a Deed Poll had given him an indisputable legal right to forget the cognomen of his father—and, incidentally, had eliminated for ever the unpleasant possibility of a deportation order, an exercise of forethought for which Mr Hayn was more than once moved to give his sagacity a pat on the back. The police knew certain things about him which made them inclined to regard him with disfavour, and they suspected a lot more, but there had never been any evidence.

He was writing letters at the big knee-hole desk in his private office at 'Danny's' when Ganning arrived. The knock on the door did not make him look up. He said, 'Come in!'—but the sound of the opening and closing of the door was, to him, sufficient indication that the order had been obeyed; and he went on to finish the letter he had been drafting.

Only when that was done did he condescend to notice the presence of his visitor.

'You're late, Snake,' he said, blotting the sheet carefully.

'Sorry, boss.'

Mr Hayn screwed the cap on his fountain-pen, replaced it in

his pocket, and raised his eyes from the desk for the first time. What he saw made him sag back with astonishment.

'Who on earth have you been picking a quarrel with?' he demanded.

The Snake certainly looked the worse for wear. A bandage round his head covered one eye, and the eye that was visible was nearly closed up. His lips were bruised and swollen, and a distinct lack of teeth made him speak with a painful lisp.

'Was it Harrigan's crowd?' suggested Hayn.

Ganning shook his head.

'A bloke we met on the train coming back from Brighton last night.'

'Were you alone?'

'Nope; Ted and Bill were with me. And Mario.'

'And what was this man trooping round? A regiment?'

'He was alone.'

Hayn blinked.

'How did it happen?'

'We thought he was a sucker,' explained Snake disgustedly. 'Smart clothes, gold cigarette-case, gold-mounted stick, gold watch—and a wad. He showed us the wad. Two-fifty, he said it was. We couldn't let that go, so we got him into a game of cards. Poker. He said he didn't know anything about the game, so it looked safe enough—he struck us as being that sort of mug. We were geeing him along nicely right up to ten minutes or so before Victoria, and we'd let him take fifty off us. He was thinking himself the greatest poker player in the world by then, you'd have said. Then we asked him to be a sport and give us a chance of getting our money back on a couple of big jackpots with a five-pound ante. He agreed, and we let him win the first one. We all threw in after the first rise. 'What about making it a tenner ante for the last deal?' I said, tipping the wink to the boys. He wasn't too keen on that, but we jollied him along, and at last he fell for it. It was his deal, but I shuffled the broads for him.'

'And your hand slipped?'

Ganning snorted.

'Slipped nothin'! My hand doesn't slip. I'd got that deck stacked better than any conjurer could have done it. And I picked up a straight flush, just as I'd fixed it. Mario chucked in right away, and Ted and Bill dropped out after the first round. That left the Mug and me, and we went on raising each other till every cent the boys and I could find between us was in the kitty. We even turned in our links and Mario's diamond pin to account for as much of the Mug's wad as possible. When we hadn't another bean to take, he saw me. I showed down my straight flush, and I was just getting set to scoop in the pool when he stopped me. 'I thought you told me this was next to unbeatable,' he says, and then he shows down five kings.'

'Five?' repeated Mr Hayn frowning.

'We were playing deuces wild, and a joker. He'd got the joker.'

'Well, didn't you know what he was holding?'

'It wasn't the hand I fixed for him to deal himself!'

Mr Hayn controlled his features.

'And then you cut up rough, and got the worst of it?'

'I accused him of cheating. He didn't deny it. He had the nerve to say: "Well, you were supposed to be teaching me the game, and I saw you were cheating all the time, so I thought it was allowed by the rules!" And he started putting away our pile. Of course we cut up rough!'

'And he cut up rougher?' suggested Mr Hayn.

'He didn't fight fair,' said Ganning aggrievedly. 'First thing I knew, he'd jabbed the point of his stick into Ted's neck before Ted had a chance to pull his cosh, so Ted was out of it. Bill was all ready for a fair stand-up fight with the knuckle-dusters, but this man kicked him in the stomach, so *he* took the count. Mario and me had to tackle him alone.'

The Snake seemed disinclined to proceed further with the description of the battle, and Hayn tactfully refrained from pressing him. He allowed the Snake to brood blackly over the memory for a few moments.

'He wasn't an amateur,' said Ganning. 'But none of us could place him. I'd give the hell of a lot to find out who he was. One of these fly mobsmen you read about, I shouldn't wonder. He'd got all the dope. Look at this,' said the Snake, producing the envelope. 'He shoved that at Ted when he got out. Said it was his receipt. I tried to get Teal to take it up—he was at the station—but he wouldn't take it seriously.'

Hayn slipped the sheet of paper out of the envelope and spread it out on his desk. Probably he had not fully grasped the purport of Ganning's description, for the effect the sight had on him was amazing.

If Ganning had been disappointed with Inspector Teal's unemotional reception of the Saint's receipt, he was fully compensated by the reaction of Mr Edgar Hayn. Hayn's pink face suddenly turned white, and he jerked away from the paper that lay on the blotter in front of him as if it had spat poison at him.

'What's it mean to you, boss?' asked the bewildered Ganning.

'This morning we got a consignment over from Germany,' Hayn said, speaking almost in a whisper. 'When Braddon opened the case, there was the same picture on top of the packing. We couldn't figure out how it came there.'

'Have· you looked the stuff over yet?' demanded the Snake, instantly alert.

Hayn shook his head. He was still staring, as though hypnotised, at the scrap of paper.

'We didn't think anything of it. There's never been a hitch yet. Braddon thought the men who packed the case must have been playing some game. We just put the marked jars away in the usual place.'

'You haven't had to touch them yet?'

Hayn made a negative gesture. He reached out a shaky hand for the telephone, while Ganning sat silently chewing over the startling possibilities that were revealed by this information.

'Hullo. . . . Regent nine double-o four seven . . . please.' Hayn fidgeted nervously as he waited for the call to be put through. It came after what seemed an eternity. 'Hullo. . . . That you, Braddon? . . . I want you to get out the marked jars that came over in the case with the paper in—you remember? . . . Never mind why!'

A minute ticked away, while Hayn kept the receiver glued to his ear and tapped out an impatient tattoo on the desk.

'Yes? . . . What's that? . . . How d'you know? . . . I see. Well, I'll be right round!'

Hayn clicked the receiver back and slewed his swivel-chair round so that he faced Snake Ganning.

'What's he say?' asked the Snake.

'There's just a tin of Keating's powder in each,' Hayn replied. 'I asked him how he knew what it was, and he said the whole tin was there, label and all, packed in with cotton-wool to make it fit. There was ten thousand pounds' worth of snow in that shipping, and this guy has lifted the lot!'

IV

'You may decant some beer, son,' said Simon Templar, stretched out in the armchair. 'And then you may start right in and tell me the story of your life. I can spare you about two minutes.'

Jerry Stannard travelled obediently over to a side table where bottles and glasses were already set out, accomplished his task with a practised hand, and travelled back again with the results.

'Your health,' said the Saint, and two foaming glasses were half-emptied in an appreciative silence.

Stannard was then encouraged to proceed. He put down his glass with a sigh and settled back at his ease, while the Saint made a long arm for the cigarette-box.

'I can't make out yet why you should have interested yourself in me,' said Stannard.

'That's my affair,' said the Saint bluntly. 'And if it comes to that, son, I'm not a philanthropic institution. I happen to want an assistant, and I propose to make use of you. Not that you won't get anything out of it. I'm sufficiently interested in you to want to help you, but you're going to pay your way.'

Stannard nodded.

'It's decent of you to think I'm worth it,' he said.

He had not forgotten—it would have been impossible to forget such an incident in two days—the occasion of his first meeting with the Saint. Stannard had been entrusted with a small packet which he had been told to take to an address in Piccadilly; and even if he had not been told what the packet contained, he could not have helped having a very shrewd idea. And, therefore, when a heavy hand had fallen suddenly on his shoulder only a few minutes after he had left Mr Hayn, he had had no hope. . . .

And then the miracle had happened, although he did not realise at the time that it was a miracle. A man had brushed against him as the detective turned to hail a taxi, and the man had turned to apologise. In that crisis, all Stannard's facilities had been keyed up to the vivid supersensitiveness which comes just before breaking-point; and that abnormal acuteness had combined with the peculiarly keen stare which had accompanied the stranger's apology, so that the stranger's face was indelibly engraved on Stannard's memory. . . .

The Saint took a little package from his pocket, and weighed it reflectively in his hand.

'Forty-eight hours ago,' he murmured, 'you assumed, quite rightly, that you were booked for five years' penal servitude. Instead of that, you're a free man. The triumphant sleuths of Vine Street found nothing on you, and had to release you with apologies. Doubtless they're swearing to make up for that bloomer, and make no mistakes about landing you with the goods next time, but that can't hurt you for the moment. And I expect you're still wondering what's going to be my price for having picked your pocket in the nick of time.'

'I've been wondering ever since.'

'I'm just going to tell you,' said the Saint. 'But first we'll get rid of this.'

He left the room with the packet, and through the open door came the sound of running water. In a few moments he was back, dusting his hands.

'That disposes of the evidence,' he said. 'Now I want you to tell me something. How did you get into this dope game?'

Stannard shrugged.

'You may as well know. There's no heroic or clever reason. It's just because I'm a waster. I was in the wrong set at Cambridge, and I knew most of the toughs in Town. Then my father died and left me without a bean. I tried to get a job, but I couldn't do anything useful. And all the time, naturally, I was mixing with the same bad bunch. Eventually they roped me in. I suppose I ought to have fought against it, but I just hadn't the guts. It was easy money, and I took it. That's all.'

There was a short silence, during which the Saint blew monotonously regular smoke rings towards the ceiling.

'Now I'll tell you something,' he said. 'I've made all the enquiries I need to make about you. I know your family history for two generations back, your early life, your school record—everything. I know enough to judge that you don't belong where you are now. For one thing, I know you're engaged to a rather nice girl, and she's worried about you. She doesn't know anything, but she suspects. And you're worried. You're not as quiet and comfortable in this crime racket as you'd like to make out. You weren't cut out for a bad man. Isn't that true?'

'True enough,' Stannard said flatly. 'I'd give anything to be out of it.'

'And you're straight about this girl—Gwen Chandler?'

'Straight as a die. Honest, Templar! But what can I do? If I drop Hayn's crowd, I shan't have a cent. Besides, I don't know that they'd let me drop out. I owe money. When I was at Cambridge, I lost a small fortune—for me—in Hayn's gambling rooms, and he's got I.O.U.s of mine for close on a thousand. I've been extravagant—I've run up bills everywhere. You can't imagine how badly in the cart I am!'

'On the contrary, son,' said the Saint calmly, 'I've a very good guess about that. That's why you're here now. I wanted an agent inside Hayn's gang, and I ran through the whole deck before I chose you.'

He rose from his chair and took a turn up and down the room. Stannard waited; and presently the Saint stopped abruptly.

'You're all right,' he said.

Stannard frowned.

'Meaning?'

'Meaning I'm going to trust you. I'm going to take you in with me for this campaign. I'll get you enough out of it to square off your debts, and at the end of it I'll find you a job. You'll keep in with Hayn, but you'll be working for me. And you'll give me your word of honour that you'll go straight for the rest of your life. That's my offer. What about it?'

The Saint leant against the mantelpiece languidly enough, but there had been nothing languid about his crisp incisive sentences. Thinking it over afterwards, it seemed to Stannard that the whole thing had been done in a few minutes, and he was left to marvel at the extraordinary force of personality which in such a short time could override the prejudice of years and rekindle a spark of decency that had been as good as dead. But at the instant, Stannard could not analyse his feelings.

'I'm giving you a chance to get out and make good,' the Saint went on. 'I'm not doing it in the dark. I believe you when you say you'd be glad of a chance to make a fresh start. I believe there's the makings of a decent man in you. Anyway, I'll take a risk on it. I won't even threaten you, though I could, by telling you what I shall do to you if you double-cross me. I just ask you a fair question, and I want your answer now.'

Stannard got to his feet.

'There's only one answer,' he said, and held out his hand.

The Saint took it in a firm grip.

'Now I'll tell you exactly where you stand,' he said.

He did so, speaking in curt sentences as before. His earlier grimness had relaxed somewhat, for when the Saint did anything he never did it by halves, and now he spoke to Stannard as a friend and an ally. He had his reward in the eager attention with which the youngster followed his discourse. He told him everything that there was any need for him to know.

'You've got to think of everything, and then a heap, if you're going to come out of this with a whole skin,' Simon concluded, with some of his former sternness. 'The game I'm on isn't the kind they play in nurseries. I'm on it because I just can't live happily ever after. I've had enough adventure to fill a dozen books, but instead of satisfying me they've only left me with a bigger appetite. If I had to live the ordinary kind of safe, civilised life, I'd die of boredom. Risks are food and drink to me. You may be different. If you are, I'm sorry about it, but I can't help it. I need some help in this, and you're going to give it to me; but it wouldn't be fair to let you whale in without showing you what you are up against. Your bunch of bad hats aren't childish enemies. Before you're through, London's likely to be just about as healthy for you as the Cannibal Islands are for a nice plump missionary. Get me?'

Stannard intimated that he had got him.

'Then I'll give you your orders for the immediate future,' said the Saint.

He did so, in detail, and had everything repeated over to him twice before he was convinced that there would be no mistake and that nothing would be forgotten.

'From now on, I want you to keep away from me till I give you the all-clear,' he ended up. 'If the Snake's anywhere round, I shan't last long in Danny's, and it's essential to keep you out of suspicion for as long as possible. So this'll be our last open meeting for some time, but you can communicate by telephone—as long as you make sure nobody can hear you.'

'Right you are, Saint,' said Stannard.

Simon Templar flicked a cigarette into his mouth and reached for the matches.

The other had a queer transient feeling of unreality. It seemed fantastic that he should be associated with such a project as that into which the Saint had initiated him. It seemed equally fantastic that the Saint should have conceived it and brought it into being. That cool, casual young man, with his faultless clothes, his clipped and slangy speech, and his quick, clear smile—he ought to have been lounging his amiable easy-going way through a round of tennis and cricket and cocktail-parties and dances, instead of . . .

And yet it remained credible—it was even, with every passing second, becoming almost an article of the reawakened Stannard's new faith. The Saint's spell was unique. There was a certain quiet assurance about his bearing, a certain steely quality that came sometimes into his blue eyes, a certain indefinable air of strength and recklessness and quixotic bravado, that made the whole fantastic notion acceptable. And Stannard had not even the advantage of knowing anything about the last eight years of the Saint's hell-for-leather career—eight years of gay buccaneering which, even allowing for exaggeration, made him out to be a man of no ordinary or drawing-room toughness.

The Saint lighted his cigarette and held out his hand to terminate the interview; and the corners of his mouth were twitching to his irresistible smile.

'So long, son,' he said. 'And good hunting!'

'Same to you,' said Stannard warmly.

The Saint clapped him on the shoulder.

'I know you won't let me down,' he said. 'There's lots of good in you, and I guess I've found some of it. You'll pull out all right. I'm going to see that you do. Watch me!'

But before he left, Stannard got a query off his chest.

'Didn't you say there were five of you?'

His hands in his pockets, teetering gently on his heels, the Saint favoured Stannard with his most Saintly smile.

'I did,' he drawled. 'Four little Saints and Papa. I am the Holy Snake. As for the other four, they are like the Great White Woolly Wugga-Wugga on the plains of Astrakhan.'

Stannard gaped at him.

'What does that mean?' he demanded.

'I ask you, sweet child,' answered the Saint, with that exasperating seraphic smile still on his lips, 'has anyone ever seen a Great White Woolly Wugga-Wugga on the plains of Astrakhan? Sleep on it, my cherub—it will keep your mind from impure thoughts.'

## V

To all official intents and purposes, the proprietor and leading light of Mr Edgar Hayn's night club in Soho was the man after whom it was named—Danny Trask.

Danny was short and dumpy, a lazy little tub of a man, with a round red face, a sparse head of fair hair, and a thin sandy moustache. His pale eyes were deeply embedded in the creases of their fleshy lids; and when he smiled—which was often, and usually for no apparent reason—they vanished altogether in a corrugating mesh of wrinkles.

His intelligence was not very great. Nevertheless, he had discovered quite early in life that there was a comfortable living to be made in the profession of 'dummy'—a job which calls for no startling intellectual gifts—and Danny had accordingly made that his vocation ever since. As a figurehead, he was all that could have been desired, for he was unobtrusive and easily satisfied. He had a type of mind common to his class of law-breaker. As long as his salary—which was not small—was paid regularly, he never complained, showed no ambition to join his employer on a more equal basis of division of profits, and, if anything went wrong, kept his mouth shut and deputised for his principal in one of His Majesty's prisons without a murmur. Danny's fees for a term of imprisonment were a flat rate of ten pounds a week, with an extra charge of two pounds a week for 'hard'. The astuteness of the CID and the carelessness of one or two of his previous employers had made this quite a profitable proposition for Danny.

He had visions of retiring one day, and ending his life in comparative luxury, when his savings had reached a sufficiently large figure; but this hope had received several setbacks of late. He had been in Mr Hayn's service for four years, and Mr Hayn's uncanny skill at avoiding the attentions of the police was becoming a thorn in the side of Danny Trask. When Danny was not in 'stir', the most he could command was a paltry seven pounds a week, and living expenses had to be paid out of this instead of out of the pocket of the Government. Danny felt that he had a personal grievance against Mr Hayn on this account.

The club theoretically opened at 6 p.m., but the food was not good, and most of its members preferred to dine elsewhere. The first arrivals usually began to drift in about 10 p.m., but things never began to get exciting before 11 o'clock. Danny spent the hours between 6 o'clock and the commencement of the fun sitting in his shirt-sleeves in his little cubicle by the entrance, sucking a foul old briar and tentatively selecting the next day's losers from an evening paper. He was incapable of feeling bored—his mind had never reached the stage of development where it could appreciate the idea of activity and inactivity. It had never been active, so it didn't see any difference.

He was engaged in this pleasant pursuit towards 8 o'clock on a certain evening when Jerry Stannard arrived.

'Has Mr Hayn come in yet, Danny?'

Danny made a pencil note of the number of pounds which he had laboriously calculated that Wilco would have in hand over Man of Kent in the Lingfield Plate, folded his paper, and looked up.

'He don't usually come in till late, Mr Stannard,' he said. 'No, he ain't here now.'

Danny's utterances always contrived to put the cart before the horse. If he had wanted to give you a vivid description of a death-bed scene, he would have inevitably started with the funeral.

'Oh, it's all right—he's expecting me,' said Stannard. 'When he arrives you can tell him I'm at the bar.'

He was plainly agitated. While he was talking, he never stopped fiddling with his signet ring; and Danny, whose shrewd glances missed very little, noticed that his tie was limp and crooked, as if it had been subjected to the clumsy wrestling of shaky fingers.

'Right you are, sir.'

It was none of Danny's business, anyway.

'Oh—and before I forget. . . .'

'Sir?'

'A Mr Templar will be here later. He's OK Send down for me when he arrives, and I'll sign him in.'

'Very good, sir.'

Danny returned to his study of equine form, and Stannard passed on.

He went through the lounge which occupied the ground floor, and turned down the stairs at the end. Facing these stairs, behind a convenient curtain, was a secret door in the panelling, electrically operated, which was controlled by a button on the desk in Hayn's private office. This door, when opened, disclosed a flight of stairs running upwards. These stairs communicated with the upstairs rooms which were one of the most profitable features of the club, for in those rooms *chemin-de-fer*, poker, and *trente-et-quarante* were played every night with the sky for a limit.

Hayn's office was at the foot of the downward flight. He had personally supervised the installation of an ingenious system of mirrors, by means of which, with the aid of a large sound-proof window let into the wall at one end of the office, without leaving his seat, he was able to inspect everyone who passed through the lounge above. Moreover, when the secret door swung open in response to the pressure of his finger on the control button, a further system of mirrors panelled up the upper flight of stairs gave him a view right up the stairway itself and round the landing into the gaming rooms. Mr Hayn was a man with a cunning turn of mind, and he was pre-eminently cautious.

Outside the office, in the basement, was the dance floor, surrounded with tables, but only two couples were dining there.

At the far end was the dais on which the orchestra played, and at the other end, under the stairs, was the tiny bar.

Stannard turned in there, and roused the white-coated barman from his perusal of *La Vie Parisienne*.

'I don't know what would meet the case,' he said, 'but I want something steep in corpse-revivers.'

The man looked him over for a moment with an expert eye, then busied himself with the filling of a prescription. The result certainly had a kick in it. Stannard was downing it when Hayn came in.

The big man was looking pale and tired, and there were shadows under his eyes. He nodded curtly to Jerry.

'I'll be with you in a minute,' he said. 'Just going to get a wash.'

It was not like Mr Hayn, who ordinarily specialised in the boisterous hail-fellow-well-met method of address, and Stannard watched him go thoughtfully.

Braddon, who had remained outside, followed Hayn into the office.

'Who's the boy friend?' he asked, taking a chair.

'Stannard?' Hayn was skimming through the letters that waited on his desk. 'An ordinary young fool. He lost eight hundred upstairs in his first couple of months. Heavens knows how much he owes outside—he'd lost a packet before I started lending him money.'

Braddon searched through his pockets for a cigar, and found one. He bit off the end, and spat.

'Got expectations? Rich papa who'll come across?'

'No. But he's got the clothes, and he'd pass anywhere. I was using him.'

'*Was?*'

Hayn was frowningly examining the postmark on one of his letters.

'I suppose I shall still,' he said. 'Don't bother me—this artistic hijacker's got me all ends up. But he's got a fiancée—I've only recently seen her. I like her.'

'Any good?'

'I shall arrange something about her.'

Hayn had slit open the letter with his thumb-nail, but he only took one glance at what it contained. He tossed it over to Braddon, and it was the manager of Laserre who drew out the now familiar sketch.

'One of those came to my house by the first post this morning,' Hayn said. 'It's as old as the hills, that game. So he thinks he's going to rattle me!'

'Isn't he?' asked Braddon, in his heavily cynical way.

'He damned well isn't!' Hayn came back savagely. 'I've got the Snake and the men who were with him prowling round the West End just keeping their eyes peeled for the man who beat them up in the Brighton train. If he's in London, he can't stay hid for ever. And when Ganning's found him, we'll soon put paid to his joke!'

Then he pulled himself together.

'I'm giving Stannard dinner,' he said. 'What are you doing now?'

'I'll loaf out and get some food, and be back later,' said Braddon. 'I thought I'd take a look upstairs.'

Hayn nodded. He ushered Braddon out of the office, and locked the door behind him, for even Braddon was not allowed to remain in that sanctum alone. Braddon departed and Hayn rejoined Stannard at the bar.

'Sorry to have kept you waiting, old man,' he apologised, with an attempt to resume his pose of bluff geniality.

'I've been amusing myself,' said Stannard, and indicated a row of empty glasses. 'Have a spot?'

Hayn accepted, and Stannard looked at his watch.

'By the way,' he said, 'there's a man due here in about an hour. I met him the other day, and he seemed all right. He said he was a South African, and he's sailing back the day after tomorrow. He was complaining that he couldn't get any real fun in England, so I dropped a hint about a private gambling club I might be able to get him into and he jumped at it. I thought he might be some use—leaving England so soon he could hardly make a kick—so I told him to join us over coffee. Is that all right?'

'Quite all right, old man.' A thought struck Mr Hayn. 'You're quite sure he wasn't one of these clever dicks?'

'Not on your life!' scoffed Stannard. 'I think I know a busy when I see one by now. I've seen enough of 'em dancing here. And this man seems to have money to burn.'

Hayn nodded.

'I meant to come to some arrangement with you over dinner,' he said. 'This bird can go down as your first job, on commission. If you're ready, we'll start.'

Stannard assented, and they walked over to the table which had been prepared.

Hayn was preoccupied. If his mind had not been simmering with other problems, he might have noticed Stannard's ill-concealed nervousness, and wondered what might have been the cause of it. But he observed nothing unusual about the younger man's manner.

While they were waiting for the grapefruit, he asked a question quite perfunctorily.

'What's this South African's name?'

'Templar—Simon Templar,' answered Jerry.

The name meant nothing at all to Mr Hayn.


VI

Over the dinner, Hayn made his offer—a twenty per cent commission on business introduced. Stannard hardly hesitated before accepting.

'You don't want to be squeamish about it,' Hayn argued. 'I know it's against the law, but that's splitting hairs. Horse-racing is just as much a gamble. There'll always be fools who want to get rich without working, and there's no reason why we shouldn't take their money. You won't have to do anything that would make you liable to be sent to prison, though some of my staff would be gaoled if the police caught them. You're quite safe. And the games are perfectly straight. We only win because the law of probabilities favours the bank.'

This was not strictly true, for there were other factors to influence the runs of bad luck which attended the players upstairs; but this sordid fact Mr Hayn did not feel called upon to emphasise.

'Yes—I'll join you,' Stannard said. 'I've known it was coming. I didn't think you went on giving and lending me money for looking decorative and doing an odd job or two for you now and again.'

'My dear fellow—'

'Dear-fellowing doesn't alter it. I know you want more of me than my services in decoying boobs upstairs. Are you going to tell me you didn't know I was caught the other day?'

Hayn stroked his chin.

'I was going to compliment you. How you got rid of that parcel of snow—'

'The point that matters is that I did get rid of it,' cut in Stannard briefly. 'And if I hadn't been able to, I should have been on remand in Brixton Prison now. I'm not complaining. I suppose I had to earn my keep. But it wasn't square of you to keep me in the dark.'

'You knew—'

'I guessed. It's all right—I've stopped kicking. But I want you to let me right in from now on, if you're letting me in at all. I'm joining you, all in, and you needn't bother to humbug me any longer. How's that?'

'That's all right,' said Mr Hayn, 'if you must put things so crudely. But you don't even have to be squeamish about the dope side of it. If people choose to make fools of themselves like that, it's their own look-out. Our share is simply to refuse to quibble about whether it's legal or not. After all, alcohol is sold legally in this country, and nobody blames the publican if his customers get drunk evey night and eventually die of D.T.s.'

Stannard shrugged.

'I can't afford to argue, anyhow,' he said. 'How much do I draw?'

'Twenty per cent—as I told you.'

'What's that likely to make?'

'A lot,' said Hayn. 'We pay higher here than anywhere else in London, and there isn't a great deal of competition in the snow market. You might easily draw upwards of seventy pounds a week.'

'Then will you do something for me, Mr Hayn? I owe a lot of money outside. I'll take three thousand flat for the first year, to pay off everybody and fit myself up with a packet in hand.'

'Three thousand pounds is a lot of money,' said Hayn judicially. 'You owe me nearly a thousand as it is.'

'If you don't think I'm going to be worth it—'

Mr Hayn meditated, but not for long. The making of quick decisions was the whole reason of his success, and he didn't mind how much a thing cost if he knew it was worth it. He had no fear that Stannard would attempt to double-cross him. Among the other purposes which it served, Danny's formed a working headquarters for the Snake's Boys; Stannard could not help knowing the reputation of the gang, and he must also know that they had worked Hayn's vengeance on traitors before. No—there was no chance that Stannard would dare to try a double-cross. . . .

'I'll give you a cheque tonight,' said Hayn.

Stannard was effusively grateful.

'You won't lose by it,' he promised. 'Templar's a speculation, granted, but I've met him only once. But there are other people with mints of money, people I've known for years, that I can vouch for absolutely. . . .'

He went on talking, but Hayn only listened with half an ear, for he was anxious to turn the conversation on to another topic, and he did so at the first opportunity.

Under pretence of taking a fatherly interest in his new agent's affairs, he plied him with questions about his private life and interests. Most of the information which he elicited was stale news to him, for he had long since taken the precaution of finding out everything of importance that there was to know about his man; but in these new enquiries Mr Hayn contrived to make Stannard's fiancée the centre of interrogation. It was very cleverly and surreptitiously done, but the fact remains that at the end of half an hour, by this process of indirect questioning, Hayn had discovered all that he wanted to know about the life and habits of Gwen Chandler.

'Do you think you could get her along here to supper on Thursday?' he suggested. 'The only time I've met her, if you remember, I think you rather prejudiced her against me. It's up to you to put that right.'

'I'll see what I can do,' said Stannard.

After that, his point won, Hayn had no further interest in directing the conversation, and they were chatting desultorily when Simon Templar arrived.

The Saint, after weighing the relative merits of full evening dress or an ordinary lounge suit for the auspicious occasion, had decided upon a compromise, and was sporting a dinner jacket; but he wore it, as might have been expected, as if he had been an Ambassador paying a State visit in full regalia.

'Hullo, Jerry, dear angel!' he hailed Stannard cheerfully.

Then he noticed Mr Hayn, and turned with outstretched hand.

'And you must be Uncle Ambrose,' he greeted that gentleman cordially. 'Pleased to meet you. . . . That's right, isn't it, Jerry? This is the uncle who died and left all his money to that Cats' Home? . . . Sorry to see you looking so well, Uncle Ambrose, old mongoose!'

Mr Hayn seemed somewhat taken aback. This man did not wear his clothes in the manner traditionally associated with raw Colonials with money to burn; and if his speech was typical of that of strong silent men from the great open spaces of that vintage, Mr Hayn decided that the culture of Piccadilly must have spread farther abroad into the British Empire than Cecil Rhodes had ever hoped in his wildest dreams. Mr Hayn had never heard of Rhodes—to him, Rhodes was an island where they bred red hens—but if he had heard of Rhodes he might reasonably have expressed his surprise like that.

He looked round to Jerry Stannard with raised eyebrows, and Stannard tapped his forehead and lifted his glass significantly.

'So we're going to see a real live gambling hell!' said the Saint, drawing up a chair. 'Isn't this fun? Let's all have a lot of drinks on the strength of it!'

He called for liqueurs, and paid for them with a huge wad of bank-notes which he tugged from his pocket. Mr Hayn's eyes lit up at the sight, and he decided that there were excuses for Templar's eccentricity. He leant forward and set himself out to be charming.

The Saint, however, had other views on the subject of the way in which the conversation should go, and at the first convenient pause, he came out with a remark that showed he had been paying little attention to what had gone before.

'I've bought a book about card tricks,' he said. 'I thought it might help me to spot sharpers. But the best part of it was the chapter on fortune-telling by cards. Take a card, and I'll tell you all your sins.'

He produced a new pack from his pocket and pushed it across the table towards Hayn.

'You first, Uncle,' he invited. 'And see that your thoughts are pure when you draw, otherwise you'll give the cards a wrong impression. Hum a verse of your favourite hymn, for instance.'

Mr Hayn knew nothing about hymns, but he complied tolerantly. If this freak had all that money, and perhaps some more, by all means let him be humoured.

'Now, isn't that sweet!' exclaimed the Saint, taking up the card Hayn had chosen. 'Jerry, my pet, your Uncle Ambrose has drawn the ace of hearts. That stands for princely generosity. We'll have another brandy with you, Uncle, just to show how we appreciate it. Waiter! . . . Three more brandies, please. Face Ache—I mean Uncle Ambrose—is paying. . . . Uncle, you must try your luck again!'

Simon Templar pored over Hayn's second card until the drinks arrived. It was noticeable that his shoulders shook silently at one time. Mr Hayn attributed this to represent hiccups, and was gravely in error. Presently the Saint looked up.

'Has an aunt on your mother's side,' he asked solemnly, 'ever suffered from a bilious attack following a meal of sausages made by a German pork butcher with a hammer-toe and three epileptic children?'

Mr Hayn shook his head, staring.

'I haven't any aunts,' he said.

'I'm so sorry,' said the Saint, as if he were deeply distressed to hear of Mr Hayn's plight of pathetic auntlessness. 'But it means the beastly book's all wrong. Never mind. Don't let's bother about it.'

He pushed the pack away. Undoubtedly he was quite mad.

'Aren't you going to tell us any more?' asked Stannard, with a wink to Hayn.

'Uncle Ambrose would blush if I went on,' said Templar. 'Look at the brick I've dropped already. But if you insist, I'll try one more card.'

Hayn obliged again, smiling politely. He was starting to get acclimatised. Clearly the secret of being on good terms with Mr Templar was to let him have his own irrepressible way.

'I only hope it isn't the five of diamonds,' said the Saint earnestly. 'Whenever I do this fortune-telling stuff, I'm terrified of somebody drawing the five of diamonds. You see, I'm bound to tell the truth, and the truth in that case is frightfully hard to tell to a comparative stranger. Because, according to my book, a man who draws the five of diamonds is liable at any moment to send an anonymous donation of ten thousand pounds to the London Hospital. Also, cards are unlucky for him, he is an abominable blackguard, and he has a repulsively ugly face.'

Hayn kept his smile nailed in position, and faced his card.

'The five of diamonds, Mr Templar,' he remarked gently.

'No—is it really?' said Simon, in most Saintly astonishment. 'Well, well, *well*! . . . There you are, Jerry—I warned you your uncle would be embarrassed if I went on. Now I've dropped another brick. Let's talk of something else, quickly, before he notices. Uncle Ambrose, tell me, have you ever seen a hot dog fighting a cat-o'-nine-tails? . . . No? . . . Well, shuffle the pack and I'll show you a conjuring trick.'

Mr Hayn shuffled and cut, and the Saint rapidly dealt off five cards, which he passed face downwards across the table.

It was about the first chance Mr Hayn had had to sidle a word in, and he felt compelled to protest about one thing.

'You seem to be suffering from a delusion, Mr Templar,' he said. 'I'm not Jerry's uncle—I'm just a friend of his. My name's Hayn—Edgar Hayn.'

'Why?' asked the Saint innocently.

'It happens to be the name I was christened with, Mr Templar,' Hayn replied with some asperity.

'Is—that—so!' drawled the Saint mildly. 'Sorry again!'

Hayn frowned. There was something peculiarly infuriating about the Saint in that particular vein—something that, while it rasped the already raw fringe of his temper, was also beginning to send a queer, indefinable uneasiness creeping up his back.

'And I'm sorry if it annoys you,' he snapped.

Simon Templar regarded him steadily.

'It annoys me,' he said, 'because, as I told you, it's my business never to make mistakes, and I just hate being wrong. The records of Somerset House told me that your name was once something quite different—that you weren't christened Edgar Hayn at all. And I believed it.'

Hayn said nothing. He sat quite still, with that tingling thrill of apprehension crawling round the base of his scalp. And the Saint's clear blue gaze never left Hayn's face.

'If I was wrong about that,' the Saint went on softly, 'I may quite easily have been wrong about other things. And that would annoy me more than ever, because I don't like wasting my time. I've spent several days figuring out a way of meeting you for just this little chat—I thought it was about time our relationship became a bit more personal—and it'd break my heart to think it had all been for nothing. Don't tell me that, Edgar, beloved—don't tell me it wasn't any use my finding out that dear little Jerry was a friend of yours—don't tell me that I might have saved myself the trouble I took scraping an acquaintance with the said Jerry just to bring about this informal meeting. Don't tell me that, dear heart!'

Hayn moistened his lips. He was fighting down an insane, unreasoning feeling of panic; and it was the Saint's quiet, level voice and mocking eyes, as much as anything, that held Edgar Hayn rooted in his chair.

'Don't tell me, in fact, that you won't appreciate the little conjuring trick I came here especially to show you,' said the Saint, more mildly than ever.

He reached out suddenly and took the cards he had dealt from Hayn's nerveless fingers. Hayn had guessed what they would prove to be, long before Simon, with a flourish, had spread the cards out face upwards on the table.

'Don't tell me you aren't pleased to see our visiting cards, personally presented!' said Simon, in his very Saintliest voice.

His white teeth flashed in a smile, and there was a light of adventurous recklessness dancing in his eyes as he looked at Edgar Hayn across five neat specimens of the sign of the Saint.

## VII

'And if it's pure prune juice and boloney,' went on the Saint, in that curiously velvety tone which still contrived somehow to prickle all over with little warning spikes—'if all that is sheer banana oil and soft roe, I shan't even raise a smile with the story I was going to tell you. It's my very latest one, and it's about a loose-living land-shark called Hayn, who was born in a barn in the rain. What he'd struggled to hide was found out when he died—there was mildew all over his brain. Now, that one's been getting a big hand everywhere I've told it since I made it up, and it'll be one of the bitterest disappointments of my life if it doesn't fetch you, sweetheart!'

Hayn's chair went over with a crash as he kicked to his feet. Strangely enough, now that the murder was out and the first shock absorbed, the weight on his mind seemed lightened, and he felt better able to cope with the menace.

'So you're the young cub we've been looking for!' he rasped.

Simon raised his hand.

'I'm called the Saint,' he murmured. 'But don't let us get melodramatic about it, son. The last man who got melodramatic with me was hanged at Exeter six months back. It don't seem to be healthy!'

Hayn looked round. The diners had left, and as yet no one had arrived to take their places; but the clatter of his chair upsetting had roused three startled waiters, who were staring uncertainly in his direction. But a review of these odds did not seem to disturb the Saint, who was lounging languidly back in his seat with his hands in his pockets and a benign expression on his face.

'I suppose you know that the police are after you,' grated Hayn.

'I didn't,' said the Saint. 'That's interesting. Why?'

'You met some men in the Brighton train and played poker with them. You swindled them right and left, and when they accused you you attacked them and pinched the money. I think that's good enough to put you away for some time.'

'And who's going to identify me?'

'The four men.'

'You surprise me,' drawled Simon. 'I seem to remember that on that very day, just outside Brighton racecourse, those same four bums were concerned in beating up a poor little coot of a lame bookie named Tommy Mitre and pinching *his* money. There didn't happen to be any policeman about—they arranged it quite cleverly—and the crowd that saw it would most likely all be too scared of the Snake to give evidence. But yours truly and a couple of souls also saw the fun. We were a long way off, and the Snake and his Boys were over the horizon by the time we got to the scene, but we could identify them all, and a few more who were not there—and we shouldn't be afraid to step into the witness-box and say our piece. No, sonnikins—I don't think the police will be brought into that. That must go down into history as a little private wrangle between Snake and me. Send one of your beauty chorus out for a Robert and give me in charge, if you like, but don't blame me if Ganning and the Boys come back at you for it. Knowing their reputations, I should say they'd get the "cat" as well as their six months' hard, and that won't make them love you a lot. Have it your own way, though.'

The argument was watertight, and Hayn realised it. He was beginning to cool down. He hadn't a kick—for the moment, the Saint had got him right down in the mud with a foot on his face. But he didn't see what good that was doing the Saint. It was a big bluff, Hayn was starting to think, and he had sense enough to realise that it wasn't helping him one bit to get all hot under the collar about it. In fact—such was the exhilarating effect of having at last found an enemy that he could see and hit back at—Hayn was rapidly reckoning that the Saint might lose a lot by that display of bravado.

Clearly the Saint didn't want the police horning in at all. It didn't even matter that the Saint knew things about Hayn, and his activities that would have interested the police. The Saint was on some lay of his own, and the police weren't being invited to interfere. Very well. So be it. The cue for Hayn was to bide his time and refuse to be rattled. But he wished the Saint hadn't got that mocking, self-possessed air of having a lot more high cards up his sleeve, just waiting to be produced. It spoilt Hayn's happiness altogether. The Saint was behaving like a fool; and yet, in some disconcertingly subtle way, he managed to do it with the condescending air of putting off a naturally tremendous gravity in order to amuse the children.

Hayn righted his chair and sat down again slowly; the alert waiters relaxed—they were a tough crowd, and selected more for their qualities of toughness than for clean fingernails and skill at juggling with plates and dishes. But as Hayn sat down his right hand went behind his chair—his back was towards the group of waiters—and with his fingers he made certain signs. One of the waiters faded away inconspicuously.

'So what do you propose to do?' Hayn said.

'Leave you,' answered the Saint benevolently. 'I know your ugly dial isn't your fault, but I've seen about as much of it as I can stand for one evening. I've done what I came to do, and now I think you can safely be left to wonder what I'm going to do next. See you later, I expect, my Beautiful Ones. . . .'

The Saint rose and walked unhurriedly to the stairs. By that time, there were five men ranged in a row at the foot of the stairs, and they showed no signs of making way for anyone.

'We should hate to lose you so soon, Mr Templar,' said Hayn.

The Saint's lounging steps slowed up, and stopped. His hands slid into his pockets, and he stood for a moment surveying the quintet of waiters with a beautiful smile. Then he turned.

'What are these?' he enquired pleasantly. 'The guard of honour, or the cabaret beauty chorus?'

'I think you might sit down again, Mr Templar,' suggested Hayn.

'And I think not,' said the Saint.

He walked swiftly back to the table—so swiftly that Hayn instinctively half-rose from his seat, and the five men started forward. But the Saint did not attack at that moment. He stopped in front of Hayn, his hands in his pockets; and although that maddening little smile still lurked on his lips, there was something rather stern about his poise.

'I said I was going to leave you, and I am,' he murmured, with a gentleness that was in amazing contrast to the intent tautness of his bearing. 'That's what I came here for, ducky—to leave you. This is just meant for a demonstration of all-round superiority; you think you can stop me—but you watch! I'm going to prove that nothing on earth can stop me when I get going. Understand, loveliness?'

'We shall see,' said Hayn.

The Saint's smile became, if possible, even more Saintly.

Somehow that smile, and the air of hair-trigger alertness which accompanied it, was bothering Edgar Hayn a heap. He knew it was all bravado—he knew the Saint had bitten off more than he could chew for once—he knew that the odds were all against a repetition of the discomfiture of the Ganning combine. And yet he couldn't feel happy about it. There was a kind of quivering strength about the Saint's lazy bearing—something that reminded Edgar Hayn of wire and whipcord and indiarubber and compressed steel springs and high explosives.

'In the space of a few minutes,' said the Saint, 'you're going to see a sample of rough-housing that'll make your bunch of third-rate hoodlums look like two cents' worth of oxtail. But before I proceed to beat them up, I want to tell you this—which you can pass on to your friends. Ready?'

Hayn spread out his hands.

'Then I'll shoot,' said the Saint. 'It's just this. We Saints are normally souls of peace and goodwill towards men. But we don't like crooks, blood-suckers, traders in vice and damnation, and other verminous excrescences of that type—such as yourself. We're going to beat you up and do you down, skin you and smash you, and scare you off the face of Europe. We are not bothered about the letter of the Law, we act exactly as we please, we inflict what punishments we think suitable, and no one is going to escape us. Ganning got hurt, but still you don't believe me. You're the next on the list, and by the time I've finished with you, you'll be an example to convince others. And it will go on. That's all I've got to say now, and when I've left you you can go forth and spread the glad news. I'm leaving now!'

He stooped suddenly, and grasped the leg of Hayn's chair and tipped it backwards with one jerking heave. As Hayn tried to scramble to his feet, the Saint put an ungentle foot in his face and upset the table on top of him.

The five tough waiters were pelting across the floor in a pack. Simon reached out for the nearest chair and sent it skating over the room at the height of six inches from the ground, with a vimful swing of his arms that gave it the impetus of a charging buffalo. It smashed across the leader's knees and shins with bone-shattering force, and the man went down with a yell.

That left four.

The Saint had another chair in his hands by the time the next man was upon him. The waiter flung up his arms to guard his head, and tried to rush into a grapple; but the Saint stepped back and reversed the swing of his chair abruptly. It swerved under the man's guard and crashed murderously into his short ribs.

Three. . . .

The next man ran slap into a sledge-hammer left that hurled him a dozen feet away. The other two hesitated, but the Saint was giving no breathing space. He leapt in at the nearest man with a pile-driving, left-right-left tattoo to the solar plexus.

As the tough crumpled up with a choking groan under that battering-ram assault, some sixth sense flashed the Saint a warning.

He leapt to one side, and the chair Hayn had swung to his head swished harmlessly past him, the vigour of the blow toppling Hayn off his balance. The Saint assisted his downfall with an outflung foot which sent the man hurtling headlong.

The last man was still coming on, but warily. He ducked the Saint's lead, and replied with a right swing to the side of the head which gingered the Saint up a peach. Simon Templar decided that his reputation was involved, and executed a beautiful feint with his left which gave him an opening to lash in a volcanic right squarely upon the gangster's nose.

As the man dropped, the Saint whipped round and caught Stannard.

'Fight, you fool!' the Saint hissed in his ear. 'This is for local colour!'

Stannard clinched, and then the Saint broke away and firmly but regretfully clipped him on the ear.

It was not one of the Saint's heftiest punches, but it was hard enough to knock the youngster down convincingly; and then the Saint looked round hopefully for something else to wallop, and found nothing. Hayn was rising again, shakily, and so were those of the five roughs who were in a fit state to do so, but there was no notable enthusiasm to renew the battle.

'Any time any of you bad cheeses want any more lessons in rough-housing,' drawled the Saint, a little breathlessly, 'you've only got to drop me a postcard and I'll be right along.'

This time, there was no attempt to bar his way.

He collected hat, gloves and stick from the cloakroom, and went through the upstairs lounge. As he reached the door, he met Braddon returning.

'Hullo, Sweetness,' said the Saint genially. 'Pass right down the car and hear the new joke the Boys of the Burg downstairs are laughing at.'

Braddon was still trying to guess the cause for and meaning of this extraordinary salutation by a perfect stranger, when the Saint, without any haste or heat, but so swiftly and deftly that the thing was done before Braddon realised what was happening, had reached out and seized the brim of Braddon's hat and forced it well down over his eyes. Then, with a playful tweak of Braddon's nose, and a cheery wave of his hand to the dumbfounded Danny, he departed.

Danny was not a quick mover, and the street outside was Saintless by the time Braddon had struggled out of his hat and reached the door.

When his vocabulary was exhausted, Braddon went downstairs in search of Hayn, and stopped open-mouthed at the wreckage he saw.

Mr Hayn, turning from watching the Saint's triumphant vanishment, had swung sharply on Stannard. The Saint's unscathed exit had left Hayn in the foulest of tempers. All around him, it seemed, an army of tough waiters in various stages of disrepair were gathering themselves to their feet with a muttered obbligato of lurid oaths. Well, if there wasn't an army of them, there were five—five bone-hard heavyweights—and that ought to have been enough to settle any ordinary man, even on the most liberal computation of odds. But the Saint had simply waded right through them, hazed and manhandled and roasted them, and walked out without a scratch. Hayn would have taken a bet that the Saint's tie wasn't even a millimetre out of centre at the end of it. The Saint had made fools of them without turning a hair.

Hayn vented his exasperation on Jerry, and even the fact that he had seen the boy help to tackle the Saint and get the worst of it in their company did not mitigate his wrath.

'You damned fool!' he blazed. 'Couldn't you see he was up to something? Are you taken in by everyone who tells you the tale?'

'I told you I couldn't guarantee him,' Stannard protested. 'But when I met him he wasn't a bit like he was tonight. Honestly, Mr Hayn—how could I have known? I don't even know what he was after yet. Those cards. . . .'

'South African grandmothers,' snarled Hayn.

Braddon intervened.

'Who was this gentleman, anyway?' he demanded.

'Gentleman' was not the word he used.

'Use your eyes, you lunatic!' Hayn flared, pointing to the table, and Braddon's jaw dropped as he saw the cards.

'You've had that guy in here?'

'What the hell d'you think? You probably passed him coming in. And from what the Snake said, and what I've seen myself, he's probably right at the top—he might even be the Saint himself.'

'So that was the gentleman!' said Braddon, only once again he described Simon Templar with a more decorative word.

Hayn snorted.

'And that fool Stannard brought him here,' he said.

'I told you, I didn't know much about him, Mr Hayn,' Stannard expostulated. 'I warned you I couldn't answer for him.'

'The kid's right,' said Braddon. 'If he put it over on the Snake, he might put it over on anybody.'

There was logic in the argument, but it was some time before Hayn could be made to see it. But presently he quieted down.

'We'll talk about this, Braddon,' he said. 'I've got an idea for stopping his funny stuff. He didn't get clean away—I put Keld on to follow him. By tonight we'll know where he lives, and then I don't think he'll last long.'

He turned to Jerry. The boy was fidgeting nervously, and Hayn became diplomatic. It wasn't any use rubbing a valuable man up the wrong way.

'I'm sorry I lost my temper, old man,' he said. 'I can see it wasn't your fault. You just want to be more careful. I ought to have warned you about the Saint—he's dangerous! Have a cigar.'

It was Mr Hayn's peace-offering. Stannard accepted it.

'No offence,' he said. 'I'm sorry I let you down.'

'We won't say anything more about it, old man,' said Hayn heartily. 'You won't mind if I leave you? Mr Braddon and I have some business to talk over. I expect you'll amuse yourself upstairs. But you mustn't play any more, you know.'

'I shan't want to,' said Stannard. 'But, Mr Hayn—'

Hayn stopped.

'Yes, old man?'

'Would you mind if I asked you for that cheque? I'll give you an I.O.U. now. . . .'

'I'll see that you get it before you leave.'

'It's awfully good of you, Mr Hayn,' said Stannard apologetically. 'Three thousand pounds it was.'

'I hadn't forgotten,' said Hayn shortly.

He moved off, cursing the damaged waiters out of his path; and Stannard watched him go, thoughtfully. So far, it had all been too easy, but how long was it going to last?

He was watching the early dancers assembling when a waiter, whose face was obscured by a large piece of sticking-plaster, came through with a sealed envelope. Stannard ripped it open, inspected the cheque it contained, and scribbled his signature to the promissory note that came with it. He sent this back to Hayn by the same waiter.

Although he had disposed of several cocktails before dinner, and during the meal had partaken freely of wine, and afterwards had done his full share in the consumption of liqueurs, his subsequent abstemiousness was remarkable. He sat with an untasted brandy-and-soda in front of him while the coloured orchestra broke into its first frenzies of syncopation, and watched the gyrating couples with a jaundiced eye for an hour. Then he drained his glass, rose, and made his way to the stairs.

Through the window of the office he saw Hayn and Braddon still engaged in earnest conversation. He tapped on the pane, and Hayn looked up and nodded. The hidden door swung open as Stannard reached it, and closed after him as he passed through.

He strolled through the gaming rooms, greeted a few acquaintances, and watched the play for a while without enthusiasm. He left the club early, as soon as he conveniently could.

The next morning, he hired a car and drove rapidly out of London. He met the Saint on the Newmarket road at a prearranged milestone.

'There was a man following me,' said the Saint happily. 'When I got out my bus, he took a taxi. I wonder if he gave it up, or if he's still toiling optimistically along, bursting the meter somewhere in the wilds of Edmonton.'

He gave Stannard a cigarette, and received a cheque in return.

'A thousand pounds,' said Stannard. 'As I promised.'

The Saint put it carefully away in his wallet.

'And why I should give it to you, I don't know,' said Stannard.

'It is the beginning of wisdom,' said the Saint. 'The two thousand that's left will pay off your debts and give you a fresh start, and I'll get your I.O.U.s back for you in a day or two. A thousand pounds isn't much to pay for that.'

'Except that I might have kept the money and gone on working for Hayn.'

'But you have reformed,' said the Saint gently. 'And I'm sure the demonstration you saw last night will help to keep you on the straight and narrow path. If you kept in with Hayn, you'd have me to deal with.'

He climbed back into his car and pressed the self-starter, but Stannard was still curious.

'What are you going to do with the money?' he asked. 'I thought you were against crooks.'

'I am,' said the Saint virtuously. 'It goes to charity. Less my ten per cent commission charged for collecting. You'll hear from me again when I want you. *Au revoir*—or, in the Spanish, *hasta la vista*—or, if you prefer it in the German, *auf Wiedersehen*!'

## VIII

About a week after the Saint's mercurial irruption into Danny's, Gwen Chandler met Mr Edgar Hayn in Regent Street one morning by accident. At exactly the same time, Mr Edgar Hayn met Gwen Chandler on purpose, for he had been at some pains to bring about that accidental meeting.

'We see far too little of you these days, my dear,' he said, taking her hand.

She was looking cool and demure in a summer frock of printed chiffon, and her fair hair peeped out under the brim of her picture hat to set off the cornflower blue of her eyes.

'Why, it seems no time since Jerry and I were having supper with you,' she said.

'No time is far too long for me,' said Mr Hayn cleverly. 'One could hardly have too much of anyone as charming as yourself, my dear lady.'

At the supper-party which she had unwillingly been induced to join, he had set himself out to be an irreproachable host, and his suave geniality had gone a long way towards undoing the first instinctive dislike which she had felt for him, but she did not know how to take him in this reversion to his earlier pose of exaggerated heartiness. It reminded her of the playful romping advances of an elephant, but she did not find it funny.

Mr Hayn, however, was for the moment as pachydermatous as the animal on whose pleasantries he appeared to have modelled his own, and her slightly chilling embarrassment was lost on him. He waved his umbrella towards the window of the shop outside which they were standing.

'Do you know that name, Miss Chandler?' he asked.

She looked in the direction indicated.

'Laserre? Yes, of course, I've heard of it.'

'I am Laserre,' said Hayn largely. 'This is the opportunity I've been waiting for to introduce you to our humble premises—and how convenient that we should meet on the very doorstep!'

She was not eager to agree, but before she could frame a suitable reply he had propelled her into the glittering red-carpeted room where the preparations of the firm were purveyed in a hushed and reverent atmosphere reminiscent of a cathedral.

A girl assistant came forward, but in a moment she was displaced by Braddon himself—frock-coated, smooth, oleaginous, hands at washing position.

'This is my manager,' said Hayn, and the frock-coated man bowed. 'Mr Braddon, be so good as to show Miss Chandler some samples of the best of our products—the very best.'

Thereupon, to the girl's bewilderment, were displayed velvet-lined mahogany trays, serried ranks of them, brought from the shelves that surrounded the room, and set out with loving care on a counter, one after another, till she felt completely dazed. There were rows upon rows of flashing crystal bottles of scent, golden cohorts of lipsticks, platoons of little alabaster pots of rouge, orderly regiments of enamelled boxes of powder. Her brain reeled before the contemplation of such a massed quantity of luxurious panderings to vanity.

'I want you to choose anything you like,' said Hayn. 'Absolutely anything that takes your fancy, my dear Miss Chandler.'

'But—I—I couldn't possibly,' she stammered.

Hayn waved her objections aside.

'I insist,' he said. 'What is the use of being master of a place like this if you cannot let your friends enjoy it? Surely I can make you such a small present without any fear of being misunderstood?

Accept the trifling gift graciously, my dear lady. I shall feel most hurt if you refuse.'

In spite of the grotesqueness of his approach, the circumstances made it impossible to snub him. But she was unable to fathom his purpose in making her the object of such an outbreak. It was a hot day, and he was perspiring freely, as a man of his build is unhappily liable to do, and she wondered hysterically if perhaps the heat had temporarily unhinged his brain. There was something subtly disquieting about his exuberance.

She modestly chose a small vanity-case and a little flask of perfume, and he seemed disappointed by her reluctance. He pressed other things upon her, and she found herself forced to accept two large boxes of powder.

'Make a nice parcel of those things for Miss Chandler, Mr Braddon,' said Hayn, and the manager carried the goods away to the back of the shop.

'It's really absurdly kind of you, Mr Hayn,' said the girl confusedly. 'I don't know what I've done to deserve it.'

'Your face is your fortune, my dear young lady,' answered Hayn, who was obviously in a brilliant mood.

She had a terrified suspicion that in a moment he would utter an invitation to lunch, and she hastily begged to be excused on the grounds of an entirely fictitious engagement.

'Please don't think me rude, hurrying away like this,' she pleaded. 'As a matter of fact, I'm already shockingly late.'

He was plainly crestfallen.

'No one can help forgiving you anything,' he said sententiously. 'But the loss to myself is irreparable.'

She never knew afterwards how she managed to keep her end up in the exchange of platitudes that followed, until the return of Braddon with a neat package enabled her to make her escape.

Hayn accompanied her out into the street, hat in hand.

'At least,' he said, 'promise me that the invitation will not be unwelcome, if I ring you up soon and ask you to suggest a day. I could not bear to think that my company was distasteful to you.'

'Of course not—I should love to—and thank you ever so much for the powder and things,' she said desperately. 'But I must fly now.'

She fled as best she might.

Hayn watched her out of sight, standing stockstill in the middle of the pavement where she had left him, with a queer gleam in his pale eyes. Then he put his hat on, and marched off without re-entering the shop.

He made his way to the club in Soho, where he was informed that Snake Ganning and some of the Boys were waiting to see him. Hayn let them wait while he wrote a letter, which was addressed to M. Henri Chastel, Poste Restante, Athens: and he was about to ring for the Snake to be admitted when there was a tap on the door and Danny entered.

'There are five of them,' said Danny helpfully.

'Five of whom?' said Hayn patiently.

'Five,' said Danny, 'including the man who pulled Mr Braddon's hat down over his eyes. They said they must see you at once.'

Mr Hayn felt in the pit of his stomach the dull sinking qualm which had come to be inseparable from the memory of the Saint's electric personality. Every morning without fail since the first warning he had received, there had been the now familiar envelope beside his plate at breakfast, containing the inevitable card; and every afternoon, when he reached Danny's, he found a similar reminder among the letters on his desk.

He had not had a chance to forget Simon Templar, even if he had wished to do so—as a matter of fact, the Snake and his Boys were at that moment waiting to receive their instructions in connection with a plot which Hayn had formed for disposing of the menace.

But the Saint's policy was rapidly wearing out Hayn's nerves. Knowing what he did, the Saint could only be refraining from passing his knowledge along to Scotland Yard because he hoped to gain more by silence, yet there had been no attempt to blackmail—only those daily melodramatic reminders of his continued interest.

Hayn was starting to feel like a mouse that has been tormented to the verge of madness by an exceptionally sportive cat. He had not a doubt that the Saint was scheming and working against him still, but his most frenzied efforts of concentration had failed to deduce the most emaciated shred of an idea of the direction from which the next assault would be launched, and seven days and nights of baffled inaction had brought Edgar Hayn to the borders of a breakdown.

Now the Saint—and the rest of his gang also, from all appearances—was paying a second visit. The next round was about to begin, and Hayn was fighting in a profounder obscurity than ever.

'Show them in,' he said in a voice that he hardly recognised as his own.

He bent over some writing, struggling to control his nerves for the bluff that was all he had to rely on, and with an effort of will he succeeded in not looking up when he heard the door opening and the soft footsteps of men filing into the room.

'Walk right in, souls,' said the Saint's unmistakable cheery accents. 'That's right. . . . Park yourselves along the wall in single rank and stand easy.'

Then Hayn raised his eyes, and saw the Saint standing over the desk regarding him affectionately.

'Good morning, Edgar,' said the Saint affably. 'How's Swan?'

'Good morning, Mr Templar,' said Hayn.

He shifted his gaze to the four men ranged beside the door. They were a nondescript quartet, in his opinion—not at all the sort of men he had pictured in his hazy attempts to visualise Templar's partners. Only one of them could have been under thirty, and the clothes of all of them had seen better days.

'These are the rest of the gang,' said the Saint. 'I noticed that I was followed home from here last time I called, so I thought it'd save you a lot of sleuthing if I brought the other lads right along and introduced them.'

He turned.

'Squad—shun!—Souls, this is dear Edgar, whom you've heard so much about. As I call your names, reading from left to right, you will each take one pace smartly to your front, bow snappily from the hips, keeping the eyebrows level and the thumb in line with the seam of the trousers, and fall in again. . . . First, Edgar, meet Saint Winston Churchill. Raise your hat, Winny. . . . On his left, Saint George Robey. Eyebrows level, George. . . . Next, Saint Herbert Hoover, President of the United States, and no relation to the vacuum cleaner. Wave your handkerchief to the pretty gentleman, Herb! Last, but not least, Saint Hannen Swaffer. Keep smiling Hannen—I won't let anyone slap your face here. . . . That's the lot, Edgar, except for myself. Meet me!'

Hayn nodded.

'That's very considerate of you, Mr Templar,' he said, and his voice was a little shaky, for an idea was being born inside him. 'Is that all you came to do?'

'Not quite, Precious,' said the Saint, settling down on the edge of the desk. 'I came to talk business.'

'Then you won't want to be hurried,' said Hayn. 'There are some other people waiting to see me. Will you excuse me while I go and tell them to call again later?'

The Saint smiled.

'By all manner of means, sonny,' said he. 'But I warn you it won't be any use telling the Snake and his Boys to be ready to beat us up when we leave here, because a friend of ours is waiting a block away with a letter to our friend Inspector Teal—and that letter will be delivered if we don't report safe and sound in ten minutes from now!'

'You needn't worry,' said Hayn. 'I haven't underrated your intelligence!'

He went out. It was a mistake he was to regret later—never before had he left even his allies alone in that office, much less a confessed enemy. But the urgency of his inspiration had, for the moment, driven every other thought out of his head. The cleverest criminal must make a slip sooner or later, and it usually proves to be such a childish one that the onlooker is amazed that it should have been made at all. Hayn made his slip then, but it must be remembered that he was a very rattled man.

He found Snake Ganning sitting at the bar with three picked Boys, and beckoned them out of earshot of the bartender.

'The Saint and the rest of his band are in the office,' he said, and Ganning let out a virulent exclamation. 'No—there won't be any rough business now. I want to have a chance to find out what his game is. But when the other four go, I want you to tail them and find out all you can about them. Report here at midnight, and I'll give you your instructions about Templar himself.'

'When I get hold of that swine,' Ganning ground out vitriolitically, 'he's going to—'

Hayn cut him short with an impatient sweep of his hand.

'You'll wait till I've finished with him,' he said. 'You don't want to charge in like a bull at a gate, before you know what's on the other side of the gate. I'll tell you when to start—you can bet your life on that!'

And in that short space of time the Saint, having shamelessly seized the opportunity provided by Hayn's absence, had comprehensively ransacked the desk. There were four or five I.O.U.s with Stannard's signature in an unlocked drawer, and these he pocketed. Hayn had been incredibly careless. And then the Saint's eye was caught by an envelope on which the ink was still damp. The name 'Chastel' stood out as if it had been spelt in letters of fire, so that Simon stiffened like a pointer. . . .

His immobility lasted only an instant. Then, in a flash, he scribbled something on a blank sheet of notepaper and folded it into a blank envelope. With the original before him for a guide, he copied the address in a staggeringly lifelike imitation of Hayn's handwriting. . . .

'I shall now be able to give you an hour, if you want it,' said Hayn, returning, and the Saint turned with a bland smile.

'I shan't take nearly as long as that, my cabbage,' he replied. 'But I don't think the proceedings will interest the others, and they've got work to do. Now you've met them, do you mind if I dismiss the parade?'

'Not at all, Mr Templar.'

There was a glitter of satisfaction in Hayn's eyes; but if the Saint noticed it, he gave no sign.

'Move to the right in column o' route—etcetera,' he ordered briskly. 'In English, hop it!'

The parade, after a second's hesitation, shuffled out with expressionless faces. They had not spoken a word from the time of their entrance to the time of their exit.

It may conveniently be recorded at this juncture that Snake Ganning and the Boys spent eleven laboriously profitless hours following a kerbstone vendor of bootlaces, a pavement artist, and a barrel-organ team of two ex-Service men, whom the Saint had hired for ten shillings apiece for the occasion; and it may also be mentioned that the quartet, assembling at a near-by dairy to celebrate the windfall, were no less mystified than were the four painstaking bloodhounds who dogged their footsteps for the rest of the day.

It was the Saint's idea of a joke—but then, the Saint's sense of humour was remarkably broad.

IX

'And now let's get down to business—as the bishop said to the actress,' murmured Simon, fishing out his cigarette-case and tapping a gasper on his thumbnail. 'I want to ask you a very important question.'

Hayn sat down.

'Well, Mr Templar?'

'What would you say,' said the Saint tentatively, 'if I told you I wanted ten thousand pounds?'

Hayn smiled.

'I should sympathise with you,' he answered. 'You're not the only man who'd like to make ten thousand pounds as easily as that.'

'But just suppose,' said Simon persuasively—'just suppose I told you that if I didn't get ten thousand pounds at once, a little dossier about you would travel right along to Inspector Teal to tell him the story of the upstairs rooms here and the inner secrets of the Maison Laserre? I could tell him enough to send you to penal servitude for five years.'

Hayn's eye fell on the calendar hung on the wall, with a sliding red ring round the date. His brain was working very rapidly then. Suddenly, he felt unwontedly confident. He looked from the calendar to his watch, and smiled.

'I should write you a cheque at once,' he said.

'And your current account would stand it?'

'All my money is in a current account,' said Hayn. 'As you will understand, it is essential for a man in my position to be able to realise his estate without notice.'

'Then please write,' murmured the Saint.

Without a word, Hayn opened a drawer, took out his chequebook, and wrote. He passed the cheque to Templar, and the Saint's eyes danced as he read it.

'You're a good little boy, son,' said the Saint. 'I'm so glad we haven't had any sordid argument and haggling about this. It makes the whole thing so crude, I always think.'

Hayn shrugged.

'You have your methods,' he said. 'I have mine. I ask you to observe the time.' He showed his watch, tapping the dial with a stubby forefinger. 'Half-past twelve of a Saturday afternoon. You cannot cash that cheque until nine o'clock on Monday morning. Who knows what may have happened by then? I say you will never pay that cheque into your bank. I'm not afraid to tell you that. I know you won't set the police on to me until Monday morning, because you think you're going to win—because you think that at nine o'clock on Monday morning you'll be sitting on the bank's doorstep waiting for it to open. I know you won't. Do you honestly believe I would let you blackmail me for a sum like that—nearly as much money as I have saved in five years?'

The crisis that he had been expecting for so long had come. The cards were on the table, and the only thing left for Edgar Hayn to wonder was why the Saint had waited so many days before making his demand. Now the storm which had seemed to be hanging fire interminably had broken, and it found Edgar Hayn curiously unmoved.

Templar looked at Hayn sidelong, and the Saint also knew that the gloves were off.

'You're an odd cove,' he said. 'Your trouble is that you're too serious. You'll lose this fight because you've no sense of humour— like all second-rate crooks. You can't laugh.'

'I may enjoy the last laugh, Templar,' said Hayn.

The Saint turned away with a smile, and picked up his hat.

'You kid yourself,' he said gently. 'You won't, dear one.' He took up his stick and swung it delicately in his fingers. The light of battle glinted in his blue eyes. 'I presume I may send your kind donation to the London Hospital anonymously, son?'

'We will decide that on Monday,' said Hayn.

The Saint nodded.

'I wonder if you know what my game is?' he said soberly. 'Perhaps you think I'm a kind of hijacker—a crook picking crooks' pockets? Bad guess, dearie. I'm losing money over this. But I'm just a born-an'-bred fighting machine, and a quiet life on the moss-gathering lay is plain hell for this child. I'm not a dick, because I can't be bothered with red tape, but I'm on the same side. I'm out to see that unpleasant insects like you are stamped on, which I grant you the dicks could do; but to justify my existence I'm going to see that the said insects contribute a large share of their ill-gotten gains to charity, which you've got to grant me the dicks can't do. It's always seemed a bit tough to me that microbes of your breed should be able to make a pile swindling, and then be free to enjoy it after they've done a month or two in stir—and I'm here to put that right. Out of the money I lifted off the Snake I paid Tommy Mitre back his rightful property, plus a bonus for damages; but the Snake's a small bug, anyway. You're big, and I'm going to see that your contribution is in proportion.'

'We shall see,' said Hayn.

The Saint looked at him steadily.

'On Monday night you will sleep at Marlborough Street Police Station,' he said dispassionately.

The next moment he was gone. Simon Templar had a knack of making his abrupt exits so smoothly that it was generally some minutes before the other party fully realised that he was no longer with them.

Hayn sat looking at the closed door without moving. Then he glanced down, and saw the envelope that lay on the blotter before him, addressed in his own hand to M. Henri Chastel. And Hayn sat fascinated, staring, for although the imitation of his hand might have deceived a dozen people who knew it, he had looked at it for just long enough to see that it was not the envelope he had addressed.

It was some time before he came out of his trance, and forced himself to slit open the envelope with fingers that trembled. He spread out the sheet of paper on the desk in front of him, and his brain went numb. As a man might have grasped a concrete fact through a murky haze of dope, Hayn realised that his back was to the last wall. Underneath the superficial veneer of flippancy, the Saint had shown for a few seconds the seriousness of his real quality and the intentness of his purpose, and Hayn had been allowed to appreciate the true mettle of the man who was fighting him.

He could remember the Saint's last words. 'On Monday night you will sleep at Marlborough Street Police Station.' He could hear the Saint saying it. The voice had been the voice of a judge pronouncing sentence, and the memory of it made Edgar Hayn's face go grey with fear.

X

The Saint read Edgar Hayn's letter in the cocktail bar of the Piccadilly, over a timely Martini, but his glass stood for a long time untasted before him, for he had not to read far before he learned that Edgar Hayn was bigger game than he had ever dreamed.

Then he smoked two cigarettes, very thoughtfully, and made certain plans with a meticulous attention to detail. In half an hour he had formulated his strategy, but he spent another quarter of an hour and another cigarette going over it again and again in search of anything that he might have overlooked.

He did not touch his drink until he had decided that his plans were as fool-proof as he could make them at such short notice.

The first move took him to Piccadilly Post Office, where he wrote out and despatched a lengthy telegram in code to one Norman Kent, who was at that time in Athens on the Saint's business; and the Saint thanked his little gods of chance for the happy coincidence that had given him an agent on the spot. It augured well for the future.

Next he shifted across from the counter to a telephone-box, and called a number. For ten minutes he spoke earnestly to a certain Roger Conway, and gave minute directions. He had these orders repeated over to him to make sure that they were perfectly memorised and understood, and presently he was satisfied.

'Hayn will have found out by now that I know about his connection with Chastel,' he concluded, 'that is, unless he's posted that letter without looking at it. We've got to act on the assumption that he *has* found out, and therefore the rule about having nothing to do with me except through the safest of safe channels is doubly in force. I estimate that within the next forty-four hours a number of very strenuous efforts will be made to bump me off, and it won't be any good shutting your eyes to it. It won't be dear Edgar's fault if I haven't qualified for Kensal Green for Monday morning.'

Conway protested, but the Saint dealt shortly with that.

'You're a heap more useful to me working unknown,' he said. 'I can't help it if your natural vanity makes you kick at having to hide your light under a bushel. There's only need for one of us to prance about in the line of fire; and since they know me all round and upside down as it is, I've bagged the job. You don't have to worry, I've never played the corpse yet, and I don't feel like starting now!'

He was in the highest of spirits. The imminent prospect of violent and decisive action always got him that way. It made his blood jingle thrillingly through his veins, and set his eyes dancing recklessly, and made him bless the perfect training in which he had always kept his nerves and sinews. The fact that his life would be charged a five hundred per cent premium by any cautious insurance company failed to disturb his cheerfulness one iota. The Saint was made that way.

The 'needle' was a sensation that had never troubled his young life. For the next few hours there was nothing that he could do for the cause that he had made his own, and he therefore proposed to enjoy those hours on his own to the best of his ability. He was completely unperturbed by the thought of the hectic and perilous hours which were to follow the interlude of enjoyment—rather, the interlude gathered an added zest from the approach of zero hour.

He could not, of course, be sure that Hayn had discovered the abstraction of the letter; but that remained a distinct probability in spite of the Saint's excellent experiment in forgery. And even without the discovery, the cheque he had obtained, and Hayn's confidence in giving it, argued that there were going to be some very tense moments before the Monday morning. Simon Templar's guiding principle, which had brought him miraculously unscathed through innumerable desperate adventures in the past, was to assume the worst and take no chances; and in this instance subsequent events were to prove that pessimistic principle the greatest and most triumphant motto that had ever been invented.

The Saint lunched at his leisure, and then relaxed amusingly in a convenient cinema until half-past six. Then he returned home to dress, and was somewhat disappointed to find no reply to his cable waiting for him at his flat.

He dined and spent the night dancing at the Kit-Cat with the lovely and utterly delightful Patricia Holm, for the Saint was as human as the next man, if not more so, and Patricia Holm was his weakness then.

It was a warm evening, and they walked up Regent Street together, enjoying the fresh air. They were in Hanover Square, just by the corner of Brook Street, when the Saint saw the first thunder-cloud, and unceremoniously caught Patricia Holm by the shoulders and jerked her back round the corner and out of sight. An opportune taxi came prowling by at that moment, and the Saint had hailed it and bundled the girl in before she could say a word.

'I'm telling him to take you to the Savoy,' he said. 'You'll book a room there, and you'll stay there without putting even the tip of your pretty nose outside the door until I come and fetch you. You can assume that any message or messenger you receive is a fake. I don't think they saw you, but I'm not risking anything. Refuse to pay any attention to anything or anybody but myself in person. I'll be round Monday lunch-time, and if I'm not you can get hold of Inspector Teal and the lads and start raising Cain—but not before.'

The girl frowned suspiciously.

'Saint,' she said, in the dangerous tone that he knew and loved, 'you're trying to elbow me out again.'

'Old darling,' said the Saint quietly, 'I've stopped trying to elbow you out and make you live a safe and respectable life. I know it can't be done. You can come in on any game I take up, and I don't care if we have to fight the massed gangs of bad hats in New York, Chicago, Berlin and London. But there's just one kind of dirty work I'm not going to have you mixed up in, and this is it. Get me, old Pat? . . . Then s'long!'

He closed the door of the taxi, directed the driver, and watched it drive away. The Saint felt particularly anxious to keep on living at that moment. . . . And then the taxi's tail-light vanished round the corner, and Patricia Holm went with it; and the Saint turned with a sigh and an involuntary squaring of the shoulders, and swung into Brook Street.

He had observed the speedy-looking closed car that stood by the kerb directly outside the entrance to his flat, and he had seen the four men who stood in a little group on the pavement beside it conversing with all apparent innocence, and he had guessed the worst. The sum total of those deceptively innocuous fixtures and fittings seemed to him to bear the unmistakable hall-mark of the Hayn confederacy; for the Saint had what he called a nasty suspicious mind.

He strolled on at a leisurely pace. His left hand, in his trouser pocket, was sorting out the key of his front door; in his right hand he twirled the stick that in those days he never travelled without. His black felt hat was tilted over to the back of his head. In everything outward and visible he wore the mildest and most Saintly air of fashionable and elegant harmlessness, for the Saint was never so cool as when everything about him was flaming with red danger-signals. And as he drew near the little group he noticed that they fell suddenly silent, all turning in his direction.

The Saint was humming a little tune. It all looked too easy—nothing but a welcome and entertaining limbering-up for the big stuff that was to follow. He had slipped the front door key off the ring and transferred it to a side pocket of his jacket, where it would be more easily found in a hurry.

'Excuse me,' said the tallest of the four, taking a step forward to meet him.

'I'm afraid I can't excuse you, Snake,' said the Saint regretfully, and swayed back from his toes as Ganning struck at him with a loaded cane.

The Saint felt the wind of the blow caress his face, and then a lightning left uppercut came rocketing up from his knees to impact on the point of Snake's jaw, and Ganning was catapulted back into the arms of his attendant Boys.

Before any of them could recover from their surprise, Templar had leapt lightly up the steps to the portico, and had slipped the key into the lock. But as he turned and withdrew it, the other three came after him, leaving their chief to roll away into the gutter, and the Saint wheeled round to face them with the door swinging open behind him.

He held his stick in both hands, gave it a half-turn, and pulled. Part of the stick stripped away, and in the Saint's right hand a long slim blade of steel glinted in the dim light. His first thrust took the leading Boy through the shoulder, and the other two checked.

The Saint's white teeth flashed in an unpleasant smile.

'You're three very naughty children,' said the Saint, 'and I'm afraid I shall have to report you to your Sunday School teacher. Go a long way away, and don't come near me again for years and years!'

The rapier in his hand gleamed and whistled, and the two Boys recoiled with gasps of agony as the supple blade lashed across their faces. And then, as they sprang blindly to attack, the Saint streaked through the door and slammed it on them.

He turned the sword back into a stick, and went unhurriedly up the stairs to his flat, which was the first floor.

Looking down from the window, he saw the four men gathered together engaged in furious deliberation. One of them was mopping about inside his coat with an insanitary handkerchief, and the Snake was sagging weakly back against the side of the car holding his jaw. There were frequent gesticulations in the direction of the Saint's windows. After a time, the four men climbed into the car and drove away.

The brief affray had left the Saint completely unruffled. If you had taken his pulse then, you would have found it ticking over at not one beat above or below its normal 75. He sauntered across the room, switched on the lights, and put away his hat and stick, still humming gently to himself.

Propped up on the table, in a prominent position, was a cable envelope. Without any hurry, the Saint poured himself out a modest whisky, lighted a cigarette, and then fetched a small black notebook from its hiding-place behind a picture. Provided with these essentials, the Saint settled down on the edge of the table, ripped up the envelope, and extracted the flimsy.

'Elephant revoke,' the message began. A little farther on was the name Chandler. And near the end of the closely-written sheet were the words: 'Caterpillar diamonds ten spades four chicane hearts knave overcall.'

'Elephant' was the code word for Hayn; Chastel was 'Caterpillar'. 'Revoke' meant 'has changed his mind.' And the Saint could almost decode the sentence which included the words 'chicane' and 'overcall' at sight.

In his little black book, against the names of every card in the pack, and every bridge and poker term, were short sentences broadly applicable to almost any purpose about which his fellowship of free-booters might wish to communicate; and with the aid of this book, and a pencil, the Saint translated the message and wrote the interpretation between the lines. The information thus gleaned was in confirmation of what he had already deduced since purloining and reading Hayn's letter to Chastel, and the Saint was satisfied.

He opened his portable typewriter, and wrote a letter. It was the Saint's first official communiqué.

To Chief Inspector Teal
Criminal Investigation Department
New Scotland Yard
SW1


Sir,

I recommend to your notice Edgar Hayn, formerly Heine, of 27, Portugal Mansions, Hampstead. He is the man behind Danny's Club in Soho, and a well-timed raid on that establishment, with particular attention to a secret door in the panelling of the ground-

*floor lounge (which is opened by an electric control in Hayn's office in the basement) will give you an interesting insight into the methods of card-sharping de luxe.*

*More important than this, Hayn is also the man behind Laserre, the Regent Street perfumiers, the difference being that George Edward Braddon, the manager, is not a figurehead, but an active partner. A careful watch kept on future consignments received from the Continent by Laserre will provide adequate proof that the main reason for the existence of Laserre is cocaine. The drug is smuggled into England in cases of beauty preparations shipped by Hayn's foreign agents and quite openly declared—as dutiable products, that is. In every case, there will be found a number of boxes purporting to contain face powder, but actually containing cocaine.*

*Hayn's European agent is a French national of Levantine extraction named Henri Chastel. The enclosed letter, in Hayn's own handwriting, will be sufficient to prove that Hayn and Chastel were up to their necks in the whole European dope traffic.*

*Chastel, who is at present in Athens, will be dealt with by my agent there. I regret that I cannot hand him over to the regular processes of justice; but the complications of nationality and extradition treaties would, I fear, defeat this purpose.*

*By the time you receive this, I shall have obtained from Hayn the donation to charity which it is my intention to extract before passing him on to you for punishment, and you may at once take steps to secure his arrest. He has a private Moth aeroplane at Stag Lane Aerodrome, Edgware, which has for some time been kept in readiness against the necessity for either himself or one of his valued agents to make a hasty getaway. A watch kept on the aerodrome, therefore, should ensure the frustration of this scheme.*

*In the future, you may expect to hear from me at frequent intervals.*

*Assuring you of my best services at all times.*

*I remain, etc.,*

THE SAINT.

With this epistle, besides Hayn's letter, Templar enclosed his artistic trade-mark. So that there should be no possibility of tracing him, he had had the paper on which it was drawn specially obtained by Stannard from the gaming rooms at Danny's for the purpose.

He addressed the letter, and after a preliminary survey of the street to make sure that the Snake had not returned or sent deputies, he walked to a near-by pillar-box and posted it. It would not be delivered until Monday morning, and the Saint reckoned that that would give him all the time he needed.

Back in his flat, the Saint called up the third of his lieutenants, who was one Dicky Tremayne, and gave him instructions concerning the protection of Gwen Chandler. Finally he telephoned another number and called Jerry Stannard out of bed to receive orders.

At last he was satisfied that everything had been done that he had to do.

He went to the window, drew the curtains aside a cautious half-inch, and looked down again. A little farther up Brook Street, on the other side of the road, a blue Furillac sports saloon had drawn up by the kerb. The Saint smiled approvingly.

He turned out the lights in the sitting-room, went through to his bedroom, and began to undress. When he rolled up his left sleeve, there was visible a little leather sheath strapped to his forearm, and in this sheath he carried a beautifully-balanced knife— a mere six inches of razor-keen, leaf-shaped blade and three inches of carved ivory hilt. This was Anna, the Saint's favourite throwing-knife. The Saint could impale a flying champagne cork with Anna at twenty paces. He considered her present place of concealment a shade too risky, and transferred the sheath to the calf of his right leg. Finally, he made sure that his cigarette-case contained a supply of a peculiar kind of cigarette.

Outside, in the street, an ordinary bulb motor-horn hooted with a peculiar rhythm. It was a prearranged signal, and the Saint did not have to look out again to know that Ganning had returned.

And then, almost immediately, a bell rang, and the indicator in the kitchen showed him that it was the bell of the front door.

'They must think I'm a mug!' murmured the Saint.

But he was wrong—he had forgotten the fire-escape across the landing outside the door of his flat.

A moment later he heard, down the tiny hall, a dull crash and a sound of splintering wood. It connected up in his mind with the ringing of the front door bell, and he realised that he had no monopoly of prearranged signals. That ringing had been to tell the men who had entered at the back that their companions were ready at the front of the building. The Saint acknowledged that he had been trapped into underrating the organising ability of Edgar Hayn.

Unthinkingly, he had left his automatic in his bedroom. He went quickly out of the kitchen into the hall, and at the sound of his coming the men who had entered with the aid of a jemmy swung round. Hayn was one of them, and his pistol carried a silencer.

'Well, well, *well!*' drawled the Saint, whose mildness in times of crisis was phenomenal, and prudently raised his hands high above his head.

'You are going on a journey with me, Templar,' said Hayn. 'We are leaving at once, and I can give no date for your return. Kindly turn round and put your hands behind you.'

Templar obeyed. His wrists were bound, and the knots tightened by ungentle hands.

'Are you still so optimistic, Saint?' Hayn taunted him, testing the bonds.

'More than ever,' answered the Saint cheerfully. 'This is my idea of a night out—as the bishop said to the actress.'

Then they turned him round again.

'Take him downstairs,' said Hayn.

They went down in a silent procession, the Saint walking without resistance between two men. The front door was opened and a husky voice outside muttered: 'All clear. The flattie passed ten minutes ago, and his beat takes him half an hour.'

The Saint was passed on to the men outside and hustled across the pavement into the waiting car. Hayn and two other men followed him in; a third climbed up beside the driver. They moved off at once, heading west.

At the same time, a man rose from his cramped position on the floor of the Furillac that waited twenty yards away. He had been crouched down there for three-quarters of an hour, without a word of complaint for his discomfort, to make it appear that the car was empty, and the owner inside the house opposite which the car stood. The self-starter whirred under his foot as he sidled round behind the wheel, and the powerful engine woke to a throaty whisper.

The car in which the Saint rode with Hayn flashed up the street, gathering speed rapidly; and as it went by, the blue sports Furillac pulled out from the kerb and purred westwards at a discreet distance in its wake.

Roger Conway drove. The fit of his coat was spoiled by the solid bulge of the automatic in one pocket, and there was a stern set to his face which would have amazed those who only knew that amiable young man in his more flippant moods.

From his place in the leading car Simon Templar caught in the driving mirror a glimpse of the following Furillac, and smiled deep within himself.

## XI

Gwen Chandler lived in a microscopic flat in Bayswater, the rent of which was paid by the money left her by her father. She did the housekeeping herself, and, with this saving on a servant, there was enough left over from her income to feed her and give her a reasonably good time. None of the few relations she had ever paid much attention to her.

She would have been happy with her friends, and she had been, but all that had stopped abruptly when she had met and fallen in love, head over heels, with Jerry Stannard.

He was about twenty-three. She knew that, for the past two years, he had been leading a reckless life, spending most of his time and money in night clubs and usually going to bed at dawn. She also knew that his extravagant tastes had plunged him into debt, and that since the death of his father he had been accumulating bigger and bigger creditors; and she attributed these excesses to his friends, for the few people of his acquaintance she had met were of a type she detested. But her advice and enquiries had been answered with such a surliness that at least she had given up the contest and nursed her anxiety alone.

But a few days ago her fiancé's grumpiness had strangely vanished. Though he still seemed to keep the same Bohemian hours, he had been smiling and cheerful whenever she met him; and once, in a burst of good spirits, he had told her that his debts were paid off and he was making a fresh start. She could get no more out of him than this, however—her eager questions had made him abruptly taciturn, though his refusal to be cross-examined had been kindly enough. He would be able to tell her all about it one day, he said, and that day would not be long coming.

She knew that it was his practice to lie in bed late on Sunday mornings—but then, it was his practice to lie in bed late on all the other six days of the week. On this particular Sunday morning, therefore, when a ring on the front door bell had disturbed her from the task of preparing breakfast, she was surprised to find that he was her visitor.

He was trying to hide agitation, but she discerned that the agitation was not of the harassed kind.

'Got any breakfast for me?' he asked. 'I had to come along at this unearthly hour, because I don't know that I'll have another chance to see you all day. Make it snappy, because I've got an important appointment.'

'It'll be ready in a minute,' she told him.

He loafed about the kitchen, whistling, while she fried eggs and bacon, and sniffed the fragrant aroma appreciatively.

'It smells good,' he said, 'and I've got the appetite of a lifetime!'

She would have expected him to breakfast in a somewhat headachy silence; but he talked cheerfully.

'It must be years since you had a decent holiday,' he said. 'I think you deserve one, Gwen. What do you say if we get married by special licence and run over to Deauville next week?'

He laughed at her bewildered protests.

'I can afford it,' he assured her. 'I've paid off everyone I owe money to, and in a fortnight I'm getting a terribly sober job, starting at five pounds a week.'

'How did you get it?'

'A man called Simon Templar found it for me. Have you ever met him, by any chance?'

She shook her head, trying to find her voice.

'I'd do anything in the world for that man,' said Jerry.

'Tell me about it,' she stammered.

He told her—of his miraculous rescue by the Saint and the interview that followed it, of the Saint's persuasiveness, of the compact they had made. He also told her about Hayn; but although the recital was fairly inclusive, it did not include the machinations of the Maison Laserre. The Saint never believed in telling anybody everything, and even Hayn had secrets of his own.

The girl was amazed and shocked by the revelation of what Stannard's life had been and might still have been. But all other emotions were rapidly submerged in the great wave of relief which swept over her when she learned that Stannard had given his word to break away, and was even then working on the side of the man who had brought him back to a sense of honour—even if that honour worked in an illegal method.

'I suppose it's crooked, in one way,' Stannard admitted. 'They're out to get Hayn and his crowd into prison, but first they're swindling them on behalf of charity. I don't know how they propose to do it. On the other hand, though, the money they've got back for me from Hayn is no more than I lost in cash at his beastly club.'

'But why did Hayn let you keep on when he knew you'd got no money left?'

Stannard made a wry grimace.

'He wanted to be able to force me into his gang. I came in, too—but that was because Templar told me to agree to anything that would make Hayn pay me that three thousand pound cheque.'

She digested the information in a daze. The revelation of the enterprise in which Jerry Stannard was accompliced to the Saint did not shock her. Womanlike, she could see only the guilt of Hayn and the undoubted justice of the punishment. Only one thing made her afraid.

'If you were caught—'

'There'll be no fuss,' said Jerry. 'Templar's promised me that, and he's the kind of man you'd trust with anything. I haven't had to do anything criminal. And it'll all be over in a day or two. Templar rang me up last night.'

'What was it about?'

'That's what he wouldn't tell me. He told me to go to the Splendide at eleven and wait for a man called Tremayne, who may arrive any time up to one o'clock, and he'll tell me the rest. Tremayne's one of Templar's gang.'

Then she remembered Hayn's peculiar behaviour of the previous morning. The parcel she had brought away from Laserre still lay unopened on her dressing-table.

Jerry was interested in the account. Hayn's association with Laserre, as has been mentioned, was news to him. But he could make nothing of the story.

'I expect he's got some foolish crush on you,' he suggested. 'It's only the way you'd expect a man like that to behave. I'll speak to Templar about it when I see him.'

He left the dining-room as soon as he had finished breakfast, and was back in a moment with his hat.

'I must be going now,' he said, and took her in his arms. 'Gwen dear, with any luck it'll all be over very soon, and we'll be able to forget it. I'll be back as soon as ever I can.'

She kissed him.

'God bless you. And be careful, my darling!'

He kissed her again, and went out singing blithely. The world was very bright for Jerry Stannard that morning.

But the girl listened to the cheerful slamming of the door with a little frown, for she was troubled with misgivings. It had all seemed so easy at the time, in the optimistic way in which he had told her the story, but reviewed in cold blood it presented dangers and difficulties in legion.

She wished, for both their sakes, that he had been able to stay with her that day, and her fears were soon to be justified.

Half an hour after he had gone, when the breakfast things had been cleared away, and she was tidying herself to go out for a walk, there was a ring on the front door bell.

She answered it; and when she saw that it was Edgar Hayn, after what Jerry had been able to tell her, she would have closed the door in his face. But he had pushed through before she could collect her wits.

He led the way into the sitting-room, and she followed in mingled fear and anger. Then she saw that there were dark rings round his eyes, and his face was haggard.

'What is it?' she asked coldly.

'The police,' he said. 'They're after me—and they're after you, too. I came to warn you.'

'But why should they be after me?' she demanded blankly.

He was in a terrible state of nerves. His hands fidgeted with his umbrella all the time he was talking, and he did not meet her eyes.

'Drugs!' he said gruffly. 'Illicit drugs. Cocaine. You know what I mean! There's no harm in your knowing now—we're both in the same boat. They've been watching me, and they saw me with you yesterday and followed you.'

'But how do you know?'

'I've got friends at Scotland Yard,' he snapped. 'It's necessary. Policemen aren't incorruptible. But my man let me down—he never gave me the tip till the last moment. They're going to raid this flat and search it this morning.'

Her brain was like a maelstrom, but there was one solid fact to hold on to.

'There's nothing for them to find.'

'That's where you're wrong! Those things I gave you—one of our other boxes got mixed up in them. I've just found that out. That's why I'm here. There's six ounces of cocaine in this flat!'

She recoiled, wide-eyed. Her heart was thumping madly. It all seemed too impossible, too fantastic. . . . And yet it only bore out and amplified what Jerry had been able to tell her. She wondered frantically if the excuse of innocence would convince a jury. Hayn saw the thought cross her mind, and shattered it.

'You know how Jerry's lived,' he said. 'No one would believe that you weren't both in it!'

He looked out of the window. She was impelled to follow his example, and she was in time to see two broad-shouldered men in bowler hats entering the house.

'They're here!' said Hayn breathlessly. 'But there may be a chance. I recognised one of the men—he's a friend of mine. I may be able to square him.'

Outside, a bell rang.

Hayn was scribbling something on a card.

'Take this,' he muttered. 'My car's outside. If I can get them away from you for a moment, slip out and show the card to the chauffeur. I've got a house at Hurley. He'll take you there, and I'll come down later and discuss how we're going to get you and Jerry out of the country.'

The bell rang again, more urgently. Hayn thrust the pasteboard into the girl's hand.

'What're you hesitating for?' he snarled. 'Do you want to stand in the dock at the Old Bailey beside your lover?'

Hardly knowing what she did, she put the card in her bag.

'Go and open the door,' Hayn commanded. 'They'll break in if you don't.'

As he spoke, there came yet a more insistent ringing, and the flat echoed with the thunder of a knocker impatiently plied.

The girl obeyed, and at the same time she was thinking furiously. Jerry—or his chief, this man Templar—would know how to deal with the crisis; but for the moment there was no doubt that Hayn's plan was the only practicable one. Her one idea was to stay out of the hands of the police long enough to make sure that Jerry was safe, and to give them time to think out an escape from the trap in which Hayn had involved them.

The two broad-shouldered men entered without ceremony as she opened the door.

'I am Inspector Baker, of Scotland Yard,' said one of them formally, 'and I have a warrant to search your flat. You are suspected of being in illegal possession of a quantity of cocaine.'

The other man took her arm and led her into the sitting-room. Hayn came forward, frowning.

'I must protest about this,' he said. 'Miss Chandler is a friend of mine.'

'That's unlucky for you,' was the curt reply.

'I'll speak to Baker about this,' threatened Hayn hotly, and at that moment Baker came in.

He was carrying a small cardboard box with the label of Laserre. 'Poudre Laserre,' the label said; but the powder was white and crystalline.

'I think this is all we need,' said Baker, and stepped up to Gwen. 'I shall take you into custody on a charge—'

Hayn came between them.

'I should like a word with you first,' he said quietly.

Baker shrugged.

'If you must waste your time—'

'I'll take the risk,' said Hayn. 'In private, please.'

Baker jerked his thumb.

'Take Chandler into another room, Jones.'

'Jones had better stay,' interrupted Hayn. 'What I have to say concerns him also. If you will let Miss Chandler leave us for a minute, I will guarantee that she will not attempt to escape.'

There was some argument, but eventually Baker agreed. Hayn opened the door for the girl, and as she went out gave her an almost imperceptible nod. She went into her bedroom and picked up the telephone. It seemed an eternity before the paging system of the Splendide found Jerry. When he answered, she told him what had happened.

'I'm going to Hayn's house at Hurley,' she said. 'It's the only way to get out at the moment. But tell Tremayne when he comes, and get hold of Templar, and do something quickly!'

He was beginning to object, to ask questions, but there was no time for that, and she hung up the receiver. She had no means of knowing what Hayn's methods of 'squaring' were, or how long the negotiations might be expected to keep the detectives occupied.

She tiptoed down the hall, and opened the door.

From the window, Hayn, Baker and Jones watched her cross the pavement and enter the car.

'She's a peach, boss,' said Baker enviously.

'You've said all I wanted you to say,' Hayn returned shortly. 'But it's worked perfectly. If I'd simply tried to kidnap her, she'd have been twice as much nuisance. As it is, she'll be only too glad to do everything I say.'

Dick Tremayne arrived two minutes after Hayn's car had driven off. He should have been there over an hour earlier, but the cussedness of Fate had intervened to baulk one of the Saint's best-laid plans. A bus had skidded into Tremayne's car in Park Lane, the consequent policeman had delayed him interminably, the arrangements for the removal of his wrecked car had delayed him longer, and when at last he had got away in a taxi a series of traffic blocks had held him up at every crossing.

Now he had to act on his own initiative.

After a second's indecision, Tremayne realised that there was only one thing to do. If Hayn and his men were already in the flat, he must just blind in and hope for the best; if they had not yet arrived, no harm would be done.

He went straight into the building, and on the way up the stairs he met Hayn and two other men coming down. There was no time for deliberation or planning a move in advance.

'You're the birds I'm looking for,' Tremayne rapped, barring the way. 'I'm Inspector Hancock, of Scotland Yard, and I shall arrest you—'

So far he got before Hayn lashed out at him. Tremayne ducked, and the next instant there was an automatic in his hand.

'Back up those stairs to the flat you've just left,' he ordered, and the men retreated before the menace of his gun.

They stopped at the door of the flat, and he told Hayn to ring. They waited.

'There seems to be no reply,' said Hayn sardonically.

'Ring again,' Tremayne directed grimly.

Another minute passed.

'There can't really be anyone at home,' Hayn remarked.

Tremayne's eyes narrowed. It was something about the tone of Hayn's sneering voice. . . .

'You swine!' said Tremayne through his teeth. 'What have you done with her?'

'With whom?' inquired Hayn blandly.

'With Gwen Chandler!'

Tremayne could have bitten his tongue off as soon as the words were out of his mouth. That fatal, thoughtless impetuosity which was always letting him down! He saw Hayn suddenly go tense, and knew that it was useless to bluff further.

'So you're a Saint!' said Hayn softly.

'Yes, I am!' Tremayne let out recklessly. 'And if you scabs don't want me to plug you full of holes—'

He had been concentrating on Hayn, the leader, and so he had not noticed the other men edging nearer. A hand snatched at his gun, and wrenched. . . . As Dicky Tremayne swung his fist to the man's jaw, Hayn dodged behind him and struck at the back of his head with a little rubber truncheon. . . .

## XII

Jerry Stannard never understood how he managed to contain himself until one o'clock. Much less did he understand how he waited the further half-hour which he gave Dicky Tremayne for grace. Perhaps no other man in the world but Simon Templar could have inspired such a blind loyalty. The Saint was working some secret stratagem of his own, Stannard argued, and he had to meet Tremayne for reasons appertaining to the Saint's tactics. In any case, if Gwen had left when she telephoned, he could not have reached the flat before she had gone—and then he might only have blundered into the police trap that she had tried to save him from.

But it all connected up now—Gwen's Laserre story, and what Stannard himself knew of Hayn, and more that he suspected—and the visions that it took only a little imagination to conjure up were dreadful.

When half-past one came, and there was still no sign of Tremayne, the suspense became intolerable. Stannard went to the telephone, and fruitlessly searched London over the wires for Simon Templar. He could learn nothing from any of the clubs or hotels or restaurants which he might have frequented, nor was he any more successful with his flat. As for Dicky Tremayne, Stannard did not even know him by sight—he had simply been told to leave his card with a page, and Tremayne would ask for him.

It was after two o'clock by that time, and Tremayne had not arrived. He tried to ring up Gwen Chandler's flat, but after an interminable period of ringing, the exchange reported 'No reply.'

Jerry Stannard took a grip on himself. Perhaps that emergency was the making of him, the final consolidation of the process that had been started by the Saint, for Stannard had never been a fighting man. He had spoken the truth when he told Templar that his weakness was lack of 'guts'. But now he'd got to act. He didn't know nearly everything about Hayn, but he knew enough not to want to leave Gwen Chandler with that versatile gentleman for a moment longer than was absolutely necessary. But if anything was going to be done, Stannard had got to do it himself.

With a savage resolution, he telephoned to a garage where he was known. While he waited, he scribbled a note for Tremayne in which he described the whole series of events and stated his intentions. It was time wasted, but he was not to know that.

When the car arrived, he dismissed the mechanic who had brought it around, and drove to Hurley.

He knew how to handle cars—it was one of his few really useful accomplishments. And he sent the Buick blazing west with his foot flat down on the accelerator for practically every yard of the way.

Even so, it was nearly five o'clock when he arrived there, and then he realised a difficulty. There were a lot of houses at Hurley, and he had no idea where Hayn's house might be. Nor had the post office, nor the nearest police.

Stannard, in the circumstances, dared not press his enquiries too closely. The only hope left to him was that he might be able to glean some information from a villager, for he was forced to conclude that Hayn tenanted his country seat under another name. With this forlorn hope in view, he made his way to the Bell, and it was there that he met a surprising piece of good fortune.

As he pulled up outside, a man came out, and the man hailed him.

'Thank the Lord you're here,' said Roger Conway without preface. 'Come inside and have a drink.'

'Who are you?' asked a mystified Jerry Stannard.

'You don't know me, but I know you,' answered the man. 'I'm one of the Saint's haloes.'

He listened with a grave face to Stannard's story.

'There's been a hitch somewhere,' he said, when Jerry had finished. 'The Saint kept you in the dark because he was afraid your natural indignation might run away with you. Hayn had designs on your girl friend—you might have guessed that. The Saint pinched a letter of Hayn's to Chastel—Hayn's man abroad—

in which, among other things, Edgar described his plot for getting hold of Gwen. I suppose he wanted to be congratulated on his ingenuity. The rough idea was to plant some cocaine on Gwen in a present of powder and things from Laserre, fake a police raid, and pretend to square the police for her. Then, if she believed the police were after you and her—Hayn was banking on making her afraid that you were also involved—he thought it would be easy to get her away with him.'

'And the Saint wasn't doing anything to stop that?' demanded Jerry, white-lipped.

'Half a minute! The Saint couldn't attend to it himself, having other things to deal with, but he put Tremayne, the man you were supposed to have met at the Splendide, on the job. Tremayne was to get hold of Gwen before Hayn arrived, and tell her the story— we were assuming that you hadn't told her anything—and then bring her along to the Splendide and join up with you. The two of you were then to take Gwen down by car to the Saint's bungalow at Maidenhead and stay down there till the trouble had blown over.'

The boy was gnawing his finger-nails. He had had more time to think over the situation on the drive down, and Conway's story had only confirmed his own deductions. The vista of consequences that it opened up was appalling.

'What's the Saint been doing all this time?'

'That's another longish story,' Conway answered. 'He'd got Hayn's cheque for five figures, and that made the risk bigger. There was only one way to settle it.'

Roger Conway briefly described the Saint's employing of the four spoof Cherubs. 'After that was found out, Simon reckoned Hayn would think the gang business was all bluff, and he'd calculate there was only the Saint against himself. Therefore he wouldn't be afraid to try on his scheme about Gwen, even though he knew the Saint knew it, because the Saint was going to be out of the way. Anyhow, Hayn's choice was between getting rid of the Saint and going to prison, and we could guess which he'd try first. The

Saint had figured out that Hayn wouldn't simply try a quick assassination, because it wouldn't help him to be wanted for murder. There had got to be a murder, of course, but it would have to be well planned. So the Saint guessed he'd be kidnapped first and taken away to some quiet spot to be done in, and he decided to play stalking-horse. He did that because if Hayn were arrested, his cheques would be stopped automatically, so Hayn had got to be kept busy till tomorrow morning. I was watching outside the Saint's flat in a fast car last night, as I'd been detailed to do, in case of accidents. The Saint was going to make a fight of it. But they got him somehow—I saw him taken out to a car they had waiting—and I followed down here. Tremayne was to be waiting at the Splendide for a phone call from me at two o'clock. I've been trying to get him ever since, and you as well, touring London over the toll line, and it's cost a small fortune. And I didn't dare to go back to London, because of leaving the Saint here. That's why I'm damned glad you've turned up.'

'But why haven't you told the police?'

'Simon'd never forgive me. He's out to make the Saint the terror of the Underworld, and he won't do that by simply giving information to Scotland Yard. The idea of the gang is to punish people suitably before handing them over to the law, and our success over Hayn depends on sending five figures of his money to charity. I know it's a terrible risk. The Saint may have been killed already. But he knew what he was doing. We were ordered not to interfere and the Saint's the head man in this show.'

Stannard sprang up.

'But Hayn's got Gwen!' he half sobbed. 'Roger, we can't hang about, not for anything, while Gwen's—'

'We aren't hanging about any longer,' said Roger quietly.

His hand fell with a firm grip on Jerry Stannard's arm, and the youngster steadied up. Conway led him to the window of the smokeroom, and pointed.

'You can just see the roof of the house, over there,' he said. 'Since last night, Hayn's gone back to London, and his car came by again about two hours ago. I couldn't see who was in it, but it must have been Gwen. Now—'

He broke off suddenly. In the silence, the drone of a powerful car could be heard approaching. Then the car itself whirled by at speed, but it did not pass too quickly for Roger Conway to glimpse the men who rode in it.

'Hayn and Braddon in the back with Dicky Tremayne between them!' he said tensely.

He was in time to catch Stannard by the arm as the boy broke away wildly.

'What the blazes are you stampeding for?' he snapped. 'Do you want to go charging madly in and let Hayn rope you in, too?'

'We can't wait!' Stannard panted, struggling.

Conway thrust him roughly into a chair and stood over him. The boy was as helpless as a child in Conway's hands.

'You keep your head and listen to me!' Roger commanded sharply. 'We'll have another drink and tackle this sensibly. And I'm going to see that you wolf a couple of sandwiches before you do anything. You've been in a panic for hours, with no lunch, and you look about all in. I want you to be useful.'

'If we phone the police—'

'Nothing doing!'

Roger Conway's contradiction ripped out almost automatically, for he was not the Saint's right-hand man for nothing. He had learnt the secret of the perfect lieutenant, which is the secret of, in any emergency, divining at once what your superior officer would want you to do. It was no use simply skinning out any old how—the emergency had got to be dealt with in a way that would dovetail in with the Saint's general plan of campaign.

'The police are our last resort,' he said. 'We'll see if the two of us can't fix this alone. Leave this to me.'

He ordered a brace of stiff whiskies and a pile of sandwiches, and while these were being brought he wrote a letter which he sealed. Then he went in search of the proprietor, whom he knew of old, and gave him the letter.

'If I'm not here to claim that in two hours,' he said, 'I want you to open it and telephone what's inside to Scotland Yard. Will you do that for me, as a great favour, and ask no questions?'

The landlord agreed, somewhat perplexedly.

'Is it a joke?' he asked good-humouredly.

'It may grow into one,' Roger Conway replied. 'But I give you my word of honour that if I'm not back at eight o'clock, and that message isn't opened and phoned punctually, the consequences may include some of the most unfunny things that ever happened!'

## XIII

The Saint had slept. As soon as they had arrived at the house at Hurley (he knew it was Hurley, for he had travelled that road many times over the course of several summers) he had been pushed into a bare-furnished bedroom and left to his own devices. These were not numerous, for the ropes had not been taken off his wrists.

A short tour of inspection of the room had shown that, in the circumstances, it formed an effective prison. The window, besides being shuttered, was closely barred; the door was of three-inch oak, and the key had been taken away after it had been locked. For weapons with which to attack either window or door there was the choice of a light table, a wooden chair, or a bedpost. The Saint might have employed any of these, after cutting himself free—for they had quite overlooked, in the search to which he had been subjected, the little knife strapped to his calf under his sock—but he judged that the time was not yet ripe for any such drastic action. Besides, he was tired; he saw strenuous times ahead of him, and he believed in husbanding his energies. Therefore, he had settled down on the bed for a good night's rest, making himself as comfortable as a man can when his hands are tied behind his back, and it had not been long before he had fallen into an untroubled sleep. It had struck him, drowsily, as being the most natural thing to do.

Glints of sunlight were stabbing through the interstices of the shutters when he was awakened by the sound of his door opening. He rolled over, opening one eye, and saw two men enter. One carried a tray of food, and the other carried a club. This concession to the respect in which the gang held him, even when bound and helpless, afforded the Saint infinite amusement.

'This is sweet of you,' he said; and indeed he thought it was, for he had not expected such a consideration, and he was feeling hungry. 'But, my angels of mercy,' he said, 'I can't eat like this.'

They sat him down in a chair and tied his ankles to the legs of it, and then the cords were taken off his wrists and he was able to stretch his cramped arms. They watched him eat, standing by the door, and the cheerful comments with which he sought to enliven the meal went unanswered. But a request for the time evoked the surly information that it was past one o'clock.

When he had finished, one of the men fastened his hands again, while the other stood by with his bludgeon at the ready. Then they untied his ankles and left him, taking the tray with them.

The searchers had also left him his cigarette-case and matches, and with some agility and a system of extraordinary contortions the Saint managed to get a cigarette into his mouth and light it. This feat of double-jointed juggling kept him entertained for about twenty minutes; but as the afternoon wore on he developed, in practice, a positively brilliant dexterity. He had nothing else to do.

His chief feeling was one of boredom, and he soon ceased to find any enjoyment in wondering how Dick Tremayne had fared in Bayswater. By five o'clock he was yawning almost continuously, having thought out seventeen original and foolproof methods of swindling swindlers without coming within reach of the law, and this and similar exercises of ingenuity were giving him no more kick at all.

He would have been a lot more comfortable if his hands had not been bound, but he decided not to release himself until there was good cause for it. The Saint knew the tactical advantage of keeping a card up his sleeve.

The room, without any noticeable means of ventilation, was growing hotter and stuffier, and the cigarettes he was smoking were not improving matters. Regretfully, the Saint resigned himself to giving up that pleasure, and composed himself on the bed again. Some time before, he had heard a car humming up the short drive, and he was hazily looking forward to Hayn's return and the renewed interest that it would bring. But the heaviness of the atmosphere did not conduce to mental alertness. The Saint found himself dozing. . . .

For the second time, it was the sound of his door opening that roused him, and he blinked his eyes open with a sigh.

It was Edgar Hayn who came in. Physically he was in much worse case than the Saint, for he had had no sleep at all since the Friday night, and his mind had been much less care-free. His tiredness showed in the pallor of his face and the bruise-like puffiness of his eyes, but he had the air of one who feels himself the master of a situation.

'Evening,' murmured Simon politely.

Hayn came over to the bedside, his lips drawn back in an unlovely smile.

'Still feeling bumptious, Templar?' he asked.

'Ain't misbehavin',' answered the Saint winningly. 'I'm savin' my love for you.'

The man who had held the bludgeon at lunch stood in the doorway. Hayn stood aside and beckoned him in.

'There are some friends of yours downstairs,' said Hayn. 'I should like to have you all together.'

'I should be charmed to oblige you—as the actress said to the bishop,' replied the Saint.

And he wondered whom Hayn could be referring to, but he showed nothing of the chill of uneasiness that had leaped at him for an instant like an Arctic wind.

He was not left long in doubt.

The bludgeon merchant jerked him to his feet and marched him down the corridor and down the stairs, Hayn bringing up the rear. The door of a room opening off the hall stood ajar, and from within came a murmur of voices which faded into stillness as their footsteps were heard approaching. Then the door was kicked wide, and the Saint was thrust into the room.

Gwen Chandler was there—he saw her at once. There were also three men whom he knew, and one of them was a dishevelled Dicky Tremayne.

Hayn closed the door and came into the centre of the room.

'Now, what about it, Templar?' he said.

'What, indeed?' echoed the Saint.

His lazy eyes shifted over the assembled company.

'Greetings, Herr Braddon,' he murmured. 'Hullo, Snake. . . . Great heavens, Snake!—what's the matter with your face?'

'What's the matter with my face?' Ganning snarled.

'Everything, honeybunch,' drawled the Saint. 'I was forgetting. You were born like that.'

Ganning came close, his eyes puckered with fury.

'I owe you something,' he grunted, and let fly with both fists.

The Saint slipped the blows, and landed a shattering kick to the Snake's shins. Then Braddon interposed a foot between the Saint's legs, and as Simon went down Ganning loosed off with both feet. . . .

'That'll do for the present,' Hayn cut in at last.

He took Templar by the collar and yanked him into a sitting position on a chair.

'You filthy blots!' Tremayne was raving, with the veins standing out purply on his forehead. 'You warts—you flaming, verminous . . .'

It was Braddon who silenced him, with a couple of vicious, backhand blows across the mouth. And Dick Tremayne, bound hand and foot, wrestled impotently with ropes that he could not shift.

'We'll hear the Haynski speech,' Simon interrupted. 'Shut up, Dicky! We don't mind, but it isn't nice for Gwen to have to watch!'

He looked across at the girl, fighting sobbingly in Hayn's hold.

'It's all right, Gwen, old thing,' he said. 'Keep smiling, for Jerry's sake. We don't worry about anything that these dregs can do. Don't let them see they can hurt you!'

Hayn passed the girl over to Braddon and Ganning, and went over to the Saint's chair.

'I'm going to ask you one or two questions, Templar,' he said. 'If you don't want to let the Snake have another go at you, you'll answer them truthfully.'

'Pleasure,' said the Saint briefly. 'George Washington was the idol of my childhood.'

Everything he had planned had suffered a sudden reversal. Gwen Chandler had been caught, and so had Dicky. Their only hope was in Roger Conway—and how long would it be before he discovered the disaster and got busy? . . . The Saint made up his mind.

'How many of you are there?'

'Seventy-six,' said the Saint. 'Two from five—just like when you were at Borstal.'

There was no one behind him. He had got his legs well back under the chair. His arms were also reaching back, and he was edging his little knife out of its sheath.

'You can save the rest of your questions,' he said. 'I'll tell you something. You'll never get away with this. You think you're going to find out all about my organisation, the plans I've made, whether I've arranged for a squeal to the police. Then you'll counter-move accordingly. Hold the line while I laugh!'

'I don't think so,' said Hayn.

'Then you don't think as much as a weevil with sleepy sickness,' said the Saint equably. 'You must think I was born yesterday! Listen, sweetheart! Last night I posted a little story to Inspector Teal, which he'll get Monday morning. That letter's in the post now— and nothing will stop it—and the letter to friend Henri I enclosed with it will make sure the dicks pay a lot of attention to the rest of the things I had to say. You haven't an earthly, Edgarvitch!'

Hayn stepped back as if he had received a blow, and his face was horribly ashen. The Saint had never imagined that he would cause such a sensation.

'I told you he'd squeak!' Braddon was raging. 'You fool—I told you!'

'I told him, too,' said the Saint. 'Oh, Edgar—why didn't you believe your Uncle Simon?'

Hayn came erect, his eyes blazing. He swung round on Braddon.

'Be quiet, you puppy!' he commanded harshly. 'We've all come to this—that's why we've got those aeroplanes. We leave tonight, and Teal can look for us tomorrow as long as he likes.'

He turned on the Saint.

'You'll come with us—you and your friend. You will not be strapped in. Somewhere in mid-Channel we shall loop the loop. You understand . . . Templar; you've undone years of work, and I'm going to make you pay for it! I shall escape, and after a time, I shall be able to come back and start again. But you—'

'I shall be flitting through Paradise, with a halo round my hat,' murmured the Saint. 'What a pleasant thought!'

And as he spoke he felt his little knife biting into the cords on his wrists.

'We lose everything we've got,' Braddon babbled.

'Including your liberty,' said the Saint softly, and the knife was going through his ropes like a wire through cheese.

They all looked at him. Something in the way he had spoken those three words, something in the taut purposefulness of his body, some strange power of personality, held them spellbound. Bound and at their mercy, for all they knew, an unarmed man, he was yet able to dominate them. There was hatred and murder flaring in their eyes, and yet for a space he was able to hold them on a curb and compel them to listen.

'I will tell you why you have lost, Hayn,' said the Saint, speaking in the same, gentle, leisured tones that nevertheless quelled them as definitely as if he had backed them up with a gun. 'You made the mistake of kidding yourself that when I told you I was going to put you in prison, I was bluffing. You were sure that I'd never throw away such an opening for unlimited blackmail. Your miserable warped temperament couldn't conceive the idea of a man doing and risking all that I did and risked for nothing but an ideal. You judged me by your own crooked standards. That's where you crashed, because I'm not a crook. But I'm going to make crooks go in fear of me. You and your kind aren't scared enough of the police. You've got used to them—you call them by their first names and swap cigarettes with them when they arrest you—it's become a game to you, with prison as a forfeit for a mistake, and bullbaiting's just the same as tiddly-winks, in your lives. But I'm going to give you something new to fear—the Unknown. You'll rave about us in the dock, and all the world will hear. And when we have finished with you, you will go to prison, and you will be an example to make others afraid. But you will tell the police that you cannot describe us, because there are still three left whom you do not know; and if we two came to any harm through you, the other three would deal with you, and they would not deal gently. You understand? You will never dare to speak. . . .'

'And do you think you will ever be able to speak, Templar?' asked Hayn in a quivering voice, and his right hand was leaping to his hip pocket.

And the Saint chuckled, a low triumphant murmur of a laugh.

'I'm sure of it!' he said, and stood up with the cords falling from his wrists.

The little throwing-knife flashed across the room like a chip of flying quicksilver, and Hayn, with his automatic half out of his pocket, felt a pain like the searing of a hot iron across his knuckles, and all the strength went out of his fingers.

Braddon was drawing at that moment, but the Saint was swift. He had Edgar Hayn in a grip of steel, and Hayn's body was between the Saint and Braddon.

'Get behind him, Snake!' Braddon shrilled; but as Ganning moved to obey, the Saint reached a corner.

'Aim at the girl, you fool!' Hayn gasped, with the Saint's hand tightening on his throat.

The Saint held Hayn with one hand only, but the strength of that hold was incredible. With the other hand, he was fumbling with his cigarette-case.

Braddon had turned his gun into Gwen Chandler's face, while Ganning pinioned her arms. And the Saint had a cigarette in his mouth and was striking a match with one hand.

'Now do you surrender?' Braddon menaced.

'Like Hell I do!' cried the Saint.

His match touched the end of his cigarette, and in the same movement he threw the cigarette far from him. It made an explosive hiss like a launched rocket, and in a second everything was blotted out in a swirl of impenetrable fog.

Templar pushed Hayn away into the opacity. He knew to a fraction of a square inch where his knife had fallen after it had severed the tendons of Hayn's hand, and he dived for it. He bumped against Tremayne's chair, and cut him free in four quick slashes.

Came, from the direction of the window, the sound of smashing glass. A shadow showed momentarily through the mist.

'Gwen!'

It was Jerry Stannard's agonised voice. The girl answered him. They sought each other in the obscurity.

A sudden draught parted the wreathing clouds of the Saint's rapid-action smoke-screen. Stannard, with the girl in his arms, saw that the door was open. The Saint's unmistakable silhouette loomed in the oblong of light.

'Very, very efficient, my Roger,' said the Saint.

'You can always leave these little things to me,' said Mr Conway modestly, leaning against the front door, with Edgar Hayn, Braddon, and Snake Ganning herded into a corner of the hall at the unfriendly end of his automatic.

## XIV

They took the three men into a room where there was no smoke.

'It was my fiancée,' pleaded Jerry Stannard.

'That's so,' said the Saint tolerantly. 'Dicky, you'll have to be content with Braddon. After all, he sloshed you when your hands were tied. But nobody's going to come between the Snake and this child!'

It lasted half an hour all told, and then they gathered up the three components of the mess and trussed them very securely into chairs.

'There were two other men,' said the Saint hopefully, wrapping his handkerchief round a skinned set of knuckles.

'I stuck them up, and Jerry dotted them with a spanner,' said Conway. 'We locked them in a room upstairs.'

The Saint sighed.

'I suppose we'll have to leave them,' he said. 'Personally, I feel I've been done. These guys are rotten poor fighters when it comes to a showdown.'

Then Conway remembered the message he had left in the landlord's hands at the Bell, and they piled hurriedly into the car in which Conway and Stannard had driven up. They retrieved the message, tidied themselves, and dined.

'I think we can call it a day,' said the Saint comfortably, when the coffee was on the table. 'The cheque will be cashed on Monday morning, and the proceeds will be registered to the London Hospital, as arranged—less our ten per cent commission, which I don't mind saying I think we've earned. I think I shall enclose one of my celebrated self-portraits—a case like this ought to finish in a worthily dramatic manner, and that opportunity's too good to miss.'

He stretched himself luxuriously, and lighted a fresh cigarette which did not explode.

'Before I go to bed tonight,' he said, 'I'll drop a line to old Teal and tell him where to look for our friends. I'm afraid they'll have a hungry and uncomfortable night, but I can't help that. And now, my infants, I suggest that we adjourn to London.'

They exchanged drinks and felicitations with the lord and master of the Bell, and it should stand to the eternal credit of that amiable gentleman that not by the twitch of an eyebrow did he signify any surprise at the somewhat battered appearance of two of the party. Then they went out to their cars.

'Who's coming back with me?' asked Tremayne.

'I'm going back without you, laddie,' said Jerry Stannard. 'Gwen's coming with me!'

They cheered the Buick out of sight; and then the Saint climbed into the back of the Furillac and settled himself at his ease.

'Mr Conway will drive,' he said. 'Deprived of my charming conversation, you will ponder over the fact that our friend is undoubtedly for it. You may also rehearse the song which I've just composed for us to sing at his funeral—I mean wedding. It's about a wicked young lover named Jerry, who had methods decidedly merry. When the party got rough, was he smart with his stuff? Oh, very! Oh, very! . . . Oh, very! . . . Take me to the Savoy, Roger. I have a date. . . . Night-night, dear old bacteria!'

# THE POLICEMAN WITH WINGS

## I

By this time all the world has heard of the Saint. It has been estimated (by those industrious gentlemen who estimate these things) that if all the columns that the newspapers have devoted to the Saint were placed end to end, they would reach from the south-east corner of the Woolworth Building, New York, to a point seventeen inches west of the commissionaire outside the Berkeley Street entrance of the May Fair Hotel, London—which, as was remarked at the time, only goes to prove that the bridging of the gulf between rich and poor can be materially helped by the vigorous efforts of a democratic Press.

It was not to be hoped, however, that the Saint could remain for ever under the shroud of anonymity in which he had made his *début*. Policemen, in spite of the libels of the mystery novelist, possess a certain amount of intelligence, and a large amount of plodding patience; and the Saint's campaign was a definite challenge. The actual episode in which Chief Inspector Teal began to suspect that Simon Templar might know more about the Saint than he told the world, is, as it happens, of no absorbing interest for the purposes of this chronicle; but it may be recorded that the Saint returned one day from one of his frequent trips abroad, and found reason to believe that unauthorised persons had entered his apartment while he was away.

The detectives who had discovered the flat in Brook Street had searched it thoroughly, as was their duty. They had found nothing, but the traces of their passage were everywhere visible.

'They might have tidied the place up after them,' remarked the Saint mildly, standing at gaze before the disorder.

Orace, the Saint's devoted servant, ran his thumb through the accumulated dust on the mantelpiece, and made strangled snuffling noises of disgust.

He was still struggling ferociously with the mess when they went to bed that night. The Saint, wandering towards his bath the next morning, caught through an open door a glimpse of a sitting-room become magically clean and shipshape, and was moved to investigate further. Eventually he came upon Orace frying eggs in the kitchen.

'I see you've been spring-cleaning,' he said.

'Yus,' said Orace, savagely. 'Brekfuss narf a minnit.'

'Good scout,' drawled the Saint, and drifted on.

The Saint refused to behave like a hunted man. He went out and about his lawful occasions, and in consequence it was five days before the police noticed his return. There are times when bare-faced effrontery is the most impenetrable disguise.

But it could not last. There are constables, and they patrol beats, and not the least of their duties is to embody in their reports an account of anything unusual they may notice. There was a night when the Saint, looking out from behind his curtains, saw two men in bowler hats staring up long and earnestly at the lighted windows, which should have been in deserted darkness; and then he knew that it would not be long before the Law reached out an enquiring hand towards him. But he said nothing at the time.

Roger Conway came in at lunch-time the following afternoon to find the Saint still in his dressing-gown. Simon Templar was smoking a thin cigar, with his feet on the sill of the open window, and Roger knew at once, from the extraordinary saintliness of his expression, that something had happened.

'Teal's been here,' said Roger, after a hawk-eyed glance round the room.

'Claud Eustace himself,' murmured the Saint, admiringly. 'How did you guess?'

'There's a discarded piece of chewing-gum in that ashtray, and that scrap of pink paper in the fireplace must once have enclosed the piece he went out with. Giving my well-known impersonation of Sherlock Holmes—'

Simon nodded.

'You look dangerously like developing an intelligence, my Roger. Yes, Teal has called. I knew he was coming, because he told me so himself.'

'Liar!' said Mr Conway, pleasantly.

'He told me over the telephone,' said the Saint calmly. 'I rang up and asked him, and he told me.'

'He didn't!'

'He did. I said I was Barney Malone of the *Clarion*, and I told him we'd heard a rumour that he was on the Saint's trail, and asked him if he could say anything about it. "Not yet," says Teal, who's pally with Barney, "but I'm going to see about it this morning. Come down after lunch and get the story." "Right," I said. And there we were.'

'You have a nerve, Simon.'

'Not so bad, sonny boy. I then proceeded to ring up my solicitors, and Uncle Elias whiffled round and held my hand while we waited for the Law, which arrived about eleven-thirty. There was some argument, and then Teal went home. I hope he doesn't wait too long for Barney,' added the Saint, piously.

Roger Conway sat down and searched for cigarettes.

'He went like a lamb?'

'Like a lamb. In all our exploits, you see, his case depends on the evidence of the injured parties—and none of the said I.P.s seem anxious to prosecute. I simply told Teal to get on with it and try to prove something—the innocent-citizen-falsely-accused stunt. Of course, he bluffed for all he was worth, but Uncle Elias and I made him see that his chance wasn't too hopeful.'

'So you parted like brothers?'

The Saint shrugged.

'I should call it an armed truce. He asked me if I was going on, and I said I hadn't anything to go on with. I said we were so good that the light of virtue glowing within us made us faintly luminous in the dark.'

'And that was that?'

'He sailed out on a note of warning, very grim and stern and law-abiding. For, of course, he didn't believe me. And yet I won't swear that he winked. Uncle Elias didn't see it, anyway. But I'm afraid Uncle Elias was rather shocked by the whole palaver. However, if you reach out and ring the bell twice, Orace will understand. . . .'

They solemnly toasted each other over the tankards which came in answer to the summons; and then Roger Conway spoke.

'There's a problem which might interest us—'

'Professionally?'

'It's quite possible. It starts with a girl I met in Torquay last summer.'

Simon sighed.

'You insist on meeting girls in these outlandish places,' he complained. 'Now, if you'd only met her in Gotham, for instance, I should have had a song all ready for you. When you came in, I was just perfecting a little song about a wild woman of Gotham, who made love to young men and then shot 'em—till she started to shoot at a hard-hearted brute, who just grabbed her and walloped her for all he was worth. But don't let that cramp your style. You were saying?'

'This girl I met in Torquay—'

'Did she think that love ought to be free?'

'My dear Mr Templar—'

'I was recalling,' said the Saint impenitently, 'another girl you met in Torquay who thought that love ought to be free. She clung to this view till she chanced to meet you—Oh, send back my bonny to me! But you were telling me about someone else.'

'She has an uncle—'

'Impossible!'

'She has an uncle, and she lives with the uncle, and the uncle has a house at Newton.'

'They have an abbot there, haven't they?'

'Newton Abbot is the place. The uncle built this house nearly seven years ago. He intended to settle down and spend the rest of his life there—and now a man insists on buying the place.'

'Insists?'

'It comes to something like that. This man—'

'Let's have it clear, sonny boy. What's uncle's name?'

'Sebastian Aldo.'

'Then he must be rich.'

'He's happy.'

'And Whiskers—the bloke who wants to buy the house?'

'We don't know his name. He sent his secretary, an oily excrescence called Gilbert Neave.'

The Saint settled deeper in his armchair.

'And the story?' he prompted.

'There's very little of it—or there was until today. Uncle refused to sell. Neave bid more and more—he went up to twenty thousand pounds, I believe—and he was so insistent that finally Uncle lost his temper and kicked him out.'

'And?'

'Three days later, Uncle was pottering about the garden when his hat flew off. When he picked it up there was a bullet hole through it. A week later he was out in his car and the steering came unstuck. He'd have been killed if he'd been driving fast. A week after that everybody in the house was mysteriously taken ill, and the analysts found arsenic in the milk. A couple of days later, Neave 'phoned up and asked if Uncle had changed his mind about selling.'

'Uncle Sebastian still give him the razz?'

'Betty says he fused the telephone wires for miles around.'

'Who's Betty?'

'His niece—the girl I met in Torquay.'

'I see. A lovely young lady named Betty, made such noises when eating spaghetti, it played absolute hell with the *maître d'hôtel*, and made sensitive waiters quite—er—self-conscious. And when did they bury Uncle?'

Roger Conway was smoothing out the evening paper which he had bought at twelve-thirty.

'Betty told me all this in her letters while we were down at Maidenhead,' he said. 'Now you can read the sequel.'

Simon took the paper.

Roger indicated the column, but that was hardly necessary. There was one heading that caught the eye—that could not have helped being the first thing to catch the eye of a man like the Saint. For by that single title an inspired sub-editor had made a sensation out of a simple mystery.

'The Policeman With Wings,' said the heading; and the point of the story was that a policeman had called on a certain Mr Sebastian Aldo three days before, a perfectly ordinary and wingless policeman, according to the testimony of the housekeeper who admitted him, but a most unusual policeman according to the testimony of subsequent events. For, after a short interview, Mr Aldo had left his house with the policeman in his car, saying that he would be back to lunch; but neither the policeman nor Mr Aldo had been heard of since, and the police of all the surrounding districts, appealed to, declared that none of their policemen were missing and certainly none had been sent to see Mr Aldo.

'I observe,' said the Saint thoughtfully, 'that Miss Aldo was in Ostend at the time, and has just returned upon hearing of her uncle's disappearance. So the paper says.'

'She told me she was going to Ostend for a week in August to stay with friends. Have you any ideas?'

'Millions,' said the Saint.

The door opened, and a head came in.

'Lunch narf a minnit,' said the head, and went out again.

The Saint rose.

'Millions of ideas, Roger, old dear,' he murmured. 'But none of them, at the moment, tells me why anyone should be so absorbingly interested in one particular house at Newton Abbot. On the other hand, if you like to sing softly to me while I dress, I may produce something brilliant over the cocktail you will be shaking up while you sing.'

He vanished, and was back again in an amazingly short space

of time to collect the Martini which Conway was decanting from the shaker as Orace came in with the soup. The Saint's speed of dressing was an unending source of envious admiration to his friends.

'We are interested,' said the Saint, holding his glass up to the light, and inspecting it with an appreciative eye, 'and we have produced a brilliant idea.'

'What's that?'

'After lunch, we will go out into the wide world and buy a nice-looking car, and in the car we will travel down to Newton Abbot this very afternoon.'

'Arriving in time to have dinner with Betty.'

'If you insist.'

'Any objections?'

'Only that, knowing you, I feel that for her sake—'

'She's a nice girl,' said Roger, reminiscently.

'She hasn't known you long,' said the Saint.

'Cheer-ho!' said Conway.

'Honk, honk!' said the Saint.

They drank.

'Further to mine of even date,' said the Saint, 'when we've bought this car, we will continue on our way through the wide world, and seek a place where we can buy you a policeman's uniform. You can grow the wings yourself.'

Roger stared.

'Uniform!' he repeated feebly. 'Wings?'

'As a Policeman with Wings,' said the Saint comfortably, 'I think you'd be a distinct hit. That's part of my brilliant idea.'

And the Saint grinned, hands on hips, tall and fresh and immaculate in grey. His dark hair was at its sleekest perfection, his clear blue eyes danced, his brown face was alight with an absurdly boyish and hell-for-leather enthusiasm.

The Saint in those days had moods in which he was unwontedly sober. He was then nearly twenty-eight, and in those twenty-eight years of his life he had seen more than most men would see in eighty years, and done more than they would have done in a hundred and eighty. And yet he had not fulfilled himself. He was then only upon the threshold of his destiny; but it seemed sometimes that he glimpsed wider visions through the opening door ahead. But this was not so much a dulling of his impetuous energy as the acquiring of a more solid foundation for it. He remained the Saint—the flippant dandy with the heart of a crusader, a fighter who laughed as he fought, the reckless, smiling swashbuckler, the inspired and beloved leader of men, the man born with the sound of trumpets in his ears. And the others followed him.

He was impatient through that lunch, but he made the meal. And after it he lighted a cigarette and set it canting up between smiling lips, and leapt to his feet as if he could contain himself no longer.

'Let's go!' cried the Saint.

He clapped Roger Conway on the shoulder, and so they went out arm in arm. Roger Conway would have followed in the same spirit if the Saint had announced that their objective was the Senate House, Timbuctoo.

And so they went.

II

If Simon Templar had been a failure, he would have been spoken of pityingly as a man born out of his time. The truth was that in all the fields of modern endeavour—except the crazy driving of high-powered cars, the suicidal stunting of aeroplanes, and the slick handling of boxing gloves—the Saint was cheerfully useless. Golf bored him. He played tennis with vigour and shameless inefficiency, erratically scrambling through weeks of rabbitry to occasional flashes of a positively Tildenesque *maestria*. He was always ready to make his duck or bowl his wides in any cricket game that happened to be going; and his prowess at baseball, on an expedition which he once made to America, brought tears to the eyes of all beholders.

But put a fencing foil in Simon Templar's hand; throw him into dangerous swimming water; invite him to slither up a tree or the side of a house; set him on the wildest horse that ever bucked; ask him to throw a knife into a visiting card or shoot the three leaves out of an ace of clubs at twenty paces; suggest that he couldn't put an arrow through a greengage held between your finger and thumb at the same range—and then you'd see something to tell your grand-children.

Of course he was born out of his time. He ought to have lived in any age but the present—any age in which his uncanny flair for all such medieval accomplishments would have brought him to the front of his fellows.

And yet you didn't notice the anachronism, because he wasn't a failure. He made for himself a world fit for himself to live in.

It is truly said that adventures are to the adventurous. Simon had about him that indefinable atmosphere of romance and adventurousness which is given to some favoured men in every age, and it attracted adventure as inevitably as a magnet attracts iron filings.

But it will be left for future generations to decide how much of the adventure which he found was made by himself. For adventure can only be born of the conflict of two adventurous men: the greatest adventurer would be baffled if he came into conflict with a dullard, and a dullard would find no adventure in meeting the greatest adventurer that ever stepped. The Saint found the seeds of adventure everywhere around him. It was the Saint himself who saw the budding of the seed before anyone else would have noticed it, and who brought the thing to a full flowering glory with the loving care of a fanatic.

With a typical genius the Saint had already touched the story of the Policeman with Wings.

'A mug,' said the Saint kindly, as he pushed the Desurio towards Devonshire with the speedometer needle off the map—'a mug, such as yourself, for instance, my beautiful,' said the Saint kindly, 'wouldn't have thought of anything like that.'

'He wouldn't,' agreed Roger fervently, as the Saint shot the Desurio between two cars with the width of a matchbox to spare on either side.

'A mug,' said the Saint kindly, 'would have thought that it was quite sufficient either (*a*) to remove Betty to the comparative safety of his maiden aunt's home at Stratford—'

'Upon the Avon.'

'Upon the Avon—or (*b*) to entrench ourselves in Uncle's house at Newton and prepare to hold the place against the enemy.'

'A mug such as myself would have thought that,' confessed Roger, humbly.

The Saint paused for a moment to slide contemptuously past a Packard that was crawling along at sixty.

'But that mug's scheme,' said the Saint, 'wouldn't get us any forrader. I grant you that if we watched vigilantly and shot straight we might very well frustrate the invading efforts of the enemy for as long as we stayed in residence—which, if Betty is all you say she is, might keep us busy for weeks. But we still shouldn't know who is the power behind Mr Neave—if it isn't Mr Neave himself.'

'Whereas you suggest—'

'That we carry the war into the enemy's camp. Consider the position of the power behind Mr Neave, whom we'll call Whiskers for short. Consider the position of Whiskers. There he's been and gone and thought out the charming scheme of abducting people by means of a fake policeman—a notable idea. No one ever suspects a policeman. I'll bet that the fake policeman simply said they'd arrested a man whom they suspected of having something to do with the doping of the milk, and would Mr Aldo come over to the station and see if the accused looked anything like Neave. And Uncle was removed without any of the fuss and bother you have when you kidnap people by force.'

'You suggest that we run a policeman of our own?'

'Obviously. Think of the publicity. A few days after the abduction of Uncle, the niece also disappears with a mysterious policeman. I'm afraid that'll make Betty out to be rather a dim bulb, but we can't help that. The fact remains that Whiskers, in his secret lair, will read of the leaf that's been taken out of his book, will wonder who's got on to his game, and will promptly arm himself to the teeth and set out to find and strafe us.'

'And we help him by leaving a trail of clues leading straight into a trap.'

The Saint sighed.

'You're getting on—as the actress said to the bishop,' he murmured. 'This brain of yours is becoming absolutely phenomenal. Now go ahead and invent the details of this trap we're going to lead Whiskers into, because I've thought enough for one day, and I'm tired.'

And the Saint languidly settled down to concentrate on the business of annihilating space; what time Roger Conway, after a few prayers, closed his eyes and proceeded with the train of thought which the Saint had initiated.

They broke the journey at Shaftesbury for liquid nourishment, and when they came out Roger approached the car unhappily. But he was always tactful.

'Shall I take a turn at the wheel?' he ventured.

'I'm not tired,' said the Saint breezily.

'You said just now you were too tired to think.'

'I don't think when I'm driving,' said the Saint.

Roger would have liked to say that he could very well believe it, but he thought of the retort too late.

They covered the next eighty-five miles in a shade under two hours, and ran up the drive of the house to which Roger pointed the way as the clocks were striking seven-thirty.

'It occurs to me,' said Simon, as he applied the brakes, 'that we ought to have sent a wire to announce ourselves. Does the girl know you're in England at all?'

Roger shook his head.

'I hadn't told her we were back.'

The Saint climbed out and stretched himself, and they walked up to the house together.

A face watched them from a ground-floor window, and before they had reached the steps the window was flung up and a voice spoke sharply and suspiciously.

'I'm sorry—Miss Aldo is out.'

The Saint stopped.

'Where's she gone?'

'She was going to the police-station.'

Simon groaned.

'Not a policeman?' he protested.

'Yes, she went with a policeman,' said the woman. 'But this one was all right. Miss Aldo rang up the police-station to make sure. They've found Mr Aldo.'

'Is he alive?' asked Roger.

'Yes, he's alive.'

The Saint was staring up intently into the sky, revolving slowly on his heels, as though following a trail in the clouds.

'Somehow,' he said gently, 'that's more than I can believe.'

Conway said: 'She telephoned to the station—'

'Yes,' said the Saint, 'she telephoned.'

By that time he had turned right round.

'Which,' he said, 'is exactly what any strategist would expect an intelligent girl to do, in the circumstances.'

'But—'

The Saint's arm went out suddenly like a sign-post.

'The telephone wire goes over those fields. And the line's cut by that group of trees over there, unless I'm mistaken. A man sitting there with an instrument—'

'My—hat!' snapped Roger, with surprising restraint.

But Simon was already on his way back to the car.

'How long ago did she leave?' he flung at the now frightened housekeeper.

'Not five minutes ago, sir, when I was just starting to serve dinner. She took her car—'

'Which way?'

The woman pointed.

The Saint let in the clutch as Roger swung into the place beside him.

'What's the betting, Roger?' he crisped. 'If they'd gone towards Exeter we'd have seen them. Therefore—'

'They've gone towards Bovey Tracey—unless they turned off towards Ashburton—'

The Saint stopped the car again so abruptly that Roger was almost lifted out of his seat.

'You can drive this car. You know the district backwards, and I don't. Take any chance you like, and never mind the damage. I'll bet they've gone towards Ashburton and Two Bridges. You can disappear on Dartmoor as well as anywhere in England.'

Conway was behind the wheel by the time Simon had reached the other side of the car. He was moving off as the Saint leapt for the running-board.

And then the Saint was lighting two cigarettes with perfect calm—one for Roger and one for himself.

'Nice of Whiskers,' said the Saint, with that irresponsible optimism which nothing could ever damp. 'He's done all the work for us, provided the policeman and everything. When I think of the money I spent on that outfit of yours—'

'*If* we catch him,' said Conway, hunched intently over the steering wheel, 'you'll be able to talk.'

'We'll catch him,' said the Saint.

If Simon Templar was a reckless driver, Roger could match him when the occasion arose. And, more valuable even than mere speed, Roger knew every inch of the road blindfolded. He sent the Desurio literally leaping over the macadam, cornering on two wheels without losing control for an instant, and cleaving a path through the other traffic without regard for anyone's nerves; but nerves were things which the Saint only knew by name.

'It's extraordinary how things happen to us,' drawled the Saint coolly, as the Desurio grazed out of what looked to be the certainty of a head-on collision. 'Perpetual melodrama—that's what we live in. Why will nobody let me live the quiet life I yearn for?'

Roger said nothing. He knew exactly why *his* life wasn't quiet. It was because he happened to be a friend of Simon Templar's, and Simon Templar was a man who couldn't help spreading melodrama all around him like an infectious disease.

III

But the Saint did not feel at all guilty about the adventure. He could not have seen, if the suggestion had been made to him, how he could possibly be blamed for any incidental melodrama therein involved. The girl was Roger's, the story so far had been Roger's, and the romantic rewards, if any, would be Roger's—therefore the whole shout was Roger's.

Anyhow, the Saint was quite happy.

He leaned back with half-closed eyes, enjoying his cigarette. Simon Templar had the gift of being able to relax instantaneously, and thereby being able to benefit to the full from the intervals of relative quiet between moments of crisis; and then, when the next crisis cropped up, he could snap back to a quivering steel-spring alertness without the loss of a second. That, he said, was the way he stayed young— by refusing to take anything quite as seriously as he should have done.

As a matter of fact, he was elaborating a really brilliant idea for a new improper story about a giraffe when Roger Conway rapped out: 'There's a car in front. . . .'

'No!' demurred the Saint, dreamily. 'Are we going to hit it?'

But his eyes were wide open, and he saw the car at once—on the crest of the next switchback.

'What kind of car?'

'A Morris—and Betty's is a Morris. A man was driving with a girl beside him, but he was wearing an ordinary soft hat—'

'Dear old ass,' said the Saint; 'naturally he'd have an ordinary coat on under his tunic, and a soft hat in his pocket, ready to transform himself on the first quiet piece of road. Policemen driving cars in uniform are so darn conspicuous. He might easily be our man. Step on it, son!'

'Damn it!' said Roger, 'the accelerator won't go down any further—unless I push it through the floor.'

'Then push it through the floor,' instructed the Saint, hopefully, and lighted another cigarette.

The car in front was out of sight then, but Roger was slamming the Desurio at the immediate slope with all the force of its eighty developed horses. Half a minute later they topped the rise and went bucketing down the subsequent slant in a roar and whistle of wind. They hurtled through the dip and slashed into the opposite grade with a deep-throated snarl. . . .

'In England,' remarked the Saint mildly, as a proposition of philosophical interest, 'there is a speed limit of twenty miles an hour.'

'Is that so?'

'Yes, that is so.'

'Then I hope it keeps fine for them.'

'Kind of you,' drawled the Saint. 'Kind of you, Mr Conway!'

The Desurio ate up the hill, whipped round the bend at the top. There was a breath-taking second in which, by a miracle that no one will ever be able to explain, they escaped being sandwiched to death between two motor-coaches moving in opposite directions; then they skimmed round the next corner into the temporary safety of a straight stretch of road, on which, for the moment, there was only the Desurio and the Morris in front—a quarter of a mile in front.

The Desurio devoured the intervening distance like a hungry beast.

'I can see the number!' came Roger's voice like the crack of a whip. 'It's Betty's car—'

'OK, Big Boy!'

But it never occurred to the Saint to abandon his half-smoked cigarette.

Another corner, taken at death-defying pace, and then another straight stretch with the Morris only thirty yards in the lead.

The Klaxon blared under Roger's hand, and the man in front signalled them to pass.

'Slacken up as you come level,' ordered the Saint. 'I'll board the galleon. Ready?'

'Yes.'

'Then we'll go!'

The Saint had the door on his side of the car open in a flash. He slipped out on to the running-board and rode there, closing the door carefully behind him as the nose of the Desurio slid past the rear wing of the Morris. And he was serenely finishing off his cigarette.

On these occasions, the Saint's *sang-froid* would have made an ice-box look like an overheated gas oven.

Then the driver of the Morris saw him in the mirror, and crowded on speed. The Saint saw the man's hand leave the wheel and dive for his pocket.

'Drop behind as soon as I'm aboard,' rapped the Saint. '*Now*!'

The Desurio came abreast, slackened, hung there.

For a second the two cars raced side by side, with a bare foot of space between them, at fifty miles an hour; and the Saint stepped across to the running-board of the Morris as one might step across a garden path.

The Desurio fell astern instantly, with a scream of overworked brakes. It was scarcely too soon, for the Morris swerved drunkenly across the road as the Saint grabbed the steering-wheel with one hand and struck twice with the other. . . .

The driver sagged sideways, and the gun slipped through his fingers and thumped to the floor.

Simon straightened the car with a steady hand. They were losing speed rapidly, for the driver's foot had come off the accelerator when he collapsed under the Saint's two crashing blows to the jaw—otherwise, they would never have been able to take the next corner.

Round the corner, twenty yards away, a lane opened off the main road. The Saint signalled the turn, and then, reaching over, used the hand-brake and spun the wheel. They ran a little way down the lane, and stopped; and Roger brought the Desurio to rest behind them.

Through all that violent and hair-raising action, the girl had never stirred. Her eyes were closed as if in sleep. The Saint looked at her thoughtfully, and thoughtfully felt in the pockets of the unconscious driver.

Roger was shaking her and called her name helplessly. He looked up at the Saint.

'They've doped her—'

'Yes,' said the Saint, thoughtfully examining a little glass hypodermic syringe that was still half-filled with a pale, straw-coloured liquid, 'they've certainly doped her.'

In the same thoughtful way, he lifted the driver's right arm, turned back the sleeve, drove the needle into the exposed flesh, and pressed home the plunger. The empty syringe went into a convenient ditch.

'I think, Roger,' said the Saint, 'we will now move with some speed. Get your bag out of the car and unload the police effects. I want to see you in those glad rags.'

'But where are we going?'

'I'll think while you're changing. The one safe bet is that we've got to go at once. The housekeeper bird will be spreading the alarm already, and we've got to get away before the roads are stopped. Jump to it, my beautiful cherub!'

The Saint sometimes said that Roger was too good-looking to be really intelligent; but there were times when Roger could get off the mark with commendable promptness, and this was one of them.

While Conway was rustling into his uniform, the Saint picked the driver out of the Morris, carried him over, and dumped him into the back of the Desurio.

'We'll do some third degree on him later,' said the Saint. 'If he recovers,' he added carelessly.

'Which way can we go?' asked Conway. 'It wouldn't be safe to go back through Newton, and we can't head out into the blue towards Land's End—'

'Why not?' drawled the Saint, who was apt to become difficult on the slightest provocation. 'Land's End sounds a good romantic place to establish a piratical base, and we must have one somewhere. Besides, it has the great advantage that nobody's ever used it before. The only alternative is to make for Tavistock and Okehampton, and either take the north coast road through Barnstaple and Minehead or chance going through Exeter.'

'I thought you wanted to be seen.'

'I do—but some place where they can't stop us. They can see us go through any village, but they can hold us up in Exeter—it's a slow place to get through at the best of times.'

'You may be right. There's nowhere for us to go if we do head east. Unless we make back for Brook Street.'

'Teal knows about Brook Street,' said the Saint. 'He's liable to drop in there any time. Your maiden aunt at Stratford upon the Avon—'

'You don't know her,' snorted Roger, testing the fit of his helmet.

'I can imagine it,' said the Saint. 'No—we'll spare the feelings of Auntie. I can understand her getting rather excited when Whiskers tools up with his gang to recapture the hostage.'

Roger picked up his discarded clothes and took them over to the Morris, and the Saint walked beside him. A barren waste of moorland stretched around them, and a hump of ground capped with gorse screened them from the main road.

'Then where can we go? Remember that anything that Whiskers gets to know through the papers will be known to the real police first. We've overlooked that.'

'Yes, we've overlooked that,' said the Saint thoughtfully; and he paused, with one foot propped up on the running-board of the Morris and his hands deep in his trouser pockets and his eyes fixed on the girl in a blank and distracted way. 'We've overlooked that,' he said.

'Well?'

Roger asked the question as if he had no hope of receiving a useful answer, yet it seemed quite natural to ask it. People naturally asked such impossible questions of the Saint.

Half an hour ago (Roger knew it was half an hour because the Saint had smoked two cigarettes, and the Saint consumed four cigarettes an hour with the regularity of clockwork) they had calmly driven up to a house in Newton Abbot in the expectation of dinner, a short convivial evening, a bath, and a well-earned night's rest before proceeding with the problem in hand.

Now—it seemed only five minutes later—they had risked their necks a dozen times in a hectic motor chase, stopped the fugitive car, laid out the driver, doped him with his own medicine, and found themselves saddled with two bodies and the necessity of putting their plans forward by twenty-four hours.

And Simon Templar was quite unperturbed, and apparently unaware that there was, or had been, any excitement whatever.

'On the other hand,' said the Saint thoughtfully, still looking at the girl, 'we might revise our strategy slightly. There's one place in the whole of England where the police will never think of looking for anybody.'

'Where's that?'

'That,' said the Saint, 'is Uncle Sebastian's house.'

Roger was beyond being startled by anything the Saint suggested. Besides, he was swift on the uptake.

'You mean we should go there now?'

'No less.'

'But the housekeeper—'

'The housekeeper, with her heart full of the fear of winged policemen, and her boots full of feet, will have shut up the house and fled to the bosom of her family and Torquay—or wherever her family keeps its official bosom. We navigate first to a pub I wot of in St Marychurch, to demand liquor and provisions—'

'Not in these trousers,' said Roger, indicating his costume.

'In those trousers,' said the Saint, 'but not in that coat and hat. You'd better stick to as much of the outfit as you can, to save time, because you'll want it later in the evening. Speed, my angel, is the order of the night. The great brain is working. . . .'

Roger, feeling somewhat dazed, but still on the spot, was starting to peel off his tunic. The Saint helped him on with his gent's jacket.

'I'll think out the further details on the way,' he said. 'I've got another colossal idea which won't work unless we get the dope bird to a quiet place before he comes to. I'll take the Desurio and the dope bird, and you take the Morris and the moll—and let's burn the road!'

He spoke the last words from his way back to the Desurio, and he was already reversing up the lane as Roger tipped his police lid into the dickey and climbed into the driving seat of the Morris.

As Conway backed round into the main road, the Desurio slid past him and the Saint leaned out.

'She's a nice girl, by appearance,' said the Saint. 'Mind you keep both hands on the steering-wheel all the way home, sonny boy!'

Then he was gone, with a gay wave of his hand, and Roger pulled out the Morris after him.

It was still daylight, for the month was August. The rays of the sun slanted softly across the purple desert; overhead, a shadow on a pale blue sky, a curlew flew towards the sunset with a weird titter; the evening air went to Roger's head like wine.

Roger had got into his stride.

He should have been concentrating exclusively on the task of keeping on the tail of the Desurio; but he was not. With both hands clinging religiously to the steering-wheel, he stole a sidelong glance at the girl. With one hand clinging religiously to the steering-wheel, he reached out the other and tugged off her small hat—in order, he told himself, that the rush of cool air might help to revive her.

Black hair, straight and sleek, framing a face that was all wrong. Eccentric eyes, an absurd nose, a ridiculous mouth—all about as wrong as they could be. But a perfect skin. She must have been tall. 'No nonsense with tall girls,' thought Roger, as an expert.

'But,' thought Roger, as an expert, 'there might be something doing. Adroitly handled . . .'

The pub at St Marychurch which both he and the Saint wotted of, where a friendly proprietor would not ask too many questions. The removal of the 'dope bird' to a quiet cellar where a ruthless interrogation could proceed without interruption. The development of the Saint's unrevealed stratagem. Then, perhaps—

It was an utterly ridiculous mouth, but rather intriguing. And if a man couldn't yank a girl out of a maze of mysterious melodrama without claiming, and getting, something in return for romantic services rendered—by what right did he call himself a man?

Roger fumbled for a cigarette and drove on, characteristically grim but quite contented.

IV

Driving straight into the garage of the Golden Eagle Hotel, St Marychurch, Conway found the Saint's Desurio there before him. The Saint was not there, but the 'dope bird' remained in the back of the car in unprotesting tenancy. His mouth was open, and he appeared to snore with distressing violence.

Roger picked the girl out of the Morris and carried her through a back entrance to the hotel adjoining the garage. He was unobserved, for the population was at dinner. Finding an empty lounge, he put the girl down in an armchair and went on his way. There was no one to question his right to leave stray unconscious females lying about the place, for Roger himself happened to be the proprietor of the pub in his spare time.

He continued down the corridor to the hall, and there found Simon Templar interviewing the manageress.

'It has been,' the Saint was saying, staggering rhythmically, 'a b-beautiful b-binge. Champagne. An' brandy. An' beer. Barrels an' barrels of it.' He giggled inanely, and flung out his arms in a wide sweep to indicate the size of the barrels. 'Barrels,' he said. 'An' we won't go home till the morning, we won't go home till the morning, we won't go home till the mor-hor-*ning*—'

He caught sight of Roger, and pointed to him with one hand

while he grasped the hand of the manageress passionately with the other.

'An' there's dear ole Roger!' he crowed. 'You ask dear ole Roger if it wasn't a b-beautiful b-binge. 'Cos we won't go home till the morning, we won't go home—'

'I'm afraid,' said Conway, advancing with solemn disapproval written all over his face, 'that my friend is rather drunk.'

The Saint wagged a wobbly forefinger at him.

'Drunk?' he expostulated, with portentous gravity. 'Roger, ole darling, that's unkind. Frightfully unkind. Now, if you'd said that about Desmond. . . . Poor ole Dismal Desmond, he's passed right out. . . . I left him in the car. An' he won't go home till the morning, he won't—'

The shocked manageress drew Roger to one side.

'We can't let him in like that, Mr Conway,' she protested, twittering. 'There are guests staying in the hotel—'

'Are there any rooms vacant?' asked Roger.

'None at all. And people will be coming out from dinner in a minute—'

'But,' carolled the Saint unmelodiously, 'we won't go home till the mor-hor-*ning*—an' so say all of us. Gimme a drink.'

The manageress looked helplessly about her.

'Are there any more of them?'

'There's one in the car, but he's dead to the world.'

'Why don't you turn them out?'

'Drink,' warbled the Saint happily. 'Thousan's of drinks. Drink to me only wi-hith thine eye-heys an' I-hi will pledge with miiiiine. . . .'

Roger glanced down the corridor. A red-faced man poked his head out of the smoke-room door and glared around to discover the source of the uproar. He discovered it, snuffled indignantly through a superb white moustache, and withdrew his head again, banging the door after it. The manageress seemed to be on the verge of hysterics.

'I,' chanted the Saint, pleasantly absorbed in his own serenade, 'sent thee late a ro-hosy wre-he-heath, not so much hon-hon'ring theeee, as giving it—'

'Can't you do something, Mr Conway?' pleaded the unfortunate manageress, almost wringing her hands.

'You can't sing without drink,' insisted the Saint throatily, as a man propounding one of the eternal verities.

Conway shrugged.

'I can't very well turn him out,' he said. 'I've known him a long time, and he was coming to stay here. Besides, he isn't often taken like this.'

'But where can we put him?'

'How about the cellar?'

'What? Among all the bottles?'

Roger had to think fast.

'There's the porter's room. I'll shove him in there to cool off. And the other man can go in with him.'

'You can't sing without drink,' insisted the Saint pathetically. 'You can't really, ole sweetheart.'

Conway took him insinuatingly by the arm.

'Then you'd better come and have another drink, old boy.'

'Good idea,' nodded the Saint, draping himself affectionately on Roger's neck. 'Less go on drinking. All night. All the silly ole night. That,' said the Saint, 'sha good idea.' He turned to blow the manageress an unsteady kiss. 'See you tomorrow, ole fruit, 'cos we're not going home till the morning, we're not—*hic*! . . . Roger, ole water-melon, why *does* this floor wave about so much? You ought to have it s-seen to. . . .'

They reached the porter's room with realistic unsteadiness, and lurched in; and then the Saint straightened up.

'Hustle Dismal Desmond along, kiddo,' he said. 'Where did you put the girl?'

'In one of the lounges. Do you *have* to act like this?'

'Obviously, my pet—to account for Dismal Desmond. Get Betty out of the way, up to one of the rooms. Pretend you're just playing the fool. I leave it to you, partner!'

He literally pushed Conway out of the room, and the muffled sounds of his discordant singing followed Roger down the corridor. Conway felt like a wolf in sheep's clothing.

He hoisted the man out of the Saint's car and carried him in, and only the simmering manageress saw him plugged into the porter's cubicle.

Through the open door came the Saint's voice:

'Why, there's dear ole Desmond! How are you, Desmond, ole pineapple? I was juss sayin'—'

Roger closed the door, and assumed an air of official efficiency.

'Did you say all the rooms were taken, Miss Cocker?'

'Number Seven's empty at the moment, sir, but there's some people due in tonight—'

'Then I'm afraid they'll be unlucky. A girl friend of mine arrived at the same time as we did, and I must give her a room. Tell these people you're awfully sorry, but you've booked the same room twice by mistake—and pass them on to some other place.'

He turned on his heel and went back up the corridor. The manageress, standing petrified, heard a short conversation in which Roger's voice was the only one audible; and then Mr Conway reappeared from the lounge with the girl in his arms.

'Cavemen,' said Mr Conway strongly, 'are all the vogue; and there'll be no nonsense from you, Betty darling—see?' He swept rapidly past the scandalised Miss Cocker, and continued towards the stairs. 'Do you like being carried about the place? Does it make you love me any more? What's that? Right. I'll teach you to sham dead. You wait till I drop you in the bath. . . .'

A bend in the staircase hid him from sight, but the conversation went on. Miss Cocker, rooted in her tracks, listened, appalled. . . .

She was standing at the foot of the stairs when Roger came down, a few minutes later, feeling as if he had blasted his reputation for ever as far as his executive staff was concerned. And he was quite right.

'Will you be taking dinner, Mr Conway?' asked the manageress frostily, and Roger knew that he might as well be jugged for a julep as a jujube.

He grinned.

'Get sandwiches cut for twenty people,' he said, 'and tell the porter to get a couple of dozen Bass. I think we're all going for a moonlight picnic on the moors—and we won't be home till the morning.'

He passed on, comforted by the moral victory; and found the Saint sitting on the porter's bed, smoking a cigarette and surveying the man sprawled out on the floor. In much the same way an introspectively-minded cat might have surveyed a sleeping mouse.

He looked up, as Roger came in, with a lift of one questioning eyebrow; and Roger shook his head.

'I left her down at the other end of the corridor. And I should like to tell you that after this, either I shall have to fire her, or I shall have to fire myself.'

'Why worry?' demanded the Saint. 'Pub-keeping is no trade for an honest criminal. Where's Betty now?'

'I got her up to Number Seven.'

'Unsuspected?'

'I think so.'

'Good boy. Now let's look at you.'

He stood up. Suddenly his hands went out and stroked down each side of Roger's chin. Conway started back.

'What the blazes—'

'Hush,' said the Saint. 'Not so much excitement.'

He showed Roger his hands. The palms were black with dust.

'You ought to make your bell-hop sweep under his bed more carefully,' he said. 'However, in this case we'll forgive him. It helps to make you look really villainous. Now—off with that collar and tie. A choker'll suit you much better. That handkerchief—'

He jerked the square of fancy silk out of Roger's pocket.

'Knot this round your neck, and you'll start to look more like yourself. And unbutton the coat and turn up the collar at the back—it'll make you look tougher. . . . And a rakish cap effect,

as worn by college chums, would make it perfect. There ought to
be a cap here somewhere—every self-respecting bell-hop has one
for his night out. . . .'

He opened the wardrobe unceremoniously, rummaged, and
found what he sought.

'Pull that on. Over one ear, and well down over the eyes. That's
the stuff!'

Roger obeyed blindly. The Saint's staccato urgency would have
overwhelmed anyone.

'But what's the idea?'

'Easy,' said the Saint. 'A real bull-dozing would make too much
noise, and we haven't a place to do it. So we take Desmond on
the bend, so to speak. I'd be the stool-pigeon myself, only he'd
recognise me, so you have the honour. Meanwhile, I'll park myself
in Betty's room and put her wise when she wakes up.'

'Yes, but—'

'I've got to leave it to your imagination what tale you tell
Desmond when he comes to. The main point is that you're one
of the gang, and you've been captured, too. You're the prisoners
of the Saint, and you don't know where you are. This room won't
tell anything.'

He pointed to the tiny window, set high up in the wall and
looking out upon nothing more informative than another blank
wall.

'Old-fashioned and unhygienic,' said the Saint, 'but useful on
this occasion. It's much too small to get out through. And I'll lock
the door and take the key with me. In half an hour's time I'll lock
myself in the service room upstairs and start watching. When
you're through, flutter your handkerchief out of this window, and
I'll see it and be right down.'

'But why the rush?' asked Conway, with what breath had not
been taken away by the Saint's machine-gun fire of directions.

'For the plan,' answered Simon. 'You have the advantage of
getting on to Desmond while he's still hazy with dope. As a friend
in the same boat as himself, you worm all you can out of him,

put two and two together, and worm again. The great thing is to find out under what name Whiskers is known to the police, and where Desmond was supposed to meet him to hand over Betty.'

Roger took the Saint's place on the bed.

'And you want to know that tonight?'

'Of course. This is the night when Whiskers is expecting Betty to join her uncle and complete the family party. And that's what she'll do, if you pull your stuff. I'll take her there myself, roughly disguised as Dismal Desmond. And as soon as Whiskers has rumbled that joke, you, old haricot, having followed closely behind in your fancy dress, will beetle in and arrest the lot of us—thereby hoisting Whiskers with his own whatnot. How's that for a funny story?'

Roger looked up with enthusiasm kindling in his face.

'It gets a laugh,' he said.

'My funny stories,' said Simon Templar modestly, 'frequently do.'

'And once we've got Whiskers—'

'Exactly. The mystery of Uncle Sebastian's house will no longer be a mystery.'

The Saint took a quick glance round him, picked up a piece of printed hotel paper off the table and stuffed it into his pocket, and then reached up and removed the single bulb from its socket.

'It's getting dark,' he explained, 'and a bad light might help you. All set?'

'You may always,' said Mr Conway tranquilly, 'leave these little things to me.'

It was one of Roger's pet expressions; and the Saint hailed it with a grin. Roger was not the star of the gang in the matter of pure abstract brains; but there could have been no greater lieutenant, when it came to the point, in the whole solar system.

The Saint opened the door cautiously, and peered out. The passage was deserted. He turned back.

'You're playing the hand,' he said. 'Don't miss any of the important tricks. And when Dismal Desmond's conversation gets boring, or if he starts to smell rats, just blip him over the head with the slop-pail and wave the flag.'

'Right you are, Saint.'

'So long, Beautiful.'

'So long, Ugly-Wugs.'

Roger heard the turning of the lock and the withdrawing of the key, but he never heard the Saint pad away down the corridor. He lighted a cigarette and stretched himself out on the bed, with one eye on the man on the floor, considering the memory of a most intriguing mouth.

V

Conway finished his cigarette, and lay for a time gazing at the ceiling. Then he tried to watch the minute-hand of his watch crawling round the dial. Time passed. The room was shrouded in a grey dusk. Roger yawned.

He wondered uneasily if the Saint had under-estimated the potency of the drug in the hypodermic syringe. True, it had been only half full when Simon found it, and Simon had promptly injected the half on the assumption that what had been sauce for the goose might very justly be made sauce for the gander—but there was nothing to show that the syringe had ever been full. Perhaps Betty had only been given a few drops, the rest being kept for a repeat dose in case of need.

Roger speculated for a moment on his chance in a murder trial. He had never been able to acquire that dispassionate valuation of human life, nor that careless contempt for the law that forbids you to bounce off your neighbour simply because you have decided that his habits are objectionable and his face an outrage, which were among the charming simplicities of Simon Templar.

But the persistent snoring of Dismal Desmond, distasteful as it might be to a sensitive man, was reassuring. Roger lighted another cigarette. . . .

Nevertheless, it was another ten minutes before the man on the floor gave any sign of returning consciousness. Then a snore was strangled into a grunt, and the grunt became a low moan.

Roger twisted over on to one shoulder to observe the recovery. The man twitched and moved one leg heavily; but after that, for some time, there seemed to be a relapse. Then another groan, and another movement more vigorous than the first.

'My head,' muttered the man foggily. 'He hit me. . . .'

Silence.

Roger shifted up on to his elbow.

'Hullo, mate,' he said.

Another silence. Then, painfully—

'Who's that?'

'They seem to have got you all right, mate,' said Roger.

'There were two men in a car. One of 'em got out an' hit me. Must have smashed us up. . . . Blast this head. . . . Why's it so dark?'

'It's night. You've been out a long time.'

Silence for a long time. Roger could sense the man's struggle to pierce the drug-fumes that still murked his brain. He would have given much for a light, even when he realised that the darkness was helping his deception. But presently the voice came again.

'Who're you, anyway?'

'They got me, too.'

'Is that Carris?'

'Yes.'

The man strained to penetrate the gloom. Roger could see his eyes.

'That's not Bill Carris's voice.'

'This is George Carris,' said Roger. 'Bill's brother.'

He swung his legs off the bed and crossed the floor. The man had writhed up into a sitting position, and Conway put an arm round his shoulders.

'Come and lie down on the bed,' he suggested. 'You'll feel better in a minute.'

The man peered closely into his face.

'You don't look like Bill.'

'I'm not Bill—I'm George.'

'You ought to look like Bill. How do you come here?'

'I was with Bill.'

'On the telephone?'

'Yes.'

'Bill said he was going alone.'

'He changed his mind and took me. D'you think you could get over to that bed if I helped you?'

'I'll try. My head's going round and round. . . .'

Roger helped the man up and more or less carried him to the bed, where he collapsed again limply. Roger sat down on the edge. He glanced at his watch; it was over half an hour since the Saint had left him.

'Who are you?' he asked.

'Why, don't you know?'

'I'm new. I don't know any of the gang except Bill.'

'You're a liar!' snarled the man. 'You're not in the gang at all. You're—'

'You fool!' retorted Roger, with an oath. 'What the—d'you think I'd be doing here if they hadn't caught me, too?'

The man appeared to cogitate this argument painfully for a time. Presently he said, as though satisfied:

'Where are we?'

'I don't know. I was laid out when they brought me here. What did you say your name was, mate?'

'My name's Dyson. "Slinky" Dyson. Who're these guys you keep talking about? Who're *they*?'

'The Saint's gang, of course.'

'The Saint—'

Dyson's voice choked on a note of fear.

'You're a liar!' he croaked.

'I tell you, it was the Saint. I saw him—'

'No one's ever seen the Saint an' got away with it.'

'But I've seen him. An' he said he was going to torture us. I'm scared. Slinky, we've got to get out of this!'

Conway felt the bed shaking.

'He can't do anything to me,' said Dyson hoarsely. 'He's got nothing on me. He can't—'

'That's all you know. He wants you most—for doping that girl. Flog the hide off your back, that's what he said he was going to do.'

'They can't—'

Roger Conway, well as he knew the superstitious terror which the name of the Saint inspired, and the legends of ruthlessness which had grown up around him, had no need to act his contempt for the whining wretch on the bed. He caught the man's shoulder and shook him roughly.

'For heaven's sake, stop blubbering!' he snapped. 'D'you think that'll get us anywhere?'

'The Boss'll do something when he finds out.'

'He's too far away to be any use,' ventured Roger.

'I was nearly there when they got me.'

Nearly there! And they had been about five miles from Two Bridges. Somewhere on the moor, then. . . . Roger's heart leapt with a thrill of triumph, and he drove in upon the opening like lightning.

'You don't know how far away we are now,' he said. 'We've both been out for over an hour. And if the Boss does find out, and knows the Saint, he'll most likely be too busy making his own getaway to bother about us.'

'That's all *you* know. You ever heard of "Spider" Sleat letting his bunch down?'

'Spider' Sleat! Point two. . . . Roger made his next remark almost with apprehension. It was a tremendous strain to keep up what he considered to be the right tone of voice, when his whole system was tingling with half-incredulous delight.

'They'll be bringing us some food soon. They said they would. I'm fitter than you are—I might make a bolt for it, if you keep them busy. And I'd fetch the Boss and the rest of the bunch along. . . . Only I can never find the way alone, out on that moor. And it'd be dark. . . .'

'How often you been there?'

'Only twice. And Bill took me each time.'

'It's easy. Where did you come from?'

'Exeter.'

'Through Okehampton?'

Something in the way the question was put—a faint, almost imperceptible hesitation, stabbed a sharp warning through Roger's flush of exultation. But he had no time to think. With his muscles tensed, he flashed back his gamble.

'No—you know that's not the way. We came through Moreton Hampstead.'

Slinky Dyson's breath came again, audibly, through his teeth.

'Sorry, chum. I had to make sure you were straight. Well, you went about ten miles past Moreton Hampstead—'

'I suppose so.'

'That put you about two miles from Two Bridges. Don't you remember the knoll with three humps, on the right of the road near where you stopped?'

'That's about all I do remember.'

'Then you can't go wrong. You make two hundred yards due north of the knoll into the dip, and follow the low ground northwest till you come to a patch of gorse in the shape of an "S", Then you strike off north-east—and you're there.'

'But it'll be dark.'

'There'll be a moon.'

Roger appeared to meditate.

'It sounds easy, the way you put it,' he said. 'But—'

'It *is* easy!' Dyson snarled. 'But I don't believe you'll do it. You're yellow! You'd just cut and run, and no one'll ever see you again for dust. You miserable little dirty quitter!'

'What the blazes are you talking about?'

'What I say. I don't believe you. You're just trying to save your own skin an' get me to help you. You might make a bolt for it, you say, while *I* keep 'em busy. Thanks for nothing! You listen here—either we both make a bolt, or we both stay. I know your sort. Bill was always a yaller dog, an' you take after him. You—'

It struck Roger that Mr Dyson's conversation was certainly becoming monotonous. And his brain was humming with other things. 'Spider' Sleat—whoever he might be—and a knoll with three humps two miles from Two Bridges on the Moreton Hampstead road. Due north—a dip—north-west to a patch of gorse in the shape of an 'S'—turn north-east. . . .

A fight, in that dark room, might have been troublesome. Dyson was no light weight—Roger had noticed that when helping him to the bed. And his strength must be returning rapidly.

The Saint, in parting, had suggested the slop-pail. But Roger had discovered something better than that—a hefty broken chair-leg, apparently used to switch off the electric light without getting out of bed. His fingers closed upon it lovingly.

VI

'Sorry to have kept you waiting,' drawled the Saint, ten minutes later, 'but your manageress is wandering about in the line of retreat looking like a flat tyre, and I didn't dare let her see me. Roger, you've blighted her young life. I know she'll never smile again.'

Conway pointed his chair-leg at the bed.

'He sleeps.'

'After laying his egg?'

'He spilled a certain amount of beans. It ought to be enough to work on.'

'Let's see what you've got—as the actress said to the bishop,' murmured Simon. 'Half a sec—we'll have some light on the subject.'

He felt for the socket, extracted the bulb from his pocket, and adjusted it. Roger switched it on.

The Saint inspected Mr Dyson with interest.

'Do you think he'll die?' he asked.

'I don't think so.'

'A pity,' said the Saint. 'It means we'll have the trouble of roping him up. Make yourself look decent, and go out and find some string. You can talk while I tie.'

Roger removed the choker and replaced his collar while the Saint employed spit-and-polish methods, with a handkerchief, to his face. Then Roger snooped off on his errand.

He met Miss Cocker in the corridor.

'I've been looking for you, Mr Conway,' said the lady ominously. 'Where have you been all this time?'

'If I told you,' said Roger truthfully, 'you'd be shocked. What's the trouble?'

'A gentleman's been complaining about the noise.'

'Let him complain.'

'He's wanting to leave at once.'

'Don't stop him. Are the sandwiches and beer ready?'

'They've been waiting half an hour. But, Mr Conway—'

'Tell the little fellows to be patient. I shan't be long now.'

He stalked away before the manageress could find her voice. But the woman was waiting for him when he came back, after a few minutes, with a couple of fathoms of stout cord in his pocket.

'Mr Conway—'

'Miss Cocker.'

'I'm not used to being treated like this, I'm not, really. I think you must be drunk yourself. I'm used to respectable hotels, I am, and I never heard of such goings on, I didn't—'

'Miss Cocker,' said Roger kindly, 'take my advice and go and look for a nice respectable hotel. Because I'm turning this one into a high-class roadside gin palace, from which people will be removed, roaring drunk, in the small hours of every morning. Bye-bye, ole geranium.'

He entered the porter's room and closed the door in her face.

The Saint looked up with his quick smile.

'Domestic strife?' he queried.

'I'm used to respectable hotels, I am, and I never heard of such goings on, I didn't.'

'And you always such a nice quiet gentleman, Mr Conway!'

'It's the only way to carry it off—to pretend I'm canned. Tomorrow I shall have to see her and apologise profusely. Here's your string.'

The Saint took the cord and bent to his task with practised efficiency, while Roger described the interview with Mr Dyson. Simon listened intently, but his memory was baulked by the name of Sleat. It had a vague familiar ring about it, but nothing more.

'Spider Sleat,' he repeated. 'Can't place it. How many men are there supposed to be on the moor?'

'I didn't find that out.'

'There's only the two of us. Dicky Tremayne took his car for a golfing tour in Scotland, and I don't know where to find him. I sent Pat and Norman off to join Terry's yachting party at Cowes.'

'You wouldn't drag her into it, anyway.'

'There wouldn't be time if I wanted to. No, my seraph—you and I must tackle this alone, and damn the odds. There's one idea. . . .'

'What's that?'

The Saint completed his last knot, tested it, and stepped back. He faced Roger.

'I hate to do it,' he said, 'but it's the most practical scheme. I know Teal's private phone number, and he'll probably be at home now. I'll ask if the name of Sleat means anything to him. Teal's got the longest memory of any man at the Yard. That means I'll have to tell him I'm on the tail of the Policeman with Wings.'

'Then he'll get on the phone to the police round here—'

'He won't. You don't know the CID like I do. They're as jealous as a mother at a baby show, and they think rather less of the country police than a Rolls chauffeur thinks of a Ford. I'll tell

Teal to come down himself by the first train in the morning to collect the specimens, and he won't say a word to a soul. Now, filter out again and remove your manageress. Take her away to a quiet place and talk to her. Apologise now, if you like, instead of tomorrow morning. But give me a clear quarter of an hour to get that trunk call through.'

Roger nodded.

'I'll see to it. But that only gives us tonight and half tomorrow.'

'It'll be enough—to get Whiskers, find out the secret of this house, and act accordingly. We've got to make this a hurry order. Off you go, son.'

'Right. Where shall I meet you?'

'Betty's room—in about half an hour. Now skate!'

Roger skated.

He found the manageress spluttering about the hall, steered her into the office, and spent a desperate twenty minutes with her. He got out at last, minus his dignity, but still blessed with a manageress; and made his way up the stairs.

Of all the Saint's little band, Roger Conway had always been Simon's especial friend. There were many men scattered over the world who held Simon Templar in a reverence bordering on idolatry; there were as many, if not more, in whose aid the Saint would not have stopped at any of the crimes in the calendar; but between Roger and the Saint was a greater bond than any of these. And Roger considered. . . .

The Saint gave his ultimate affection to two people only—one man and one girl. The man was Roger Conway. The girl was Patricia Holm. She was the cream in his coffee. And those three, like the Three Musketeers, had come together out of infinitely diverse worlds—and stuck.

And Roger considered, soberly for him, because he realised that the girl he had seen, in sleep only, that afternoon, and she almost a stranger, had moved him far more than it is safe for a man to be moved. Suppose she came to make a fourth inseparable, would the bonds that held the rest of them together hold as firmly? It was a fantastic castle to build in the air, but he had been moved, and he knew it.

Therefore he considered, in that brief breathing-space, and came to the girl's room in a subdued mood.

She was powdering her nose.

'Hullo, Roger darling,' she said. 'How are you?'

'I'm very fit,' said Roger. 'How are you?'

Commonplace. But comforting. He lighted a cigarette, and sat down on the bed where he could see her face in the dressing-table mirror.

They talked. He described, for the second time, the Dyson episode—and other matters. She said she thought it was clever of him to think of carrying her up the stairs as if she were teasing and he ragging. Roger preened himself visibly. She looked nicer with her eyes open, he thought.

'Your friend's very nice,' she said.

'Who—the Saint?'

'Is that what you call him? He said his name was Simon.'

'Everyone calls him the Saint.'

'He's a sheik.'

Roger eased up on the preening.

She was plainly frightened by her adventure, but he thought she bore up remarkably well. Her nerves were palpably fluttered, but there was no hint of hysterics in her voice. She explained the doping.

'I was driving, and I felt something prick my leg. He showed me a pin sticking out of the upholstery, and said it must have been that. But a minute or so later I began to feel horribly dizzy, and I had to stop the car. My leg seemed to have swollen up and gone numb. That's all I remember until I woke up here and found Simon—or the Saint—sitting in the armchair. He made me put my head under the cold tap, and then he made me lie down again and told me all about it.'

The minutes seemed to fly. She sat down beside him, and he took her hand absent-mindedly and went on talking. She didn't seem to mind—he recalled that afterwards. But he had hardly got started when he was interrupted by a gentle tap on the door, and Simon Templar came in.

Roger was acutely conscious of his eccentric garb, for he was still wearing his police trousers with his ordinary coat, and his face was still somewhat soiled from the Saint's improvised make-up. Roger felt depressingly unlike a sheik; and the Saint was as offensively sleek and Savile Row and patent-leather as a man can possibly be.

'Sorry to have to barge in like this, boys and girls,' he said breezily, 'but I thought you ought to know that I've had a heart-toheart chat with Teal over the long-distance wire—and worked the trick. He'll be at Exeter tomorrow afternoon to stand us a drink and remove the exhibits. But there'll be no sleep for the just between now and then, Roger!'

'Did you find out about Sleat?'

'And how.' The Saint swung round to the girl. 'Tell me, old dear—when did Uncle Sebastian start building that house?'

'I can tell you exactly,' said Betty, 'because it was a week before my birthday. I was staying with him in Torquay, and he took me over to see the foundations being dug.'

'You, all legs and pigtails, on your holidays,' said the Saint. 'I know. And when is this birthday?'

'The third of August.'

'Five days ago—and to think you didn't invite us to the party! But a week before that would be the twenty-seventh of July, seven years ago, makes it nineteen twenty-two. . . . Roger, my archangel, it's too good to be true!'

'Why?'

'Because on the fifth of July, nineteen twenty-two, Harry Sleat, known as Spider Sleat, was arrested at Southampton. On the first of August, nineteen twenty-two, he was convicted at the Old Bailey and sent down for seven years for busting the strong-room of the *Presidential* and getting away at Plymouth with fifty thousand pounds' worth of diamonds that were on their way over to America.

All that from the marvellous memory of our one and only Claud Eustace Teal.'

Roger forgot his clothes in the absorption of this cataract of facts. But his mind seized instantly on one clear idea.

'They never found the diamonds?'

'Never in all these days. But Whiskers was on the loose with the sparklers *before* Uncle Sebastian started to build his house. And Whiskers was in this district before they nobbled him—he must have been. *And* Whiskers, being an insubordinate convict, had to serve almost his full term. He came out on the eighth of June. What's he do first?'

Roger leapt into the breach, momentarily oblivious of the bewildered girl.

'He tries to buy the house. Then, when Uncle won't sell, he tries to scare him out. Then, when Uncle won't be scared, he kidnaps Uncle and follows through with kidnapping Betty—'

'Because Betty is Uncle's heir, and if Uncle merely vanishes the house goes to Betty—'

'So that Whiskers has to pinch them both, force them to sign a deed of sale dated some weeks before their disappearance—'

'And kill them—or otherwise keep them out of the way—while he takes possession, disinters the loot, and slithers off in the general direction of the tall timber. Roger, my pet, we're next to the goods this time!'

The girl was staring blankly at them.

'I haven't the least idea what you're talking about,' she said.

The Saint slapped his thigh.

'But it's marvellous!' he cried. 'It's the maddest merriest story that every brought the roof down. Think of it! Whiskers, having got clean away with his fifty thousand quids' worth of crystallised carbon, with the dicks hard on his heels, comes upon a field in the dead of night, and buries the diamonds deep down.'

Roger chipped in: 'Then they catch him—'

'And he goes to jail quite cheerfully, knowing where he can find his fortune when he comes out. And he comes out, all ready to make a splash and enjoy himself—and finds somebody's bought his field and built a house on top of the treasure. Oh, *Baby*! Can you beat it?'

The girl gasped. It was a perfect story. As an explanation of the whole mystery, it was the only possible one that was convincing at the same time—and even then it read like the creation of some imaginative novelist's brain. It wanted some digesting.

But the two men before her seemed to find it sufficiently accredited. The Saint, hands on hips, was shaking with silent laughter. Roger, always less effervescent by nature than the Saint, was grinning delightedly.

'It sounds good,' he said.

'It's the caterpillar's spats! Now, this is where we take the spring-board for the high dive. Is there provender ready for the troops?'

'Yes.'

'Load it up in the Desurio. We'll park most of it at Betty's for future reference, on the way over, and just take what we need for supper to drink in the car as we go along. We'll leave the Morris, because the police'll be looking for it. You and Betty can go out quite openly, and I'll sneak along to the best bathroom—that's the one looking out on to the garage drive, isn't it?—and drop out of the window and meet you there.'

'What about Dyson? We can't leave him in the porter's room.'

'Toddle along and give him another clip over the ear. Then he won't yelp or struggle, and you can carry him out to the car. We'll take him with us. I couldn't bear to be parted from Dismal Desmond, even for an hour.'

'I ought to be able to do that,' said Conway. 'There's a door leading into the garden right opposite the porter's room, and it's dark enough now for no one to notice, if I'm quick.'

'That's fine! Betty, old sweetheart—'

The Saint's rattling volley of instructions was cut short as if by the turning off of a tap. He turned to the dazed girl with his most winning smile.

'Betty, old sweetheart, will you do it?'

'What do you want me to do?' she asked dazedly. 'I've hardly understood a word of what you've been saying.'

The Saint seemed wilted by her denseness. Unused (as in his sober moments he was always ready to confess) to the less mercurial habits of ordinary folk, he was invariably taken aback by anyone showing the least surprise at anything he did or said. The limitations of the ordinary person's outlook on life were to him a never-ending source of hurt puzzlement.

'My dear old peach-blossom—'

Roger, who was of a commoner humanity, and who knew by his own experience what a shock a first meeting with Simon Templar in such a mood could be, intervened sympathetically.

'Leave this to me, old boy.'

In language less picturesquely volcanic than the Saint would have employed, but language nevertheless infinitely more intelligible to a lay audience, he summarised the main features of the situation and what he knew of the plot, while the Saint listened with undisguised admiration. Simon had never ceased to admire and envy, without being able to imitate, Roger's gift for meeting every known species of human life on its own ground. People had to adapt themselves to the Saint; Roger was able to adapt himself to people.

He explained, and the girl understood. Then he came to the Saint's question, and he could see an automatic refusal starting to her lips.

The Saint stepped in again—but in this he was sure of himself. He had his own particular brand of parlour tricks, had Simon Templar.

'Betty, darling—'

This time it was Roger who listened in envious admiration.

It would be useless to attempt to record what the Saint said. The bare words, bereft of the magical charm of voice which the Saint could assume on occasion with such deadly ease, would appear banal, if not ridiculous. But the Saint spoke. He was pleading; he was friendly; he was masterful; he was confidential; he was flippant; he was romantic; he was impudent. And change followed effortless change with a crazily kaleidoscopic speed that would have left any girl battered into submission—and probably mazily wondering why she submitted.

And it was all done in a few minutes, and the girl was looking at him with wide eyes and saying, 'Do you really think I ought to do it?'

'I really do,' said the Saint, as if the fate of worlds depended on it.

She hesitated, looked helplessly at Roger. Then—

'All right,' she said. 'I'll go. But I don't mind telling you I'm terrified. Honestly. After this evening—'

'That's a good girl,' said the Saint, and brazenly hugged her.

Roger felt morosely pleased that he was shortly going to be able to give Mr Dyson another clip over the ear. Anyone else would have done equally well, but if it had to be Mr Dyson. . . .

## VII

'That,' said the Saint, 'should be the place.'

He lay full length in the long damp grass, peering over the crest of a convenient hummock at the house.

When you have as extensive a wardrobe as the Saint's, you can afford to maltreat a Savile Row poem in light grey fresco by stretching it out full length in long damp grass. Roger Conway, mindful of the dignity of his police uniform, contented himself with sinking to a squatting position. The girl was a little way behind them.

They could see the cottage, a stumpy black bulk in the moonlight, with two windows sharply cut out in yellow luminance. The sky was as clear as a bowl of dark glass; and in spite of Mr Dyson's confident assurance, the fragment of moon that rode low down in the sky had been less help to them in their journey than the stars. A mile out, just off the road, the Desurio was parked with all its lights out.

The Saint squirmed down a little so that the flame of his match would not be visible to any watchers outside the cottage, and lighted a cigarette in his cupped hands.

'We might as well start now,' he murmured. 'Where's the girl?'

They crept back together to rejoin her.

'On the mark, kid?'

A clammy breath of wind had been born on the moor. She shivered in her thin coat.

'The sooner you get it over, the better I'll be pleased.'

'You'll soon be happy,' said the Saint.

His teeth gleamed in a smile—it was all they could distinguish of his expression in the gloom. But the faint tremor of eagerness in his voice was perceptible without the aid of eyes.

'All got your pieces ready to say?' he asked.

She said, nervously: 'I don't know what I've got to do—'

'Nor would you if you'd really been kidnapped. That's your piece. Anyhow, you're supposed to be dead to the world, having assimilated the second instalment of that syringeful. Roger, you've got your gun?'

Conway slapped his pocket for answer.

'Haven't you got a gun, Saint?' asked the girl.

Simon was heard to chuckle softly.

'Ask Roger if I ever carry guns,' he said. 'No—I leave them to other people. Personally, I can't stand the noise. I have my own copyright armoury, which is much more silent—and just as useful. So we're ready?'

'Yes.'

'Fine! Roger, we expect you to make your dramatic entrance in ten minutes. S'long.'

'So long, Saint. . . . So long, Betty!'

Roger felt for the girl's hand and gave it a reassuring pressure. A moment later he was alone.

The Saint, with one arm round the girl's waist to steady her, picked their way over the uneven ground with the uncanny sure-footedness of a cat. It was dark enough for his clothes to be unnoticeable. He wore Mr Dyson's soft hat pulled well down over his eyes, and he had turned up the collar of his coat to assist the crude disguise. Even before they were near the cottage, he was walking with knees bent and shoulders stooped so as to approximate more to the height of Mr Dyson.

Mr Dyson himself slept peacefully in the Desurio, roped hand and foot and gagged with his own handkerchief.

The Saint was not bothering to take precautions. He felt a thread snap across his chin, and knew he had sprung a trip-alarm, but he went on unabashed. Only the lights in the two windows went out suddenly. . . .

He had no idea where the door of the cottage would be, but his preternaturally keen ears heard it creak open when he was still twenty yards away. Instantly it stopped, and his grip on the girl tightened. She felt his lips brush her ear.

'Now go dead,' he whispered. 'And don't worry. We win this game!'

He stooped quickly, and lifted her in his arms like a child. It seemed as if there was a rustling in the grass around him that was not of the wind; and the Saint grinned invisibly. He moved forward again, with slower steps. . . .

Then, directly in front of him, the darkness was split by a probing finger of light.

The Saint halted.

His coat collar shrouded his chin; the girl he carried helped to cover his body, he lowered his head so that the hat-brim obscured most of his face, and kept his eyes away from the blinding beam of the torch.

There was a second's pause, broken only by the rustling of the grass; and then, from behind a light, a harsh voice spoke—half-startled, half-relieved.

'Dyson!'

'Who did you think it was?' Simon snapped back hoarsely. 'Put out that light!'

The light winked, and went out. The voice spoke again.

'Why didn't you give the signal?'

'Why should I?'

In the shadowy mass of the cottage, an upright oblong of light was carved out abruptly. That was the door. Just inside, a man was kindling an oil lamp. His back was turned to the Saint.

Simon straightened up, and walked in. He set the girl down on her feet, and in three quick smooth movements he took off his borrowed hat, turned down his collar, and settled his coat. But the man was still busy with the lamp, and the shout came from behind the Saint—from outside the door.

'That's not Dyson!'

The man spun round with a smothered exclamation.

Simon, standing at his elegant ease, was lighting a second cigarette.

'No, this isn't Dyson, dear heart,' he murmured. 'But, if you remember, I never said it was. I should like to maintain my reputation for truthfulness for a few minutes longer.'

He looked up blandly, waving his match gently in the air to extinguish it, and saw the men crowding in behind him. One— two—three—four . . . and two of them displaying automatics. Slightly bigger odds than the Saint had seriously expected. Simon Templar's face became extraordinarily mild.

'Well, well, *well*!' he drawled. 'Look at all the flies, Spider—I congratulate you on the collection.'

The man by the lamp took a pace forward. The movement was queerly lopsided—the shuffling forward of one twisted foot, and the dragging of another twisted foot after it. Simon understood at once the origin of the nickname. The man was almost a dwarf, though tremendously broad of shoulder, with short deformed legs and long ape-like arms. In a small wrinkled face, incredibly faded blue eyes blinked under shaggy eyebrows.

'One of these matinée idols we read about,' thought the Saint in his mild way, and felt the girl's shoulder shudder against his.

The man took another slithering step towards them, peering at them crookedly. Then—

'Who are you?' he asked, in that harsh cracked voice.

'His Royal Highness, the Prince What's-it of I-forget-where,' said the Saint. 'And you're Mr Sleat. Pleased to have you meet me. The introductions having been effected, do you curtsy first or do I? I'm afraid I hocked my table of precedence two seasons ago. . . .'

'And this—lady?'

'Miss Betty Aldo. I believe you wanted to see her, so I brought her along. The escort you provided was unfortunately—er—unable to continue the journey. I'm afraid he hit his head on a piece of wood, or something. Anyway, the poor fellow was quite incapacitated, so I thought I'd better take his place.'

The pale eyes stared back horribly.

'So you've met Dyson?'

'"Slinky"—I believe—is what his friends call him. But I call him Dismal Desmond. Yes, I think I can say that we—er—made contact.'

Sleat looked round.

'Close that door.'

Simon saw the door shut and barred.

'Do you know,' he said conversationally, 'when I didn't know you so intimately as this, I used to call you Whiskers. And now I find you've shaved, it's terribly disappointing. However, to talk of pleasanter things—'

'Talk them in here.'

'To talk of pleasanter things,' continued the Saint affably, taking Betty's hand and following without protest into the room where the dwarf led the way with the lamp—'don't you find the air up here very bracing? And we've been having such lovely weather lately. My Auntie Ethel always used to say—'

Sleat turned with a snarl that bared a row of yellow teeth.

'That'll do, for a minute—'

'But I'm not nearly satisfied yet—as the actress said in one of her famous conversations with the bishop,' remarked Simon. 'Like the actress, I want more and more. For instance, what are your favourite indoor sports? Halma, ludo, funny faces—'

Without the least warning, the dwarf reached up and struck him, flat-handed, across the mouth.

Once before in Simon's life a man had dared to do that. And this time, as before, for one blinding second, Simon saw red.

There were two men covering him with automatics, and two men standing by with heavy sticks; but not even a battery of artillery and a land mine would have stopped the Saint in such a mood. His fist had leapt like a cannon-ball from his shoulder before he had consciously aimed the blow.

And the next second he was again as cool as ice, and the dwarf was picking himself off the floor with a trickle of blood running down from his smashed lips. Nobody else had moved.

'A distinct loss of temper,' murmured the Saint regretfully, flicking the ash from his cigarette. 'All the same, I shouldn't do that again if I were you, Beautiful—you might get hurt more next time. A joke's a joke, as Auntie Ethel used to say.'

'You—'

'Hush!' said the Saint. 'Not before the Bible class. They might misunderstand you. And if you want to know why they didn't shoot me, the answer is that they never had the nerve. . . . Isn't that so, honeybunch?'

He swung round on one of the armed men—and, without the least haste or heat, flicked him under the nose. He saw the man's finger tighten on the trigger, and threw up his hands.

'One moment!' he rapped. 'Hear my speech before you decide to shoot—or you may be sorry later. You, too, my pretty one!'

He turned to crack the warning at Sleat, whose right hand was sneaking down to his hip. There was a blaze of fury in the dwarf's eyes, and for a moment Simon thought he would shoot—without waiting to listen. Simon stood quite still.

'Who are you?' rasped Sleat.

'I am Inspector Maxwell, of Scotland Yard, and I've come to get y—'

Sleat's hand came up, deliberately.

'. . . your views on the much-disputed question, Why was

Bernard Shaw? . . . And—seriously—I'll advise you to be careful with that pop-gun, because my men are all round this house, and anyone who's going to get through that cordon will have to be thinner than a lath before breakfast. You can't laugh that off, Rudolph!'

'I've a good mind—'

'To shoot and chance the consequences. I know. But I shouldn't. I shouldn't, really. Because if you do, you'll quite certainly be hanged by the neck until you're so dead that it'll be practically impossible to distinguish you from a corpse. Not that a little more length in the neck wouldn't improve your beauty, but the way they do the stretching—'

One of the armed guard cut in savagely: 'Dyson's squealed—'

'It was a good squeak,' said the Saint meditatively, 'as squeaks go. But the sweet pea had no choice. When we started to singe his second ear—'

'You're clever!' grated Sleat.

'Very,' agreed the Saint modestly. 'My Auntie Ethel always said—'

The sentence merged into a thunderous pounding on the outer door, and the Saint broke off with a smile.

'My men are getting anxious about me. It's my fault, for getting so absorbed in this genial chit-chat. But tell me, Spider,' said the Saint persuasively, 'is this or is this not entitled to be called a cop?'

Sleat drew back a pace.

His eyes fled round the room, like the eyes of a hunted animal seeking an avenue of escape. And yet—there was something about the eyes that was not surrendering. Pale, expressionless eyes in a mask-like wrinkled face. Something about the eyes that told Simon, with a weird certainty, that it was not going to be called a cop. . . .

The guard stood like statues. Or like three statues—for the fourth was staring at Simon with a wild intentness.

Sleat's eyes came back to the Saint, palely, expressionlessly. It was an eerie effect, that sudden paling out of their blaze of fury into a blind cold emptiness. Simon gripped the girl's arm to steady her, and felt her trembling.

'Don't look at me like that!' she mouthed sharply, shakily. 'It's horrible. . . .'

'Bear up, old dear,' encouraged the Saint. 'He can't help it. If you had a face like that—'

Again the thunder on the door.

And Sleat came to life. He motioned back the two armed men of the guard.

'Behind those curtains! You take the girl—you take the man. And if they try to give one word of warning—if you hear them say anything that might have a double meaning—you'll shoot! Understand?'

The men nodded dumbly, moving to obey. Sleat turned to the other two, indicating each in turn with a jerky pointing finger.

'You stay here. You go and open the door. And you—'

He swung round on the Saint.

'You—you heard the orders I gave. They'll be carried out. So you'll dismiss your men, on any excuse you can invent—'

'Shall I, dear angel?'

'You will—unless you want to die where you stand, and the girl with you. If you had been alone, I might have been afraid that your sense of duty might have outweighed your discretion. But you have a—responsibility. I think you will be discreet. Now—'

The Saint heard the unbarring of the outer door, and the measured step of heavy feet. The curtains three yards away from him reached to the floor. They had settled down, and there was nothing to betray the presence of the men behind them. The third man, standing in one corner, was still staring at him.

Sleat's hands, with the automatic, had gone behind him.

Then Roger Conway walked in and saluted, and Simon's face was terribly Saintly.

'Yes, constable?'

'Beg pardon, sir,' said Roger stiffly, 'but your time's up. Sergeant Jones sent me in to see if you were all right.'

'Quite all right, thanks,' said the Saint. 'As a matter of fact—'

And then, out of the tail of his eye, Simon saw a strange light dawn in the face of the third man, the man in the corner, the man who had been staring.

'Boss—'

Sleat craned round at the exclamation, with a malignant threat in his face that should have silenced the man. But the man was not silenced. He was pointing at the Saint with a shaking hand.

'Boss, dat ain't no bull! De foist time I see him was when he stuck up de Paradiso, back of Nassau Street, in Noo Yoik, four years back. Dat guy wid de goil's de Saint!'

Sleat spun back with his gun hand leaping into view, but the Saint's hands were high in the air.

'OK, buddy!' he drawled. 'You take the Memory Prize. Roger, take that hand away from your pocket. There's a whole firing squad got the drop on you at this moment, and they mightn't believe you were only going to produce your birth certificate. . . . Boys and girls, you may take it from me. This is our night out!'

## VIII

Conway saw the gun in Sleat's hand even as the Saint warned him, and his hands went up slowly as he moved over to join the Saint. Then the curtains moved, and the hidden men came out.

'So!' said Sleat harshly. 'I thought you were a fraud from the first words you spoke. I've known a good many busies—'

'And you'll know a lot more before you're finished,' said the Saint equably. 'You've heard of me?'

'I have.'

'Then you'll know I have—friends. Three of them are outside this house now. Unless you leave as my prisoners, you'll never pass them. They'll stalk you over the moor, in the dark, and take you one by one. Not one of you will reach the road alive. Those were my orders. You can smile at that one, sonny boy!'

'You men don't kill.'

'They killed Chastel—you've heard of him? And there are others who've never been heard of. And for me they would kill you with as little compunction as they'd kill any other poisonous spider. If you don't believe me, send one of your men outside and see if he comes back.'

It was bluff—blind, desperate bluff. But it was the only card Simon could find in his hand at that moment. At least it gave him a few seconds' respite to think. . . .

Sleat looked at him, his head on one side, as though seeking the first flaw in voice or manner. But the Saint stood as coldly solid as an iceberg, and his voice was as smooth and hard as polished steel.

'You think they'll obey your orders?' said Sleat.

'In anything.'

The dwarf nodded.

'Then you'll give me a key to let myself out of your trap. It used to be said that the Saint was clever, but it seems that he also makes his mistakes. You will call them in here—please.'

Simon laughed shortly.

'You have a hope!'

'Otherwise. . . . Fetch me a rope, Wells.'

One of the men left the room.

'He's bluffing,' said Roger tensely.

'Of course he is,' murmured the Saint. 'But don't spoil his fun, if it amuses him. A plain man of simple amusements, our Whiskers. He reminds me of—'

'In a moment we shall see who's bluffing,' said Sleat.

He turned as the man came back with a length of rope. Sleat took it and tied it in a short loop.

'Just now,' he said, as he worked, 'you spoke to me of a way of stretching necks. Personally, I prefer to compress them horizontally.'

He tightened his knot carefully. The loop was just big enough to pass over a man's head. He passed it back to the man who had brought it.

'That rope, Wells, and the poker. You understand the principle of the garotte? . . . You put the loop round the man's neck, put the poker through the loop, and twist so that the rope tightens slowly. Very slowly, you understand, Wells. . . . No—'

He broke off, and a gleam of venomous ferocity came into his faded eyes.

'No,' said Sleat. 'I made a mistake. Not round the man's neck. Round the girl's.'

Roger started forward, and instantly an armed man barred his way menacingly. Conway, helpless before the automatic that drove into his chest, raved like a maniac: 'You filthy scum—'

'My shout, Roger!'

The Saint's voice came very quietly. A stick of dynamite may also be quiet for a long time.

Simon was facing Sleat.

'I admit the argument. And the answer is—there's no one outside. That's the truth.'

'I see—another bluff!'

'We don't get you, Funny Face.'

'Was his face as funny as that before you hit him?' asked Roger insultingly.

'No,' said the Saint. 'Before that, it was a tragedy.'

Sleat stepped forward, his face contorted in a spasm of rage. The Saint thought for a second that Sleat was going to strike him again, and braced himself for the shock; but with a tremendous effort the man controlled himself.

'I could deal with your humour more comfortably, Templar,' he said malevolently, 'if you were tied up. Some more rope, Wells.'

'Another of these brave men,' snapped Roger.

The Saint smiled. There had never been a time when the Saint could not smile.

'He's got a weak heart,' said the Saint, 'and his grandmother told him never to leave off his woollen drawers and never to risk the shock of being hit back. He forgot it just now, and he might have been killed. Wouldn't that have been dreadful?'

Then the man came back, this time with a great coil of rope over his arm. Two of the others seized the Saint.

'Search him,' said Sleat, 'and tie him up.'

The Saint was searched, but he had no fear of that. He never carried such obvious things as firearms—only the two little knives which he could throw with such supernatural skill. And they were where only one who knew the secret would ever have dreamed of searching—Anna, his favourite, in a sheath strapped to his left forearm, and Belle, the second, in a similar sheath strapped to his right calf under his sock.

Then they brought up a chair, and he sat down willingly. To have struggled would have been simply a useless waste of energy. They bound his hands behind his back, and roped his ankles to the legs of the chair. Simon encouraged them.

'This is the twenty-seventh time I've been tied up like this,' he said pleasantly, 'and every time I've got away somehow. Just like the hero of numberless hectic adventures in a story-book. But don't let that depress you. Just try and do better than your predecessors. . . . I'm afraid, though, your technique rather reminds me of the technique of the twenty-second man who did this. I called him Halfred the Hideous, and Auntie Ethel never took very kindly to him, either. He died, unhappily. I had to push him off the top of the house a few hours later. He fell into the orchard, and next season all the trees grew blood oranges. . . .'

The Saint's voice was as calm as if he had been discussing the following day's race-card, and as cheerfully optimistic as if he had been discussing it in the spirit of having collected a packet over a twenty-to-one winner that afternoon. He did it, as much as anything, to lighten the hearts of the others—and particularly the girl's. But he would probably have behaved in the same way, for his own entertainment, if he had been alone. The Saint never believed in getting all hot under the collar about anything. It was so bad for the smartness of the collar. . . .

Sleat stood by the wall in silence, his automatic in his hand.

His fury had settled down into something horribly soft and deadly, like gently simmering vitriol. To anyone less reckless than the Saint, that sudden restraint might have been more paralysing to the tongue than any show of violence. Even Simon felt a chilly tingle slide up his spine like the touch of a clammy hand, and smiled more seraphically than ever.

Sleat spoke.

'Now the other man.'

'Roger—'

The girl's control broke for an instant, in that involuntary cry. Conway, forced into a chair like the Saint, with the men rapidly pinioning his arms and legs, answered her urgently: 'Don't worry, darling. These blistered rats can't do anything I care about. And when I get near that misshapen blot on the landscape, over by that wall, I'll—'

'You shall have the job of killing him, Roger,' said the Saint dispassionately. 'I promise you that. And I should recommend a sharply-pointed barge-pole. You wouldn't want to touch the skunk with anything shorter.'

The girl stifled a sob. She was white and shaking.

'But what are they going to do?'

'Nothing,' said Roger brusquely.

Sleat put his automatic away in his pocket.

'Now the girl,' he said.

Roger strained at his bonds in agony.

'You're even afraid of her, are you?' he blazed. 'That's sensible of you! New-born babes would be about your fighting mark, you white-livered—'

'Why get excited, son?' Simon's voice drawled in. 'You'll only scare the girl. Whereas there's really nothing—'

'All right, boss.'

Wells spoke. The roping was finished.

Sleat moved twistedly off the wall. 'Pale blue eyes,' thought the Saint. 'Pale blue eyes. All ruthless men—murderers and great generals—have them. This is our evening!' And Sleat picked up his loop of rope from the floor where it had fallen, and shuffled forward again.

He halted in front of the Saint.

'You are the professional humorist of the party, I believe, Templar?' he said, and his cracked voice was high-pitched and uneven.

Simon looked him steadily in the eyes.

'Quite right,' he said. 'At least, that's my reputation. And you're the monstrosity from the touring menagerie, aren't you? Let me know when you're ready to start your turn.'

Then he saw what was going to happen, and his voice ripped out again in a desperate command.

'Don't look, Betty! Whiskers is going to make one of his funny faces, and you might die laughing!'

'I dislike your kind of humour,' said Sleat, in the same tone as before, and swung the loose end of the rope.

The girl screamed once, and closed her eyes.

Roger swore foully, impotently.

Sleat babbled: '. . . that . . . and that . . . and that . . . and that . . . and that!' He paused, panting. 'And if you've any more humorous remarks to make, Templar—'

'Only,' said the Saint, with nothing but the least tremor in his voice, 'that my Auntie Ethel had a very good joke about an incorrigible bimetallist of Salt Lake City whose hobby was collecting freaks. He was quite happy until one day he noticed that all pigs had short curly tails. He went quite mad, and wore himself to a shadow touring all the pig-farms in the States looking for a pig with a long straight tail. For all I know, he's searching still, and it occurred to me that perhaps your tail—'

Sleat, with the face of a fiend, lifted his rope's end again.

'Then you can add that . . . and that . . .'

It was Roger who interrupted, with an unprintable profanity which, for some reason, found its mark.

The dwarf turned on him.

'Another humorist?' he sneered. 'Then—'

He struck once, twice. . . .

'You fool!' sobbed the girl hysterically. 'That won't help you! There aren't any men outside, I tell you—'

Sleat paused with his hand raised again—and slowly lowered it. And as slowly as that slow movement, the flush of madness froze under the surface of his face, leaving it grey and twitching.

'There aren't any men outside,' he muttered. 'That's what I wanted to be sure about, in case he was trying to make me walk out into a trap. But there aren't any men outside. . . .'

He dropped the rope.

'Oh, Roger—Saint—'

The girl was sobbing weakly in her chair.

Conway called to her, insistently: 'Don't cry, dear—don't cry, please! It'll only make that walking ulcer think he's won. I'm not hurt. Don't cry!'

'You beasts—you beasts!'

Sleat shambled over to her and tilted back her head brutally.

'How did they come here?' he demanded.

'In a car—it's by the road—and your man's in it—'

'You little fool,' broke in the Saint's bitter voice. 'You're smashing the game to glory! Why don't you go down on your knees and beg the scab to spare us? That'd finish it splendidly.'

Sleat turned.

'Unless you want some more rope, Templar—'

'Thanks,' said the Saint clearly, with his head held high and the blood running down to stain his collar—'that hurts me a lot less than the thought of all the clean mud you must have soiled by crawling through it.'

The dwarf lifted his hand; and then he mastered himself.

'I know all I want to know,' he said. 'And I have things to attend to at once.'

'Disposing of the body of Sebastian Aldo, for instance?' suggested the Saint insolently.

'Yes—I shall do that at the same time as I dispose of yours.'

'So he's dead?' said Roger.

'He died of heart failure.'

'When he saw you, I suppose?'

The girl said: 'You cowards! You murdered him—'

'I said he died of heart failure,' snarled the dwarf. 'Why should I trouble to lie, when none of you will ever be able to use anything I tell you? The shock killed him.'

'That is sufficient for me,' said the Saint. 'For that alone I shall be justified in ordering your execution. And the sentence will be carried out.'

Sleat shook his head. His eyes shifted over to the Saint, and a slow malevolent leer came into his wrinkled face.

'You will order nothing,' he said.

Only the dim yellow light of the oil lamp on the table illuminated that macabre scene. The four guards stood motionless around the walls. Simon, Roger and Betty, in their chairs, were ranged in a rough crescent. In the centre of the room stood Sleat, with a queer light flickering in his pale eyes, and his face twisted and ghoulish.

There was a moment's silence.

Conway sat grimly still. His face was white, save for two thick red weals that ran across either cheek, and behind his eyes burned a dull fire. He looked at the Saint, and saw the Saint's head thrown back with its old unconquerable mocking arrogance, and the Saint's face bruised and bloody. He looked at the girl, and met her eyes. Her quick breathing was then the only sound in that moment's silence.

'I warn you,' said the Saint clearly, 'that whatever you do—whether you fly to the end of the world, or hide yourself at the bottom of the sea—my friends will follow you and find you. And you will die.'

Again Sleat shook his head. It was like the wagging of the head of a grotesque doll.

'You will order nothing,' he repeated. 'Because you—and these two friends of yours—will die—tonight.'

A window rattled in the wind, and the flame of the lamp flickered like a tired soul.

The Saint felt the atmosphere weighing down as if with a tense, dark, evil heaviness. And he laughed the laugh of a boy, and shattered that evil cloud with a breath.

'Very dramatic!' he mocked, in a voice that slipped through that murky room like a shaft of sunlight. 'But a shade theatrical, my pet. Never mind. We don't object to sharing your simple fun. That infectious gaiety is the most charming thing about you. And after Roger's killed you, I shall commemorate it in a snappy little epitaph which I've just made up. It's all about "a handsome young hero named Sleat, whose pleasures were simple but sweet. He'd be happy for hours just gathering flowers, or removing his whiskers with Veet." That ought to look well in marble. . . .'

'With a memorial statue over a refuse heap,' added Roger.

Sleat leered and shuffled away.

He went into one corner, and dragged aside a box that stood there. Stooping, he picked up what looked like two ends of black cord, and came a little forward again, trailing them behind him.

'I've been to prison once,' he said, 'and I swore then that I'd never be taken again. I prepared this place so that if the police ever came here I could blow them all to blazes—and myself with them. You see these fuses?'

No one answered.

'This one—marked with a piece of thread—is fast. It burns in about three seconds. The other is slow. It should burn for about eight minutes. And under this floor there are twenty pounds of dynamite. In the next room'—the vacant eyes focused on the girl—'is your uncle. He is dead. You will soon join him. And there will be no trace—nothing but a crater in the moor—in eight minutes' time. I light the slow fuse, you understand. . . .'

The eyes moved along the short line of bound figures, studied, with a ghastly delight, the girl, sitting numbed with horror, and the two men, sitting erect and unflinching.

'The slow fuse,' said Sleat harshly. 'I don't want to blow myself up as well. So you will have a little leisure in which to meditate your folly. I shall hear the explosion as I drive away, and I shall laugh. . . .'

He laughed then, a short raucous cackle.

'So easy,' he said, 'and so quick, after the first eight minutes. Some matches, Wells. . . . And you may go. You may all go. Find his car, and wait for me with it on the road. . . . I light the slow fuse—'

The match was sizzling up between his fingers as the men filed out. He touched the match to the fuse, and blew on the glowing end so that it shone like a tiny glow-worm. He held it up.

'You see?' he cackled. 'I've lighted the fuse!'

'Yes,' said Simon mechanically, 'you've lighted the fuse!'

And, now that there was no longer anyone behind him, the Saint was reaching his bound hands down and round behind the chair, twisting them till the cords ate into his wrists. It was impossible to reach the knife on his leg; but if he could only loosen the ropes on his wrists sufficiently—the merest trifle would do— enough to enable the fingers of his right hand to reach the hilt of the little knife on his left forearm. . . .

Sleat dropped the lighted fuse and came over to the Saint. He thrust his face down to within a few inches of Simon's.

'And you die!' he gloated. 'While I go and collect the diamonds for which I gave seven years of my life. You knew about the diamonds? . . . I thought you did. You know too much, my friend. And you are too funny—'

He lashed out at the Saint's face, but Simon dropped his head and took the blow on his forehead. Sleat did not seem to notice it. He turned to the girl, and took her face between his hands.

'You are beautiful,' he said, and she looked him in the eyes.

'I'm not afraid of you,' she flashed back.

'It is a pity that you should die with your beauty,' said the dwarf, in the same unemotional way. 'But you are like the others— you know too much. So I bid you farewell—like this—'

He bent suddenly and kissed her full on the mouth; and Roger Conway's chair creaked with his mad struggling.

'You disgusting blot! You foul, slimy, crawling—'

Sleat let go the girl and shuffled across to him.

'As for you,' he croaked, 'you also know too much. And you also are too funny. I bid *you* farewell—like this—'

His fist struck Roger on the mouth, half-stunning him; but through a reeling red haze Roger heard the Saint's voice ring out like the voice of a trumpet.

'Wait, Sleat! You lose!'

Sleat limped round. And the glowing end of the fuse was stealing across the bare floor like the eye of a retreating worm.

'Why do I lose?'

'Because you do,' taunted the Saint. 'Why? I'll tell you in about six minutes—just before the fuse blows up. You'll have the satisfaction of knowing, before you die with us!'

To Roger it was all like a nightmare, from which he could have believed that he would wake up in a moment—if it had not been for the pain which racked his face from brow to chin. He could only guess what the Saint must have been suffering, for Simon had never shown it by the flicker of an eyelid.

The atom of red light seemed to be racing across the floor at lightning speed. Unless Sleat had underestimated the length of his fuse—or unless there was more of it concealed under the boards . . .

He could see the Saint's hands behind his chair. The Saint was wrestling with his wrists, but Roger could not see the knife. The Saint's fingers were in his left sleeve, groping and straining, but nothing seemed to happen.

Then Roger saw the Saint's fingers stop moving—saw the Saint's fingers relax and his hands sink limply down behind his back—and understood.

*The Saint could not reach his knife.*

For once the trick had failed. The ropes had been tied too tightly, or else the knife had slipped round. . . .

And the Saintly smile had never been sweeter.

'Why do I lose?' asked Sleat again.

'Wouldn't you like to know?' jeered the Saint.

Sleat's face convulsed with a spasm of rage. He stared about him, and saw the discarded piece of rope. He started to move towards it. 'And if you think that'll help you,' came Simon's voice steadily, 'you've got another guess due, sweetheart. Torture doesn't make me whine. You ought to have found that out—'

The smouldering end of the fuse was only a few inches from the hole in the floor. Four inches at the most . . . three. . . .

Roger's head swam. The Saint could only be doing one thing. His trump card had been snatched from him, and he was taking the only revenge that was left. To waste time, distract Sleat's attention—to take Sleat with them into eternity. . . .

Roger shouted. He knew he was shouting, because he heard his own voice like the voice of another man across an infinite emptiness. He shouted: 'Betty—'

Her answer came to him as from a vast distance. There was nothing real—nothing. And the glow-worm was slipping into the hole in the floor.

'Why can't you hold me?' sobbed the girl pitifully.

Roger groaned.

'I can't,' he said in a whisper. 'I can't. They've tied me too tight. I can't move. My dear—'

A few feet away, on the other side of the earth, he saw her. And he saw Spider Sleat, moving with what seemed to be an unbelievable slowness, picking up the rope. And he saw the Saint smiling his indomitable smile.

And again the shaft of sunlight, that was the Saint's voice, leapt through the air. And this time it seemed to fall on a bright banner of triumph.

'You're too late!' cried the Saint. 'It's too late even for torture— because you can't put out the fuse! It's gone. It's been gone for a minute now. You can't reach it unless you tear up the floor—and you haven't the time for that. You've less than four minutes—'

And the Saint's heart was singing with a wild hope.

It was true—Roger's surmise had been right at first. The Saint had been playing for time, fighting to make Sleat forget the lighting of the fuse and the flight of time, with the grim intention of keeping Sleat there to be hurled with his victims into the black sky. He had played for time—but he had won.

He had seen a way out. The wraith of a chance, but . . .

'About three minutes now, I should say, Sleat. And you'll never see your diamonds. I'll tell you that, dear one!'

Sleat's lips curled back in a dreadful grimace.

'The diamonds—'

'I found them. I dug them up before I came here. Did you think I'd be such a fool as to forget that? They're where you'll never find them—not if you hunt for the rest of your days. And three minutes isn't enough to make me talk—even if you dared stay to try—'

Sleat was at the hole in the floor. His hand was through it. He was trying to force in his arm, but the aperture was far too small. He was scrabbling at the boards with the nails of his other hand, but the boards were fast.

It was a gruesome sight. The man was blubbering and slavering at the mouth like an animal.

'It's no good, Sleat,' the Saint mocked him. 'You've left it too long. You can't reach the fuse—you can't stop the balloon going up—and you'll go with it unless you're quick! But you'll never see those diamonds. Unless—'

Sleat writhed more madly, and then for a moment he lay still, huddled on the floor. Then he drew his hand out of the hole and crawled slowly up on his knee. His eyes seemed blank and sightless.

'Unless what?' he uttered.

Not for a second did the Saint pause, for he recognised the cunning of Sleat's madness. The slightest faltering would have been fatal, but the Saint did not falter. He played his card—the card which had been sent to him out of the blue by whatever beneficent deity guarded him in all his ways—the wildest, most inspired bluff of his career—and played it without batting an eyelid, as casually as he might have gambled a bluff in a poker game with a quarter limit.

147

'Unless you cut us loose, and get us away from here, in two and a half minutes,' said the Saint steadily.

## X

Roger heard the words, and his brain throbbed crazily. He understood—he understood at once—but. . . . Surely the Saint couldn't—the Saint couldn't possibly be betting on such a barefaced bluff! Even if it was their only chance, the Saint couldn't imagine that Sleat would fall for a lie like that!

And an observer with a stop-watch would have noted that there was a silence of fifteen seconds, but to Roger Conway it seemed like fifteen minutes.

Roger thought, in his nightmare: 'He might bring it off. He might bring it off. Only the Saint could do it, but he might bring it off. He's got Sleat half demented. That was done at the beginning, and the man must be almost insane, anyway. And since he lighted the fuse, the Saint's never stopped baiting him, tantalising him, making stinging rings round him like a wasp round a mad bull. He might have got Sleat hazed enough to fall. He might bring it off. . . .'

And Sleat was getting up.

And again the wasp stung.

'Seven years of your life!' it gibed. 'And a lot of good it's done you, beloved—when you've just arranged to kill the only man who could ever have taken you to your diamonds. Smoke! I'd give a pile for the rest of the boys to be able to hear that funny story. Another two minutes, pretty Sleating, and. . . . Oh, isn't it rich? I ask you—if you've got a sense of humour—isn't it rich?'

And the Saint laughed, as if he hadn't a care in the world—as if they were all a thousand miles away from a landmine that was timed to smithereen them out of life in one hundred and twenty seconds.

Roger thought: 'He might have brought it off, but he's left it too late now. He hasn't a hope in hell—'

Then he saw Sleat's face working, saw it with a startling clarity, as if through a powerful lens, saw the trembling eyelids and the thin trickle of saliva running down from the corner of his mouth, saw . . .

*Saw Sleat jerk a clasp-knife from his pocket and fling himself at the Saint's chair.*

Sleat was mad. He must have been. The Saint's barbed taunts, on top of the belief that the Saint had really taken the diamonds and alone knew where they were hidden, must have snapped the last withered, shred of reason in his brain. Otherwise Sleat would never have bought the joke. Otherwise Sleat would never have dared take the risk.

If he had been in his senses, he would have known that he hadn't a chance of cutting the Saint free and guarding himself at the same time—even with a gun in his other hand—when his guard had been sent out of hearing. Or did he, in his madness, which the Saint had played on with such a superb touch, think that he could achieve the impossible?

The girl, and Roger, and Simon himself, knew that they would never know.

But the Saint's hands were free, and the Saint's right hand was flying to his left sleeve, and Sleat was freeing the Saint's right foot. And the Saint's right foot was free. And Sleat, on his knees in front of the chair, was hacking wildly at the ropes that held the Saint's left ankle. The Saint's left foot was. . . .

Simon jerked back his right foot, and sent it forward again. The girl gasped.

And Sleat, overbalanced and almost knocked out by the kick, was groping blindly for his gun, which he had dropped, when the Saint kicked it aside and snatched it up.

Roger's breath came through his teeth in one long sigh.

The Saint's knife was out, and he was beside Conway's chair. Three swift slashes of the razor-keen blade, and Roger rose to his feet, free, as the dwarf came at them with clawing fingers.

'Yours, partner,' drawled the Saint, as if they were playing a friendly game of tennis, and reached the girl's side in two steps.

The cords fell away in a moment; and, as she came stiffly to her feet, the Saint took her arm and hustled her out of the room. The outer door stood open, and the Saint pointed straight ahead across the dark moor.

'Carry on, old dear,' he said. 'We'll catch you up in the dip in about one and a half shakes.'

'But Roger—'

Simon showed his teeth.

'Roger's killing a man,' he said, 'and he never looks his best when he's doing that sort of thing. You oughtn't to see it, for the sake of the romance. But I'll fetch him right along. See you in a minute, kid.'

Then she was alone.

The Saint went back, and went straight through the room they had left to the room that opened off it. There was a man on the bed, and he did not stir when the Saint came in. Simon folded him in a blanket, and carried him out.

Roger was climbing shakily to his feet.

'Who's that?' he asked huskily.

'Uncle Sebastian.' Simon glanced at the thing in the corner. 'Is he—'

Conway passed a hand across his eyes.

'Yes. I killed him.'

Simon looked into Roger's face, and saw the grim reaction there. He spoke for commonplace comfort.

'Careless of you, now I come to think of it,' he remarked lightly. 'It means we'll have to look for the diamonds. Still—we can't stop to weep here. Let's go!'

They went quickly, stumbling over tufts and hummocks in the darkness. Even the Saint, with his instinctive sense of country, tripped once and fell to one knee; but he was up again almost without a check.

A shadow loomed up in the obscurity.

'Is that you?'

Betty's voice.

'This is we,' answered the Saint grammatically, and walked down into the hollow.

Roger was beside him no longer as he laid down his burden.

'If I may interrupt,' said the Saint apologetically, 'I should advise you to lie down, cover your heads, shut your mouths, and stop your ears. If you can do all that in each other's arms, so much the better; but there's some disturbance about due—'

And as he finished speaking, the earth seemed to billow shudderingly under them, like a giant in torment; and with that the giant roared with pain, with a voice like a hundred thunders. And in front of them the darkness was split with a flash of amethyst fire; and it seemed as if a colossal black mushroom blotted out the cowering stars as the echoes of the detonation rang from end to end of the sky.

Then the black mushroom became a cloud, and the cloud burst in a torrent of pelting black rain.

Some seconds later the Saint scrambled to his feet and tried to shake the earth off his clothes.

'Some balloon, you quiet fellow, some balloon,' he murmured appreciatively. 'If we'd been in that, I reckon we should just about be on our way down.'

They went on with their own thoughts, the Saint with his load, and Roger's arm about the girl's waist.

After a while Simon stopped, and they stopped with him. He was peering into the blackness at something they could not see. Then he bent slowly, and when he straightened up again there was nothing in his arms.

He touched Roger on the shoulder.

'Sorry to interrupt again,' he said softly, 'but between us and the car there are some specimens, I promised to take home for Chief Inspector Teal. If you'll just wait here a sec, I'll ripple over and complete the bag.'

He disappeared as silently and swiftly as a hunting panther.

The four men, with Mr Dyson, were standing in a little group by the car, talking in low voices, when the Saint came towards them in the starlight with Sleat's automatic in his hand.

Simon hated firearms, as has been related, but in the circumstances. . . .

'Good evening,' he remarked affably.

Silence fell on the group like a pall. Then, slowly and fearfully, they turned and saw him only a couple of yards away.

Shrilly, one man blasphemed. The others were mute, staring, dumb with a superstitious terror. And the Saint smiled like an angel through the dried blood on his face.

'I am the ghost of Julius Caesar,' he said sepulchrally, 'and unless you all immediately put up your hands, I shall turn you into little frogs.'

He came a little nearer, so that they could see him more plainly. And slowly their hands went up. Whatever doubts they might have had of his reality, the gun he displayed was real enough. But the fear of death was in their faces.

Then the laughter faded from Simon's eyes, leaving them bleak and merciless.

'You were accessories to torture,' he said, 'and you might well have been accessories to murder. Therefore in due course you will go to prison according to the law. But when you come out—in about three years, I should say—you will remember this night, and you will tell your friends. Let it help to teach you that the Saint cannot be beaten. But if I meet you again—'

He paused for a moment.

'If I meet you again,' he said, and waved one hand towards the moor, 'you may go to the place where your leader has already gone. I dislike your kind. . . .

'Meanwhile,' said the Saint, 'you may step forward one by one and take off your coats and braces, keeping up your trousers by faith and hope. Move!'

While his apparently eccentric commands were being carried out, he called Roger and directed him. One by one, the men's braces were used to fasten their hands securely behind their backs, and their coats, knotted by the sleeves, hobbled their legs.

'Not a bad day's work,' said the Saint, when it was done, 'but—'

Roger shot a quick glance of comprehension at him, and the girl's hand went out.

'I'd forgotten, old boy—'

'A good day's work, but tough,' said the Saint weakly, and leaned against the car.

Conway drove them back.

The prisoners were decanted at the police station in Torquay, there to await the morrow and the pleasure of Inspector Teal. There followed a call on a sympathetic physician on the road to St Marychurch. Finally, they were at the Golden Eagle Hotel, with the Saint clamouring for beer.

The manageress was still waiting up.

'Mr Conway—'

'Miss Cocker.'

'I thought. . . . Why, whatever—'

'No, indeed to goodness,' said Roger. 'If I have to tell that story again tonight, I shall scream.'

'And I shall burst into tears and ask to be taken away,' said the Saint, sinking into the first chair he encountered. 'The blithering idiots at the police station nearly sent me pots with their fool questions. I'm still wondering how we persuaded them not to lock us up as well. Fetch me some beer, somebody, for the love of Mike!'

It took some time to convince the manageress that the Saint had recovered sufficiently to be allowed a drink, but it was done. Simon made a quart look like a gill in hot weather, and then he rose to his feet with a yawn.

'Roger,' he said, 'if you'll hurry up and tuck Betty into bed, we'll go.'

Roger stared. He said:

'Go?'

'Go,' said the Saint. 'You know. The opposite of "come." There's something I particularly want to do tonight.'

'As the bishop said to the actress,' murmured the girl.

Gravely the Saint regarded her. Then—

'Betty, old girl,' he said, 'you'll do. I shall allow Roger to fall in love with you if he wants to. Those seven words prove you One of Us. I may say that for a girl who's been through all you've been through tonight—'

'But,' said Roger, 'you don't mean to go on to Newton Abbot now?'

Simon turned.

'When else?' he demanded. 'Teal's due tomorrow. Anyhow, we couldn't assault that garden with spades in broad daylight, looking like retired coal-miners on a busman's holiday, when the place is supposed to be closed down. It's tonight or never, son—and I feel we've earned those diamonds. Forty-five thousand to charity, and the odd ten per cent. fee for collection—which is one thousand two hundred and fifty pounds apiece—to Dicky Tremayne, Norman Kent, you and me. What price glory?'

Now, it should be recorded that at exactly 4.17 a.m. that morning, the Saint's spade struck upon something hard yet yielding, and his hail brought Roger across the garden at a run. Together they opened the soft leather bag, and examined the stones in the light of a torch.

At exactly 4.19 a.m., their own light was eclipsed by another that leapt on them from out of the darkness, and a familiar voice said: 'This is early for you to be up, Mr Templar.'

The Saint closed the bag and rose from the ground with a sigh.

'Late,' he said, 'is what you mean. Teal, you have an admirable faculty for being on the spot.'

'I couldn't wait,' said Chief Inspector Teal slumbrously. 'I was kept awake wondering what you boys were up to. So I got out my car and came right down. Let's go into the house and have a chat.'

'Yes, let's,' said the Saint, without enthusiasm.

They went into the house, and Simon had to fight his battle over again. Teal listened—he was a good listener—champing his favourite sweetmeat monotonously. He did not interrupt until the end of the story.

'And what happened to Sleat?'

Simon looked him in the eyes.

'When he saw Roger properly,' he said, 'Sleat was so overcome by Roger's beauty that he had a heart attack, and died all over the place. It was most distressing. However, we hadn't time to remove him, so he went up with the balloon, and all you're likely to find of him is his boots and his back stud. Sorry, I'm sure. It'll be difficult for the coroner.'

Teal nodded like a mandarin.

'I believe you,' he said sleepily. 'Thousands wouldn't, but I will. There's no evidence.'

'No,' said the Saint comfortably. 'There's no evidence.'

Teal got to his feet mountainously, and looked out of the window. The first wan silver of dawn was in the sky.

'I think,' he said, 'we might go over to Mr Conway's hotel and see if we can find some early breakfast.'

And further, as a matter of history, which the Press has had no opportunity to record, it should be noted that Teal himself, in the Saint's company, deposited the bag of diamonds at the police station in Exeter, at the same time as he transferred the Saint's prisoners there to await their trial at the next assizes, the following afternoon.

'You're not going back today?' asked the Saint solicitously.

'Not until tomorrow,' said Teal grimly. 'That's why it occurred to me to leave the diamonds here. If I kept them at the Golden Eagle, you boys might sleep-walk. I'm going to ask your Mr Conway if I can keep my room on for tonight—there's the explosion to investigate, and one or two other details I must get. I hope it won't inconvenience anyone.'

'We shall be delighted,' said the Saint truthfully.

At precisely 9 a.m. the following morning, a man in the uniform of the Metropolitan Police marched smartly into the Exeter Police Station.

'Detective-Constable Hawkins, of Scotland Yard,' he reported to the inspector. 'I came down with Mr Teal the night before last on the Policeman case. He's just sent me over to fetch the diamonds he left here and meet him at the railway station.'

'Have you an order?'

The policeman produced a paper. The inspector read it; and then he opened his safe and handed over the bag.

'Better take care of it,' he advised. 'It's supposed to be worth fifty thousand pounds.'

'Blimey!' said the policeman, in understandable awe.

The following morning, Simon Templar was holding a breakfast-party when Chief Inspector Teal was admitted.

'Have an egg,' invited the Saint hospitably. 'In fact, have two eggs. Don't go, Orace—we may want you.'

Teal sank into a chair and unwrapped a fresh wafer of gum.

'I'll have some diamonds,' he said.

'Sorry,' said the Saint, 'but Hatton Garden is still where it was, and Brook Street remains free of that sordid commerce. You must have got on the wrong bus.'

'Your friend Mr Conway—'

'Has temporarily left us. He's met a girl. You know what these young men are. But if there's any message I can give him—'

'You two are supposed to have come up to London on Friday night, aren't you?' said Teal sluggishly.

Simon raised his eyebrows.

'Why "supposed"?' he demanded innocently.

'Does anyone else know it except yourselves?'

The Saint leaned back in his chair.

'At eight ack emma on Saturday morning, yesterday,' he said, 'a party of us breakfasted here together. That is a ceremony which we observe religiously on every fourth anniversary of the death of Sir Richard Arkwright. After breakfast, we walk out in straw hats and football boots, and go and sail paper boats in the Round Pond. That's part of the ceremony.'

'Yes?' prompted the torpid Mr Teal.

'At this breakfast,' said the Saint, 'there were present Mr Conway and Miss Aldo, who aren't here today to answer for themselves, and also those whom you see repeating the performance this morning—Miss Patricia Holm and Mr Richard Tremayne. Orace served us. You ask them if that isn't true.'

'I see,' said Mr Teal, as if he didn't see at all.

'Therefore,' said the Saint speciously, 'we couldn't possibly have been in Exeter at nine o'clock on Saturday morning, which I understand is the time when the mysterious policeman removed the swag from the police station with a forged order.'

'How did you know about that?' asked Teal, quickly for him.

'About what?'

'About the policeman taking the diamonds.'

'Why,' said the Saint indignantly, 'I never said anything about a policeman or about the diamonds. Did I, Pat? . . . Did I, Dicky? . . . Did I, Orace? . . .'

Solemnly the three persons appealed to shook their heads.

'There!' said the Saint. 'You must be dreaming, Teal!'

Very slowly, Chief Inspector Teal inclined his head.

'I see,' he said, in his monumentally tired way—'I see. The technical name for that is an alibi.'

'Do we call it a day, Teal?' said the Saint insinuatingly.

Mr Teal's jaws continued to oscillate rhythmically, and his round head had not stopped nodding. He seemed, as he always did at such moments, on the point of falling off to sleep from sheer boredom.

'It's a day,' said Mr Teal wearily. 'It's a day!'

I

For a law-breaker, in the midst of his law-breaking, to be attempting at the same time to carry on a feud with a Chief Inspector of Police, might be called heroically quixotic. It might equally well be called pure blame-foolishness of the most suicidal variety—according to the way you look at these things.

Simon Templar found it vastly entertaining.

Chief Inspector Claud Eustace Teal, of the Criminal Investigation Department, New Scotland Yard, that great detective (and he was nearly as great in mere bulk as he was in reputation) found it an interesting novelty.

Teal was reputed to have the longest memory of any man at the Yard. It was said, perhaps with some exaggeration, that if the Records Office happened to be totally destroyed by fire, Teal could personally have rewritten the entire dossier of every criminal therein recorded, methods, habits, haunts, and notable idiosyncrasies completely included—and added thereto a rough but reliable sketch of every set of fingerprints therewith connected. Certainly, he had a long memory.

He distinctly remembered a mysterious Policeman, whom an enterprising journalist called the Policeman with Wings, who was strangely reincarnated some time after the originator and (normal) patentee of the idea had departed to Heaven—or some other place beginning with the same letter—on top of a pile of dynamite, thereby depriving Teal of the pleasure of handing over to his Commissioner fifty thousand pounds' worth of diamonds which had been lost for seven years.

Mr Teal suspected—not without reason—that Simon Templar's fertile brain had given birth to the dénouement of that gentle jest. And Mr Teal's memory was long.

Therefore the secret activities of the Saint came to be somewhat hampered by a number of massive gentlemen in bowler hats, who took to patrolling Brook Street in relays like members of a Scottish clan mounting guard over the spot where their chieftain is sure he had dropped a sixpence.

The day arrived when Simon Templar tired of this gloomy spectacle, and, having nothing else to do, armed himself with a stout stick and sallied forth for a walk, looking as furtive and conspiratorial as he knew how.

He was as fit as a fiddle, and shouting for exercise. He walked westward through London, and crossed the Thames by Putney Bridge. He left Kingston behind him. Continuing south-west, he took Esher and Cobham in his stride. He walked fast, enjoying himself. Not until he reached Ripley did he pause, and there he swung into a convenient hostel towards six o'clock, after twenty-three brisk miles had been spurned by his Veldtschoen.

The afternoon had been sunny and warm. Simon knocked back a couple of pints of beer as if he felt he had earned every drop of them, smoked a couple of cigarettes, and then started back to the road with a refreshed spring in his step.

On his way out, in another bar, he saw a man with a very red face. The man had a bowler hat on the seat beside him, and he appeared to be melting steadily into a large spotted handkerchief.

Simon approached him like an old friend.

'Are you ready to go on?' he asked. 'I'm making for Guildford next. From there, I make for Winchester, where I shall have dinner, and I expect to sleep in Southampton tonight. At six-thirty tomorrow morning I start for Liverpool, via Land's End. Near Manchester, I expect to murder a mulatto gas-fitter with a false nose. After which, if you care to follow me to John o' Groats—'

The rest of the conversation was conducted, on one side at least, in language which might have made a New York stevedore feel slightly shocked.

Simon passed on with a pained expression, and went on his way.

A mile farther on, he slowed his pace to a stroll, and was satisfied that Red Face was no longer bringing up the rear. Shortly afterwards, a blue sports saloon swept past him with a rush and stopped a few yards away. As he reached it, a girl leaned out, and Simon greeted her with a smile.

'Hullo, Pat darling,' he said. 'Let's go and have a cocktail and some dinner.'

He climbed in, and Patricia Holm let in the clutch.

'How's the market in bowler hats?' she asked.

'Weakening,' murmured the Saint. 'Weakening, old dear. The bulls weren't equal to the strain. Let's change the subject. Why are you so beautiful, Pat?'

She flung him a dazzling smile.

'Probably,' she said, 'because I find I'm still in love with you—after a whole year. And you're still in love with me. The combination's enough to make anyone beautiful.'

It was late when they got back to London.

At the flat in Brook Street, Roger Conway and Dicky Tremayne were drinking the Saint's beer.

'There was some for you,' said Roger, 'only we drank it in case it went flat.'

'Thoughtful of you,' said the Saint.

He calmly annexed Mr Conway's tankard, and sank into a chair.

'Well, soaks,' he remarked, 'how was the English countryside looking this afternoon?'

'I took the North Road,' said Roger. 'My little Mary's lamb petered out at St Alban's, and Dicky picked me up just beyond. Twenty-one miles by the clock—in five hours forty-five minutes Fahrenheit. How's that?'

'Out,' said the Saint. 'I did twenty-three miles in five and a half hours dead. My sleuth was removed to hospital on an asbestos stretcher, and when they tried to revive him with brandy he burst into flames. We shall hear more of this.'

Nevertheless, the following morning, Orace, bringing in his master's early tea, reported that a fresh detachment of bowler hats had arrived in Brook Street, and the Saint had to devote his ingenuity to thinking out other means of evading their vigilance.

In the next fortnight, the Saint sent £9,000 to charity, and Inspector Teal, who knew that to obtain that money the Saint must have 'persuaded' someone to write him a cheque for £10,000, from which had been deducted the 10 per cent commission which the Saint always claimed according to his rules, was annoyed. His squad, interrogated, were unable to make any suggestions as to the source of the gift. No, Simon Templar had done nothing suspicious. No, he had not been seen visiting or associating with any suspicious characters. No, he . . .

'You're as much use as so many sick headaches,' said Teal unkindly. 'In fact, less use. You can stop watching that house. It's obviously a waste of your time—not,' he added sweetly, 'that the Department has missed you.'

The climax came a few days later, when a cocaine smuggler whom Teal had been watching for months was at last caught with the goods as he stepped ashore at Dover. Teal, 'acting on information received,' snapped the bracelets on his wrists in the Customs House, and personally accompanied his prisoner on the train to London, sitting alone in a reserved compartment with his captive.

He did not know that Simon Templar was on the train until they were fifteen minutes out of Victoria Station, when the Saint calmly walked in and hailed him joyfully.

'Can you read?' asked Teal.

'No,' said the Saint.

Teal pointed to the red labels pasted on the windows.

'R-E-S-E-R-V-E-D,' he spelt out. 'Do you know the word?'

'No,' said the Saint.

He sat down, after one curious glance at the man at Teal's side, and produced a gold cigarette-case.

'I believe I owe you an apology for walking one of your men off his feet a while ago,' he said. 'Really, I think you asked for it, but I'm told you're sore. Can't we kiss and be friends?'

'No,' said Teal.

'Have a cigarette?'

'I don't smoke cigarettes.'

'A cigar, then?'

Teal turned warily.

'I've had some of your jokes,' he said. 'Does this one explode, or is it the kind that blows soot all over your face when you light it?'

Simon handed over the weed. It was unmistakably excellent. Teal wavered, and bit off the end absent-mindedly.

'Maybe I was unreasonable,' he conceded, puffing. 'But *you* asked for something before I ever did. And one day you'll get it. See this bright boy?'

He aimed his cigar at the prisoner, and the Saint nodded.

'I've been after him for the best part of a year. And he's had plenty of laughs off me before I got him. Now it's my turn. It'll be the same with you. I can wait. One day you'll go too far, you'll make a mistake, and—'

'I know that man,' said the Saint.

He looked across the compartment with cold eyes.

'He is a blackmailer and a dealer in drugs. His name is Cyril Farrast, and he is thirty-two years old. He had one previous .conviction.'

Teal was surprised, but he concealed it by lowering his eyelids sleepily. He always looked most bored when he was most interested.

'I know all that,' he said. 'But how do you know?'

'I've been looking for him,' said the Saint simply, and the man stared. 'Even now, I still want him. Not for the dope business—I see you're going to take care of that—but for a girl in Yorkshire. There are thousands of stories like it, but this one happened to come to my notice. He'll recognise her name—but does he know who I am?'

'I'll introduce you,' said Teal, and turned to his captive. 'Cyril, this is Simon Templar. You've heard of him. He's known as the Saint.'

The man shrank away in horror, and Simon grinned gently.

'Oh, no,' he drawled. 'That's only Teal's nasty suspicious mind. . . .
But if I *were* the Saint, I should want you, Cyril Farrast, because
of Elsa Gordon, who committed suicide eleven days ago. I ought
to kill you, but Teal has told me to be good. So, instead—'

Farrast was white to the lips. His mouth moved, but no sound
came. Then—

'It's a lie!' he screamed, 'you can't touch me—'

Teal pushed him roughly back, and faced the Saint.

'Templar, if you think you're going to do anything funny—'

'I'm sure of it.' Simon glanced at his watch. 'That cigar, for
instance, is due to function about now. No explosives, no soot. A
much better joke than that. . . .'

Teal was holding the cigar, staring at it. He felt very weak. His
head seemed to have been aching for a long time.

With a sudden convulsive effort he pitched the cigar through
the window, and his hand began to reach round to his hip pocket.
Then he sprawled limply sideways.

A porter woke him at Victoria.

That night there were warrants out for the arrest of Simon
Templar and all his friends. But the flat in Brook Street was shut
up, and the janitor stated that the owners had gone away for a
week—destination unknown.

The Press was not informed. Teal had his price.

Three days later, a large coffin, labelled FRAGILE—HANDLE
CARELESSLY—ANY OLD SIDE UP, was delivered at New
Scotland Yard, addressed to Chief Inspector Teal. When examined,
it was heard to tick loudly, and the explosives experts opened it
at dead of night in some trepidation in the middle of Hyde Park.

They found a large alarm clock—and Cyril Farrast.

He was bound hand and foot, and gagged. And his bare back
showed that he had been terribly flogged.

Also in the coffin was a slip of paper bearing the sign of the
Saint. And in a box, carefully preserved in tissue paper and
corrugated cardboard, was a cigar.

When Teal arrived home that night he found Simon Templar patiently waiting on his doorstep.

'I got your cigar,' Teal said grimly.

'Smoke it,' said the Saint. 'It's a good one. If you fancy the brand, I'll mail you the rest of the box tomorrow.'

'Come in,' said Teal.

He led the way, and the Saint followed. In the tiny sitting-room, Teal unwrapped the cigar, and the Saint lighted a cigarette.

'Also,' said Teal, 'I've got a warrant for your arrest.'

'And no case to use it on,' said Simon. 'You've got your man back.'

'You flogged him.'

'He's the only man who can bring that charge against me. You can't.'

'If you steal something and send it back, that doesn't dispose of the charge of theft—if we care to prosecute.'

'But you wouldn't,' smiled the Saint, watching Teal light the cigar. 'Frankly, now, between ourselves, would it be worth it? I notice the papers haven't said anything about the affair. That was wise of you. But if you charged me, you couldn't keep it out of the papers. And all England would be laughing over the story of how the great Claud Eustace Teal'—the detective winced—'was caught on the bend with the old, old doped cigar. Honestly—wouldn't it be better to call it a day?'

Teal frowned, looking straight at the smiling young man before him.

From the hour of his first meeting with the Saint, Teal had recognised an indefinable superiority. It lay in nothing that the Saint did or said. It was simply there. Simon Templar was not common clay; and Teal, who was of the good red earth earthy, realised the fact without resentment.

'Seriously, then, Templar,' said Teal, 'don't you see the hole you put me in? You took Farrast away and flogged him—that remains. And he saw you talking to me in the train. If he liked, he could say in Court that we were secretly aiding and abetting you. The police are in the limelight just now, and a lot of the mud would stick.'

'Farrast is dumb,' answered Simon. 'I promise you that. Because I told him that if he breathed a word of what had happened, I should find him and kill him. And he believes it. You see, I appreciated your difficulty.'

Teal could think fast. He nodded.

'You win again,' he said. 'I think the Commissioner'll pass it—this once—since you've sent the man back. But another time—'

'I never repeat myself,' said the Saint. 'That's why you'll never catch me. But thanks, all the same.'

He picked up his hat; but he turned back at the door.

'By the way—has this affair, on top of the diamonds, put you in bad with the Commissioner?'

'I won't deny it.'

The Saint looked at the ceiling.

'I'd like to put that right,' he said. 'Now, there's a receiver of stolen goods living in Notting Hill, named Albert Handers. Most of the big stuff passes through his hands, and I know you've been wanting him for a longish while.'

Teal started.

'How the deuce—'

'Never mind that. If you really want to smooth down the Commissioner, you'll wait for Handers at Croydon Aerodrome tomorrow morning, when he proposes to fly to Amsterdam with the proceeds of the Asheton robbery. The diamonds will be sewn into the carrying handle of his valise. I wonder you've never thought of that, the times you've stopped him and searched him. . . . Night-night, sonny boy!'

He was gone before the plump detective could stop him; and that night the Saint slept again in Brook Street.

But the information which the Saint had given came from Dicky Tremayne, another of the gang, and it signalled the beginning of the end of a coup to which Tremayne had devoted a year of patient preparation.

II

Dicky Tremayne walked into the Saint's flat late one night, and found the Saint in pyjamas. Dicky Tremayne was able to walk in at any hour, because, like Roger Conway, he had his own key. Dicky Tremayne said: 'Saint, I feel I'm going to fall in love.'

The Saint slewed round, raising his eyes to heaven.

'What—not again?' he protested.

'Again,' snapped Dicky. 'It's an infernal nuisance, but there you are. A man must do something.'

Simon put away his book and reached for a cigarette from the box that stood conveniently open on the table at his elbow.

'Burn it,' said Simon. 'I always thought Archie Sheridan was bad enough. Till he went and got married, I used to spend my spare time wondering why he never got landed. But since you came out of your hermitage, and we let you go and live unchaperoned in Paris—'

'I know,' snapped Dicky. 'I can't help it. But it may be serious this time.'

Match in hand, Simon regarded him.

Norman Kent was the most darkly attractive of the Saints; Archie Sheridan had been the most delightfully irresponsible; Roger Conway was the most good-looking; but Dicky . . .

Dicky Tremayne was dark and handsome in the clean, keen-faced way which is the despairing envy of the Latin, and with it Dicky's elegance had a Continental polish and his eye a wicked Continental gleam. Dicky was what romantic maidens call a sheik—and yet he was unspoiled. Also he had a courage and a cheerfulness which never failed him. The Saint had a very real affection for Dicky.

'Who is it this time, son?' he asked.

Tremayne walked to the window and stared out.

'Her house in Park Lane was taken in the name of the Countess Anusia Marova,' he said. 'So was the yacht she's chartered for the season. But she was born in Boston, Mass., twenty-three years ago, and her parents called her Audrey Perowne. She's had a lot of names since then, but the Amsterdam police knew her best as "Straight" Audrey. You know who I mean.'

'And you—'

'You know what I've done. I spent all my time in Paris working in with Hilloran, who was her right-hand man in the States, because we were sure they'd get together sooner or later, and then we'd make one killing of the pair. And they *are* together again, and I'm in London as a fully accredited member of the gang. Everything's ready. And now I want to know why we ever bothered.'

Simon shrugged.

'Hilloran's name is bad enough, and she's made more money—'

'Why do they call her "Straight" Audrey?'

'Because she's never touched or dealt in dope, which is considered eccentric in a woman crook. And because it's said to be unhealthy to get fresh with her. Apart from that, she's dabbled in pretty well everything—'

Dicky nodded helplessly.

'I know, old man,' he said. 'I know it all. You're going to say that she and Hilloran, to us, were just a pair of crooks who'd made so much out of the game that we decided to make them contribute. We'd never met her. And it isn't as if she were a man—'

'And yet,' said the Saint, 'I remember a woman whom you wanted to kill. And I expect you'd have done it, if she hadn't died of her own accord.'

'She was a—'

'Quite. But you'd 've treated her exactly the same as you'd 've treated a man engaged in the same traffic.'

'There's nothing like that about Audrey Perowne.'

'You're trying to argue that she's really hardly more of a crook than we are. Her crime record's pretty clean, and the men she's robbed could afford to lose.'

'Isn't that so?'

Simon studied his cigarette-end.

'Once upon a time,' he observed, 'there was a rich man named John L. Morganheim. He died at Palm Beach—mysteriously. And Audrey Perowne was—er—keeping him company. You understand? It had to be hushed up, of course. His family couldn't have a scandal. Still—'

Tremayne went pale.

'We don't know the whole of that story,' he said.

'We don't,' admitted the Saint. 'We only know certain facts. And they mayn't be such thundering good facts, anyhow. But they're there—till we know something better.'

He got to his feet, and laid a hand on Dicky's shoulder.

'Let's have some straight talk, Dicky,' he suggested. 'You're beginning to feel you can't go through with the job. Am I right?'

Tremayne spread out his hands.

'That's about the strength of it. We've got to be sure—'

'Let's be sure, then,' agreed the Saint. 'But meanwhile, what's the harm in carrying on? You can't object to the thrashing of Farrast. You can't feel cut up about the shopping of Handers. And you can't mind what sort of a rise we take out of Hilloran. What we do about the girl can be decided later—when we're sure. Till then, where's the point in chucking in your hand?'

Tremayne looked at him.

'There's sense in that.'

'Of course there's sense in it!' cried the Saint. 'There's more in the gang than one girl. We want the rest. We want them like I want the mug of beer you're going to fetch me in a minute. Why shouldn't we have 'em?'

Dicky nodded slowly.

'I knew you'd say that. But I felt you ought to know. . . .'

Simon slapped him on the back.

'You're a great lad,' he said. 'And now, what about that beer?'

Beer was brought, and tasted with a fitting reverence. The discussion was closed.

With the Saint, momentous things could be brought up, argued, and dismissed like that. With Roger Conway, perhaps, the argument would have been pursued all night—but that was only because Roger and the Saint loved arguing. Dicky was reserved. Rarely did he throw off his reserve and talk long and seriously. The Saint understood, and respected his reticence. Dicky understood also. By passing on so light-heartedly to a cry for beer, the Saint did not lose one iota of the effect of sympathy; rather, he showed that his sympathy was complete.

Dicky could have asked for nothing more; and when he put down his tankard and helped himself to a cigarette, the discussion might never have raised its head between them.

'To resume,' he said, 'we leave on the twenty-ninth.'

Simon glanced at the calendar on the wall.

'Three days,' he murmured. 'And the cargo of billionaires?'

'Complete.' Dicky grinned. 'Saint, you've got to hand it to that girl. Seven of 'em—with their wives. Of course, she's spent a year dry-nursing them. Sir Esdras Levy—George Y. Ulrig—Matthew Sankin—'

He named four others whose names could be conjured with in the world of high finance.

'It's a peach of an idea.'

'I can't think of anything like it,' said the Saint. 'Seven bloated perambulating gold-mines with diamond studs, and their wives loaded up with enough jewellery to sink a battleship. She gets them off on the rolling wave—knowing they'll have all their sparklers ready to make a show at the ports they touch—on a motor yacht manned by her own crew—'

'Chief Steward, J. Hilloran—'

'And the first thing the world'll know of it will be when the cargo is found marooned on the Barbary coast, and the *Corsican Maid* has sailed off into the blue with the whichnots. . . . Oh, boy! As a philosophic student, I call that the elephant's tonsils.'

Dicky nodded.

'The day after tomorrow,' he said, 'we leave by special train to join the yacht at Marseilles. You've got to say that girl does her jobs in style.'

'How do you go?'

'As her secretary. But—how do you go?'

'I haven't quite made up my mind yet. Roger's taking a holiday—I guess he deserves it. Norman and Pat are still cruising the Mediterranean. I'll handle this one from the outside alone. I leave the inside to you—and that's the most important part.'

'I mayn't be able to see you again before we leave.'

'Then you'll have to take a chance. But I think I shall also be somewhere on the ocean. If you have to communicate, signal in Morse out of a porthole, with an electric torch, either at midnight or four in the morning. I'll be on the look-out at those times. If. . . .'

They talked for two hours before Tremayne rose to go. He did so at last.

'It's the first real job I've had,' he said. 'I'd like to make it a good one. Wish me luck, Saint!'

Simon held out his hand.

'Sure—you'll pull it off, Dicky. All the best, son. And about that girl—'

'Yes, about that girl,' said Dicky shortly. Then he grinned ruefully. 'Good night, old man.'

He went, with a crisp handshake and a frantic smile. He went as he had come, by way of the fire escape at the back of the building, for the Saint's friends had caution thrust upon them in those days.

The Saint watched him go in silence, and remembered that frantic smile after he had gone. Then he lighted another cigarette and smoked it thoughtfully, sitting on the table in the centre of the room. Presently he went to bed.

Dicky Tremayne did not go home to bed at once. He walked round to the side street where he had left his car, and drove to Park Lane.

The lights were still on in an upper window of the house outside which he stopped; and Tremayne entered without hesitation, despite the lateness of the hour, using his own key. The room in which he had seen the lights was on the first floor; it was used as a study and communicated with the Countess Anusia Marova's bedroom. Dicky knocked, and walked in.

'Hullo, Audrey,' he said.

'Make yourself at home,' she said, without looking up.

She was in a rich blue silk kimono and brocade slippers, writing at a desk. The reading lamp at her elbow struck gold from her hair.

There was a cut-glass decanter on the side table, glasses, a siphon, an inlaid cigarette-box. Dicky helped himself to a drink and a cigarette, and sat down where he could see her.

The enthusiastic compilers of the gossip columns in the daily and weekly Press had called her the most beautiful hostess of the season. That in itself would have meant little, seeing that fashionable hostesses are always described as 'beautiful'—like fashionable brides, bridesmaids and débutantes. What, therefore, can it mean to be the most beautiful of such a galaxy?

But in this case something like the truth might well have been told. Audrey Perowne had grave grey eyes and an enchanting mouth. Her skin was soft and fine without the help of beauty parlours. Her colour was her own. And she was tall, with the healthy grace of her kind; and you saw pearls when she smiled.

Dicky feasted his eyes.

She wrote. She stopped writing. She read what she had written, placed the sheet in an envelope, and addressed it. Then she turned.

'Well?'

'I just thought I'd drop in,' said Dicky. 'I saw the lights were on as I came past, so I knew you were up.'

'Did you enjoy your golf?'

Golf was Dicky's alibi. From time to time he went out in the afternoon, saying that he was going to play a round at Sunningdale. Nearly always, he came back late, saying that he had stayed late playing cards at the club. Those were the times when he saw the Saint.

Dicky said that he had enjoyed his golf.

171

'Give me a cigarette,' she commanded.

He obeyed.

'And a match. . . . Thanks. . . . What's the matter with you, Dicky? I shouldn't have had to ask for that.'

He brought her an ashtray and returned to his seat.

'I'm hanged if I know,' he said. 'Too many late nights, I should think. I feel tired.'

'Hilloran's only just left,' she said, with deceptive inconsequence.

'Has he?'

She nodded.

'I've taken back his key. In future, you'll be the only man who can stroll in here when and how he likes.' Dicky shrugged, not knowing what to say. She added: 'Would you like to live here?'

He was surprised.

'Why? We leave in a couple of days. Even then, it hadn't occurred to me—'

'It's still occurring to Hilloran,' she said, 'even if we are leaving in a couple of days. But you live in a poky little flat in Bayswater, while there are a dozen rooms going to waste here. And it's never occurred to you to suggest moving in?'

'It never entered my head.'

She smiled.

'That's why I like you, Dicky,' she said. 'And it's why I let you keep your key. I'm glad you came tonight.'

'Apart from your natural pleasure at seeing me again—why?'

The girl studied a slim ankle.

'It's my turn to ask questions,' she said. 'And I ask you—why are you a crook, Dicky Tremayne?'

She looked up at him quickly as she spoke, and he met her eyes with an effort.

The blow had fallen. He had seen it coming for months—the day when he would have to account for himself. And he had dreaded it, though he had his story perfectly prepared. Hilloran had tried to deliver the blow; but Hilloran, shrewd as he was, had been easy. The girl was not easy.

She had never broached the subject before, and Dicky had begun to think that Hilloran's introduction had sufficiently disposed of questions. He had begun to think that the girl was satisfied, without making enquiries of her own. And that delusion was now rudely shattered.

He made a vague gesture.

'I thought you knew,' he said. 'A little trouble in the Guards, followed by the O.B.E. You know. Order of the Boot—Everywhere. I could either accept the licking, or fight back. I chose to fight back. On the whole, it's paid me.'

'What's your name?' she asked suddenly.

He raised his eyebrows.

'Dicky Tremayne.'

'I meant—your real name.'

'Dicky is real enough.'

'And the other?'

'Need we go into that?'

She was still looking at him. Tremayne felt that the grim way in which he was returning her stare was becoming as open to suspicion as shiftiness would have been. He glanced away, but she called him back peremptorily.

'Look at me—I want to see you.'

Brown eyes met grey steadily for an intolerable minute. Dicky felt his pulse throbbing faster, but the thin straight line of smoke that went up from his cigarette never wavered.

Then, to his amazement, she smiled.

'Is this a joke?' he asked evenly.

She shook her head.

'I'm sorry,' she said. 'I wanted to make sure if you were straight—straight as far as I'm concerned, I mean. You see, Dicky, I'm worried.'

'You don't trust me?'

She returned his gaze.

'I had my doubts. That's why I had to make sure—in my own way. I feel sure now. It's only a feeling, but I go by feelings. I feel that you wouldn't let me down—now. But I'm still worried.'

'What about?'

'There's a squeaker in the camp,' she said. 'Somebody's selling us. Until this moment, I was prepared to believe it was you.'

### III

Tremayne sat like an image, mechanically flicking the ash from his cigarette. Every word had gone through him like a knife, but never by a twitch of a muscle had he shown it.

He said calmly enough: 'I don't think anyone could blame you.'

'Listen,' she said. 'You ask for it—from anyone like me. Hilloran's easy to fool. He's cleverer than most, but you could bamboozle him any day. I'm more inquisitive—and you're too secretive. You don't say anything about your respectable past. Perhaps that's natural. But you don't say anything about your disreputable past, either—and that's extraordinary. If it comes to the point, we've only got your word for it that you're a crook at all.'

He shook his head.

'Not good enough,' he replied. 'If I were a dick, sneaking into your gang in order to shop you—first, I'd have been smart enough to get Headquarters to fix me up with a convincing list of previous convictions, with the co-operation of the Press, and, second, we'd have pulled in the lot of you weeks ago.'

She had taken a chair beside him. With an utterly natural gesture, that nevertheless came strangely and unexpectedly from her, she laid a hand on his arm.

'I know, Dicky,' she said. 'I told you I trusted you—now. Not for any logical reasons, but because my hunch says you're not that sort. But I'll let you know that if I hadn't decided I could trust you—I'd be afraid of you.'

'Am I so frightening?'

'You were.'

He stirred uncomfortably, frowning.

'This is queer talk from you, Audrey,' he said, rather brusquely. 'Somehow, one doesn't expect any sign of weakness—or fear—from you. Let's be practical. What makes you so sure there's a squeaker?'

'Handers. You saw he was taken yesterday?' Dicky nodded. 'It wasn't a fluke. I'll swear Teal would never have tumbled to that valise-handle trick. Besides, the papers said he was "acting on information received." You know what that means?'

'It sounds like a squeal, but—'

'The loss doesn't matter so much—ten thousand pounds and three weeks' work—when we're set to pull down twenty times that amount in a few days. But it makes me wonder what's going to happen to the big job.'

Tremayne looked at her straightly.

'If you don't think I'm the squeaker,' he said, 'who do you think it is?'

'There's only one other man, as far as I know, who was in a position to shop Handers.'

'Namely?'

'Hilloran.'

Dicky stared.

The situation was grotesque. If it had been less grotesque, it would have been laughable; but it was too grotesque even for laughter. And Dicky didn't feel like laughing.

The second cut was overwhelming. First she had half accused him of being the traitor; and then, somehow, he had convinced her of a lie without speaking a word, and she had declared that she trusted him. And now, making him her confidant, she was turning the eye of her suspicion upon the man who had been her chief lieutenant on the other side of the Atlantic.

'Hilloran,' objected Dicky lamely, 'worked for you—'

'Certainly. And then I fired him—with some home truths in lieu of notice. I patched it up and took him back for this job because he's a darned useful man. But that doesn't say he's forgiven and forgotten.'

'You think he's out to double-cross you, and get his own back and salve his vanity?'

'It's not impossible.'

'But—'

She interrupted with an impatient movement.

'You don't get the point. I thought I'd make it plain. Apart from anything else, Hilloran seems to think I'd make a handsome ornament for his home. He's been out for that lay ever since I first met him. He was particularly pressing tonight, and I sent him away with several large fleas in each ear. I'll admit he was well oiled, and I had to show him a gun—'

Dicky's face darkened.

'As bad as that?'

She laughed shortly.

'You needn't be heroic about it, Dicky. The ordinary conventions aren't expected to apply in our world. Being outside the pale, we're reckoned to be frankly ruddy, and we usually are. However, I just happen to be funny that way—Heaven knows why. The point is that Hilloran's as sore and spiteful as a coyote on hot tiles, and if he didn't know it was worth a quarter of a million dollars to keep in with me—'

'He might try to sell you?'

'Even now,' said the girl, 'when the time comes, he mightn't be content with his quarter share.'

Dicky's brain was seething with this new spate of ideas. On top of everything else, then, Hilloran was playing a game of his own. That game might lead him to laying information before the police on his own account, or, far more probably, to the conception of a scheme for turning the entire proceeds of the 'big job' into his own pocket.

It was a factor which Tremayne had never considered. He hadn't yet absorbed it properly. And he had to get the main lines of it hard and clear, get the map of the situation nailed out in his mind in a strong light, before—

Zzzzzzz . . . zzzzzzzz. . . .

'What's that?'

'The front door,' said the girl, and pointed. 'There's a buzzer in my bedroom. See who it is.'

Dicky went to a window and peered out from behind the curtains. He came back soberly.

'Hilloran's back again,' he said. 'Whatever he's come about, he must have seen my car standing outside. And it's nearly four o'clock in the morning.' She met his eyes. 'Shall we say it's difficult?'

She understood. It was obvious, anyway.

'What would you like me to do?' asked Dicky.

The buzzer sounded again—a long, insistent summons. Then the smaller of the two telephones on the desk tinkled.

The girl picked up the receiver.

'Hullo. . . . Yes. He can come up.'

She put down the instrument and returned to her armchair.

'Another cigarette, Dicky.'

He passed her the box, and struck a match.

'What would you like me to do?' he repeated.

'Anything you like,' she said coolly. 'If I didn't think your gentlemanly instincts would be offended, I'd suggest that you took off your coat and tried to look abandoned, draping yourself artistically on the arm of this chair. In any case you can be as objectionable as Hilloran will be. If you can help him to lose his temper, he may show some of his hand.'

Dicky came thoughtfully to his feet, his glass in his hand.

Then the girl raised her voice, clearly and sweetly.

'Dicky—darling—'

Hilloran stood in the doorway, a red-faced giant of a man, swaying perceptibly. His dinner jacket was crumpled, his tie askew, his hair tousled. It was plain that he had had more to drink since he left the house.

'Audrey—'

'It is usual,' said the girl coldly, 'to knock.'

Hilloran lurched forward. In his hand he held something which he flung down into her lap.

'Look at that!'

The girl picked up the cards languidly.

'I didn't know you were a proud father,' she remarked. 'Or have you been taking up art yourself?'

'Two of 'em!' blurted Hilloran thickly. 'I found one pinned to my door when I got home. The other I found here—pinned to your front door—since I left! Don't you recognise it—the warning? It means that the Saint has been here tonight!'

The girl's face had changed colour. She held the cards out to Dicky.

Hilloran snatched them viciously away.

'No, you don't!' he snarled. 'I want to know what you're doing here at all, in this room, at this hour of the morning.'

Audrey Perowne rose.

'Hilloran,' she said icily, 'I'll thank you not to insult my friend in my own house.'

The man leered at her.

'You will, will you? You'd like to be left alone with him, when you know the Saint's sitting round waiting to smash us. If you don't value your own skin, I value mine. You're supposed to be the leader—'

'I am the leader.'

'Are you? ... Yes, you lead. You've led me on enough. Now you're leading him on. You little—'

Tremayne's fist smashed the word back into Hilloran's teeth.

As the man crashed to the floor, Dicky whipped off his coat.

Hilloran put a hand to his mouth, and the same came away wet and red. Then he shot out a shaky forefinger.

'You—you skunk—I know you! You're here making love to Audrey, crawling in like a snake—and all the time you're planning to squeal on us. Ask him, Audrey!' The pointing finger stiffened, and the light of drunken hate in the man's eyes was bestial. '*Ask him what he knows about the Saint!*'

Dicky Tremayne stood perfectly still.

He knew that the girl was looking at him. He knew that Hilloran could have no possible means of substantiating his accusation. He knew also how a seed sown in a bed of panic could grow, and realised that he was very near death.

And he never moved.

'Get up, Hilloran,' he said quietly. 'Get up and have the rest of your teeth knocked out.'

Hilloran was scrambling to his feet.

'Yes, I'll get up!' he rasped, and his hand was making for his pocket. 'But I've my own way of dealing with rats—'

And there was an automatic in his hand. His finger was trembling over the trigger. Dicky saw it distinctly.

Then, in a flash, the girl was between them.

'If you want the police here,' she said, 'you'll shoot. But I shan't be here to be arrested with you.'

Hilloran raved: 'Out of the way, you—'

'Leave him to me,' said Dicky.

He put her aside, and the muzzle of the automatic touched his chest. He smiled into the flaming eyes.

'May I smoke a cigarette?' he asked politely. His right hand reached to his breast pocket in the most natural way in the world.

Hilloran's scream of agony shattered the silence.

Like lightning, Dicky's right hand had dropped and gripped Hilloran's right hand, at the same instant as Dicky's left hand fastened paralysingly on Hilloran's right arm just above the elbow. The wrench that almost broke Hilloran's wrist was made almost in the same movement.

The gun thudded into the carpet at their feet, but Tremayne took no notice. Retaining and strengthening his grip, he turned Hilloran round and forced him irresistibly to his knees. Tremayne held him there with one hand.

'We can talk more comfortably now,' he remarked.

He looked at the girl, and saw that she had picked up the fallen automatic.

'Before we go any further, Audrey,' he said, 'I should like to know what you think of the suggestion—that I might be a friend of the Saint's. I needn't remind you that this object is jealous as well as drunk. I won't deny the charge, because that wouldn't cut any ice. I'd just like your opinion.'

'Let him go, first.'

'Certainly.'

With a twist of his hand, Dicky released the man and sent him toppling over on to his face.

'Hilloran, get up!'

'If you—'

'*Get up!*'

Hilloran stumbled to his feet. There was murder in his eyes, but he obeyed. No man of his calibre could have challenged that command. Dicky thought, 'A crook—and she can wear power like a queen. . . .'

'I want to know, Hilloran,' observed the girl frostily, 'why you said what you said just now.'

The man glared.

'He can't account for himself, and he doesn't look or behave like one of us. We know there's a squeaker somewhere—someone who squealed on Handers—and he's the only one—'

'I see.' The contempt in the girl's voice had the quality of concentrated acid. 'What I see most is that because I prefer his company to yours, you're ready to trump up any wild charge against him that comes into your head—in the hope of putting him out of favour.'

'And *I* see,' sneered Hilloran, 'that *I'm* the one who's out of favour—because he's taken my place. He's—'

'Either,' said the girl, 'you can walk out on your own flat feet, or you can be thrown out. Take your choice. And whichever way you go, don't come back here till you're sober and ready to apologise.'

Hilloran's fists clenched.

'You're supposed to be bossing this gang—'

'I am,' said Audrey Perowne. 'And if you don't like it, you cut out as soon as you like.'

Hilloran swallowed.

'All right—'

'Yes?' prompted Audrey silkily.

'One day,' said Hilloran, staring from under black brows, 'you're going to be sorry for this. We know where we are. You don't want to fire me before the big job, because I'm useful. And I'll take everything lying down for the same time, because there's a heap of money in it for me. Yes, I'm drunk, but I'm not too drunk to be able to see that.'

'That,' said the girl sweetly, 'is good news. Have you finished?'

Hilloran's mouth opened, and closed again deliberately. The knuckles showed whitely in his hands.

He looked at the girl for a long time. Then, for a long time, in exactly the same way, he looked at Tremayne, without speaking.

At last—

'Good night,' he said, and left the room without another word.

From the window, Tremayne watched him walk slowly up the street, his handkerchief to his mouth. Then Dicky turned, and found Audrey Perowne beside him. There was something in her eyes which he could not interpret.

He said: 'You've proved that you trust me—'

'He's crazy,' she said.

'He's mad,' said Dicky. 'Like a mad dog. We haven't heard the last of this evening. From the moment you step on board the yacht, you'll have to watch him night and day. You understand that, don't you?'

'And what about you?'

'A knowledge of Ju-jitsu is invaluable.'

'Even against a knife in the back?'

Dicky laughed.

'Why worry?' he asked. 'It doesn't help us.'

The grey eyes were still holding his.

'Before you go,' she said, 'I'd like your own answer—from your own mouth.'

'To what question?'

'To what Hilloran said.'

He was picking up his coat. He put it down, and came towards her. A madness was upon him. He knew it, felt everything in him rebelling against it; yet he was swept before it out of reason, like a leaf before the wind. He held out his hand.

'Audrey,' he said, 'I give you my word of honour that I'd be burnt alive sooner than let you down.'

The words were spoken quite simply and calmly. The madness in him could only prompt them. He could still keep his face impassive and school the intensest meaning out of his voice.

Her cool fingers touched his, and he put them to his lips with a smile that might have meant anything—or nothing.

A few minutes later he was driving home with the first streaks of dawn in the sky, and his mouth felt as if it had been seared with a hot iron.

He did not see the Saint again before they left for Marseilles.

IV

Three days later, Dicky Tremayne, in white trousers, blue reefer, and peaked cap, stood at the starboard rail of the *Corsican Maid* and stared moodily over the water.

The sun shone high overhead, turning the water into a sea of quicksilver, and making of the Château d'If a fairy castle. The *Corsican Maid* lay in the open roadstead, two miles from Marseilles Harbour; for the Countess Anusia Marova, ever thoughtful for her guests, had decided that the docks, with their grime and noise and bustle, were no place for holiday-making millionaires and their wives to loiter, even for a few hours. But over the water, from the direction of the harbour, approached a fussy little tender. Dicky recognised it as the tender that had been engaged to bring the millionaires, with their wives and other baggage, to the Countess's yacht, and watched it morosely.

That is to say that his eyes followed it intently; but his mind was in a dozen different places.

The situation was rapidly becoming intolerable—far too rapidly.
That, in fact, was the only reflection which was seriously concerned
with the approach of the tender. For every yard of that approach
seemed, in a way, to entangle him ten times more firmly in the
web that he had woven for himself.

The last time he had seen the Saint, Dicky hadn't told him the
half of it. One very cogent reason was that Dicky himself, at the
time, hadn't even known the half well enough to call it Dear Sir
or Madam. Now, he knew it much too well. He called it by its
first name now—and others—and it sat back and grinned all over
its ugly face at him. Curse it. . . .

When he said that he *might* fall in love with Audrey Perowne,
he was underestimating the case by a mile. He *had* fallen in love
with her, and there it was. He'd done his level best not to; and,
when it was done, he'd fought for all he was worth against admitting
it even to himself. By this time, he was beginning to see that the
struggle was hopeless.

And if you want to ask why the pink parakeets he should put
up a fight at all, the answer is that that's the sort of thing men
of Dicky Tremayne's stamp do. If everything had been different—
if the Saint had never been heard of—or, at least, if Tremayne
had only known him through his morning newspaper—the problem
would never have arisen. Say that the problem, having arisen,
remains a simple one—and you're wrong. Wrong by the first
principles of psychological arithmetic.

The Saint might have been a joke. The Press, at first, had
suggested that he must be a joke—that he couldn't, reasonably,
be anything else. Later, with grim demonstrations thrust under
their bleary eyes, the Press admitted that it was no joke. In spite
of which, the jest might have stood, had the men carrying it out
been less under the Saint's spell.

There exists a loyalty among men of a certain type which defies
instinct, and which on occasion can rise above the limitations of
mere logic. Dicky Tremayne was of that breed. And he didn't find
the problem simple at all.

He figured it out in his own way.

'She's a crook. On the other hand, as far as that goes, so am I—though not the way she thinks of it. She's robbing people who can afford to stand the racket. Their records, if you came to examine them closely, probably wouldn't show up any too clean. In fact, she's on much the same ground as we are ourselves. Except that she doesn't pass on ninety per cent of the profits to charity. But that's only a private sentimentality of our own. It doesn't affect the main issue.

'Hilloran isn't the same proposition. He's a real bad *hombre*. I'd be glad to see him go down.

'The snag with the girl is the late John L. Morganheim. She probably murdered him. But then, there's not one of our crowd that hasn't got blood on his hands. What matters is why the blood was shed. We don't know anything about Morganheim, and action's going to be forced on me before I've time to find out.

'In a story, the girl's always innocent. Or, if she's guilty, she's always got a cast-iron reason to be. But I'm not going to be led away. I've seen enough to know that that kind of story is mostly based on vintage boloney, according to the recipe. I'm going to look at it coldly and sanely, till I find an answer or my brain busts. Because—

'Because, in fact, things being as they are, I've as good as sworn to the Saint that I'd bring home the bacon. Not in so many words, but that's what he assumes. And he's got every right to assume it. He gave me the chance to cry off if I wanted to—and I turned it down. I refused to quit. I dug this perishing pitfall, and it's up to me to fight my own way out—and no whining. . . .'

Thus Dicky Tremayne had balanced the ledger, over and over again, without satisfying himself.

The days since the discomfiture of Hilloran had not made the account any simpler.

Hilloran had come round the next morning, and apologised. Tremayne had been there—of course. Hilloran had shaken his hand heartily, boisterously disclaimed the least animosity, declared that it had been his own silly fault for getting canned, and taken Dicky and Audrey out to lunch. Dicky would have had every excuse for being deceived—but he wasn't. That he pretended to be was nobody's business.

But he watched Hilloran when he was not being watched himself; and from time to time he surprised in Hilloran's eyes a curiously abstracted intentness that confirmed his misgivings. It lasted only for a rare second here and there; and it was swallowed up again in a fresh flood of open-handed good humour so quickly that a less prejudiced observer might have put it down to imagination. But Dicky understood, and knew that there was going to be trouble with Hilloran.

Over the lunch, the intrusion of the Saint had been discussed, and a decision had been reached—by Audrey Perowne.

'Whoever he is, and whatever he's done,' she said, 'I'm not going to be scared off by any comic-opera threats. We've spent six thousand pounds on ground bait, and we'd be a cheap lot of pikers to leave the pitch without a fight. Besides, sooner or later, this Saint's going to bite off more than he can chew, and this may very well be the time. We're going to be on the broad Mediterranean, with a picked crew, and not more than twenty per cent of them can be double-crossing us. That gives us an advantage of four to one. Short of pulling out a ship of their own and making a pitched battle of it, I don't see what the Saint can do. I say we go on—with our eyes twice skinned.'

The argument was incontestable.

Tremayne, Hilloran and Audrey had left London quietly so as to arrive twelve hours before their guests were due. Dicky had spent another evening alone with the girl before the departure.

'Do you believe in Hilloran's apology?' he had asked.

She had answered, at once: 'I don't.'

'Then why are you keeping him on?'

'Because I'm a woman. Sometimes, I think, you boys are liable to forget that. I've got the train, but it takes a man to run a show like this, with a crew like mine to handle. You're the only other man I'd trust it to, but you—well, Dicky, honestly, you haven't the experience, have you?'

It had amazed him that she could discuss a crime so calmly. Lovely to look upon, exquisitely dressed, lounging at her ease in a deep chair, with a cigarette between white fingers that would have served the most fastidious sculptor for a model, she looked as if she should have been discussing, delightfully—anything but that.

Of his own feelings he had said nothing. He kept them out of his face, out of his eyes, out of his voice and manner. His dispassionate calm rivalled her own.

He dared hold no other pose. The reeling tumult of his thoughts could only be masked by the most stony stolidness. Some of the turmoil would inevitably have broken through any less sphinx-like disguise.

He was trying to get her in her right place—and, in the attempt, he was floundering deeper and deeper in the mire of mystification. There was about her none of the hard flashiness traditionally supposed to brand the woman criminal. For all her command, she remained completely feminine, gentle of voice, perfectly gracious. The part of the Countess Anusia Marova, created by herself, she played without effort; and, when she was alone, there was no travesty to take off. The charmingly broken English disappeared—that was all. But the same woman moved and spoke.

If he had not known, he would not have believed. But he knew—and it had rocked his creed to its foundations.

There had only been one moment, that evening, when he had been in danger of stumbling.

'If we bring this off,' she had said, 'you'll get your quarter share of course. Two hundred and fifty thousand dollars. Fifty thousand pounds of your money. You need never do another job as long as you live. What will you do?'

'What will you do with yours?' he countered.

She hesitated, gazed dreamily into a shadowy corner as though she saw something there. Then:

'Probably,' she said lightly, 'I'll buy a husband.'

'I might buy a few wives,' said Dicky, and the moment was past.

Now he looked down into the blue Mediterranean and meditated that specimen of repartee with unspeakable contempt. But it had been the only thing that had come into his head, and he'd had to say something promptly.

'Blast it all,' thought Dicky, and straightened up with a sigh.

The tender had nosed up to the gangway, and Sir Esdras Levy, in the lead, was helping Lady Levy to the grating.

Mr George Y. Ulrig stood close behind. Dicky caught their eye. He smiled with his mouth, and saluted cheerily.

He ought to have known them, for he himself had been the means of introducing them to the house in Park Lane. That had been his job, on the Continent, under Hilloran, for the past three months—to travel about the fashionable resorts, armed with plenty of money, an unimpeachable wardrobe, and his natural charm of manner, and approach the Unapproachables when they were to be found in holiday moods with their armour laid aside.

It had been almost boringly simple. A man who would blow up high in the air if addressed by a perfect stranger in the lounge of the Savoy Hotel, London, may be addressed by the same stranger with perfect impunity in the lounge of the Heliopolis Hotel, Biarritz. After which, to a man of Dicky Tremayne's polished worldliness, the improvement of the shining hour came automatically.

Jerking himself back to the realities of immediate importance, he went down to help to shepherd his own selected sheep to the slaughter.

Audrey Perowne stood at the head of the gangway, superbly gowned in a simple white skirt and coloured jumper—superbly gowned because she wore them. She was welcoming her guests inimitably, with an intimate word for each, while Hilloran, in uniform, stood respectfully ready to conduct them to their cabins.

'Ah, Sir Esdras, ve 'ardly dare expec' you. I say, "'E vill not com to my seely leetle boat." But 'e is nize, and 'e come to be oncomfortable to pleasse me. . . . And Lady Levy. My dear, each day you are more beautiful.' Lady Levy, who was a fat fifty, glowed audibly. 'And Mrs Ulrig. Beefore I let you off my boat, you shall tell me 'ow eet iss you keep zo sleem.' The scrawny and faded Mrs George Y. Ulrig squirmed with pleasure. 'George Y.,' said the Countess, 'I see you are vhat zey call a sheek. Ozairvize you could not 'ave marry 'er. And Mrs Sankin. . . .'

Dicky's task was comparatively childish. He had only to detach Sir Esdras Levy, Mr George Y. Ulrig, and Matthew Sankin from their respective spouses, taking them confidentially by the arm, and murmur that there were cocktails set out in the saloon.

Luncheon, with Audrey Perowne for hostess, could not have been anything but a success.

The afternoon passed quickly. It seemed no time before the bell rung by the obsequious Hilloran indicated that it was time to dress for dinner.

Tremayne went below with the rest to dress. It was done quickly; but the girl was already in the saloon when he arrived. Hilloran was also there, pretending to inspect the table.

'When?' Hilloran was asking.

'Tomorrow night. I've told them we're due at Monaco about half-past six. We shan't be near the place, but that doesn't matter. We'll take them in their cabins when they go below to change.'

'And afterwards?' questioned Dicky.

'We make straight across to Corsica during the night, and land them near Calvi the next morning. Then we make round the south of Sicily, and lose ourselves in the Greek Archipelago. We should arrive eventually at Constantinople—repainted, rechristened, and generally altered. There we separate. I'll give the immediate orders tomorrow afternoon. Come to my cabin about three.'

Hilloran turned to Dicky.

'By the way,' he said, 'this letter came with the tender. I'm afraid I forgot to give it to you before.'

Dicky held the man's eyes for a moment, and then took the envelope. It was postmarked in London. With a glance at the flap, he slit it open.

The letter was written in a round feminine hand.

*Darling,*

*This is just a line to wish you a jolly good time on your cruise.*

*You know I'll miss you terribly. Six weeks seems such a long time for you to be away. Never mind. I'm going to drown my sorrows in barley-water.*

*I refuse to be lonely. Simple Simon, the man I told you about, says he'll console me. He wants me to go with a party he's taking to the Ægean Islands. I don't know yet if I shall accept, but it sounds awfully thrilling. He's got a big aeroplane, and wants us to fly all the way.*

*If I go, I shall have to leave on Saturday. Won't you be jealous?*

*Darling, I mustn't pull your leg any more. You know I'm always thinking of you, and I shan't be really happy till I get you back again.*

*Here come all my best wishes, then. Be good, and take care of yourself.*

*It's eleven o'clock, and I'm tired. I'm going to bed to dream of you. It'll be twelve by the time I'm there. My eyes are red from weeping for you.*

*You have all my love. I trust you.*

*PATRICIA.*

Tremayne folded the letter, replaced it in its envelope, and put it in his pocket.

'Does she still love you?' mocked Audrey Perowne, and Dicky shrugged.

'So she says,' he replied carelessly. 'So she says.'

V

Much later that night, in the privacy of his cabin, Dicky read the letter again.

The meaning to him was perfectly obvious.

The Saint had decided to work his end of the business by aeroplane. The reference to the Ægean Islands, Tremayne decided, had no bearing on the matter—the Saint could have had no notion that the *Corsican Maid's* flight would take her to that quarter. But Saturday—the next day—was mentioned, and Dicky took that to meant that the Saint would be on the look-out for signals from Saturday onwards.

'Take care of yourself,' was plain enough.

The references to 'eleven o'clock' and 'twelve' were ambiguous. 'It'll be twelve by the time I'm there' might mean that, since the aeroplane would have to watch for signals from a considerable distance, to avoid being betrayed by the noise of the engines, it would be an hour from the time of the giving of the signal before the Saint could arrive on the scene. But why 'eleven o'clock' and 'twelve' instead of 'twelve o'clock' and 'one'—since they had previously arranged that signals were to be made either at midnight or four o'clock in the morning?

Dicky pondered for an hour; and decided that either he was trying to read too much between the lines, or that a signal given an hour before the appointed time, at eleven o'clock instead of twelve, would not be missed.

'My eyes are red from weeping for you.' He interpreted that to mean that he was to signal with a red light if there seemed to be any likelihood of their having cause to weep for him. He had a pocket flash-lamp fitted with colour screens, and that code would be easy to adopt.

It was the last sentence that hit him fairly between the eyes.

'I trust you.'

A shrewd blow—very shrewd. Just an outside reminder of what he'd been telling himself for the past three days.

Simon couldn't possibly understand. He'd never met Audrey

Perowne. And, naturally, he'd do his level best to keep Dicky on the lines.

Dicky crumpled the paper slowly into a ball, rolling it thoughtfully between his two palms. He picked up the envelope, and rolled that into the ball also. Hilloran had steamed open that envelope and sealed it again before delivering the letter—Dicky was sure of that.

He went to the porthole and pitched the ball far out into the dark waters.

He undressed and lay down in his bunk, but he could not compose his mind to sleep. The night was close and sultry. The air that came through the open porthole seemed to strike warm on his face, and to circulate that torrid atmosphere with the electric fan was pointless. He tried it, but it brought no relief.

For an hour and a half he lay stifling; and then he rose, pulled on his slippers and a thin silk dressing-gown, and made his way to the deck.

He sprawled in a long cane chair, and lighted a cigarette. Up there it was cooler. The ghost of a breeze whispered in the rigging and fanned his face. The soft hiss and wash of the sea cleft by the passage of their bows was very soothing. After a time, he dozed.

He awoke with a curious sensation forcing itself through his drowsiness. It seemed as if the sea was rising, for the chair in which he lay was lurching and creaking under him. Yet the wind had not risen, and he could hear none of the thrash of curling waves which he should have been able to hear.

All this he appreciated hazily, roused but still half-asleep. Then he opened one eye, and saw no rail before him, but only the steely glint of waters under the moon. Looking upwards and behind him he saw the foremast light riding serenely among the stars of a cloudless sky.

The convulsive leap he made actually spread-eagled him across the rail; and he heard his chair splash into the sea below as he tumbled over on to the deck.

Rolling on his shoulder, he glimpsed a sea-boot lashing at his head. He ducked wildly, grabbed, and kept his hold. All the strength he could muster went into the wrench that followed, and he heard the owner of the boot fall heavily with a strangled oath. An instant later he was on his feet—to find Hilloran's face two inches from his own.

'Would you!' snapped Dicky.

He slipped the answering punch over his left shoulder, changed his feet, and crammed every ounce of his weight into a retaliatory jolt that smacked over Hilloran's heart and dropped the man as if his legs had been cut away from beneath him.

Dicky turned like a whirlwind as the man he had tripped up rose from the ground and leapt at him with flailing fists.

Scientific boxing, in that light, was hopeless. Dicky tried it, and stopped a right swing with the side of his head. Three inches lower, and it would probably have put an end to the fight. As it was, it sent him staggering against the rail, momentarily dazed, and it was more by luck than judgment that his shoulder hunched in the way of the next blow. He hit back blindly, felt his knuckles make contact, and heard the man grunt with pain.

Then his sight cleared.

He saw the seaman recover his balance and gather himself for a renewed onslaught. He saw Hilloran coming unsteadily off the deck, with the moonlight striking a silvery gleam from something in his right hand. And he understood the issue quite plainly.

They had tried to dump him overboard, chair and all, while he slept. A quiet and gentle method of disposing of a nuisance— and no fuss or mess. That having failed, however, the execution of the project had boiled down to a free fight for the same end. Dicky had a temporary advantage, but the odds were sticky. With the cold grim clarity of vision that comes to a man at such moments, Dicky Tremayne realised that the odds were very sticky indeed.

But not for a second could he consider raising his voice for help. Apart from the fact that the battle was more or less a duel of honour between Hilloran and himself—even if Hilloran didn't

choose to fight his side single-handed—it remained to be assumed
that, if Hilloran had one ally among the crew, he was just as likely
to have half a dozen. The whole crew, finally, were just as likely
to be on Hilloran's side as one. The agreement had been that
Audrey, Hilloran and Dicky were to divide equally three-quarters
of the spoil, and the crew were to divide the last quarter. Knowing
exactly the type of man of which the crew was composed, Tremayne
could easily reckon the chance of their falling for the bait of a
half share to divide instead of a quarter, when the difference
would amount to a matter of about four thousand pounds per
man.

And that, Tremayne realised, would be a pretty accurate guess
at the position. He himself was to be eliminated, as Audrey
Perowne's one loyal supporter and a thorn in Hilloran's side. The
quarter share thus saved would go to bribe the crew. As for
Hilloran's own benefit, Audrey Perowne's quarter share . . .

Dicky saw the whole stark idea staring him in the face, and
wondered dimly why he'd never thought of it before. Audrey
Perowne's only use, for Hilloran, had been to get the millionaires
on board the yacht and out to sea. After that, he could take his
own peculiar revenge on her for the way she had treated him,
revenge himself also on Tremayne for similar things, and make
himself master of the situation and half a million dollars instead
of a quarter. A charming inspiration. . . .

But Dicky didn't have to think it all out like that. He saw it in
a flash, more by intuition than by logic, in the instant of rest that
he had while he saw also the seaman returning to the attack and
Hilloran rising rockily from the deck with a knife in his hand.

And therefore he fought in silence.

The darkness was against him. Dicky Tremayne was a strong
and clever boxer, quicker than most men, and he knew more than
a little about ju-jitsu; but those are arts for which one needs the
speed of vision that can only come with a clear light. The light
he had was meagre and deceptive—a light that was all on the side
of sheer strength and bulk, and all against mere speed and skill.

He was pretty well cornered. His back was against the rail. Hilloran was on his left front, the huge seaman on his right. There was no room to pass between them, no room to escape past either of them along the rail. There was only one way to fight: their own way.

The seaman was nearest, and Dicky braced himself. It had to be a matter of give and take, the only question being that of who was to take the most. As the seaman closed in, Tremayne judged his distance, dropped his chin, and drove with a long left.

The sailor's fist connected with Dicky's forehead, knocking back his head with a jar that ricked his neck. Dicky's left met something hard that seemed to snap under the impact. Teeth. But Dicky reeled, hazed by the sickening power of the two tremendous blows he had taken; and he could hardly see for the red and black clouds that swam before his eyes.

But he saw Hilloran and dropped instinctively to one knee. He rose again immediately under Hilloran's knife arm, taking the man about the waist. Summoning all his strength, he heaved upwards, with some mad idea of treating Hilloran to some of his own pleasant medicine—or hurling the man over the rail into the glimmering black sea. And almost at once he realised that he could not do it—Hilloran was too heavy, and Dicky was already weakened. Nor was there time to struggle, for in another moment Hilloran would lift his right arm again and drive the knife into Dicky's back.

But Tremayne, in that desperate effort, had Hilloran off his feet for a second. He smashed him bodily against the rail, hoping to slam the breath out of him for a momentary respite, and broke away.

As he turned, the seaman's hands fastened on his throat, and Dicky felt a sudden surge of joy.

Against a man who knows his ju-jitsu, that grip is more than futile: it is more than likely to prove fatal to the man who employs it. Particularly was this fact proven then. For most of the holds in ju-jitsu depend on getting a grip on a wrist or hand—which, of course, are the hardest parts of the body to get a grip on, being the smallest and most swift-moving. Dicky had been hampered all along by being unable to trust himself to get his hold in that light, when the faintest error of judgment would have been fatal. But now there could be no mistake.

Dicky's hands went up on each side of his head, and closed on the seaman's little fingers. He pulled and twisted at the same time, and the man screamed as one finger at least was dislocated. But Dicky went on, and the man was forced sobbing to his knees.

The surge of joy in Dicky's heart rose to something like a shout of triumph—and died.

Out of the tail of his eye, he saw Hilloran coming in again.

Tremayne felt that he must be living a nightmare. There were two of them, both far above his weight, and they were wearing him, gradually, relentlessly. As fast as he gained an advantage over one, the other came to nullify it. As fast as he was able temporarily to disable one, the other came back refreshed to renew the struggle. It was his own stamina against their combined consecutive staminas—and either of them individually was superior in brute strength to himself, even if one left the knife out of the audit.

Dicky knew the beginning of despair.

He threw the seaman from him, sideways, across Hilloran's very knees, and leapt away.

Hilloran stumbled, and Dicky's hand shot out for the man's knife wrist, found its mark, twisted savagely. The knife tinkled into the scuppers.

If Dicky could have made a grip with both hands, he would have had the mastery, but he could only make it with one. His other hand, following the right, missed. A moment later he was forced to release his hold. He swung back only just in time to avoid the left cross that Hilloran lashed out at his jaw.

Then both Hilloran and the sailor came at him simultaneously, almost shoulder to shoulder.

Dicky's strength was spent. He was going groggy at the knees, his arms felt like lead, his chest heaved terribly to every panting breath he took, his head swirled and throbbed dizzily. He was taking his licking.

He could not counter the blows they both hurled at him at once. Somehow, he managed to duck under their arms, with some hazy notion of driving between them and breaking away into the open, but he could not do it. They had him cold.

He felt himself flung against the rail. The sailor's arms pinioned his own arms to his side; Hilloran's hands were locked about his throat, strangling him to silence, crushing out life. His back was bent over the rail like a bow. His feet were off the ground.

The stars had gone out, and the moon had fallen from the sky. His chest was bound with ever-tightening iron bands. He seemed to be suspended in a vast void of utter blackness, and, though he could feel no wind, there was the roaring of a mighty wind in his ears.

And then, through the infinite distances of the dark gulf in which he hung, above even the great howling of that breathless wind, a voice spoke as a silver bell, saying: 'What's this, Hilloran?'

VI

Dicky seemed to awake from a hideous dream.

The fingers loosened from his throat, the iron cage that tortured his chest relaxed, the rushing wind in his ears died down to a murmur. He saw a star in the sky; and, as he saw it, a moon that had not been there before seemed to swim out of the infinite dark, back to its place in the heavens. And he breathed.

Also, he suddenly felt very sick.

These things happened almost immediately. He knew that they must have been almost immediate, though they seemed to follow one another with the maddening slowness of the minute hand's pursuit of the hour hand round the face of the clock. He tried to whip them to a greater speed.

He could not pause to savour the sensations of this return to life. His brain had never lost consciousness. Only his body was dead, and that had to be forced back to activity without a pause.

One idea stood out distinctly from the clearing fog that blurred his vision. Audrey Perowne was there, and she had caused an interruption that was saving him; but he was not safe yet. Neither was she.

She slept, he remembered, in a cabin whose porthole looked out on to the very stretch of deck where they had been fighting, and the noise must have roused her. But, in that light, she could have seen little but a struggling group of men, unless she had watched for a time before deciding to intervene—and that was unlikely. *And she must not be allowed to know the true reason for the disturbance.*

Tremayne now understood exactly how things were.

If Hilloran was prepared to dispose of him, he was prepared to dispose of the girl as well—Dicky had no doubt of that. But that would require some determination. The habit of obedience would remain, and to break it would require a conscious effort. And that effort, at all costs, must not be stimulated by any provocation while Hilloran was able to feel that he had things mostly his own way. All this Dick Tremayne understood, and acted upon it in an instant, before his senses had fully returned.

His feet touched the deck; and he twisted and held the seaman in his arms as he himself had been held a moment earlier. Then he looked across and saw Audrey Perowne.

She stood by a bulkhead light, where they could see her clearly, and the light glinted on an automatic in her hand. She said again: 'Hilloran—'

And by the impatient way she said it, Dicky knew that she could not have been waiting long for her first question to be answered.

'It's all right,' said Dicky swiftly. 'One of the men's gone rather off his rocker, and he was trying to chuck himself overboard. Hilloran and I stopped him, and he fought. That's all.'

The girl came closer, and neither Hilloran nor the seaman spoke.

Now it was all a gamble. Would they take the lead he had offered them, and attest the lie? Or, rather, would Hilloran?—for the other man would take the cue from him.

It was a pure toss-up—with Audrey's automatic on Dicky's side. If Hilloran had a weapon—which he probably had—he would not dare to try and reach it when he was already covered, unless he had a supreme contempt for the girl's intelligence and straight shooting. And Dicky had surmised that the man was not yet prepared for open defiance.

But there was a perceptible pause before Hilloran said:

'That's so, Audrey.'

She turned to the sailor.

'Why did you want to throw yourself overboard?'

Sullenly, the man said: 'I don't know, miss.'

She looked closely at him.

'They seemed to have been handling you pretty roughly.'

'You should have seen the way he struggled,' said Dicky. 'I've never seen anyone so anxious to die. I'm afraid I did most of the damage. Here—'

He took the man's hand.

'I'm going to put your finger back,' he said. 'I'll hurt. Are you ready?'

He performed the operation with a sure touch; and then he actually managed a smile.

'I should take him below and lock him up, Hilloran,' he remarked. 'He'll feel better in the morning. It must have been the heat. . . .'

Leaning against the rail, he watched Hilloran, without a word, take the man by the arm and lead him away. He felt curiously weak, now that the crisis was past and he hadn't got to fight any more. The blessing was that the girl couldn't see the bruises that must have been rising on his forehead and the side of his head.

But something must have shown in his face that he didn't know was showing, or the way he leaned against the rail must have been rather limp, for suddenly he found her hand on his shoulder.

'It strikes me,' she said softly, 'that that man wasn't the only one who was roughly handled.'

Dicky grinned.

'I got some of the knocks, of course,' he said.

'Did Hilloran?' she asked quietly.

He met her eyes, and knew then that she was not deceived. But he glanced quickly up and down the deck before he answered.

'Hilloran took some knocks, too,' he answered, 'but it was a near thing.'

'They tried to bump you off.'

'That, I believe, was the general idea.'

'I see.' She was thoughtful. 'Then—'

'I was trying to sleep on deck,' said Dicky suddenly, 'Hilloran was here when I arrived. We saw the man come along and try to climb over the rail—'

He broke off as Hilloran's shadow fell between them.

'I've locked him up,' said Hilloran, 'but he seems quite sensible now.'

'Good,' said the girl casually. 'I suppose you'd got the better of him by the time I came out. We'll discuss what's to be done with him in the morning. Dicky, you might take a turn round the deck with me before we go back to bed.'

She carried off the situation with such an utter naturalness that Hilloran was left with no answer. Her arm slipped through Dicky's, and they strolled away.

They went forward, rounded the deck-house, and continued aft, saying nothing; but when they came to the stern she stopped and leaned over the taffrail, gazing absorbedly down into the creaming wake.

Dicky stopped beside her. Where they stood, no one could approach within hearing distance without being seen.

He took cigarettes and matches from his dressing-gown pocket. They smoked. He saw her face by the light of the match as he held it to her cigarette, and she seemed rather pale. But that might have been the light.

'Go on telling me about it,' she ordered.

He shrugged.

'You've heard most of it. I woke up when they were about to tip me over the side. There was some trouble. I did my best, but I'd have been done if you hadn't turned up when you did.'

'Why did you lie to save them?'

He explained the instinctive reasoning which had guided him.

'Not that I had time to figure it out as elaborately as that,' he said, 'but I'm still certain that it was a darned good guess.'

'It's easily settled,' she said. 'We'll put Hilloran in irons—and you'll have to do the best you can in his place.'

'You're an optimist,' said Dicky sardonically. 'Haven't I shown you every necessary reason why he should have the crew behind him to a man? They aren't the kind that started the story about honour among thieves.'

She turned her head.

'Are you suggesting that I should quit?'

He seemed to see his way clearly.

'I am. We haven't an earthly—short of outbribing Hilloran, which 'ud mean sacrificing most of our own shares. We aren't strong enough to fight. And we needn't bank on Hilloran's coming back into the fold like a repentant sheep, because we'd lose our bets. He's got nothing to lose, and everything to gain. We've served our purpose. He can handle the hold-up just as well without us, and earn another quarter of a million dollars for the shade of extra work. I don't say I wouldn't fight it out if I were alone. I would. But I'm not alone, and I suspect that Hilloran's got a nasty mind. If he's only thinking of taking your *money*—I'll be surprised.'

She said coolly: 'In that case, it doesn't look as if we'd gain anything by quitting.'

'I could guarantee to get you away.'

'How?'

'Don't ask me, Audrey. But I know how.'

She appeared to contemplate the glowing end of her cigarette as though it were a crystal in which she could see the solution of all problems.

Then she faced him.

She said: 'I don't quit.'

'I suppose,' said Dicky roughly, 'you think that's clever. Let me tell you that it isn't. If you know that the decision's been framed against you right from the first gong, you don't lose caste by saving yourself the trouble of fighting.'

'The decision on points may have been framed against you,' she said, 'but you can get round that one. You can win on a knock-out.'

'Possibly—if that were the whole of it. But you're forgetting something else, aren't you?'

'What's that?'

'The Saint.'

He saw the exaggerated shrug of kimono'd shoulders.

'I should worry about him. I'll stake anything he isn't among the passengers. I've had the ship searched from end to end, so he isn't here as a stowaway. And I haven't taken many chances with the crew. What is he going to do?'

'I don't know. But if the people he's beaten before now had known what the Saint was going to do—they wouldn't have been beaten. We aren't the first people who've been perfectly certain they were safe. We aren't the only clever crooks in the world.'

Then she said again: 'I've told you—I don't quit.'

'All right—'

'This is the biggest game I've ever played!' she said, with a kind of savage enthusiasm. 'It's more—it's one of the biggest games that ever *has* been played. I've spent months preparing the ground. I've sat up night after night planning everything out to the smallest detail, down to the last item of our getaways. It's a perfect machine. I've only got to press the button, and it'll run from tomorrow night to safety—as smoothly as any human machine ever ran. And you ask me to give that up!'

A kind of madness came over Dicky Tremayne. He turned, and

his hands fell on her shoulders, and he forced her round with unnecessary violence.

'All right!' he snapped. 'You insist on keeping up this pose that you think's so brave and clever. You're damned pleased with yourself about it. Now listen to what I think. You're just a spoilt, silly little fool—'

'Take your hands off me!'

'When I've finished. You're just a spoilt, silly little fool that I've a good mind to spank here and now, as I'd spank any other child—'

The moonlight gleamed on something blue-black and metallic between them.

'Will you let me go?' she asked dangerously.

'No. Go ahead and shoot. I say you ought to be slapped and, by the Lord. . . . Audrey, Audrey, why are you crying?'

'Damn you,' she said, 'I'm not crying.'

'I can see your eyes.'

'Some smoke—'

'You dropped your cigarette minutes ago.'

His fierce grip had slackened. She moved swiftly, and flung off his hands.

'I don't want to get sentimental,' she said shakily. 'If I'm crying, it's my own business, and I've got my own good reasons for it. You're quite right, I *am* spoilt. I *am* a fool. I want that quarter of a million dollars, and I'm going to have it—in spite of Hilloran—in spite of you, too, if you want to take Hilloran's side—'

'I'm not taking Hilloran's side. I'm—'

'Whose side are you taking, then? There's only two sides to this.'

The moment had passed. He had chanced his arm on a show of strength—and failed. He wasn't used to bullying a girl. And through the dispersal of that shell-burst of madness he was aware again of the weakness of his position.

A barefaced bluffer like the Saint might still have carried it off, but Dicky Tremayne couldn't. He dared not go too far. He was tied hand and foot. It had been on the tip of his tongue to throw up the game then—to tell the truth, present his ultimatum, and damn the consequences. Prudence—perhaps too great a prudence—had stopped him. In that, in a way, he was like Hilloran. Hilloran was in the habit of obedience; Tremayne was in the habit of loyalty; neither of them could break his habit on the spur of the moment.

'I'm taking your side,' said Dicky.

And he wondered, at the same time, whether he oughtn't to have given way to the impulse of that moment's loss of temper.

'Then what's the point of all this?' she demanded.

'I'm taking your side,' said Dicky, 'better than you know. But we won't go into that any more—not just now, anyway. Let it pass. Since you're so clever—what's your idea for dealing with the situation?'

'Another cigarette.'

He gave her one, lighted it, and turned to stare moodily over the sea. It was a hopeless dilemma. 'I wonder,' he thought bitterly, 'why a man should cling so fanatically to his word of honour? It's sheer unnatural lunacy, that's what it is.' He knew that was what it was. But he was on parole, and he would have no chance to take back his parole until the following night at the earliest.

'What do you think Hilloran'll do now?' she asked. 'Will he try again tonight, or will he wait till tomorrow?'

The moment was very much past. It might never have been.

Dicky tried to concentrate, but his brain seemed to have gone flabby.

'I don't know,' he said vaguely. 'In his place, I'd probably try again tonight. Whether Hilloran has that type of mind is another matter. You know him better than I do.'

'I don't think he has. He's had one chance tonight to make the stand against me, and he funked it. That's a setback, psychologically, that'll take him some time to get over. I'll bet he doesn't try again till tomorrow. He'll be glad to be able to do some thinking, and there's nothing to make him rush it.'

'Will you have any better answer tomorrow than you have now?'

She smiled.

'I shall have slept on it,' she said carelessly. 'That always helps. . . . Good night, Dicky. I'm tired.'

He stopped her.

'Will you promise me one thing?'

'What is it?'

'Lock your door tonight. Don't open to anyone—on any excuse.'

'Yes,' she said. 'I should do that, in any case. You'd better do the same.'

He walked back with her to her cabin. Her hair stirred in the breeze, and the moon silvered it. She was beautiful. As they passed by a bulkhead light, he was observing the serenity of her proud lovely face. He found that he had not lost all his madness.

They reached the door.

'Good night, Dicky,' she said again.

'Good night,' he said.

And then he said, in a strange strained voice: 'I love you, Audrey. Good night, my dear.'

He was gone before she could answer.

## VII

Dicky dreamed that he was sitting on Hilloran's chest, with his fingers round Hilloran's throat, banging Hilloran's head on the deck. Every time Hilloran's head hit the deck, it made a lot of noise. Dicky knew that this was absurd. He woke up lazily, and traced the noise to his cabin door. Opening one eye, he saw the morning sunlight streaming in through his porthole.

Yawning, he rolled out of the bunk, slipped his automatic from under the pillow, and went to open the door.

It was a white-coated steward, bearing a cup of tea. Dicky thanked the man, took the cup, and closed the door on him, locking it again.

He sat on the edge of the bunk, stirring the tea thoughtfully.

He looked at it thoughtfully, smelt it thoughtfully, got up thoughtfully, and poured it thoughtfully out of the porthole. Then he lighted a cigarette.

He went to his bath with the automatic in his dressing-gown pocket and his hand on the automatic. He finished off with a cold shower, and returned to his cabin to dress, with similar caution, but feeling better.

The night before, he had fallen asleep almost at once. Dicky Tremayne had an almost Saintly faculty for carrying into practice the ancient adage that the evil of the day is sufficient thereto; and, since he reckoned that he would need all his wits about him on the morrow, he had slept. But now the morrow had arrived, he was thoughtful.

Not that the proposition in front of him appeared any more hopeful in the clear light of day. Such things have a useful knack of losing many of their terrors overnight, in the ordinary way—but this particular specimen didn't follow the rules.

It was true that Dicky had slept peacefully, and, apart from the perils that might have lurked in the cup of tea which he had not drunk, no attempt had been made to follow up the previous night's effort. That fact might have been used to argue that Hilloran hadn't yet found his confidence. In a determined counter-attack, such trifles as locked doors would not for long have stemmed his march; but the counter-attack had not been made. Yet this argument gave Dicky little reassurance.

An estimated value of one million dollars' worth of jewellery was jay-walking over the Mediterranean in that yacht, and every single dollar of that value was an argument for Hilloran—and others. Audrey Perowne had described her scheme as a fool-proof machine. So it was—granted the trustworthiness of the various cogs and bearings. And that was the very snag on which it was liable to take it into its head to seize up.

The plot would have been excellent if its object had been monkey nuts or hot dogs—things of no irresistible interest to anyone but an incorrigible collector. Jewels that were readily convertible into real live dollars were another matter. Even then, they might have been dealt with in comparative safety on dry land. But when they and their owners were more or less marooned in the open sea, far beyond the interference of the policeman at the street corner, with a crew like that of the *Corsican Maid*, each of those dollars became not only an argument but also a very unstable charge of high explosive.

Thus mused Dicky Tremayne while he dressed, while he breakfasted, and while he strolled round the deck afterwards with Sir Esdras Levy and Mr Matthew Sankin. And the question that was uppermost in his mind was how he could possibly stall off the impending explosion until eleven or twelve o'clock that night.

He avoided Audrey Perowne. He saw her at breakfast, greeted her curtly, and plunged immediately into a discussion with Mr George Y. Ulrig on the future of the American negro—a point of abstract speculation which interested Dicky Tremayne rather less than the future of the Patagonian paluka. Walking round the deck, he had to pass and re-pass the girl, who was holding court in a shady space under an awning. He did not meet her eye, and was glad that she did not challenge him. If she had, she could easily have made him feel intolerably foolish.

The madness of the night before was over, and he wondered what had weakened him into betraying himself. He watched her out of the tail of his eye each time he passed. She chattered volubly, joked, laughed delightfully at each of her guests' clumsy sallies. It was amazing—her impudent nerve, her unshakable self-possession. Who would have imagined, he asked himself, that before the next dawn she was proposing that those same guests that she was then entertaining so charmingly should see her cold and masterful behind a loaded gun?

And so to lunch. Afterwards . . .

It was hot. The sun, a globe of eye-aching fire, swung naked over the yard-arm in a burnished sky. It made the tar bubble between the planks of the open deck, and turned the scarcely rippling waters to a sheet of steel. With one consent, guests and their wives, replete, sought long chairs and the shade. Conversation suffocated—died.

At three o'clock, Dicky went grimly to the rendezvous. He saw Hilloran entering as he arrived, and was glad that he had not to face the girl alone.

They sat down on either side of the table, with one measured exchange of inscrutable glances. Hilloran was smoking a cigar. Dicky lighted a cigarette.

'What have you done about that sailor?' asked Audrey.

'I let him out,' said Hilloran. 'He's quite all right now.'

She took an armchair between them.

'Then we'll get to business,' she said. 'I've got it all down to a time-table. We want as little fuss as possible, and there's going to be no need for any shooting. While we're at dinner, Hilloran, you'll go through all the cabins and clean them out. Do it thoroughly. No one will interrupt you. Then you'll go down to the galley and serve out—this.'

She held up a tiny flask of a yellowish liquid.

'Butyl,' she said, 'and it's strong. Don't overdo it. Two drops in each cup of coffee. With the last two good ones for Dicky and me. And there you are. It's too easy—and far less trouble than a gun hold-up. By the time they come to, they'll be tied hand and foot. We drop anchor off the Corsican coast near Calvi at eleven, and put them ashore. That's all.'

Dicky arose.

'Very neat,' he murmured. 'You don't waste time.'

'We haven't to do anything. It all rests with Hilloran, and his job's easy enough.'

Hilloran took the flask and slipped it into his pocket.

'You can leave it to me,' he said; and that reminder of the favourite expression of Dicky's friend, Roger Conway, would have made Dicky wince if his face hadn't been set so sternly.

'If that's everything,' said Dicky, 'I'll go. There's no point in anyone having a chance to notice that we're both absent together.'

It was a ridiculous excuse, but it was an excuse. She didn't try to stop him.

Hilloran watched the door close without making any move to follow. He was carefully framing a speech in his mind, but the opportunity to use it was taken from him.

'Do you trust Dicky?' asked the girl.

It was so exactly the point he had himself been hoping to lead up to that Hilloran could have gasped. As it was, some seconds passed before he could trust himself to answer.

'It's funny you should say that now,' he remarked. 'Because I remember that when *I* suggested it, you gave me the air.'

'I've changed my mind since last night. As I saw it—mind you, I couldn't see very well because it was so dark—but it seemed to me that the situation was quite different from the way you both described it. It seemed,' said the girl bluntly, 'as if Dicky was trying to throw *you* overboard, and the sailor was trying to stop him.'

'That's the truth,' said Hilloran blindly.

'Then why did you lie to save him?'

'Because I didn't think you'd believe me if I told the truth.'

'Why did the sailor lie?'

'He'd take his tip from me. If I chose to say nothing, it wasn't worth his while to contradict me.'

The girl's slender fingers drummed on the table.

'Why do you think Dicky should try to kill you?'

Hilloran had an inspiration. He couldn't stop to give thanks for the marvellous coincidence that had made the girl play straight into his hands. The thanksgiving could come later. The immediate thing was to leap for the heaven-sent opening.

He took a sheet of paper from his pocket and leaned forward.

'You remember me giving Dicky a letter yesterday evening, before dinner?' he asked. 'I opened it first and took a copy. Here it is. It looks innocent enough, but—'

'Did you test it for invisible ink?'

'I made every test I knew. Nothing showed up. But just read

the letter. Almost every sentence in it might be a hint to anyone who knew how to take it.'

The girl read, with a furrow deepening between her brows. When she looked up, she was frowning.

'What's your idea?'

'What I told you before. I think Dicky Tremayne is one of the Saint's gang.'

'An arrangement—'

'That can't be right. I don't know much about the Saint, but I don't imagine he'd be the sort to send a man off on a job like this and leave his instructions to a letter delivered at the last minute. The least delay in the post, and he mightn't have received the letter at all.'

'That's all very well, but—'

'Besides, whoever sent this letter, if it's what you think it is, must have guessed that it might be opened and read. Otherwise the instructions would have been written in plain language. Now, these people are clever. The hints may be good ones. They may just as probably be phoney. I wouldn't put it above them to use some kind of code that anyone might tumble to—and hide another code behind it. You think you've found the solution—in the hints, if you can interpret them—but I say that's too easy. It's probably a trap.'

'Can you find any other code?'

'I'm not a code expert. But that doesn't say there isn't one.'

Hilloran scowled.

'I don't see that that makes any difference,' he said. 'I say that that letter's suspicious. If you agree with me, there's only one thing to be done.'

'Certainly.'

'He can go over the side, where he might have put me last night.'

She shook her head.

'I don't like killing, Hilloran. You know that. And it isn't necessary.' She pointed to his pocket. 'You have the stuff. Suppose there was only *one* coffee without it after dinner tonight?'

Hilloran's face lighted up with a brutal eagerness. He had a struggle to conceal his delight. It was too simple—too utterly, utterly sitting. Verily, his enemies were delivered into his hands. . . . But he tried to make his acknowledgment of the idea restrained and calculating.

'It'd be safer,' he conceded. 'I must say I'm relieved to find you're coming round to my way of thinking, Audrey.'

She shrugged, with a crooked little smile.

'The more I know you,' she said, 'the more I realise that you're usually right.'

Hilloran stood up. His face was like the thin crust of a volcano, under which fires and horrible forces boil and batter for release.

'Audrey—'

'Not now, Hilloran—'

'I've got a first name,' he said slowly. 'It's John. Why don't you ever use it?'

'All right—John. But please. . . . I want to rest this afternoon. When all the work's done, I'll—I'll talk to you.'

He came closer.

'You wouldn't try to double-cross John Hilloran, would you?'

'You know I wouldn't!'

'I want you!' he burst out incoherently. 'I've wanted you for years. You've always put me off. When I found you were getting on too well with that twister Tremayne, I went mad. But he's not taking you in any more, is he?'

'No—'

'And there's no one else?'

'How could there be?'

'You little beauty!'

'Afterwards, Hilloran. I'm so tired. I want to rest. Go away now—'

He sprang at her and caught her in his arms, and his mouth found her lips. For a moment she stood passively in his embrace. Then she pushed him back, and dragged herself away.

'I'll go now,' he said unsteadily.

She stood like a statue, with her eyes riveted on the closing door, till the click of the latch snapping home seemed to snap also the taut cord that held her rigid and erect. Then she sank limply back into her chair.

For a second she sat still. Then she fell forward across the table, and buried her face in her arms.

## VIII

'Ve vere suppose,' said the Countess Anusia Marova, 'to come to Monaco at nine o'clock. But ve are delay, and ze captayne tell me ve do nod zere arrive teel ten o'clock. So ve do nod af to urry past dinair to see ourselves come in ze port.'

Dicky Tremayne heard the soft accents across the saloon, above the bull-voiced drawl of Mr George Y. Ulrig, who was holding him down with a discourse on the future of the Japanese colony in California. Dicky was rather less interested in this than he would have been in a discourse on the future of the Walloon colony in Cincinnati. A scrap of paper crumpled in the pocket of his dinner-jacket—or Tuxedo (George Y. Ulrig)—seemed to be burning his side.

The paper had come under his cabin door while he dressed. He had been at the mirror, fidgeting with his tie, and he had seen the scrap sliding on to the carpet. He had watched it, half-hypnotised, and it had been some time before he moved to pick it up. When he had read it, and jerked open the door, the alleyway outside was deserted. Only, at the end, he had seen Hilloran, in his uniform, pass across by the alley athwartships without looking to right or to left.

The paper had carried one line of writing in block letters:

## DON'T DRINK YOUR COFFEE.

Nothing else. No signature, or even an initial. Not a word of explanation. Just that. But he knew that there was only one person on board who could have written it.

He had hurried over the rest of his toilet in the hope of finding Audrey Perowne in the saloon before the other guests arrived, but she had been the last to appear. He had not been able to summon up the courage to knock on the door of her cabin. His desire to see her and speak to her again alone, on any pretext, was tempered by an equal desire to avoid giving her any chance to refer to his last words of the previous night.

'This Jap is a good citizen,' George Y. Ulrig droned on, holding up his cocktail-glass like a sceptre. 'He has few vices, he's clean, and he doesn't make trouble. On the other hand, he's too clever to trust. He. . . . Say, boy, what's eatin' you?'

'Nothing,' denied Dicky hastily. 'What makes you think the Jap's too clever to trust?'

'Now, the Chinaman's the honestest man in this world, whatever they say about him,' resumed the drone. 'I'll tell you a story to illustrate that. . . .'

He told his story at leisure, and Dicky forced himself to look interested. It wasn't easy.

He was glad when they sat down to dinner. His partner was the less eagle-eyed Mrs George Y. Ulrig, who was incapable of noticing the absent-minded way in which he listened to her detailed description of her last illness.

But half-way through the meal he was recalled to attention by a challenge, and for some reason he was glad of it.

'Deeky,' said the girl at the end of the table.

Dicky looked up.

'Ve are in ze middle of an argument,' she said.

'Id iss this,' interrupted Sir Esdras Levy. 'Der Gountess asks, if for insdance you vos a friendt off mine, and I hat made a business teal mit odder friendts off mine, ant bromised to tell nobody nothing, ant I see you vill be ruined if you don't know off der teal, ant I know der teal vill ruined be if you know off it—vot shoot I to?'

This lucid exposition was greeted with a suppressed titter which made Sir Esdras whiffle impatiently through his beard. He waved his hands excitedly.

'I say,' he proclaimed magisterially, 'dot a man's vort iss his pond. I am sorry for you, but i must my vort keep.'

''Owever,' chipped in Mr Matthew Sankin, and, catching his wife's basilisk eye upon him, choked redly. '*How*-ever,' said Mr Matthew Sankin, 'I 'old by the British principle that a man oughter stick by his mates—friends—an' he ain't—asn't—*hasn't* got no right to let 'em down. None of 'em. That's wot.'

'Matthew, deah,' said Mrs Sankin silkily, 'the Countess was esking Mr Tremayne the question, Ay believe. Kaindly give us a chance to heah his opinion.'

'What about a show of hands?' suggested Dicky. 'How many of you say that a man should stand by his word—whatever it costs him?'

Six hands went up. Sankin and Ulrig were alone among the male dissenters.

'Lost by one,' said Dicky.

'No,' said the Countess. 'I do not vote. I make you ze chairman, Deeky, and you 'ave ze last word. 'Ow do you say?'

'In this problem, there's no chance of a compromise? The man couldn't find a way to tell his friend so that it wouldn't spoil the deal for his other friends?'

'Ve hof no gompromises,' said Sir Esdras sternly.

Dicky looked down the table and met the girl's eyes steadily.

'Then,' he remarked, 'I should first see my partners and warn them that I was going to break my word, and then I should go and do it. But the first condition is essential.'

'A gompromise,' protested Sir Esdras. 'Subbose you hof nod der dime or der obbortunity?'

'How great is this friend?'

'Der greatest friendt you hof,' insisted the honourable man vehemently. 'Id mags no tifference.'

'Come orf it,' urged Mr Sankin. 'A Britisher doesn't let 'is best pal dahn.'

'Wall,' drawled George Y. Ulrig, 'does an American?'

'You say I am nod Briddish?' fumed Sir Esdras Levy, whiffling. 'You hof der imberdinence—'

'Deeky,' said the girl sweetly, 'you should make up your mind more queekly. Ozairvise ve shall 'ave a quarrel. Now, 'ow do you vote?'

Dicky looked round the table. He wondered who had started that fatuous argument. He could have believed that the girl had done it deliberately, judging by the way she was thrusting the casting vote upon him so insistently. But, if that were so, it could only mean. . . .

But it didn't matter. With zero hour only a few minutes away, a strange mood of recklessness was upon him. It had started as simple impatience—impatience with the theories of George Y. Ulrig, impatience with the ailments of Mrs Ulrig. And now it had grown suddenly to a hell-for-leather desperation.

Audrey Perowne had said it. 'You should make up your mind more quickly.' And Dicky knew that it was true. He realised that he had squandered all his hours of grace on fruitless shilly-shallying which had taken him nowhere. Now he answered in a kind of panic.

'No,' he said. 'I'm against the motion. I'd let down my partners, and smash the most colossal deal under the sun, rather than hurt anyone I loved. Now you know—and I hope you're satisfied.'

And he knew, as the last plates were removed, that he was fairly and squarely in the cart. He was certain then that Audrey Perowne had engineered the discussion, with intent to trap him into a statement. Well, she'd got what she wanted.

He was suspect. Hilloran and Audrey must have decided *that* after he'd left her cabin that afternoon. Then why the message before dinner? They'd decided to eliminate him along with the rest. That message must have been a weakness on her part. She must have been banking on his humanity—and she'd inaugurated the argument, and brought him into it, simply to satisfy herself that her shirt was on a stone-cold certainty.

All right. . . .

That was just where she'd wrecked her own bet. A grim, vindictive resentment was freezing his heart. She chose to trade on the love he'd confessed—and thereby she lost it. He hated her now, with an increasing hatred. She'd almost taken him in. Almost she'd made him ready to sacrifice his honour and the respect of his friends to save her. And now she was laughing at him.

When he'd answered, she'd smiled. He'd seen it—too late—and even then the meaning of that smile hadn't dawned on him immediately. But he understood it all now.

'*Fool! Fool! Fool!*' he cursed himself savagely, and the knowledge that he'd so nearly been seduced from his self-respect by such a waster was like a worm in his heart.

'But she doesn't get away with it,' he swore savagely to himself. 'By God, she doesn't get away with it!'

And savagely that vindictive determination lashed down his first fury to an intensely simmering malevolence. Savagely he cursed the moment's panic that had made him betray himself—speaking from his heart without having fully reckoned all that might be behind the question. And then suddenly he was very cold and watchful.

The steward was bringing in the tray of coffee.

As if from a great distance, Dicky Tremayne watched the cups being set before the guests. As each guest accepted his cup, Dicky shifted his eyes to the face above it. He hated nearly all of them. Of the women, Mrs Ulrig was the only one he could tolerate—for all her preoccupation with the diseases which she imagined afflicted her. Of the men, there were only two whom he found human: Matthew Sankin, the henpecked Cockney who had, somehow, come to be cursed rather than blessed with more money than he knew how to spend, and George Y. Ulrig, the didactic millionaire from the Middle West. The others he would have been delighted to rob at any convenient opportunity—particularly Sir Esdras Levy, an ill-chosen advertisement for a frequently noble race.

Dicky received his cup disinterestedly. His right hand was returning from his hip pocket. Of the two things which it brought with it, he hid one under his napkin: the cigarette-case he produced, and offered.

The girl caught his eye, but his face was expressionless.

An eternity seemed to pass before the first cup was lifted.

The others followed. Dicky counted them, stirring his own coffee mechanically. Three more to go . . . two more. . . .

Matthew Sankin drank last. He alone dared to comment.

'Funny taste in this cawfy,' he said.

'It tastes good to me,' said Audrey Perowne, having tasted.

And Dicky Tremayne, watching her, saw something in her eyes which he could not interpret. It seemed to be meant for him but he hadn't the least idea what it was meant to be. A veiled mockery? A challenge? A gleam of triumph? Or what? It was a curious look. Blind. . . .

Then he saw Lady Levy half rise from her chair, clutch at her head, and fall sprawling across the table.

'Fainted,' said Matthew Sankin, on his feet. 'It's a bit stuffy in here—I've just noticed. . . .'

Dicky sat still, and watched the man's eyes glaze over with a state of comical perplexity—watched his mouth open, and saw him fall before he could speak again.

They fell one by one, while Dicky sat motionless, watching, with the sensation of being a spectator at a play. Dimly he appreciated the strangeness of the scene, dimly he heard the voices, and the smash of crockery swept from the table; but he himself was aloof, alone with his thoughts, and his right hand held his automatic pistol hidden under his napkin. He was aware that Ulrig was shaking him by the shoulder, babbling again and again: 'Doped—that coffee was doped—some goldurned son of a coot!'—until the American in his turn crumbled to the floor. And then Dicky and the girl were alone, she standing at her end of the table, and Dicky sitting at his end with the gun on his knee.

That queer blind look was still in her eyes. She said, in a hushed voice: 'Dicky—'

'I should laugh now,' said Dicky. 'You needn't bother to try and keep a straight face any longer. And in a few minutes you'll have nothing to laugh about—so I should laugh now.'

'I only took a sip,' she said.

'I see the rest was spilt,' said Dicky. 'Have some of mine.'

She was working round the table towards him, holding on to the backs of the swivel chairs. He never moved.

'Dicky, did you mean what you answered—just now?'

'I *did*. I suppose I might mean it still, if the conditions were fulfilled. You'll remember that I said—*Anyone I loved*. That doesn't apply here. Last night, I said I loved you. I apologise for the lie. I don't love you. I never could. But I thought—' He paused, and then drove home the taunt with all the stony contempt that was in him: 'I thought it would amuse me to make a fool of you.'

He might have struck her across the face. But he was without remorse. He still sat and watched her, with the impassivity of a graven image, till she spoke again.

'I sent you that note—'

'Because you thought you had a sufficient weapon in my love. Exactly. I understand that.'

She seemed to be keeping her feet by an effort of will. Her eyelids were drooping, and he saw tears under them.

'Who are you?' she asked.

'Dicky Tremayne is my real name,' he said, 'and I am one of the Saint's friends.'

She nodded so that her chin touched her chest.

'An—I—suppose—you—doped—my coffee,' she said, foolishly, childishly, in that small hushed voice that he had to strain to hear; and she slid down beside the chair she was holding, and fell on her face without another word.

Dicky Tremayne looked down at her in a kind of numb perplexity, with the ice of a merciless vengefulness holding him chilled and unnaturally calm. He looked down at her, at her crumpled dress, at her bare white arms, at the tousled crop of golden hair tumbled disorderly over her head by the fall, and he was like a figure of stone.

But within him something stirred and grew and fought with the foundations of his calm. He fought back at it, hating it, but it brought him slowly up from his chair at last, till he stood erect, still looking down at her, with his napkin fallen to his feet and the gun naked in his right hand.

'Audrey!' he cried suddenly.

His back was to the door. He heard the step behind him, but he could not move quicker than Hilloran's tongue.

'Stand still!' rapped Hilloran.

Dicky moved only his eyes.

These he raised to the clock in front of him, and saw that it was twenty minutes past nine.

## IX

'Drop that gun,' said Hilloran.

Dicky dropped the gun.

'Kick it away.'

Dicky kicked it away.

'Now you can turn round.'

Dicky turned slowly.

Hilloran, with his own gun in one hand and Dicky's gun in the other, was leaning back against the bulkhead by the door with a sneer of triumph on his face. Outside the door waited a file of seamen. Hilloran motioned them in.

'Of course, I was expecting this,' said Dicky.

'Mother's Bright Boy, you are,' said Hilloran.

He turned to the seamen, pointing with his gun.

'Frisk him and tie him up.'

'I'm not fighting,' said Dicky.

He submitted to the search imperturbably. The scrap of paper in his pocket was found and taken to Hilloran, who waved it aside after one glance at it.

'I guessed it was something like that,' he said. 'Dicky, you'll be glad to hear that I saw her slip it under your door. Lucky for me!'

'Very,' agreed Dicky dispassionately. 'She must have come as near fooling you as she was to fooling me. We ought to get on well together after this.'

'Fooling *you*!'

Dicky raised his eyebrows.

'How much did you hear outside that door?'

'Everything.'

'Then you must have understood—unless you're a born fool.'

'I understand that she double-crossed me, and warned you about the coffee.'

'Why d'you think she did that? Because she thought she'd got me under her thumb. Because she thought I was so crazy about her that I was as soundly doped that way as I could have been doped by a gallon of "knock-out". And she was right—then.'

The men were moving about with lengths of rope, binding wrists and ankles with methodical efficiency. Already pinioned himself, Dicky witnessed the guests being treated one by one in similar fashion, and remained outwardly unmoved. But his brain was working like lightning.

'When they're all safe,' said Hilloran, with a jerk of one gun, 'I'm going to ask you some questions—Mr Dicky Tremayne! You'd better get ready to answer right now, because I sha'n't be kind to you if you give trouble.'

Dicky stood in listless submission. He seemed to be in a kind of stupor. He had been like that ever since Hilloran had disarmed him. Except for the movements of his mouth, and the fact that he remained standing, there might have been no life in him. Everything about him pointed to a paralysed and fatalistic resignation.

'I sha'n't give any trouble,' he said tonelessly. 'Can't you understand that I've no further interest in anything—after what I've found out about her?'

Hilloran looked at him narrowly, but the words, and Dicky's slack pose, carried complete conviction. Tremayne might have been half-chloroformed. His apathetic, benumbed indifference was beyond dispute. It hung on him like a cloak of lead.

'Have you any friends on board?' asked Hilloran.

'No,' said Dicky flatly. 'I'm quite alone.'

'Is that the truth?'

For a moment Tremayne seemed stung to life.

'Don't be so damned dumb!' he snapped. 'I say I'm telling you the truth. Whether you believe me or not, you're getting just as good results this way as you would by torture. You've no way of proving my statements—however you obtain them.'

'Are you expecting any help from outside?'

'It was all in the letter you read.'

'By aeroplane?'

'Seaplane.'

'How many of your gang?'

'Possibly two. Possibly only one.'

'At what time?'

'Between eleven and twelve, any night from tonight on. Or at four o'clock any morning. I should have called them by flashing— a red light.'

'Any particular signal?'

'No. Just a regular intermittent flash,' said Dicky inertly. 'There's no catch in it.'

Hilloran studied his face curiously.

'I'd believe you—if the way you're surrendering wasn't the very opposite of everything that's ever been said about the Saint's gang.'

Tremayne's mouth twitched.

'For heaven's sake!' he burst out seethingly. 'Haven't I told you, you poor blamed boob? I'm fed up with the Saint. I'm fed up with everything. I don't give another lonely damn for anything anyone does. I tell you, I was mad about that double-crossing little slut. And now I see what she's really worth, I don't care what happens to her or to me. You can do what you like. Get on with it!'

Hilloran looked round the saloon. By then, everyone had been securely bound except the girl, and the seamen were standing about uncertainly, waiting for further instructions.

Hilloran jerked his head in the direction of the door.

'Get out,' he ordered. 'There's two people here I want to interview—alone.'

Nevertheless, when the last man had left the room, closing the door behind him, Hilloran did not immediately proceed with the interview. Instead, he pocketed one gun, and produced a large bag of soft leather. With this he went round the room, collecting necklaces, ear-rings, brooches, rings, studs, bracelets, wallets—till the bag bulged and weighed heavy.

Then he added to it the contents of his pockets. More and more jewels slipped into the bag like a stream of glittering hailstones. When he had finished, he had some difficulty in tightening the cords that closed the mouth of it.

He balanced it appreciatively in the palm of his hand.

'One million dollars,' he said.

'You're welcome,' said Dicky.

'Now I'll talk,' said Hilloran.

He talked unemotionally, and Dicky listened without the least sign of feeling. At the end, he shrugged.

'You might shoot me first,' he suggested.

'I'll consider it.'

No sentence of death could ever have been given or received more calmly. It was a revelation to Dicky, in its way, for he would have expected Hilloran to bluster and threaten luridly. Hilloran, after all, had a good deal to be vindictive about. But the man's restraint was inhuman.

Tremayne's stoicism matched it. Hilloran promised death as he might have promised a drink: Dicky accepted the promise as he might have accepted a drink. Yet he never doubted that it was meant. The very unreality of Hilloran's command of temper made his sincerity more real than any theatrical elaboration could have done.

'I should like to ask a last favour,' said Dicky calmly.

'A cigarette?'

'I shouldn't refuse that. But what I should appreciate most

would be the chance to finish telling—her—what I was telling her when you came in.'

Hilloran hesitated.

'If you agree,' added Dicky callously, 'I'd advise you to have her tied up first. Otherwise, she might try to untie me in the hope of saving her own skin. Seriously—we haven't been melodramatic about this tonight, so you might go on in the same way.'

'You're plucky,' said Hilloran.

Tremayne shrugged.

'When you've no further interest in life, death loses its terror.'

Hilloran went and picked up a length of rope that had been left over. He tied the girl's wrists behind her back; then he went to the door and called, and two men appeared.

'Take those two to my cabin,' he said. 'You'll remain on guard outside the door.' he turned back to Dicky. 'I shall signal at eleven. At any time after that, you may expect me to call you out on deck.'

'Thank you,' said Dicky quietly.

The first seaman had picked up Audrey Perowne, and Dicky followed him out of the saloon. The second brought up the rear.

The girl was laid down on the bunk in Hilloran's cabin. Dicky kicked down the folding seat and made himself as comfortable as he could. The men withdrew, closing the door.

Dicky looked out of the porthole and waited placidly. It was getting dark. The cabin was in twilight; and, beyond the porthole, a faintly luminous blue-grey dusk was deepening over the sea.

Sometimes he could hear the tramp of footsteps passing over the deck above. Apart from that, there was no sound but the murmuring undertone of slithering waters slipping past the hull, and the vibration, felt rather than heard, of the auxiliary engines. It was all strangely peaceful. And Dicky waited.

After a long time, the girl sighed and moved. Then she lay still again. It was getting so dark that he could hardly see her face as anything but a pale blur in the shadow.

But presently she said, softly: 'So it worked.'

'What worked?'

'The coffee.'

He said. 'I had nothing to do with that.'

'Almost neat butyl, it was,' she said. 'That was clever. I guessed my own coffee would be doped, of course. I put the idea into Hilloran's head, because it's always helpful to know how you're going to be attacked. But I didn't think it'd be as strong as that. I thought it'd be safe to sip it.'

'Won't you believe that I didn't do it, Audrey?'

'I don't care. It was somebody clever who thought of catching me out with my own idea.'

He said: 'I didn't do it, Audrey.'

Then for a time there was a silence.

Then she said: 'My hands are tied.'

'So are mine.'

'He got you as well?'

'Easily. Audrey, how awake are you?'

'I'm quite awake now,' she said. 'Just very tired. And my head's splitting. But that doesn't matter. Have you got anything else to say?'

'Audrey, do you know who I am?'

'I know. You're one of the Saint's gang. You told me. But I knew it before.'

'You knew it before?'

'I've known it for a long time. As soon as I noticed that you weren't quite an ordinary crook, I made enquiries—on my own, without anyone knowing. It took a long time, but I did it. Didn't you meet at a flat in Brook Street?'

Dicky paused.

'Yes,' he said slowly. 'That's true. Then why did you keep it quiet?'

'That,' she said, 'is my very own business.'

'All the time I was with you, you were in danger—yet you deliberately kept me with you.'

'I chose to take the chance. That was because I loved you.'

'You what?'

'I loved you,' she said wearily. 'Oh, I can say it quite safely now. And I will, for my own private satisfaction. You hear me, Dicky Tremayne? I loved you. I suppose you never thought I could have the feelings of an ordinary woman. But I did. I had it worse than an ordinary woman has it. I've always lived recklessly, and I loved recklessly. The risk was worth it—as long as you were with me. But I never thought you cared for me, till last night. . . .'

'Audrey, you tell me that!'

'Why not? It makes no difference now. We can say what we like—and there are no consequences. What exactly is going to happen to us?'

'My friends are coming in a seaplane. I told Hilloran, and he proposed to double-cross the crew. He's got all the jewels. He's going to give my signal. When the seaplane arrives, he's going to row out with me in a boat. My friends will be told that I'll be shot if they don't obey. Naturally, they'll obey—they'll put themselves in his hands, because they're that sort of fool. And Hilloran will board the seaplane and fly away—with you. He knows how to handle an aeroplane.'

'Couldn't you have told the crew that?'

'What for? One devil's better than twenty.'

'And what happens to you?'

'I go over the side with a lump of lead tied to each foot. Hilloran's got a grudge to settle—and he's going to settle it. He was so calm about it when he told me that I knew he meant every word. He's a curious type,' said Dicky meditatively. 'I wish I'd studied him more. Your ordinary crook would have been noisy and nasty about it, but there's nothing like that about Hilloran. You'd have thought it was the same thing to him as squashing a fly.'

There was another silence, while the cabin grew darker still. Then she said: 'What are you thinking, Dicky?'

'I'm thinking,' he said, 'how suddenly things can change. I loved you. Then, when I thought you were trading on my love, and laughing at me up your sleeve all the time, I hated you. And then, when you fell down in the saloon, and you lay so still, I knew nothing but that I loved you whatever you did, and that all the hell you could give me was nothing because I had touched your hand and heard your blessed voice and seen your smile.'

She did not speak.

'But I lied to Hilloran,' he said. 'I told him nothing more than that my love had turned to hate, and not that my hate had turned back to love again. He believed me. I asked to be left alone with you before the end, to hurl my dying contempt on you—and he consented. That again makes him a curious type—but I knew he'd do it. That's why we're here now.'

'Why did you do that?'

'So that I could tell you the truth, and try to make you tell me the truth—and, perhaps, find some way out with you.'

The darkness had become almost the darkness of night.

She said, far away: 'I couldn't make up my mind. I kept on putting myself off and putting myself off, and in order to do that I *had* to trade on your love. But I forced you into that argument at dinner to find out how great your love could be. That was a woman's vanity—and I've paid for it. And I told Hilloran to dope your coffee, and told you not to drink it, so that you'd be ready to surprise him and hold him up when he thought you were doped. I was going to double-cross him, and then leave the rest in your hands, because I couldn't make up my mind.'

'It's a queer story, isn't it?' said Dicky Tremayne.

'But I've told you the truth now,' she said. 'And I tell you that if I can find the chance to throw myself out of the boat, or out of the seaplane, I'm going to take it. Because I love you.'

He was silent.

'I killed Morganheim,' she said, 'because I had a sister—once.'

He was very quiet.

'Dicky Tremayne,' she said, 'didn't you say you loved me—once?'

He was on his feet. She could see him.

'That was the truth.'

'Is it—still—true?'

'It will always be true,' he answered; and he was close beside her, on his knees beside the bunk. He was so close beside her that he could kiss her on the lips.

X

Simon Templar sat at the controls of the tiny seaplane, and stared thoughtfully across the water.

The moon had not yet risen, and the parachute flares he had thrown out to land by had been swallowed up into extinction by the sea. But he could see, a cable's length away, the lights of the yacht riding sulkily on a slight swell; and the lamp in the stern of the boat that was stealing darkly across the intervening stretch of water was reflected a thousand times by a thousand ripples, making a smear of dancing luminance across the deep.

He was alone. And he was glad to be alone, for undoubtedly something funny was going to happen.

He had himself, after much thought, written Patricia's letter to Dicky Tremayne, and he was satisfied that it had been explicit enough. 'My eyes are red from weeping for you.' It couldn't have been plainer. Red light—danger. A babe in arms couldn't have missed it.

And yet, when he had flown nearer, he had seen that the yacht was not moving; and his floats had hardly licked the first flurry of spray from the sea before the boat he was watching had put off from the ship's side.

He could not know that Dicky had given away that red signal deliberately, hoping that it would keep him on his guard and that the inspiration of the moment might provide for the rest. All the same, the Saint was a good guesser, and he was certainly on his guard. He knew that something very fishy was coming towards him across that piece of fish-pond, and the only question was—what?

Thoughtfully the Saint fingered the butt of the Lewis gun that was mounted on the fuselage behind him. It had not been mounted there when he left San Remo that evening; for the sight of private seaplanes equipped with Lewis guns is admittedly unusual, and may legitimately cause comment. But it was there now. The Saint had locked it on to its special mounting as soon as his machine had come to rest. The tail of the seaplane was turned towards the yacht; and, twisting round in the roomy cockpit, the Saint could comfortably swivel the gun round and keep the sights on the approaching boat.

The boat, by that time, was only twenty yards away.

'Is that you, sonny boy?' called the Saint sharply.

The answering hail came clearly over the water:

'That's me, Saint.'

In the dark, the cigarette between the Saint's lips glowed with the steady redness of intense concentration. Then he took his cigarette from his mouth and sighted carefully.

'In that case,' he said, 'you can tell your pals to heave to, Dicky Tremayne. Because, if they come much nearer, they're going to get a lead shower-bath.'

The sentence ended in a stuttering burst from the gun; and five tracer bullets hissed through the night like fire-flies and cut the water in a straight line directly across the boat's course. The Saint heard a barked command, and the boat lost way; but a laugh followed at once, and another voice spoke.

'Is that the Saint?'

The Saint only hesitated an instant.

'Present and correct,' he said, 'complete with halo. What do your friends call you, honeybunch?'

'This is John Hilloran speaking.'

'Good evening, John,' said the Saint politely.

The boat was close enough for him to be able to make out the figure standing up in the stern, and he drew a very thoughtful bead upon it. A Lewis gun is not the easiest weapon in the world to handle with a microscopic accuracy, but his sights had been picked out with luminous paint, and the standing figure was silhouetted clearly against the reflection in the water of one of the lights along the yacht's deck.

'I'll tell you,' said Hilloran, 'that I've got your friend at the end of my gun—so don't shoot any more.'

'Shoot, and be damned to him!' snapped in Dicky's voice. 'I don't care. But Audrey Perowne's here as well, and I'd like her to get away.'

'My future wife,' said Hilloran, and again his throaty chuckle drifted through the gloom.

Simon Templar took a long pull at his cigarette, and tapped some ash fastidiously into the water.

'Well—what's the idea, big boy?'

'I'm coming alongside. When I'm there, you're going to step quietly down into this boat. If you resist, or try any funny business, your friend will pass in his checks.'

'Is—that—so?' drawled Simon.

'That's so. I want to meet you—Mr Saint!'

'Well, well, *well*!' mocked the Saint alertly.

And there and then he had thrust upon him one of the most desperate decisions of a career that continued to exist only by cool swift making of desperate decisions.

Dicky Tremayne was in that boat, and Dicky Tremayne had somehow or other been stung. That had been fairly obvious ever since the flashing of that red signal. Only the actual details of the stinging had been waiting to be disclosed. Now the Saint knew.

And, although the Saint would willingly have stepped into a burning fiery furnace if he thought that by so doing he could help Dicky's getaway, he couldn't see how the principle applied at that moment. Once the Saint stepped down into that boat, there would be two of them in the *consommé* instead of one—and what would have been gained?

What, more important, would Hilloran have gained? Why should J. Hilloran be so anxious to increase his collection of Saints?

The Saint thoughtfully rolled his cigarette-end between his finger and thumb, and dropped it into the water.

'Why,' ruminated the Saint—'because the dear soul wants this blinkin' bus what I'm sitting in. He wants to take it and fly away into the wide world. Now, again—why? Well, there were supposed to be a million dollars' worth of jools in that there hooker. It's quite certain that their original owners haven't got them any longer—it's equally apparent that Audrey Perowne hasn't got them, or Dicky wouldn't have said that he wanted her to get away— and, clearly, Dicky hasn't got them. Therefore, Hilloran's got them. And the crew will want some of them. We don't imagine Hilloran proposes to load up the whole crew on this airyplane for their getaway: therefore, he only wants to load up himself and Audrey Perowne—leaving the ancient mariners behind to whistle for their share. Ha! Joke. . . .'

And there seemed to be just one solitary way of circumventing the opposition.

Now, Hilloran wasn't expecting any fight at all. He'd had several drinks, for one thing, since the hold-up, and he was very sure of himself. He'd got everyone cold—Tremayne, Audrey, the crew, the Saint, and the jewels. He didn't see how anyone could get out of it.

He wasn't shaking with the anticipation of triumph, because he wasn't that sort of crook. He simply felt rather satisfied with his own ingenuity. Not that he was preening himself. He found it as natural to win that game as he would have found it natural to win a game of stud poker from a deaf, dumb, and blind imbecile child. That was all.

Of course, he didn't know the Saint except by reputation, and mere word-of-mouth reputations never cut much ice with Hilloran. He wasn't figuring on the Saint's uncanny intuition of the psychology of the crook, nor on the Saint's power of lightning logic and lightning decision. Nor had he reckoned on that quality of reckless audacity which lifted the Saint as far above the rut of ordinary adventurers as Walter Hagen is above the man who has taken up golf to amuse himself in his old age—a quality which infected and inspired also the men whom the Saint led.

There was one desperate solution to the problem, and Hilloran ought to have seen it. But he hadn't seen it—or, if he had, he'd called it too desperate to be seriously considered. Which was where he was wrong to all eternity.

He stood up in the stern of the boat, a broad dominant figure in black relief against the shimmering waters, and called out again: 'I'm coming alongside now, Saint, if you're ready.'

'I'm ready,' said the Saint; and the butt of the Lewis gun was cuddled in to his shoulder as steadily as if it had lain on a rock.

Hilloran gave an order, and the sweeps dipped again. Hilloran remained standing.

If he knew what happened next, he had no time to co-ordinate his impressions. For the harsh stammer of the Lewis gun must have merged and mazed his brain with the sharp tearing agony that ripped through his chest, and the numbing darkness that blinded his eyes must have been confused with the numbing weakness that sapped all the strength from his body, and he could not have heard the choking of the breath in his throat, and the cold clutch of the waters that closed over him and dragged him down could have meant nothing to him at all . . .

But Dicky Tremayne, staring stupidly at the widening ripples that marked the spot where Hilloran had been swallowed up by the sea, heard the Saint's hail.

'Stand by for the mermaids!'

And at once there was a splash such as a seal makes in plunging from a high rock, and there followed the churning sounds of a strong swimmer racing through the water.

The two men who were the boat's crew seemed for a moment to sit in a trance; then, with a curse, one of them bent to his oars. The other followed suit.

Dicky knew that it was his turn.

He came to his feet and hurled himself forward, throwing himself anyhow across the back of the man nearest to him. The man was flung sideways and over on to his knees, so that the boat lurched perilously. Then Dicky had scrambled up again, somehow, with bruised shins, and feet that seemed to weigh a ton, and launched himself at the back of the next man in the same way.

The first man whom he had knocked over struck at him, with an oath, but Dicky didn't care. His hands were tied behind his back, but he kicked out, swung his shoulders, butted with his head—fought like a madman. His only object was to keep the men from any effective rowing until the Saint could reach them.

And then, hardly a foot from Dicky's eyes, a hand came over the gunwale, and he lay still, panting. A moment later the Saint had hauled himself over the side, almost overturning the boat as he did so.

'OK, sonny boy!' said the Saint, in that inimitable cheerful way that was like new life to those who heard it on their side, and drove his fist into the face of the nearest man.

Then the other man felt the point of a knife prick his throat.

'You heard your boss telling you to row over to the seaplane,' remarked the Saint gently, 'and I'm very hot on carrying out the wishes of the dead. Put your back into it!'

He held the knife in place with one hand, with the other hand he reached for the second little knife which he carried strapped to his calf.

'This way, Dicky boy, and we'll have you loose in no time.'

It was so. And then the boat was alongside the seaplane and Dicky had freed the girl.

The Saint helped them up, and then went down to the stern of the boat and picked up the bag which lay fallen there. He tossed it into the cockpit, and followed it himself.

From that point of vantage he leaned over to address the crew of the boat.

'You've heard all you need to know,' he said. 'I am the Saint. Remember me in your prayers. And when you've got the yacht to a port, and you're faced with the problem of accounting for all that's happened to your passengers—remember me again. Because tomorrow morning every port in the Mediterranean will be watching for you, and on every quay there'll be detectives waiting to take you away to the place where you belong. So remember the Saint!'

And Simon Templar roused the engine of the seaplane and began to taxi out over the water as the first shot spat out from the yacht's deck and went whining over the sea.

A week later, Chief Inspector Teal paid another visit to Brook Street.

'I'm very much obliged to you, Mr Templar,' he said. 'You'll be interested to hear that *Indomitable* picked up the *Corsican Maid* as she was trying to slip through the Straits of Gibraltar last night. They didn't put up much of a scrap.'

'You don't say!' murmured the Saint mockingly. 'But have some beer.'

Mr Teal sank ponderously into the chair.

'Fat men,' he declined, 'didn't ought to drink—if you won't be offended. But listen, sir—what happened to the girl who was the leader of the gang? And what happened to the jewels?'

'You'll hear today,' said the Saint happily, 'that the jewels have been received by a certain London hospital. The owners will be able to get them back from there, and I leave the reward they'll contribute to the hospital to their own consciences. But I don't think public opinion will let them be stingy. As for the money that was collected in cash, some twenty-five thousand dollars. I—er—well, that's difficult to trace, isn't it?'

Mr Teal nodded sleepily.

'And Audrey Perowne, *alias* the Countess Anusia Marova?'

'Were you wanting to arrest her?'

'There's a warrant—'

The Saint shook his head sadly.

'What a waste of time, energy, paper, and ink! You ought to have told me that before. As it is, I'm afraid I—er—that is, she was packed off three days ago to a country where extradition doesn't work—I'm afraid I shouldn't know how to intercept her. Isn't that a shame?'

Teal grimaced.

'However,' said the Saint, 'I understand that she's going to reform and marry and settle down, so you needn't worry about what she'll do next.'

'How do you know that?' asked Teal suspiciously.

The Saint's smile was wholly angelic.

He flung out his hand.

'A little Dicky bird,' he answered musically, 'a little Dicky bird told me so this morning.'

I

Before the world at large had heard even one lonely rumour about the gentleman who called himself, among other things, the Scorpion, there were men who knew him in secret. They knew him only as the Scorpion, and by no other name; and where he came from and where he lived were facts that certain of them would have given much to learn.

It is merely a matter of history that one of these men had an unassailable legal right to the name of Montgomery Bird, which everyone will agree was a very jolly sort of name for a bloke to have.

Mr Montgomery Bird was a slim and very dapper little man; and although it is true he wore striped spats there were even more unpleasant things about him which were not so noticeable but which it is the chronicler's painful duty to record. He was, for instance, the sole proprietor of a night club officially entitled the Eyrie, but better and perhaps more appropriately known as the Bird's Nest, which was a very low night club. And in this club, on a certain evening, he interviewed the Scorpion.

That Simon Templar happened to be present was almost accidental.

Simon Templar, in fact, having for some time past cherished a purely business-like interest in the affairs of Mr Montgomery Bird, had decided that the time was ripe for that interest to bear its fruit.

The means by which he became a member of the Eyrie are not known. Simon Templar had his own private ways of doing these things. It is enough that he was able to enter the premises unchallenged. He was saluted by the doorkeeper, climbed the steep stairs to the converted loft in which the Eyrie had its being, collected and returned the welcoming smile of the girl at the reception desk, delivered his hat into the keeping of a liveried flunkey, and passed on unquestioned. Outside the glass doors that separated the supper-room from the lounge he paused for a moment, lighting a cigarette, while his eyes wandered lazily over the crowd. He already knew that Mr Bird was in the habit of spending the evening among his guests, and he just wanted to make sure about that particular evening. He made sure; but his subsequent and consequent movements were forced to diverge slightly from schedule, as will be seen.

Mr Bird had met the Scorpion before. When a waiter came through and informed him that a gentleman who would give no name was asking to speak to him, Mr Bird showed no surprise. He went out to the reception desk, nodded curtly to the visitor, signed him under the name of J. N. Jones, and led the way into his private office without comment.

He walked to his desk; and there he stopped and turned.

'What is it now?' he asked shortly, and the visitor shrugged his broad shoulders.

'Must I explain?'

Mr Bird sat down in his swivel chair, rested his right ankle on his left knee, and leaned back. The fingers of one carefully manicured hand played a restless tattoo on the desk.

'You had a hundred pounds only last week,' he said.

'And since then you have probably made at least three hundred,' replied the visitor calmly.

He sat on the arm of another chair, and his right hand remained in the pocket of his overcoat. Mr Bird, gazing at the pocket, raised one cynical eyebrow.

'You look after yourself well.'

'An elementary precaution.'

'Or an elementary bluff.'

The visitor shook his head.

'You might test it—if you are tired of life.'

Mr Bird smiled, stroking his small moustache.

'With that—and your false beard and smoked glasses—you're an excellent imitation of a blackguard,' he said.

'The point is not up for discussion,' said the visitor smoothly. 'Let us confine ourselves to the object of my presence here. Must I repeat that I know you to be a trader in illicit drugs? In this very room, probably, there is enough material evidence to send you to penal servitude for five years. The police, unaided, might search for it in vain. The secret of your ingenious little hiding-place under the floor in that corner might defy their best efforts. They do not know that it will only open when the door of this room is locked and the third and fifth sections of the wainscoting on that wall are slid upwards. But suppose they were anonymously informed—'

'And then found nothing there,' said Montgomery Bird, with equal suavity.

'There would still be other suggestions that I could make,' said the visitor.

He stood up abruptly.

'I hope you understand me,' he said. 'Your offences are no concern of mine, but they would be a great concern of yours if you were placed in the dock to answer for them. They are also too profitable for you to be ready to abandon them—yet. You will therefore pay me one hundred pounds a week for as long as I choose to demand it. Is that sufficiently plain?'

'You—'

Montgomery Bird came out of his chair with a rush.

The bearded man was not disturbed. Only his right hand, in his overcoat pocket, moved slightly.

'My—er—elementary bluff is still waiting your investigation,' he said dispassionately, and the other stopped dead.

With his head thrust a little forward, he stared into the tinted lenses that masked the big man's eyes.

'One day I'll get you—you—swine.'

'And until that day, you will continue to pay me one hundred pounds a week, my dear Mr Bird,' came the gentle response. 'Your next contribution is already due. If it is not troubling you too much—'

He did not bother to complete the sentence. He simply waited.

Bird went back to the desk and opened a drawer. He took out an envelope and threw it on the blotter.

'Thank you,' said the visitor.

His fingers had just touched the envelope when the shrill scream of a bell froze him into immobility. It was not an ordinary bell. It had a vociferous viciousness about it that stung the eardrums—something like the magnified buzzing of an infuriated wasp.

'What is that?'

'My private alarm.'

Bird glanced at the illuminated clock on the mantelpiece; and the visitor, following the glance, saw that the dial had turned red.

'A police raid?'

'Yes.'

The big man picked up the envelope and thrust it into his pocket.

'You will get me out of here,' he said.

Only a keen ear would have noticed the least fraying of the edges of his measured accents; but Montgomery Bird noticed it, and looked at him curiously.

'If I didn't—'

'You would be foolish—very foolish,' said the visitor quietly.

Bird moved back, with murderous eyes. Set in one wall was a large mirror; he put his hands to the frame of it and pushed it bodily sideways in invisible grooves, revealing a dark rectangular opening.

And it was at that moment that Simon Templar, for his own inscrutable reasons, tired of his voluntary exile.

'Stand clear of the lift gates, please,' he murmured.

To the two men, wheeling round at the sound of his voice like a pair of marionettes whose control wires have got mixed up with a dynamo, it seemed as if he had appeared out of the fourth dimension. Just for an instant. And then they saw the open door of the capacious cupboard behind him.

'Pass right down the car, gents,' he murmured, encouragingly.

He crossed the room. He appeared to cross it slowly, but that, again, was an illusion. He had reached the two men before either of them could move. His left hand shot out and fastened on the lapels of the bearded man's coat—and the bearded man vanished. It was the most startling thing that Mr Montgomery Bird had ever seen; but the Saint did not seem to be aware that he was multiplying miracles with an easy grace that would have made a Grand Lama look like a third-rate three-card man. He calmly pulled the sliding mirror back into place, and turned round again.

'No—not you, Montgomery,' he drawled. 'We may want you again this evening. Back-pedal, comrade.'

His arm telescoped languidly outwards, and the hand at the end of it seized the retreating Mr Bird by one ear, fetching him up with a jerk that made him squeak in muted anguish.

Simon steered him firmly but rapidly towards the open cupboard.

'You can cool off in there,' he said; and the next sensations that impinged upon Montgomery Bird's delirious consciousness consisted of a lot of darkness and the sound of a key turning in the cupboard lock.

The Saint straightened his coat and returned to the centre of the room.

He sat down in Mr Bird's chair, put his feet on Mr Bird's desk, lighted one of Mr Bird's cigars, and gazed at the ceiling with an expression of indescribable beatitude on his face; and it was thus that Chief Inspector Claud Eustace Teal found him.

Some seconds passed before the detective recovered the use of his voice; but when he had done this, he made up for lost time.

'What,' he snarled, 'the blankety blank blanking blank-blanked blank—'

'Hush,' said the Saint.

'Why?' snarled Teal, not unreasonably.

Simon held up his hand.

'Listen.'

There was a moment's silence; and then Teal's glare re-calorified.

'What am I supposed to be listening to?' he demanded violently; and the Saint beamed at him.

'Down in the forest something stirred—it was only the note of a bird,' he explained sweetly.

The detective centralised his jaw with a visible effort.

'Is Montgomery Bird another of your fancy names?' he inquired, with a certain lusciousness.

'Because, if it is—'

'Yes, old dear?'

'If it is,' said Chief Inspector Teal grimly, 'you're going to see the inside of a prison at last.'

Simon regarded him imperturbably.

'On what charge?'

'You're going to get as long as I can get you for allowing drinks to be sold in your club after hours—'

'And then—?'

The detective's eyes narrowed.

'What do you mean?'

Simon flourished Mr Bird's cigar airily.

'I always understood that the police were pretty bone-headed,' he remarked genially, 'but I never knew before that they'd been reduced to employing Chief Inspectors for ordinary drinking raids.'

Teal said nothing.

'On the other hand, a dope raid is quite a different matter,' said the Saint.

He smiled at the detective's sudden stillness, and stood up, knocking an inch of ash from his cigar.

'I must be toddling along,' he murmured. 'If you really want to find some dope, and you've any time to spare after you've finished cleaning up the bar, you ought to try locking the door of this room and pulling up bits of wainscoting. The third and fifth sections—I can't tell you which wall. Oh, and if you want Montgomery, he's simmering down in the Frigidaire . . . See you again soon.'

He patted the crown of Mr Teal's bowler hat affectionately, and was gone before the detective had completely grasped what was happening.

The Saint could make those well-oiled exits when he chose; and he chose to make one then, for he was a fundamentally tactful man. Also, he had in one pocket an envelope purporting to contain one hundred pounds, and in another pocket the entire contents of Mr Montgomery Bird's official safe; and at such times the Saint did not care to be detained.

II

Simon Templar pushed back his plate.

'Today,' he announced, 'I have reaped the first-fruits of virtue.'

He raised the letter he had received, and adjusted an imaginary pair of pince-nez. Patricia waited expectantly. The Saint read:

'*Dear Mr Templar,*

*Having come across a copy of your book 'The Pirate' and having nothing to do I sat down to read it. Well, the impression it gave me was that you are a writer with no sense of proportion. The reader's sympathy owing to the faulty setting of the first chapter naturally goes all the way with Kerrigan, even though he is a crook. It is not surprising that this book has not gone to a second edition. You do not evidently understand the mentality of an English reading public. If instead of Mario you had selected for your hero an Englishman or an American, you would have written a fairly readable and a passable tale—but a lousy Dago who works himself out of impossible difficulties and situations is too much. It is not convincing. It does not appeal. In a word it is puerile.*

*I fancy you yourself must have a fair amount of Dago blood in you—*'

He stopped, and Patricia Holm looked at him puzzledly.

'Well?' she prompted.

'There is no more,' explained the Saint. 'No address—no signature—no closing peroration—nothing. Apparently words failed him. At that point he probably uttered a short sharp yelp of intolerable agony, and began to chew pieces out of the furniture. We may never know his fate. Possibly, in some distant asylum—'

He elaborated on his theory.

During a brief spell of virtue some time before, the Saint had beguiled himself with the writing of a novel. Moreover, he had actually succeeded in finding a home for it; and the adventures of Mario, a super-brigand of South America, could be purchased at any bookstall for three half-crowns. And the letter that he had just read was part of his reward.

Another part of the reward had commenced six months previously.

'Nor is this all,' said the Saint, taking another document from the table. 'The following billet-doux appears to close some entertaining correspondence:

*Previous applications for payment of the under-mentioned instalment for the year 1931–1932, due from you on the 1st day January, 1932, having been made to you without effect, **Personal Demand** is now made for payment, and I **Hereby Give You Final Notice** that if the amount be not paid or remitted to me at the above address within **Seven Days** from this date, steps will be taken for recovery by Distraint, with costs.*

*Lionel Delborn, Collector.'*

In spite of the gloomy prognostications of the anonymous critic, The Pirate had not passed utterly unnoticed in the spate of sensational fiction. The Intelligence Department ('A beautiful name for them,' said the Saint) of the Inland Revenue had observed its appearance, had consulted their records, and had discovered that the author, the notorious Simon Templar, was not registered as a contributor towards the expensive extravagances whereby a modern boobocracy does its share in encouraging the survival of the fattest. The Saint's views about his liabilities in this cause were not invited:

he simply received an assessment which presumed his income to be six thousand pounds per annum, and he was invited to appeal against it if he thought fit. The Saint thought fit, and declared that the assessment was bad in law, erroneous in principle, excessive in amount, and malicious in intent. The discussion that followed was lengthy and diverting; the Saint, conducting his own case with remarkable forensic ability and eloquence, pleaded that he was a charitable institution and therefore not taxable.

'If,' said the Saint, in his persuasive way, 'you will look up the delightful words of Lord Macnaghten, in *Income Tax Commissioners v. Pemsel*, 1891, A.C. at p. 583, you will find that charitable purposes are there defined in four principal divisions, of which the fourth is "trusts for purposes beneficial to the community, not falling under any of the preceding heads." I am simply and comprehensively beneficial to the community, which the face of the third Commissioner from the left definitely is not.'

We find from the published record of the proceedings that he was overruled; and the epistle he had just quoted was final and conclusive proof of the fact.

'And that,' said the Saint, gazing at the formidable red lettering gloomily, 'is what I get for a lifetime of philanthropy and self-denial.'

'I suppose you'll have to pay,' said Patricia.

'Someone will,' said the Saint significantly.

He propped the printed buff envelope that had accompanied the Final Demand against the coffee-pot, and his eyes rested on it for a space with a gentle thoughtfulness—amazingly clear, devil-may-care blue eyes with a growing glimmer of mischief lurking somewhere behind the lazily drooping lids.

And slowly the old Saintly smile came to his lips as he contemplated the address.

'Someone will have to pay,' repeated the Saint thoughtfully; and Patricia Holm sighed, for she knew the signs.

And suddenly the Saint stood up, with his swift soft laugh, and took the Final Demand and the envelope over to the fireplace. On the wall close by hung a plain block calendar, and on the mantelpiece lay an old Corsican stiletto. '*Che la mia ferita sia mortale*,' said the inscription on the blade.

The Saint rapidly flicked over the pages of the calendar and tore out the sheet which showed in solid red figures the day on which Mr Lionel Delborn's patience would expire. He placed the sheet on top of the other papers, and with one quick thrust he drove the stiletto through the collection and speared it deep into the panelled overmantel.

'Lest we forget,' he said, and turned with another laugh to smile seraphically into Patricia's outraged face. 'I just wasn't born to be respectable, lass, and that's all there is to it. And the time has come for us to remember the old days.'

As a matter of fact, he had made that decision two full weeks before, and Patricia had known it; but not until then had he made his open declaration of war.

At eight o'clock that evening he was sallying forth in quest of an evening's innocent amusement, and a car that had been standing in the darkness at the end of the cul-de-sac of Upper Berkeley Mews suddenly switched on its headlights and roared towards him. The Saint leapt back and fell on his face in the doorway, and he heard the plop of a silenced gun and the thud of a bullet burying itself in the woodwork above his head. He slid out into the mews again as the car went past, and fired twice as it swung into Berkeley Square, but he could not tell whether he did any damage.

He returned to brush his clothes, and then continued calmly on his way; and when he met Patricia later he did not think it necessary to mention the incident that had delayed him. But it was the third time since the episode chez Bird that the Scorpion had tried to kill him, and no one knew better than Simon Templar that it would not be the last attempt.

III

For some days past, the well-peeled eye might at intervals have observed a cadaverous and lantern-jawed individual protruding about six and a half feet upwards from the cobbled paving of Upper Berkeley Mews. Simon Templar, having that sort of eye, had in fact noticed the apparition on its first and in all its subsequent visits; and anyone less well-informed than himself might pardonably have suspected some connection between the lanky boulevardier and the recent disturbances of the peace. Simon Templar, however, was not deceived.

'That,' he said once, in answer to Patricia's question, 'is Mr Harold Garrot, better known as Long Harry. He is a moderately proficient burglar; and we have met before, but not professionally. He is trying to make up his mind to come and tell me something, and one of these days he will take the plunge.'

The Saint's deductions were vindicated twenty-four hours after the last firework display.

Simon was alone. The continued political activities of a certain newspaper proprietor had driven him to verse, and he was covering a sheet of foolscap with the beginning of a minor epic expressing his own views on the subject:

> Charles Charleston Charlemagne St Charles
> Was wont to utter fearful snarls
> When by professors he was pressed
> To note how England had progressed
> Since the galumptious, gory days
> Immortalised in Shakespeare's plays.
> For him, no Transatlantic flights,
> Ford motor-cars, electric lights,
> Or radios at less than cost
> Could compensate for what he lost
> By chancing to coagulate
> About five hundred years too late.
> Born in the only days for him

He would have swung a sword with vim,
Grown ginger whiskers on his face,
And mastered, with a knobbly mace,
Men who wore hauberks on their chests
Instead of little woollen vests.
And drank strong wine among his peers
Instead of pale synthetic beers.

At this point, the trend of his inspiration led the Saint on a brief excursion to the barrel in one corner of the room. He replenished his tankard, drank deeply, and continued:

Had he not reason to be glum
When born in nineteen umpty-um?

And there, for the moment, he stuck; and he was cogitating the possible developments of the next stanza when he was interrupted by the zing! of the front door bell.

As he stepped out into the hall, he glanced up through the fanlight above the door at the mirror that was cunningly fixed to the underneath of the hanging lantern outside. He recognised the caller at once, and opened the door without hesitation.

'Come in, Harry,' invited the Saint cordially, and led the way back to the sitting-room. 'I was busy with a work of art that is going to make Milton look like a distant relative of the gargle, but I can spare you a few minutes.'

Long Harry glanced at the sheet half-covered with the Saint's neat handwriting.

'Poetry, Mr Templar? We used to learn poetry at school,' he said reminiscently.

Simon looked at him thoughtfully for two or three seconds, and then he beamed.

'Harry, you hit the nail on the head. For that suggestion, I pray that your shadow may always be jointed at the elbows. Excuse me one moment.'

He plumped himself back in his chair and wrote at speed. Then he cleared his throat, and read aloud:

> 'Eton and Oxford failed to floor
> The spirit of the warrior;
> Though ragged and bullied, teased and hissed,
> Charles stayed a Medievalist;
> And even when his worldly Pa
> (Regarding him with nausea)
> Condemned him to the dismal cares
> Of sordid trade in stocks and shares,
> Charles, in top-hat and Jaeger drawers,
> Clung like a limpet to his Cause,
> Believing, in a kind of trance,
> That one day he would have his Chance.'

He laid the sheet down reverently.

'A mere pastime for me, but I believe Milton used to sweat blood over it,' he remarked complacently. 'Soda or water, Harry?'

'Neat, please, Mr Templar.'

Simon brought over the glass of Highland cream, and Long Harry sipped it, and crossed and uncrossed his legs awkwardly.

'I hope you don't mind my coming to see you, sir,' he ventured at last.

'Not at all,' responded the Saint heartily. 'Always glad to see any Eton boys here. What's the trouble?'

Long Harry fidgeted, twiddling his fingers and corrugating his brow. He was the typical 'old lag', or habitual criminal, which is to say that outside of business hours he was a perfectly ordinary man of slightly less than average intelligence and rather more than average cunning. On this occasion he was plainly and ordinarily ill at ease, and the Saint surmised that he had only begun to solve his worries when he mustered up the courage to give that single, brief, and symptomatic ring at the front door bell.

Simon lighted a cigarette and waited impassively, and presently his patience reaped its harvest.

'I wondered—I thought maybe I could tell you something that might interest you, Mr Templar.'

'Sure.' The Saint allowed a thin jet of smoke to trickle through his lips, and continued to wait.

'It's about . . . it's about the Scorpion, Mr Templar.'

Instantaneously the Saint's eyes narrowed, the merest fraction of a millimetre, and the inhalation that he drew from his cigarette was long and deep and slow. And then the stare that he swivelled round in the direction of Long Harry was wide blue innocence itself.

'What Scorpion?' he inquired blandly.

Long Harry frowned.

'I thought you'd've known about the Scorpion, of course, Mr Templar, you being—'

'Yeah?'

Simon drawled out the prompting diphthong in a honeyed slither up a gently persuasive G-string; and Long Harry shuffled his feet uncomfortably.

'Well, you remember what you used to be, Mr Templar. There wasn't much you didn't know in those days.'

'Oh, yes—once upon a time. But now—'

'Last time we met, sir—'

The Saint's features relaxed, and he smiled.

'Forget it, Harold,' he advised quietly. 'I'm now a respectable citizen. I was a respectable citizen the last time we met, and I haven't changed. You may tell me anything you like, Harry—as one respectable citizen to another—but I'd recommend you to forget the interview as you step over the front door mat. I shall do the same—it's safer.'

Long Harry nodded.

'If you forget it, sir, it'll be safer for me,' he said seriously.

'I have a hopeless memory,' said the Saint carefully. 'I've already forgotten your name. In another minute, I shan't be sure that you're here at all. Now shoot the dope, son.'

'You've got nothing against me, sir?'

'Nothing. You're a professional burglar, housebreaker, and petty larcenist, but that's no concern of mine. Teal can attend to your little mistakes.'

'And you'll forget what I'm going to say—soon as ever I've said it?'

'You heard me.'

'Well, Mr Templar—' Long Harry cleared his throat, took another pull at his drink, and blinked nervously for some seconds. 'I've worked for the Scorpion, Mr Templar,' he said suddenly.

Simon Templar never moved a muscle.

'Yes?'

'Only once, sir—so far.' Once having left the diving-board, Long Harry floundered on recklessly. 'And there won't be a second time—not if I can help it. He's dangerous. You ain't never safe with him. I know. Sent me a message he did, through the post. Knew where I was staying, though I'd only been there two days, an' everything about me. There was five one-pound notes in the letter, and he said if I met a car that'd be waiting at the second milestone north of Hatfield at nine o'clock last Thursday night there'd be another fifty for me to earn.'

'What sort of car was it?'

'I never had a chance to notice it properly, Mr Templar. It was a big, dark car, I think. It hadn't any lights. I was going to tell you—I was a bit suspicious at first. I thought it must be a plant, but it was that talk of fifty quid that tempted me. The car was waiting for me when I got there. I went up and looked in the window, and there was a man there at the wheel. Don't ask me what he looked like—he kept his head down, and I never saw more than the top of his hat. "Those are your instructions," he says, pushing an envelope at me, he says, "and there's half your money. I'll meet you here at the same time tomorrow." And then he drove off. I struck a match, and found he'd given me the top halves of fifty pound notes.'

'And then?'

'Then—I went an' did the job, Mr Templar.'

'What job?'

'I was to go to a house at St Albans and get some papers. There was a map, an' a plan, an' all about the locks an' everything. I had my tools—I forgot to tell you the first letter said I was to bring them—and it was as easy as the orders said it would be. Friday night, I met the car as arranged, and handed over the papers, and he gave me the other halves of the notes.'

Simon extended a lean brown hand.

'The orders?' he inquired briefly.

He took the cheap yellow envelope, and glanced through the contents. There was, as Long Harry had said, a neatly-drawn map and plan; and the other information, in a studiously characterless copperplate writing, covered two more closely written sheets.

'You've no idea whose house it was you entered?'

'None at all, sir.'

'Did you look at these papers?'

'Yes.' Long Harry raised his eyes and looked at the Saint sombrely. 'That's the one reason why I came to you, sir.'

'What were they?'

'They were love-letters, sir. There was an address—64 Half Moon Street. And they were signed—"Mark".'

Simon passed a hand over his sleekly perfect hair.

'Oh yes?' he murmured.

'You saw the Sunday papers, sir?'

'I did.'

Long Harry emptied his glass, and put it down with clumsy fingers.

'Sir Mark Deverest shot 'imself at 64 'Alf Moon Street, on Saturday night,' he said huskily.

When he was agitated, he occasionally lost an aspirate and it was an index of his perturbation that he actually dropped two in that one sentence.

'That's the Scorpion's graft, Mr Templar—blackmail. I never touched black in my life, but I'd heard that was his game. An' when he sent for me, I forgot it. Even when I was looking through those letters, it never seemed to come into my head why he wanted them. But I see it all now. He wanted 'em to put the black on Deverest, an' Deverest shot himself instead of paying up. And—I 'elped to murder 'im, Mr Templar. Murder, that's what it was. Nothing less. An' I 'elped!' Long Harry's voice fell to a throaty whisper, and his dull eyes shifted over the clear-etched contours of the Saint's tanned face in a kind of panic of anxiety. 'I never knew what I was doing, Mr Templar, sir—strike me dead if I did—'

Simon reached forward and crushed out his cigarette in an ashtray.

'Is that all you came to tell me?' he asked dispassionately; and Long Harry gulped.

'I thought you'd be laying for the Scorpion, sir, knowing you always used to be—'

'Yeah?'

Again that mellifluous dissyllable, in a voice that you could have carved up with a wafer of butter.

'Well, sir, what I mean is, if you were the Saint, sir, and if you hadn't forgotten that you might ever have been him, you might—'

'Be hunting scorpions?'

'That's the way I thought it out, sir.'

'And?'

'I was hanging around last night, Mr Templar, trying to make up my mind to come and see you, and I saw the shooting.'

'And?'

'That car—it was just like the car that met me out beyond Hatfield, sir.'

'And?'

'I thought p'raps it was the same car.'

'And?'

Simon prompted him for the fourth time from the corner table where he was replenishing Long Harry's glass. His back was turned, but there was an inconspicuous little mirror just above the level of the eyes—the room was covered from every angle by those inconspicuous little mirrors. And he saw the twitching of Long Harry's mouth.

'I came because I thought you might be able to stop the Scorpion getting me, Mr Templar,' said Long Harry, in one jerk.

'Ah!' The Saint swung round. 'That's more like it! So you're on the list, are you?'

'I think so.' Long Harry nodded. 'There was a shot aimed at me last night, too, but I suppose you wouldn't've noticed it.'

Simon Templar lighted another cigarette.

'I see. The Scorpion spotted you hanging around here, and tried to bump you off. That's natural. But, Harry, you never even started hanging around here until you got the idea you might like to tell me the story of your life—and still you haven't told me where that idea came from. Sing on, Harry—I'm listening, and I'm certainly patient.'

Long Harry absorbed a gill of Maison Dewar in comparative silence, and wiped his lips on the back of his hand.

'I had another letter on Monday morning, telling me to be at the same place at midnight tomorrow.'

'And?'

'Monday afternoon I was talking to some friends. I didn't tell 'em anything, but I sort of steered the conversation around, not bringing myself in personal. You remember Wilbey?'

'Found full of bullets on the Portsmouth Road three months ago? Yes—I remember.'

'I heard—it's just a story, but I heard the last job he did was for the Scorpion. He talked about it. The bloke shot himself that time, too. An' I began thinking. It may surprise you, Mr Templar, but sometimes I'm very si-chick.'

'You worked it out that as long as the victims paid up, everything was all right. But if they did anything desperate, there was always a chance of trouble; and the Scorpion wouldn't want anyone who could talk running about without a muzzle. That right?'

Long Harry nodded, and his prominent Adam's apple flickered once up and down.

'Yes, I think if I keep that appointment tomorrow I'll be—what's that American word?—on the spot. Even if I don't go—' The man broke off with a shrug that made a feeble attempt at bravado. 'I couldn't take that story of mine to the police, Mr Templar, as you'll understand, and I wondered—'

Simon Templar settled a little deeper into his chair and sent a couple of perfect smoke-rings chasing each other up towards the ceiling.

He understood Long Harry's thought processes quite clearly. Long Harry was a commonplace and more or less peaceful yegg, and violence was not among the most prominent interests of his life. Long Harry, as the Saint knew, had never even carried so much as a life-preserver . . . The situation was obvious.

But how the situation was to be turned to account—that required a second or two's meditation. Perhaps two seconds. And then the little matter of spoon-feeding that squirming young pup of a plan up to a full-sized man-eating carnivore hopping around on its own pads . . . maybe five seconds more. And then—

'We deduce,' said the Saint dreamily, 'that our friend had arranged for you to die tomorrow; but when he found you on the outskirts of the scenery last night, he thought he might save himself a journey.'

'That's the way I see it, Mr Templar.'

'From the evidence before us, we deduce that he isn't the greatest snap shot in the world. And so—'

'Yes, Mr Templar?'

'It looks to me, Harry,' said the Saint pleasantly, 'as if you'll have to die tomorrow after all.'


IV

Simon was lingering over a cigarette and his last breakfast cup of coffee when Mr Teal dropped in at half-past eleven next morning.

'Have you breakfasted?' asked the Saint hospitably. 'I can easily hash you up an egg or something—'

'Thanks,' said Teal, 'I had breakfast at eight.'

'A positively obscene hour,' said the Saint.

He went to an inlaid smoking-cabinet, and solemnly transported a new and virginal packet of spearmint into the detective's vicinity.

'Make yourself at home, Claud Eustace. And why are we thus honoured?'

There was a gleaming automatic, freshly cleaned and oiled, beside the breakfast-tray, and Teal's sleepy eyes fell on it as he undressed some Wrigley. He made no comment at that point, and continued his somnambulation round the room. Before the papers pinned to the overmantel, he paused.

'You going to contribute your just share towards the expenses of the nation?' he inquired.

'Someone is going to,' answered the Saint calmly.

'Who?'

'Talking of scorpions, Teal—'

The detective revolved slowly, and his baby eyes suddenly drooped as if in intolerable ennui.

'What scorpions?' he demanded, and the Saint laughed.

'Pass it up, Teal, old stoat. That one's my copyright.'

Teal frowned heavily.

'Does this mean the old game again, Saint?'

'Teal! Why bring that up?'

The detective gravitated into a pew.

'What have you got to say about scorpions?'

'They have stings in their tails.'

Teal's chewing continued with rhythmic monotonousness.

'When did you become interested in the Scorpion?' he questioned casually.

'I've been interested for some time,' murmured the Saint. 'Just recently, though, the interest's become a shade too mutual to be healthy. Did you know the Scorpion was an amateur!' he added abruptly.

'Why do you think that?'

'I don't think it—I know it. The Scorpion is raw. That's one reason why I shall have to tread on him. I object to being shot up by amateurs—I feel it's liable to lower my stock. And as for being finally killed by an amateur . . . Teal, put it to yourself!'

'How do you know this?'

The Saint renewed his cigarette at leisure.

'Deduction. The Sherlock Holmes stuff again. I'll teach you the trick one day, but I can give you this result out flat. Do you want chapter and verse?'

'I'd be interested.'

'OK.' The Saint leaned back. 'A man came and gave me some news about the Scorpion last night, after hanging around for three days—and he's still alive. I was talking to him on the phone only half an hour ago. If the Scorpion had been a real professional, that man would never even have seen me—let alone have been alive to ring me up this morning. That's one point.'

'What's the next?'

'You remember the Portsmouth Road murder?'

'Yes.'

'Wilbey had worked for the Scorpion, and he was a possible danger. If you'll consult your records, you'll find that Wilbey was acquitted on a charge of felonious loitering six days before he died. It was exactly the same with the bird who came to see me last night. He had also worked for the Scorpion, and he was discharged at Bow Street only two days before the Scorpion sent for him. Does that spell anything to you?'

Teal crinkled his forehead.

'Not yet, but I'm trying.'

'Let me save you the trouble.'

'No—just a minute. The Scorpion was in court when the charges were dismissed—'

'Exactly. And he followed them home. It's obvious. If you or I wanted someone to do a specialised bit of crime—say burglary, for instance—in thirty hours we could lay our hands on thirty men we could commission. But the genuine aged-in-the-wood amateur hasn't got those advantages, however clever he may be. He simply hasn't got the connections. You can't apply for cracksmen to the ordinary labour exchange, or advertise for them in *The Times*, and if you're a respectable amateur you haven't any among your intimate friends. What's the only way you can get hold of them?'

Teal nodded slowly.

'It's an idea,' he admitted. 'I don't mind telling you we've looked over all the regulars long ago. The Scorpion doesn't come into the catalogue. There isn't a nose on the pay-roll who can get a whiff of him. He's something right outside our register of established clients.'

The name of the Scorpion had first been mentioned nine months before, when a prominent Midland cotton-broker had put his head in a gas-oven and forgotten to turn off the gas. In a letter that was read at the inquest occurred the words: 'I have been bled for years, and now I can endure no more. When the Scorpion stings, there is no antidote but death.'

And in the brief report of the proceedings:

The Coroner: Have you any idea what the deceased meant by that reference to a scorpion?

Witness: No.

Is there any professional blackmailer known to the police by that name?—I have never heard it before.

And thereafter, for the general run of respectable citizens from whom the Saint expressly dissociated Teal and himself, the rest had been a suavely expanding blank . . .

But through that vast yet nebulous area popularly called 'the underworld' began to voyage vague rumours, growing more and more wild and fantastic as they passed from mouth to mouth, but still coming at last to the respective ears of Scotland Yard with enough credible vitality to be interesting. Kate Allfield, 'the Mug', entered a railway carriage in which a Member of Parliament was travelling alone on a flying visit to his constituency: he stopped the train at Newbury and gave her in charge, and when her counter-charge of assault broke down under ruthless cross-examination she 'confessed' that she had acted on the instigation of an unknown accomplice. Kate had tried many ways of making easy money, and the fact that the case in question was a new one in her history meant little. But round the underworld travelled two words of comment and explanation, and those two words said simply 'The Scorpion'.

'Basher' Tope—thief, motor-bandit, brute, and worse—was sent for. He boasted in his cups of how he was going to solve the mystery of the Scorpion, and went alone to his appointment. What happened there he never told; he was absent from his usual haunts for three weeks, and when he was seen again he had a pink scar on his temple and a surly disinclination to discuss the matter. Since he had earned his nickname, questions were not showered upon him; but once again the word went round . . .

And so it was with half a dozen subsequent incidents; and the legend of the Scorpion grew up and was passed from hand to hand in queer places, unmarked by sensation-hunting journalists, a mystery for police and criminals alike. Jack Wilbey, ladder larcenist, died and won his niche in the structure; but the newspapers noted his death only as another unsolved crime on which to peg their perennial criticisms of police efficiency, and only those who had heard other chapters of the story linked up that murder with the suicide of a certain wealthy peer. Even Chief Inspector Teal, whose finger was on the pulse of every unlawful activity in the Metropolis, had not visualised such a connecting link as the Saint had just forged before his eyes; and he pondered over it in a ruminative silence before he resumed his interrogation.

'How much else do you know?' he asked at length, with the mere ghost of a quickening of interest in his perpetually weary voice.

The Saint picked up a sheet of paper.

'Listen,' he said.

'His faith was true: though once misled
By an appeal that he had read
To honour with his patronage

Crusades for better Auction Bridge
He was not long deceived; he found
No other paladins around
Prepared to perish, sword in hand,
While storming in one reckless band

Those strongholds of Beelzebub

The portals of the Portland Club.
His chance came later; one fine day
Another paper blew his way:
Charles wrote; Charles had an interview;

And Charles, an uncrowned jousting Blue,
Still spellbound by the word Crusade,
Espoused the cause of Empire Trade.'

'What on earth's that?' demanded the startled detective.

'A little masterpiece of mine,' said the Saint modestly. 'There's rather an uncertain rhyme in it, if you noticed. Do you think the Poet Laureate would pass patronage and Bridge? I'd like your opinion.'

Teal's eyelids lowered again.

'Have you stopped talking?' he sighed.

'Very nearly, Teal,' said the Saint, putting the paper down again. 'In case that miracle of tact was too subtle for you, let me explain that I was changing the subject.'

'I see.'

'Do you?'

Teal glanced at the automatic on the table and then again at the papers on the wall, and sighed a second time.

'I think so. You're going to ask the Scorpion to pay your income tax.'

'I am.'

'How?'

The Saint laughed. He pointed to the desecrated overmantel.

'One thousand three hundred and thirty-seven pounds, nineteen and five-pence,' he said. 'That's my sentence for being a useful wage-earning citizen instead of a prolific parasite, according to the laws of this spavined country. Am I supposed to pay you and do your work as well? If so, I shall emigrate on the next boat and become a naturalised Venezuelan.'

'I wish you would,' said Teal, from his heart.

He picked up his hat.

'Do you know the Scorpion?' he asked suddenly.

Simon shook his head.

'Not yet. But I'm going to. His donation is not yet assessed, but I can tell you where one thousand three hundred and thirty-eight pounds of it are going to travel. And that is towards the offices of Mr Lionel Delborn, collector of extortions—may his teeth fall out and his legs putrefy! I'll stand the odd seven-pence out of my own pocket.'

'And what do you think you're going to do with the man himself?'

The Saint smiled.

'That's a little difficult to say,' he murmured. 'Accidents sort of—er—happen, don't they? I mean, I don't want you to start getting back any of your naughty old ideas about me, but—'

Teal nodded; then he met the Saint's mocking eyes seriously.

'They'd have the coat on my back if it ever got round,' he said, 'but between you and me and these four walls, I'll make a deal—if you'll make one too.'

Simon settled on the edge of the table, his cigarette slanting quizzically upwards between his lips, and one whimsically sardonic eyebrow arched.

'What is it?'

'Save the Scorpion for me, and I won't ask how you paid your income tax.'

For a few moments the Saint's noncommittal gaze rested on the detective's round red face; then it wandered back to the impaled memorandum above the mantelpiece. And then the Saint looked Teal in the eyes and smiled again.

'OK,' he drawled. 'That's OK with me, Claud.'

'It's a deal?'

'It is. There's a murder charge against the Scorpion, and I don't see why the hangman shouldn't earn his fiver. I guess it's time you had a break, Claud Eustace. Yes—you can have the Scorpion. Any advance on four-pence?'

Teal nodded, and held out his hand.

'Fourpence half-penny—I'll buy you a glass of beer at any pub inside the three-mile radius on the day you bring him in,' he said.

V

Patricia Holm came in shortly after four-thirty. Simon Templar had lunched at what he always referred to as 'the pub round the corner'—the Berkeley—and had ambled elegantly about the purlieus of Piccadilly for an hour thereafter; for he had scarcely learned to walk two consecutive steps when his dear old grandmother had taken him on her knee and enjoined him to 'eat, drink, and be merry, for tomorrow is Shrove Tuesday.'

He was writing when she arrived, but he put down his pen and surveyed her solemnly.

'Oh, there you are,' he remarked. 'I thought you were dead, but Teal said he thought you might only have taken a trip to Vladivostok.'

'I've been helping Eileen Wiltham—her wedding's only five days away. Haven't you any more interest in her?'

'None,' said the Saint callously. 'The thought of the approaching crime makes my mind feel unbinged—unhinged. I've already refused three times to assist Charles to select pyjamas for the bridal chamber. I told him that when he'd been married as often as I have—'

'That'll do,' said Patricia.

'It will, very nearly,' said the Saint.

He cast an eye over the mail that she had brought in with her from the letter-box.

'Those two envelopes with half-penny stamps you may exterminate forthwith. On the third, in spite of the deceptive three-half-penny *Briefmarke*. I recognise the clerkly hand of Anderson and Sheppard. Add it to the holocaust. Item four'—he picked up a small brown-paper package and weighed it calculatingly in his hand—'is much too light to contain high explosive. It's probably the new gold-mounted sock-suspenders I ordered from Asprey's. Open it, darling, and tell me what you think of them. And I will read you some more of the *Hideous History of Charles*.'

He took up his manuscript.

'With what a zest did he prepare
For the first meeting (open-air)!
With what a glee he fastened on

His bevor and his morion

His greaves, his ventail, every tace,
His pauldrons and his rerebrace!
He sallied forth with martial eye,
Prepared to do, prepared to die,

But not prepared—by Bayard! not
For the reception that he got.
Over that chapter of the tale
It would be kind to draw a veil:
Let it suffice that in disdain,
Some hecklers threw him in a drain,
And plodding home—

'Excuse me,' said the Saint.

His right hand moved like lightning, and the detonation of his heavy automatic in the confined space was like a vindictive thunderclap. It left the girl with a strange hot sting of powder on her wrist and a dull buzzing in her ears. And through the buzzing drifted the Saint's unruffled accents:

> 'And plodding home, all soaked inside,
> He caught pneumonia—and died.'

Patricia looked at him, white-faced.

'What was it?' she asked, with the faintest tremor in her voice.

'Just an odd spot of scorpion,' answered Simon Templar gently. 'An unpleasant specimen of the breed—the last time I saw one like that was up in the hills north of Puruk-jahu. Looks like a pal of mine has been doing some quick travelling, or . . . Yes.' The Saint grinned. 'Get on the phone to the Zoo, old dear, and tell 'em they can have their property back if they care to send round and scrape it off the carpet. I don't think we shall want it any more, shall we?'

Patricia shuddered.

She had stripped away the brown paper and found a little cardboard box such as cheap jewellery is sometimes packed in. When she raised the lid, the tiny blue-green horror, like a miniature deformed lobster, had been lying there in a nest of cotton-wool; while she stared at it, it had rustled on to her and . . .

'It—wasn't very big,' she said, in a tone that tried to match the Saint's for lightness.

'Scorpions run to all sizes,' said the Saint cheerfully, 'and as often as not their poisonousness is in inverse ratio to their size in boots. Mostly, they're very minor troubles—I've been stung myself, and all I got was a sore and swollen arm. But the late lamented was a member of the one and only sure-certain and no-hokum family of homicides in the species. Pity I bumped it off so quickly— it might have been really valuable stuffed.'

Patricia's finger-tips slid mechanically around the rough edges of the hole that the nickel-cased .45 bullet had smashed through the polished mahogany table before ruining the carpet and losing itself somewhere in the floor. Then she looked steadily at the Saint.

'Why should anyone send you a scorpion?' she asked.

Simon Templar shrugged.

'It was the immortal Paragot who said: "In this country the unexpected always happens, which paralyses the brain". And if a real man-sized Scorpion can't be expected to send his young brothers to visit his friends as a token of esteem, what can he be expected to do?'

'Is that all?'

'All what?'

'All you propose to tell me.'

The Saint regarded her for a moment. He saw the tall slim lines of reposeful strength in her body, the fine moulding of the chin, the eyes as blue and level as his own. And slowly he screwed the cap on his fountain pen; and he stood up and came round the table.

'I'll tell you as much more as you want to know,' he said.

'Just like in the mad old days?'

'They had their moments, hadn't they?'

She nodded.

'Sometimes I wish we were back in them,' she said wistfully. 'I didn't fall in love with you in a pair of Anderson and Sheppard trousers—'

'They were!' cried the Saint indignantly. 'I distinctly remember—'

Patricia laughed suddenly. Her hands fell on his shoulders.

'Give me a cigarette, boy,' she said, 'and tell me what's been happening.'

And he did so—though what he had to tell was little enough. And Chief Inspector Teal himself knew no more. The Scorpion had grown up in darkness, had struck from the darkness, and crawled back deeper into the dark. Those who could have spoken dared not speak, and those who might have spoken died too soon . . .

But as he told his tale, the Saint saw the light of all the mad old days awakening again in Patricia's eyes, and it was in a full and complete understanding of that light that he came to the one thing that Chief Inspector Teal would have given his ears to know.

'Tonight, at nine—'

'You'll be there?'

'I shall,' said the Saint, with the slightest tightening of his lips. 'Shot up by a bloody amateur! Good God! Suppose he'd hit me! Pat, believe papa—when I pass out, there's going to be a first-class professional, hall-marked on every link, at the thick end of the gun.'

Patricia, in the deep armchair, settled her sweet golden head among the cushions.

'What time do we start?' she asked calmly.

For a second, glancing at him sidelong. She saw the old stubborn hardening of the line of his jaw. It happened instinctively, almost without his knowing it; and then suddenly he swung off the arm of the chair in the breath of an even older Saintly laughter.

'Why not?' he said. 'It's impossible—preposterous—unthinkable—but why not? The old gang have gone—Dicky, Archie, Roger—gone and got spliced on to women and come over all bowlerhat. There's only you left. It'd make the vicar's wife let out one piercing squawk and swallow her knitting-needles, but who cares? If you'd really like to have another sniff at the old brew—'

'Give me the chance!'

Simon grinned.

'And you'd flop after it like a homesick walrus down a water-chute, wouldn't you?'

'Faster,' she said.

'And so you shall,' said the Saint. 'The little date I've got for tonight will be all the merrier for an extra soul on the side of saintliness and soft drinks. And if things don't turn out exactly according to schedule, there may be an encore for your especial entertainment. Pat, I have a feeling that this is going to be our week!'

## VI

It was one of the Saint's most charming characteristics that he never hurried and never worried. He insisted on spending an idle hour in the cocktail bar of the May Fair Hotel, and seven-thirty had struck before he collected his car, inserted Patricia, and turned the Hirondel's long silver nose northwards at an unwontedly moderate speed. They dined at Hatfield, after parking the Hirondel in the hotel garage, and after dinner the Saint commanded coffee and liqueurs and proceeded to incinerate two enormous cigars of a plutocratically delicate bouquet. He had calculated exactly how long it would take to walk out to location, and he declined to start one moment before his time-table demanded it.

'I am a doomed man,' he said sombrely, 'and I have my privileges. If necessary, the Scorpion will wait for me.'

Actually he had no intention of being late, for the plan of campaign that he had spent the nicotinised interval after dinner adapting to Patricia's presence required them to be at the rendezvous a shade in advance of the rest of the party.

But this the Scorpion did not know.

He drove up slowly, with his headlights dimmed, scanning the dark shadows at the side of the road. Exactly beside the point where his shaded lights picked up the grey-white blur of the appointed milestone, he saw the tiny red glow of a cigarette-end, and applied his brakes gently. The cigarette-end dropped and vanished under an invisible heel, and out of the gloom a tall dark shape stretched slowly upwards.

The Scorpion's right hand felt the cold bulk of the automatic pistol in his pocket as his other hand lowered the nearside window. He leaned over towards the opening.

'Garrot?'

The question came in a whisper to the man at the side of the road, and he stepped slowly forward and answered in a throaty undertone.

'Yes, sir?'

The Scorpion's head was bent low, so that the man outside the car could only see the shape of his hat.

'You obeyed your orders. That is good. Come closer . . .'

The gun slipped silently out of the Scorpion's pocket, his forefinger curling quickly round the trigger as he drew it. He brought it up without a sound, so that the tip of the barrel rested on the ledge of the open window directly in line with the chest of the man twelve inches away. One lightning glance to left and right told him that the road was deserted.

'Now there is just one thing more—'

'There is,' agreed Patricia Holm crisply. 'Don't move!'

The Scorpion heard, and the glacial concentration of dispassionate unfriendliness in her voice froze him where he sat. He had not heard the noiseless turning of the handle of the door behind him, nor noticed the draught of cooler air that trickled through the car; but he felt the chilly hardness of the circle of steel that pressed into the base of his skull, and for a second he was paralysed. And in that second his target vanished.

'Drop that gun—outside the car. And let me hear it go!'

Again that crisp, commanding voice, as inclemently smooth as an arctic sea, whisked into his eardrums like a thin cold needle. He hesitated for a moment, and then, as the muzzle of the gun behind his neck increased its pressure by one warning ounce, he moved his hand obediently and relaxed his fingers. His automatic rattled on to the running board, and almost immediately the figure that he had taken for Long Harry rose into view again, and was framed in the square space of window.

But the voice that acknowledged the receipt of item, Colts, automatic, scorpions, for the use of, one, was not the voice of Long Harry. It was the most cavalier, the most mocking, the most cheerful voice that the Scorpion had ever heard—he noted those qualities about it subconsciously, for he was not in a position to revel in the discovery with any hilariously wholehearted abandon.

'OK . . . And how are you, my Scorpion?'

'Who are you?' asked the man in the car.

He still kept his head lowered, and under the brim of his hat his eyes were straining into the gloom for a glimpse of the man who had spoken; but the Saint's face was in shadow. Glancing away to one side, the Scorpion could focus the head of the girl whose gun continued to impress his cervical vertebræ with the sense of its rocklike steadiness; but a dark close-fitting hat covered the upper part of her head, and a scarf that was loosely knotted about her neck had been pulled up to veil her face from the eyes downwards.

The Saint's light laugh answered the question.

'I am the world's worst gunman, and the lady behind you is the next worst, but at this range we can say that we never miss. And that's all you need to worry about just now. The question that really arises is—who are you?'

'That is what you have still to discover,' replied the man in the car impassively. 'Where is Garrot?'

'Ah! That's what whole synods of experts are still trying to discover. Some would say that he was simply rotting, and others would say that that was simply rot. He might be floating around the glassy sea, clothed in white samite, mystic, wonderful, with his new regulation nightie flying in the breeze behind; or he might be attending to the central heating plant in the basement. I was never much of a theologian myself—'

'Is he dead?'

'Very,' said the Saint cheerfully. 'I organised the decease myself.'

'You killed him?'

'Oh, no! Nothing like that about me. I merely arranged for him to die. If you survive to read your morning paper tomorrow, you may be informed that the body of an unknown man has been fished out of the Thames. That will be Long Harry. Now come out and take your curtain, sweetheart!'

The Saint stepped back and twitched open the door, pocketing the Scorpion's gun as he did so.

And at the same moment he had a queer feeling of futility. He knew that that was not the moment when he was destined to lay the Scorpion by the heels.

Once or twice before, in a life which had only lasted as long as it had by reason of a vigilance that never blinked for one split second, and a forethought that was accustomed to skid along half a dozen moves ahead of the opposition performers in every game with the agility of a startled streak of lightning zipping through space on ball bearings with the wind behind it, he had experienced the same sensation—of feeling as if an intangible shutter had guillotined down in front of one vitally receptive lens in his alertness. Something was going to happen—his trained intuition told him that beyond all possibility of argument, and an admixture of plain horse-sense told him what would be the general trend of that forthcoming event, equally beyond all possibility of argument—but exactly what shape that event would take was more than any faculty of his could divine.

A tingling stillness settled upon the scene, and in the stillness some fact that he should have been reckoning with seemed to hammer frantically upon that closed window in his mind. He knew that that was so, but his brain produced no other response. Just for that fractional instant of time a cog slipped one pinion, and the faultless machine was at fault. The blind spot that roams around somewhere in every human cerebral system suddenly broke its moorings, and drifted down over the one minute area of co-ordinating apparatus of which Simon Templar had most need; and no effort of his could dislodge it.

'Step out, Cuthbert,' snapped the Saint, with a slight rasp in his voice.

In the darkness inside the car, a slight blur of white caught and interested Simon's eye. It lay on the seat beside the driver. With that premonition of failure dancing about in his subconscious and making faces at his helpless stupidity, the Saint grabbed at the straw. He got it away—a piece of paper—and the Scorpion, seeing it go, snatched wildly but not soon enough.

Simon stuffed the paper into his coat pocket, and with his other hand he took the Scorpion by the neck.

'Step!' repeated the Saint crisply.

And then his forebodings were fulfilled—simply and straightforwardly, as he had known they would be.

The Scorpion had never stopped the engine of his car—that was the infinitesimal yet sufficient fact that had been struggling ineffectively to register itself upon the Saint's brain. The sound was scarcely anything at all, even to the Saint's hypersensitive ears—scarcely more than a rhythmic pulsing disturbance of the stillness of the night. Yet all at once—too late—it seemed to rise and racket in his mind like the thunder of a hundred dynamos; and it was then that he saw his mistake.

But that was after the Scorpion had let in the clutch. In the blackness, his left hand must have been stealthily engaging the gears; and then, as a pair of swiftly growing lights pin-pointed in his driving-mirror, he unleashed the car with a bang.

The Saint, with one foot in the road and the other on the running-board, was flung off his balance. As he stumbled, the jamb of the door crashed agonisingly into the elbow of the arm that reached out to the driver's collar, and something like a thousand red-hot needles prickled right down his forearm to the tip of his little finger and numbed every muscle through which it passed.

As he dropped back into the road, he heard the crack of Patricia's gun.

The side of the car slid past him, gathering speed, and he whipped out the Scorpion's own automatic. Quite casually, he plugged the off-side back tyre; and then a glare of light came into the tail of his eye, and he stepped quickly across to Patricia.

'Walk on,' he said quietly.

They fell into step and sauntered slowly on, and the headlights of the car behind threw their shadows thirty yards ahead.

'That jerk,' said Patricia ruefully, 'my shot missed him by a yard. I'm sorry.'

Simon nodded.

'I know. It was my fault. I should have switched his engine off.'

The other car flashed past them, and Simon cursed it fluently.

'The real joy of having the country full of automobiles,' he said, 'is that it makes gunning so easy. You can shoot anyone up anywhere, and everyone except the victim will think it was only a backfire. But it's when people can see the gun that the deception kind of disintegrates.' He gazed gloomily after the dwindling tail light of the unwelcome interruption. 'If only that four-wheeled gas-crocodile had burst a blood-vessel two miles back, we mightn't have been on our way home yet.'

'I heard you shoot once—'

'And he's still going—on the other three wheels. I'm not expecting he'll stop to mend that leak.'

Patricia sighed.

'It was short and sweet, anyway,' she said. 'Couldn't you have stopped that other car and followed?'

He shook his head.

'Teal could have stopped it, but I'm not a policeman. I think this is a bit early for us to start gingering up our publicity campaign.'

'I wish it had been a better show, boy,' said Patricia wistfully, slipping her arm through his; and the Saint stopped to stare at her.

In the darkness, this was not very effective, but he did it.

'You bloodthirsty child!' he said.

And then he laughed.

'But that wasn't the final curtain,' he said. 'If you like to note it down, I'll make you a prophecy: the mortality among Scorpions is going to rise one unit, and for once it will not be my fault.'

They were back in Hatfield before she had made up her mind to ask him if he was referring to Long Harry, and for once the Saint did not look innocently outraged at the suggestion.

'Long Harry is alive and well, to the best of my knowledge

and belief,' he said, 'but I arranged the rough outline of his decease with Teal over the telephone. If we didn't kill Long Harry, the Scorpion would; and I figure our method will be less fatal. But as for the Scorpion himself—well, Pat, I'm dreadfully afraid I've promised to let them hang him according to the law. I'm getting so respectable these days that I feel I may be removed to Heaven in a fiery chariot at any moment.'

He examined his souvenir of the evening in a corner of the deserted hotel smoking-room a little later, over a final and benedictory tankard of beer. It was an envelope, postmarked in the South-Western district at 11 a.m. that morning, and addressed to Wilfred Garniman, Esq., 28, Mallaby Road, Harrow. From it the Saint extracted a single sheet of paper, written in a feminine hand.

Dear Mr Garniman,
    Can you come round for dinner and a game of bridge on Tuesday next? Colonel Barnes will be making a fourth. Yours sincerely
    (Mrs) R. Venables.

For a space he contemplated the missive with an exasperated scowl darkening the beauty of his features; then he passed it to Patricia, and reached out for the consolation of draught Bass with one hand and for a cigarette with the other. The scowl continued to darken.

Patricia read, and looked at him perplexedly.

'It looks perfectly ordinary,' she said.

'It looks a damned sight too ordinary!' exploded the Saint. 'How the devil can you blackmail a man for being invited to play bridge?'

The girl frowned.

'But I don't see. Why should this be anyone else's letter?'

'And why shouldn't Mr Wilfred Garniman be the man I want?'

'Of course. Didn't you get it from that man in the car?'

'I saw it on the seat beside him—it must have come out of his pocket when he pulled his gun.'

'Well?' she prompted.

'Why shouldn't this be the beginning of the Scorpion's triumphal march towards the high jump?' asked the Saint.

'That's what I want to know.'

Simon surveyed her in silence. And, as he did so, the scowl faded slowly from his face. Deep in his eyes a pair of little blue devils roused up, executed a tentative double-shuffle, and paused with their heads on one side.

'Why not?' insisted Patricia.

Slowly, gently, and with tremendous precision, the Saintly smile twitched at the corners of Simon's lips, expanded, grew, and irradiated his whole face.

'I'm blowed if I know why not,' said the Saint seraphically. 'It's just that I have a weakness for getting both feet on the bus before I tell the world I'm travelling. And the obvious deduction seemed too good to be true.'


VII

Mallaby Road, Harrow, as the Saint discovered, was one of those jolly roads in which ladies and gentlemen live. Lords and ladies may be found in such places as Mayfair, Monte Carlo, and St Moritz; men and women may be found almost anywhere; but Ladies and Gentlemen blossom in their full beauty only in such places as Mallaby Road, Harrow. This was a road about two hundred yards long, containing thirty of the stately homes of England, each of them a miraculously preserved specimen of Elizabethan architecture, each of them exactly the same as the other twenty-nine, and each of them surrounded by identical lawns, flower-beds, and atmospheres of overpowering gentility.

Simon Templar, entering Mallaby Road at nine o'clock—an hour of the morning at which his vitality was always rather low—felt slightly stunned.

There being no other visible distinguishing marks or peculiarities about it, he discovered No. 28 by the simple process of looking at the figures on the garden gates, and found it after inspecting thirteen other numbers which were not 28. He started on the wrong side of the road.

To the maid who opened the door he gave a card bearing the name of Mr Andrew Herrick and the official imprint of the *Daily Record*. Simon Templar had no right whatever to either of these decorations, which were the exclusive property of a reporter whom he had once interviewed, but a little thing like that never bothered the Saint. He kept every visiting card that was ever given him and a few that had not been consciously donated, and drew appropriately upon his stock in time of need.

'Mr Garniman is just finishing breakfast, sir,' said the maid doubtfully, 'but I'll ask him if he'll see you.'

'I'm sure he will,' said the Saint, and he said it so winningly that if the maid's name had been Mrs Garniman the prophecy would have passed automatically into the realm of sublimely concrete certainties.

As it was, the prophecy merely proved to be correct.

Mr Garniman saw the Saint, and the Saint saw Mr Garniman. These things happened simultaneously, but the Saint won on points. There was a lot of Mr Garniman.

'I'm afraid I can't spare you very long, Mr Herrick,' he said. 'I have to go out in a few minutes. What did you want to see me about?'

His restless grey eyes flittered shrewdly over the Saint as he spoke, but Simon endured the scrutiny with the peaceful calm which only the man who wears the suits of Anderson and Shepphard, the shirts of Harman, the shoes of Lobb, and self-refrigerating conscience can achieve.

'I came to ask you if you could tell us anything about the Scorpion,' said the Saint calmly.

Well, that is one way of putting it. On the other hand, one

could say with equal truth that his manner would have made a sheet of plate glass look like a futurist sculptor's impression of a bit of the Pacific Ocean during a hurricane. And the innocence of the Saintly face would have made a Botticelli angel look positively sinister in comparison.

His gaze rested on Mr Wilfred Garniman's fleshy prow with no more than a reasonable directness; but he saw the momentary flicker of expression that preceded Mr Garniman's blandly puzzled frown, and wistfully wondered whether, if he unsheathed his sword-stick and prodded it vigorously into Mr Garniman's immediate future, there would be a loud pop, or merely a faint sizzling sound. That he overcame this insidious temptation, and allowed no sign of the soul-shattering struggle to register itself on his face, was merely a tribute to the persistently sobering influence of Mr Lionel Delborn's official proclamation and the Saint's sternly practical devotion to business.

'Scorpion?' repeated Mr Garniman, frowning. 'I'm afraid I don't quite—'

'Understand. Exactly. Well, I expected I should have to explain.'

'I wish you would. I really don't know—'

'Why we should consider you an authority on scorpions. Precisely. The Editor told me you'd say that.'

'If you'd—'

'Tell you the reason for this rather extraordinary procedure—'

'I should certainly see if I could help you in any way, but at the same time—'

'You don't see what use you could be. Absolutely. Now, shall we go on like this or shall we sing the rest in chorus?'

Mr Garniman blinked.

'Do you want to ask me some questions?'

'I should love to,' said the Saint heartily. 'You don't think Mrs Garniman will object?'

'Mrs Garniman?'

'Mrs Garniman.'

Mr Garniman blinked again.

'Are you—'

'Certain—'

'Are you certain you haven't made a mistake? There is no Mrs Garniman.'

'Don't mention it,' said the Saint affably.

He turned the pages of an enormous notebook.

'"Interviewed Luis Cartaro. Diamond rings and Marcel wave. Query—Do Pimples Make Good Mothers? Said—"

Sorry, wrong page ... Here we are: "Memo. See Wilfred Garniman and ask the big—ask him about scorpions. 28 Mallaby Road, Harrow." That's right, isn't it?'

'That's my name and address,' said Garniman shortly. 'But I have still to learn the reason for this—er—'

'Visit,' supplied the Saint. He was certainly feeling helpful this morning.

He closed his book and returned it to his pocket.

'As a matter of fact,' he said, 'we heard that the Saint was interested in you.'

He was not even looking at Garniman as he spoke. But the mirror over the mantelpiece was in the tail of his eyes, and thus he saw the other's hands, which were clasped behind his back, close and unclose—once.

'The Saint?' said Garniman. 'Really—'

'Are you sure I'm not detaining you?' asked the Saint, suddenly very brisk and solicitous. 'If your staff will be anxious . . .'

'My staff can wait a few minutes.'

'That's very good of you. But if we telephoned them—'

'I assure you—that is quite unnecessary.'

'I shouldn't like to think of your office being disorganised—'

'You need not trouble,' said Garniman. He moved across the room. 'Will you smoke?'

'Thanks,' said the Saint.

He had just taken the first puff from a cigarette when Garniman turned round with a carved ebony box in his hand.

'Oh,' said Mr Garniman, a trifle blankly.

'Not at all,' said the Saint, who was never embarrassed. 'Have one of mine?'

He extended his case, but Garniman shook his head.

'I never smoke during the day. Would it be too early to offer you a drink?'

'I'm afraid so—much too late,' agreed Simon blandly.

Garniman returned the ebony box to the side table from which he had taken it. Then he swung round abruptly.

'Well?' he demanded. 'What's the idea?'

The Saint appeared perplexed.

'What's what idea?' he inquired innocently.

Garniman's eyebrows came down a little.

'What's all this about scorpions—and the Saint?'

'According to the Saint—'

'I don't understand you. I thought the Saint had disappeared long ago.'

'Then you were grievously in error, dear heart,' murmured Simon Templar coolly. 'Because I am myself the Saint.'

He lounged against a book-case, smiling and debonair, and his lazy blue eyes rested mockingly on the other's pale plump face.

'And I'm afraid you're the Scorpion, Wilfred,' he said.

For a moment Mr Garniman stood quite still. And then he shrugged.

'I believe I read in the newspapers that you had been pardoned and had retired from business,' he said, 'so I suppose it would be useless for me to communicate your confession to the police. As for this scorpion that you have referred to several times—'

'Yourself,' the Saint corrected him gently, and Garniman shrugged again.

'Whatever delusion you are suffering from—'

'Not a delusion, Wilfred.'

'It is immaterial to me what you call it.'

The Saint seemed to lounge even more languidly, his hands deep in his pockets, a thoughtful and reckless smile playing lightly about his lips.

'I call it a fact,' he said softly. 'And you will keep your hands away from that bell until I've finished talking ... You are the Scorpion, Wilfred, and you're probably the most successful blackmailer of the age. I grant you that—your technique is novel and thorough. But blackmail is a nasty crime. Your ingenuity has already driven two men to suicide. That was stupid of them, but it was also very naughty of you. In fact, it would really give me great pleasure to peg you in your front garden and push this highly desirable residence over on top of you; but for one thing. I've promised to reserve you for the hangman and for another thing I've got my income tax to pay, so—Excuse me one moment.'

Something like a flying chip of frozen quicksilver flashed across the room and plonked crisply into the wooden panel around the bell-push towards which Garniman's fingers were sidling. It actually passed between his second and third fingers, so that he felt the swift chill of its passage and snatched his hand away as if he had received an electric shock. But the Saint continued his languid propping up of the *Encyclopaedia Britannica*, and he did not appear to have moved.

'Just do what you're told, Wilfred, and everything will be quite all right—but I've got lots more of them there missiles packed in my pants,' murmured the Saint soothingly, warningly, and untruthfully—though Mr Garniman had no means of perceiving this last adverb. 'What was I saying? ... Oh yes. I have my income tax to pay—'

Garniman took a sudden step forward, and his lips twisted in a snarl.

'Look here—'

'Where?' asked the Saint excitedly.

Mr Garniman swallowed. The Saint heard him distinctly.

'You thrust yourself in here under a false name—you behave like a raving lunatic—then you make the most wild and fantastic accusations—you—'

'Throw knives about the place—'

'What the devil,' bellowed Mr Garniman, 'do you mean by it?'

'Sir,' suggested the Saint mildly.

'What the devil,' bellowed Mr Garniman, 'do you mean—"sir"?'

'Thank you,' said the Saint.

Mr Garniman glared. 'What the—'

'OK,' said the Saint pleasantly. 'I heard you the second time. So long as you go on calling me "sir", I shall know that everything is perfectly respectable and polite. And now we've lost the place again. Half a minute . . . Here we are: "I have my income tax to pay—"'

'Will you get out at once,' asked Garniman, rather quietly, 'or must I send for the police?'

Simon considered the question.

'I should send for the police,' he suggested at length.

He hitched himself off the book-case and sauntered leisurely across the room. He detached his little knife from the bell panel, tested the point delicately on his thumb, and restored the weapon to the sheath under his left sleeve; and Wilfred Garniman watched him without speaking. And then the Saint turned.

'Certainly—I should send for the police,' he drawled. 'They will be interested. It's quite true that I had a pardon for some old offences; but whether I've gone out of business, or whether I'm simply just a little cleverer than Chief Inspector Teal, is a point that is often debated at Scotland Yard. I think that any light you could throw on the problem would be welcomed.'

Garniman was still silent; and the Saint looked at him, and laughed caressingly.

'On the other hand—if you're bright enough to see a few objections to that idea—you might prefer to push quietly on to your beautiful office and think over some of the other things I've said. Particularly those pregnant words about my income tax.'

'Is that all you have to say?' asked Garniman, in the same low voice; and the Saint nodded.

'It'll do for now,' he said lightly. 'And since you seem to have decided against the police, I think I'll beetle off and concentrate on the method by which you're going to be induced to contribute to the Inland Revenue.'

The slightest glitter of expression came to Wilfred Garniman's eyes for a moment, and was gone again. He walked to the door and opened it.

'I'm obliged,' he said.

'After you, dear old reed-warbler,' said the Saint courteously.

He permitted Garniman to precede him out of the room, and stood in the hall adjusting the piratical slant of his hat.

'I presume we shall meet again?' Garniman remarked.

His tone was level and conversational. And the Saint smiled.

'You might even bet on it,' he said.

'Then—*au revoir*.'

The Saint tilted back his hat and watched the other turn on his heels and go up the stairs.

Then he opened the door and stepped out; and the heavy ornamental stone flower-pot that began to gravitate earthwards at the same moment actually nicked the brim of his Stetson before it split thunderously on the flagged path an inch behind his right heel.

Simon revolved slowly, his hands still in his pockets, and cocked an eyebrow at the debris; and then he strolled back under the porch and applied his forefinger to the bell.

Presently the maid answered the door.

'I think Mr Garniman has dropped the aspidistra,' he murmured chattily, and resumed his interrupted exit before the bulging eyes of an audience of one.

## VIII

'But what on earth,' asked Patricia helplessly, 'was the point of that?'

'It was an exercise in tact,' said the Saint modestly.

The girl stared.

'If I could only see it,' she begun; and then the Saint laughed.

'You will, old darling,' he said.

He leaned back and lighted another cigarette.

'Mr Wilfred Garniman,' he remarked, 'is a surprisingly intelligent sort of cove. There was very little nonsense—and most of what there was was my own free gift to the nation. I grant you he added to his present charge-sheet by offering me a cigarette and then a drink; but that's only because, as I've told you before, he's an amateur. I'm afraid he's been reading too many thrillers, and they've put ideas into his head. But on the really important point he was most professionally bright. The way the calm suddenly broke out in the middle of the storm was quite astonishing to watch.'

'And by this time,' said Patricia, 'he's probably going on being calm a couple of hundred miles away.'

Simon shook his head.

'Not Wilfred,' he said confidently. 'Except when he's loosing off six-shooters and throwing architecture about, Wilfred is a really first-class amateur. And he is so rapid on the uptake that if he fell off the fortieth floor of the Empire Building he would be sitting on the roof before he knew what had happened. Without any assistance from me, he divined that I had no intention of calling in the police. So he knew he wasn't very much worse off than he was before.'

'Why?'

'He may be an amateur, as I keep telling you, but he's efficient. Long before his house started to fall to pieces on me, he'd begun to make friendly attempts to bump me off. That was because he'd surveyed all the risks before he started in business, and he figured that his graft was exactly the kind of graft that would make me sit up and take notice. In which he was darned right. I just breezed in and proved it to him. He told me himself that he was unmarried; I wasn't able to get him to tell me anything about his lawful affairs, but the butcher told me that he was supposed to be "something in the City"—so I acquired two items of information. I also verified his home address, which was the most important thing; and I impressed him with my own brilliance and charm of personality, which was the next most important. I played the perfect clown, because that's the way these situations always get me, but in the intervals between laughs I did everything that I set out to do. And he knew it—as I meant him to.'

'And what happens next?'

'The private war will go on,' said the Saint comfortably.

His deductions, as usual, were precisely true; but there was one twist in the affairs of Wilfred Garniman of which he did not know, and if he had known of it he might not have taken life quite so easily as he did for the next few days. That is just possible.

On the morning of that first interview, he had hung around in the middle distances of Mallaby Road with intent to increase his store of information; but Mr Garniman had driven off to his righteous labours in a car which the Saint knew at a glance it would be useless to attempt to follow in a taxi. On the second morning, the Saint decorated the same middle distances at the wheel of his own car, but a traffic jam at Marble Arch baulked him of his quarry. On the third morning he tried again, and collected two punctures in the first half-mile; and when he got out to inspect the damage he found sharp steel spikes strewn all over the road. Then, fearing that four consecutive seven-o'clock breakfasts might affect his health, the Saint stayed in bed on the fourth morning and did some thinking.

One error in his own technique he perceived quite clearly.

'If I'd sleuthed him on the first morning, and postponed the backchat till the second, I should have been a bright lad,' he said. 'My genius seems to have gone off the boil.'

That something of the sort had happened was also evidenced by the fact that during those four days the problem of evolving a really agile method of inducing Mr Garniman to part with a proportion of his ill-gotten gains continued to elude him.

Chief Inspector Teal heard the whole story when he called in on the evening of that fourth day to make inquiries, and was almost offensive.

The Saint sat at his desk after the detective had gone, and contemplated the net result of his ninety-six hours' cerebration moodily. This consisted of a twelve-line epilogue to the *Epic History of Charles*.

> His will was read. His father learned
> Charles wished his body to be burned.
>
> With huge heroic flames of fire
> Upon a Roman funeral pyre.
>
> But Charles's pa, sole legatee,
> Averse to such publicity,
> Thought that, his bidding might be done
> Without disturbing anyone,
>
> And, in a highly touching scene,
> Cremated him at Kensal Green.
>
> And so Charles has his little shrine
> With cavalier and concubine.

Simon Templar scowled sombrely at the sheet for some time; and then, with a sudden impatience, he heaved the inkpot out of the window and stood up.

'Pat,' he said, 'I feel that the time is ripe for us to push into a really wicked night club and drown our sorrows in iced ginger-beer.'

The girl closed her book and smiled at him.

'Where shall we go?' she asked; and then the Saint suddenly shot across the room as if he had been touched with a hot iron.

'Holy Petal!' he yelled. 'Pat—old sweetheart—old angel—'

Patricia blinked at him.

'My dear old lad—'

'Hell to all dear old lads!' cried the Saint recklessly.

He took her by the arms, swung her bodily out of her chair, put her down, rumpled her hair, and kissed her.

'Paddle on,' he commanded breathlessly. 'Go on—go and have a bath—dress—undress—glue your face on—anything. Sew a gun into the cami-whatnots, find a butterfly net—and let's go!'

'But what's the excitement about?'

'We're going entomo-botanising. We're going to prowl around the West End fishing for beetles. We're going to look at every night club in London—I'm a member of them all. If we don't catch anything, it won't be my fault. We're going to knock the L out of London and use it to tie the Home Secretary's ears together. The voice of the flatfooted periwinkle shall be heard in the land—'

He was still burbling foolishly when Patricia fled; but when she returned he was resplendent in Gents' Evening Wear and wielding a cocktail-shaker with a wild exuberance that made her almost giddy to watch.

'For heaven's sake,' she said, catching his arm, 'pull yourself together and tell me something!'

'Sure,' said the Saint daftly. 'That nightie of yours is a dream. Or is it meant to be a dress? You can never tell, with these long skirts. And I don't want to be personal, but are you sure you haven't forgotten to put on the back or posterior part? I can see all your spine. Not that I mind, but . . . Talking of swine—spine—there was a very fine specimen at the Embassy the other night. Must have measured at least thirty-two inches from snout to—They say the man who landed it played it for three weeks. Ordinarily trout line and gaff, you know . . .'

Patricia Holm was almost hysterical by the time they reached the Carlton, where the Saint had decided to dine. And it was not until he had ordered an extravagant dinner, with appropriate wines, that she was able to make him listen to a sober question. And then he became the picture of innocent amazement.

'But didn't you get me?' he asked. 'Hadn't you figured it out for yourself? I thought you were there long ago. Have you forgotten my little exploit at the Bird's Nest? Who d'you think paid for that bit of coloured mosquito-net you're wearing? Who bought these studs I'm wearing? Who, if it comes to that, is standing us this six-course indigestion? . . . Well, some people might say it was Montgomery Bird, but personally—'

The girl gasped. 'You mean that other man at the Bird's Nest was the Scorpion?'

'Who else? . . . But I never rumbled to it till tonight! I told you he was busy putting the black on Montgomery when Teal and I butted in. I overheard the whole conversation, and I was certainly curious. I made a mental note at the time to investigate that bearded battleship, but it never came into my head that it must have been Wilfred himself—I'm damned if I know why!'

Patricia nodded.

'I'd forgotten to think of it myself,' she said.

'And I must have been fast asleep the whole time! Of course it was the Scorpion—and his graft's a bigger one than I ever dreamed. He's got organisation, that guy. He probably has his finger in half the wicked pies that are being cooked in this big city. If he was on to Montgomery, there's no reason why he shouldn't have got on to a dozen others that you and I can think of; and he'll be drawing his percentage from the whole bunch. I grant you I put Montgomery out of business, but—'

'If you're right,' said Patricia, 'and the Scorpion hasn't done a bunk, we may find him anywhere.'

'Tonight,' said the Saint. 'Or, if not tonight, some other night. And I'm prepared to keep on looking. But my income tax has got to be paid tomorrow, and so I want the reunion to be tonight.'

'Have you got an idea?'

'I've got a dozen,' said the Saint. 'And one of them says that Wilfred is going to have an Evening!'

His brain had suddenly picked up its stride again. In a few minutes he had sketched out a plan of campaign as slick and agile as anything his fertile genius had ever devised. And once again he was proved a true prophet, though the proceedings took a slight twist which he had not foreseen.

For at a quarter past eleven they ran Wilfred Garniman to earth at the Golden Apple Club. And Wilfred Garniman certainly had an Evening.

He was standing at the door of the ballroom, sardonically surveying the clientele, when a girl walked in and stopped beside him. He glanced round at her almost without thinking. Having done which, he stayed glancing—and thought a lot.

She was young, slim, fair-haired, and exquisite. Even Wilfred Garniman knew that. His rather tired eyes, taking in other details of her appearance, recognised the simple perfection of a fifty-guinea gown. And her face was utterly innocent of guile—Wilfred Garniman had a shrewd perception of these things also. She scanned the crowd anxiously, as though looking for someone, and in due course it became apparent that the someone was not present. Wilfred Garniman was the last man she looked at. Their glances met, and held for some seconds; and then the faintest ripple of a smile touched her lips.

And exactly one hour later, Simon Templar was ringing the bell at 28, Mallaby Road, Harrow.

He was not expecting a reply, but he always liked to be sure of his ground. He waited ten minutes, ringing the bell at intervals; and then he went in by a ground-floor window. It took him straight into Mr Garniman's study. And there, after carefully drawing the curtains, the Saint was busy for some time. For thirty-five minutes by his watch, to be exact.

And then he sat down in a chair and lighted a cigarette.

'Somewhere,' he murmured thoughtfully, 'there is a catch in this.'

For the net result of a systematic and expert search had panned out at precisely nil.

And this the Saint was not expecting. Before he left the Carlton, he had propounded one theory with all the force of an incontestable fact.

'Wilfred may have decided to take my intrusion calmly, and trust that he'll be able to put me out of the way before I managed to strafe him good and proper; but he'd never leave himself without at least one line of retreat. And that implies being able to take his booty with him. He'd never have put it in a bank, because there'd always be the chance that someone might notice things and get curious. It will have been in a safe deposit; but it won't be there now.'

Somewhere or other—somewhere within Wilfred Garniman's easy reach—there was a large quantity of good solid cash, ready and willing to be converted into all manner of music by anyone who picked it up and offered it a change of address. It might have been actually on Wilfred Garniman's person; but the Saint didn't think so. He had decided that it would most probably be somewhere in the house at Harrow; and as he drove out there he had prepared to save time by considering the potential hiding-places in advance. He had thought of many, and discarded them one by one, for various reasons; and his final judgment had led him unhesitatingly into the very room where he had spent thirty-five fruitless minutes . . . and where he was now getting set to spend some more.

'This is the Scorpion's sacred lair,' he figured, 'and Wilfred wouldn't let himself forget it. He'd play it up to himself for all it was worth. It's the inner sanctum of the great ruthless organisation that doesn't exist. He'd sit in that chair in the evenings—at that desk—there—thinking what a wonderful man he was. And he'd look at whatever innocent bit of interior decoration hides his secret cache, and gloat over the letters and dossiers that he's got hidden there, and the money they've brought in or are going to bring in—the fat, slimy, wallowing slug . . .'

Again his eyes travelled slowly round the room. The plainly papered walls could have hidden nothing, except behind the pictures, and he had tried every one of those. Dummy books he had ruled out at once, for a servant may always take down a book; but he had tested the back of every shelf—and found nothing. The whole floor was carpeted, and he gave that no more than a glance: his analysis of Wilfred Gamiman's august meditations did not harmonise with the vision of the same gentleman crawling about on his hands and knees. And every drawer of the desk was already unlocked, and not one of them contained anything of compromising interest.

And that appeared to exhaust the possibilities. He stared speculatively at the fireplace—but he had done that before. It ignored the exterior architecture of the building and was a plain modern affair of blue tiles and tin, and it would have been difficult to work any grisly gadgets into its bluntly bourgeois lines. Or, it appeared, into the lines of anything else in that room.

'Which,' said the Saint drowsily, 'is absurd.'

There remained of course, Wilfred Garniman's bedroom—the Saint had long since listed that as the only feasible alternative. But, somehow, he didn't like it. Plunder and pink poplin pyjamas didn't seem a psychologically satisfactory combination— particularly when the pyjamas must be presumed to surround something like Wilfred Garniman must have looked like without his Old Harrovian tie. The idea did not ring a bell. And yet, if the boodle and etceteral appurtenances thereof and howsoever were not in the bedroom, they must be in the study—some blistered whereabouts or what not . . .

'Which,' burbled the Saint, 'is absluly posrous . . .'

The situation seemed less and less annoying . . . It really didn't matter very much . . . Wilfred Garniman, if one came to think of it, was even fatter than Teal . . . and one made allowances for detectives . . . Teal was fat, and Long Harry was long, and Patricia played around with Scorpions; which was all very odd and amusing, but nothing to get worked up about before breakfast, old dear . . .

IX

Somewhere in the infinite darkness appeared a tiny speck of white. It came hurtling towards him; and as it came it grew larger and whiter and more terrible, until it seemed as if it must smash and smother and pulp him into the squashed wreckage of the whole universe at his back. He let out a yell, and the upper half of the great white sky fell back like a shutter, sending a sudden blaze of dazzling light into his eyes. The lower bit of white touched his nose and mouth damply, and an acrid stinging smell stabbed right up into the top of his head and trickled down his throat like a thin stream of condensed fire. He gasped, coughed, choked—and saw Wilfred Garniman.

'Hullo, old toad,' said the Saint weakly.

He breathed deeply, fanning out of his nasal passages the fiery tingle of the restorative that Garniman had made him inhale. His head cleared magically, so completely that for a few moments it felt as if a cold wind had blown clean through it; and the dazzle of the light dimmed out of his eyes. But he looked down, and saw that his wrists and ankles were securely bound.

'That's a pretty useful line of dope, Wilfred,' he murmured huskily. 'How did you do it?'

Garniman was folding up his handkerchief and returning it to his pocket, working with slow meticulous hands.

'The pressure of your head on the back of the chair released the gas,' he replied calmly. 'It's an idea of my own—I have always been prepared to have to entertain undesirable visitors. The lightest pressure is sufficient.'

Simon nodded.

'It certainly is a great game,' he remarked. 'I never noticed a thing, though I remember now that I was blithering to myself rather inanely just before I went under. And so the little man works off his own bright ideas . . . Wilfred, you're coming on.'

'I brought my dancing partner with me,' said Garniman, quite casually.

He waved a fat indicative hand; and the Saint, squirming over to follow the gesture, saw Patricia in another chair. For a second or two he looked at her; then he turned slowly round again.

'There's no satisfying you jazz fiends, is there?' he drawled. 'Now I suppose you'll wind up the gramophone and start again . . . But the girl seems to have lost the spirit of the thing . . .'

Garniman sat down at the desk and regarded the Saint with the heavy inscrutable face of a great gross image.

'I had seen her before, dancing with you at the Jericho, long before we first met—I never forget a face. After she had succeeded in planting herself on me, I spent a little time assuring myself that I was not mistaken; and then the solution was simple. A few drops from a bottle that I am never without—in her champagne— and the impression was that she became helplessly drunk. She will recover without our assistance, perhaps in five minutes, perhaps in half an hour—according to her strength.' Wilfred Garniman's fleshy lips loosened in the travesty of a smile. 'You underestimated me, Templar.'

'That,' said the Saint, 'remains to be seen.' Mr Garniman shrugged.

'Need I explain that you have come to the end of your interesting and adventurous life?'

Simon twitched an eyebrow, and slid his mouth mockingly sideways.

'What—not again?' he sighed, and Garniman's smooth forehead crinkled.

'I don't understand.'

'But you haven't seen so many of these situations through as I have, old horse,' said the Saint. 'I've lost count of the number of times this sort of thing has happened to me. I know the tradition demands it, but I think they might give me a rest sometimes. What's the programme this time—do you sew me up in the bath and light the geyser, or am I run through the mangle and buried under the billiard-table? Or can you think of something really original?'

Garniman inclined his head ironically. 'I trust you will find my method satisfactory,' he said. He lighted a cigarette, and rose from the desk again; and as he picked up a length of rope from the floor and moved across to Patricia, the Saint warbled on in the same tone of gentle weariness.

'Mind how you fix those ankles, Wilfred. That gauzy silk stuff you see on the limbs costs about five pounds a leg, and it ladders if a fly settles on it. Oh, and while we're on the subject: don't let's have any nonsense about death or dishonour. The child mightn't want to die. And besides, that stuff is played out, anyway . . .'

Garniman made no reply.

He continued with his task in his ponderous methodical way, making every movement with immensely phlegmatic deliberation. The Saint, who had known many criminals, and who was making no great exaggeration when he said that this particular situation had long since lost all its pristine charm for him, could recall no one in his experience who had ever been so dispassionate. Cold-blooded ruthlessness, a granite impassivity, he had met before; but through it all, deep as it might be, there had always run a perceptible taut thread of vindictive purpose. In Wilfred Garniman there showed nothing of this. He went about his work in the same way that he might have gone about the setting of a mouse-trap—with elephantine efficiency, and a complete blank in the teleological compartment of his brain. And Simon Templar knew with an eerie intuition that this was no pose, as it might have been in others. And then he knew that Wilfred Garniman was mad.

Garniman finished, and straightened up. And then, still without speaking, he picked Patricia up in his arms and carried her out of the room.

The Saint braced his muscles.

His whole body tightened to the effort like a tempered steel spring, and his arms swelled and corded lip until the sleeves were stretched and strained around them. For an instant he was absolutely motionless, except for the tremors of titanic tension that shuddered down his frame like wind-ripples over a quiet pool . . . And then he relaxed and went limp, loosing his breath in a great gasp. And the Saintly smile crawled a trifle crookedly over his face.

'Which makes things difficult,' he whispered—to the four unanswering walls.

For the cords about his wrists still held him firmly.

Free to move as he chose, he could have broken those ropes with his hands; but bound as he was, he could apply scarcely a quarter of his strength. And the ropes were good ones—new, half-inch, three-ply Manila. He had made the test; and he relaxed. To have struggled longer would have wasted valuable strength to no purpose. And he had come out without Belle, the little knife that ordinarily went with him everywhere, in a sheath strapped to his left forearm—the knife that had saved him on countless other occasions such as this.

Clumsily he pulled himself out of the chair, and rolled the few yards to the desk. There was a telephone there; he dragged himself to his knees and lifted the receiver. The exchange took an eternity to answer. He gave Teal's private number, and heard the preliminary buzz in the receiver as he was connected up; and then Wilfred Garniman spoke behind him, from the doorway.

'Ah! You are still active, Templar?'

He crossed the room with quick lumbering strides, and snatched the instrument away. For a second or two he listened with the receiver at his ear; then he hung it up and put the telephone down at the far end of the desk.

'You have not been at all successful this evening,' he remarked stolidly.

'But you must admit we keep on trying,' said the Saint cheerfully.

Wilfred Garniman took the cigarette from his mouth. His expressionless eyes contemplated the Saint abstractedly.

'I am beginning to believe that your prowess was overrated. You came here hoping to find documents or money—perhaps both. You were unsuccessful.'

'Er—temporarily.'

'Yet a little ingenuity would have saved you from an unpleasant experience—and shown you quite another function of this piece of furniture.'

Garniman pointed to the armchair. He tilted it over on its back, prised up a couple of tacks, and allowed the canvas finishing of the bottom to fall away. Underneath was a dark steel door, secured by three swivel catches.

'I made the whole chair myself—it was a clever piece of work,' he said; and then he dismissed the subject almost as if it had never been raised. 'I shall now require you to rejoin your friend, Templar. Will you be carried, or would you prefer to walk?'

'How far are we going?' asked the Saint cautiously.

'Only a few yards.'

'I'll walk, thanks.'

Garniman knelt down and tugged at the ankle ropes. A strand slipped under his manipulations, giving an eighteen-inch hobble.

'Stand up.'

Simon obeyed. Garniman gripped his arm and led him out of the room. They went down the hall, and passed through a low door under the stairs. They stumbled down a flight of narrow stone steps. At the bottom, Garniman picked up a candlestick from a niche in the wall and steered the Saint along a short flagged passage.

'You know, Wilf,' murmured the Saint conversationally, 'this has happened to me twice before in the last six months.

'And each time it was gas. Is it going to be gas again this time, or are you breaking away from the rules?'

'It will not be gas,' replied Garniman flatly.

He was as heavily passionless as a contented animal. And the Saint chattered on blithely.

'I hate to disappoint you—as the actress said to the bishop— but I really can't oblige you now. You must see it, Wilfred. I've got such a lot more to do before the end of the volume, and it'd wreck the whole show if I went and got bumped off in the first story. Have a heart, dear old Garbage-man!'

The other made no response; and the Saint sighed. In the matter of cross-talk comedy, Wilfred Garniman was a depressingly feeble performer. In the matter of murder, on the other hand, he was probably depressingly efficient; but the Saint couldn't help feeling that he made death a most gloomy business.

And then they came into a small low vault; and the Saint saw Patricia again.

Her eyes were open, and she looked at him steadily, with the faintest of smiles on her lips.

'Hullo, boy.'

'Hullo, lass.'

That was all.

Simon glanced round. In the centre of the floor there was a deep hole, and beside it was a great mound of earth. There was a dumpy white sack in one corner, and a neat conical heap of sand beside it.

Wilfred Garniman explained, in his monotonously apathetic way.

'We tried to sink a well here, but we gave it up. The hole is only about ten feet deep—it was not filled up again. I shall fill it up tonight.'

He picked up the girl and took her to the hole in the floor. Dropping on one knee at the edge, he lowered her to the stretch of his arms and let go . . . He came back to the Saint, dusting his trousers.

'Will you continue to walk?' he inquired.

Simon stepped to the side of the pit, and turned. For a moment he gazed into the other man's eyes—the eyes of a man empty of the bowels of compassion. But the Saint's blue gaze was as cold and still as a polar sea.

'You're an over-fed, pot-bellied swamp-hog,' he said; and then Garniman pushed him roughly backwards.

Quite unhurriedly, Wilfred Garniman took off his coat, unfastened his cuff-links, and rolled his sleeves up above his elbows. He opened the sack of cement and tipped out its contents into a hole that he trampled in the heap of sand. He picked up a spade, looked about him, and put it down again. Without the least variation of his heavily sedate stride he left the cellar, leaving the candle burning on the floor. In three or four minutes he was back again, carrying a brimming pail of water in either hand; and with the help of these he continued his unaccustomed labour, splashing gouts of water on his materials and stirring them carefully with the spade.

It took him over half an hour to reduce the mixture to a

consistency smooth enough to satisfy him, for he was an inexperienced worker and yet he could afford to make no mistake. At the end of that time he was streaming with sweat, and his immaculate white collar and shirt-front were grubbily wilting rags; but those facts did not trouble him. No one will ever know what was in his mind while he did that work. Perhaps he did not know himself, for his face was blank and tranquil.

His flabby muscles must have been aching, but he did not stop to rest. He took the spade over to the hole in the floor. The candle sent no light down there, but in the darkness he could see an irregular blur of white—he was not interested to gloat over it. Bending his back again, he began to shovel the earth back into the hole. It took an astonishing time, and he was breathing stertorously long before he had filled the pit up loosely level with the floor. Then he dropped the spade and tramped over the surface, packing it down tight and hard.

And then he laid over it the cement that he had prepared, finishing it off smoothly level with the floor.

Even then he did not rest—he was busy for another hour, filling the pails with earth and carrying them up the stairs and out into the garden and emptying them over the flower-beds. He had a placidly accurate eye for detail and an enormous capacity for taking pains, had Mr Wilfred Garniman; but it is doubtful if he gave more than a passing thought to the eternal meaning of what he had done.

X

To Mr Teal, who in those days knew the Saint's habits almost as well as he knew his own, it was merely axiomatic that breakfast and Simon Templar coincided somewhere between the hours of 11 a.m. and 1 p.m.; and therefore it is not surprising that the visit which he paid to 7, Upper Berkeley Mews on one historic morning resulted in a severe shock to his system. For a few moments after the door had been opened to him he stood bovinely rooted to the mat, looking like some watcher of the skies who has just seen the Great Bear turn a back-somersault and march rapidly over the horizon in column of all fours. And when he had pulled himself together, he followed the Saint into the sitting-room with the air of a man who is not at all certain that there is no basin of water balanced over the door to await his entrance.

'Have some gum, old dear,' invited the Saint hospitably; and Mr Teal stopped by the table and blinked at him.

'What's the idea?' he demanded suspiciously.

The Saint looked perplexed.

'What idea, brother?'

'Is your clock fast, or haven't you been to bed yet?'

Simon grinned.

'Neither. I'm going to travel, and Pat and I have got to push out and book passages and arrange for international overdrafts and all that sort of thing.' He waved towards Patricia Holm, who was smoking a cigarette over The Times. 'Pat, you have met Claud Eustace, haven't you? Made his pile in Consolidated Gas. Mr Teal, Miss Holm. Miss Holm, Mr Teal. Consider yourselves divorced.'

Teal picked up the packet of spearmint that sat sedately in the centre of the table, and put it down again uneasily. He produced another packet from his own pocket.

'Did you say you were going away?' he asked.

'I did. I'm worn out, and I feel I need a complete rest—I did a couple of hours' work yesterday, and at my time of life . . .'

'Where were you going?'

The Saint shrugged.

'Doubtless Thomas Cook will provide. We thought of some nice warm islands. It may be the Canaries, the Balearic or Little by Little—'

'And what about the Scorpion?'

'Oh yes, the Scorpion . . . Well, you can have him all to yourself now, Claud.'

Simon glanced towards the mantelpiece, and the detective

followed his gaze. There was a raw puncture in the panelling where a stiletto had recently reposed, but the papers that had been pinned there were gone. The Saint took the sheaf from his pocket.

'I was just going to beetle along and pay my income tax,' he said airily. 'Are you walking Hanover Square way?'

Teal looked at him thoughtfully, and it may be recorded to the credit of the detective's somnolently cyclopean self-control that not a muscle of his face moved.

'Yes, I'll go with you—I expect you'll be wanting a drink,' he said; and then his eyes fell on the Saint's wrist.

He motioned frantically at it.

'Did you sprain that trying to get the last drops out of the barrel?' he inquired.

Simon pulled down his sleeve.

'As a matter of fact, it was a burn,' he said.

'The Scorpion?'

'Patricia.'

Teal's eyes descended one millimetre. He looked at the girl, and she smiled at him in a seraphic way which made the detective's internal organs wriggle. Previously, he had been wont to console himself with the reflection that that peculiarly exasperating kind of sweetness in the smile was the original and unalienable copyright of one lone face out of all the faces in the wide world. He returned his gaze to the Saint.

'Domestic strife?' he queried, and Simon assumed an expression of pained reproach.

'We aren't married,' he said.

Patricia flicked her cigarette into the fireplace and came over. She tucked one hand into the belt of her plain tweed suit, and laid the other on Simon Templar's shoulder. And she continued to smile seraphically upon the detective.

'You see, we were being buried alive,' she explained simply.

'All down in the—er—what's-its of the earth,' said the Saint.

'Simon hadn't got his knife, but he remembered his cigarette-lighter just in time. He couldn't reach it himself, so I had to do it. And he never made a sound—I never knew till afterwards—'

'It was a minor detail,' said the Saint.

He twitched a small photograph from his pocket and passed it to Teal.

'From the Scorpion's passport,' he said. 'I found it in a drawer of his desk. That was before he caught me with as neat a trick as I've come across—the armchairs in his study will repay a sleuth-like investigation, Claud. Then, if you pass on to the cellars, you'll find a piece of cement flooring that had only just begun to floor. Pat and I are supposed to be under there. Which reminds me—if you decide to dig down in the hope of finding us, you'll find my second-best boiled shirt somewhere in the depths. We had to leave it behind. I don't know if you've ever noticed it, but I can give you my word that even the most pliant rubber dickey rattles like a suit of armour when you're trying to move quietly.'

For a space the detective stared at him.

Then he took out a notebook.

It was, in its way, one of the most heroic things he ever did.

'Where is this place?' he asked.

'Twenty-eight, Mallaby Road, Arrer. The name is Wilfred Garniman. And about that shirt—if you had it washed at the place where they do yours before you go toddling round the night clubs, and sent it on to me at Palma. I expect I could find a place to burn it. And I've got some old boots upstairs which I thought maybe you might like—'

Teal replaced his notebook and pencil.

'I don't want to ask too many questions,' he said. 'But if Garniman knows you got away—'

Simon shook his head.

'Wilfred does not know. He went out to fetch some water to dilute the concrete, and we moved while he was away. Later on I saw him carting out the surplus earth and dumping it on the gardening notes. When you were playing on the sands of Southend in a pair of pink shrimping drawers, Teal, did you ever notice that you can always dig more out of a hole than you can put back in it? Wilfred had quite enough mud left over to make him happy.'

Teal nodded.

'That's all I wanted,' he said, and the Saint smiled.

'Perhaps we can give you a lift,' he suggested politely.

They drove to Hanover Square in the Saint's car. The Saint was in form. Teal knew that by the way he drove. Teal was not happy about it. Teal was even less happy when the Saint insisted on being escorted into the office.

'I insist on having police protection,' he said. 'Scorpions I can manage, but when it comes to tax collectors . . . Not that there's a great difference. The same threatening letters, the same merciless bleeding of the honest toiler, the same bleary eyes—'

'All right,' said Teal wearily.

He climbed out of the car, and followed behind Patricia; and so they climbed to the general office. At the high counter which had been erected to protect the clerks from the savage assaults of their victims the Saint halted, and clamoured in a loud voice to be ushered into the presence of Mr Delborn.

Presently a scared little man came to the barrier.

'You wish to see Mr Delborn, sir?'

'I do.'

'Yes, sir. What is your business, sir?'

'I'm a burglar,' said the Saint innocently.

'Yes, sir. What did you wish to see Mr Delborn about, sir?'

'About the payment of my income tax, Algernon. I will see Mr Delborn himself and nobody else; and if I don't see him at once, I shall not only refuse to pay a penny of my tax, but I shall also take this hideous office to pieces and hide it in various drains belonging to the London County Council. By the way, do you know Chief Inspector Teal? Mr Teal, Mr Veal. Mr Veal—'

'Will you take a seat, sir?'

'Certainly,' said the Saint.

He was half-way down the stairs when Teal caught him.

'Look here, Templar,' said the detective, breathing heavily

through the nose, 'I don't care if you have got the Scorpion in your pocket, but if this is your idea of being funny—'

Simon put down the chair and scratched his head.

'I was only obeying instructions,' he said plaintively. 'I admit it seemed rather odd, but I thought maybe Lionel hadn't got a spare seat in his office.'

Teal and Patricia between them got him as far as the top of the stairs where he put the chair down, sat on it, and refused to move.

'I'm going home,' said Patricia finally.

'Bring some oranges back with you,' said the Saint. 'And don't forget your knitting. What time do the early doors open?'

The situation was only saved by the return of the harassed clerk.

'Mr Delborn will see you, sir.'

He led the way through the general office and opened a door at the end.

'What name, sir?'

'Ghandi,' said the Saint, and stalked into the room.

And there he stopped.

For the first time in his life, Simon Templar stood frozen into a kind of paralysis of sheer incredulous startlement.

In its own genre, that moment was the supremely flabbergasting instant of his life. Battle, murder, and sudden death of all kinds and varieties notwithstanding, the most hectic moments of the most earth-shaking cataclysms in which he had been involved paled their ineffectual fires beside the eye-shrivelling dazzle of that second. And the Saint stood utterly still, with every shadow of expression wiped from his face, momentarily robbed of even his facile power of speech, simply staring.

For the man at the desk was Wilfred Garniman.

Wilfred Garniman himself, exactly as the Saint had seen him on that very first expedition to Harrow—black-coated, black-tied, the perfect office gentleman with a fifty-two-inch waist. Wilfred Garniman sitting there in a breathless immobility that matched

298

the Saint's, but with the prosperous colour draining from his face and his coarse lips going grey.

And then the Saint found his voice.

'Oh, it's you, Wilfred, is it?' The words trickled very softly into the deathly silence. 'And this is Simon Templar speaking—not a ghost. I declined to turn into a ghost, even though I was buried. And Patricia Holm did the same. She's outside at this very moment, if you'd like to see her. And so is Chief Inspector Teal—with your photograph in his pocket . . . Do you know that this is very tough on me, sweetheart? I've promised you to Teal, and I ought to be killing you myself. Buried Pat alive, you did—or you meant to . . . And you're the greasy swine that's been pestering me to pay your knock-kneed taxes. No wonder you took to Scorping in your spare time. I wouldn't mind betting you began in this very office, and the capital you started with was the things you wormed out of people under the disguise of official inquiries . . . And I came in to give you one thousand, three hundred and thirty-seven pounds, nineteen and five-pence of your own money, all out of the strong-box under that very interesting chair, Wilfred—'

He saw the beginning of the movement that Garniman made, and hurled himself sideways. The bullet actually skinned one of his lower ribs, though he did not know it until later. He swerved into the heavy desk, and got his hands under the edge. For one weird instant he looked from a range of two yards into the eyes of Wilfred Garniman, who was in the act of rising out of his chair. Garniman's automatic was swinging round for a second shot, and the thunder of the first seemed to still be hanging in the air. And behind him Simon heard the rattle of the door.

And then—to say that he tipped the desk over would be absurd. To have done anything so feeble would have been a sentence of death pronounced simultaneously upon Patricia Holm and Claud Eustace Teal and himself—at least. The Saint knew that.

But as the others burst into the room, it seemed as if the Saint gathered up the whole desk in his two hands, from the precarious hold that he had on it, and flung it hugely and terrifically into the wall; and Wilfred Garniman was carried before it like a great bloated fly before a cannon-ball . . . And, really, that was that . . .

The story of the Old Bailey trial reached Palma about six weeks later, in an ancient newspaper which Patricia Holm produced one morning.

Simon Templar was not at all interested in the story; but he was vastly interested in an illustration thereto which he discovered at the top of the page. The Press photographer had done his worst; and Chief Inspector Teal, the hero of the case, caught unawares in the very act of inserting some fresh chewing gum in his mouth as he stepped out on to the pavement of Newgate Street, was featured looking almost libellously like an infuriated codfish afflicted with some strange uvular growth.

Simon clipped out the portrait and pasted it neatly at the head of a large plain postcard. Underneath it he wrote:

> Claud Eustace Teal, when overjoyed,
> Wiggled his dexter adenoid;
> For well-bred policemen think it rude
> To show their tonsils in the nude.

'That ought to come like a ray of sunshine into Claud's dreary life,' said the Saint, surveying his handiwork.

He may have been right; for the postcard was delivered in error to an Assistant Commissioner who was gifted with a particularly acid tongue, and it is certain that Teal did not hear the last of it for many days.

I

Simon Templar's mail, like that of any other celebrity, was a thing of infinite variety. Perhaps it was even more so than that of most celebrities, for actors and authors and the other usual recipients of fan mail are of necessity a slightly smaller target for the busy letter-writer than a man who has been publicised at frequent intervals as a twentieth-century Robin Hood, to the despair and fury of the police officials at whose expense the publicity has been achieved. Of those correspondents who approached him under his better-known *nom de guerre* of 'The Saint', about half were made up of people who thought that the nickname should be taken literally, and half of people who suspected that it stood for the exact opposite.

There were, of course, the collectors of autographs and signed photos. There were the hero-worshipping schoolboys whose ideas of a future profession would have shocked their fathers, and the romantic schoolgirls whose ideals of a future husband would have made their mothers swoon. There were also romantic maidens who were not so young, who supplied personal data of sometimes startling candour, and whose propositions were correspondingly more concrete.

And then there were the optimists who thought that the Saint would like to finance a South American revolution, a hunt for buried treasure on the Spanish Main, a new night club, or an invention for an auxiliary automatic lighter to light automatic lighters with. There were the plodding sportsmen who could find a job in some remote town, thereby saving their wives and children from imminent starvation, if only the Saint would lend them the fare. There were the old ladies who thought that the Saint might be able to trace their missing Pomeranians, and the old gentlemen who thought that he might be able to exterminate the damned

Socialists. There were crooks and cranks, fatheads and fanatics, beggars, liars, romancers, idiots, thieves, rich men, poor men, the earnest, the flippant, the gay, the lonely, the time-wasters and the genuine tragedies, all that strange and variegated section of humanity that writes letters to total strangers; and then sometimes the letters were not from one stranger to another, but were no less significant, like a letter that came one morning from a man named Marty O'Connor:

*I should have written you before but I didn't want you to think I was asking for a handout. I stuck at that stable in Ireland and we were doing fine. I thought we were all set but the guy was betting on the horses. I didnt know he was such a mug, so the next thing is hes bust, the stable is sold up and Im out of a job. I could not get nothing else there, but I hear the heat is off in London now so me and Cora come back, I got a job as chaufer and hold that 3 weeks til the dame hears I got a police record, she wont believe Im going strait now. I got thrown out and havent found nothing since, but Cora does odd jobs and I may get a job any day. When I do you got to come see us again, we never fergot what you done for us and would do the same for you anytime if we burn for it . . .*

That was a reminder of two people whom he had helped because he liked them and because he thought they were worth helping, in one of those adventures that made all his lawlessness seem worth while to him, whatever the moralists might say. Marty O'Connor, who put off writing to his friend for fear of being suspected of begging, was a very different character from many others who wrote with no such scruples and with less excuse— such as the Countess Jannowicz, whose letter came in the same mail.

The smile which Simon had had for Marty's letter turned cynical as he read it. On the face of it, it was a very genteel and dignified epistle, tastefully engraved under an embossed coronet, and printed on expensive hand-made paper. The Countess Jannowicz, it said, requested the pleasure of Mr Simon Templar's company at a dinner and dance to be held at the Dorchester on the twentieth of that month, in aid of the National League for the Care of Incurables, RSVP.

That in itself would have been harmless enough; but the catch came in very small copperplate at the foot of the invitation, in the shape of the words 'Tickets Five Guineas'—and in the accompanying printed pamphlet describing the virtues of the League and its urgent need of funds.

Simon had heard from her before, as had many other people in London, for she was a busy woman. Born as Maggie Oaks in Bermondsey, resplendent later as Margaretta Olivera in a place of honour in the nuder tableaux of the Follies, she had furred her nest with a notable collection of skins, both human and animal, up to the time when she met and married Count Jannowicz, a Polish boulevardier of great age and reputedly fabulous riches. Disdaining such small stuff as alimony, she had lived with him faithfully and patiently until the day of his death, which in defiance of all expectations he had postponed for an unconscionable time through more and more astounding stages of senility, only to discover after the funeral that he had been living for all that time on an annuity which automatically ceased its payments forthwith, so that after nineteen years of awful fidelity his widowed Countess found herself the proud inheritor of a few more furs, a certain amount of jewellery, a derelict castle already mortgaged for more than its value, and some seventeen kopeks in hard cash.

Since she was then forty-four, and her outlines had lost the voluptuousness which had once made them such an asset to the more artistic moments of the Follies, many another woman might have retired to the companionable obscurity of her fellow unfortunates in some small Riviera *pension*. Not so Maggie Oaks, who had the stern marrow of Bermondsey in her bones. At least she had the additional intangible asset of a genuine title, and during her spouse's doggedly declining years she had wiled away the time consolidating the social position which her marriage had given her; so that after some sober consideration which it would have educated a bishop to hear, she was able to work out a fairly satisfactory solution to her financial problems.

Unlike Mr Elliot Vascoe, of whom we have heard before, who used charity to promote his social ambitions, she used her social position to promote charities. What the charities were did not trouble her much, as long as they paid her the twenty-five per cent of the proceeds which was her standard fee: she had been known to sponsor, in the same day, a luncheon in aid of the Women's Society for the Prosecution of Immorality, and a ball in aid of the Free Hospital for Unmarried Mothers. As a means of livelihood, it had been a triumphant inspiration. Social climbers fought to serve, expensively, on her committees; lesser snobs scrambled to attend her functions to get their names in the papers in such distinguished company; charitable enterprises, struggling against depressions, were only too glad to pass over some of the labour of extracting contributions from the public to such a successful organiser; and the Countess Jannowicz, nee Maggie Oaks, lived in great comfort on Park Lane and maintained a chauffeur-driven Daimler out of her twenty-five per cents, eked out by other percentages which various restaurants and hotels were only too glad to pay her for bringing them the business.

The Saint had had his piratical eye on her for a long time; and now, with the apt arrival of that last invitation at a period when he had no other more pressing business on his hands, it seemed as if the discounting of the charitable Countess was a pious duty which could no longer be postponed.

He called on her the same afternoon at her apartment, for when once the Saint had made up his mind to a foray the job was as good as done. A morning's meditation had been enough for him to sketch out a plan of campaign, and after that he saw no good reason to put it aside while it grew whiskers.

But what the plan was is of no importance, for he never used it. He had sent in a card bearing his venerable alias of Sebastian

Tombs; but when the Countess sailed into the luxuriously modernistic drawing-room in which the butler had parked him, she came towards him with outstretched hand and a grim smile that promised surprises a split second before she spoke.

'Mr Templar?' she said coolly. 'I'm sorry I had to keep you waiting.'

It would be unfair to say that the Saint was disconcerted—in a buccaneer's life nothing could be foreseen, and you had to be schooled to the unexpected. But a perceptible instant went by before he answered.

'Why, hullo, Maggie,' he murmured. 'I was going to break it to you gently.'

'A man with your imagination should have been able to do better. After all, Mr Sebastian Tombs is getting to be almost as well known as the great Simon Templar—isn't he?'

The Saint nodded, admitting his lapse, and making a mental note that the time had come to tear himself finally away from the *alter ego* to which he had clung with perverse devotion for too many years.

'You keep pretty well up to date,' he remarked.

'Why not?' she returned frankly. 'I've had an idea for some time that I'd be getting a visit from you one day.'

'Would that be the voice of conscience?'

'Just common sense. Even you can't have a monopoly on thinking ahead.'

Simon studied her interestedly. The vats of champagne which had sparkled down her gullet in aid of one charity or another over the past six years had left their own thin dry tang in her voice, but few of her other indulgences had left their mark. The cargoes of caviar, the schools of smoked salmon, the truck-loads of *foie gras*, the coveys of quail, the beds of oysters and the regiments of lobsters which had marched in eleemosynary procession through her intestines, had resolved themselves into very little solid flesh. Unlike most of her kind, she had not grown coarse and flabby: she had aged with a lean and arid dignity. At fifty, Maggie Oaks, late of Bermondsey and the Follies, really looked like a Countess, even if it was a rather tart and desiccated Countess. She looked like one of those brittle fish-blooded aristocrats who stand firm for kindness to animals and discipline for the lower classes. She had hard bright eyes and hard lines cracked into the heavy layers of powder and enamel on her face, and she was a hard bad woman in spite of her successful sophistication.

'At least that saves a lot of explanations,' said the Saint; and she returned his gaze with her coldly quizzical stare.

'I take it that I was right—that you've picked me for your next victim.'

'Let's call it "contributor",' suggested the Saint mildly.

She shrugged.

'In plain language, I'm either to give you, or have stolen from me, whatever sum of money you think fit to assess as a fine for what you would call my misdeeds.'

'Madam, you have a wonderful gift of coming to the point.'

'This money will be supposedly collected for charity,' she went on, 'but you will take your commission for collecting it before you pass it on.'

'That was the general idea, Maggie.'

She lighted a cigarette.

'I suppose I shouldn't be allowed to ask why it's a crime for me to make a living in exactly the same way as you do?'

'There is a difference. I don't set myself up too seriously as a public benefactor. As a matter of fact, most people would tell you that I was a crook. If you want that point of view, ask a policeman.'

Her thin lips puckered with watchful mockery.

'That seems to make me smarter than you are, Mr Templar. The policeman would arrest you, but he'd tip his hat to me.'

'That's possible,' Simon admitted imperturbably. 'But there are other differences.'

'Meaning what?'

'Mathematical ones. A matter of simple economy. When I collect money, unless I'm trying to put things right for someone else who's been taken for a mug, between seventy-five and ninety per cent of it really does go to charity. Now suppose you collect a thousand pounds in ticket sales for one of your parties. Two hundred and fifty quid go straight into your pocket—you work on the gross. Other organising expenses take up at least a hundred pounds more. Advertising, prizes, decorations, publicity, and what not probably cost another ten per cent. Then there's the orchestra, hire of rooms and waiters, and the cost of a lot of fancy food that's much too good for the people who eat it—let's say four hundred pounds. And the caterers give you a fifty pound cut on that. The net result is that you take in three hundred pounds and a nice big dinner, and the good cause gets maybe a hundred and fifty. In other words, every time one of your suckers buys one of your five-guinea tickets, to help to save fallen women or something like that, he gives you twice as much as he gives the fallen women, which might not be exactly what he had in mind. So I don't think we really are in the same class.'

'You don't mean that I'm in a better class?' she protested sarcastically.

The Saint shook his head.

'Oh, no, he said. 'Not for a moment. . . . But I do think that some of these differences ought to be adjusted.'

Her mouth was as tight as a trap.

'And how will that be done?'

'I thought it'd be an interesting change if you practised a little charity yourself. Suppose we set a donation of ten thousand pounds—'

'Do you really think I'd give you ten thousand pounds?'

'Why not?' asked the Saint reasonably. 'Other people have. And the publicity alone would be almost worth it. Ask your Press agent. Besides, it needn't really even cost you anything. That famous diamond necklace of yours, for instance—even in the limited markets I could take it to, it'd fetch ten thousand quid easily. And if you bought yourself a good imitation hardly anyone would know the difference.'

For a moment her mouth stayed open at the implication of what he was saying; and then she burst into a deep cackle of laughter.

'You almost scared me,' she said. 'But people have tried to bluff me before. Still, it was nice of you to give me the warning.' She stood up. 'Mr Templar, I'm not going to threaten you with the police, because I know that would only make you laugh. Besides, I think I can look after myself. I'm not going to give you ten thousand pounds, of course, and I'm not going to let you steal my necklace. If you can get either, you'll be a clever man. Will you come and see me again when you've hatched a plot?'

The Saint stood up also, and smoothed the clothes over his sinewy seventy-four inches. His lazy blue eyes twinkled.

'That sounds almost like a challenge.'

'You can take it as one if you like.'

'I happen to know that your necklace isn't insured—no company in the country will ever carry you for a big risk since that fraudulent claim that got you a suspended sentence when you were in the Follies. Insurance company black lists don't fade.'

Her thin smile broadened.

'I got two thousand pounds, just the same, and that's more than covered any losses I've had since,' she said calmly. 'No, Mr Templar, I'm not worried about insurance. If you can get what you're after I'll be the first to congratulate you.'

Simon's brows slanted at her with an impudent humour that would have given her fair warning if she had been less confident. He had completely recovered from the smithereening of his first ingenious plans, and already his swift imagination was playing with a new and better scheme.

'Is that a bet?' he said temptingly.

'Do you expect me to put it in writing?'

He smiled back at her.

'I'll take your word for it. . . . We must tell the newspapers.'

He left her to puzzle a little over that last remark but by the time she went to bed she had forgotten it. Consequently she had a second spell of puzzlement a couple of mornings later when she listened to the twittering voice of one of her society acquaintances on the telephone.

'My *dear*, how *too* original! Quite the *cleverest* thing I ever heard of! . . . Oh, now you're just playing innocent! Of *course* it's in all the papers! And on the front page, too! . . . How *did* you manage it? My dear, I'm *madly* jealous! The Saint could steal anything I've got, and I mean *anything*! He must be the most fascinating man—isn't he?'

'He is, darling, and I'll tell him about your offer,' said the Countess instinctively.

She hung up the microphone and said: 'Silly old cow!' There had been another ball the night before, in aid of a seamen's mission or a dogs' hospital or something, and she had had to deal with the usual charitable ration of champagne and brandy: at that hour of the morning after, her reactions were not as sharp as they became later in the day. Nevertheless, a recollection of the Saint's parting words seeped back into her mind with a slight shock. She took three aspirins in a glass of whisky and rang for some newspapers.

She didn't even have to open the first one. The item pricked her in the eyes just as the sheet was folded:

## SAINT WILL ROB COUNTESS
## FOR CHARITY

### 'IT'S A BET,' SAYS SOCIETY HOSTESS

LONDON, October 12.—Simon Templar, better known as 'The Saint', famous twentieth-century Robin Hood, added yesterday to his long list of audacities by announcing that he had promised to steal for charity the £20,000 necklace of Countess Jannowicz, the well-known          Society          leader.

But for once the police have not been asked to prevent the intended crime. Templar called on the Countess personally last Tuesday to discuss his scheme, and was told that she would be the first to congratulate him if he could get away with it.

The twist in the plot is that Countess Jannowicz is herself an indefatigable worker for charity, and the organiser of countless social functions through which thousands of pounds are annually collected for various hospitals and humane societies.

Those who remember the Countess' many triumphs in roping in celebrities as a bait for her charities believe that she has surpassed herself with her latest 'catch'. It was whispered that the sensational stunt launching of                    some                    new

(*continued on page nine*)

The Countess read it all through; and then she put her head back on the pillows and thought about it some more, and began to shake with laughter. The vibration made her feel as if the top of her head was coming off, but she couldn't stop it. She was still quivering among her curlers when the telephone exploded again.

'It's someone from Scotland Yard,' reported her maid. 'Inspector Teal.'

'What the hell does he want?' demanded the Countess.

She took over the instrument.

'Yes?' she squawked.

'This is Inspector Teal speaking,' clacked the diaphragm. 'I suppose you've seen that story about the Saint and yourself in the papers?'

'Oh, yes,' said the Countess sweetly. 'I was just reading it. Isn't it simply delightful?'

'That isn't for me to say,' answered the detective in a laboured voice. 'But if this is a serious threat we shall have to take steps to protect your property.'

'Take steps— Oh, but I don't want to make it *too* easy for him. He always seems to get away with everything when the police are looking out for him.'

There was a strangled pause at the other end of the wire. Then: 'You mean that this really is only a publicity stunt?'

'Now, now,' said the Countess coyly. 'That would be telling, wouldn't it? Goodbye, Inspector.'

She handed the telephone back to her maid.

'If that damn flatfoot calls again, tell him I'm out,' she said. 'Get me some more aspirin and turn on my bath.'

It was typical of her that she dismissed Teal's offer without a moment's uneasiness. After she had bathed and swallowed some coffee, however, she did summon the sallow and perspiring Mr Ullbaum who lived a feverish life as her Press agent and vaguely general manager.

'There'll be some reporters calling for interviews,' she said. 'Some of 'em have been on the phone already. Tell 'em anything that comes into your head, but keep it funny.'

Mr Ullbaum spluttered, which was a habit of his when agitated, which was most of the time.

'But what's so funny if he does steal the necklace?'

'He isn't going to get the necklace—I'll take care of that. But I hope he tries. Everybody he's threatened to rob before has gone into hysterics before he's moved a finger, and they've been licked before he starts. I'm going to lick him and make him look as big as a flea at the same time—and all without even getting out of breath. We'll treat it as a joke now; and after he's made a fool of himself and it really *is* a joke, it'll be ten times funnier. For God's sake go away and use your own brain. That's what I pay you for. I've got a headache.'

She was her regal self again by cocktail time, when the Saint saw her across the room at the May Fair with a party of friends, immaculately groomed from the top of her tightwaved head to the toes of her tight-fitting shoes, and looking as if she had just stepped out of an advertisement for guillotines. He sauntered over in answer to her imperiously beckoning forefinger.

'I see your Press agent didn't waste any time, Mr Templar.'

'I don't know,' said the Saint innocently. 'Are you sure you didn't drop a hint to your own publicity man?'

She shook her head.

'Mr Ullbaum was quite upset when he heard about it.'

The Saint smiled. He knew the permanently flustered Mr Ullbaum.

'Then it must have been my bloke,' he murmured. 'How did you like the story?'

'I thought it was rather misleading in places, but Mr Ullbaum is going to put that right. . . . Still, the police are quite interested. I had a phone call from a detective this morning before I was really awake.'

A faint unholy glimmer crossed the Saint's eyes.

'Would that be Inspector Teal, by any chance?'

'Yes.'

'What did you tell him?'

'I told him to leave me alone.'

Simon seemed infinitesimally disappointed; but he grinned.

'I was wondering why he hadn't come paddling around to see me and add some more fun to the proceedings. I'm afraid I'm going to miss him. But it's nice to play with someone like you who knows the rules.'

'I know the rules, Mr Templar,' she said thinly. 'And the first rule is to win. Before you're finished you're going to wish you hadn't boasted so loudly.'

'You're not worried?'

She moved one jewel-encrusted hand indicatively.

'Did you notice those two men at that table in the corner?'

'Yes—have they been following you? I'll call a cop and have them picked up if you like.'

'Don't bother. Those are my bodyguard. They're armed, and they have orders to shoot at the drop of a hat. Are you sure *you* aren't worried?'

He laughed.

'I never drop my hat.' He buttoned his coat languidly, and the impudent scapegrace humour danced in his eyes like sunlight on blue water. 'Well—I've got to go on with my conspiring, and I'm keeping you from your friends. . . .'

There was a chorus of protest from the other women at the table, who had been craning forward with their mouths open, breathlessly eating up every word.

'Oh, *no*—'

'Countess, you *must* introduce us—'

'I've been *dying* to meet him—'

The Countess's lips curled.

'Of course, my dears,' she said, with the sugariness of arsenic. 'How rude of me!' She performed the introductions. 'Lady Instock was telling me only this morning that you could steal *anything* from her,' she added spikily.

'*Anything*,' confirmed Lady Instock, gazing at the Saint rapturously out of her pale protruding eyes.

Simon looked at her thoughtfully.

'I won't forget it,' he said.

As he returned to his own table he heard her saying to a unanimous audience: 'Isn't he the most *thrilling*—'

Countess Jannowicz watched his departure intently, ignoring the feminine palpitations around her. She had a sardonic sense of humour, combined with a scarcely suppressed contempt for the climbing sycophants who crawled around her, that made the temptation to elaborate the joke too attractive to resist. Several times during the following week she was impelled to engineer opportunities to refer to 'that Saint person who's trying to steal my necklace'; twice again, when their paths crossed in fashionable restaurants, she called him to her table for the express pleasure of twitting him about his boast. To demonstrate her contempt for his reputation by teasing him on such friendly terms, and at the same time to enjoy the awed reactions of her friends, flattered something exhibitionistic in her that gave more satisfaction than any other fun she had had for years. It was like having a man-eating tiger for a pet and tweaking its ears.

This made nothing any easier for Mr Ullbaum. The Countess was already known as a shrewd collector of publicity, and the seeds of suspicion had been firmly planted by the opening story. Mr Ullbaum tried to explain to groups of sceptical reporters that the Saint's threat was perfectly genuine, but that the Countess was simply treating it with the disdain which it deserved; at the same time he tried to carry out his instructions to 'keep it funny,' and the combination was too much for his mental powers. The cynical cross-examinations he had to submit to usually reduced him to ineffectual spluttering. His disclaimers were duly printed, but in contexts that made them sound more like admissions.

The Countess, growing more and more attached to her own joke, was exceptionally tolerant.

'Let 'em laugh,' she said. 'I'll make it all the funnier when he flops.'

She saw him a third time at supper at the Savoy, and invited him to join her party for coffee. He came over, smiling and immaculate, as much at ease as if he had been her favourite nephew. While she introduced him—a briefer business now, for he had met some of the party before—she pointedly fingered the coruscating rope of diamonds on her neck.

'You see I've still got it on,' she said as he sat down.

'I noticed that the lights seemed rather bright over here,' he admitted. 'You've been showing it around quite a lot lately, haven't you? Are you making the most of it while you've got it?'

'I want to make sure that you can't say I didn't give you plenty of chances.'

'Aren't you afraid that some ordinary grab artist might get it first? You know I have my competitors.'

She looked at him with thinly veiled derision.

'I'll begin to think there is a risk of that, if you don't do something soon. And the suspense is making me quite jittery. Haven't you been able to think of a scheme yet?'

Simon's eyes rested on her steadily for a moment while he drew on his cigarette.

'That dinner and dance you were organising for Friday—you sent me an invitation,' he said. 'Is it too late for me to get a ticket?'

'I've got some in my bag. If you've got five guineas—'

He laid ten pounds on the table.

'Make it two—I may want someone to help me carry the loot.'

Her eyes went hard and sharp for an instant before a buzz of excited comment from her listening guests shut her off from him. He smiled at them all inscrutably, and firmly changed the subject while he finished his coffee and smoked another cigarette. After he had taken his leave, she faced a bombardment of questions with stony preoccupation.

'Come to the dance on Friday,' was all she would say. 'You may see some excitement.'

Mr Ullbaum, summoned to the Presence again the next morning, almost tore his hair.

'Now you will tell the police?' he gibbered.

'Don't be so stupid,' she snapped. 'I'm not going to lose anything, and he's going to look a bigger fool than he has for years. All I want you to do is see that the papers hear that Friday is the day— we may sell a few more tickets.'

Her instinct served her well in that direction at least. The stories already published, vague and contradictory as they were, had boosted the sale of tickets for the Grand Ball in aid of the National League for the Care of Incurables beyond her expectations, and the final announcement circulated to the Press by the unwilling Mr Ullbaum caused a flurry of last-minute buying that had the private ballroom hired for the occasion jammed to overflowing by eight o'clock in the evening of the twentieth. It was a curious tribute to the legends that had grown up around the name of Simon Templar, who had brought premature grey hairs to more police officers than could easily have been counted. Everyone who could read knew that the Saint had never harmed any innocent person; and there were enough sensation-seekers with clear consciences in London to fill the spacious suite beyond capacity.

Countess Jannowicz, glittering with diamonds, took her place calmly at the head table beside the chairman. He was the aged and harmlessly doddering bearer of a famous name who served in the same honorary position in several charitable societies and boards of directors, without ever knowing much more about them than was entailed in presiding over occasional public meetings convened by energetic organisers like the Countess; and he was almost stone deaf, an ailment which was greatly to his advantage in view of the speeches he had to listen to.

'What's this I read about some fella goin' to steal your necklace?' he mumbled, as he shakily spooned his soup.

'It wouldn't do you any good if I told you, you dithering old goat,' said the Countess, with a gracious smile.

'Oh, yes. Hm. Ha. Extraordinary.'

She was immune to the undercurrents of excitement that ebbed and flowed through the room like leakages of static electricity. Her only emotion was a slight anxiety lest the Saint should cheat her after all by simply staying away. After all the build-up, that would certainly leave her holding the bag. But it would bring him no profit, and leave him deflated on his own boast at the same time: it was impossible to believe that he would be satisfied with such a cheap anti-climax as that.

What else he could do and hope to get away with, on the other hand, was something that she had flatly given up trying to guess. Unless he had gone sheerly cuckoo, he couldn't hope to steal so much as a spoon that night, after his intentions had been so widely and openly proclaimed, without convicting himself on his own confession. And yet the Saint had so often achieved things that seemed equally impossible that she had to stifle a reluctant eagerness, to see what his uncanny ingenuity would devise. Whatever that might be, the satisfaction of her curiosity could cost her nothing—for one very good reason.

The Saint might have been able to accomplish the apparently impossible before, but he would literally have to perform a miracle if he was to open the vaults of the Vandrick National Bank. For that was where her diamond necklace lay that night, and where it had lain ever since he paid his first call on her. The string she had been wearing ever since was a first-class imitation, worth about ten guineas. That was her answer to all the fanfaronading and commotion—a precaution so obvious and elementary that no one else in the world seemed to have thought of it, so flawless and unassailable that the Saint's boast was exploded before he even began, so supremely ridiculously simple that it would make the whole earth quake with laughter when the story broke.

Even so, ratcheted notch after notch by the lurking fear of a fiasco, tension crept up on her as the time went by without a sign of the Saint's elegant slender figure and tantalising blue eyes. He was not there for the dinner or the following speeches, nor did he show up during the interval while some of the tables were being whisked away from the main ballroom to make room for the dancing. The dancing started without him, went on through long-drawn expectancy while impatient questions leapt at the Countess spasmodically from time to time like shots from ambush.

'He'll come,' she insisted monotonously, while news photographers roamed restively about with their fingers aching on the triggers of their flash-lights.

At midnight the Saint arrived.

No one knew how he got in; no one had seen him before; but suddenly he was there.

The only announcement of his arrival was when the music stopped abruptly in the middle of a bar. Not all at once, but gradually, in little groups, the dancers shuffled to stillness, became frozen to the floor as the first instinctive turning of eyes towards the orchestra platform steered other eyes in the same direction.

He stood in the centre of the dais, in front of the microphone. No one had a moment's doubt that it was the Saint, although his face was masked. The easy poise of his athletic figure in the faultlessly tailored evening clothes was enough introduction, combined with the careless confidence with which he stood there, as if he had been a polished master of ceremonies preparing to make a routine announcement. The two guns he held, one in each hand, their muzzles shifting slightly over the crowd, seemed a perfectly natural part of his costume.

'May I interrupt for a moment, ladies and gentlemen?' he said.

He spoke quietly, but the loud speakers made his voice audible in every corner of the room. Nobody moved or made any answer. His question was rather superfluous. He *had* interrupted, and everyone's ears were strained for what he had to say.

'This is a hold-up,' he went on, in the same easy conversational tone. 'You've all been expecting it, so none of you should have heart failure. Until I've finished, none of you may leave the room— a friend of mine is at the other end of the hall to help to see that this order is carried out.'

A sea of heads screwed round to where a shorter, stockier man, in evening clothes that seemed too tight for him, stood blocking the far entrance, also masked, and also with two guns in his hands.

'So long as you all do exactly what you're told, I promise that nobody will get hurt. You two'—one of his guns flicked towards the Countess's bodyguard, who were standing stiff-fingered where they had been caught when they saw him—'come over here. Turn your backs, take out your guns slowly, and drop them on the floor.'

His voice was still quiet and matter-of-fact, but both the men obeyed like automatons.

'OK. Now turn round again and kick them towards me. . . . That's fine. You can stand where you are, and don't try to be heroes if you want to live to boast about it.'

A smile touched his lips under the mask. He pocketed one of his guns, and picked up a black gladstone bag from the dais and tossed it out on to the floor. Then he put a cigarette between his lips and lighted it with a match flicked on the thumbnail of the same hand.

'The hold-up will now proceed,' he remarked affably. 'The line forms on the right, and that means everybody except the waiters.

Each of you will put a contribution in the bag as you pass by. Lady Instock, that's a nice pair of earrings—'

Amazed, giggling, white-faced, surly, incredulous, according to their different characters, the procession began to file by and drop different articles into the bag under his directions. There was nothing much else that they could do. Each of them felt that gently waving gun centred on his own body, balancing its bark of death against the first sign of resistance. To one red-faced man who started to bluster, a waiter said tremulously: 'Better do what he says. Tink of all da ladies. Anybody might get hit if he start shooting.' His wife shed a pearl necklace and hustled him by. Most of the gathering had the same idea. Anyone who had tried to be a hero would probably have been mobbed by a dozen others who had no wish to die for his glory. Nobody really thought much beyond that. This wasn't what they had expected, but they couldn't analyse their reactions. Their brains were too numbed to think very much.

Two brains were not numbed. One of them belonged to the chairman, who had lost his glasses, adding dim-sightedness to his other failings. From where he stood he couldn't distinguish anything as small as a mask or a gun, but somebody seemed to be standing up on the platform and was probably making a speech. The chairman nodded from time to time with an expression of polite interest, thinking busily about the new corn plaster that somebody had recommended to him. The other active brain belonged to the Countess Jannowicz, but there seemed to be nothing useful that she could do with it. There was no encouraging feeling of enterprise to be perceived in the guests around her, no warm inducement to believe that they would respond to courageous leadership.

'Can't you see he's bluffing?' she demanded in a hoarse bleat. 'He wouldn't dare to shoot!'

'I should be terrified,' murmured the Saint imperturbably, without moving his eyes from the passing line. 'Madam, that looks like a very fine emerald ring—'

Something inside the Countess seemed to be clutching at her

319

stomach and shaking it up and down. She had taken care to leave her own jewels in a safe place, but it hadn't occurred to her to give the same advice to her guests. And now the Saint was robbing them under her nose—almost under her own roof. Social positions had been shattered overnight on slighter grounds.

She grabbed the arm of a waiter who was standing near.

'Send for the police, you fool!' she snarled.

He looked at her and drew down the corners of his mouth in what might have been a smile or a sneer, or both; but he made no movement.

Nobody made any movement except as the Saint directed. The Countess felt as if she were in a nightmare. It was amazing to her that the hold-up could have continued so long without interruption—without some waiter opening a service door and seeing what was going on, or someone outside in the hotel noticing the curious quietness and giving the alarm. But the ballroom might have been spirited away on to a desert island.

The last of the obedient procession passed by the Saint and left its contribution in the bag, and joined the silent, staring throng of those who had already contributed. Only the chairman and the Countess had not moved—the chairman because he hadn't heard a word and didn't know what was going on.

The Saint looked at her across the room.

'I've been saving Countess Jannowicz to the last,' he said, 'because she's the star turn that you've all been waiting for. Will you step up now, Countess?'

Fighting a tangle of emotions, but compelled by a fascination that drove her like a machine, she moved towards the platform. And the Saint glanced at the group of almost frantic photographers.

'Go ahead, boys,' he said kindly. 'Take your pictures. It's the chance of a lifetime. . . . Your necklace, Countess.'

She stood still, raised her hands a little way, dropped them, raised them again, slowly to her neck. Magnesium bulbs winked and splashed like a barrage of artificial lightning as she unfastened the clasp and dropped the necklace on top of the collection in the bag.

'You can't get away with this,' she said whitely.

'Let me show you how easy it is,' said the Saint calmly. He turned his gun to the nearest man to the platform. 'You, sir—would you mind closing the bag, carefully, and taking it down to my friend at the other end of the room? Thank you.' He watched the bag on its way down the room until it was in the hands of the stocky man at the far entrance. 'OK, partner,' he said crisply. 'Scram.'

As if the word had been a magical incantation, the man vanished.

A kind of communal gasp like a sigh of wind swept over the assembly, as if the final unarguable physical disappearance of their property had squeezed the last long-held breath out of their bodies. Every eye had been riveted on it in its last journey through their midst, every eye had blinked to the shock of its ultimate vanishment; and then every eye dragged itself dazedly back to the platform from which those catastrophes had been dictated.

Almost to their surprise, the Saint was still standing there. But his other gun had disappeared, and he had taken his mask off. In some way, the aura of subtle command that had clung to him before in spite of his easy casualness had gone, leaving the easy casualness alone. He was still smiling.

For an instant the two bodyguards were paralysed. And then with muffled choking noises they made a concerted dive for their guns.

The Saint made no move except a slight deprecating motion of the hand that held his cigarette.

'Ladies and gentlemen,' he said into the microphone, 'I must now make my apologies, and an explanation.'

The bodyguards straightened up, with their guns held ready. And yet something in his quiet voice, unarmed as he was, gripped them in spite of themselves, as it had gripped everyone else in the room. They looked questioningly towards the Countess.

She gave them no response. She was rigid, watching the Saint with the first icy grasp of an impossible premonition closing in on her.

Somehow the Saint was going to get away with it. She knew it, with a horrible certainty, even while she was wildly trying to guess what he would say. He could never have been so insane as to believe that he could pull a public holdup like that without being arrested an hour after he left the hotel, unless he had had some trick up his sleeve to immobilise the hue and cry. And she knew that she was now going to hear the trick she had not thought of.

'You have just been the victims of a hold-up,' he was saying. 'Probably to nearly all of you that was a novel experience. But it is something that might happen to any of you tonight, tomorrow, at any time—so long as there are men at large to whom that seems like the best way of making a living.

'You came here tonight to help the National League for the Care of Incurables. That is a good and humane work. But I have taken this opportunity—with the kind co-operation of Countess Jannowicz—to make you think of another equally good, perhaps even more constructive work: the care of Curables.

'I am talking about a class of whom I may know more than most of you—a section of those unfortunates who are broadly and indiscriminatingly called criminals.

'Ladies and gentlemen, not every lawbreaker is a brutalised desperado, fit only for swift extermination. I know that there are men of that kind, and you all know that I have been more merciless with them than any officer of the law. But there are others.

'I mean the men who steal through ignorance, through poverty, through misplaced ambition, through despair, through lack of better opportunity. I mean also men who have been punished for their crime, and who are now at the crossroads. One road takes them deeper and deeper into crime, into becoming real brutalised desperadoes. The other road takes them back to honesty, to regaining their self-respect, to becoming good and valuable citizens. All they need is the second chance which society is so often unwilling to give them.

'To give these men their second chance, has been founded the

Society for the Rehabilitation of Delinquents—rather an elaborate name for a simple and straightforward thing. I am proud to be the first president of that Society.

'We believe that money spent on this object is far cheaper than the money spent on keeping prisoners in jail, and at the same time is less than the damage that these men would do to the community if they were left to go on with their crimes. We ask you to believe the same thing, and to be generous.

'Everything that has been taken from you tonight can be found tomorrow at the office of the Society, which is in the Devonshire Bank Building on Piccadilly. If you wish to leave your property there, to be sold for the benefit of the Society, we shall be grateful. If it has too great a sentimental value to you, and you wish to buy it back, we shall be glad to exchange it for a cheque. And if you object to us very seriously, and simply want it back, we shall of course have to give it back. But we hope that none of you will demand that.

'That is why we ventured to take the loot away tonight. Between now and tomorrow morning, we want you to have time to think. Think of how different this hold-up would have been if it had been real. Think of your feelings when you saw your jewellery vanishing out of that door. Think of how little difference it would really make to your lives'—he looked straight at the Countess—'if you were wearing imitation stones, while the money that has been locked up idly in the real ones was set free to do good and useful work. Think, ladies and gentlemen, and forgive us the melodramatic way in which we have tried to bring home our point.'

He stepped back, and there was a moment of complete silence.

The chairman had at last found his glasses. He saw the speaker retiring with a bow from the microphone. Apparently the speech was over. It seemed to be the chairman's place to give the conventional lead. He raised his hands and clapped loudly.

It is things like that that turn tides and start revolutions. In another second the whole hall was clattering with hysterical applause.

'My dear, how *do* you think of these things?'

'The most *divinely* thrilling—'

'I was really *petrified* . . .'

The Countess Jannowicz wriggled dazedly free from the shrill jabber of compliments, managed somehow to snatch the Saint out of a circle of clamorous women of which Lady Instock was the most gushing leader. In a comparatively quiet corner of the room she faced him.

'You're a good organiser, Mr Templar. The head waiter tells me that Mr Ullbaum telephoned this afternoon and told the staff how they were to behave during the hold-up.'

He was cheerfully appreciative.

'I must remember to thank him.'

'Mr Ullbaum did no such thing.'

He smiled.

'Then he must have been impersonated. But the damage seems to be done.'

'You know that for all your talking you've still committed a crime?'

'I think you'd be rather a lonely prosecutor.'

Rage had made her a little incoherent.

'I shall not come to your office. You've made a fool of yourself. My necklace is in the bank—'

'Countess,' said the Saint patiently. 'I'd guessed that much. That's why I want you to be sure and bring me the real one. Lady Instock is going to leave her earrings and send a cheque as well, and all the rest of your friends seem to be sold on the idea. You're supposed to be the Number One patron. What would they think of you if after all the advertising you let yourself out with a ten-guinea string of cut glass?'

'I can disclaim—'

'I know you can. But your name will still be Mud. Whereas at the moment you're tops. Why not make the best of it and charge it to publicity?'

She knew she was beaten—that he had simply turned a trick

with the cards that for days past she had been busily forcing into his hand. But she still fought with the bitterness of futility.

'I'll have the police investigate this phoney charity—'

'They'll find that it's quite legally constituted, and so long as the funds last they'll be administered with perfect good faith.'

'And who'll get the benefit of them beside yourself?'

Simon smiled once again.

'Our first and most urgent case will be a fellow named Marty O'Connor. He helped me with the collection tonight. You ought to remember him—he was your chauffeur for three weeks. Anyone like yourself, Countess,' said the Saint rather cruelly, 'ought to know that charity begins at home.'

# THE STAR PRODUCERS

I

Mr Homer Quarterstone was not, to be candid, a name to conjure with in the world of the Theatre. It must be admitted that his experience behind the footlights was not entirely confined to that immortal line: 'Dinner is served'— as a matter of fact, he had once said, 'The Baron is here' and 'Will there be anything further, Madam?' in the same act; and in another never-to-be-forgotten drama which had run for eighteen performances in the West End, he had taken part in the following classic dialogue:

NICK: Were you here?
JENKINS: (*Mr Homer Quarterstone*): No, sir.
NICK: Did you hear anything?
JENKINS: No, sir.
NICK: A hell of a lot of use you are.
JENKINS: Yes, sir.
(*Exit, carrying tray.*)

In the executive line, Mr Quarterstone's career had been marked by the same magnanimous emphasis on service rather than personal glory. He had not actually produced any spectacles of resounding success, but he had contributed his modest quota to their triumph by helping to carry chairs and tables on to the stage and arrange them according to the orders of the scenic director. And although he had not actually given his personal guidance to any of the financial manoeuvres associated with theatrical production, he had sat in the box office at more than one one-night stand, graciously controlling the passage over the counter of those fundamental monetary items without which the labours of more egotistical financiers would have been fruitless.

Nevertheless, while it is true that the name of Quarterstone had never appeared in any headlines, and that his funeral cortège would never have attracted any distinguished pall-bearers, he had undoubtedly found the Theatre more profitable than many other men to whom it had given fame.

He was a man of florid complexion and majestic bearing, with a ripe convexity under his waistcoat and a forehead that arched glisteningly back to the scruff of his neck; and he had a taste for black homburgs and astrakhan-collared overcoats which gave an impression of great artistic prosperity. This prosperity was by no means illusory; for Mr Homer Quarterstone, in his business capacity, was now the principal, president, director, owner and twenty-five per cent of the staff of Supremax Academy of Dramatic Art, which according to the frequent advertisements had been the training ground, the histrionic hot-house, so to speak, of many stars whose names were now household words from the igloos of Greenland to the tents of the wandering Bedouin. And the fact that Mr Quarterstone had not become the principal, president, director, owner, etc., of the Supremax Academy until several years after the graduation of those illustrious personages, when in a period of unaccustomed affluence and unusually successful borrowing he had purchased the name and goodwill of an idealistic but moribund concern, neither deprived him of the legal right to make that claim in his advertising nor hampered the free flow of his imagination when he was expounding his own experience and abilities to prospective clients.

Simon Templar, who sooner or later made the acquaintance of practically everyone who was collecting too much money with too little reason, heard of him first from Rosalind Hale, who had been one of those clients; and she brought him her story for the same reason that many other people who had been foolish would often come to Simon Templar with their troubles, as if the words 'The Saint', had some literally supernatural significance, instead of being merely the nickname with which he had once incongruously been christened.

'I thought it was only the sensible thing to do—to get some proper training—and his advertisements looked genuine. You wouldn't think those film stars would let him use their names for a fraud, would you . . . ? I suppose I was a fool, but I'd played in some amateur things, and people who weren't trying to flatter me said I was good, and I really believed I'd got it in me, sort of instinctively. And *some* of the people who believe they've got it in them must be right, and they must do something about it, or else there wouldn't be any actors and actresses at all, would there . . . ? And really I'm—I—well, I don't make you shudder when you look at me, do I?'

This at least was beyond argument, unless the looker was a crusted misogynist, which the Saint very firmly was not. She had an almost childishly heart-shaped face, with small features that were just far enough from perfection to be exciting, and her figure had just enough curves in just the right places.

The Saint smiled at her without any cynicism.

'And when you came into this money—'

'Well, it looked just like the chance I'd been dreaming about. But I still wanted to be intelligent about it, and not go dashing off to Hollywood to turn into a waitress, or spend my time sitting in producers' waiting-rooms hoping they'd notice me, and just looking dumb when they asked if I had any experience, or anything like that. That's why I went to Quarterstone. And he said I'd got everything, and I only wanted a little schooling. I paid him a hundred pounds for a course of lessons, and then another hundred for an advanced course, and then another hundred for a movie course, and by that time he'd been talking to me so that he'd found out all about that legacy, and that was when his friend came in, and they got me to give them eight hundred pounds to put that play on.'

'In which you were to play the lead.'

'Yes, and—'

'The play never did go on.'

She nodded, and the moistness of her eyes made them shine

like jewels. She might not have been outstandingly intelligent, she might or might not have had any dramatic talent, but her own drama was real. She was crushed, frightened, dazed, wounded in the deep and desperate way that a child is hurt when it has innocently done something disastrous, as if she was still too stunned to realise what she had done.

Some men might have laughed, but the Saint didn't laugh. He said, in his quiet, friendly way: 'I suppose you checked up on your legal position?'

'Yes. I went to see a solicitor. He said there wasn't anything I could do. They'd been too clever. I couldn't *prove* that I'd been swindled. There really was a play, and it could have been put on, only the expenses ran away with all the money before that, and I hadn't got any more, and apparently that often happens, and you couldn't prove it was a fraud. I just hadn't read the contracts and things properly when I signed them, and Urlaub—that's Quarterstone's friend—was entitled to spend all that money, and even if he was careless and stupid you couldn't prove it was criminal. . . . I suppose it was my own fault, and I've no right to cry about it, but it was everything I had, and I'd given up my job as well, and—well, things have been pretty tough. You know.'

He nodded, straightening a cigarette with his strong brown fingers.

All at once the consciousness of what she was doing now seemed to sweep over her, leaving her tongue-tied. She had to make an effort to get out the last words that everything else had inevitably been leading up to.

'I know I'm crazy and I've no right, but could you—could you think of anything to do about it?'

He went on looking at her thoughtfully for a moment; and then, incredulously, she suddenly realised that he was smiling, and that his smile was still without satire.

'I could try,' he said.

He stood up, long immaculately tailored legs gathering themselves with the lazy grace of a tiger, and all at once she found something in his blue eyes that made all the legends about him impossible to question. It was as if he had lifted all the weight off her shoulders without another word when he stood up.

'One of the first things I should prescribe is a mansized lunch,' he said. 'A diet of sandwiches and malted milk never produced any great ideas.'

When he left her it was still without any more promises, and yet with a queer sense of certainty that was more comforting than any number of promises.

The Saint himself was not quite so certain; but he was interested, which perhaps meant more. He had that impetuously human outlook which judged an adventure on its artistic quality rather than on the quantity of boodle which it might contribute to his unlawful income. He liked Rosalind Hale, and he disliked men such as Mr Homer Quarterstone and Comrade Urlaub sounded as if they would be; more than that, perhaps, he disliked rackets that preyed on people to whom a loss of eight hundred pounds was utter tragedy. He set out that same afternoon to interview Mr Quarterstone.

The Supremax Academy occupied the top floor and one room on the street level of a sedate old-fashioned building in Soho; but the entrance was so cunningly arranged and the other intervening tenants so modestly unheralded that any impressionable visitor who presented himself first at the ground-floor room labelled 'Inquiries', and who was thence whisked expertly into the elevator and upwards to the rooms above, might easily have been persuaded that the whole building was taken up with various departments of the Academy, a hive buzzing with ambitious Thespian bees. The brassy but once luscious blonde who presided in the Inquiry Office lent tone to this idea by saying that Mr Quarterstone was busy, very busy, and that it was customary to make appointments with him some days in advance; when she finally organised the interview it was with the regal generosity of a slightly flirtatious goddess performing a casual miracle for an especially favoured and deserving suitor—

a beautifully polished routine that was calculated to impress prospective clients from the start with a gratifying sense of their own importance. Simon Templar was always glad of a chance to enjoy his own importance; but on this occasion he regretfully had to admit that so much flattery was undeserved, for instead of his own name he had given the less notorious name of Tombs. This funereal anonymity, however, cast no shadow over the warmth of Mr Quarterstone's welcome.

'My dear Mr Tombs! Come in. Sit down. Have a cigarette.'

Mr Quarterstone grasped him with large warm hands, wrapped him up, transported him tenderly, and installed him in an armchair like a collector enshrining a priceless piece of fragile glass. He fluttered anxiously around him, pressing a cigarette into the Saint's mouth and lighting it before he retired reluctantly to his own chair on the other side of the desk.

'And now, my dear Mr Tombs,' said Mr Quarterstone at last, clasping his hands across his stomach, 'how can I help you?'

Simon looked at his hands, his feet, the carpet, the wall, and then at Mr Quarterstone.

'Well,' he said bashfully. 'I wanted to inquire about some dramatic lessons.'

'Some—ah—oh, yes. You mean a little advanced coaching. A little polishing of technique?'

'Oh, no,' said the Saint hastily. 'I mean, you know your business, of course, but I'm only a beginner.'

Mr Quarterstone sat up a little straighter and gazed at him.

'You're only a beginner?' he repeated incredulously.

'Yes.'

'You mean to tell me you haven't any stage experience?'

'No. Only a couple of amateur shows—'

'You're not joking?'

'Of course not.'

'Well!'

Mr Quarterstone continued to stare at him as if he were something rare and strange. The Saint twisted his hat-brim uncomfortably. Mr Quarterstone sat back again, shaking his head.

'That's the most extraordinary thing I ever heard of,' he declared.

'But why?' Simon asked, with not unreasonable surprise.

'My dear fellow, anyone would take you for a professional actor! I've been in the theatrical business all my life—I was in the West End for ten years, played before the Royal Family, produced hundreds of shows—and I'd have bet anyone I could pick out a professional actor every time. The way you walked in, the way you sat down, the way you use your hands, even the way you're smoking that cigarette—it's amazing! Are you *sure* you're not having a little joke?'

'Absolutely.'

'May I ask what is your present job?'

'Until a couple of days ago,' said the Saint ingenuously, 'I was working in a bank. But I'd always wanted to be an actor, so when my uncle died and left me four thousand pounds I thought it was a good time to start. I think I could play parts like William Powell,' he added, looking sophisticated.

Mr Quarterstone beamed like a cat full of cream.

'Why not?' he demanded oratorically. 'Why ever not? With that natural gift of yours . . .' He shook his head again, clicking his tongue in eloquent expression of his undiminished awe and admiration. 'It's the most amazing thing! Of course, I sometimes see fellows who are nearly as good-looking as you are, but they haven't got your manner. Why, if you took a few lessons—'

Simon registered the exact amount of glowing satisfaction which he was supposed to register.

'That's what I came to you for, Mr Quarterstone. I've seen your advertisements—'

'Yes, yes!'

Mr Quarterstone got up and came round the desk again. He took the Saint's face in his large warm hands and turned it this way and that, studying it from various angles with increasing astonishment. He made the Saint stand up and studied him from

a distance, screwing up one eye and holding up a finger in front
of the other to compare his proportions. He stalked up to him
again, patted him here and there, and felt his muscles. He stepped
back again and posed in an attitude of rapture.

'Marvellous!' he said. 'Astounding!'

Then, with an effort, he brought himself out of his trance.

'Mr Tombs,' he said firmly, 'there's only one thing for me to
do. I must take you in charge myself. I have a wonderful staff
here, the finest staff you could find in any dramatic academy in
the world, past masters, every one of 'em—but they're not good
enough. I wouldn't dare to offer you anything but the best that
we have here. I offer you myself. And because I only look upon
it as a privilege—nay, a sacred duty, to develop this god-given
talent you have, I shall not try to make any money out of you. I
shall only make a small charge to cover the actual value of my
time. Charles Laughton paid me a thousand pounds for one hour's
coaching in a difficult scene. John Barrymore took me to
Hollywood and paid me fifteen thousand dollars to criticise him
in four rehearsals. But I shall only ask you for enough to cover
my out-of-pocket expenses—let us say, two hundred pounds—for
a course of ten special, personal, private, exclusive lessons. . . .
No,' boomed Mr Quarterstone, waving one hand in a magnificent
gesture, 'don't thank me! Were I to refuse to give you the benefit
of all my experience, I should regard myself as a traitor to my
calling, a very—ah—Ishmael!'

If there was one kind of acting in which Simon Templar had
graduated from a more exacting academy than was dreamed of
in Mr Quarterstone's philosophy, it was the art of depicting the
virgin sucker yawning hungrily under the baited hook. His
characterisation was pointed with such wide-eyed and unsullied
innocence, such eager and open-mouthed receptivity, such a
succulently plastic amenability to suggestion, such a rich response
to flattery—in a word, with such a sublime absorptiveness to the
old oil—that men such as Mr Quarterstone, on becoming conscious
of him for the first time, had been known to wipe away a furtive

tear as they dug down into their pockets for first mortgages on the Tower of London and formulæ for extracting radium from old toothpaste tubes. He used all of that technique on Mr Homer Quarterstone, so effectively that his enrolment in the Supremax Academy proceeded with the effortless ease of a stratospherist returning to terra firma a short head in front of his punctured balloon. Mr Quarterstone did not actually brush away an unbidden tear; but he did bring out an enormous leather-bound ledger and enter up particulars of his newest student with a gratifying realisation that Life, in spite of the pessimists, was not wholly without its moments of unshadowed joy.

'When can I start?' asked the Saint, when that had been done.

'Start?' repeated Mr Quarterstone, savouring the word. 'Why, whenever you like. Each lesson lasts a full hour, and you can divide them up as you wish. You can start now if you want to. I had an appointment—'

'Oh.'

'But it is of no importance, compared with this.' Mr Quarterstone picked up the telephone. 'Tell Mr Urlaub I shall be too busy to see him this afternoon,' he told it. He hung up. 'The producer,' he explained, as he settled back again. 'Of course you've heard of him. But he can wait. One day he'll be waiting on your doorstep, my boy.' He dismissed Mr Urlaub, the producer, with a majestic *ademán*. 'What shall we take first— elocution?'

'You know best, Mr Quarterstone,' said the Saint eagerly.

Mr Quarterstone nodded. If there was anything that could have increased his contentment, it was a pupil who had no doubt that Mr Quarterstone knew best. He crossed his legs and hooked one thumb in the armhole of his waist-coat.

'Say "Eee".'

'Eee.'

'Ah.'

Simon went on looking at him expectantly.

'Ah,' repeated Mr Quarterstone.

'I beg your pardon?'

'I said "Ah".'

'Oh.'

'No, ah.'

'Yes, I—'

'Say it after me, Mr Tombs. '*Aaaah*.' Make it ring out. Hold your diaphragm in, open your mouth, and bring it up from your chest. This is a little exercise in the essential vowels.'

'Oh. *Aaaah*.'

'Oh.'

'Oh.'

'I.'

'I.'

'*Ooooo*.'

'*Ooooo*.'

'Wrong.'

'I'm sorry—'

'Say "wrong", Mr Tombs.'

'Wrong.'

'Right,' said Mr Quarterstone.

'Right.'

'Yes, yes,' said Mr Quarterstone testily. 'I—'

'Yes, yes, I.'

Mr Quarterstone swallowed.

'I don't mean you to repeat *every* word I say,' he said. 'Just the examples. Now let's try the vowels again in a sentence. Say this: "Faaar skiiies loooom O-ver meee".'

'Faaar skiiies loooom O-ver meee.'

'Daaark niiight draaaws neeear.'

'The days are drawing in,' Simon admitted politely.

Mr Quarterstone's smile became somewhat glassy, but whatever else he may have been he was no quitter.

'I'm afraid he is a fraud,' Simon told Rosalind Hale when he saw her the next day. 'But he has a beautiful line of sugar for the flies. I was the complete gawky goof, the perfect bank clerk with dramatic ambitions—you could just see me going home and leering at myself in the mirror and imagining myself making love to Greta Garbo—but he told me he just couldn't believe how anyone with my poise couldn't have had any experience.'

The girl's white teeth showed on her lower lip.

'But that's just what he told me!'

'I could have guessed it, darling. And I don't suppose you were the first, either. . . . I had two lessons on the spot, and I've had another two today; and if he can teach anyone anything worth knowing about acting, then I can train ducks to write shorthand. I was so dumb that anyone with an ounce of artistic feeling would have thrown me out of the window, but when I left him this afternoon he almost hugged me and told me he could hardly wait to finish the course before he rushed out to get me a part.'

She moved her head a little, gazing at him with big sober eyes.

'He was just the same with me, too. Oh, I've been such a fool!'

'We're all fools in our own way,' said the Saint consolingly. 'Boys like Homer are my job, so they don't bother me. On the other hand, you've no idea what a fool I can be with soft lights and sweet music. Come on to dinner and I'll show you.'

'But now you've given Quarterstone two hundred pounds, and what are you going to do about it?'

'Wait for the next act of the stirring drama.'

The next act was not long in developing. Simon had two more of Mr Quarterstone's special, personal, private, exclusive lessons the next day, and two more the day after—Mr Homer Quarterstone was no apostle of the old-fashioned idea of making haste slowly, and by getting in two lessons daily he was able to double his temporary income, which then chalked up at the very pleasing figure of forty pounds per diem, minus the overhead, of which the brassy blonde was not the smallest item. But this method of gingering up the flow of revenue also meant that its duration was reduced from ten days to five, and during a lull in the next day's first hour (Diction, Gesture and Facial Expression) he took the opportunity of pointing out that Success, while already certain, could never be too certain or too great, and therefore that a supplementary series of lessons in the Art and Technique of the Motion Picture, while involving only a brief delay, could only add to the magnitude of Mr Tombs's ultimate inevitable triumph.

On this argument, for the first time, Mr Tombs disagreed.

'I want to see for myself whether I've mastered the first lessons,' he said. 'If I could get a small part in a play, just to try myself out—'

He was distressingly obstinate; and Mr Quarterstone, either because he convinced himself that it would only be a waste of time, or because another approach to his pupil's remaining three thousand eight hundred pounds seemed just as simple, finally yielded. He made an excuse to leave the studio for a few minutes, and Simon knew that the next development was on its way.

It arrived in the latter part of the last hour (Declamation with Gestures, Movement and Facial Expression—The Complete Classical Scene).

Mr Quarterstone was demonstrating.

'To be,' trumpeted Mr Quarterstone, gazing ceilingwards with an ecstatic expression, the chest thrown out, the arms slightly spread. 'Or not to be.' Mr Quarterstone ceased to be. He slumped, the head bowed, the arms hanging listlessly by the sides, the expression doleful. 'That—is the question.' Mr Quarterstone pondered it, shaking his head. The suspense was awful. He elaborated the idea.

'Whether 'tis nobler'—Mr Quarterstone drew himself nobly up, the chin lifted, the right arm turned slightly across the body, the forearm parallel with the ground—'in the mind'—he clutched his brow, where he kept his mind—'to suffer'—he clutched his heart, where he did his suffering—'the slings'—he stretched out his left hand for the slings—'and arrows'—he flung out his right hand for the arrows—'of outrageous fortune'—Mr Quarterstone rolled the insult lusciously around his mouth and spat it out with defiance—'or to take arms'—he drew himself up again, the shoulders squared, rising slightly on tiptoes—'against a sea of troubles'—his right hand moved over a broad panorama, undulating symbolically—'and by opposing'—the arms rising slightly from the elbow, fists clenched, shoulders thrown back, chin drawn in—'end them!'—the forearms striking down again with a fierce chopping movement, expressive of finality, and knocking a calendar off the table.

'Excuse me,' said the brassy blonde, with her head poking round the door. 'Mr Urlaub is here.'

'Tchah!' said Mr Quarterstone, inspiration wounded in midflight. 'Tell him to wait.'

'He said—'

Mr Quarterstone's eyes dilated. His mouth opened. His hands lifted a little from his sides, the fingers tense and parted rather like plump claws, the body rising. He was staring at the Saint.

'Wait!' he cried. 'Of course! The very thing! The very man you've got to meet! One of the greatest producers in the world today! Your chance!'

He leapt a short distance off the ground and whirled on the blonde, his arm flung out, pointing quiveringly.

'Send him in!'

Simon looked wildly breathless.

'But—but will he—'

'Of course he will! You've only got to remember what I've taught you. And sit down. We must be calm.'

Mr Quarterstone sank into a chair, agitatedly looking calm, as Urlaub bustled in. Urlaub trotted quickly across the room.

'Ah, Homer.'

'My dear Waldemar! How is everything?'

'Terrible! I came to ask for your advice—'

Mr Urlaub leaned across the desk. He was a smallish, thin, bouncy man with a big nose and sleek black hair. His suit fitted him as tightly as an extra skin, and the stones in his tie-pin and in his rings looked enough like diamonds to look like diamonds. He moved as if he were hung on springs, and his voice was thin and spluttery like the exhaust of an anæmic motor cycle.

'Niementhal has quit. Let me down at the last minute. He wanted to put some goddam gigolo into the lead. Some ham that his wife's got hold of. I said to him, "Aaron, your wife is your business and this play is my business." I said, "I don't care if it hurts your wife's feelings and I don't care if she gets mad at you, I can't afford to risk my reputation in the West End and my investment in this play by putting that ham in the lead." I said, "Buy her a box of chocolates or a diamond bracelet or anything or send her to Paris or something, but don't ask me to make her happy by putting that gigolo in this play." So he quit. And me with everything set, and the rest of the cast ready to start rehearsing next week, and he quits. He said, "All right, then use your own money." I said, "You know I've got ten thousand pounds in this production already, and all you were going to put in is three thousand, and for that you want me to risk my money and my reputation by hiring that ham. I thought you said you'd got a good actor." "Well, you find yourself a good actor and three thousand pounds," he says, and he quits. Cold. And I can't raise another cent—you know how I just tied up half a million to save those aluminium shares.'

'That's tough, Waldemar,' said Mr Quarterstone anxiously. 'Waldemar, that's tough! . . . Ah—by the way—pardon me—may I introduce a student of mine? Mr Tombs . . .'

Urlaub turned vaguely, apparently becoming aware of the Saint's presence for the first time. He started forward with a courteously extended hand as the Saint rose.

But their hands did not meet at once. Mr Urlaub's approaching movement died slowly away, as if paralysis had gradually overtaken him, so that he finally came to rest just before they met, like a clockwork toy that had run down. His eyes became fixed, staring. His mouth opened.

Then, very slowly, he revived himself. He pushed his hand onwards again, and grasped the Saint's as if it were something precious, shaking it slowly and earnestly.

'A pupil of yours, did you say, Homer?' he asked in an awestruck voice.

'That's right. My star pupil, in fact. I might almost say—'

Mr Urlaub paid no attention to what Quarterstone might almost have said. With his eyes still staring, he darted suddenly closer, peered into the Saint's face, took hold of it, turned it from side to side, just as Quarterstone had once done. Then he stepped back and stared again, prowling round the Saint like a dog prowling round a tree. Then he stopped.

'Mr Tombs,' he said vibrantly, 'will you walk over to the door, and then walk back towards me?'

Looking dazed, the Saint did so.

Mr Urlaub looked at him and gulped. Then he hauled a wad of typescript out of an inside pocket, fumbled through it, and thrust it out with one enamelled fingernail dabbing at a paragraph.

'Read that speech—read it as if you were acting it.'

The Saint glanced over the paragraph, drew a deep breath, and read with almost uncontrollable emotion.

'No, do not lie to me. You have already given me the answer for which I have been waiting. I am not ungrateful for what you once did for me, but I see now that that kind act was only a part of your scheme to ensnare my better nature in the toils of your unhallowed passions, as though pure love were a thing that could be bought with merchandise. Ah, yes, I loved you, but I did not know that that pretty face was only a mask for the corruption beneath. How you must have laughed at me! Ha, ha. I brought you a rose, but you turned it into a nest of vipers in my bosom. They have stabbed my heart! (Sobs.)'

Mr Urlaub clasped his hands together. His eyes bulged and rolled upwards.

'My God,' he breathed hoarsely.

'What?' said the Saint.

'Why?' said Mr Quarterstone.

'But it's like a miracle!' squeaked Waldemar Urlaub. 'He's the man! The type! The face! The figure! The voice! The manner! He is a genius! Homer, where did you find him? The women will storm the theatre.' He grasped the Saint by the arm, leaning as far as he could over the desk and over Mr Quarterstone. 'Listen. He must play that part. He must. He is the only man. I couldn't put anyone else in it now. Not after I've seen him. I'll show Aaron Niementhal where he gets off. Quit, did he? Okay. He'll be sorry. We'll have a hit that'll make history!'

'But Waldemar—'

Mr Urlaub dried up. His clutching fingers uncoiled from Simon's arm. The fire died out of his eyes. He staggered blindly back and sank into a chair and buried his face in his hands.

'Yes,' he whispered bitterly. 'I'd forgotten. The play can't go on. I'm sunk, Homer—just for a miserable three thousand pounds. And now, of all times, when I've just seen Mr Tombs!'

'You know I'd help you if I could, Waldemar,' said Mr Quarterstone earnestly. 'But I just bought my wife a fur coat, and she wants a new car, and that yacht we just bought set me back twenty thousand.'

Mr Urlaub shook his head.

'I know. It's not your fault. But isn't it just the toughest break?'

Quarterstone shook his head in sympathy. And then he looked at the Saint.

It was quite a performance, that look. It started casually, beheld inspiration, blazed with triumph, winked, glared significantly, poured out encouragement, pleaded, commanded, and asked and answered several questions, all in a few seconds. Mr Quarterstone had not at any period in his career actually held down the job of prompter, but he more than made up with enthusiasm for any lack of experience. Only a man who had been blind from birth could have failed to grasp the idea that Mr Quarterstone was suggesting; and the Saint had not strung along so far in order to feign blindness at the signal for his entrance.

Simon cleared his throat.

'Er—did you say you only needed another three thousand pounds to put on this play?' he asked diffidently, but with a clearly audible note of suppressed excitement.

After that he had to work no harder than he would have had to work to get himself eaten by a pair of hungry lions. Waldermar Urlaub, once the great light had dawned on him, skittered about like a pea on a drum in an orgy of exultant planning. Mr Tombs would have starred in the play anyhow, whenever the remainder of the necessary wind had been raised—Urlaub had already made up his mind to that—but if Mr Tombs had three thousand pounds as well as his genius and beauty, he would be more than a star. He could be co-producer as well, a sharer in the profits, a friend and an equal, in every way the heir to the position which the great Aaron Niementhal would have occupied. His name would go on the billing with double force—Urlaub grabbed a piece of paper and a pencil to illustrate it:

SEBASTIAN TOMBS
and
WALDEMAR URLAUB
*present*
SEBASTIAN TOMBS
in
LOVE—THE REDEEMER

There would also be lights on the theatre, advertisements, photographs, newspaper articles, news items, gossip paragraphs, parties, movie rights, screen tests, Hollywood, New York, beautiful and adoring women. . . . Mr Urlaub built up a luminous picture of fame, success and fortune, while Mr Quarterstone nodded benignly and slapped everybody on the back and beamed at the Saint at intervals with a sublimely smug expression of 'I told you so.'

'And they did all that to me, too,' said Rosalind Hale wryly. 'I was practically Sarah Bernhardt when they'd finished. . . . But I told you just how they did it. Why do you have to let yourself in for the same mess that I got into?'

'The easiest way to rob a bank is from the inside,' said the

Saint cryptically. 'I suppose you noticed that they really have got a play?'

'Yes. I read part of it—the same as you did.'

'Did you like it?'

She made a little grimace.

'You've got a right to laugh at me. I suppose that ought to have been warning enough; but Urlaub was so keen about it, and Quarterstone had already made me think he was a great producer, so I couldn't say that I thought it was awful. And then I wondered if it was just because I didn't know enough about plays.'

'I don't know much about plays myself,' said the Saint. 'But the fact remains that Comrade Urlaub has got a complete play, with three acts and everything, god-awful though it is. I took it away with me to read it over, and the more I look at it the more I'm thinking that something might be done with it.'

Rosalind was aghast.

'You don't mean to say you'd really put your money into producing it?'

'Stranger things have happened,' said the Saint thoughtfully. 'How bad can a play be before it becomes good? And how much sense of humour is there in the movie business? Haven't you seen those reprints of old two-reelers that they show sometimes for a joke, and haven't you heard the audience laughing itself sick? . . . Listen. I only wish I knew who wrote *Love—the Redeemer*. I've got an idea . . .'

Mr Homer Quarterstone could have answered his question for him, for the truth was that the author of *Love—the Redeemer* resided under the artistic black homburg of Mr Homer Quarterstone. It was a matter of considerable grief to Mr Quarterstone that no genuine producer had ever been induced to see eye to eye with him on the subject of the superlative merits of that amorous masterpiece, so that after he had grown weary of collecting rejections Mr Quarterstone had been reduced to the practical expedient of using his *magnum opus* as one of the props in the more profitable but by no means less artistic drama from

343

which he and Mr Urlaub derived their precarious incomes; but his loyalty to the child of his brain had never been shaken.

It was therefore with a strange squirmy sensation in the pit of his stomach that Mr Quarterstone sat in his office a few mornings later and gazed at a card in the bottom left-hand corner of which were the magic words 'Paragon Pictures, Inc., Hollywood, Calif.' A feeling of fate was about him, as if he had been unexpectedly reminded of a still-cherished childhood dream.

'Show her in,' he said, with husky magnificence.

The order was hardly necessary, for she came in at once, shepherded by a beaming Waldemar Urlaub.

'Just thought I'd give you a surprise, Homer,' he explained boisterously. 'Did your heart jump when you saw that card? Well, so did mine. Still, it's real. I fixed it all up. Sold her the play. "You can't go wrong," I said. "With one of the greatest dramas ever written—"'

Mrs Wohlbreit turned her back on him coldly and inspected Mr Quarterstone. She looked nothing like the average man's conception of a female from Hollywood, being gaunt and masculine with a sallow lined face and gold-rimmed glasses and mousey hair plastered back above her ears; but Mr Quarterstone had at least enough experience to know that women were used in Hollywood in executive positions which did not call for the decorative qualities of more publicised employees.

She said, in her cold masculine voice: 'Is this your agent?'

Mr Quarterstone swallowed.

'Ah—'

'Part owner,' said Mr Urlaub eagerly. 'That's right, isn't it, Homer? You know our agreement, fifty-fifty in everything. Eh? Well, I've been working on this deal—'

'I asked you,' said Mrs Wohlbreit penetratingly, 'because I understand that you're the owner of this play we're interested in. There are so many chisellers in this business that we make it our policy to approach the author first direct—if he wants to take any ten-per-centers in afterwards, that's his affair. I am the representative of Paragon Pictures in London. A Mr Tombs brought me the play first, and told me he had an interest in it. I found out that he got it from Mr Urlaub, so I went to him. Mr Urlaub told me that you were the original author. Now, who am I to talk business with?'

Mr Quarterstone saw his partner's mouth opening for another contribution.

'With—with us,' he said weakly.

It was not what he might have said if he had had time to think, but he was too excited to be particular.

'Very well,' said Mrs Wohlbreit. 'We've read this play, *Love—the Redeemer*, and we think it would make a grand picture. If you haven't done anything yet about the movie rights—'

Mr Quarterstone drew himself up. He felt as if he was in a daze from which he might be rudely awakened at any moment; but it was a beautiful daze. His heart was thumping, but his brain was calm and clear. It was, after all, only the moment with which he had always known that his genius must ultimately be rewarded.

'Ah—yes,' he said, with resonant calm. 'The movie rights are, for the moment, open to—ah—negotiation. Naturally, with a drama of such quality, dealing as it does with a problem so close to the lives of every member of the thinking public, and appealing to the deepest emotions and beliefs of every intelligent man and woman—'

'We thought it would make an excellent farce,' said Mrs Wohlbreit blandly. 'It's just the thing we've been looking for for a long time.' But before the stricken Mr Quarterstone could protest, she had added consolingly: 'We could afford to give you six thousand pounds for the rights.'

'Ah—quite,' said Mr Quarterstone bravely.

By the time that Mrs Wohlbreit had departed, after making an appointment for the contract to be signed and the cheque paid over at the Paragon offices the following afternoon, his wound had healed sufficiently to let him take Mr Urlaub in his arms, as soon as the door closed, and embrace him fondly in an impromptu rumba.

'Didn't I always tell you that play was a knock-out?' he crowed.

'It's taken 'em years to see it, but they had to wake up in the end. Six thousand pounds! Why, with that money I can—' He sensed a certain stiffness in his dancing partner, and hastily corrected himself: 'I mean, we—we can—'

'Nuts,' said Mr Urlaub coarsely. He disengaged himself and straightened the creases out of his natty suit. 'What you've got to do now is sit down and figure out a way to crowbar that guy Tombs out of this.'

Mr Quarterstone stopped dancing suddenly, and his jaw dropped.

'Tombs?'

'Yeah!' said Mr Urlaub, who had always imagined that it would be in keeping with his character to talk like a Broadway producer would. 'He wasn't so dumb. He had the sense to see that that play of yours was the funniest thing ever written. When we were talking about it in here, he must have thought we thought it was funny too.'

Mr Quarterstone was appalled as the idea of duplicity struck him.

'Waldemar—d'you think he was trying to—'

'No. I pumped the old battle-axe on the way here. He told her he only had a part interest, but he wanted to do something for the firm and give us a surprise—he thought he could play the lead in the picture, too.'

'Has she told him—'

'Not yet. You heard what she said. She gets in touch with the author first. But we got to get him before he gets in touch with her. Don't you remember those contracts we signed yesterday? Fifty per cent of the movie rights for him!'

Mr Quarterstone sank feebly on to the desk.

'Three thousand pounds!' he groaned. Then he brightened tentatively. 'But it's all right, Waldemar. He agreed to put three thousand pounds into producing the play, so we just call it quits and we don't have to give him anything.'

'You great, fat, lame-brained slob,' yelled Mr Urlaub affectionately. 'Quits! Like hell it's quits! D'you think I'm not going to put that play on, after this? It took that old battle-axe to see it, but she's right. They'll be rolling in the aisles!' He struck a Quarterstone-ish attitude. '"*I brought you a rose*,"' he uttered tremulously, '"*but you turned it into a nest of vipers in my bosom. They have stabbed my heart!*" My God! It's a natural! I'm going to put it on in the West End whatever we have to do to raise the dough—but we aren't going to cut that mug Tombs in on it.'

Mr Quarterstone winced.

'It's all signed up legal,' he said dolefully. 'We'll have to spend our own dough and buy him out.'

'Get your hat,' said Mr Urlaub shortly. 'We'll cook up a story on the way.'

When Rosalind Hale walked into the Saint's apartment at Cornwall House that afternoon, Simon Templar was counting crisp new twenty-pound notes into neat piles.

'What have you been doing?' she said. 'Burgling a bank?'

The Saint grinned.

'The geetus came out of a bank, anyway,' he murmured. 'But Comrades Quarterstone and Urlaub provided the cheques. I just went out and cashed them.'

'You mean they bought you out?'

'After a certain amount of haggling and squealing—yes. Apparently Aaron Niementhal changed his mind about backing the show, and Urlaub didn't want to offend him on account of Aaron offered to cut him in on another and bigger and better proposition at the same time; so they gave me two thousand quid to tear up the contracts, and the idea is that I ought to play the lead in Niementhal's bigger and better show.'

She pulled off her hat and collapsed into a chair. She was no longer gaunt and masculine and forbidding, for she had changed out of a badly fitting tweed suit and removed her sallow make-up and thrown away the gold-rimmed glasses and fluffed out her hair again so that it curled in its usual soft brown waves around her face, so that her last resemblance to anyone by the name of Wohlbreit was gone.

'Two thousand pounds,' she said limply. 'It doesn't seem possible. But it's real. I can see it.'

'You can touch it, if you like,' said the Saint. 'Here.'

He pushed one of the stacks over the table towards her. 'Three hundred that you paid Quarterstone for tuition.' He pushed another. 'Eight hundred that you put into the play.' He drew a smaller sheaf towards himself. 'Two hundred that I paid for my lessons. Leaving seven hundred drops of gravy to be split two ways.'

He straightened the remaining pile, cut it in two, and slid half of it on to join the share that was accumulating in front of her. She stared at the money helplessly for a second or two, reached out and touched it with the tip of her fingers; and then suddenly she came round the table and flung herself into his arms. Her cheek was wet where it touched his face.

'I don't know how to say it,' she said shakily. 'But you know what I mean.'

'There's only one thing bothering me,' said the Saint, some time later, 'and that's whether you're really entitled to take back those tuition fees. After all, Homer made you a good enough actress to fool himself. Maybe he was entitled to a percentage, in spite of everything.'

His doubts, however, were set at rest several months afterwards, when he had travelled a long way from London and many other things had happened, when one day an advertisement in a London paper caught his eye:

---

14th Week!
Sold out 3 months ahead!
The Farce Hit of the Season:

**LOVE—THE REDEEMER**

by Homer Quarterstone
Imperial Theatre.
A Waldemar Urlaub Production

---

Simon Templar was not often at a loss for words, but on this occasion he was tongue-tied for a long time. And then, at last, he lay back and laughed helplessly.

'Oh, well,' he said. 'I guess they earned it.'

I

Chief Inspector Claud Eustace Teal unfolded the paper wrapping from a leaf of chewing-gum with slow-moving pudgy fingers, and the sleepy china-blue eyes in his pink chubby face blinked across the table with the bland expressionlessness of a doll.

'Of course I know your point of view,' he said flatly. 'I'm not a fool. I know that you've never done anything which I could complain about if I were just a spectator. I know that all the men you've robbed and . . .' the somnolent eyes steadied themselves deliberately for a moment—'and killed,' he said, 'they've all deserved it—in a way. But I also know that, technically, you're the most dangerous and persistent criminal outside of prison. I'm a police officer, and my job is technicalities.'

'Such as pulling in some wretched innkeeper for selling a glass of beer at the wrong time, while the man who floats a million-pound swindle gets away on a point of law,' Simon Templar suggested gently; and the detective nodded.

'That's my job,' he said, 'and you know it.'

The Saint smiled.

'I know it, Claud,' he murmured. 'But it's also the reason for my own career of crime.'

'That, and the money you make out of it,' said the detective, with a tinge of gloomy cynicism in his voice.

'And, as you say, the boodle,' Simon agreed shamelessly.

Mr Teal sighed.

In that stolid, methodical, honest, plodding, unimaginative and uninspired mechanism which was his mind, there lingered the memory of many defeats—of the countless times when he had gone up against that blithe and bantering buccaneer, and his long-suffering tail had been mercilessly pulled, stretched, twisted, strung with a pendant of tin-cans and fireworks, and finally nailed firmly down between his legs; and it was not a pleasant reflection. Also in his consciousness was the fact that the price of his dinner had undoubtedly been paid out of the boodle of some other buccaneering foray, and the additional disturbing fact that he had enjoyed his dinner immensely from the first moment to the last. It was very hard for him to reconcile those three conflicting emanations from his brain; and his heavy-lidded eyes masked themselves even deeper under their perpetual affectation of weariness as he rolled the underwear of his spearmint ration into a small pink ball and flicked it across the restaurant tablecloth. He might even have been phrasing some suitable reply which should have comprehended all the opalescent facets of his paradox in one masterly sentence; but at that moment a waiter came to the table.

The chronicler, a conscientious and respectable citizen whose income-tax payments are never more than two years in arrears, hesitates over those last ten words. He bounces, like an inexpert matador on the antlers of an Andalusian bull, upon the horns of a dilemma. All his artistic soul, all that lumescent literary genius which has won him the applause and reverence of the reading world, rises in shuddering protest against that scant dismissal. He feels that this waiter, who rejoiced in the name of Bassanio Quinquapotti, should have more space. He is tempted to elaborate at much greater length the origin and obscure beginnings of this harbinger of fate, this dickey-bird of destiny; to expatiate in pages of elegant verbiage upon the psychological motivations which put him into permanent evening dress, upon his feverish sex life, and upon the atrophied talent which made him such a popular performer on the sackbut at informal Soho soirées. For this waiter, who came to the table, was the herald of five million golden pounds, the augur of one of the Saint's most satisfactory adventures, and the outrider of yet another of the melancholy journeys of Mr Teal. With all these things in mind, the sensitive psyche of the historian revolts from that terse unceremonious description—'a waiter came to the table.' And only the bloodthirsty impatience of editors and publishers forces him to press on.

'Excuse me, sir,' said this waiter (whose name, we insist on recording, was Bassanio Quinquapotti), 'but are you Mr Teal?'

'That's right,' said the detective.

'You're wanted on the telephone, sir,' said the waiter (Bassanio Quinquapotti).

Mr Teal got up and left the table. Ulysses, at some time or another, must have got up and left a table with the same limpid innocence, undreaming of the odyssey which lay before him . . . And the Saint lighted a cigarette and watched him go.

It was one of those rare occasions when Simon Templar's conscience carried no load; when his restless brain was inevitably plotting some fresh audacious mischief, as it always was, but there was no definite incident in the daily chronicles of London crime which could give Scotland Yard cause to inquire interestedly into his movements; and Chief Inspector Teal was enjoying a brief precarious interlude of peace. At those times the Saint could beguile Mr Teal into sharing a meal with him, and Mr Teal would accept it with an air of implacable suspicion; but they would both end their evening with a vague feeling of regret.

On this particular occasion, however, thanks to the egregious Mr Quinquapotti, the feeling of regret was doomed on one side to be the reverse of vague; but this vision of the future was hidden from Claud Eustace Teal.

He wedged himself into the telephone booth in the foyer of the restaurant with the pathetic trustfulness of a guinea-pig trotting into a vivisectionist's laboratory, and took up the receiver.

'Teal speaking,' he said.

The familiar voice of his assistant at the Yard clacked back at him through the diaphragm. It uttered one sentence. It uttered another.

The voice of Mr Teal's assistant went on uttering, and the mouth of Mr Teal opened wider as the recital went on. The milk of human kindness, always an unstable element in Mr Teal's sorely tried cosmogony, curdled while he listened. By the time his assistant had finished, it would, if laid aside in a cool place, have turned itself gradually into a piece of cheese.

'All right,' he said thickly, at the end. 'I'll call you back.'

He hung up the receiver and levered himself out of the cabinet. Squeezing his way between the tables on his way back across the restaurant, he was grimly conscious of the Saint's face watching his approach. It was a face that inevitably stood out among the groups of commonplace diners, a lean and darkly handsome face which would have arrested any wandering glance; but it was no less inevitably the face of an Elizabethan buccaneer, lacking only the beard. The lean relaxed figure struck the imagination like a sword laid down among puddings; and for the same reason it was indescribably dangerous. The very clear and humorous blue eyes had a mocking recklessness which could never have stood in awe of man or devil; and Mr Teal knew that that also was true. The detective's mind went back once again over the times when he had confronted that face, that debonair immaculate figure, those gay piratical blue eyes; and the remembrance was no more comforting than it had been before. But he went back to the table, and sat down.

'Thanks for the dinner, Saint,' he said.

Simon blew a smoke-ring.

'I enjoyed it, too,' he remarked. 'Call it a small compensation for the other times when everything hasn't been so rosy. I often feel that if only our twin souls, freed from the contagion of this detectivitis which comes over you sometimes—'

'It's a pity you didn't complete the party,' Teal said with a certain curious shortness.

The Saint raised his eyebrows.

'How?'

'That American gunman you've been going about with, for instance—what's his name?'

'Hoppy Uniatz? He's gone to the Ring to have a look at some wrestling. Ran into some Yankee grunter he knew over on the other side, who's doing a tour over here; so Hoppy felt he'd better go and root for him.'

'Yes?' Teal was jerkily unwrapping a fresh slice of gum, although the wad in his mouth was still putting forth flavour in a brave endeavour to live up to its advertising department. 'He wouldn't have gone there alone, of course.'

'I think he went with this wriggler's manager and a couple of his clutching partners,' said the Saint.

Mr Teal nodded. Something was happening to his blood pressure—something which had begun its deadly work while he was listening to the voice of his assistant on the telephone. He knew all the symptoms. The movements with which he folded his wafer of naked spearmint and stuffed it into his mouth had a stupendous slothfulness which cost him a frightful effort to maintain.

'Or your girl friend, perhaps—Patricia Holm?' Teal articulated slowly. 'What's happened to her?'

'She came over all evening dress and went to a party—one of these Mayfair orgies. Apart from that she's quite normal.'

'She'd have a good time at a party, wouldn't she?' Teal said ruminatively.

The Saint swilled liqueur brandy around in the bowl of a pear-shaped glass.

'I believe lots of young men do get trampled to death in the stampede when she turns up,' he admitted.

'But there'd be enough survivors left to be able to swear she'd been dancing or sitting out with one or other of 'em from the time she arrived till well after midnight—wouldn't there?' Teal insisted. Simon sat up. For one or two minutes past he had been aware that a change had come over the detective since he returned to the table, and there had been a sudden grittiness in the way that last question mark had been tagged on which he couldn't have missed if he had been stone deaf. He looked Teal over with thoughtful blue eyes.

'Claud!' he exclaimed accusingly. 'I believe there's something on your mind!'

For a moment Teal's windpipe tied itself into a knot of indignation which threatened to strangle him. And then, with a kind of dogged resolution, he untied it and waded on.

'There's plenty on my mind,' he said crunchily. 'And you know what it is. I suppose you've been laughing yourself sick ever since you sat down at the table. I suppose you've been wondering if there were any limits on earth to what you could make me swallow. Well, I've bought it. I've given you your rope. And now suppose you tell me why you think it isn't going to hang you?'

'Claud?' The Saint's voice was wicked. 'Are you sure you haven't had too much of this brandy? I feel that your bile is running away with you. Is this—'

'Never mind my bile!' Teal got out through his teeth. 'I'm waiting for you to talk about something else. And before you start, let me tell you that I'm going to tear this alibi to pieces if it takes me the rest of my life!'

Simon raised his eyebrows. 'Alibi?' he repeated gently.

'That's what I said.'

'I don't know what you're talking about.'

'No?' Teal meant to be derisive, but the word plopped out of his mouth like a cork out of a bottle. 'I'm talking about this precious alibi of yours which accounts for everything that fellow Uniatz and that girl Patricia Holm have been doing all the evening— and probably accounts for all your other friends as well. I mean this alibi you think you've framed me into giving you—'

'What on earth are you talking about?' asked the Saint patiently; and Teal drew another laboured breath.

'I mean,' he said—and all the cumulative rancour of five years of that unequal duel was rasping through his voice like a red-hot file—'I mean that you must be thinking it was damned clever of you to get me to have dinner with you on this night of all nights, and keep me here with you from seven o'clock till now, when a dead man was picked up on the Brighton road half an hour ago with your mark on him!'

II

Simon stared at him blankly. And even while he did so, he realised that he was letting the opportunity of a lifetime of Teal-baiting dawdle past him and raise its hat as it went by, without so much as lifting a hand to grab it. To be accused for once of a crime of which he was as innocent as an unborn Eskimo, and to have a made-to-measure alibi presented to him on a plate at the same time, should have presented vistas of gorgeous possibility to warm the heart. But he didn't even see them. He was too genuinely interested.

'Say that again,' he suggested.

'You've heard me already,' retorted the detective gratingly. 'It's your turn now. Well, I'm waiting for it. I like your fairy-tales. What is it this time? Did he commit suicide and tie your mark round his neck for a joke? Did the Emperor of Abyssinia do it for you, or was it arranged by the Sultan of Turkey? Whatever your story is, I'll hear it!'

It has been urged by some captious critics of these records that Chief Inspector Teal has rarely been observed in them to behave like a normal detective. This charge the scribe is forced to admit. But he points out that there are very few of these chronicles in which Chief Inspector Teal has had any chance to be a normal detective. Confronted with the slow smile and bantering blue eyes of the Saint, something went haywire inside Mr Teal. He was not himself. He was overwrought. He gave way. He behaved, in fact, exactly as a man who had been burned many times might have been expected to behave in the presence of fire. But it wasn't his fault; and the Saint knew it.

'Now wait a minute, you prize fathead,' Simon answered quite pleasantly, 'I didn't kill this bloke—'

'I know you didn't,' said Teal in an ecstasy of elephantine sarcasm. 'You've been sitting here talking to me all the time. This fellow just died. He drew your picture on a piece of paper, and had heart failure when he looked at it.'

'Your guess is as good as mine, Claud,' drawled the Saint lazily. 'But personally I should say that some low crook is trying to frame me.'

'You would, eh? Well, if I were looking for this low crook—'

'You'd come to my address.' Simon pushed his cigarette into

an ashtray, finished his drink, and spread money on the table to pay the bill. 'Well, here I am. You gave me the murder and you gave me the alibi. You thought of this game. Why don't you get on with it? Am I arrested?'

Teal gulped and swallowed a piece of gum.

'You'll be arrested as soon as I know some more about this murder. I know where to find you—'

The Saint smiled.

'I seem to have heard words to that effect before,' he said. 'But it hasn't always worked out quite that way. My movements are so erratic. Why take a chance? Let me arrest myself. My car's just round the corner, and the night is before us. Let's go and find out some more about this murder of mine.'

He stood up; and for some unearthly reason Teal also rose to his feet. An exasperating little bug of uncertainty was hatching out in the detective's brain and starting to dig itself in. He had been through these scenes before, and they had lopped years off his expectation of life. He had known the Saint guilty of innumerable felonies and breaches of the peace, beyond any possible shadow of human doubt, and had got nothing out of it—nothing, but a smile of infuriating innocence, and a glimmer of mocking amusement in the Saint's eyes which was not evidence. He was used to being outwitted, but it had never occurred to him that he might be wrong. Until that very moment, when the smile of infuriating innocence was so startlingly absent . . . He didn't believe it even then—he had reached the stage when nothing that Simon Templar said or did could be taken at its face value—but the germ of preposterous doubt was brooding in his mind, and he followed the Saint out into the street in silence, without understanding why he did it.

'Where did this news come from?' Simon inquired, as he slid in behind the wheel of the great shining Hirondel which was parked close by.

'Horley,' Teal replied curtly, and couldn't help adding: 'You ought to know.'

The Saint made no retort; and that again was unusual. The

tiny maggot of incertitude in Teal's brain laid another egg, and he chewed steadily on his remaining sludge of spearmint in self-defensive taciturnity while the long thrumming nose of the car threaded its way at breath-taking speed through the thinning traffic of South London.

Simon kindled a fresh cigarette from the lighter on the dash and thrust the Hirondel over the southward artery with one hand on the wheel and the speedometer quivering around seventy, driving automatically and thinking about other things. Before that, he had sometimes wondered why such a notorious scapegoat as himself should have been passed over for so long by the alibi experts of the underworld, and he had only been able to surmise that the fear of attracting his own attention was what had deterred them. The man who had set a new precedent this night must either have been very confident or very rash; and the Saint wanted to know him. And there was an edge of quiet steel in the Saint's narrowed eyes as they followed the road in the blaze of his sweeping headlights which indicated that he would have an account to settle with his unauthorised substitute when they met . . .

Perhaps it was because he was very anxious to learn something more which might help to bring that meeting nearer, or perhaps it was only because the Saint never felt really comfortable in a car unless it was using the king's highway for a race-track, but it was exactly thirty-five minutes after they left the restaurant when he swung the car round the last two-wheeled corner and switched off the engine under the blue lamp of Horley Police Station. For the latter half of the journey Mr Teal had actually forgotten to chew; but he released his hold on his bowler hat and climbed out phlegmatically enough. Simon followed him up the steps, and heard Teal introduce himself to the night sergeant.

'They're in the inspector's office, sir,' said the man.

Simon went in at Teal's shoulder, and found three men drinking coffee in the bare distempered room. One of them, from his typical bulk and the chair he occupied at the desk, appeared to be the inspector; the second, a grey-haired man in pince-nez and an overcoat, was apparently the police surgeon; the third was a motorcycle patrol in uniform.

'I thought I'd better come down at once,' Teal said laconically.

The inspector, who shared the dislike of all provincial inspectors for interference from Scotland Yard, but accepted it as an unfortunate necessity, nodded no less briefly and indicated the motorcycle patrol.

'He can tell you all about it.'

'There ain't much to tell, sir,' said the patrol, putting down his cup. 'Just about two mile from here, it was, on the way to Balcombe. I was on me way home when I saw a car pulled up by the side of the road an' two men beside it carryin' what looked like a body. Well, it turned out it was a body. They said they saw it lyin' in the road an' thought it was someone been knocked down by another car, but when I had a look I saw the man had been shot. I helped 'em put the body in their car and rode in alongside of 'em to the police station here.'

'What time was this?' Teal asked him.

'About half-past ten, sir, when I first stopped. It was exactly a quarter to eleven when we got here.'

'How had this man been shot?'

It was the doctor who answered.

'He was shot through the back of the head at close range— probably with an automatic or a revolver. Death must have been instantaneous.'

Mr Teal rolled his gum into a spindle, pushed his tongue into the middle to shape a horseshoe, and chewed it back into a ball.

'I was told you'd found the Saint's mark on the body,' he said. 'When was that?'

The inspector turned over the papers on his desk.

'That was when we were going through his things. It was in his outside breast pocket.'

He found a scrap of paper and handed it over. Teal took it and smoothed it out. It was a leaf torn from a cheap pocket diary; and on one side of it had been drawn, in pencil, a squiggly skeleton figure whose round blank head was crowned with a slanting elliptical halo.

Teal's heavy eyes rested on the drawing for a few seconds, and then he turned and held it out to the Saint.

'And I suppose you didn't do that?' he said.

There was a sudden stillness of incomprehension over the other men in the room, who had accepted Simon without introduction as an assistant of the Scotland Yard man; and Teal glanced back at them with inscrutable stolidity.

'This is the Saint,' he explained.

A rustle of astonishment stirred the local men, and Teal bit on his gum and met it with his own soured disillusion: 'No, I haven't done anything clever. He's been with me all the evening. He hasn't been out of my sight from seven o'clock till now—not for five minutes.'

The police surgeon blew a bubble in his coffee-cup and wiped his lips on his handkerchief, gaping at him stupidly.

'But that's impossible!' he spluttered. 'The body was still warm when I saw it, and the pupils dilated with atropine. He couldn't have been dead three hours at the outside!'

'I expected something like that,' said the detective, with sweltering restraint. 'That's all it wanted to round off the alibi.'

Simon put the torn scrap of paper back on the inspector's desk. It had given him a queer feeling looking at that crude sketch on it. He hadn't drawn it; but it was his. It had become too well known for him to be able to use it very often now, for the precise reason which Mr Teal had overlooked—that when that little drawing was found anywhere on the scene of a crime, there was only one man to search for. But it still had its meaning. That childish haloed figure had stood for an ideal, for a justice that struck swiftly where the Law could not strike, a terror which could not be turned aside by technicalities: it had never been used wantonly . . . The three local men were staring at him inquisitively, more like morbid sightseers at a sensational trial than professional sifters of crime; but the Saint's gaze met them with an arctic calm.

'Who was this man?' he asked.

The inspector did not answer at once, until Teal's shifting glance repeated the question. Then he turned back to the things on his desk.

'He had a Spanish passport—nothing seems to have been stolen from him. The name is—here it is—Enrique. Manuel Enrique. Age thirty; domicile, Madrid.'

'Occupation?'

The inspector frowned over the booklet.

'Aviator,' he said.

Simon took out his cigarette-case, and his eyes travelled thoughtfully back to the drawing which was not his. It was certainly rather squiggly.

'Who were these men who picked him up on the road?'

Again the inspector hesitated, and again Teal's attitude repeated the interrogation. The inspector compressed his lips. He disapproved of the proceedings entirely. If he'd had his way, the Saint would have been safely locked away in a cell in no time— not taking up a cross-examination of his own. With the air of a vegetarian being forcibly fed with human flesh, he picked up a closely-written report sheet.

'Sir Hugo Renway, of March House, Betfield, near Folkestone, and his chauffeur, John Kellard,' he recited tersely.

'I suppose they didn't stay long?'

The inspector leaned back so that his chair creaked.

'Do you think I ought to have arrested them?' he inquired ponderously.

The doctor smirked patronisingly, and said: 'Sir Hugo is a Justice of the Peace and a permanent official of the Treasury.'

'Wearing top hat and spats?' asked the Saint dreamily.

'He was not wearing a top hat.'

The Saint smiled; and it was a smile which made Mr Teal queerly uneasy. The little beetle of dubiety in his mind laid another clutch of eggs and sat on them. In some way he felt that he was losing his depth, and the sensation lifted his temperature a degree nearer to boiling point.

'Well, Claud,' the Saint was saying, 'we're making progress. I arrested myself to come down here, and I'm always ready to go on doing your work for you. Shall I charge myself, search myself, and lock myself up in a cell? Or what?'

'I'll think it over and let you know,' said the detective jaggedly.

'Go on a fish diet and give your brain a chance,' Simon advised him.

He trod on his cigarette-end and buttoned his coat; and his blue eyes went back to Mr Teal with a level recklessness of challenge which was like a draught of wind on the embers of Teal's temper.

'I'm telling you again that I don't know a thing about this bird Manuel Enrique, beyond what I've heard here. I don't expect you to believe me, because you haven't that much intelligence; but it happens to be the truth. My conscience is as clean as your shirt was before you put it on—'

'You're a liar,' brayed the detective.

'Doubtless you know your own laundry best,' said the Saint equably; and then his eyes chilled again. 'But that's about all you do know. You're not a detective—you're a homing pigeon. When in doubt, shove it on the Saint—that's your motto. Well, Claud, just for this once, I'm going to take the trouble to chew you up. I'm going to get your man. I've got a quarrel with anyone who takes my trade-mark in vain; and the lesson'll do you some good as well. And then you're going to come crawling to me on your great fat belly—'

In a kind of hysteria, Teal squirmed away from the sinewy brown forefinger which stabbed at his proudest possession.

'Don't do it!' he blared.

'—and apologise,' said the Saint; and in spite of himself, in spite of every obdurately logical belief he held, Chief Inspector Teal thought for a moment that he would not have liked to stand in the shoes of the man who ventured to impersonate the owner of that quiet satirical voice.

III

March House, from one of the large-scale ordnance maps of which Simon Templar kept a complete and up-to-date library, appeared to be an estate of some thirty acres lying between the village of Betfield and the sea. Part of the southern boundary was formed by the cliffs themselves, and a secondary road from Betfield to the main Folkestone highway skirted it on the north-west. The Saint sat over his maps with a glass of sherry for half an hour before dinner the following evening, memorising the topography— he had always been a firm believer in direct action, and, wanting to know more about a man, nothing appealed to him with more seductive simplicity than the obvious course of going to his house and taking an optimistic gander at the scenery.

'But whatever makes you think Renway had anything to do with it?' asked Patricia Holm.

'The top hat and spats,' Simon told her gravely. He smiled. 'I'm afraid I haven't got the childlike faith of a policeman, lass, and that's all there is to it. Claud Eustace would take the costume as a badge of respectability, but to my sad and worldly mind it's just the reverse. From what I could gather, Hugo wasn't actually sporting the top hat at the time, but he seems to have been that kind of man. And the picture they found on the body was rather squiggly— as it might have been if a bloke had drawn it in a car, travelling along . . . I know it's only one chance in a hundred, but it's a chance. And we haven't any other clue in the whole wide world.'

Hoppy Uniatz had no natural gift for subtlety, but he did understand direct action. Out of the entire panorama of human endeavour, it was about the only thing which really penetrated through all the layers of bullet-proof ivory which protected his brain. Detaching his mouth momentarily from a tumbler of gin, nominally diluted with ginger-ale, he said: 'I'll come wit' ya, boss.'

'Is it in your line?' asked the Saint.

'I dunno,' Hoppy confessed frankly. 'I ain't never done no boiglary. Whadda we have to wear dis costume for?'

Patricia looked at him blankly. 'What costume?'

'De top hat an' spats,' said Hoppy Uniatz.

The Saint covered his eyes.

Six hours later, braking the Hirondel to a smooth standstill under an overarching elm where the road touched the north-west boundary of March House, Simon felt more practically cautious about accepting Hoppy's offer of assistance. On such an expedition as he had undertaken, a sportive elephant would certainly have been less use; but not much less. All the same, he had no wish to offend Mr Uniatz, whose proud spirit was perhaps unduly sensitive on such points. He swung himself out into the road, detached the spare wheel, and opened up the tool-kit, while Hoppy stared at him puzzledly.

'This is where you come in,' the Saint told him flatteringly. 'You're going to be an unfortunate motorist with a puncture, toiling over the wheel.'

Mr Uniatz blinked at him dimly.

'Is dat part of the boiglary?' he asked.

'Of course it is,' said the Saint unscrupulously. 'It's probably the most important part. You never know when some village slop may come paddling around these parts, and if he saw a car standing by the road with nobody in it he'd naturally be suspicious.'

Hoppy reached round for his hip flask, and nodded.

'OK, boss,' he said. 'I get it. If de cop comes while you're gone, I give him de woiks.'

'You don't do anything of the sort,' said the Saint wearily. 'They don't allow you to kill policemen in this country. What you do is to give your very best imitation of a guy fixing a flat. You might possibly get into conversation with him. Talk sentimentally about the little woman at home, waiting for her man. Make him feel homesick, and encourage him to push on. But you don't give him de woiks.'

'OK, boss,' repeated Hoppy accommodatingly. 'I'll fix it.'

'God help you if you don't,' said the Saint harrowingly, and left him to it.

The frontier of the March House estate at that point consisted of a strong board fence about eight feet high, topped with three lines of barbed-wire carried on spiked iron brackets beetling outwards at an angle: the arrangement was effective enough to have checked any less experienced and determined trespasser than the Saint, and even Simon might have wasted some time over it if it had not been for the overhanging elm under which he had thoughtfully stopped his car. But by balancing himself precariously on the side of the tonneau and leaping upwards, he was able to get a fingerhold on one of the lower branches; and he swung himself up on to it as if Tarzan had been his grandfather.

Finding his way through the tree, in the dark, was not quite so easy; but he managed it more or less silently, and dropped from another branch on to a mat of short undergrowth on the inside of the fence.

From there, while the muffled mutterings of Hoppy Uniatz wrestling with a wheel drifted faintly to his ears, he surveyed the lie of the land ahead of him. He was in a spinney of young trees and brushwood, barred here and there with the holes of older trees similar to the one by which he had made his entrance; a half-moon, peeping fitfully between squadrons of cirrus cloud, gave his night-hunter's eyes enough light to make out that broad impression and at the same time suggested an open space some distance farther on beyond the coppice. The house itself stood roughly in the same direction, according to his map-reading; and with a fleeting smile for the complete craziness of his intentions he began to pick his way through the scrub towards it.

A small bird let out a startled squeak at his feet and went whirring away into the dark, and from time to time he heard the rustlings of diminutive animal life scurrying away from his approach; but he encountered no pitfalls or tripwires or other unpleasant accidents. The clear space ahead was farther away

THE BEST OF THE SAINT

than he had thought at first, and as he went on he seemed to make very little progress towards it. Presently he understood why, when he broke out through a patch of thinner shrubbery into what seemed to be a long narrow field laid out broadside to his route: twenty yards away, on the other side, was a single rank of taller trees linked by what appeared to be another fence—it was this wall of shadow and line of lifting tree-trunks which he had never seemed to come any nearer to as he threaded his way through the spinney.

As he crossed the field and came close to this inner boundary, he saw that it was not a fence, but a loosely grown hedge about six feet high. He was able to see this without any difficulty, because when he was still a couple of yards away the pattern of it was suddenly thrown up in silhouette by the kindling of a light behind it. At first his only impression was that the moon had chosen that moment for one of its periodical peeps from behind the drifting flotillas of cloud. Then, very quickly, the light flared up brighter. He saw the patchwork shadow of the hedge printed on his own clothes, and instinctively ducked behind the sheltering blackness of the nearest tree. And as he did so he became aware that the humming noise he had been hearing had grown much louder.

It was a noise which had been going on, very faintly, for some time; but he had thought nothing of it. A car passing on another road half a mile away might have caused it, and a subconscious suggestion of the same car drawing nearer had prevented him paying much attention to the first increase in its volume. But at this moment it had swelled into a steady drone that was too powerful and unvarying for any ordinary car to make, rising to the indefinable border-line of assertiveness at which his sense of hearing was jolted into sitting up and taking notice. He listened to it, frowning, while it grew to a sharp roar—and then stopped altogether.

The Saint remained as still as the tree beside which he stood, as if he had been an integral part of it, and looked out over the hedge at the field where the light was. Rising a little on his toes, he was able to get a clear view of it and see the cause of the light.

A double row of flares was being kindled in the field, like a file of tiny brilliant bonfires. With a sudden jerk of understanding, he remembered other days in his life, and knew what they were. Mounds of cotton waste soaked in petrol or paraffin. Even while he watched, the last of them was lighted: a reddish glow danced in the dark, licked up into a tentative flame, and sprang suddenly into blazing luminance. The shadow of the man who had lit it stretched out in a sudden long bar of blackness into the surrounding gloom where the light exhausted itself. The twin rank of flares was complete, forming a broad lane of light from north-west to south-east, six flares to each side, two hundred yards long at a rough guess. The dimension of the field beyond that was lost in the darkness which lapped the light.

Over his head there was a rush of air and a dying hiss of wind as though a monstrous bird sighed across the sky. Looking upwards, he saw a shadow like a great black cross diving against the hazy luminousness of the clouds, barely skimming the tree-tops: it plunged into the lane of light, gathering shape and detail—flattened out, bumped once, and landed.

Almost at the same moment the nearer flares began to flicker and die down. One of them went out; then another . . .

'Never again, so long as I live, will I be rude to Luck,' the Saint said to Patricia Holm, much later. 'For every dozen minor troubles the little lady gives us, somehow or other she manages to let you draw three to a straight flush and fill your hand—once or twice in a lifetime.'

He stood, fascinated, and watched the flares going out. Fifteen minutes earlier, he might have run into no end of trouble, without profit to himself or anybody else; fifteen minutes later, there might have been nothing whatever to see; only the blind gods of chance had permitted him to arrive at the exact moment when things were happening. In the outer glow of the farthest flare he saw a man attaching himself to the tail of the aeroplane and beginning to push it farther into the darkness; in a few seconds he was joined by the pilot, unidentifiable in helmet and goggles and leather coat. The engine had been switched off as the ship touched the deck, and the last scene of the drama was played out in utter silence. The two men wheeled the machine away, presumably into some invisible hangar: the last flare wavered and blinked, and the fitful gloom of the night came down once again upon the scene.

Simon Templar drew a long deep breath, and stepped back out of the shadow of his tree. Of all the sins which he might have accused the top hat and spats of Sir Hugo Renway of camouflaging, ordinary smuggling was the last; but he was always accessible to new ideas.

In this case, the most obvious course which presented itself was a further and yet more sleuth-like investigation into the topography and individual peculiarities of March House; and with the sublime abandon of the congenitally insane he proposed to pursue the said course without delay. The last flare was finally extinguished, and the peaceful darkness settled once more upon the field. As far as anyone outside the estate could have told, the aeroplane had flown on across the Channel—if any reflected glow of light had been visible beyond the belt of woodland through which he had passed, and the high fence beside the road, it could hardly have attracted any ordinary citizen's attention, and it had lasted such a short time that there would have been nothing particularly remarkable about it anyway. But to anyone who had been privileged to witness the performance from the inside, the whole thing was highly furtive and irregular, especially at the country house of a Justice of the Peace and permanent Treasury official; and the Saint could see nothing for it but to intrude.

And it was at this psychological moment that the moon, to whose coy tactics we have already had occasion to refer, elected once again to say peekaboo to the slumbering world.

Simon Templar had owed his life to many queer things, from opening a window to dropping a cigarette, but he had never owed it before to such a rustic combination of items as a flirtatious moon and a rabbit. The rabbit appeared about one second after the moon, by lolloping out of a bush into the pool of twilight which the moon provided between two trees. The Saint had been so absolutely immobile in his observation post by the tree-trunk that it could never even have noticed him: it had simply been attracted by the lighting effects provided in the adjoining field, and, being a bunny of scientific appetites and an inquisitive turn of mind, it had suspended its foraging for a space to explore this curious phenomenon. Simon saw the moving blur of it out of the corner of his eye before he realised what it was, and froze instinctively back into motionlessness almost before he had begun to move. Then he saw the rabbit clearly, and moved again. A dry leaf rustled under his foot, and the rabbit twitched its nose and decided to abandon its cosmic investigations for that evening.

But it didn't lollop back into the bush from which it had emerged. Perhaps it had a date with some loose-moralled doe in the next parish, and had merely paused to admire the wonders of nature on its way to more serious business; or perhaps it had only heard news of some fresh, young lettuces sprouting in the kitchen gardens of March House; only its reincarnation in the shape of a theosophist will ever tell. But at all events, it pushed on instead of turning back. It made a rapid hopping dive for the nearest gap in the hedge through which Simon himself had been preparing to pass.

And it died.

There was a momentary flash of blue flame, and the rabbit kicked over backwards in a dreadful leap and lay twitching in the patch of moonlight.

## IV

Simon turned it over with his foot: it was indubitably one of the deadest rabbits in the county of Kent. Then he took a tiny flashlight from his pocket and examined the hedge with great caution. There were lines of gleaming copper wire strung through it at intervals of about six inches and rising to a height of six feet above the ground—if he had not stopped to watch the rabbit he could not have helped touching one of them.

The Saint pushed a hand somewhat unsteadily across his forehead, and turned his attention to the tree. But there was no chance there of repeating his Tarzan impersonation, for there were similar copper wires coiled round the trunk to a greater height than he could reach. Without rubber gloves and insulated wire-cutters he could go no farther; and he had no doubt that the same high-voltage circuit continued all the way round the landing-field and enclosed everything else that might be interesting to look at.

Twenty minutes later he dropped out of another tree into the road beside his car, and found Hoppy Uniatz sitting on the running-board and gazing disconsolately at an inadequate hip-flask which had long since run as dry as a Saharan water-hole.

'Hi, boss,' said Mr Uniatz, rising stiffly from his unprofitable meditations. 'Dijja get de dough?'

Simon shook his head, lighting a cigarette in his cupped hands.

'I didn't get to first base,' he said. 'A rabbit stopped me.' He saw a vacuous expression of perplexity appear on Mr Uniatz's homely dial, and extinguished his lighter with a faint grin. 'Never mind, Hoppy. Pass it up. I'll tell you all about it next year. Let's get back to London.'

He slid into the driving seat; and Mr Uniatz put his flask away and followed him more slowly, glancing back doubtfully over his shoulder with a preoccupied air. As Simon pressed the starter, he coughed.

'Boss,' said Mr Uniatz diffidently. 'Is it oke leavin' de cop here?'

'Leaving the which?' ejaculated the Saint limply.

'De cop,' said Mr Uniatz.

Simon pushed the gear lever back into neutral and gazed at him.

'What are you talking about?' he inquired.

'Ya see, boss,' said Mr Uniatz, with the manner of Einstein solving a problem in elementary arithmetic, 'de tyre wasn't flat.'

'What tyre?' asked the Saint heroically.

'De tyre you told me to change,' explained Hoppy. 'Ya told me to fix de flat, but it wasn't.'

The Saint struggled with his vocabulary in an anguished silence, seeking words in which he might deal suitably with the situation; but before he had counted all the syllables in the phrases he proposed to use, Mr Uniatz was ploughing on, as if determined, now that he had started, to make a clean breast of the matter.

'Well, boss, I put back de wheel an' sat down to wait for de cop. After a bit he rides up on a bicycle. "Hi-yah, guy," he says, "whaddaya doin' here?" So I tells him I was fixin' a flat, but it wasn't. "Well, whaddaya waitin' for?" he says. So I remember what ya tells me, boss, an' I says: "I'm t'inkin' of de little woman back home, waitin' for her man." "Ya big bum," he says, "ya drunk."'

'I'll bet he didn't,' said the Saint.

'Well, it was sump'n like dat,' said Hoppy, dismissing the quibble, 'only he talked wit' an accent.'

'I see what you mean,' said the Saint. 'And what did you do?'

'Well, boss, I hauls off an' gives him a poke in de jaw.'

'And what does he say to that?'

'He don't say nut'n, boss.' Mr Uniatz jerked a nicotine-stained thumb backwards at an indistinguishable quarter of the night. 'I tucks him up in de bushes an' leaves him. Dat's what I mean, is it oke leavin' him here,' said Hoppy, harking back to his original problem.

Simon Templar fought with his soul for a short time without speaking. If he had followed his most primitive instincts, there would probably have been a late lamented Mr Uniatz tucked up in the bushes alongside the sleeping rural constable; but the Saint's sense of civic responsibility was improving.

'I guess we'll leave him,' he said at length. 'It can't make things any worse.'

He drove back to London in a thoughtful frame of mind. It was one of those times when the hundredth chance turned up in magnificent vindication of all hare-brained enterprises; and when the established villain was a man in the position of Sir Hugo

Renway the Saint was inclined to have a few things to think about. There were only two forms of smuggling in which the rewards were high and the penalties heavy enough to justify such extreme measures as the murdered airman on the Brighton Road and that lethally electrified wire fence at March House—it is curious that the Saint was still far from reading the real interpretation into the facts he knew.

The wandering policeman whom Hoppy Uniatz had 'poked in de jaw' was a complication which had not been allowed for in his plan of campaign as seriously as it might; and he was not expecting the repercussions of it to reach him quite so quickly as they did.

He put the Hirondel back in its garage at about a quarter to four, and walked round to his apartment on Piccadilly. A sleepy night porter took them up in the lift: he was a new employee of the building whom the Saint had not seen before, and Simon made a mental note to learn more about him at an early date—he had found it a very sound principle to enlist the sympathies of the employees in any such building where he lived, for there were other detectives besides Mr Teal who had visualised a cast-iron arrest of the Saint as a signpost to promotion. But he was not thinking of doing anything about it at that hour, and his mind was too much occupied with other matters to notice that the man looked at him with more than ordinary curiosity as he got in.

His apartment lay at the end of a short corridor. He strolled innocently towards it, taking out his key, with Hoppy following him; and he was on the point of putting the key in the lock when a voice that was only too familiar spoke behind him. 'Do you mind if we come in?'

The Saint turned rather slowly on his heel, and looked at the two men who had appeared from somewhere to bar the way back along the corridor—there was something rather solid and purposeful about the way they stood shoulder to shoulder so as to fill the passage, something which put the glint of steel back in his eyes and set his heart ticking a fraction faster. Hoppy's hand was leaping automatically to his hip; but Simon caught it by the wrist, and smiled.

'You know you're always welcome, Claud,' he murmured. 'But you do choose the most Bohemian hours for your visits.'

He turned back to the door and unlocked it, and led the way into the living-room, spinning his hat on to a peg in the hall as he passed through. He took a cigarette from the box on the table and lighted it, facing round with one hand in his pocket and that thoughtful smile still on his lips.

'Well, what's the fun, boys?' he inquired genially. 'Has somebody pinched the north side of Oxford Street and do you think I did it, or have you just dropped in to sing carols?'

'Where have you been tonight?' asked Mr Teal. His manner was not the manner of a man who had dropped in to sing carols. Even in his wildest flights of whimsy, the Saint had never thought of Chief Inspector Teal as the Skylark of Scotland Yard, but he had known him to look more like an embryonic warbler than he did just then. Simon smiled even more genially and even more thoughtfully, and trickled out a lungful of blue smoke.

'We've been on a pub-crawl with Andrew Volstead and Lady Astor, and Hoppy came along to carry the bromo-seltzer.' Teal did not smile.

'If you've got another alibi,' he said; 'I'd like to hear it. But it had better be a good one.' The Saint pondered for a moment.

'You are getting particular,' he said. 'A story like that would always have kept you amused for hours in the old days. I suppose you've been taking a correspondence course in this detective business ... All right. We haven't been on a pub-crawl. We've been splitting hairs on the dome of St Paul's and looking for needles in the Haymarket.'

Mr Teal's hands remained in his pockets, but his whole attitude suggested that they were grasping something as heavy as a steamroller.

'Is that all you've got to say?' he demanded hoarsely.

'It'll do for the time being,' said the Saint calmly. 'That's what I say we've been doing; and what the hell does it matter to you?'

The detective appeared, somehow, in spite of his mountainous immobility, to approach the verge of gibbering. It may seem unkind of the chronicler to mention this, but he is conscientiously concerned to deal only with the bare facts, without apology or decoration. And yet he must admit that Mr Teal had lately suffered much.

'Now listen,' Mr Teal got out through his teeth. 'About half-past eleven tonight the watchman at Hawker's factory, down at Brooklands, was knocked on the head by someone he found prowling around the sheds. When he woke up and raised the alarm, one of the hangars had been forced open and an aeroplane had been stolen!'

Simon tapped his cigarette on the edge of an ashtray. His brain was starting to turn over like an electric motor responding to the touch of a switch, but no hint of that sudden mental commotion could have been seen in his face. His gaze went back to the detective from under quizzically slanting eyebrows.

'It sounds pretty ambitious,' he remarked. 'But what makes you think I'd be interested?'

'I don't have to think—'

'I know, Claud, You just chew a thistle and your ears flap.'

'I don't have to think,' Teal said grimly, 'when you leave your mark behind you.' The Saint raised one eyebrow a little farther.

'Meaning?'

'When the watchman woke up, there was a piece of paper pinned to his coat. There was a drawing on it. It was the same drawing that was found in the pocket of that dead airman last night— Manuel Enrique. It was your mark!'

'Dear me!' said the Saint.

The detective's china-blue eyes were as hard and bright as porcelain. His mouth had disappeared altogether—it was a mere slit in the hardened round chubbiness of his face.

'I suppose you can explain that away,' he snapped.

'Of course I can,' said the Saint easily. 'The same low criminal who was taking my name in vain on the Brighton Road last night—'

'Is that all the alibi you've got this time?' Teal asked, with a kind of saw-edged note in his voice.

'More or less,' said the Saint. He watched the detective take a second grip on himself, watched a glimmer of tentative relief and triumph creep hesitantly into the angry baby-blue eyes, watched the thinned mouth begin to open for an answer—and added, with a seraphically apologetic smile, at the very last and most devastating instant: 'Oh, yes, there was something I forgot to mention. On the way from St Paul's to the Haymarket I did stop at the Lex Garage off Piccadilly to collect my car; and now I come to think of it, Claud, it must have been exactly half-past eleven.'

Mr Teal blinked. It was not the nervous bashful blink of a gentle botanist being rudely confronted with the facts of mammalian reproduction: it was the dizzy blink of a bather who has made unwary contact with an electric eel. His chest appeared to deflate; then it swelled up again to a point where his coat was straining on its seams.

'You expect me to believe that?' he blared.

'Of course not,' said the Saint. 'You haven't enough intelligence to save yourself that much time. But you can verify it. Go to the garage and find out. Their records'll show what time I checked out. The night staff'll remember me. Go and ask 'em. Push off and amuse yourself. But if that's all that's on your mind tonight, I'm going to bed.'

'You can wait a little longer,' retorted Teal. 'Half-past eleven isn't the only time I want you to account for.'

The Saint sighed.

'What's the rest of it?'

'You seemed rather interested in Sir Hugo Renway last night,' Teal said waspily, 'so I asked the police down there to keep an eye on his place. I know your methods pretty well by now, and I had an idea you might go there. At half-past one this morning the constable was cycling round the estate when he saw your car—and`him!'

'What—Brother Uniatz?' drawled Simon. 'Did you see a cop, Hoppy?'

Mr Uniatz, who had been trying to unlock the cellaret with a piece of bent wire, turned round vacantly.

'Yes, boss,' he said.

'Ha!' barked Mr Teal. It may sound improbable, but that is a close approximation to the noise he made.

'I see one only yesterday,' Hoppy elaborated hastily, with the Saint's blue stare scorching through him. 'In de Haymarket.'

Chief Inspector Teal did not burst. Perhaps it is not actually possible for the human organism to become so inflated with spleen that it explodes into small fragments—the chronicler is inclined to take this as the only plausible reason why his favourite detective did not stand there and pop. But there was something about him which suggested that even the point of a joke might have punctured him into the power of performing that impossible disintegration. He glared at the Saint again with reddening eyes.

'This constable was also knocked on the head,' he went on, getting the words out somehow through his contracting larynx; 'and when he woke up—'

'The garden gate had been forced open and March House had been stolen,' murmured Simon. 'I know. The bloke flew off with it in the aeroplane.'

'He reported to the local station, and they telephoned me. The other thing I want to know is what you were doing at that time.'

'We were driving round and round Regent's Park; and I'll give you half a million pounds if you can prove we weren't!'

The detective bit on his long-forgotten chewing-gum with a force that almost fractured his jaw.

'Do you think you can make a monkey out of me?' he roared.

Simon shook his head.

'Certainly not,' he replied solemnly. 'I wouldn't try to improve on God's creation.'

The chronicler has already submitted, perhaps somewhat rashly, his opinion that the human organism is not capable of literally expanding into small and separate pieces under no other influence than the dilation of its own wrath. But he has, fortunately, offered the suggestion that some outside prod might succeed in procuring this phenomenal disruption.

Mr Teal did not burst, physically. But he performed the psychological equivalent. Moved by a cosmic passion which stronger men than he might have failed lamentably to control, he grasped destiny in both his quivering hands. He did something which he had never in all his life contrived to do before.

'All right,' he said throatily. 'I've heard all I want to hear tonight. You can tell the rest of it to a jury. I'm arresting you on charges of common assault, burglary, and wilful murder.'

V

Simon extinguished his cigarette in an ashtray. The ticking of his heart was going faster, but not so very much faster. It was curious how Teal's ultimate explosion surprised him; curious also that it did not find him unprepared. Perhaps, in his heart of hearts, he had always known that something of the kind must happen some day. The gay career of Teal-baiting could not go on for ever: it had gone on for a long time, but Mr Teal was human. There was no more concrete evidence now than there had ever been; but the Saint had a good deal of belated psychological understanding. In Teal's place he would probably have done the same.

The detective was still speaking, with the same rather frantic restraint and rather frantic consciousness of the awful temerity of what he was going to do.

'I caution you that anything you say now will be taken down and may be used in evidence at your trial.'

The Saint smiled. He understood. He deeply sympathised. In Teal's place, he would probably have done the same. But he was not in Teal's place.

'If you want to make a fool of yourself, Claud, I can't stop you,' he said; and his left fist leapt out and crashed like a cannon-ball into the furrow between Chief Inspector Teal's first and second chins.

The expression of compressed wrathfulness vanished startlingly from the detective's face. For a moment it was superseded by a register of grotesque surprise; and then every other visible emotion was smudged out by a vast blank sleepiness which for once was entirely innocent of pose. Mr Teal's legs folded up not ungracefully beneath him; he lay down on the floor, and went to sleep.

Mr Teal's mute equerry was starting forward, and his mouth was opening: it is possible that at any moment some human sound might have emerged from that preternaturally silent man, but Simon gave it no chance. The man was grabbing for his wrists, and the Saint obligingly permitted him to get his hold. Then he planted his left foot firmly in the detective's stomach, and rolled over backwards, pushing his foot vimfully upwards as he pulled his wrists down. The man sailed over his head in an *adagio* flying somersault and hit the carpet with an explosive 'wuff!' which any medium-sized dog could have vocalised much better; and Simon somersaulted after him more gently and sat astride his chest. He grasped the man's coat collar in his hands and twisted his knuckles scientifically into the carotid arteries—unconsciousness can be produced in two or three seconds by that method, when employed by a skilful exponent, and Sergeant Barrow's resistance had been considerably impaired already by the force with which his shoulder-blades had landed on the floor. It was all over in far less time than it takes to describe; and Simon looked up at Mr Uniatz, who was prancing about like a puppy with his revolver reversed in his hand.

'Fetch me a towel from the bathroom, Hoppy,' he ordered. 'And for Heaven's sake put that blasted cannon away. How many more times have I got to tell you that this is the close season for policemen?'

While he was waiting, he handcuffed the two detectives with

their own bracelets; and when the towel arrived he tore it into two strips and gagged them.

'Get your hat,' he said, when the job was finished. 'We're going to travel.'

Mr Uniatz followed him obediently. It may be true, as we have acknowledged, that the higher flights of philosophy and metaphysics were for ever beyond the range of Mr Uniatz's bovine intellect; but he had an incomparable grip on the fundamentals of self-preservation. Experience had taught him that after an active encounter with the police the advantages of expeditious travelling could be taken for granted—a fact which relieved his brain of much potentially painful exertion.

As they turned into Berkeley Square, he followed a little more hesitantly; and eventually he plucked at the Saint's sleeve.

'Where ya goin', boss?' he asked. 'Dis ain't de way to de garage.'

'It's the way to the garage we're going to,' answered the Saint.

He had automatically ruled out the Hirondel as a conveyance for that getaway—the great red and cream speedster was far too conspicuous and far too well known, and it was the car whose description would be immediately broadcast by Mr Teal as soon as that hapless sleuth had worked the gag out of his mouth and reached the telephone. Simon had another and more commonplace car in reserve, in another garage and another name, which he had laid up some weeks ago with a far-sighted eye to just such a complication as this; and he was inclined to flatter himself on his forethought without undertaking the herculean labour of hammering the idea into Hoppy's armour-plated skull.

Whether any net was actually spread out for him in time to cross his path, he never knew; certainly he slipped through London without incident, making excellent time over the almost deserted roads in spite of several detours at strategic points where he might have been stopped. He abandoned the car outside the entrance of Vickers' factory on the Byfleet road, where there would soon be a score of other cars parked around it, and one more modest saloon might easily pass unnoticed for days; and walked through the woods to his house as the dawn was breaking. There was no hope that Teal would fail to draw that covert as soon as he had reorganised his forces; but it was a temporary haven, and the Saint had a few items of personal equipment there which he wanted to pick up.

There were sounds of movement in the kitchen when he let himself in at the front door, and in another moment the belligerent walrus-moustached visage of Orace appeared on the opposite side of the hall. Simon threw his hat at him and smiled.

'What's our chance of breakfast, Orace?' he asked.

'Narf a minnit,' said Orace expressionlessly, and vanished again.

Over the bacon and eggs, golden brown toast, and steaming coffee which Orace produced necromantically in very little more than the time he had promised, the Saint's brain was working overtime. For the time being, Teal had been dealt with; but that past tense had no more permanent stability than the haven in which Simon Templar was eating his breakfast. Ahead of those transient satisfactions lay the alternatives of penal servitude or a completed getaway; and he had no spontaneous leaning towards either. He turned them over in his mind like small beetles discovered under a log, and decided that he liked them even less. But there was a third solution which took him longer to think over—which, in fact, kept him wrapped in silent concentration until his plate was pushed away and he was smoking a cigarette over a second cup of coffee, and Mr Uniatz intruded his bashful personality again.

Hoppy's brain had not been working overtime, because the hours between one breakfast and the following bedtime were rarely long enough to let it do much more than catch up with where it had left off the previous night. Nevertheless, the wheels, immersed in the species of thick soup in which nature had asked them to whizz round, had been doggedly trying to revolve.

'Boss,' said Hoppy Uniatz, articulating with some indistinctness through a slice of toast, two ounces of butter, a rasher of bacon, and half an egg, 'de cops knows you got dis house.'

Simon harked back over some leagues of his own cerebrations, and recognised the landmark which Hoppy had contrived to reach.

'That's perfectly true,' he remarked admiringly. 'Now don't go doing any more of that high-pressure thinking—give your brain a minute to cool off, because I want you to listen to me.'

He rang the bell and smoked quietly until Orace answered. Mr Uniatz, happily absolved from further brain work, engulfed the rest of the food within his reach and cast longing eyes at a decanter of whisky on the sideboard.

'Orace,' said the Saint, 'I'm afraid Claud Eustace is after us again.'

'Yessir,' said Orace phlegmatically.

'You might sound more sympathetic about it,' Simon complained. 'One of the charges is wilful murder.'

'Well, it's yer own thunderin' fault, ain't it?' retorted Orace, unmoved.

The Saint sighed.

'I suppose you're right,' he admitted. 'Anyway, Hoppy's idea is that we ought to pull the pin.'

'Dat means to take it on de lam,' explained Hoppy, clarifying the point.

Orace's faded eyes lost none of their ferocity, but his overhanging moustache twitched.

'If yer can wite 'arf a minnit, sir,' he said, 'I'll go wiv yer.'

The Saint laughed softly, and stood up. His hand fell on Orace's shoulder.

'Thanks a lot, you old humbug; but it isn't necessary. You see, Hoppy's wrong. And you ought to know it, after all the years you've been around with me.' He leaned back against the mantelpiece, one hand in his pocket, and looked at the two men with eyes that were beginning to twinkle again. 'Hoppy reminds me that Teal knows all about this house, but he's forgotten that Teal also knows I know it. Hoppy thinks we ought to pack our keisters and take it on the lam, but he's forgotten that that's the very thing Teal is expecting us to do. After all, Claud Eustace has seen me hang it on the limb before ... Are you there, Hoppy?'

'Yes, boss,' said Mr Uniatz, after glancing around to reassure himself of the fact.

'It's quite true that you'll probably see some cops skating up the drive before long; but somehow I don't think Claud Eustace will be with them. It'll be almost a formality. They may browse around looking for incriminating relics, but they won't be seriously looking for me—or Hoppy. And that's why none of 'em will ever be great detectives, because this is exactly where Hoppy is going to be—lying snug and low in the secret room off the study, which is one of the things they still don't know about this house.'

'Cheese!' said Mr Uniatz, in pardonable awe. Dijja t'ink of all dat while ya was eatin' breakfast?'

The Saint smiled.

'That, and some more; but I guess that's enough for your head to hold at one time.' He looked at his watch. 'You'd better move into your new quarters, now—Orace will bring you food and drink from time to time, and I'll know where to find you when I want you.'

He steered Hoppy across the hall and into the study, slid back the bookcase beside the desk, and pushed him through the gap in the wall behind it. Framed in the narrow opening, Mr Uniatz blinked out at him pleadingly.

'Boss,' he said, 'it's going to be toisty waitin'.'

'Hoppy,' said the Saint, 'if I think you're going to have to wait long, I'll tell Orace to have a pipeline laid from a distillery right into the room. Then you can just lie down under the tap and keep your mouth open—and it'll be cheaper than buying it in bottles.'

He slammed the bookcase into place again, and turned round on the last puff of his cigarette as Orace came in.

'You've got to be an Orphan of the Storm, and draw the fire,' he said. 'But it shouldn't be very dangerous. They've nothing against you. The one thing you must do is get in touch with Miss Holm—let her know all the latest news, and tell her to keep in contact. There may be fun and games for all before this party's over.'

'Addencha better 'ide in there yerself, sir?' asked Orace threateningly. 'I can look after everythink for yer.'

The Saint shook his head.

'You can't look after what I'm going to look after,' he said gently. 'But I can tell you some more. It won't mean much to you, but you can pass it on to Miss Holm in case she's curious, and remember it yourself in case anything goes wrong.'

He caught Orace by the shoulders and swung him round. The mocking blue eyes were reckless and wicked; the Saintly smile was as blithe and tranquil as if he had been setting out on a picnic— which, according to his own scapegrace philosophy, he was.

'Down at Betfield, near Folkestone,' he said, 'there's a place called March House, where a guy called Sir Hugo Renway lives. The night before last, this guy murdered a Spanish airman named Manuel Enrique, on the Brighton Road—and left my mark on him. Last night, this same guy pinched an aeroplane out of the Hawker factory over the road—and left my mark on the night watchman. And in the small hours of this morning, an aeroplane which may or may not have been the one that was pinched landed in the grounds of March House. I was there, and I saw it. A few hours back, Claud Eustace Teal tried to run me in for both those efforts.

'I wasn't responsible for either of 'em, but Teal doesn't believe it. Taking things by and large, you can't exactly blame him. But I know better, even if he doesn't; and I'm just naturally curious. I want to know what all this jolly carnival is about that Renway's trying to tack on to me. And there's one thing you'll notice, Orace, with that greased-lightning brain of yours, which ties all these exciting goings-on together. What is it, Orace?'

The warlike moustache of his manservant bristled.

'Hairyplanes,' said Orace brilliantly; and Simon smote him on the back.

'You said it, Horatio. With that sizzling brain of yours, you biff the ailnay on the okobay. Hairyplanes it is. We've got to get to the bottom of this, as the bishop said to the actress; and it strikes me that if I were to fetch out the old Gilette and go hairyplaning—if I blundered into March House as a blooming aviator waiting to be pruned—'

The peremptory zing of the front door bell interrupted him, and he looked up with mischief hardening on his lips. Then he chuckled again.

'I expect this is the deputation. Give them my love, Orace—and some of those exploding cigarettes. I'll be seein' ya!'

He reached the window in a couple of strides, and swung himself nimbly through. Orace watched him disappear into the dell of bracken at the other end of the lawn, and strutted off, glowering, to answer the front door.

## VI

There is believed to exist a happy band of half-wits whose fondest faith it is that the life of a government official, the superman to whom they entrust their national destiny, is one long treadmill of selfless toil from dawn to dusk. They picture the devoted genius labouring endlessly over reports and figures, the massive brain steaming, the massive stomach scarcely daring even to call a halt for food. They picture him returning home at the close of the long day, his shoulders still bowed beneath the cares of state, to fret and moil over their problems through the night watches. They are, we began by explaining, a happy band of half-wits.

The life of a government official is very far from that; particularly if he is of the species known as 'Permanent', which means that he is relieved even of the sordid obligation of being heckled from time to time by audiences of weary electors. His job is safe. Only death, the Great Harvester, can remove him; and even when he dies, the event may pass unnoticed until the body begins to fall apart. Until then, his programme is roughly as follows:

```
10:30 a.m.  Arrive at office in Whitehall. Read
            newspaper. Discuss night before with
            fellow officials. Talk to secretary. Pick
            up correspondence tray. Put down again.
11:30 a.m.  Go out for refreshment.
12.30 p.m.  Return to office. Practise short putts
            on H.M. carpet.
1:00 p.m.   Go out to lunch.
3:00 p.m.   Back from lunch. Pick up correspondence
            tray. Refer to other department.
3:30 p.m.   Sleep in armchair.
4:00 p.m.   Tea.
4:30 p.m.   Adjourn to club. Go home.
```

As a matter of fact, Sir Hugo Renway was not thinking of his office at all at half-past nine that morning. He was discussing the ravages of the incorrigible green-fly with his gardener; but he was not really thinking of that, either.

He was a biggish thin-lipped man, with glossily brushed grey hair and a slight squint. The squint did not make him look sinister: it made him look smug. He was physically handicapped against looking anyone squarely in the face; but the impression he managed to convey was not that he couldn't, but that he didn't think it worthwhile. He was looking at the gardener in just that way while they talked, but his air of well-fed smugness was illusory. He was well fed, but he was troubled. Under that smooth supercilious exterior, his nerves were on edge; and the swelling drone of an aeroplane coming up from the Channel harmonised curiously well with the rasp of his thoughts.

'I don't think none of them new-fangled washes is any good, zir, if you aarsk me,' the man was reiterating in his grumbling brogue; and Renway nodded, and noticed that the steady drone had suddenly broken up into an erratic popping noise.

The man went on grumbling, and Renway went on pretending to listen, in his bored way. Inwardly he was cursing—cursing the stupidity of a man who was dead, whose death had transformed the steady drone of his own determination into the erratic popping which was going through his nerves.

The aeroplane swept suddenly over the house. It was rather low, wobbling indecisively; and his convergent stare hardened on it with an awakening of professional interest. The popping of the engine had slackened away to nothing. Then, as if the pilot had seen sanctuary at that moment, the machine seemed to pull itself together. Its nose dipped, and it rushed downwards in a long glide, with no other accompaniment of sound than the whining thrum of the propeller running free. Instinctively Renway ducked; but the plane sideslipped thirty feet over his head and fishtailed down to a perfect three-point landing in the flat open field beyond the rose garden.

Renway turned round and watched it come to a standstill. He knew at once that the helmeted figure in the cockpit had nothing left to learn about the mastery of an aeroplane. That field was a devil to get into, he had learned from experience; but the unknown pilot had dumped his ship in it with a dead stick as neatly as if he had had a whole prairie to choose from. Enrique had been the same—a swarthy daredevil who could land on a playing-card and make an aeroplane do anything short of balancing billiard balls on its tail, whose nerveless brilliance had been so maddeningly beyond the class of all Renway's own taut-strung efforts . . . Renway's hands tensed involuntarily at his sides for a moment while he went on thinking; and then he turned away and began minutely examining some buds of rose-crimson Papa Gontiers as the pilot walked under a rustic arch and came towards him.

'I'm terribly sorry,' said the aviator, 'but I'm afraid I've had a forced landing in your grounds.'

Renway looked at him for a moment. He had a dangerous devil-may-care sort of mouth, which showed very white teeth when he smiled. Enrique had had a smile very much like that.

'So I see,' said Renway, and returned to his study of rose-buds.

His voice was an epitome of all that mincing rudeness which the English lower classes have been so successfully trained to regard as a symbol of superiority. The Saint would have liked to hit him with a spanner; but he restrained himself.

'I'm terribly sorry,' he repeated. 'My oil pressure started to drop rather quickly, and I had to come down where I could. I don't think I've done any damage. If you can direct me to the village, I'll arrange to get the machine moved as quickly as possible.'

'One of the servants will show you the way.'

Renway looked up with his complacent squint, and glanced at the gardener, who put away his pruning-knife and dusted his hands.

'It's very good of you,' said the Saint; and then an unfortunate accident happened.

He was carrying a valise in one hand, which he had taken out of the machine and brought with him. It could not have been very securely fastened, for at that moment it fell open. A cascade of shirts, socks, pyjamas, shaving tackle, and similar impedimenta might not have distracted Renway for more than a couple of seconds from his horticultural absorption; but nothing of the kind fell out. Instead, the valise emptied itself of a heavy load of small square tins such as cough lozenges are sold in. The tins did, in fact, carry printed labels proclaiming their contents to be cough lozenges; but one of them burst open in its fall and scattered a small snowfall of white powder over the path.

Simon dropped on his knees and shovelled the tins back with rather unsteady hands, forcing them into the attaché-case with more haste than efficiency. He scraped the white powder clumsily back into the one which had burst open; and when Renway touched him on the shoulder he jumped.

'Pardon my curiosity,' said Renway, with unexpected suaveness, 'but you have the most unusual luggage.'

Simon laughed somewhat shortly.

'Yes, I suppose it is. I'm the Continental traveller for—er—some patent medicine manufacturers—'

'I see.'

Renway looked back at the aeroplane again; and again his hands tensed involuntarily at his sides. And then, once more, he looked at the Saint, Simon forced the last tin into his case, crammed the locks together, and straightened up.

'I'm awfully sorry to give you so much trouble,' he said.

'Not at all.' Renway's voice was dry, unnatural. He was aghast at himself, sweating coldly under the arms at the realisation of what he was doing; but he spoke without any conscious volition. The jangling of his nerves forced him on, provided the motive power for the fantastic inspiration which had seized him. 'In fact, my chauffeur can drive into Folkestone himself and make the necessary arrangements, while you stay here. You can give him instructions; and it's sure to mean a good deal of waiting about. I suppose the authorities will have to be notified . . .'

He was watching the pilot closely when he uttered that last sentence, although the cast in his eye made him appear to be staring past him; and he did not miss the slight instantaneous tightening of the dangerous mouth.

'Oh, I couldn't possibly let you do that,' Simon protested. 'I've given you quite enough trouble as it is—'

'Not a bit of it,' insisted Renway, still watching him.

He was quite sure now. The pilot stiffened almost imperceptibly—Renway saw the shift of his eyes and the whitening of his knuckles on the hand which clutched the valise, and went on with more pronounced assurance: 'It's no trouble at all to me, and my chauffeur has far too little to do. Besides, that landing must have given you one or two bad moments; and I'm sure you wouldn't refuse a drink. Come along up to the house, my dear fellow, and let me see what I can find for you.'

He took the Saint's arm and led him away with a grim cordiality which it would have been difficult to resist—even if Simon had wanted to. They went through a small rockery up to the tennis lawn, across the lawn to a paved terrace, through open french windows into a rather stuffy library.

'Will you have a cigarette—or is it too early for a cigar?'

Simon took a cigarette, and lighted it while Renway rang the bell.

'Sit down, Mr—er—'

'Tombs.'

'Sit down, Mr Tombs.'

The Saint sat on the edge of a plush armchair and smoked in silence until the butler answered the bell. Renway ordered drinks, and the butler went out again. The silence went on. Renway went over to a window and stood there, humming unmusically to himself.

'Awkward thing to have happen to you,' ventured the Saint.

Renway half turned his head.

'I beg your pardon?'

'I said, it's an awkward thing to have happen to you—oil pressure going down.'

'Quite,' said Renway, and went on humming.

The butler came in with a tray, put it down, and departed. Renway crossed over to it and poured whisky into two glasses.

'Soda?'

'Thanks.'

Renway worked the siphon, and handed over the drink. Then he took up his own glass; and abruptly, as if he was blurting out something which he had been mustering his determination to say for several minutes, he snapped: 'I suppose you don't think I believe that story of yours about being a patent-medicine salesman?'

'Don't you?' said the Saint evasively.

'Of course not. I know cocaine when I see it.'

Simon, who had carefully filled all his tins with boracic, wanted to smile. But he glanced apprehensively at the valise, which he had put down beside his chair, and then hardened his face into an ineffective mask.

'But don't worry,' said Renway. 'I'm not going to tell the police. It's none of my business. I'm only wondering why a fellow like you—clever, daring, a good pilot—why you should waste your time over small stuff like that.'

Simon licked his lips.

'It isn't so very small. And what else is there for me to do? There aren't so many jobs going these days for an out-of-work ace. You know yourself that war heroes are two a penny nowadays. I'm desperate enough to take the risk; and I want the money.'

'You'll never make a million out of it.'

'If you know anything that I can make a million out of, I'll do it.'

Renway swallowed another gulp of whisky and put down his glass. In the last few moments, the jangling of his nerves seemed to have risen to a pitch at which anything might crack. And yet it was without the tense wearing raggedness that he had felt before—he had a crazy breathless presentiment of success, waiting for him to grasp it if he risked the movement. It had come miraculously, incredibly, literally out of the blue; and it was all personified in the broad-shouldered blue-eyed shape of the dangerous young man whose leather coat filled his armchair. Renway wiped his mouth on a silk handkerchief and tucked it away.

'Tomorrow morning,' he said, 'an aeroplane will leave Croydon for Paris with about ten tons of gold on board—as a matter of fact, the value will be exactly three million pounds. It is going to be shot down over the Channel, and the gold is going to be stolen. If you were desperate enough, you would be the man to do it.'

## VII

Simon Templar did not need to act. The peculiar stillness that settled over him called for no simulation. It was as starkly genuine as any expression his face had ever worn.

And way back in the dim detached recesses of consciousness he was bowing down before the everlasting generosity of fortune. He had taken that wide sweep out over the sea and choked his engine over the cliffs at the southern boundary of March House, staged his whole subsequent demonstration of guilt and truculence, rolled the dice down the board from beginning to end with nothing more substantial behind the play than a vast open-minded optimism; but the little he knew and the little he had guessed, the entire nebulous theory which had given him the idea of establishing himself as a disreputable airman, was revealed to be so grotesquely inadequate that he was temporarily speechless. His puerile stratagem ought to have gained him nothing more than a glimpse of March House from the inside and a quick passage to the nearest police station; instead of which, it had flung doors wide open into something which even now he could scarcely believe in cold blood.

'It couldn't be done,' he said at length.

'It can be done by a few men with the courage to take big chances for a share in three million pounds,' said Renway. 'I have all the necessary information. I have everything organised. The only thing I need to make it certain is the perfect pilot.'

Simon tapped his cigarette.

'I should have thought that was the first thing.'

'It was the first thing.' Renway drank again. He was speaking with more steadiness now, with a conviction that was strengthening through every sentence; his faded stare weaved endlessly over the Saint's face, changing from one eye to the other. 'I had the ideal man; but he—met with an accident. There wasn't time to find anyone else. I was going to try it myself, but I'm not an expert pilot. I have no fighting experience. I might have bungled it. You wouldn't.'

Meeting the gaze of those unequally staring eyes, Simon had an eerie intuition that Renway was mad. He had to make a deliberate effort to separate a part of his mind from that precognition while he pieced his scanty facts together again in the light of what Renway had said.

There had been a pilot. That would have been Manuel Enrique, who died on the Brighton Road. A new pilot swooped down out of the sky, and within twenty minutes was being offered the vacant post. With all due deference to the gods of luck, it seemed as if that new aviator was having a remarkable red carpet laid out for him.

'You don't only need a pilot,' said the Saint mechanically. 'You need a proper fighting ship, with geared machine-guns and all the rest of it.'

'There is one,' said Renway. 'I took it from Hawker's factory last night. It's one of a new flight they're building for the Moravian Government. The one I took had been out on range tests, and the guns were still fitted. I also took three spare drums of ammunition. I flew it over here myself—it was the first night landing I've ever made.'

It had not been a particularly clean one, Simon remembered; and then he saw the continual tensing and twitching of Renway's hands, and suddenly understood much more.

There had been a pilot; but he had—met with an accident. And yet the plot in which he had a vital role could not be given up. Therefore it had grown in Renway's mind to the dimensions of an obsession, until the point had been reached where it loomed up as the needle's eye of an insanely conceived salvation. Although Enrique was dead, the aeroplane had still been stolen: Renway had flown it himself, and the ordeal of that untutored night flight had cut into the marrow of his nerves. Still the goal could not be given up. The new pilot arrived at the crisis of an eight hours' sleepless nightmare of strain—a solution, an escape, a straw which he could clutch even while preserving the delusion that he was a superman irresistibly turning a chance tool to his need. Simon recalled Renway's abrupt defiant plunge into the subject after that long awkward silence, and hypothesis merged into certainty. It was queer, he reflected, how that superman complex, that delusion of being able to enslave human instruments body and soul by the power of a hypnotic personality which usually existed only in the paranoiac's own grandiose imagination, had been the downfall of so many promising criminals.

'You did that?' said the Saint, in a tone which contained exactly the right blend of incredulous admiration and sober awe.

'Of course.'

Simon put out his cigarette and helped himself to a second.

'That's a beginning,' he said. 'But the pilots will be armed—they're in touch with the shore by radio all the way—'

'What is the good of that?' asked Renway calmly. 'The conditions aren't the same as they would be in war-time. They aren't really expecting to be attacked. They see another aeroplane overtaking them, that's all—there's always plenty of traffic on that route, and they wouldn't think anything of it. Then you dive. With your experience, they'd be an easy target. It ought to be finished in a couple of bursts—long before they could wireless any alarm to the shore. And as soon as their wireless stops, I shall carry on with their report. I have a short-wave transmitter installed in this house, and I have a record of every signal that's been sent out by cross-Channel aircraft for the last month. I know all the codes. The shore stations will never know what's happened until the aeroplane fails to arrive.'

The Saint blew out a flick of smoke, and kept his eyes on Renway's pale complacent face. It was dawning on him that if Renway was a lunatic, he was the victim of a very thorough and methodical kind of madness.

'There isn't only traffic in the air,' he said. 'There's also shipping. Suppose a ship sees what happens?' Renway made a gesture of impatience.

'My good fellow, you're going over ground that I covered two months ago. I could raise more objections than you know yourself. For instance, all the time the aeroplane is over the Channel, there will be special motor-boats cruising off the French and English coasts. One or more of them may possibly reach the scene. It will be part of your job to keep them at a distance by machinegun fire from the air until all the gold has been secured.'

'How do you propose to do that?' persisted the Saint. 'You can't lift ten tons of gold out of a wrecked aeroplane in five minutes.'

A sudden sly look hooded Renway's eyes.

'That has also been arranged,' he said.

He refilled his glass and drank again, sucking in his lips after the drink. As if wondering whether he had betrayed too much already, he said: 'You need only be concerned with your own share in the proceedings. Do you feel like taking a part?'

Simon thought for a moment, and nodded.

'I'm your man,' he said.

Renway remained looking at him for a while longer, and the Saint fancied he could almost see the man's nerves relaxing in the sedative glow of conquest.

'In that case, I shall not need to send for my chauffeur.'

'What about my machine?' asked the Saint.

'You can keep it here until you require it again. I have plenty of accommodation, and one of my mechanics can find out the cause of your trouble and put it right.'

For a second the Saint's eyes chilled, for no mechanic would take long to discover that there was nothing whatever the matter with the machine in which he had landed. But he answered easily enough.

'That's very good of you.'

Renway picked up his valise and took it to a big built-in safe at one end of the room, into which he locked it. He came back blandly, rubbing his hands.

'Your—er—samples will be quite safe there until you need them. Shall we go and attend to your aeroplane?'

They walked out again in the strengthening sunshine, down through the rose garden and across the small field where the Saint had made his landing. Simon felt the dead weight of the automatic in his pocket bumping his hip as he walked, and felt unexpectedly glad of its familiar comfort; the nervous twitching of Renway's hands had finished altogether now, and there was an uncanny inert calm about his sauntering bulk which was frightful to study— the unnatural porcine opaqueness of a man whose mind has ceased to work like other men's minds . . .

Renway went on talking, in the same simpering monotone, as if he had been describing the layout of an asparagus bed: 'I shall know the number of the transport plane and the time it leaves Croydon five minutes after it takes off—you'll have plenty of time to be waiting for it in the air.'

On the other side of the field there was a big tithe barn with the hedge laid up to one wall. Renway knocked on a small door, and it opened three inches to show a narrow strip of the grimy face and figure of a man in overalls. After the first pause of identification it opened wider, and they went in.

The interior was cool and spacious, dimly lit in contrast with the sunlight outside by a couple of naked bulbs hung from the high ridge. Simon's first glance round was arrested by the grey bull-nosed shape of the Hawker pursuit plane at the far end of the shed. In another two or three hours he would have found it less easy to recognise, except by the long gleaming snouts of the machine-guns braced forward from the pilot's cockpit, for another overalled man mounted on a folding ladder was even then engaged in painting out the wing cocardes with a layer of neutral-grey dope. But the national markings on the empennage were still untouched—if the Saint had ever been tempted to wonder whether he had lost himself in a fantastic dream, the sight of those shining strips of colour was the last thing that was needed to show him that he was in touch with nothing more fantastic than astounding reality.

He fished out his case and selected another cigarette while he surveyed the other details of his surroundings. While he was in the air he had guessed that the field adjoining the one in which he had landed was the one where he had watched the Hawker ship land some hours ago, and a glimpse of other and wider doors outlined in cracks of light on the opposite wall of the barn was his confirmation. There was a stack of petrol cans in one corner, and a work-bench and lathe in another. He saw the spare drums of ammunition which Renway had referred to under the workbench, and some curious pear-shaped objects stacked in a wooden rack beside it—in another moment he realised that they were bombs.

He indicated them with a slight movement of his thumb.

'For use on the rescue boats?' he queried; and Renway nodded.

Simon left the cigarette between his lips, but thoughtfully refrained from lighting it.

'Isn't it a bit risky?' he suggested. 'I mean, having everything here where anybody might get in and see it?'

Renway's mouth widened slightly. If another muscle of his face had moved it might have been a smile, but the effect of the surrounding deadness of flesh was curiously horrible.

'I have two kinds of servants—those who are in my confidence, and those who are merely menials. With the first kind, there is no risk—although it was a pity that Enrique met with an accident . . .' He paused for a moment, with his faded eyes wandering inharmoniously over the Saint; and then he pointed to a big humming engine bedded down in the concrete floor on his right. 'To the second kind, this is simply the building which houses our private electric light plant. The doors are kept locked, and there is no reason for them to pry further. And all of them are having a special holiday tomorrow.'

He continued to watch the Saint satirically, as if aware that there was another risk which might have been mentioned; but Simon knew the answer to that one. The case of 'samples' which his host had locked up in the library safe, so long as they remained there, must have constituted a reasonably sound security for the adventurous aviator's faithful service—from Renway's point of view. The Saint was acquiring a wholesome respect for the Treasury Pooh-ba's criminal efficiency; and his blue eyes were rather quiet and metallic as he watched the two mechanics wheel his machine through a gate in the hedge and bring it through the broad sliding doors into the barn.

As they strolled back to the house again, Renway pulled out his watch.

'I shall have to attend to some business now,' he said. 'You'll be able to spend your time making the acquaintance of the other men who are helping me.'

They entered the house by another door, and went down a long dark low-ceilinged corridor which led into a large panelled room lighted by small leaded windows. Simon ducked his head automatically, but found that he could just stand upright under the black oak beams which crossed the ceiling. There was a billiard table in the centre with a strip of carpet laid round it, and an open brick fireplace at one side; but the room had the musty dampness of disuse.

'March House is rather an architectural scrap-heap,' Renway explained impersonally. 'You're in the oldest part of it now, which goes back to the fifteenth century. I discovered this quite by accident—'

'This' was a section of panelling, about five and a half feet by three, which sprang open on invisible hinges—Simon could not see exactly what the other did to open it. Renway fumbled in the dark aperture and switched on a light.

'I don't know where the passage originally went to,' he said, as they groped their way down a flight of rickety wooden stairs. 'At present it leads into the cellars. There used to be an ordinary entrance from a more modern part of the house, where the kitchen is now, but I had that bricked up.'

At the foot of the stairway there was a narrow stone-flagged tunnel. Renway switched on another light and they went on, bent almost double in the cramped space. At intervals there was a rough wooden buttress to carry a weak section of the roof, but for the most part the upper curve of the burrow consisted of nothing but the natural chalk.

Simon Templar, who had seen the inner workings of more secret doors, rooms, and passages than any other living man, had never managed to lose the first primitive schoolboy thrill of such subterranean accessories of adventure. He followed Renway with whole-hearted enthusiasm; but there was an equally whole-hearted vigilance about him nevertheless, for the thought had crossed his mind that Sir Hugo Renway might be even more clever and efficient than he had yet begun to believe, and he had no overpowering ambition to be suddenly pushed down a well and left there to contemplate the follies of over-optimism until hunger and thirst put an end to contemplation.

After about fifteen yards Renway turned a right-angled corner and disappeared; and Simon crept up in his tracks with that knife-bladed vigilance honed to a razor edge. Rounding the corner, he found himself stepping out into a fairly large stone chamber illuminated by several electric bulbs. At the distant end there was a row of beds; a cheap square of carpet was laid out on the floor, and the room was sketchily furnished with a bare wooden table in the centre, a couple of wash-stands, and a heterogeneous selection of chairs. Four of the men in the room were congregated at one end of the table over a game of cards; the fifth was stitching a button on his coat; the sixth was reading a newspaper. They were all turned rigidly towards the end of the tunnel; and the Saint carefully set his hands on his hips—where one of them would be within handy diving range of his gun.

'Gentlemen,' Renway's high-pitched BBC voice was saying, 'this is Mr—er—Tombs, who is taking Enrique's place.'

None of the flat fish-like eyes acknowledged the introduction by so much as a flicker.

Renway turned to the Saint.

'You must meet Mr Petrowitz,' he said; 'Mr Jeddy—Mr Pargo—'

He ran through a list of names, indicating their owners with curt movements of his head; and Simon, looking them over, decided that they were the ugliest gang of cut-throats that even the most rabid Bolshevik could ever hope to find gathered together in a strategic position under the house of an English aristocrat.

His decision embodied something more than pure artistic comment. The sight of those staring immobile men added the last touch to his grim understanding that if Sir Hugo Renway was mad, he was a maniac with the cold logical resolution that was needed to carry out his insane scheme.

His glance fell on the newspaper which the sixth man had put down. The black-type banner line across the top of the page leapt to his eye.

## SAINT STEALS ARMED AEROPLANE

It reminded him that he had not yet inquired the name of his new employer.

'Are you the Saint?' he asked. Renway's lids drooped. 'Yes,' he said.

### VIII

According to his watch, Simon Templar stayed in that secret cellar for about eighteen hours: without that evidence, he could have been fairly easily persuaded that it was about eighteen days.

It was so completely removed from the sense of reality, as well as from the ordinary change of lights and movements of the outer world, that time had very little meaning. At intervals, one of the men would go to a cupboard in the corner and dig out a loaf of bread and a slab of cheese, a tin of beans, or a bottle of beer: those who felt inclined would join him in a sketchy meal or a drink. One of the card players got up from the table, lay down on one of the beds, and went to sleep, snoring. Another man shuffled the cards and looked flat-eyed at the Saint.

'Want a game?'

Simon took the vacant chair and a stack of chips. Purely as an antidote to boredom, he played blackjack for two hours, and finished five chips down.

'That's five hundred pounds,' said Pargo, writing figures with a half-inch stub of pencil on a soiled scrap of paper.

'I haven't got five hundred pounds on me,' said the Saint.

The man grinned like a rat.

'Nor have any of us,' he said. 'But you will have after tomorrow.'

Simon was impressed without being pleased. He had watched Jeddy rake up a stack of chips that must have represented about three thousand pounds at that rate of exchange, without any sign of emotion; and Mr Jeddy was a man whose spiritual niche in the Buddy-can-you-spare-a-dime class was as obvious as the fact that he had not shaved for three days.

The others were not vastly different. Their physical aspects ranged from the bearded and faintly odorous burliness of Mr Petrowitz to the rat-faced and yellow-toothed scrawniness of Mr Pargo; but all of them had the same dominant characteristic in common. It was a characteristic with which the Saint had become most familiar on the west side of the Atlantic, although it was confined to no single race or nationality; a characteristic which Hoppy Uniatz, who couldn't have spelt the word to save his life, would have been the first to recognise: the peculiar cold lifelessness of the eye which brands the natural killer. But there are grades in killers, just as there are in singers; and the men in that cellar were not in the Grand Opera class, the class that collects diamonds and expensive limousines. They were men who did their stuff at street corners and in dingy alleys for a chance coin or two; the crude hacks of their profession. And they were the men whom Renway had inspired with so much confidence in the certainty of his scheme that they were calmly gambling their hypothetical profits in hundred-pound units.

God alone knew how Renway had gathered them together—neither the Saint nor Teal ever found out. But they constituted six more amazing eye-openers for the Saint to add to his phenomenally growing collection—six stony-faced witnesses to the fact that Sir Hugo Renway, whom Simon Templar would never have credited with the ability to lead anything more piratical than a pompous secession from the Conservative Party, had found the trick of organising what might have been one of the most outstanding robberies in the history of crime.

The men took him for granted. Their conversation, when they spoke at all, was grumbling, low-voiced, monosyllabic. They asked Simon no questions, and he had a sure intuition that they would have been surprised and hostile if he had asked them any. The business for which they were collected there was never mentioned—either it had already been discussed so much that there was nothing left to say on the subject, or they were too fettered by habitual suspicion for any discussion to have a chance of getting under way. Simon decided that in addition to being the ugliest, they were also the dullest assortment of thugs he had ever come across.

The man who had been reading the newspaper put it down and added himself to the increasing company of sleepers, and Simon reached out for the opportunity of getting acquainted with the latest lurid accounts of his own entirely mythical activities. They were more or less what he would have expected; but there was a sub-heading with the words 'Scotland Yard Active' which made him smile. Scotland Yard was certainly active—by that hour. It must have been hopping about like a young and healthy flea— but he would have given much to see its face if it could have been miraculously enabled to find him at that moment.

As it turned out, that pleasure, or a representative part of it, was not to cost him anything.

'Put those damn lights out,' a voice from one of the beds growled at last; and Simon stretched himself out on a hard mattress and continued his meditations in the dark, while the choral symphony of snores gained new and individual artistes around him. After a while he fell asleep himself.

When he woke up the lights were on again, and men were pulling on their coats and gulping cups of hot tea. One by one they began to slouch off into the tunnel; and Simon splashed cold water on his face from a basin and joined in the general move with a re-awakening of vitality. A glance at his watch showed him that it was half-past four, but it might have been morning or afternoon for all the sense of time he had left. When he came up the creaking stair ladder into the billiard-room, however, he saw that it was still dark. Renway, in a light overcoat, was standing close to the panel watching the men as they emerged; he beckoned the Saint with a slight backward tilt of his head.

'How are you getting on?' he asked.

Simon glanced at the last two men as they stumbled through

the panel and followed their companions across the room and out by the more conventional door.

'I have been in more hilarious company,' he murmured.

Renway did not appear to hear his answer—the impression was that his interest in Mr Tombs' social progress was merely formal. He did something to the woodwork at the level of his shoulder, and the secret panel closed with a slight click.

'You'd better know some more about our arrangements,' he said.

They went out of the house by the same route as they had finally come in the previous morning. The file of men who had preceded them was already trudging southwards over the rough grass as if on a journey that had become familiar by routine— the Saint saw the little dabs of light thrown by their electric torches bobbing over the turf. A pale strip of silver in the east promised an early dawn, and the cool sweetness of the air was indescribably delicious after the acrid frowstiness of the cellar. Renway produced a flashlight of his own, and walked in flat-footed taciturnity. They reached the edge of the cliffs and started down a narrow zigzag path. Half-way down it, the Saint suddenly missed the dancing patches of torchlight ahead: he was wondering whether to make any comment when Renway touched his arm and halted.

'This way.'

The oval imprint of Renway's flashlight flickered over the dark spludge of a shrub growing in a cleft beside the path; suddenly Renway's own silhouette appeared in the shrinking circle of light, and Simon realised that the Treasury was going down on all fours and beginning to wriggle into the bush, presenting a well-rounded posterior which might have proved an irresistible and fatal temptation to an aggrieved ex-Service Civil Servant. The Saint, however, having suffered no especial unkindness from the Government, followed him dutifully in the same manner, and discovered that he could stand upright again on the other side of the opening in the cliff. At the same time he saw the torches of the other men again, heading downwards into the dark as if on a long stairway.

Thirty feet lower down the steps levelled off into an uneven floor. Simon saw the gleam of dark waters in the light of Renway's torch, and realised that he was at the foot of a huge natural cave. The lights of the other men were clustered a few yards away— Simon heard a clunk of wood and metal and the soft splash of an oar.

'The only other way to the sea is under water,' Renway explained, his thin voice echoing hollowly. 'You can see it at low neap tides, but at this time of year it's always covered.'

It was on the tip of the Saint's tongue to make some facetious remark about submarines when Renway lifted his torch a little, and Simon saw a shining black whaleback of steel curving out of the water a couple of dozen feet from where they stood, and knew that his flippancy could only have seemed ridiculous beside the truth.

'Did you catch that with a rod and line?' he asked, after a considerable silence.

'It was ostensibly purchased by a French film company six months ago,' Renway said prosaically.

'And who's going to run it?'

'Petrowitz—he was a U-boat officer during the war. The rest of the crew had to be trained. It was more difficult to obtain torpedoes—In case anything should come to the rescue which was too big for you to drive off, you understand. But we succeeded.'

The Saint put his hands in his pockets. His face was chiselled bronze masked by the dark.

'I get it,' he said softly. 'The gold is taken on board that little beauty. And then you go down to the bottom and nobody ever sees you any more. And then when you turn up again somewhere in South America—'

'We come back here,' said Renway. 'There are certain reasons why this is one of the last places where anyone would ever expect to find us.'

Simon admitted it. From Renway's point of view, it must have loomed out as one of the most cunning certainties of crime. And the Saint was quite cold-bloodedly aware that if he failed to separate himself from the picnic in time, it would still be true.

The party of men in the rowboat had reached the submarine and were climbing out.

'My information is that the gold will be leaving Croydon about eight o'clock,' Renway said in a matter-of-fact tone. 'Perhaps you'd like to check over your aeroplane—there are one or two things I want to talk over with Petrowitz.'

The Saint did not want to check over any aeroplane, but there was something else he very much wanted to do. He found his way back up the stairway with Renway's torch and wriggled out again through the hole in the cliff—the last glimpse he had of that strange scene was the lights glinting on the water far below him and the shadows moving over the dull sheen of the submarine's arched back. Renway had certainly spared no effort or expense to provide all the most modern and sensational accessories of melodrama, he reflected as he retraced his tracks to the house, what with electrified wire fences, stolen aeroplanes, landing by night, bombs, secret panels, caves, submarines, and unshaven desperadoes; but he found the actuality less humorous than he would have found the same recital in a book. Simon had long had a theory that the most dangerous criminal would be a man who helped himself to some of the vast fund of daring ingenuity expended upon his problems by hordes of detective-story writers; and Sir Hugo Renway's establishment looked more like a detective story come to life than anything the Saint had ever seen.

The dawn was lightening as he found his way into the library and went directly to the safe. He knelt down in front of it and unrolled a neat leather wallet which he took from a pocket in his voluminous flying-coat—the instruments in that wallet were the latest and most ingenious in the world, and would in themselves have been sufficient to earn him a long term of imprisonment, without any other evidence, if Mr Teal had caught him with them. The safe was also one of the latest and most useful models, but it was at a grave disadvantage. Being an inanimate object, it couldn't change its methods of defence so nimbly as the Saint could vary his attack. Besides which, the Saint was prepared to boast that he could make any professional peterman look like a two-year-old infant playing with a rubber crowbar when it came to safe-opening. He worked with unhurried speed and had the door open in twenty minutes; and then he carefully rolled up his kit and put it away again before he turned to an examination of the interior.

He had already charted out enough evidence within the thirty-acre confines of March House to have hanged a regiment, but there were still one or two important items missing. He found one useful article very quickly in a small heap of correspondence on one of the shelves—it was a letter which in itself was no evidence of anything but it was addressed to Sir Hugo Renway and signed by Manuel Enrique. Simon put it away in his pocket and went on with his search. He opened a japanned deed-box and found it crammed with banknotes and bearer bonds: that was not evidence at all, but it was the sort of thing which Simon Templar was always pleased to find, and he was just tipping it out when he heard the rattle of the doorhandle behind him.

The Saint moved like a cat touched with a high-voltage wire. In what seemed like one connected movement, he scooped the bundle of currency and bonds into his pocket, shoved the deed-box back on its shelf, swung the door of the safe, and leapt behind the nearest set of curtains; and then Renway came into the room.

He walked straight across to the safe, fishing out the key from his waistcoat pocket; but the door opened as soon as he touched the handle, and he froze into an instant's dreadful immobility. Then he fell on his knees and dragged out the empty deed-box . . .

Simon stepped quietly out from behind the curtains, so that he was between Renway and the door.

'Don't cry, Mother Hubbard,' he said.

## IX

Renway got to his feet, and looked down the barrel of the Saint's gun. His face was pasty, but the lipless gash of a mouth was almost inhumanly steady.

'Oh, it's you,' he whispered.

'It is I,' said the Saint, with impeccable grammar. 'Come here, Hugo—I want to see what you've got on you.'

He plunged his left hand swiftly and dexterously into the other's inner breast pocket, and found the second thing he had been looking for. It was a cheap pocket diary, and he knew without examining it that it was the one on which his forged trade-marks had been drawn. Renway must have been insanely confident of his immunity from suspicion to keep it on him.

'What ho!' drawled Simon contentedly. 'Stand back again, Hugo, while I see if you've been compromising yourself.'

He stepped back himself, and barely had time to feel the foot of the man behind him under his heel before a brawny arm shot over his shoulder and grasped his gun wrist in a grip like a twisting clamp of iron. Simon started to turn, but in the next split second another brawny arm whipped round his neck and pinned him.

The wrenching hand on his wrist forced him to drop his gun— it had begun to twist too long before he began resisting. Then he let himself go completely limp, while his left hand felt for the knees of the man behind him. His arm locked round them and he heaved himself backwards with a sudden jerk of his thighs. They fell heavily together, and the grips on his waist and neck were broken. Simon squirmed over, put a knee in the man's stomach, and sprang up and away; and then he saw that Renway had snatched up the automatic and was covering him.

Simon Templar, who knew the difference between certain death and a sporting chance, put up his hands quickly.

'OK, boys,' he said. 'Now you think of a game.'

Renway's forefinger weighed on the trigger.

'You fool!' he said almost peevishly.

'Admitted,' said the Saint. 'Nobody ought to walk backwards without eyes in the back of his head.'

Renway had also picked up the diary, which Simon had dropped in the struggle. He put it back in his pocket.

The Saint's brain was turning over so fast that he could almost hear it hum. He still had Enrique's letter—and the bundle of cash. There was still no reason for Renway to suspect him of anything more than ordinary stealing: his taking of the diary was not necessarily suspicious. And Simon understood very clearly that if Renway suspected him of anything more than ordinary stealing, he could, barring outrageous luck, only leave March House in one position. Which would be depressingly and irrevocably horizontal.

Even then, there might be no alternative attitude; but it was worth trying. Simon had a stubborn desire to hang on to that incriminating letter as long as possible. He took out the sheaf of bonds and banknotes and threw them on the desk.

'There's the rest of it,' he said cynically. 'Shall we call it quits?'

Renway's squinting eyes wandered over him.

'Do you always expect to clear yourself so easily?' he asked like a schoolmaster.

'Not always,' said the Saint. 'But you can't very well hand me over to the police this time, can you? I know too much about you.'

In the next moment he knew he had made a mistake. Renway's convergent gaze turned on to Petrowitz, who was massaging his stomach tenderly.

'He knows too much,' Renway repeated.

'I suppose there's no chance of letting bygones be bygones and still letting me fly that aeroplane?' Simon asked shrewdly.

The nervous twitch which he had seen before went over Renway's body, but the thin mouth only tightened with it.

'None at all, Mr Tombs.'

'I was afraid so,' said the Saint.

'Let me take him,' Petrowitz broke in with his thick gruff voice. 'I will tie iron bars to his legs and fire him through one of the torpedo tubes. He will not talk after that.'

Renway considered the suggestion, and shook his head.

'None of the others must know. Any doubt or fear in their minds may be dangerous. He can go back into the cellar. Afterwards, he can take the same journey as Enrique.'

Probably for much the same offence, Simon thought grimly; but he smiled.

'That's very sweet of you, Hugo,' he remarked; and the other looked at him.

'I hope you will continue to be satisfied.'

He might have been going to say more, but at that moment the telephone began to ring. Renway sat down at the desk.

'Hullo . . . Yes . . . Yes—speaking.' He drew a memorandum block towards him and took up a pencil from a glass tray. With the gun close to his hand, he jotted down letters and figures. 'Yes, G-EZQX. At seven . . . Yes . . . Thank you.' He sat for a little while staring at the pad, as if memorising his note and rearranging his plans. Then he pressed the switch of a microphone which stood on the desk beside the ordinary post office instrument. 'Kellard?' he said. 'There is a change of time. Have the Hawker outside and warmed up by seven o'clock.'

He picked up the automatic again and rose from the desk.

'They're leaving an hour earlier,' he said, speaking to Petrowitz. 'We haven't any time to waste.'

The other man rubbed his beard.

'You will be flying yourself?'

'Yes,' said Renway, as if defying contradiction. He motioned with his gun towards the door. 'Petrowitz will lead the way, Mr Tombs.'

Simon felt that he was getting quite familiar with the billiard-room, and almost suggested that the three of them should put aside their differences and stop for a game; but Renway had the secret panel open as soon as the Saint reached it. With the two men watching him, Simon went down the shaky wooden stair and heard the spring door close behind him.

He sat down on the bottom step, took out his cigarette-case, and computed that if all the cellars in which he had been imprisoned as an adjunct or preliminary to murder had been dug one underneath the other, they would have provided the shaft of a diametric subway between England and the Antipodes. But his jailers had not always been so generous as to push him into the intestines of the earth without searching him; and his blue eyes were thoughtful as he took out his portable burgling kit again. Renway must have been going to pieces rapidly, to have overlooked such an obvious precaution as that; but this meant, if anything, that for a few mad hours he would be more dangerous than before. The attack on the gold plane would still be made, Simon realised, unless he got out in time to stop it. It was not until some minutes after he had started work on the door that he discovered that the panel which concealed it was backed by a solid plate of case-hardened steel . . .

It was a quarter past six when he started work, by his wrist watch; it was five minutes past seven when he got out. He had to dig his way through twelve inches of solid brick with a small screwdriver before he could get the claw of his telescopic jemmy behind the steel panel and break the lock inwards. Anyone who had come that way must have heard him; but in that respect his luck held flawlessly. Probably neither Renway nor Petrowitz had a doubt in their minds that the tempered steel plate would be enough to hold him.

He was tired and sweating when he got out, and his knuckles were raw in several places from accidental blows against the brickwork which they had suffered unnoticed in his desperate haste; but he could not stop. He raced down the long corridor and found his way through the house to the library. Nobody crossed his path. Renway had said that the regular servants would all be away, and the gang were probably busy at their appointed stations; but if anyone had attempted to hinder him, Simon with his bare hands would have had something fast and savage to say to the interference. He burst recklessly into the library, and looked out of the French windows in time to see the grey shape of the Hawker pursuit plane skimming across the far field like a bullet and lofting airily over the trees at the end.

Simon lighted another cigarette very quietly, and watched the grey ship climbing swiftly into the clear morning sky. If there was something cold clutching at his heart, if he was tasting the sourest narrowness of defeat, no sign of it could have been read on the tanned outline of his face.

After a second or two he sat down at the desk and picked up the telephone.

'Croydon 2720,' he called, remembering the number of the aerodrome.

The reply came back very quickly.

'I'm sorry—the line is out of order.'

'Then get me Croydon Police Station.'

'I'm afraid we can't get through to Croydon at all. All the lines seem to have gone wrong.'

Simon bit his lip.

'Can you get me Scotland Yard?'

He knew the answer to that inquiry also, even before he heard it, and realised that even at that stage of the proceedings he had underestimated Sir Hugo Renway. There would be no means of establishing rapid communication with any vital spot for some hours—that was because something might have gone wrong with the duplicate wireless arrangements, or one of the possible rescue ships might have managed to transmit a message.

The Saint blew perfect smoke-rings at the ceiling, and stared at the opposite wall. There was only one other wild solution. He had no time to try any other avenues. There would first be the business of establishing his bona fides, then of convincing an impenetrably sceptical audience, then of getting word through by personal messenger to a suitable headquarters—and the transport plane would be over the Channel long before that. But he remembered Renway's final decision—'None of the others must know'—and touched the switch of the table microphone.

'Kellard?' he said. 'This is Tombs. Get my machine out and warmed up right away.'

'Yessir,' said the mechanic, without audible surprise; and

Simon Templar felt as if a great load had been lifted from his shoulders.

Probably he still had no chance, probably he was still taking a path to death as certain as that which he would have trodden if he had stayed in the cellar; but it was something to attempt— something to do.

Of course, there was a radio station on the premises. Renway had said so. But undoubtedly it was well hidden. He might spend half an hour and more looking for it . . .

No—he had taken the only way. And if it was a form of spectacular suicide, it ought to have its diverting moments before the end.

It was only natural that in those last few moments he should think of Patricia. He took up the telephone again and called his own number at St George's Hill. In ten seconds the voice of Orace, who never seemed to sleep, answered him. 'They've gorn,' Orace informed him, with a slight sinister emphasis on the pronoun. 'Miss 'Olm says she's sleepin' at Cornwall 'Ouse. Nobody's worried 'er.'

Simon called another number.

'Hullo, sweetheart,' he said; and the Saintly voice had never been more gentle, more easy and light-hearted, more bubbling over with the eager promise of an infinite and adventurous future. 'Why, I'm fine . . . No, there hasn't been any trouble. Just an odd spot of spontaneous combustion in the withered brain-cells of Claud Eustace Teal—but we've had that before. I've got it all fixed . . . Never mind how, darling. You know your Simon. This is much more important. Now listen carefully. D'you remember a guy named George Wynnis, that I've talked about soaking some time? . . . Well, he lives at 366 South Audley Street. He never gets up before ten in the morning, and he never has less than two thousand quid in his pockets. Phone Hoppy to join you, and go get that dough—now! And listen. Leave my mark behind!'

'You're crazy,' she said; and he laughed.

'I am and I'm not,' he said. 'But this time I have the perfect alibi; and I want to get you every cent I can lay hold of before I cash in my chips.' The lilt in his voice made it impossible to take him literally. 'God bless you, keed,' he said. 'Be seein' ya!'

He hung up the handpiece and leaned back in his chair, inhaling the last puffs of his cigarette. Surely, this time, he had the perfect and immutable alibi. A dry sardonic smile touched his lips; but the fine-cut sapphires in his eyes were twinkling. It would give Claud Eustace something more to think about, anyway . . . He looked out of the windows, down the long gentle slope that was just being gilded by the sun, and he saw his own Tiger Moth standing beside the old tithe barn, the propeller lost in a swirling circle of light, the mechanic's hair fluttering in the cockpit, a thin plume of haze drifting back from the exhaust. The sky was a pale crystalline eggshell-blue, clear and still as a dream, a sky that could give a man pleasant memories to carry with him into the long dark . . .

Without conscious thought, he hauled out his helmet from a side pocket, pulled it over his head, buckled the strap, and adjusted the goggles on his forehead. And he was doing that when a shadow fell across the desk and he looked up.

A broad-shouldered portly form, with a round cherubic pink face and small baby-blue eyes, crowned with an incongruous black bowler hat of old-fashioned elevation, was filling the open French doors. It was Chief Inspector Teal.

X

Simon sprang up impetuously.

'Claud!' he cried. 'I never thought I should be glad to see your huge stomach—'

'I thought you might be here,' said the detective stiffly.

He came on into the room, but only far enough to allow Sergeant Barrow to follow him through the window. With that end accomplished, he kept his distance. There was still a puffy tenderness in his jaw to remind him of a fist like a chunk of stone driven by a bolt of lightning, which had reached him once already when he came too near.

'It must be this deductive business that Scotland Yard is taking up,' Simon remarked more slowly.

Teal nodded without relaxing.

'I knew you were interested in Renway, and I knew you'd been here once before—when Uniatz knocked out the policeman. It occurred to me that it'd be just like you to come back, in spite of everything.'

'In spite of hell and high water,' Simon murmured with a faint smile, 'we keep on doing our stuff. Well, it's not a bad reputation to have . . . But this time I've got something more important to say to you.'

'I've got the same thing to say to you as I had last time,' said the detective, iron-jawed. 'I want you, Saint.'

Simon started round the desk.

'But this is serious!'

'So is this,' said Teal implacably. He took his right hand out of his pocket, and there was a gun in it. 'I don't want to have to use it, but I'm going to take you back this time if it's the last thing I do.'

The Saint's eyes narrowed to shreds of flint.

'You're damn right it'll be the last thing you do!' he shot back. And then his tensed lips moved into the thinnest of dim smiles. 'Now listen to me, you great oaf. You want me for being mixed up with a guy named Hoppy Uniatz who smacked a cop on the button outside here the other night. Guilty. But you also want me for the murder of Manuel Enrique and the knocking off of an aeroplane from Hawker's. Not guilty and not guilty. That's what I wanted to see you for. That's the only reason on earth why I couldn't have been more glad to see anything else walk in here than your fatuous red face. I want to tell you who you really do want!'

'I know who I want,' answered Teal stonily.

'Yeah?' The Saint's voice was one vicious upward swoop of

derision. 'Then did you know you were standing inside his house right now?'

Mr Teal blinked. His eyes began a fractional widening; his mouth began an infinitesimal opening.

'Renway?' he said. And then the baleful scepticism came back into his face with a tinge of colour. 'Is that your new alibi?' he jeered.

'That's my new alibi,' said the Saint, rather quickly and quietly; 'and you'd better listen to it. Did you know that Renway was the man who stole that aeroplane from Hawker's?'

'I didn't. And I don't know it yet.'

'He brought it here and landed it here, and I watched him. Go down to that field out there and have a look at the scars in the grass where he had his flares, if you're too dumb to believe me. Did you know that he had a submarine in a cave in the cliffs, with live torpedoes on board?'

'Did I know—?'

'Did you know that the crew of the submarine have been sleeping in a secret room under this house for months? Did you know they were the toughest bunch of hoodlums I've seen in England for years?'

'Did I—'

'Did you know,' asked the Saint in a final rasp, 'that three million pounds in gold is on its way flying from Croydon to Paris right now while you're getting in my hair with your blathering imitation of a bum detective—and Renway has got everything set to shoot it down and set up a crime record that'll make Scotland Yard look more half-witted than it's ever looked since I started taking it apart?'

The detective swallowed. There was an edge of savage sincerity in the Saint's voice which bit into the leathery hide of his incredulity. He suffered a wild fantastic temptation to begin to listen, to take in the preposterous story that the Saint was putting up, to consider the items of it soberly and seriously. And he was sure he was making a fool of himself. He gulped down the ridiculous impulse and plunged into defensive sarcasm.

'Of course I didn't know all that,' he almost purred. 'Is Einstein going to prove it for you, or will Renway admit it himself?'

'Renway will admit it himself,' said the Saint grimly. 'But even that won't be necessary. Did you know that these ten tons of gold were being shipped on aeroplane G-EZQX, which took off from Croydon at seven?' He ripped the top sheet off the memorandum block on the desk, and thrust it out. 'Do you know that that's his handwriting, or will you want his bank manager to tell you?'

Teal looked at the sheet.

'It doesn't matter much whether it's his writing, or your version of it,' he said, with an almost imperceptible break in the smoothness of his studied purr. 'As a Treasury official, Renway has a perfect right to know anything like that.'

'Yeah?' Simon's voice was suddenly so soft that it made Teal's laboured suaveness sound like the screech of a circular saw. 'And I suppose he had a perfect right to know Manuel Enrique, and not say anything about it when he brought him into the police station at Horley?'

'Who says he knew Enrique?'

The Saint smiled.

'Not me, Claud. If I tell you he did, it'll just make you quite sure he didn't. This is what says so.'

He put his hand in his pocket and took out the letter which he had found in the safe. 'Or maybe I faked this, too?' he suggested mildly.

'You may have done,' said Teal dispassionately; but his baby-blue eyes rested with a rather queer intensity on Simon's face.

'Come for a walk, Claud,' said the Saint gently, 'and tell me if I faked this.'

He turned aside quite calmly under the muzzle of Teal's gun, and walked to the door. For no earthly reason that he could have given in logical terms, Mr Teal followed him. And all the time he had a hot gnawing fear that he was making a fool of himself.

Sergeant Barrow followed Mr Teal because that was his job.

He was a fool anyway, and he knew it. Mr Teal had often told him so.

In the billiard-room, Simon pointed to the panel sagging loose on its hinges as he had torn it off—the hole he had chipped through the wall, the wooden stairway going steeply down into the chalk.

'That's where those six men have been living, so that the ordinary servants never knew there was anything going on. You'll find their beds, and everything. That's where I was shut up when they got wise to who I was; and that's where I've just got out of.'

Teal said nothing for several seconds. And then the most significant thing was not what he said, but what he did.

He put his gun back in his pocket, and looked at the Saint almost helplessly. No one will ever know what it cost him to be as natural as that. But whatever his other failings may have been, Chief Inspector Teal was a kind of sportsman. He could take it, even when it hurt.

'What else do you know?' he asked.

'That the submarine is out in the Channel now, waiting for the aeroplane to come down. That Renway's up over here in that Hawker ship, with loaded machine-guns to shoot down the gold transport, and a packet of bombs to drop on any boat that tries to go to the rescue. That all the telephone lines to Croydon Aerodrome, and between the coast and London, have been cut. That there's a radio transmitter somewhere in this place—I haven't found it yet—which is just waiting to carry on signalling when the transport plane stops. That there isn't a hope in hell of getting a warning through to anywhere in time to stop the raid.'

Teal's pink face had gone curiously pale.

'Isn't there anything we can do?' he said.

'There's only one thing,' answered the Saint. 'Down on the landing-field you probably saw a Tiger Moth warming up. It's mine. It's the ship I came here in—but that's another story. With your permission, I can go up in it and try to keep Renway off.

416

Don't tell me it's suicide, because I know all that. But it's murder for the crew of that transport plane if I don't try.'

The detective did not answer for a moment. He stared at the floor, avoiding the Saint's straight blue gaze.

'I can't stop you,' he said at last; and Simon smiled.

'You can forget about Hoppy hitting that policeman, if you're satisfied with the other evidence,' he said. He had a sudden absurd thought of what would shortly be happening to a certain George Wynnis, and a shaft of the old mockery touched his smile like sunlight. 'And next time I tell you that some low criminal is putting his stuff on to me, Claud,' he said, 'you mayn't be so nasty and disbelieving.'

His forefinger prodded Mr Teal's stomach in the old maddening way; but his smile was only reminiscent. And without another word he went out of the billiard-room, down the long dark corridor to the open air.

As he climbed into the cockpit of his ship he looked back towards the house, and saw Mr Teal standing on the terrace watching him. He waved a gay arm, while the mechanic dragged away the chocks from under the wheels; and then he settled down and opened the throttle. The stick slid forward between his knees, the tail lifted, and he went roaring down the field to curve upwards in a steep climbing turn over the trees.

He had left it late enough; and if the wind had been in the north instead of in the south, he might have been too late. Winding up the sky in smoothly controlled spirals, he saw the single wide span of a big monoplane coming up from the northern horizon, and knew that it must be the transport plane for which Renway was waiting—no other ship of that build would have been flying south at that hour. He looked for Renway, and saw a shape like a big square-tipped seagull swinging round in a wide circle over the Channel, six thousand feet up in the cloudless blue . . .

Renway! The Saint's steady fingers moved on the stick, steepening the angle of climb by a fraction; and his lips settled in a grim reckless line at the reminder that those fingers had no Bowden trips under them, as Renway's had. He looked ahead through the propeller between a double rank of dancing valve-springs instead of between the foreshortened blued jackets of a pair of guns. He was taking on a duel in which nothing but his own skill of hand and eye could be matched against the spitting muzzles of Renway's guns—and whatever skill Renway could bring to the handling of them. And suddenly the Saint laughed—a devilish buccaneering laugh that bared his teeth and edged the chilled steel in his eyes, and was drowned to soundlessness in the smashing howl of his engine and whipped away in the tearing sting of the wind.

Renway! The man who had taken his name in vain. The man who had murdered Enrique, and put the Saint's mark on him. The man who had stolen the very aeroplane which he was now going up to fight—and had put the Saint's mark on the theft. The over-fed, mincing, nerve-ridden, gas-choked, splay-footed, priggish, yellow-bellied, pompous great official sausage who had had the everlasting gall to say that to himself—he—was the Saint!

Simon Templar glanced at the altimeter, and edged the stick forward again along his right thigh. Five thousand feet . . . A gentle pressure of his right foot on the rudder, and the Tiger Moth swung round and levelled off. The country beneath him was flattened out like a painted map, the light green of fields, the darker green of woods, white ribbons of road, and a white ribbon of surf along the edge of the grey-green sea. The transport plane was slipping across the map half a mile under him, cruising at ninety miles an hour air-speed—a lumbering slow-motion cargo boat of the skies. His eagle's eyesight picked out the letters painted across the upper fabric of the wing. G-EZQX. His own air-speed indicator showed a hundred and eighty. It went through his mind that Renway must have watched him coming up. Renway must have seen the Tiger Moth warming up outside the barn, and seen it take off. Renway must have guessed that something had gone wrong—must, even then, have been staring down with glazed eyes and twitching fingers, realising that there was an obstacle in his path that must be blotted out.

Simon wondered when the attack would come.

And at that moment it came.

His machine quivered slightly, and he saw an irregular line of punctures sewing itself diagonally across his left wing. Even above the roar of his own engine he heard the Hawker's guns cackling their fierce challenge down the sky. He kicked the rudder and hauled the stick back into his groin, and grinned mirthlessly at the downward drag of his bowels as the nose of the Moth surged upwards, skew-eyed, like the prow of a ship in a terrific sea, and whipped over in a flick roll that twisted into the downward half of a tight loop.

XI

Renway came about in a skidding turn and plunged after him. Screwed round to watch him over the tail, Simon led him down in a shallow dive, weaving deftly from side to side against the efforts of the Hawker's nose to follow him. Little hiccoughs of orange flame danced on the muzzles of Renway's guns; gleaming squirts of tracer went rocketing past the Moth, now wide on the right, now wide on the left. The Saint went on smiling. Aiming an aeroplane is a fine art, and Renway hadn't had the practice—it was the only factor which Simon could count on his side.

A chance swerve of the Hawker sprayed another line of pock-marks across the fuselage; and Simon drew back on the stick and went over in a sudden loop. Renway shot past under his tail and began to pull round in a belated vertical bank. The Saint put a curve in the fall of his loop and went to meet him. They raced head-on for a collision. Simon held his course till the last split second, lifted his nose slightly for a hint, and zoomed over the Hawker's prop on the upturn of a switchback that carried him clear of death by shaved inches.

He looked down on the swing-over of the stalling turn that ended his zoom, and saw Renway's ship sloping down, wobbling erratically. And his fine-drawn hell-for-leather smile glinted wickedly as he opened out the throttle and went down on the Hawker again in a shrieking power dive.

Down . . . down . . . The engine howling and the wires moaning shriller and shriller as the air-speed indicator climbed over three hundred and twenty miles an hour. His whole body tensed and waiting fearfully for the first vibration, the first shiver of the wing-tips that would spell the break-up of the machine. The Tiger Moth wasn't built for that sort of work. It was the latest, strongest, fastest thing of its kind in the air; but it wasn't designed for fighting aerobatics. He saw the Hawker dodging in hesitant clumsy efforts to escape; saw Renway's white goggled face staring back over the empennage, leaping up towards him at incredible speed. He set his teeth and pulled back the stick . . . Now! The Moth seemed to squat down in the air, momentarily blinding him as the frightful centrifugal force sucked the blood down from his head; but the wings held. He peered over the side and saw the Hawker diving again, veering wildly in the trembling control of its pilot.

Simon looped off the top of his zoom and went down again.

That was the only thing he could do, the only hope he had of beating the Hawker's guns. Dive and zoom, loop and dive again. Wipe the Moth's undercarriage across the Hawker's upper wing every time. Split-arch and dive again. Ride the Hawker down by sheer reckless flying. Wing-over and dive again, wires screaming and engine thundering. Smash down on Renway from every angle of the sky, pitting nerve against nerve, judgment against judgment; make him duck and push the stick forward a little more, every time, with the wheels practically rolling over his head with every hairbreadth miss. Beat him down five hundred feet, a thousand, fifteen hundred. Loop and dive again . . .

The Saint flew as he had never flown before. He did things that couldn't be done, took chances that could never come off, tore his machine through the air under strains that no ship of its class could possibly survive—and kept on flying. If Renway had been able to fly half as well, it couldn't have gone on.

But Renway couldn't fly half as well. For minutes at a time, his guns never had a target within forty-five degrees of them; and when he brought them round, the target had gone. And each time, a little more of his nerve went with it. He was losing height faster and faster, losing it foot by foot to that nerveless demon of the sky who seemed to have made up his mind to lock their machines together and send them crashing to earth in a single shroud of flame . . . The Saint smiled with merciless blue eyes like chips of frozen sea-water; and dived again . . . He was going to win. He knew it. He could see the Hawker wobbling more wildly at every moment, plunging more panickily downwards at every effort to escape, sprawling more clumsily on every amateurish manoeuvre.

He saw Renway's white face looking round again, saw a gloved fist impotently shaken at him, saw the mouth open and heard in his imagination the scream of fury that was ripped to fragments in the wind; and he laughed. He could divine what was in Renway's mind—divine the trembling twitching fear that was shuddering through his flabby limbs, the clammy sweat that must have been breaking out on the soft body—and he laughed through a mask of merciless bronze and swept the Moth screeching down again to whisk its wheels six inches over Renway's helmet. Renway, the snivelling jelly who had called himself the Saint.

Then, for the first time in a long while, he looked down to see what else was happening, and saw that the dog-fight had carried them about a mile out over the sea, and the transport plane was just passing over the cliffs.

Renway must have seen it too. Suddenly, in a frantic vertical bank which almost went into a power spin, he turned and dived on it, his guns rattling.

Simon pushed the stick into the dash, flung the throttle wide, and went down like a plummet.

The sobbing growl of the motor wailed up to an eldritch shriek as the ship slashed through the air. Down and down; with a wind greater than anything in nature slapping his face and plucking at his goggles, while the transport plane curled away in a startled bank and Renway twisted after it. Down and down, in the maddest plunge of that fantastic combat. Fingers cool and steady on the stick, feet as gentle on the rudder bar as the hands of a horseman on the reins, every coordinated nerve and muscle holding the ship together like a living creature. Bleak eyes following every movement of his quarry. Lips parted and frozen in a deadly smile. Down and down, till he saw the bulk of the Imperial Airways monoplane leap upwards past the tail of his eye, and realised that Renway had shot down past his mark without scoring a hit. Downwards still, while Renway flattened out in a slow turn and began to climb again.

Finish it now—before Renway got in another burst which might be lucky enough to score.

Down . . . But there wasn't a civil aeroplane built which could squat down out of a dive like that without leaving its wings behind. It would have to be fairly gentle—and that would be bad enough. As coolly as if he had been driving a car at twenty miles an hour, the Saint judged his margin and felt the resistance on the stick. For one absurd instant he realised that Renway's cockpit was coming stone-cold into the place where the sights would have been if the Moth had been armed . . .

Crash!

The Moth shuddered under him in an impact like the explosion of a big gun. The painted map whirled across his vision while he fought to get the ship under control. He glanced out to right and left—both wings were still there, apparently intact. The nose of the machine began to lift again, steadily, across the flat blue water and the patchwork carpet, until at last it reached the horizon.

Simon looked down.

The Hawker was going down, five hundred feet below him, in a slow helpless spin. Its tail section was shattered as if a giant club had hit it, and tangled up with it were some splintered spars which looked as if they had belonged to his own landing gear. He had glimpses of Renway struggling wildly in the cockpit, wrestling with the useless controls, and felt a momentary twinge of pity which did not show in his face. After all, the man must have been mad . . . And even if he had killed and tried to kill, he was not going to the most pleasant of all deaths.

Then Simon remembered the bombs which the Hawker was supposed to carry, and realised that the end might be quick.

He watched the Hawker with a stony fascination. If it fell in the sea, the bombs might not go off. But it was very near the cliffs, bobbing and fluttering like a broken grey leaf . . . For several seconds he thought it would miss the land.

And then, in one of those queer freaks of aero-dynamics which every airman knows, it steadied up. For an instant of time it seemed to hang poised in the air. And then, with the straight clean swoop of a paper dart, it dived into the very rim of the surf which was creaming along the foot of the white cliffs. There was a split second of horrible suspense; and then the wreckage seemed to lift open under the thrust of a great tongue of orange-violet flame.

Simon Templar tasted his sherry, and lighted a cigarette.

'It was fairly easy after that,' he said. 'I did a very neat pancake on the water about fifty yards off-shore, and a motor-boat brought me in. I met Teal half-way up the cliff and showed him the entrance of the cave. We took a peek inside, and damn if Petrowitz and his crew weren't coming up the steps. Renway had crashed right on top of the underwater exit and blown it in—and the sub was bottled up inside. Apparently the crew had seen our scrap and guessed that something had gone wrong, and scuttled back for home. They were heading for the last round-up with all sail set, and since they could only get out one at a time we didn't lose any weight helping them on their way.'

Patricia Holm was silent for a moment.

'You didn't deserve to come out of it with a whole skin,' she said.

'I came out of it with more than that, old darling,' said the Saint, with impenitent eyes. 'I opened the safe again before I left, and collected Hugo's cash-box again. It's outside in the car now.'

Hoppy Uniatz was silent somewhat longer. It is doubtful whether he had any clear idea of what all the excitement had ever been about; but he was able to grasp one point in which he seemed to be involved.

'Boss,' he said tentatively, 'does it mean I ain't going to take no rap for smackin' de cop?'

The Saint smiled.

'I guess you can put your shirt on it, Hoppy.'

'Jeez,' said Mr Uniatz, reaching for the whisky with a visible revival of interest, 'dat's great! Howja fix it?'

Simon caught Patricia's eye, and sighed. And then he began to laugh.

'I got Claud to forget it for the sake of his mother,' he said. 'Now suppose you tell your story. Did you catch Wynnis?'

The front door bell rang on the interrogation, and they listened in a pause of silence, while Hoppy poured himself out half a pint of undiluted Scotch. They heard Orace's limping tread crossing the hall, and the sounds of someone being admitted; and then the study door was opened and Simon saw who the visitor was.

He jumped up.

'Claud!' he cried. 'The very devil we were talking about! I was just telling Hoppy about your mother.'

Mr Teal came just inside the room, and settled his thumbs in the belt of his superfluous overcoat. His china-blue eyes looked as if they were just about to close in the sleep of unspeakable boredom; but that was an old affectation. It had nothing to do with the slight heliotrope flush in his round face, or the slight compression of his mouth. In the ensuing hiatus, an atmosphere radiated from him which was nothing like the sort of atmosphere which should have radiated from a man who was thinking kindly of his mother.

'Oh, you were, were you?' he said, and his voice broke on the words in a kind of hysterical bark. 'Well, I didn't come down from London to hear about my mother. I want to hear what you know about a man called Wynnis, who was held up in his flat at half-past eight this morning—'

I

There was nothing unusual about the fact that when Simon Templar landed in England he was expecting trouble. Trouble was his chosen vocation; the last ten years of his life had held enough of it to satisfy a couple of dozen ordinary men for three or four lifetimes, and it would have been surprising if after so many hectic events he had contemplated a future of rustic quietude, enlivened by nothing more thrilling than wild gambles on the laying abilities of leghorns. But it was perhaps more unusual that the particular trouble which he was expecting on this occasion could not be blamed on any fault of his.

He came down the gangway of the Transylvania with a light step in the summer sunlight, with a soft grey hat canted rakishly over one eye, and a raincoat slung carelessly over his shoulder. There was death in his pocket and peril of an even deadlier kind under his arm; but he faced the Customs officer across his well-labelled luggage with an easy smile, and ran a humorous glance down the list of dutiable and prohibited articles presented for his inspection.

'Yes,' he said, 'I'm carrying large quantities of silk, perfume, wines, spirits, tobacco, cut flowers, watches, embroidery, eggs, type writers, and explosives. I also have some opium and a couple of howitzers—'

'You don't have to be funny about it anyway,' grunted the official, and scrawled the cryptic hieroglyphics that passed him through with his two guns into England.

He sauntered on through the bleak echoing shed, waving casual *adieus* to his acquaintances of the voyage. An American banker from Ohio, who had lost three thousand dollars to him over the poker-table, buttonholed him without malice.

'See you look me up next time you're in Wapakoneta,' he said.

'I won't forget,' Simon answered gravely.

There was a girl with raven hair and deep grey eyes. She was very good to look upon, and Simon had sat out with her on the boat deck under the moon.

'Perhaps you'll be coming to Sacramento one day,' she said.

'Maybe I will,' he said with a quick smile; and the deep grey eyes followed him rather wistfully out of sight.

Other eyes followed the tall lean figure as it swung by, and carried their own pictures of the brown fighting face and the smile that touched the strong reckless mouth and the gay blue eyes. They belonged to a Miss Gertrude Tinwiddle, who had been seasick all the way over, and who would never have been taken on to the boat deck anyhow.

'Who is that man?' she asked.

'His name is Templar,' said her neighbour, who knew everything. 'And you mark my words, there's something queer about him. I shouldn't be surprised if he was a sort of gangster.'

'He looks like a—a sort of cavalier,' said Miss Tinwiddle timidly.

'Pish!' said her companion testily, and returned to the grim task of trying to convince a cynical Customs officer that twenty-four silk dresses would have been a beggarly allowance even for a week-end traveller.

At the end of the shed, Detective-Sergeant Harry Jepson of the Southampton CID said to Police Constable Ernest Potts:

'You see the tall fellow in the grey tweeds coming this way? Handsome devil, isn't he? Well, you'd better remember that face.'

'Who is he?' asked Police Constable Potts.

'That,' said Sergeant Jepson, 'is Mr Simon Templar, alias the Saint; and you aren't likely to see a smarter crook than him in your time. At least, I hope not. He's committed every blooming crime there is from murder downwards, and he'll tell you so himself, but nobody's ever been able to hang a thing on him. And to look at him you'd think he had a conscience like a new-born babe.'

In which utterance Detective-Sergeant Harry Jepson was as close to eternal truth as he was ever likely to get; for the Saint had never been sure that he had a conscience at all, but if he had one there was certainly nothing on it. He looked the two officers shamelessly in the eye as he approached, and as he strolled past them his right hand waved a quizzical salute that had no regard whatever for the affronted majesty of the law.

'D'you ever hear of such blooming sauce?' demanded Mr Jepson indignantly.

But Simon Templar, who was called the Saint, neither heard nor cared. He stood on the railroad platform, tapping a cigarette on a thin platinum case, and panned a thoughtful and quietly vigilant eye along the whole length of the train. He was expecting somebody to meet him, but he knew that it would not be anyone whose welcome would be friendly; and he had the additional disadvantage of not even being able to guess what the welcomer might look like. The Saint's vocation was trouble, but he had contrived to stay alive for thirty-two years only because of an unceasing devotion to the business of divining where the trouble would come from, and meeting it on his toes.

'Wantcher luggidge in the van, sir?' asked the porter who was wheeling his barrow.

The Saint's gaze travelled round to measure up two suitcases and a wardrobe trunk.

'I think so, George,' he murmured. 'I shouldn't be able to run very far with that load, should I?'

He took over his small overnight bag, and saw the rest of his impedimenta registered through to his apartment on Piccadilly. He was still carrying the black book under his arm, and it occurred to him that there were more convenient forms of camouflage for it than the slung raincoat by which it was temporarily hidden. He paused at the bookstall and glanced over the volumes of fiction offered for the entertainment of the traveller. In the circumstances, his choice had to be dictated by size rather than subject-matter.

'I'll take this,' he said brazenly and the assistant's eyes bulged slightly as he paid over three half-crowns for a copy of an opus entitled *Her Wedding Secret*.

A signpost adjoining the bookstall invited gentlemen to enter and make themselves at home, and the Saint drifted through with his purchase. No other gentlemen were availing themselves of the Southern Railway's hospitality at the time, and it was the work of a moment to slip the intriguing jacket from the volume he had just bought and transfer it to the black book from under his arm, where it fitted quite comfortably. He pitched the unknown lady's wedding secret dextrously through the skylight, and went out again with the newly-jacketed black book conspicuously flaunted in his hand—no one who had been watching him would have had any reason to suspect that there had been any change in the contents of that artistically suggestive wrapper.

There were several minutes left before the train was due to leave, and the Saint strolled unhurriedly along the platform with his bag, as though selecting a carriage. If the welcomer or welcomers that he expected were there, he wanted to help them in every possible way. He covered the whole length of the train before he turned back, and then made his choice of an empty smoker. Pushing his suitcase up on to the rack, and dumping his raincoat and book on a corner seat, he leaned out of the window and slid another idly thoughtful glance over the scene.

A military-looking man of about forty-five, with a strongly aquiline nose, and a black guardee moustache, came slowly down the platform. He passed the window without looking round, walked on a little way, and turned. He stood there for a while, teetering toe to heel and gazing vacantly over the gallery of posters plastered on the opposite wall; then he came back, past the Saint's window again, circumnavigated a farewell party congregated outside the next carriage and did the same thing on the other side.

The Saint's cool blue eyes never once looked directly at him; his brown keen-cut face never changed its expression from one of languid patience, but he had seen every movement of the military-looking man's manoeuvres. And Simon Templar knew, beyond a shadow of doubt, that this was at least one of the welcomers whom he had been expecting.

Along the train came a bustle of belated activity, the banging of doors, the scream of the guard's whistle. Simon remained in his window, finishing his cigarette, and saw the military-looking man climb into an adjoining compartment. The engine let out a hiss of steam, and the platform began to slip back under his eyes.

Simon dropped his cigarette and settled back into his corner. He turned the pages of the black book in its new wrapper, refreshing his memory. The action was more automatic than deliberate, only different in degree from a nervous person's gesture in twiddling his thumbs while waiting on tenterhooks for some anticipated event to happen. The Saint already knew almost every line of that amazing volume by heart—he had had plenty of time to study it from cover to cover on the voyage over. The odds were about fifty to one that the military-looking man was mentioned somewhere in its pages; but it was rather difficult to decide, out of the available names, which one he was most likely to bear.

The conductor came round and collected tickets; and then fifteen minutes passed before the door of the Saint's compartment slid back again. Simon closed his book and looked up with exactly the conventional nuance of irritated curiosity, which darkens the distinguished features of the railroad passenger who has contrived to secure a compartment to himself and who finds his privacy illegitimately invaded at the last moment; but the military-looking man put his back to the door and stared at him with a grimness that was by no means conventional.

'Come on,' he said grimly. 'Give me that book!'

'What, this?' said the Saint in innocent surprise, raising *Her Wedding Secret*. 'You're welcome to it when I've finished, brother, but I hardly think it's in your line. I've only got to the part where she discovers that the man she has married is a barbarian lover—'

The intruder pushed the unoffending volume roughly aside.

'I don't mean that,' he said shortly. 'You know perfectly well what book I mean.'

'I'm afraid I don't,' said the Saint.

'And you know perfectly well,' continued the intruder, 'what I'm going to do to you if I don't get it.'

Simon shook his head.

'I can't guess that one either,' he remarked mildly. 'What is it—slap my wrist and tell me to stand in the corner?'

The man's mouth was working under his moustache. He came further into the compartment, past the Saint, and jerked a small automatic from his pocket. It was an almost pathetically amateurish movement—Simon could have forestalled it easily, but he wanted to see how far the other would go.

'Very well,' grated the man. 'I'll have to take it myself. Put 'em up!'

'Up what?' asked the Saint, doing his best to understand.

'Put your hands up. And don't think of any more of that funny stuff, or you'll be sorry for it.'

Simon put his hands up lazily. His bag was on the rack directly over his head, and the handle was within an inch of his fingers.

'I suppose the keepers will be along to collect you in a minute, old fruit?' he drawled. 'Or do you fancy yourself as a sort of highwayman?'

'Now listen, you,' came the snarling answer. 'I'm going to allow you five seconds to give me that book. If I haven't got it in that time, I'm going to shoot. I'll start counting now. One . . . two . . .'

There was a crazy red glare in the intruder's eyes, and although the gun was shaking unsteadily, something told Simon that he had permitted the melodrama to go far enough.

'You know all the rules, don't you, brother?' he said gently, and his fingers grasped the handle of his bag and hurled it full into the other's face.

The man reeled back with the force of the impact, and went crashing against the outside door. It flew open under his weight; and the Saint's blue eyes turned to sudden ice as he realised that it could not have been properly latched when he got in. For one awful instant the man's fingers clawed at the frame; and then with a choking gasp he was gone, and there was only the drab streaked wall of the cutting roaring by the door . . .

Simon's hand reached up instinctively towards the communication cord. And then it drew back.

The intruder, whoever he was, had asked for it: he had taken his own chances. And although Simon Templar had only done what was justified in self-defence, he knew his own reputation at Scotland Yard too well to believe for a moment that it would be a brief and simple task to impress that fact upon the suspicious hostility of the CID. To stop the train would achieve nothing more helpful than his own immediate arrest; and of all the things which might happen to him while he had that black book in his possession, an interlude behind bars in Brixton Prison was the least exhilarating.

He caught the swinging door and closed it again, and then restored his suitcase to the rack. The unknown casualty's gun had gone out with him—there was no other evidence that he had ever entered the compartment.

The Saint lighted a cigarette and sat down again, listening to the rhythmic thrum and rattle of the wheels pounding over the metals towards London. There was nothing unusual about the fact that he was expecting trouble when he returned to Europe, or even about the fact that a fair sample of that trouble should have greeted him within such a short time of setting foot in England.

But it was perhaps more unusual that the particular trouble he was expecting could not be blamed on any fault of his. And the queerest thing of all was that everything should hinge around the black book on his knee which was the legacy of Rayt Marius— the strangest and deadliest gift that any man ever received.

II

He was one of the first passengers to alight from the train at Waterloo, with his raincoat slung over his shoulder and the book in his hand; but he did not take the first available taxi. He allowed six to go by him, and boarded the seventh after taking a good look at it.

'Hyde Park Corner,' he directed it clearly, and watched the traffic out of the rear window as they drove away.

Another taxi swung in behind them, and he noted the number.

Five minutes later he looked again, and it was still there. Simon pressed the button of the telephone.

'Turn right round at Hyde Park Corner and go back the way we've come,' he said.

He waited a short time after his instructions had been carried out, and looked back for the third time. The other taxi was plugging patiently along three yards behind, and the Saint's teeth gleamed in a thin smile. Coincidence of destination was one thing, but coincidence of such a radical change of direction as he had ordered his driver to carry out was quite another matter.

'Now we'll go through the Green Park and up St James's Street,' he said through the telephone.

The driver was so moved that he opened the door an inch and performed incredible contortions to yell back through it.

'Wot is this?' he demanded. 'A game of 'ide-and-seek?'

'You have no idea,' said the Saint.

The apartment he was heading for was in the north side of Piccadilly, overlooking the Green Park. It was only one of many addresses that he had had at various times, to several of which he still owned the keys; but it was the one which had been prepared for his return, and he had no intention of being prevented from going there. The only question was how the shadowing party was to be shaken off.

As they ran up St James's Street he looked at the meter and counted off the necessary change to pay the fare with a substantial tip. When the next frame light reddened against them he stretched a long arm through the window and thrust the money into the driver's hand.

'I shall be leaving you any minute now, Alphonse,' he said. 'But don't let that stop you. Keep right on your way, and don't look back till you get to Hyde Park Corner. And have a bob on Samovar for the Derby.'

He had the door on the latch as they passed the Ritz, and his steel-blue eyes were watching the traffic intently. Three buses were taking on passengers at the stop just west of the hotel, and as they went past the leader was edging out into the stream. Simon looked back and saw it cut out close behind him, baulking the following taxi; and that was his chance. In a flash he was out of his cab, dropping nimbly to the road, and the red side of the bus thundered by a couple of inches from his shoulder. It hid him perfectly from whoever was trailing him in the other cab, which was trying to pass the obstruction and catch up again; and he stood on the sidewalk and watched the whole futile procession trundling away westwards with a relentless zeal that brought an irresponsible twinkle of sheer urchin mischief into his eyes.

A few minutes later he was sauntering into his apartment building and nodding cheerily to the janitor.

'Anybody called while I've been away, Sam?' he asked, as if he had only been away for a weekend.

Sam Outrell's beam of delight gave way to a troubled gravity. He looked furtively about him.

'There was two detectives here the other day, sir,' he said.

The Saint frowned at him thoughtfully for a moment. Although Sam Outrell was nominally employed by the management of the building, he was on Simon Templar's private pay-roll as well; but no stipend could have bought the look of almost dog-like devotion with which he waited anxiously for the Saint's reaction. Simon looked up at him again and smiled.

'I expect they were the birds I hired to try and find a collar-stud that went down the waste pipe,' he said, and went whistling on his way to the lift.

He let himself into his apartment noiselessly. There were sounds of someone moving about in the living-room, and he only stopped to throw his hat and coat on to a chair before he went through and opened the second door.

'Hullo, Pat,' he said softly. 'I thought you'd be here.'

Across the room, a tall slender girl with fair golden hair gazed at him with eyes as blue as his own. There was the grace of a pagan goddess in the way she stood, caught in surprise as she was by the sound of his voice, and the reward of all journeys in the quiver of her red lips.

'So you have come back,' she said.

'After many adventures,' said the Saint, and took her into his arms.

She turned away presently, keeping his arm round her, and showed him the table.

'I got in a bottle of your favourite sherry,' she said rather breathlessly, 'in case you came.'

'In case!' said the Saint.

'Well, after you wired me not to meet you at Southampton—'

He laughed, a quiet lilt of laughter that had rung in her memory for many weeks.

'Darling, that was because I was expecting another deputation of welcome at the same time, and it might have spoilt the fun for both of us. The deputation was there, too—but you shall hear about that presently.'

He filled the two glasses which stood beside the bottle and carried one of them over to an armchair. Over the rim of his glass he regarded her, freshening the portrait which he had carried with him ever since he went away. So much had happened to him, so many things had touched him and passed on into the illimitable emptiness of time, but not one line of her had changed. She was the same as she had been on the day when he first met her, the same as she had been through all the lawless adventures that they had shared since she threw in her lot irrevocably with his. She looked at him in the same way.

'You're older,' she said quietly.

He smiled.

'I haven't been on a picnic.'

'And there's something about you that tells me you aren't on a picnic even now.'

He sipped the golden nectar from his glass and delved for a cigarette. When she said that he was older she could not have pointed to a grey hair or a new line on his face to prove her statement. And at that moment she felt that the clock might well have been put back five years. The fine sunburnt devil-may-care face, the face of a born outlaw, was in some subtle way more keenly etched than ever by the indefinable inward light that came to it when trouble loomed up in his buccaneering path. She knew him so well that the lazy quirk of the unscrupulous freebooter's mouth told a story of its own, and even the whimsical smile that lurked on in his eyes could not deceive her.

'It isn't my fault if you develop these psychic powers, old sweetheart,' he said.

'It's your fault if you can't even stay out of trouble for a week now and again,' she said, and sat on the arm of his chair.

He shook his head, and took one of her hands.

'I tried to, Pat, but it just wasn't meant to happen. A wicked ogre with a black guardee moustache hopped through a window and said "Boo!" and my halo blew off. If I wanted to, I could blame it all on you.'

'How?'

'For just managing to catch me in Boston before I sailed, with that parcel you forwarded!'

Patricia Holm puckered her sweet brow.

'Parcel? . . . Oh, I think I remember it. A thing about the size of a book—it came from Monte Carlo, didn't it?'

'It came from Monte Carlo,' said the Saint carefully, 'and it was certainly about the size of a book. In fact, it was a book. It was the most amazing book I've ever read—maybe the most amazing book that was ever written. There it is!'

He pointed to the volume which he had put down on the table, and she stared at it and then back at him in utter perplexity.

'*Her Wedding Secret*?' she said. 'Have you gone mad, or have I?'

'Neither of us,' said the Saint. 'But you wouldn't believe how many other people are mad about it.'

She looked at him in bewildered exasperation. He was standing up again, a debonair wide-shouldered figure against the sunlight that streamed in through the big windows and lengthened the evening shadows of the trees in the Green Park. She felt the spell of his dare-devil delight as irresistible as it had always been, the absurd glamour which could even take half the sting from his moments of infuriating mysteriousness. He smiled, and his hands went to her shoulders.

'Listen, Pat,' he said. 'That book is a present from an old friend, and he knew what he was doing when he sent it to me. When I show it to you, you'll see that it's the most devilishly clever revenge that ever came out of a human brain. But before we go any further, I want you to know that there's more power in that book for the man who's got it than anyone else in England has today, and for that very reason—'

The sharp trill of the telephone bell cut him off. He looked at the instrument for a moment, and then lifted the receiver.

'Hullo,' he said.

'This is Outrell, sir,' said an agitated voice. 'Those two detectives I told you about—they've just bin here again. They're on their way up to you now, sir.'

Simon gazed dreamily at the ceiling for a second or two, and his finger-tips played a gently syncopated tattoo on the side table.

'OK, Sam,' he said. 'I'll give them your love.'

He replaced the instrument and stood with his hand on it, looking at Patricia. His level blue eyes were mocking and enigmatic, but this time at least she knew enough of his system to read beyond them.

'Hadn't you better hide the book?' she said.

'It is hidden,' he answered, touching the gaudy wrapper. 'And we may as well have a look at these sleuths.'

The ringing of another bell put a short stop to further discussion, and with a last smile at her he went out to open the door. The trouble was coming thick and fast, and there were tiny chisellings at the corners of his mouth to offset the quiet amusement in his eyes. But he only stopped long enough in the little hall to transfer the automatic from his hip pocket to a pocket in his raincoat, and then he opened the door wide with a face of seraphic tranquillity.

Two men in dark suits stood on the mat outside. Both of them wore bowler hats; neither of them carried sticks or gloves.

'Mr Simon Templar?' queried one of them, in a voice of astounding refinement.

Simon nodded, and they moved determinedly through the door with a concerted solidity which would certainly have obstructed any attempt he might have made to slam it in their faces.

'I am Inspector Nassen,' said the genteel spokesman, 'and I have a warrant to search your flat.'

'Bless my soul,' ejaculated the Saint, with his juiciest lisp. 'So you're one of our new public school policemen. How perfectly sweet!'

The other's lips tightened.

'We'll start with searching you,' he said shortly.

His hands ran over the Saint's pockets in a few efficient movements which were sufficient to assure him that Simon had no lethal weapon on his person. The Saint restrained a natural impulse to smack him on the nose, and smiled instead.

'This is a great game, Snowdrop, isn't it?' he said. 'Personally I'm broad-minded, but if you did these things to a lady she might misunderstand you.'

Nassen's pale face flushed wrathfully, and an unholy gleam came into the Saint's eye. Of all the detectives who ought never to have called upon him, one who was so easily baited was booked for a rough passage before he ever set out.

'We'll go over the flat now,' he said.

Simon led them into the living-room and calmly set about refilling his sherry glass.

'Pat,' he explained casually, 'these are two little fairies who just popped through the keyhole. They seem to want to search the place and see if it's all cleany-weeny. Shall we let them get on with it?'

'I suppose so,' said Patricia tolerantly. 'Did they wipe their tootsy-wootsies before they came in?'

'I'm afraid not,' said the Saint. 'You see, they aren't very well-bred little fairies. But when you have a beautiful Oxford accent you aren't supposed to need manners as well. You should just hear Snowdrop talking. Sounds as if all his teeth were loose . . .'

He went on in the same vein throughout the search, with an inexhaustible resource of wicked glee, and it was two very red and spluttering men who faced him after they had ransacked every room under the running commentary with which he enlivened their tour.

'Get your hat,' Nassen said. 'You're coming along with us.'

Simon put down his glass—they were back in the living-room.

'On what charge, Snowdrop?' he inquired.

'The charge is being in possession of information contrary to the Official Secrets Act.'

'It sounds a mouthful,' Simon admitted. 'Shall I pack my powder-puffs as well, or will you be able to lend me one?'

'Get your hat!' Nassen choked out in a shaking voice.

The Saint put a cigarette between his lips and stroked a thumb over the cog of his lighter. He looked at Patricia through the first feather of smoke, returning the lighter to his pocket, and the careless twinkle in his eyes might or might not have been an integral part of the smile that flitted across his brown face.

'It looks as if we shall have to finish our talk later, old darling,' he murmured. 'Snowdrop is in a hurry. Save some sherry for me, will you?—I shan't be long.'

Almost incredulously, but with a sudden leap of uncomprehending fear, she watched him saunter serenely from the room, and through the open door she saw him pick up his raincoat from the hall chair and pause to adjust his soft hat to its correct piratical angle before he went out. Long after he had gone, she was still trying to make herself believe that she had seen Simon

Templar, the man who had tantalised all the forces of law and order in the world for more years than any of them liked to be reminded of, arrested as easily as that.

III

Riding in a taxi between the two detectives, the Saint looked at his watch and saw that he had been in England less than four hours, and he had to admit that the pace was fairly rapid even by his exacting standards. One whiskered hold-up merchant, an unidentified shadower in a taxi, and two public school detectives, worked out at a reasonably hectic average for the time involved; but Simon knew that that was only a preliminary sample of the kind of attention he could expect while he remained the holder of *Her Wedding Secret.*

On either side of him, Nassen and the other sleuth licked their sores in silence. Whether they were completely satisfied with the course of events so far is not known, nor does the chronicler feel that posterity will greatly care. Simon thought kindly of other possible ways of adding to their martyrdom; but before he had made his final choice of the various forms of torment at his disposal the taxi was stopped by a traffic light at the corner of St James's Street, and the Saint looked through the window from a range of less than two yards full into the chubby face and sleepy eyes of the man without whom none of his adventures were really complete.

Before either of the other two could stop him, he had slung himself forward and loosed a delighted yell through the open window.

'Claud Eustace, by the bed-socks of Dr Barnardo!' cried the Saint joyfully.

The man's drowsy optics revolved towards the source of the sound, and, having located it, widened with indescribable eloquence. For a second or two he actually stopped chewing on his gum. His jaws seized up, and his portly bowler-hatted figure halted statuesquely.

There were cogent and fundamental reasons for the tableau—reasons which were carved in imperishable letters across the sluggish coagulation of emotions which Chief Inspector Claud Eustace Teal himself would have been much too diffident to call his soul. They were reasons which went way back through the detective's life to those almost unimaginably distant blissful days before anyone in England had ever heard of the Saint—the days when a policeman's lot had been a reasonably happy one, moving through well-ordered grooves to a stolid and methodical percentage of success, and there had been no such incalculable filibuster sweeping at intervals into the peaceful scene to tie all averages in knots and ride such rings round the wrath and vengeance of Scotland Yard as had never been ridden before. They were reasons which could have been counted one by one on Mr Teal's grey hairs; and all of them surged out of his memory in a solid phalanx at such moments as that, when the Saint returned to England after an all too brief absence, and Mr Teal saw him in London again and knew that the tale was no nearer its end than it had ever been.

All these things came back to burden Mr Teal's overloaded heart in that moment's motionless stare; and then with a sigh he stepped to the window of the taxi-cab and faced his future stoically.

'Hullo,' he said.

The Saint's eyebrows went up in a rising slant of mockery.

'Claud!' he protested. 'Is that kind? I ask you, is that a brotherly welcome? Anyone might think you weren't pleased to see me.'

'I'm not,' said Mr Teal dourly. 'But I shall have to see you.'

The Saint smiled.

'Hop in,' he invited hospitably. 'We're going your way.'

Teal shook his head—that is the simplest way of describing the movement, but it was such a perfunctory gesture that it simply looked as if he had thought of making it and had subsequently decided that he was too tired.

'Thanks,' he said. 'I've got another job to do just now. And you seem to be in good company.' His baby blue eyes, restored to their habitual affectation of sleepiness, moved over the two embarrassed men who flanked the Saint. 'You know who you're with, boys,' he told them. 'Watch him.'

'Pardon me,' said the Saint hastily. 'I forgot to do the honours. This specimen on my left is Snowdrop, the Rose of Peckham—'

'All right,' said Teal grimly. 'I know them. And I'll bet they're going to wish they'd never known you—if they haven't begun wishing it already.' The traffic light was at green again, and the hooting of impatient drivers held up behind made the detective step back from the window. 'I'll see you later,' he said, and waved the taxi on.

The Saint grinned and settled back again, as the cab turned south towards the Park. That chance encounter had set the triumphal capstone on his homecoming: it was the last familiar chord of the old opening chorus, his guarantee that the old days had finally come back in all their glory. The one jarring note was in the sinister implications of Teal's parting speech. Ever frank and open, the Saint sought to compare opinions on the subject.

'It sounds,' he murmured, 'almost as if Claud Eustace had something on his mind. Didn't it sound that way to you, Snowdrop?'

Nassen was wiping his forehead with a large white handkerchief; and he seemed deaf to the advance. His genteel sensitive soul had been bruised, and he had lost the spirit of such candid camaraderie. He put his handkerchief away and slipped an automatic from his pocket. Simon felt the muzzle probe into his ribs, and glanced down at it with one satirical eyebrow raised.

'You know, you could kill someone with that,' he said reprovingly.

'I wish it could be you,' said the Rose of Peckham in a tone of passionate earnestness, and relapsed into morbid silence.

Simon chuckled and lighted another cigarette. The gun in his own raincoat pocket rested comfortingly across his thigh, but he saw no need to advertise his own armoury. He watched their route with patient interest—they emerged at Parliament Square, but instead of turning down to the Embankment they circled the square and went back up Victoria Square.

'I suppose you know this isn't the way to Scotland Yard, Snowdrop?' he remarked helpfully.

'This is the way you're going first,' Nassen told him. The Saint shrugged. They turned quickly off Victoria Street, and pulled up shortly afterwards outside a house in one of those almost stupefyingly sombre and respectable squares in the district known to its residents as Belgravia but to the vulgar public, less pretentiously, as Pimlico.

Nassen's colleague got out and went up the steps to ring the bell, and the Saint followed under the unnecessarily aggressive propulsion of Nassen's gun.

The door was opened by one of the most magnificently majestic butlers that the Saint had ever seen. He seemed to be expecting them, for he stood aside immediately, and the Saint was led quickly through the hall into a spacious library on the ground floor.

'I will inform his lordship of your arrival,' said the butler, and left them there.

Simon Templar, who had been taking in his surroundings with untroubled interest, turned round as the door closed.

'You ought to have told me we were going to visit a lord, Snowdrop,' he said reproachfully. 'I'd have put on my Old Etonian suspenders and washed my neck, I know you washed your neck today, because I can see the line where you left off.'

Nassen tugged at his lower lip and simmered audibly, but his woes had passed beyond the remedy of repartee. And he was still smouldering pinkly when Lord Iveldown came in.

Lord Iveldown's name will not go down to history in the company of Gladstone, Disraeli, or the Earl of Chatham. Probably it will not go down to history at all. He was a minor statesman whose work had never been done in the public eye, which was at least a negative blessing for a public eye which has far too much to put up with already. In plain language, which tradition forbids any statesman to use, he was one of those permanent Government officials who do actually run the country while the more publicised politicians are talking about it. He was a big man inclined to paunchiness, with thin grey hair and pince-nez and the aura of stupendous pomposity by which the permanent Government official may instantly be recognised anywhere; and the Saint, whose portrait gallery of excrescences left very little ground uncovered, recognised him at once.

He came in polishing his pince-nez, and took up a position with his back to the fireplace.

'Sit down, Mr Templar,' he said brusquely, and turned to Nassen. 'I take it that you failed to find what you were looking for?'

The detective nodded.

'We turned the place inside out, your lordship, but there wasn't a sign of it. He might have sewn it up inside a mattress or in the upholstery of a chair, but I don't think he would have had time.'

'Quite,' muttered Lord Iveldown. 'Quite.' He took off his pince-nez, polished them again, and looked at the Saint. 'This is a serious matter, Mr Templar,' he said. 'Very serious.'

'Apparently,' agreed the Saint blandly. 'Apparently.'

Lord Iveldown cleared his throat, and wagged his head once or twice.

'That is why I have been obliged to adopt extraordinary measures to deal with it,' he said.

'Such as sending along a couple of fake detectives to turn my rooms inside out?' suggested the Saint languidly.

Lord Iveldown started, peered down at him, and coughed.

'Ah-hum,' he said. 'You knew they were—ah—fakes?'

'My good ass,' said the Saint, lounging more snugly in his armchair, 'I knew that the Metropolitan police had lowered itself a lot by enlisting public school men and what not, but I couldn't quite believe that it had sunk so low as to make inspectors out of herbaceous borders like Snowdrop over there. Besides, I'm never arrested by ordinary inspectors—Chief Inspector Teal himself always comes to see me.'

'Then why did you allow Nassen to bring you here?'

'Because I figured I might as well take a gander at you and hear what you had to say. The gander,' Simon admitted frankly, 'is not quite the greatest thrill I've had since I met Dietrich.'

Lord Iveldown cleared his throat again and expanded his stomach, clasping his hands behind his back under his coat-tails and rocking slightly in the manner of a schoolmaster preparing to deal with a grave breach of the public school code.

'Mr Templar,' he said heavily, 'this is a serious matter. A very serious matter. A matter, I might say, of the utmost gravity. You have in your possession a volume which contains certain—ah—statements and—ah—suggestions concerning me—statements and suggestions which, I need scarcely add, are wholly without foundation—'

'As, for instance,' said the Saint gently, 'the statement or suggestion that when you were Under-Secretary of State for War you placed an order for thirty thousand Lewis guns with a firm whose tender was sixty per cent higher than any other, and enlarged your own bank balance immediately afterwards.'

'Gross and damnable falsehoods,' persisted Lord Iveldown more loudly.

'As, for instance,' said the Saint, even more gently, 'the gross and damnable falsehood that you accepted on behalf of the Government a consignment of one million gas-masks which technical experts had already condemned in the strongest language as worse than useless—'

'Foul and calumnious imputations,' boomed Lord Iveldown in a trembling voice, 'which can easily be refuted, but which if published would nevertheless to some degree smirch a name which hitherto has not been without honour in the annals of this nation. It was only for that reason, and not because I feared that my public and private life could not stand the light of any inquiry whatever that might be directed into it, that I consented to—ah—grant you this interview.'

Simon nodded.

'Since your synthetic detectives had failed to steal that book from me,' he murmured, 'it was—ah—remarkably gracious of you.'

His sardonic blue eyes, levelled over the shaft of a cigarette that slanted from between his lips like the barrel of a gun, bored into Lord Iveldown with a light of cold appraisal which made the nobleman shift his feet awkwardly.

'It was an extraordinary situation,' repeated his Lordship in a resonant voice, 'which necessitated extraordinary measures.' He cleared his throat, adjusted his pince-nez, and rocked on his heels again. 'Mr Templar,' he said, 'let us not beat about the bush any longer. For purely personal reasons—merely, you understand, because I desire to keep my name free from common gossip—I desire to suppress these base insinuations which happen to have come into your possession; and for that reason I have accorded you this personal interview in order to ascertain what—ah—value you would place on this volume.'

'That's rather nice of you,' said the Saint guardedly.

'If, for example,' said Lord Iveldown throatily, 'a settlement of, shall we say—ah—two thousand pounds—'

He broke off at that point because suddenly the Saint had begun to laugh. It was a very quiet, very self-contained laugh—a laugh that somehow made the blood in Lord Iveldown's hardened arteries run colder as he heard it. If there was any humour in the laugh, it did not reach the Saint's eyes.

'If you mentioned two hundred thousand,' said the Saint coolly, 'you would have been right on my figure.'

There was a long terrific silence in which the mere rustle of a coat-sleeve would have sounded like the crash of doom. Many seconds went by before Lord Iveldown's dry cough broke the stillness like a rattle of musketry.

'How much did you say?' he articulated hoarsely.

'I said two hundred thousand pounds.'

Those arctic blue eyes had never shifted from Lord Iveldown's faintly empurpled face. Their glacial gaze seemed to go through him with the cold sting of a rapier blade—seemed to strip away all his bulwarks of pomposity like tissue, and hold the naked soul of the man quivering on the point like a grub on a pin.

'But that,' said Lord Iveldown tremblingly—'that's impossible! That's blackmail!'

'I'm afraid it is,' said the Saint.

'You sit there, before witnesses—'

'Before all the witnesses you like to bring in. I don't want you to miss the idea, your lordship. Witnesses don't make any difference. In any ordinary case—yes. If I were only threatening to advertise your illicit love affairs, or anything like that, you could bring me to justice and your own name would quite rightly be suppressed. But in a case like this even the Chief Commissioner couldn't guarantee you immunity. This isn't just ordinary haughtiness. This is high treason.'

Simon tapped the ash from his cigarette and blew a smoke-ring towards the ceiling; and once again his relentless eyes went back to Lord Iveldown's face. Nassen and the other detective, staring at the Saint in sullen silence, felt as if an icy wind blew through the room and goose-fleshed their skin in spite of the warmth of the evening. The bantering buffoon who had goaded them to the verge of apoplexy had vanished as though he had never existed, and another man spoke with the same voice.

'The book you're talking about,' said the Saint, in the same level dispassionate tones, 'is a legacy to me, as you know, from Rayt Marius. And you know what made him a millionaire. His money was made from war and the instruments of war. All those amazing millions—the millions out of which you and others like you were paid, Lord Iveldown—were the wages of death and destruction and wholesale murder. They were coined out of blood and dishonour and famine, and the agony of peaceful nations. Men—and women and children, too—were killed and tortured and maimed to find that money—the money out of which you were paid, Lord Iveldown.'

Lord Iveldown licked his lips, and opened his mouth to speak. But that clear ruthless voice went on, cleaving like a sword through his futile attempt at expostulation.

'Since I have that book, I had to find a use for it. And I think my idea is a good one. I am organising the Simon Templar Foundation, which will be started with a capital of one million pounds—of which your contribution will be a fifth. The Foundation will be devoted to the care and comfort of men maimed and crippled in war, to helping the wives and children of men killed in war, and to the endowment of any cause which has a chance of doing something to promote peace in the future. You must agree that the retribution is just.'

Iveldown's bluff had gone. He seemed to have shrunk, and was not teetering pompously on the hearth any more. His blotched face was working, and his small eyes had lost all their dominance—they were the mean shifty eyes of a man who was horribly afraid.

'You're mad!' he said, and his voice cracked. 'I can't listen to anything like that. I won't listen to it! You'll change your tune, before you leave here, by God! Nassen—'

The two detectives started forward, roused abruptly from their trance; and in the eyes of the Rose of Peckham particularly Simon saw the dawn of a sudden vengeful joy. He smiled, and moved his raincoat a little to uncover the gun in his hand.

'Not just now, Snowdrop,' he said smoothly, and the two men stopped. 'I have a date, and you've kept me too long already. A little later, I think, you'll get your chance.' His gaze roved back to Lord Iveldown's sickly features, on which the fear was curdling to a terrible impotent malevolence; and the Saintly smile touched his lips again for a moment. 'I shall expect that two hundred thousand pounds by Saturday midnight,' he said. 'I haven't the least doubt that you'll do your best to kill me before then, but I'm equally sure that you won't succeed. And I think you will pay your share . . .'

IV

Simon Templar was not a light sleeper, by the ordinary definition. Neither was he a heavy one. He slept like a cat, with the complete and perfect relaxation of a wild animal, but with the same wild animal's gift of rousing into instant wakefulness at the slightest sound which might require investigation. A howling thunderstorm would not have made him stir, but the stealthy slither of a cautiously opened drawer brought him out of a dreamless untroubled slumber into tingling consciousness.

The first outward sign of awakening touched nothing more than his eyelids—it was a trick he had learned many years ago, and it had saved his life more than once. His body remained still and passive, and even a man standing close beside his bed could have detected no change in the regular rate of his breathing. He lay staring into the dark, with his ears strained to pick up and locate the next infinitesimal repetition of the noise which had awoken him.

After a few seconds he heard it again, a sound of the identical quality but from a different source—the faint scuff of a rubber sole moving over the carpet in his living-room. The actual volume of sound was hardly greater than a mouse might have made, but it brought him out of bed in a swift writhing movement that made no sound in response.

And thereafter the blackness of the bedroom swallowed him up like a ghost. His bare feet crossed the floor without the faintest whisper of disturbance, and his fingers closed on the doorknob as surely as if he could have seen it. He turned the knob without a rattle, and moved noiselessly across the hall.

The door of the living-room was ajar—he could see the blackness ahead of him broken by a vague nimbus of light that glowed from the gap and shifted his position erratically. He came up to the door softly, and looked in.

The silhouette of a man showed against the darkened beam of an electric torch with the aid of which he was silently and systematically going through the contents of the desk; and the Saint showed his teeth for a moment as he sidled through the doorway and closed the door soundlessly behind him. His fingers found the switch beside the door, and he spoke at the same time.

'Good morrow, Algernon,' he murmured.

The man swung round in the sudden blaze of light. At the very moment when he started to turn Simon saw the gun in his hand, and thanked his immortal deities that he had not removed his fingers too promptly from the switch. In a split second he had clicked the lever up again, and the darkness fell again with blinding intensity after that one dazzling instant of luminance.

The Saint's voice floated once more out of the blackness.

'So you pack a rod, do you, Algernon? You must know that rods aren't allowed in this respectable city. I shall have to speak to you severely about that presently, Algernon—really I shall . . .'

The beam of the intruder's torch stabbed out again, printing a white circle of light on the door; but Simon was not inside the circle. The Saint had no rooted fear of being cold-bloodedly shot down in that apartment—the chances of a clean getaway for the shooter were too remote—but he had a very sound knowledge of what a startled burglar, amateur or professional, may do in a moment of panic; and what had been visible of the intruder's masked face as he spun round had not been tender or sentimental.

Simon heard the man's heavy breathing as the ray of the flashlight moved to left and right of the door and then began with a wilder haste to dance over the other quarters of the room. For the space of about half a minute it was a game of deadly hide-and-seek: the door appeared to be unguarded, but something told the intruder that he would be walking into a trap if he attempted to make a dash for liberty that way. At the end of that time his nerve broke and he plunged desperately for the only visible path of escape, and in so doing found that his suspicions had been almost clairvoyantly accurate.

A weight of teak-like bone and muscle landed on his back with a cat-like spring; steel fingers fastened on his gun hand, and another equally strong hand closed round his throat, driving him remorselessly to the floor. They wrestled voicelessly on the ground, but not for long. Simon got the gun away without a single shot being fired, and flung himself clear of his opponent with an acrobatic twist of his body. Then he found his way to the switch and turned on the lights again.

The burglar looked up at him from the floor, breathing painfully: and Simon permitted the muzzle of the captured gun to settle into a steady aim on the centre of the man's tightly tailored torso.

'You look miserable, Algernon,' he remarked affably. 'But you couldn't expect to have all the fun to yourself, could you? Come on, my lad—take that old sock off your head and let's see how your face is put together.'

The man did not answer or obey, and Simon stepped forward and whipped off the mask with a deft flick of his hand.

Having done which, he remained absolutely motionless for several ticks of the clock.

And then, softly, helplessly, he started to laugh.

'Suffering snakes,' he wailed. 'If it isn't good old Hoppy Uniatz!'

'Fer cryin' out loud,' gasped Mr Uniatz. 'If it ain't de Saint!'

'You haven't forgotten that time, when you took a dive through the window of Rudy's joint on Mott Street?'

'Say, an' dat night you shot up Angie Paletta an' Russ Kovari on Amsterdam Avenue?'

'And you got crowned with a chair and locked in the attic—you remember that?'

Mr Uniatz fingered his neck gingerly, as though the aches in it brought back memories.

'Say,' he protested aggrievedly, 'whaddaya t'ink I got for a memory—a sieve?' He beamed again, reminiscently; and then another thought overcast his homely features with a shadow of retrospective alarm. 'An' I might of killed you!' he said in an awed voice.

The Saint smiled.

'If I'd known it was you, I mightn't have thought this gun was quite so funny,' he admitted. 'Well, well, well, Hoppy—this is a long way from little old New York. What brings you here?'

Mr Uniatz scrambled up from the floor, and scratched his head.

'Well, boss,' he said, 't'ings never were de same after prohibition went out, over dere. I bummed around fer a while, but I couldn't get in de money. Den I hoid dey was room fer guys like me to start up in London, so I come over. But, hell, boss, dese Limeys dunno what it's all about, fer God's sake. Why, I asks one mob over here what about gettin' a coupla typewriters, an' dey t'ink I'm nuts.' Mr Uniatz frowned for a moment, as if the incapability of the English criminal to appreciate the soverign uses of machine-guns was still preying on his mind. 'I guess I must of been given a bum steer,' he said.

Simon nodded sympathetically, and strolled across to the table for a cigarette. He had known Hoppy Uniatz many years ago as a seventh-rate gunman of the classical Bowery breed, and had never been able to regard him with the same distaste as he viewed other hoodlums of the same species. Hoppy's outstanding charm was a skull of almost phenomenal thickness, which, while it had protected his brain from fatal injury on several occasions, had by its disproportionate density of bone left so little space for the development of grey matter that he had been doomed from the beginning to linger in the very lowest ranks even of that unintellectual profession; but at the same time it lent to Hoppy's character a magnificent simplicity which the Saint found irresistible. Simon could understand that Hoppy might easily have been lured across the Atlantic by exaggerated rumours of an outbreak of armed banditry in London; but that was not all he wanted to know.

'My heart bleeds for you, Hoppy,' he murmured. 'But what made you think I had anything worth stealing?'

'Well, boss,' explained Mr Uniatz apologetically, 'it's like dis. I get interdooced to a guy who knows anudder guy who's bein' blackmailed, an' dis guy wants me to get back whatever it is he's bein' blackmailed wit' an' maybe bump off de guy who's got it. So I'm told to rent an apartment here, an' I got de one next door to you—it's a swell apartment, wit' a bathroom an' everyt'ing. Dat's how I'm able to come in de buildings wit'out de janitor stoppin' me an' askin' who I wanna see.'

Simon blew out a thoughtful streamer of smoke—he had overlooked that method of slipping through his defences.

'Didn't they tell you my name?' he asked.

'Sure. But all dey tell me is it's a Mr Templar. When I hear it, I feel somehow I oughta remember de name,' said Mr Uniatz, generously forgetting the indignation with which he had received a recent aspersion on his memory, 'but I never knew it was you. Honest, Saint, if I'd of known it was you, it'd of been ixnay on de job, for mine. Ya wouldn't believe anyt'ing else, woujja, boss?'

The Saint shook his head

'You know, Hoppy,' he said slowly, 'I don't think I would.'

An idea was germinating in his mind—one of those sublimely fantastic ideas that sometimes came to him, an idea whose gorgeous simplicity, even in embryo, brought the ghost of a truly Saintly smile back to his lips. He forgot his interrupted beauty sleep.

'Could you do with a drink, old man?' he asked.

Hoppy Uniatz allowed the breath to hiss between his teeth, and a light of childlike beatitude irradiated his face.

'Boss,' he replied, 'what couldn't I do wit' a drink?'

Simon refrained from suggesting any answers to the conundrum. He poured out a liberal measure, and saved his soda-water. Mr Uniatz took the glass, sniffed it, and sucked his saliva for a moment of disciplined anticipation.

'Don't get me wrong, boss,' he said earnestly. 'Dose t'ings I said about Limeys wasn't meant poisonal. I ain't never t'ought about you as a Limey. You've been in New York, an' you know what it's all about. I know we had some arguments over dere, but over on dis side it don't seem de same. Say, I been so lonesome here it makes me feel kinda mushy to have a little fight like we had just now wit' a guy like you, who knows what a Roscoe's for. I wish you an' me could of teamed up before, boss.'

The Saint had helped himself to a more modest dose of whisky. He stretched himself out on the davenport, and waved Mr Uniatz to an armchair.

'Maybe it's not too late even now, Hoppy,' he said; and he had much more to talk about, which kept him out of bed for another two hours.

V

Chief Inspector Teal arrived while the Saint was finishing a belated breakfast. Simon Templar's breakfasts were usually belated, for he had never been able to appreciate the spiritual rewards of early rising; but on this particular morning the lateness was not entirely his fault. He had already been interrupted twice during the meal, and the bell which heralded the third interruption made him finally abandon a cup of coffee which had abandoned all pretension of being even lukewarm.

'Mr Teal is here, sir,' said Sam Outrell's voice on the telephone; and the Saint sighed.

'OK, Sam. Send him up.' He replaced the microphone and turned back to Mr Uniatz, who was engulfing quantities of toast with concentrated gusto, 'I'm afraid you've got to blow again, Hoppy,' he said. 'I'll see you later.'

Mr Uniatz rose wearily. He had been shot out of the Saint's apartment to make room for other visitors so often that morning that he had grave fears for his digestion. There was one slice of toast left for which even his gargantuan mouth was temporarily unable to find room. In order to eliminate any further risks of having his meal disturbed, he put the slice in his pocket and went out obediently; and he was the first thing that Teal saw when Simon opened the door.

'Hi, Claud,' said Mr Uniatz amiably, and drifted on towards the sanctity of his own quarters.

'Who the deuce is that?' demanded the startled detective, staring after Hoppy's retreating rear.

The Saint smiled.

'A friend of mine,' he said. 'Come along in, Claud, and make yourself uncomfortable. This is just like old times.'

Mr Teal turned round slowly and advanced into the apartment.

The momentary human surprise which Hoppy's greeting had given him faded rather quickly out of his rubicund features. The poise of his plump body as he came to rest in the living-room, the phlegmatic dourness of his round pink face under its unfashionable bowler hat, was exactly like old times. It was Chief Inspector Teal paying an official call: Chief Inspector Teal, with the grim recollection of many such calls haunting his mind, trundling doggedly out once again to take up his hopeless duel with the smiling young freebooter before him. The sum of a score of interviews like that drummed through his head, the memory of a seemingly endless sequence of failures and the bitter presentiment of many more to come was in his brain; but there was no hint of weakness or evasion in the somnolent eyes that rested on the Saint's brown face.

'Well,' he said, 'I told you I'd be coming to see you.'

Simon nodded pleasantly.

'It was nice of you to make it so soon, Claud,' he murmured. 'And what do you think is going to win the Derby?'

He knew as well as the Chief Commissioner himself that Mr Teal would never have called on him to enjoy small talk and racing gossip; but it was not his business to make the first move. A faint smile of humorous challenge stayed on his lips, and under the light of that smile Teal rummaged in his pockets and pulled out a folded sheet of paper.

'Do you know anything about that?' he asked. Simon took the sheet and flattened it out. It was his own note-heading, and there was certainly no surprise for him in the words which were written on it; but he read the document through obligingly.

*The Rt. Hon. Leo Farwill,*
*384, Hanover Square,*
*London, W.1.*
*Dear Sir,*

*As you have probably been informed, I have in my possession a volume of unique international interest in which your own distinguished name happens to be mentioned.*

*I have decided to sell this volume, in sections, for the benefit of the Simon Templar Foundation, which I am founding. This foundation will exist for the purpose of giving financial and other assistance to the needy families of men who were killed or deprived of their livelihood in the last war, to the care of the incurably crippled wounded, and to the endowment of any approved cause which is working to prevent a repetition of that outbreak of criminal insanity.*

*The price to you, of the section in which your name appears, is £200,000; and, knowing your interest in literature, I am sure you will decide that the price is reasonable—particularly as the Simon Templar Foundation will in its way work towards the promise of 'a land fit for heroes to live in' with which you once urged men to military service, death, and disablement, and which circumstances (always, of course, beyond your control) have since made you unable to fulfil.*

*In expecting your cheque to reach me before next Saturday midnight, I am, I feel sure, my dear honourable Leo, only anticipating your own natural urgent desire to benefit such a deserving charity.*

*Yours faithfully,*
*Simon Templar.*


'Very lucid and attractive, I think,' said the Saint politely. 'What about it?'

Teal took the letter back from him.

'It's signed with your name, isn't it?' he asked.

'Certainly,' said the Saint.

'And it's in your handwriting?'

'Beyond a doubt.'

'So that it looks very much as if you wrote it.'

Simon nodded.

'That Sherlock Holmes brain of yours goes straight to the point, Claud,' he said. 'Faced with such keen deductive evidence, I can't deceive you. I did write it.'

Teal folded the letter again and put it back in his pocket. His mouth settled into a relentless line. With any other man than the one who faced him, he would have reckoned the interview practically over; but he had crossed swords with the Saint too often ever to believe that of any interview—had seen too many deadly thrusts picked up like the clumsy lunges of an amateur on the rapier-like brilliance of the Saint's brain, and tossed aside with a smile that was more deadly than any riposte. But the thrust had to be made.

'I suppose you know that's blackmail,' Teal said flatly.

The Saint frowned slightly.

'Demanding money with menaces?' he asked.

'If you want the technical charge,' Teal said stubbornly, 'yes.'

And it came—the cool flick of the rapier that carried his point wide and aimless.

'Where,' asked the Saint puzzledly, 'are the menaces?'

Teal swallowed an obstruction in his throat. The game was beginning all over again—the futile hammering of his best blades on a stone wall that was as impalpable as ether, the foredoomed pursuit of the brigand who was easier to locate than any other lawbreaker in London, and who was more elusive than a will-o'-the-wisp even when he was most visible in the flesh. All the wrath that curdled his milk of human kindness was back in the detective at that moment, all the righteous anger against the injustice of his fate; but he had to keep it bottled up in his straining chest.

'The menaces are in the letter,' he said bluntly.

Simon stroked his chin in a rendering of ingenuous perplexity that acted on Teal's blood-pressure like a dose of strychnine.

'I may be prejudiced,' he remarked, 'but I didn't see them. It seemed a very respectable appeal to me, except for a certain unconventional familiarity at the end, where Leo's Christian name was used—but these are free and easy days. Otherwise I thought it was a model of restrained and touching eloquence. I have a book, of which it occurs to me that Leo might like to buy the section in which his name appears—you know what publicity-hounds most of these politicians are. Therefore I offer to sell it to him, which I'm sure must be strictly legal.'

'Mr Farwill's statement,' retorted Teal, 'is that the part of the book you're referring to is nothing but a collection of libellous lies.'

Simon raised his eyebrows.

'He must have a guilty conscience,' he murmured. 'But you can't put me in jail for that. I didn't say anything in my letter to give him that impression. I defy you to find one threat, one word of abuse, one questionable insinuation. The whole epistle,' Simon said modestly, 'is couched in the most flattering and even obsequious terms. In expecting his cheque to reach me before next Saturday midnight, I am, I feel sure, only anticipating his own natural urgent desire to benefit such a deserving charity. Leo may have turned out to be not quite the eager philanthropist I took him for,' said the Saint regretfully, 'but I still hope he'll see the light of godliness in the end; and I don't see what you've got to do with it, Claud.'

Mr Teal gulped in a breath that hurt him as it went down his windpipe.

'Oh, you don't, don't you?' he bit out.

'I'm afraid I don't, Claud,' said the Saint. 'Leo may have been caught in a hysterical moment, but other blokes have had the identical letter without feeling that way about it. Look at this.'

He picked up a slip of tinted paper from beside the coffee-pot, and held it out so that the detective could read the words. It was a cheque on the City & Continental Bank, dated that day, and it was made out for two hundred thousand pounds.

'Sir Barclay Edingham came here at half-past nine to give me that—he was in such a hurry to do his share. Major-General Sir Humbolt Quipp blew in at half-past ten—he grumbled and thundered a bit about the price, but he's gone away again to think it over, and I'm sure he'll pay it in the end. The other contributors will be coming through in the next day or two, and I wouldn't mind betting that Leo will be one of them as soon as he comes out of his tantrum. You ought to have another talk with him, Claud—it might help him to see the path of duty.'

'Never you mind what I ought to do,' Teal said hotly. His baby blue eyes, with all the sleepiness knocked out of them, were goggling like young balloons at the cheque which Simon was dangling under his nose, as if his brain had flatly refused to believe their message and they had swollen to twice their normal size with proper indignation at the insult. With a genuine physical effort he averted them from the astounding figures. 'Sir Barclay Edingham gave you that?' he repeated incredulously.

Simon inclined his head.

'And he was glad to. Sir Barclay Edingham has a very keen appreciation of literature. The pages I sold him are now his most treasured possession, and you couldn't buy them off him for twice as much as he gave me.'

He folded the cheque carefully, and put it away in his wallet; and the detective straightened up.

'Where is this book?' he demanded.

The Saint's eyebrows shifted again fractionally. It was a gesture that Teal knew better than any other of the Saint's bar one, and that almost imperceptible change of alignment carried more meaning than a thousand words of description could convey.

'It's in England,' he answered.

'That's good,' said Teal grimly, 'because I want to see it.'

The Saint picked up a cigarette, spun it into the air, and caught it in his mouth without moving his head. He snapped a flame from his lighter and blew out a long feather of smoke.

'Do you?' he murmured interestedly.

'Yes, I do!' barked the detective. 'And I mean to see it before I go. I mayn't be much of a critic, but I'll soon find out whether this literary work is worth two hundred thousand pounds a chapter. I'll get my own ideas about whether it's libellous. Now, are you going to show me that book or am I going to look for it?'

'Where's your search warrant?' inquired Simon imperturbably.

Teal gritted his teeth.

'I don't need a search-warrant. You're a suspected person—'

'Only in your wicked suspicious mind, Claud. And I'm telling you that you do need a search-warrant. Or, if you're going to take my home apart without one, you need three or four strong men with you. Because if you try to do it yourself, I shall pick you up by the scruff of your neck and the seat of your pants and throw you over the Ritz, and there's no magistrate in England who could give you a comeback!'

The Saint was smiling; but Mr Teal had no illusions about that smile. It was not a smile of simple-hearted bonhomie and goodwill towards policemen. It was a smile that could have been worn by no one but that lean dangerous privateer who was never more dangerous than when he smiled.

And Mr Teal knew that he hadn't got a leg to stand on. The Saint had tied him in a knot again. There were no menaces, no threats of any kind, in the letter with which the Honourable Leo Farwill had gone to Scotland Yard—it was a pleasant polite epistle with no unlawful insinuations whatsoever, and any fairly clever advocate could have convinced a normally half-witted jury that the suspicions attached to it arose from nothing but the notorious Simon Templar's signature at the end. And without a definite charge of blackmail, there were no grounds at all for demanding an inspection of the literary work on which the whole case hinged.

Mr Teal knew all these things as well as anyone—and knew also that in spite of the strictly legal appearances no man had ever given the Saint two hundred thousand pounds except as the reward of some devilish and unlawful cunning that had been born in that gay unscrupulous brain. He knew all these things as well as he knew his own birthday; but they did not cheer him. And Simon Templar's forefinger went out and tapped him on the stomach in the Saintly gesture that Mr Teal knew and hated best of all.

'You're too full of naughty ideas and uncharitable thoughts these days,' said the Saint. 'I was hoping that after I'd been away for a bit you might have got over them; but it seems as if you haven't. You're having one of your relapses into detectivosis, Claud; and it offends me. You stand there with your great stomach wobbling—'

'It doesn't wobble!' yapped the detective furiously.

'It wobbles when I poke it with my finger,' said the Saint coldly, and proceeded to demonstrate.

Teal struck his hand aside.

'Now listen,' he brayed. 'You may be able to twist the law around to suit yourself for a while—'

'I can twist the law around to suit myself as long as I like,' said the Saint cheerfully; 'and when I fall down on it, it will be soon enough for you to come and see me again. Now you've completely spoiled my breakfast; and I've got an important appointment in ten minutes, so I can't stop to play with you any more. Drop in again next time you wake up, and I'll have some more to say to you.'

Chief Inspector Teal settled his bowler hat. The wrath and righteous indignation were steaming together under his waistcoat; but with a terrific effort he recovered his pose of torpid weariness.

'I'll have some more to say to you,' he replied curtly, 'and it'll keep you out of trouble for several years.'

'Let me know when you're ready,' murmured the Saint, and opened the door for him with old-world courtesy.

A couple of minutes later, with his wide-brimmed felt hat tipped challengingly over his right eye, he was knocking at the door of the adjoining apartment.

'Come along, Hoppy,' he said. 'We've left it late enough already—and I can't afford to miss this date.'

Mr Uniatz put down a bottle of whisky regretfully and took up his hat. They left the building by the entrance in Stratton Street; and as they came out on to the pavement a shabby and ancient touring car pulled away from the kerb and went past. Simon felt as if a gust of wind plucked at his swashbuckling headgear and carried it spinning: the crack that went with the gust of wind might have been only one of the many backfires that a big city hears every hour.

## VI

Simon collected his hat and dusted it thoughtfully. The bullet hole made a neat puncture in the centre of the crown—the only mistake in the aim had been the elevation.

The attack surprised him seriously. He had allowed himself to believe that during his possession of *Her Wedding Secret* his life at least was safer than it had ever been—that while the opposition would go to any lengths to obtain that classic work, they would be extraordinarily solicitous about his own bodily health. He turned to Mr Uniatz, and had a sudden spasm of alarm when he saw that enterprising warrior standing out on the edge of the sidewalk with an automatic waving towards the retreating car. Simon made a grab at the gun and whipped it under his coat.

'You everlasting fathead!' he said. 'Where the blazes d'you think you are?'

Mr Uniatz scratched his head and looked around him.

'I t'ink we're in Stratton Street, boss,' he said anxiously. 'Ain't dat right? I can't seem to find my way around dis town. Why ja grab de Betsy off of me?—I could of plugged dat guy easy.'

The Saint sighed. By some miracle the street had been practically deserted, and no one appeared to have noticed the brief flourish of gangland armaments.

'Because if you'd plugged that guy you'd have had us both in the hoosegow before you knew what had happened, you poor sap,' he said tersely, and slipped the lethal weapon cautiously back into its owner's pocket. 'Now keep that Betsy of yours buttoned up until I tell you to let it out—and try to remember which side of the Atlantic you're on, will you?'

They walked round to the garage where Simon kept his car, with Mr Uniatz preserving a silence of injured perplexity. The ways of the old world were strange to him; and his brain had never been geared to lightning adaptability. If one guy could take a shot at another guy and get away with it, but the other guy couldn't take a shot back at the first guy without being clapped in the hoosegow, what the hell sort of country was this England, for God's sake?

There was just no percentage in trying to hold down a racket in those parts, reflected Hoppy Uniatz, and laboured over the subtleties of this sociological observation for twenty minutes, while Simon Templar whisked the huge purring Hirondel through the traffic to the south-west.

Simon had a different problem to ponder, and he was inclined to share it.

'Tell me, Hoppy,' he said. 'Suppose a bloke had some papers that he was blackmailing you with—papers that would be the end of you if they ever came out. Suppose he'd got your signed confession to a murder, or something like that. What would you do about it?'

Mr Uniatz rubbed his nose.

'Dat's easy, boss. I'd bump de guy off, sure.'

'I'm afraid you would,' said the Saint. 'But suppose you did bump him off—those papers would still be around somewhere, and you wouldn't know who was going to get hold of them next.'

This had not occurred to Mr Uniatz. He frowned gloomily for a while; and then he brightened again as the solution struck him like a ray of sunshine.

'Why, boss,' he said, 'I know what I'd do. After I'd bumped him off, I'd look for de papers.'

'And where would you look for them?' asked the Saint.

'In de guy's pocket,' said Mr Uniatz promptly.

'And suppose they weren't there?'

Hoppy sighed. The corrugations of worried thought returned to his brow. Thinking had never been his greatest talent—it was one of the very few things that were capable of hurting his head.

Simon shot the Hirondel between a lorry and an omnibus

with the breadth of a finger to spare on either side, and tried to assist.

'I mean, Hoppy,' he said, 'you might have thought: "Suppose I bump this guy off. Suppose he isn't carrying the papers in his pocket." Well, when a guy's bumped off, one of the first things the cops want to know is who did it. And one of the ways of finding that out is to find out who might have had a reason to do it. And one of the ways of finding that out is to go through his letters and anything else like that you can get hold of. So if you'd thought all that out, Hoppy, you might have decided that if you bumped him off the cops might get hold of the papers, and that wouldn't be too healthy for you.'

Mr Uniatz ruminated over this point for two or three miles, and finally he shrugged.

'I dunno,' he said. 'It looks like we better not bump off dis guy, at dat. Whadda you t'ink, boss?'

Simon realised that he would have to be content with his own surmises, which were somewhat disturbing. He had been prepared to bank heavily on his immunity from death, if not from organised discomfort, so long as the ungodly were in doubt about the concurrent fate of *Her Wedding Secret*; but the recent episode was a considerable discouragement to his faith. Leaving aside the possibility that Lord Iveldown had gone completely and recklessly berserk, it meant that the ungodly were developing either a Satanic cunning or a denseness of cranium equalled only by that of Hoppy Uniatz.

He made a rough summary of the opposition. They had been five in number originally, and it was only to be expected that out of those five a solid percentage would have been non-resisters. Sir Barclay Edingham had paid. Major-General Sir Humbolt Quipp would pay. The active dissenters consisted of Lord Iveldown, who had already declared his hand, a certain Mr Neville Yorkland, M.P., with whom the Saint was going to have an interview, and perhaps the Honourable Leo Farwill, who might jump either way. But none of these three gentlemen, undesirable citizens though they might be, could lightly be accused of excessive denseness of cranium. Neither, as a matter of fact, had the Saint been prepared to credit them with talents of satanic cunning; but on that score it was dawning on him that he might do well to maintain an open mind.

The inevitable triangle possessed a third corner—if anything so nearly spherical could be described as a corner—in the rotund shape of Chief Inspector Claud Eustace Teal. Whatever his other errors may have been, Simon Templar was not guilty of kidding himself that he had finally and eternally disposed of that menace in the brief *tête-à-tête* they had enjoyed that morning.

The Saint, it must be confessed, had sometimes been guilty of deceiving Chief Inspector Teal. He had not always unbosomed all his secrets as Mr Teal would have liked him to. At times, even, he had deliberately and grievously misled that persistent enforcer of the Law—a breach of the public school code which all English gentlemen will undoubtedly deplore.

He had misled Mr Teal that morning when telling him that he had an appointment in ten minutes. As a matter of fact, the Saint's appointment was not until that evening, and he had merely been promising himself an idle day in the country on the way, with which he did not propose to allow Scotland Yard to interfere. It was a casual and almost pointless untruth; but he might have thought more about it if he had foreseen its results.

Mr Teal brooded all day over his problem. In the course of the afternoon he had a second interview with the Honourable Leo Farwill; and that estimable politician's reaction to his report, far from consoling him, made him still more uneasy.

Later that evening he saw the Assistant Commissioner.

'There's something darned funny going on, sir,' he summarised his conclusions tentatively.

The Assistant Commissioner sniffed. He had a sniff which annoyed Mr Teal almost as much as Simon Templar's irreverently prodding forefinger.

'I, in my humble way, had reached the same conclusion,' said the Commissioner sarcastically. 'Has Farwill said any more?'

'He was just wooden,' said Teal. 'That's what I don't like about it. If he'd gone off the deep end, ranted about the inefficiency of the police and the questions he was going to ask in Parliament— all the usual stuff, you know—I'd have felt happier about it. That was what I was expecting him to do, but he didn't do it. He seemed to go back into a sort of shell.'

'You mean you got the impression that he was rather regretting having gone to the police with that letter?'

Teal nodded.

'It did seem like that. I've seen it happen before, when the Saint's on a job. The fellow may kick up a fuss at first, but pretty soon he shuts down like a clam. Either he pays, or he tries to deal with the Saint on his own. He doesn't ask us to interfere again.'

'And yet you haven't the faintest idea why solid and respectable people—public men like Farwill, for instance—crumple up like frightened babies just because this man writes them a letter,' remarked the Assistant Commissioner acidly.

The detective twiddled a button on his coat.

'I have got the faintest idea, sir,' he said redly. 'I've got more than a faint idea. I know why they do it. I know why they're doing it now. It's blackmail.'

'Do you know, I really believe you've solved the mystery,' said the Commissioner, with a mildness that singed the air.

'If I've done that, I've done more than anyone else in this building,' retorted Teal heatedly. 'But there are plenty of people sitting in their offices criticising me who couldn't have got half as far as I have, even if that isn't saying much.' He glared at his chief stubbornly, while all the accumulated wrath and resentment of a score of such conferences rose up recklessly in his breast and strangled his voice for a moment. 'Everybody knows that it's some kind of blackmail, but that doesn't help. We can't prove it. When I produced that letter, Templar simply laughed at me. And he was right. There wasn't a line of blackmail in it—except to anyone who knew what was in that book he mentions.'

'Which you failed to find out,' said the Commissioner.

'Which I failed to find out,' agreed Teal feverishly, 'because I'm not a miracle worker, and I never said I was.'

The Assistant Commissioner picked up his pen.

'Do you want a search-warrant—is that what all these hysterics are about?' he inquired icily.

Teal gulped.

'Yes, I want a search-warrant!' he exploded defiantly. 'I know what it means. The Saint'll probably get around that somehow. When I get there, the book will have disappeared, or it'll turn out to be a copy of *Fairy Tales for Little Children*, or something. And Edingham and Quipp will get up and swear it was never anything else.' Goaded beyond endurance though he was, the detective checked for an instant at the horrific potentialities of his prophecy; but he plunged on blindly. 'I've seen things like that happen before, too. I've seen the Saint turn a cast-iron conviction into a cast-iron alibi in ten seconds. I'm ready to see it happen again, I'm ready to see him give the newspapers a story that'll make them laugh themselves sick for two months at my expense. But I'll take that search-warrant!'

'I'll see that you have it in half an hour,' said the Assistant Commissioner coldly. 'We will discuss your other remarks on the basis of what you do with it.'

'Thank you, sir,' said Chief Inspector Teal, and left the room with the comfortless knowledge that the last word on that subject was a long way from having been said.

## VII

'Gents,' announced Mr Uniatz, from a chest swelling with proper pride, 'dis here is my pal Mr Orconi. Dey calls him Peter de Blood. He's de guy youse guys is lookin' for. He'll fix t'ings . . .'

From that moment, with those classic words, the immortal gorgeousness of the situation was established for all time. Simon Templar had been in many queer spots before, had cheerfully allowed his destiny to be spun giddy in almost every conceivable whirlpool of adventure, but never before had he entered such a portentous conclave to solemnly discuss the manner in which he should assassinate himself; and the sheer ecstatic pulchritude of the idea was prancing balmily through his insides in a hare-brained saraband which only a delirious sense of humour like the Saint's could have appreciated to the full.

He stood with his hands in his pockets surveying the two other members of the conference with very clear blue eyes, and allowing the beatific fruitiness of the scheme which Mr Uniatz had made possible to squirm rapturously through his system.

'Pleased to meet ya,' he drawled, with a perfect gangster intonation that had been learned in more perilous and unsavoury surroundings than a fire-proof air-conditioned movie theatre.

Mr Neville Yorkland, M.P., fidgeted with his tie and looked vaguely about the room. He was a broad tubby little man, who looked something like a cross between a gentleman farmer and a dilettante artist—an incongruous soufflé of opposites, with a mane of long untidy hair crowning a vintage-port complexion.

'Well,' he said jerkily, 'let's sit down. Get to business. Don't want to waste any time.'

The Honourable Leo Farwill nodded. He was as broad as York-land, but longer; and he was not fussy. His black brows and heavy black moustache were of almost identical shape and dimensions, so that his face had a curiously unfinished symmetry, as if its other features had been fitted quite carelessly into the decisive framework of those three arcs of hair.

'An excellent idea,' he boomed. 'Excellent. Perhaps we might have a drink as well. Mr—ah—Orconi—'

'Call me Pete,' suggested the Saint affably, 'and let's see your liquor.'

They sat, rather symbolically, on opposite sides of the long table in Farwill's library. Hoppy Uniatz gravitated naturally to the Saint's elbow, while Yorkland pulled up a chair beside Farwill.

The Honourable Leo poured sherry into four glasses from a crystal decanter.

'Mr—er—Uniatz gives us to understand that you are what is known as a—ah—gunman, Mr Orconi.'

'Pete,' said the Saint, sipping his drink.

'Ah—Pete,' Farwill corrected himself, with visible distaste.

Simon nodded gently.

'I guess that's right,' he said. 'If there's anyone horning in on your racket, you've come to the guy who can stop him.'

'Sure,' echoed Hoppy Uniatz, grasping his opportunity and swallowing it in one gulp. 'We'll fix him.' Farwill beamed laboriously, and produced a box of cigars.

'I presume that Mr Uniatz has already acquainted you with the basic motives of our proposition,' he said.

'Hoppy told me what you wanted—if that's what you mean,' said the Saint succinctly, stripping the band from his selected Corona. 'This guy Templar has something on you, an' you want him taken off.'

'That—ah—might be a crude method of expressing it,' rumbled the Honourable Leo. 'However, it is unnecessary to go into the diplomatic niceties of the dilemma. I will content myself with suggesting to you that the situation is one of, I might almost say, national moment.'

'Tremendous issues involved,' muttered Mr Neville Yorkland helpfully. 'World-wide catastrophe. The greatest caution is called for. Tact. Secrecy. Emergency measures.'

'Exactly,' concluded Farwill. 'Emergency measures. The ordinary avenues are closed to us by the exigencies of the crisis. You would, in fact, find yourself in the position of an unofficial secret service agent—taking your own risks, fighting your own battles, knowing that in the event of failure you will be disowned by your employers. The situation, in short, calls for a man who is able to take care of himself, who is prepared to endanger his life for a reasonable reward, who—who—'

'I get it,' said the Saint blandly. 'This guy Templar has something on you, an' you want him taken off.' Farwill compressed his lips.

'At this stage of developments, I feel called upon neither to confirm that statement nor repudiate it,' he said with the fluency of many years in Parliament. 'The points at issue are, first, whether you are a suitable man for the mission—'

'Nuts,' said the Saint tersely. 'You want a guy like me, an' I'm the guy you want. When do you cut the cackle an' come to the hosses?'

The Honourable Leo glanced despairing at Yorkland, as if appealing to the Speaker on a point of order. Yorkland twiddled his thumbs. 'Should be all right,' he mumbled. 'Looks the type. Vouched for by Mr Uniatz. Been to America myself. Can't pick and choose. Got to decide.'

'Ah, yes,' admitted Farwill despondently, as if the very idea violated all his dearest principles. 'We have got to decide.' He inflated his chest again for the only outlet of oratory that was left to him. 'Well, Mr Orconi—ah—Pete, you are doubtless familiar with the general outline of the engagement. This book, of which Mr Uniatz must have told you, must be recovered—whether by guile or force is immaterial. Nothing must be permitted to obstruct a successful consummation of the undertaking. If, in the course of your work, it should prove necessary to effect physical injuries upon this man Templar, or even to—er—expedite his decease, humanitarian considerations must not influence our firmness. Now, I would suggest that a fee of two hundred pounds—'

Simon straightened up in his chair and laughed rudely.

'Say, whaddaya think I'm lookin' for?' he demanded. 'Chicken-feed?'

The Honourable Leo drew further breath for eloquence, and the argument was on. It would scarcely be profitable to record it in detail. It went on for a long time, conducted on the Parliamentary side in rounded periods which strayed abstractedly to every other subject on earth except the one in hand and nearly sent the Saint to sleep. But Simon Templar had a serene determination of his own which could even survive the soporific flatulence of Farwill's long-winded verbiage; he was in no hurry, and he was still enjoying himself hugely. Hoppy Uniatz, endowed with a less vivid appreciation of the simple jests of life, did actually fall into a doze.

At long last a fee of two thousand pounds was agreed on; and the Saint helped himself to a fifth glass of sherry.

'OK, boys,' he murmured. 'We'll get that guy.'

'Sure,' echoed Mr Uniatz, rousing with a snort. 'We'll get him.'

Yorkland shuffled about on the edge of his seat, buttoned and unbuttoned his coat, and got up.

'Very well,' he stuttered. 'That's settled. Glad it's all fixed up. Now I must get back to town. Late already. Important meetings.' His restless eyes glanced at the other member of his side. 'Count on me for my share, Farwill.'

The Honourable Leo nodded.

'Certainly,' he reverberated. 'Certainly. You may leave it to me to arrange the details.' He drew the sherry decanter towards him and replaced the stopper unobtrusively but firmly. 'I think we owe a vote of thanks to Mr Uniatz for the—er—introduction.'

Simon Templar surveyed him dispassionately over a second Corona.

'You owe more than that, fella,' he said.

Farwill coughed.

'I thought the—er—honorarium was payable when the commission had been—ah—executed.'

'Half of it is,' agreed the Saint pleasantly. 'The first half is payable now. I done business with politicians before. You make so many promises in your job, you can't expect to remember 'em all.'

'Sure,' seconded Hoppy Uniatz heartily. 'Cash wit' order is de rule in dis foim.'

Farwill drew out his wallet grudgingly; but it was stocked with a supply of currency which indicated that some such demand had not been unforeseen. He counted out a number of bank-notes with reluctant deliberation; and Yorkland watched the proceeding with a hint of hollowness in his round face.

'Well,' he said with a sigh, 'that's done. Send you a cheque tonight, Farwill. Thanks. Really must be off now. Excuse me. Goodbye.'

He shook hands all round, with the limp perfunctory grip of the professional handshaker, and puttered out of the room; and they heard his car scrunching away down the drive.

The Saint smiled to himself, and raked in the money. He counted it into two piles, pushed one towards Hoppy Uniatz, and folded the other into his pocket. There were five hundred pounds in his own share—it was a small enough sum as the Saint rated boodle, but there were circumstances in which he could take a fiver with just as much pleasure as he would have taken five thousand. It was not always the amount of the swag, it was the twist of the game by which it was collected; and beyond all doubt the twist by which that five hundred had been pulled in ranked high in the scale of pure imponderable delights. On such an occasion, even a purely nominal allowance of loot was its own reward; but still the Saint had not achieved everything that had been in his mind when he set out on that soul-satisfying jag.

One other riddle had been working in his brain ever since he left his apartment that morning, and he led up to it with studied casualness.

'The job's as good as done, Leo,' he said.

'Sure,' echoed the faithful Mr Uniatz. 'De guy is dead an' buried.'

'Excellent,' responded Farwill formally. 'Ah—excellent.'

He had almost got the decanter away when Simon reached it with a long arm. Farwill winced, and averted his eyes.

'This ain't such bad stuff, Leo,' the Saint commented kindly, emptying his glass and refilling it rapidly. He spilt an inch of ash from his cigar on to the carpet, and cocked one foot on to the polished table with a callous disregard for his host's feelings which he felt would go well with the imaginary character of Pete de Blood, and which soothed his own sleepless sense of mischief at the same time. 'About this guy, Templar,' he said. 'Suppose I do have to rub him out?'

'Rub him out?' repeated Farwill dubiously. 'Ah—yes, yes. Suppose you have to kill him.' His eyes shifted for a moment with the hunted look of the politician who scents an attempt to commit him to a definite statement. 'Well, naturally it is understood that you will look after yourself.'

'Aw, shucks,' said the Saint scornfully. 'I can look after myself. That ain't what I mean, I mean, suppose he was rubbed out, then there wouldn't be any way to find out where the book was, an' the cops might get it.'

Farwill finally collared the decanter and transported it in an absent-minded way to the cellaret, which he locked with the same preoccupied air. He turned round and clasped his hands under his coat-tails.

'From our point of view, the problem might be simplified,' he said.

The Saint rolled his cigar steadily between his finger and thumb. The question with which he had taxed the imagination of Mr Uniatz had been propounded again where it might find a more positive reply; but the Saint's face showed no trace of his eagerness for a solution. He tipped the dialogue over the brink of elucidation with a single impassive monosyllable.

'How?'

'The Saint has a—ah—confederate,' said Farwill, looking at the ceiling. 'A young lady. We understand that she shared his confidence in all his—ah—enterprises. We may therefore assume that she is cognisant of the whereabouts of the volume in question. If the Saint were—ah—removed, therefore,' Farwill suggested impersonally, 'one would probably have a more—ah—tractable person with whom to deal.'

A flake of ash broke from the Saint's cigar and trickled a dusty trail down his coat; but his eyes did not waver.

'I get you,' he said.

The simplicity of the argument hit him between the eyes with a force that almost staggered him. Now that it had been put forward, he couldn't understand how he had failed to see it himself from the beginning. It was so completely and brutally logical. The Saint was tough: everyone knew it, everyone admitted it. And he held the whip-hand. But he could be—ah—removed; and the whip would pass into the hands of one lone girl. Undoubtedly, the problem might be simplified. It would be reduced to an elementary variant of an old game of which the grim potentialities were still capable of sending a cold trickle down his spine. He should have seen it at once. His hat hung in the hall with a bullet-punched ventilation through the crown which was an enduring testimony that the opposition had neither gone berserk nor sunk into the depths of imbecility: without even charting the pinnacles of satanic cunning, they had merely grasped at the elusive obvious—which he himself had been too wooden-headed to see.

'That's a great idea,' said the Saint softly. 'So after we've rubbed out this guy Templar, we go after his moll.'

'Ah—yes,' assented Farwill, staring into the opposite corner as if he were not answering the question at all. 'If that should prove necessary—ah—yes.'

'Sure,' chirped Mr Uniatz brightly, anticipating his cue. 'We'll fix de goil.'

The Saint silenced him with a sudden lift of ice-blue eyes. His voice became even softer, but the change was too subtle for Farwill to notice it.

'Who thought of that great idea?' he asked.

'It was jointly agreed,' said the Honourable Leo evasively. 'In such a crisis, with such issues at stake, one cannot be sentimental. The proposition was received with unanimous approval. As a matter of fact, I understand that an abortive attempt has already been made in that direction—I should perhaps have explained that there is another member of our—er—coalition who was unfortunately unable to be present at our recent discussion. I expect him to arrive at any moment, as he is anxious to make your acquaintance. He is a gentleman who has already done valuable independent work towards this—ah—consummation which we all desire.'

The Saint's eyebrows dropped one slow and gentle quarter-inch over his steady eyes.

'Who is he?'

Farwill's mouth opened for another elaborate paragraph; but before he had voiced his preliminary 'Ah' the headlights of a car swept across the drawn blinds and the gravel, scraped again outside the windows. Footsteps and voices sounded in the hall, and the library door opened to admit the form of the Honourable Leo's butler.

'Lord Iveldown,' he announced.


VIII

Simon Templar's cigar had gone out. He put it down carefully in an ashtray, and took out his cigarette-case. It stands as a matter of record that at that moment he did not bat an eyelid, though he knew that the show-down had arrived.

'Delighted to see you, Iveldown,' the Honourable Leo was exclaiming. 'Yorkland was unfortunately unable to stay. However, you are not too late to make the acquaintance of our new—ah—agents. Mr Orconi . . .'

Farwill's voice trailed hesitantly away. It began to dawn on him that his full-throated flow of oratory was not carrying his audience with him. Something, it seemed, was remarkably wrong.

Standing in front of the door which had closed behind the retiring butler, Lord Iveldown and Mr Nassen were staring open-mouthed at the Saint with the aspect of a comedy unison dance team arrested in mid-flight. The rigidity of their postures, the sag of their lower jaws, the glazed bulging of their eyes, and the suffusion of red in their complexions, were so ludicrously identical that they might have been reflections of each other. They looked like two peas who had fallen out of their pod and were still trying to realise what had hit them; and the Honourable Leo looked from them to the Saint and back again with a frown of utter bewilderment.

'Whatever is the matter?' he demanded, startled into uttering one of the shortest sentences of his life; and at the sound of his question Lord Iveldown came slowly and painfully out of his paralysis.

He turned, blinking through his pince-nez.

'Is that—that—the American gunman you told me about?' he queried awfully.

'That is what I have been—ah—given to understand,' said Farwill, recovering himself. 'We are indebted to Mr Uniatz for the introduction. I am informed that he has had an extensive career in the underworld of—ah—Pittsburg. Do you imply that you are already acquainted?'

His lordship swallowed.

'You bumptious blathering ass!' he said.

Simon Templar uncoiled himself from his chair with a genial smile. The spectacle of two politicians preparing to speak their minds candidly to one another was so rare and beautiful that it grieved him to interrupt; but he had his own part to play. It had been no great effort to deny himself the batting of an eyelid up to that point—the impulse to bat eyelids simply had not arisen to require suppressing. Coming immediately on the heels of Leo Farwill's revelation, he was not sorry to see Lord Iveldown.

'What ho, Snowdrop,' he murmured cordially. 'Greetings, your noble lordship.'

Farwill gathered himself together.

'So you are already acquainted,' he rumbled with an effort of heartiness. 'I thought—'

'Do you know who that is?' Iveldown asked dreadfully.

Some appalling intuition made Farwill shake his head; and the Saint smiled encouragingly.

'You tell him, Ivelswivel,' he urged. 'Relieve the suspense.'

'That's the Saint himself!' exploded Iveldown.

There are times when even this talented chronicler's genius stalls before the task of describing adequately the reactions of Simon Templar's victims. Farwill's knees drooped and his face took on a greenish tinge; but in amplification of those simple facts a whole volume might be written in which bombshells, earthquakes, dynamite, mule-kicks, and other symbols of devastating violence would reel through a kaleidoscope of similes that would still amount to nothing but an anaemic ghost of the sight which rejoiced Simon Templar's eyes. And the Saint smiled again, and lighted his cigarette.

'Of course we know each other,' he said. 'Leo and I were just talking about you, your lordship. I gather that you're not only the bird who suggested bumping me off so that you'd only have Patricia Holm to deal with, but your little pal Snowdrop was the bloke who tried it on this morning, and wrecked a perfectly good hat with his rotten shooting. I shall have to add a fiver on to your account for that, brother; but the other part of your brilliant idea isn't so easily dealt with.'

Farwill's face was turning from green to grey.

'I seem to have made a mistake,' he said flabbily.

'A pardonable error,' said the Saint generously. 'After all, Hoppy Uniatz didn't exactly give you an even break. But you didn't make half such a big mistake as Comrade Iveldown over there—'

Out of the corner of his eye he saw Nassen make a slight movement, and his hand had flashed to his pocket before he remembered that he had set out to enjoy his joke with so much confidence that he had not even gone heeled. But even if there had been a gun there, he would have reached it too late. Nassen had a hand in his coat pocket already; and there was a protuberance under the cloth whose shape Simon knew only too well.

He looked round and saw the reason for it. The ponderous thought processes of Hoppy Uniatz had at last reduced the situation to terms which he could understand. In his slow but methodical way, Mr Uniatz had sifted through the dialogue and action, and arrived at the conclusion that something had gone amiss. Instinct had made him go for his gun; but the armchair in which he was ensconced had impeded his agility on the draw, and Nassen had forestalled him. He sat with his right hand still tangled in his pocket, glaring at the lanky stillness of Iveldown's private detective with self-disgust written all over his face. 'I'm sorry, boss,' he growled plaintively. 'De guy beat me to it.'

'Never mind,' said the Saint. 'It's my fault.' Iveldown came forward, with his mouth twitching.

'The mistake could have been worse,' he said. 'At least we have the Saint. Where is Yorkland?' Farwill chewed his lower lip.

'I believe he could be intercepted. When he first arrived, he told me that he had meant to call on Lady Bredon at Camberley on his way down, but he had not had time. He intimated that he would do so on his way back—'

'Telephone there,' snapped Iveldown.

He strode about the room, rubbing his hands together under his coat-tails, while Farwill made the call. He looked at the Saint frequently, but not once did he meet Simon's eyes. Simon Templar never made the mistake of attributing that avoidance of his gaze to fear: at that moment, Iveldown had less to fear than he had ever had before. Watching him with inscrutable blue eyes, the Saint knew that he was looking at a weak pompous egotistical man whom fear had turned into a jackal at bay.

'What message shall I leave?' asked Farwill, with his hand over the transmitter.

'Tell them to tell him—we've caught our man,' said Iveldown.

The Saint blew a smoke-ring.

'You seem very sure about that, brother,' he remarked. 'But Snowdrop doesn't look too happy about that gun. He looks as if he was afraid it might go off—and do you realise, Snowdrop, that if it did go off it'd burn a hole in your beautiful Sunday suit, and Daddy would have to smack you?'

Nassen looked at him whitely.

'Leave him to me,' he said. 'I'll make him talk.'

Simon laughed shortly.

'You might do it if you're a ventriloquist,' he said contemptuously. 'Otherwise you'd be doing good business if you took a tin cent for your chance. Get wise to yourself, Snowdrop.

You've lost your place in the campaign. You aren't dealing with a girl yet. You're talking to a man—if you've any idea what that means.'

Lord Iveldown stood aside, with his head bowed in thought, as if he scarcely heard what was going on. And then suddenly he raised his eyes and looked at the Saint again for the first time in a long while; and, meeting his gaze, Simon Templar read there the confirmation of his thoughts. His fate lay in the hands of a creature more ruthless, more vindictive, more incalculable than any professional killer—a weak man, shorn of his armour of pomposity, fighting under the spur of fear.

'The mistake could have been worse,' Iveldown repeated.

'You ought to be thinking about other things,' said the Saint quietly. 'This is Friday evening; and the sun isn't standing still. By midnight tomorrow I have to receive your contribution to the Simon Templar Foundation—and yours also, Leo. And I'm telling you again that whatever you do and whatever Snowdrop threatens, wherever I am myself and whether I'm alive or dead, unless I've received your cheques by that time Chief Inspector Teal will get something that at this moment he wants more than anything else you could offer him. He'll get a chance to read the book which I wouldn't let him see this morning.'

'But meanwhile we still have you here,' said Lord Iveldown, with an equal quietness that contrasted strangely with the nervous flickers that jerked across his mottled face. He turned to his host. 'Farwill, we must go to London at once. Miss Holm will be—ah—concerned to hear the news.'

'She has a great sense of humour,' said the Saint metallically, but his voice sounded oddly in his own ears.

Iveldown shrugged.

'That remains to be seen. I believe that it will be comparatively easy to induce her to listen to reason,' he said thoughtfully; and the Saint's blood went cold.

'She won't even listen to you,' he said, and knew that he lied.

Lord Iveldown must have known it too, for he paid no attention.

He turned away without answering, gathering his party like a schoolmaster rallying a flock of boys.

'Nassen, you will remain here and guard these two. When Mr Yorkland arrives, explain the developments to him, and let him do what he thinks best . . . Farwill, you must find some pretext to dismiss your servants for the night. It will avoid difficulties if Nassen is compelled to exercise force. We will leave the front door open so that Yorkland can walk in . . .'

'Mind you don't catch cold,' said the Saint in farewell.

He smoked his cigarette through, and listened to the hum of Lord Iveldown's car going down the drive and fading away into the early night.

Not for a moment since Iveldown walked into the room had he minimised his danger. Admittedly it was easier to be distantly responsible for the deaths of ten thousand unknown men than to directly order the killing of one; yet Simon knew that Lord Iveldown, who had done the first many years ago, had in the last two days slipped over a borderline of desperation to the place where he would be capable of the second. The fussiness, the pretentious speech, the tatters of pomposity which still clung to him and made him outwardly ridiculous, made no difference. He would kill like a sententious ass; but still he would kill. And something told the Saint that the Rose of Peckham would not be unwilling to do the job at his orders.

He lighted another cigarette and paced the room with the smooth nerveless silence of a cat. It was queer, he thought, how quickly and easily, with so little melodrama, an adventurer's jest could fall under the shadow of death; and he knew how utterly false to human psychology were the ranting bullying villains who committed the murders in fiction and films. Murder was so rarely done like that. It was done by heavy, grandiose, flabby, frightened men—like Lord Iveldown or the Honourable Leo Farwill or Mr Neville Yorkland, M.P. And it made no difference that Simon Templar, who had often visualised himself being murdered, had a futile angry objection to being murdered by pettifogging excrescences of that type.

They would have no more compunction in dealing with Patricia. Perhaps less.

That was the thought which gnawed endlessly at his mind, infinitely more than any consideration of his own danger. The smooth nerveless silence of his own walking was achieved only by a grim effort of will. His muscles strained against it; a savage helplessness tore at his nerves while the minutes went by. Farwill and Iveldown had seventy-five miles to go; and with every minute his hope of overtaking them, even with his car and brilliant driving, was becoming more and more forlorn.

He glanced at Hoppy Uniatz. Mr Uniatz was sitting hunched in his chair, his fists clenched, glowering at Nassen with steady unblinking malevolence. In Hoppy's philosophy, there could be only one outcome to what had happened and his own failure on the draw. There was no point in revolving schemes of escape; the chance to put them into practice was never given. The only question to be answered was—how long? His wooden nerves warping under the strain of the long silence, he asked it.

'Well,' he growled, 'when do we go for dis ride?'

'I'll tell you when the time comes,' said Nassen.

The Saint pitched away his cigarette and lighted yet another. Nassen was alone. There were two of them; and nobody had thought to take Hoppy's gun away. If Hoppy could only get a second chance to draw—if Nassen's nerves could be played on, skilfully and relentlessly, until it became a question of which side could outlast the other . . .

'What does it feel like to be monarch of all you survey, Snowdrop?' he asked. 'Doesn't it make your little heart go pit-a-pat? I mean, suppose Hoppy and I suddenly decided we didn't love you any more, and we both jumped up together and slapped you?'

'You'd better not try,' said Nassen. 'I'd be glad of the excuse.'

He spoke with a cold stolidity that made the Saint stop breathing for a moment. Not until then, perhaps, had he admitted to himself how hopeless was the idea which had crossed his mind—hopeless, at least, to achieve any results in time for it to be worth the effort.

He halted in front of Nassen, gazing at him over the gun between them. So there was only one way left. Nassen could not possibly miss him; but he might be held long enough to give Hoppy Uniatz a chance. And after that, Hoppy would have to carry the flag . . .

'You know that would be murder, don't you, Snowdrop?' he said slowly, without a flinch of fear in his bleak watchful eyes.

'Would it?' said Nassen mincingly. 'For all anyone would ever know, you're a couple of armed burglars caught red-handed. Your record at Scotland Yard will do the rest. Don't forget whose house this is—'

He broke off.

Another pair of headlights had flashed across the windows; and a car, frantically braked, skidded on the gravel outside. A bell rang in the depths of the house; the knocker hammered impatiently; then came the slight creak of the front door opening. Every movement of the man outside could be pictured from the sounds. The unlatched door moved when he plied the knocker; he looked at it for a moment in indecision—took the first hesitant step into the hall—hurried on . . .

Nassen was listening too. And suddenly the Saint realised that the chance he had never looked for, the chance he had never thought of, had been given him. Nassen's attention was distracted—he, too, had been momentarily fascinated by the imaginary picture that could be deduced from the sequence of sounds. But he recovered less quickly than the Saint. And Simon's fist had already been clenched for a desperate blow when the interruption came.

The Saint launched it.

Snowdrop, the Rose of Peckham, was never very clear in his mind about what happened. He was not by nature addicted to physical violence of the cruder sort; and no experience of that kind had ever come his way before to give him a standard of comparison. He saw a bony fist a few inches from his face, travelling towards him with appalling speed; and his mouth opened. The fist shut it again for him, impacting on the point of his chin with a crack that seemed to jar his brain against the roof of his skull. And beyond that there was nothing but a great darkness filled with the hum of many dynamos . . .

Simon caught him by the coat lapels and eased him silently to the floor, gathering up the automatic as he did so. And then the door burst open and the rounded rabbit features of Mr Neville Yorkland looked into the room.

'Hullo,' he stuttered. 'What's happened? Got Lord Iveldown's message. Said he'd caught our man.' His weak blinking eyes travelled all over the room and came to rest on the prostrate form of the slumbering Nassen. He pursed his lips. 'Oh. I see. Is this—'

The Saint straightened up; and a slow godless gleam came into his blue gaze.

'That's the guy,' he said, in the accents of Pete the Blood. 'Hoppy an' me was just waitin' to see ya before we scram. We gotta get on to London—Lord Iveldown wants us there!'

IX

Patricia Holm was waiting for the Saint when the telephone bell rang to announce the penultimate round of that adventure.

'It's that detective again, miss,' said Sam Outrell hoarsely. 'Mr Teal. An' he's got another detective with him. They wouldn't wait for me to ask if they could go up.'

The girl's heart missed a beat; and then she answered quite quietly:

'All right, Sam. Thanks. Tell Mr Templar as soon as you see him—if they haven't gone before he comes in.'

She put down the receiver, and picked up the cigarette which she had been about to light. She looked about the room while she put a match to it—her hand was steady, but her breath was coming a little faster. She had walked with Simon Templar in the ways of lawlessness too long to be flung into panic; but she knew that she was on trial. The Saint had not come back, and he had sent no message: his habits had always been too erratic for a thing like that to frighten her, but this time she was left to hold the fort alone, with no idea of what he had done or was doing or what his plans might be. The only thing she could be sure of was that Chief Inspector Teal had not arrived for the second time that day, bringing another detective with him, on a purely social call.

The book, *Her Wedding Secret*, lay on the table. Patricia picked it up. She had to think—to think quickly and calmly, building up deduction and prophecy and action, as the Saint himself would have done. Simon had left the book there. He had not troubled to move it when Nassen came. But Teal—Teal and another man ... The bell of the apartment rang while she was still trying to reach a conclusion. There was an open bookcase beside the fireplace, and with a sudden tightening of her lips she thrust the book in among the row of novels on the bottom shelf. She had no time to do anything more; but she was desperately conscious of the inadequacy of what she had done.

Chief Inspector Teal did not know it. He looked across the threshold with affectedly weary eyes at the slim startling beauty of the girl who, even to his phlegmatic unimpressionable mind was more like a legendary princess than any woman he had ever seen; who for reasons not utterly beyond his understanding had chosen to give up the whole world that she might have queened to become the companion in outlawry of a prince of buccaneers; and he saw in her blue eyes, so amazingly like the Saint's own, the same light of flickering steel with which Simon Templar had greeted him so many times.

'Good evening, Miss Holm,' he said sleepily. 'I think you know me; and this is Sergeant Barrow. We have a warrant to search this apartment.'

He held out the paper; and she glanced at it and handed it back.

'Mr Templar isn't in,' she said coolly. 'Hadn't you better call back later?'

'I don't think so,' said Mr Teal, and walked past her into the hall.

She closed the door and followed the two detectives into the living-room. Mr Teal took off his bowler hat and put it on the table—it was the only concession he made to her presence.

'We may as well start here,' he said to Barrow. 'Go over the usual places first.'

'Would you like to borrow the vacuum cleaner,' inquired Patricia sweetly, 'or will you just use your heads?'

'We'll manage,' said Teal dourly.

He was more keyed up than he would have cared to admit. The Assistant Commissioner's parting speech still rang in his ears; the resentment of many other similar interviews rang carillons through his brain. He was a man of whom Fate had demanded many martyrdoms. In doing his duty he had to expose himself to the stinging shafts of Saintly irreverence, and afterwards he had to listen to the acidulated comments of the Assistant Commissioner; and there were days when he wondered whether it was worth it. Sometimes he wished that he had never been a policeman.

Patricia stood around and watched the progress of the search with a trip-hammer working under her ribs and a sinking sensation in her stomach. And in a frightful hopeless way she realised that it was not going to fail. It was not a hurried haphazard ransacking of drawers and cupboards like Nassen and his colleague had conducted. It was thorough, systematic, scientific, ordered along the rigid lines of a training that had reduced hiding-places to a tabulated catalogue. It would not glance at the cover of a book and pass on . . .

She knew that even before Barrow came to the bookcase and began to pull out the books one by one, opening them and flicking over the pages without looking at the titles . . .

What would the Saint have done?

Patricia didn't know. Her face was calm, almost unnaturally calm; but the trip-hammer under her ribs was driving her into the clutches of a maddening helplessness that had to be fought off with all her will power. There was an automatic in the bedroom: if she could only put over some excuse to reach it . . . But the Saint would never have done that. Teal had his warrant. He was within his rights. Violence of any kind would achieve nothing— nothing except to aggravate the crash when it came.

Barrow had reached the second row of books. He was half-way through it. He had finished it. The first two shelves were stripped . . . and the books were heaped up untidily on the floor. He was going on to the third.

What would the Saint have done?

If only he could arrive! If only the door would open, and she could see him again, smiling and unaccountable and debonair, grasping the situation with one sweep of lazy blue eyes and finding the riposte at once! It would be something wild and unexpected, something swift and dancing like sunlight on open water, that would turn everything upside down in a flash and leave him mocking in command with his forefinger driving gaily and unanswerably into Teal's swelling waistcoat; she knew that, but she could not think what it would be. She only knew that he had never been at a loss—that somehow, madly, magnificently, he could always retrieve the lost battle and snatch victory from under the very scythe of defeat.

Barrow was down to the third shelf.

On the table were the bottle of beer and the glass which she had set out ready for him—the glass over which his eyes should have been twinkling while he harried the two detectives with his remorseless wit. Her hands went out and took up the bottle and the opener, as she would have done for the Saint if he had walked in.

'Would you care for a drink?' she asked huskily.

'No, thank you, Miss Holm,' said Teal politely, without looking at her.

She had the opener fitted on the crown cap. The bottle opened with a soft hiss before she fully realised that she had done it. She tried to picture the Saint standing on the other side of the table—to make herself play the scene as he would have played it.

'Excuse me if I have one,' she said.

The full glass was in her hand. She sipped it. She had never cared for beer, and involuntarily she grimaced . . .

Teal heard a gasp and a crash behind him, and whirled round. He saw the glass in splinters on the table, the beer flowing across the top and pattering down on the carpet, the girl clutching her throat and swaying where she stood, with wide horrified eyes.

'What's the matter?' he snapped.

She shook her head, and swallowed painfully before she spoke.

'It . . . burns,' she got out in a whisper. 'Inside . . . Must have been something in it . . . Meant for . . . Simon . . .'

Then her knees crumpled and she went down.

Teal went to her with surprising speed. She was writhing horribly, and her breath hissed sobbingly through her clenched teeth. She tried to speak again, but she could not form the words.

Teal picked her up and laid her on the chesterfield.

'Get on the phone,' he snarled at Barrow with unnatural harshness. 'Don't stand there gaping. Get an ambulance.'

He looked about him awkwardly. Water—that was the first thing. Dilute the poison—whatever it was. With a sudden setting of his lips he lumbered out of the room.

Patricia saw him go.

Sergeant Barrow was at the telephone, his back towards her. And the bookcase was within a yard of her. Writhing as she was, the sound of one movement more or less would not be noticed. There was no need for stealth—only for speed.

She rolled over and snatched *Her Wedding Secret* from its place in the bottom shelf. Barrow had been too practical—too methodical. He had not looked at titles. With a swift movement she lifted the first three volumes of one of the inspected piles which he had stacked on the floor, and thrust the book underneath . . .

'Thank you,' said Teal's drowsy voice.

He was standing in the doorway with a grim gleam of triumph in his eyes; and he had not even got a glass of water in his hand. She realised that he had never gone for one. He had thought too fast.

Barrow was gaping at him stupidly.

'You can cancel that call,' said Teal shortly.

Patricia sat up and watched him cross the room and pick the book out of the pile. The trip-hammer under her ribs had stopped work abruptly; and she knew the fatalistic quiet of ultimate defeat. She had played and lost. There was no more to do.

Mr Teal opened the book with hands that were not quite steady.

The realisation of success made him fumble nervously—it was a symptom which amazed himself. He learned then that he had never really hoped to succeed; that the memory of infinite failures had instilled a subconscious presentiment that he never could succeed. Even with the book in his hands, he could not quite believe that the miracle had happened.

It was in manuscript—he saw that in a moment. Manuscript written in a minute pinched hand that crowded an astonishing mass of words on to the page. Methodically he turned to the beginning.

The first page was in the form of a letter.

*Villa Philomène,*
*Nice,*
*A.M.*

*My dear Mr Templar,*
 *It is some time now since we last met, but I have no fear that you will have forgotten the encounter. Lest it should have slipped my mind at the time, let me immediately pay you the tribute of saying that you are the only man in the world who has successfully frustrated my major plans on two occasions, and who has successfully circumvented my best efforts to exterminate him.*

*It is for this reason that, being advised that I have not many more months to live, I am sending you this small token of esteem in the shape of the first volume of my memoirs.*

*In my vocation of controller of munition factories, and consequently as the natural creator of a demand for their products, I have had occasion to deal with other Englishmen, fortunately in a more amicable manner than you would permit me to deal with you. In this volume, which deals with certain of my negotiations in England before and during the last world war, you will find detailed and fully documented accounts of a few notable cases in which prominent countrymen of yours failed to view my activities with that violent and unbusinesslike distaste which you yourself have more than once expressed to me.*

*The gift has, of course, a further object than that of diminishing any insular prejudices you may have.*

*At the same time as this book is sent to you, there will be sent, to the gentlemen most conspicuously mentioned in these notes, letters which will inform them into whose hands the book has fallen. After reading it yourself, you will see that this cannot fail to cause them great perturbation.*

*Nevertheless, while it would be simple for you to allay their alarm, and assure your own safety from molestation, I cannot foresee that a man such as I recall you to be would so tamely surrender such a unique opportunity to apply moral pressure towards the righting of what you consider to be wrongs.*

*I therefore hope to leave behind me the makings of a most diverting contest which my experiments in international diplomacy may have excelled in dimension but can scarcely have excelled in quality. And you will understand, I am sure, my dear Mr Templar, that I can hardly be blamed for sincerely trusting that these gentlemen, or their agents, will succeed where I have failed.*

*Very truly yours,*
*Rayt Marius.*

Teal read the letter through, and looked up with an incredulous half-puzzled frown. Then, without speaking, he began to read it through again. Patricia stood up with a little sigh, straightened her dress, and began to comb out her hair. Sergeant Barrow shifted from one foot to the other, and compared his watch with the clock on the mantelpiece—it would be the fourth consecutive night that he had been late home for dinner, and his wife could scarcely be blamed for beginning to view his explanations with suspicion.

Mr Teal was half-way through his second reading when the telephone rang. He hesitated for a moment, and then nodded to the girl.

'You can answer it,' he said.

Patricia took up the instrument.

'There are two gentlemen here to see you, miss,' said Sam Outrell. 'Lord Iveldown and Mr Farwill.'

'Send them up,' she said recklessly.

She had no idea why those two should have called to see her, but she was also beyond caring.

'Lord Iveldown and the Home Secretary are on their way,' she told Teal, as she put down the telephone. 'You're holding quite a gathering here, aren't you?'

The detective blinked at her dubiously. He was unable to accept her statement at its face value, and he was unable for the moment to discover either an insulting witticism or the opening of another trap in it. He returned to his reading with only half his mind on it; and he had just finished when the buzz of the door-bell took her from the room.

He closed the book and changed his position so that he could see the hall.

'. . . so unceremoniously, Miss Holm,' Lord Iveldown was saying as he entered the room. 'But the matter is urgent—most urgent.' He stopped as he saw Teal. 'And private,' he added. 'I did not know that you were entertaining.'

'It must have been kept a secret,' said the girl ironically.

She moved aside to shut the door; and as she did so Mr Teal

and the Honourable Leo Farwill saw each other at the same time. There was a moment's dead silence; and then Farwill coughed.

'Ah—Inspector,' he said heavily. 'I hope we are not—ah—disturbing you.'

'No, sir,' said Teal, looking at him curiously. He added: 'I think you'll be glad to know, sir, that as far as I can see we've got all the evidence we need.'

Farwill's hand went to his moustache. His face had gone puffy and grey, and there was a dry hoarseness in his voice.

'Ah—evidence,' he repeated. 'Ah—quite. Quite. Ah—evidence. That book—'

'Have you read it?' asked Iveldown raspingly.

'Only the first page, my lord,' said Teal. 'The first page is a letter—it's rather involved, but I think that book will turn out to be the one we were looking for.'

His heavy-lidded china-blue eyes were fixed on the Home Secretary perplexedly and with a trace of subconscious hostility. There was a kind of gritty strain in the atmosphere which he could not understand; and, not understanding it, it bothered him. His second reading of the letter had definitely been distracted, and he had not yet clearly sorted its meaning out of the elaborate and unfamiliar phrases in which it was worded. He only knew that he held triumph in his hands, and that for some unaccountable reason the Honourable Leo Farwill, who had first put him on the trail, was not sharing his elation.

'Let me see the book,' said Farwill.

More or less hypnotised, Teal allowed it to be taken out of his hand; and when it was gone a kind of wild superstitious fear that was beyond logic made him breathe faster, as if the book had actually dissolved into thin air between his fingers.

Farwill opened the book at the first page and read the letter.

'Ah—quite,' he said short-windedly. 'Quite. Quite.'

'Mr Farwill was going to say,' put in Lord Iveldown, 'that we came here for a special purpose, hoping to intercept you, Inspector. Critical international developments—'

'Exactly,' boomed Farwill throatily. 'The matter is vital. I might almost say—ah—vital.' He tucked the book firmly under his arm. 'You will permit me to take complete charge of this affair, Inspector. I shall have to ask you to accompany Lord Iveldown and myself to Scotland Yard immediately, where I shall explain to the Chief Commissioner the reasons of State which obviously cannot be gone into here—ah—and your own assiduous efforts, even if misdirected, will be suitably recognised—'

The gentle click of a latch behind him made everyone spin round at once; and Patricia gave a little choking cry.

'Well, well, well!' breathed the smiling man who stood just inside the door. 'That's great stuff, Leo—but how on earth do you manage to remember all those words without notes?'

It was the Saint.

## X

He stood with his hands in his pockets and a freshly lighted cigarette tilting between his lips, with his hair blown awry by the sixty miles an hour he had averaged, and the sparkle of the wind in his eyes; and Hoppy Uniatz stood beside him. According to their different knowledge, the others stared at him with various emotions registering on their dials; and the Saint smiled at them all impartially and came on in.

'Hullo, Pat,' he murmured. 'I didn't know you'd asked the YMCA to move in. Why didn't you tell me?' His keen blue eyes, missing nothing, came to rest on the gaudily covered volume that Farwill was clutching under his arm. 'So you've taken up literature at last, Leo,' he said. 'I always thought you would.'

To say that Farwill and Iveldown were looking at him as if they had seen a ghost would be a trite understatement. They were goggling at him as if he had been the consolidated incarnation of all the spooks and banshees that ever howled through a maniac's nightmare. Their prosperous paunches were caving in like rubber balloons punctured with a sharp instrument; and it seemed as though all the inflation that escaped from their abdomens was going straight into their eyeballs. There was a sick blotchy pallor in their faces which suggested that they had been mentally spirited away on to the deck of a ship that was wallowing through all the screaming furies of the Horn.

It was Farwill who first found his voice. It was not much of a voice—it was more like the croak of a strangling frog—but it produced words.

'Inspector,' it said, 'arrest that man.'

Teal's somnolent eyes opened a little, and there was a gleam of tentative exhilaration in them. So, after all, it seemed as if he had been mistaken. He was not to be cheated of his triumph. His luck had turned.

'I was going to,' he said, and started forward.

'On what charge?' asked the Saint.

'The same charge,' said Teal inexorably. 'Blackmail.'

The Saint nodded.

'I see,' he said, and shrugged his shoulders. 'Oh, well—no game can go on for ever, and we've had lots of fun.' His gaze watched the advancing detective with a hint of wicked banter in it that belied the rueful resignation of his features; but Teal did not see that at once. 'It'll be a sensational case,' said the Saint. 'Let me give you an idea.'

And without warning, with a flow of movements too swift to follow, he took a couple of paces sideways and aimed a punch at what was left of the Honourable Leo's prosperous corporation. Farwill instinctively jerked up his hands; and with a quick smile Simon turned the feint into a deft reach of his hand that caught *Her Wedding Secret* as it fell.

Barrow and Teal plunged towards him simultaneously; and the Saint moved rapidly back—past the automatic that had appeared like magic in the hand of a Mr Uniatz who this time had not been artificially obstructed on the draw.

'Stay back, youse guys!' barked Hoppy, in a voice quivering with exultation at his achievement; and involuntarily the two detectives checked.

The two politicians, equally involuntarily taking the lead in any popular movement, went further. They went back as far as the confines of the room would allow them.

'You know your duty, Inspector,' said the Home Secretary tremblingly. 'I order you to arrest those men!'

'Don't order a good man to commit suicide,' said the Saint curtly. 'Nobody's going to get hurt—if you'll all behave yourselves for a few minutes. I'm the bloke who's being arrested, and I want to enjoy it. Readings by the Public Prosecutor of extracts from this book will be the high spot of the trial, and I want to have a rehearsal.'

He turned the pages and quickly found a place.

'Now here's a juicy bit that'll whet your appetites,' he remarked. 'It must have something to do with those reasons of State which you were burbling about, Leo. 'On May 15th I dined again with Farwill, then Secretary of State for War. He was inclined to agree with me about the potentialities of the Aix-la-Chapelle incident for increasing the friction between France and Germany; and on my increasing my original offer to fifty thousand pounds he agreed to place before the Cabinet—'

'Stop!' shouted Farwill shrilly. 'It's a lie!'

The Saint closed his book and put it down; and very slowly the smile returned to his lips.

'I shouldn't be so melodramatic as that,' he said easily. 'But of course it's a joke. I suppose it's really gone a bit too far.'

There was another long silence; and then Lord Iveldown cleared his throat.

'Of course,' he said in a cracked voice. 'A joke.'

'A joke,' repeated Farwill hollowly. 'Ah—of course.'

Simon flicked his cigarette through the open window, and a rumble of traffic went by in the sudden quiet.

'And not, I'm afraid,' he murmured, 'in the best of taste.'

His eyes strayed back to the staring gaze of Chief Inspector Teal.

Of all those persons present, Mr Teal did not seem the most

happy. It would be inaccurate to say that he realised exactly what was going on. He didn't. But something told him that there was a catch in it. Somewhere in the undercurrents of that scene, he knew, there was something phony—something that was preparing to gyp him of his triumph at the very moment of victory. He had only the dimmest idea of how it was being worked; but he had seen it happen too many times before to mistake the symptoms.

'What the heck is this joke?' he demanded.

'Leo will tell you,' said the Saint.

Farwill licked his lips.

'I—ah—the joke was so—ah—silly that I—ah ... Well, Inspector, when Mr Templar approached us with the offer of this—ah—literary work, and—ah—knowing his, if I may say so, notorious—ah—character, I—ah—that is, we—thought that it would be humorous to play a slight—ah—practical joke on him, with your—ah—unwitting assistance. Ah—'

'Whereas, of course, you meant to buy it all the time,' Simon prompted him gently.

'Ah—yes,' said the Honourable Leo chokingly. 'Buy it. Ah—of course.'

'At once,' said Lord Iveldown quaveringly, taking out his cheque-book.

'Ah—naturally,' moaned the Honourable Leo, feeling for his pen. 'At once.'

'Two hundred thousand pounds, was it not, Mr Templar?' said Lord Iveldown.

The Saint shook his head.

'The price has gone up a bit,' he said. 'It'll cost you two hundred and fifty thousand now—I need a new hat, and the Simon Templar Foundation isn't intended to pay for that.'

With his head swimming and the blood drumming in his ears, Chief Inspector Claud Eustace Teal watched the cheques being made out and blotted and handed over. He would never really know how the trick was turned. He only knew that Simon Templar was back; and anything could happen . . .

The parting words with which the Saint shepherded the gathering out of the door did nothing to enlighten him.

'By the way, Leo,' said the Saint, 'you must remember to tell Neville to send on his share. If you toddle straight back home you'll find him waiting for you. He's standing guard over the Rose of Peckham, with a great big gun—and for some reason or other he thinks Snowdrop is me.'

'Sir Humbolt Quipp came in and left a cheque,' said Patricia Holm uncertainly.

Simon took it and added it to his collection. He fanned out the four precious scraps of paper and brought the Honourable Leo Farwill's contribution to the top. Then he removed this one from the others and gazed at it for a long time with a rather rueful frown.

'I'm afraid we let Leo off too lightly,' he said. 'When I begin to think what a splendiferous orgy of Teal-baiting we could have had with the Home Secretary permanently under our thumb, I almost wonder whether the Simon Templar Foundation is worth it.'

But later on he brightened.

'It would have made life damned dull,' he said.

# THE HIGH FENCE

Apart from the fact that neither of them was a productive or useful member of the community, Johnny Anworth and Sunny Jim Fasson had very little in common. They did not own allegiance to the same Dear Old School; they had no meeting-ground in a passion for the poems of William Wordsworth, no shared devotion to collecting birds' eggs or the rarer kinds of cheese. But the circumstances in which they ceased to adorn their usual places in the files of Records Office at New Scotland Yard had a connecting link, which must be the chronicler's excuse for reciting them in quick succession.

Johnny Anworth entered a jeweller's shop in Bond Street during the Easter holidays of that year, and omitted to pay for what he took out. He entered through the ceiling, from an apartment on the floor above which he had rented temporarily. It was a pretty neat job, for Johnny was a sound worker in his line; but it had his personality written all over it, and Headquarters put out the routine dragnet and in twenty-four hours duly brought him in.

He was taken to Market Street police station, where he was seen by the Divisional Inspector. The awkward part of it from Johnny's point of view was that he had most of the proceeds of his burglary on him when he was caught—at any rate he had all the precious stones, which had been prised out of their settings, carefully packed in a small cardboard box, and done up with brown paper and string. What he had not had time to do was to write an address on the package, and for this reason the DI was very gentle with him.

'You were going to send that stuff to the High Fence, weren't you, Johnny?' he said.

'I dunno wot yer talkin' abaht, guv'nor,' answered Johnny

mechanically. 'I fahnd the stuff lyin' in the gutter in Leicester Square, an' I did it up to send it to the Lost Property Office.'

The Divisional Inspector continued to be gentle.

'You've been in stir six times already,' he said, consulting a memorandum on his desk. 'If we wanted to be hard on you now, we could have you sent to the Awful Place. You could go to the Moor for seven years, and then have three years' preventive detention waiting for you. On the other hand, if you told us who you were going to send this parcel to, we might forget about those previous convictions and put in a word for you.'

Johnny considered this. There is honour among thieves, but it is not designed to resist bad weather.

'Orl right, guv'nor,' he said philosophically. 'I'll squeal.'

This story might have ended there if the station shorthand writer had been available. But he had already gone out to lunch; and the Divisional Inspector was also hungry.

They put Johnny Anworth back in his cell with instructions to order anything he wanted to eat at the DI's expense, and an appointment to make his statement at two o'clock. His lunch, which consisted of roast beef and cabbage, was delivered from a near-by restaurant by an errand-girl who deposited it in the charge-room. Almost as soon as she had gone, after some flirtatious exchanges with the charge-sergeant, it was picked up by the gaoler, who carried it in to Johnny. He was the last man who saw the talented Mr Anworth alive.

The girl had taken the tray from the chef in the kitchen, and no one had stopped her or spoken to her on the way. The chef had had no unusual visitors. The only people in the charge-room when the girl delivered the tray were the gaoler, the charge-sergeant, and Inspector Pryke. And yet, somehow, somewhere on the short journey which Johnny Anworth's last meal had taken, someone had contrived to dope the horseradish sauce with which his plate of roast beef was garnished with enough cyanide to kill a regiment.

The murder was a nine days' wonder which provoked its inevitable quota of headlines, newspaper criticisms, and questions in Parliament. Every inquiry seemed to lead to a dead end. But the Criminal Investigation Department has become phlegmatically accustomed to dead ends; and Chief Inspector Teal was still working methodically on the case, six weeks later, when Mr James Fasson clicked to the tune of five thousand pounds' worth of gems to which he had no legal right whatsoever.

The assets of Sunny Jim Fasson were a smile which made children and hard-boiled business men trust him instinctively, a wardrobe of prosperous-looking clothes, some high-class American luggage plastered with a wonderful collection of expensive cosmopolitan labels, enough ready cash to create an impression of affluence at any hotel where he stayed, and a girl-friend who posed as his wife, sister, niece, or old widowed mother with equal success and distinction.

On this occasion he stayed at the Magnificent, a hotel which he had not previously honoured with his presence. He was a wealthy American on his honeymoon; and for a few days he and his charming wife were quite happy seeing the sights and making a round of the theatres. One day, however, a small rift appeared in their marital bliss.

'I guess she's feelin' kinda homesick, or something,' Sunny Jim confided to a clerk at the inquiry desk. 'Whaddaya do when your wife gets moody, son?'

'I don't really know, sir,' confessed the clerk, who was not employed to answer that kind of inquiry.

'Y'know, I always think a woman wants some kinda kick outa life when she feels that way,' mused Sunny Jim. Some lil thing that makes her feel good with herself. A noo hat, or a fur coat, or—a diamond bracelet . . . That's what she wants!' he cried, recognising divine inspiration when it breathed on him. 'A diamond bracelet! Say, what's the best store in this town to buy a diamond bracelet?'

'Peabody's, in Regent Street, are very good, sir,' said the clerk, after a moment's thought.

Sunny Jim beamed.

'Ring 'em up and tell 'em to send some of their best diamond bracelets around,' he said. 'I'll have the man take 'em right up to her room, and she can pick what she likes. Say, I bet that'll put everything right.' Whether it put everything right or not is a question that the various parties concerned might have answered differently. The hotel was glad enough to oblige such a lavish guest; and Mr Peabody, the jeweller, was so impressed with their brief account of Mr James Fasson that he hurried round in person with six diamond bracelets in his bag. After a short discussion, Mrs Fasson chose the most expensive, a mere trifle valued at a thousand pounds; and Mr Fasson rang for a pageboy to take his cheque for that amount round to the bank to be cashed.

'You must have a drink while you're waitin' for your money,' said Sunny Jim, turning to a bottle and a siphon which stood on a side table.

Mr Peabody had a very small drink; and remembered nothing more for another hour, at the end of which time Mr and Mrs Fasson had left the Magnificent for ever, taking all his six diamond bracelets with them. Nor did Mr Peabody's afternoon look any brighter when the bank on which Mr Fasson's cheque had been drawn rang up the hotel to mention that they had never carried an account for anybody of that name.

This episode was the subject of a hurriedly assembled conference in the Assistant Commissioner's room at New Scotland Yard.

The other two men present were Chief Inspector Claud Eustace Teal and Junior Inspector Pryke. Mr Teal, who was responsible for the conference, explained his point of view very briefly.

'Anworth and Fasson used to be fairly well acquainted, and if Anworth was using the High Fence there's a good chance that Fasson will be using him too. I know exactly where I can lay my hands on Sunny Jim, and I want permission to try and get a squeal out of him unofficially.'

'What is your objection to having him arrested and questioned in the ordinary way?' asked the Commissioner.

'He'd have to be taken to Market Street, wouldn't he?' meditated Teal aloud. His baby blue eyes hid themselves under studiously sleepy lids. 'Well,' he said dryly, 'because I don't want him murdered.'

Junior Inspector Desmond Pryke flushed. He was one of the first graduates of Lord Trenchard's famous Police College, and he usually gave the impression of being very well satisfied with his degree. He was dark, slim, and well-manicured; and the inventor of that classic experiment for turning gentlemen into detectives could certainly have pointed to him as a product who looked nothing like the traditional idea of a policeman. Mr Teal had been heard to thank God that there was no possibility of confusing them, but there were obvious reasons why Mr Teal was irrevocably prejudiced in favour of the old order.

'It's in your manor, Pryke,' said the Assistant Commissioner. 'What do you think?'

'I don't see what there is to be gained by it,' said the other. 'If Fasson hasn't been too frightened by the murder of Anworth to talk anyhow—'

'What does Fasson know about the murder of Anworth?' demanded Teal quickly, for the official statements to the Press had contained certain deliberate gaps.

Pryke looked at him.

'I don't suppose he definitely knows any more than any other outsider, but it's common gossip in the underworld that Anworth was murdered because he was going to turn informer.'

'You look as if you spent a lot of your time picking up gossip from the underworld,' retorted Teal sarcastically. He caught the Assistant Commissioner's chilly eye on him, and went on more politely: 'In any case, sir, that's only another reason why I don't want to take him to a police station. I want to try and prevent him thinking that any squeal could be traced back to him.'

There was some further discussion, through which Teal sat stolidly chewing a worn-out lump of spearmint, with his round pink face set in its habitual mask of weary patience, and eventually gained his point.

'Perhaps you had better take Inspector Pryke with you,' suggested the Commissioner, when he gave his permission.

'I should like to, sir,' said Mr Teal, with great geniality, 'but I don't know whether this can wait long enough for him to go home and change.'

Pryke adjusted the set of his coat delicately as he rose. It was undoubtedly part of a resplendent suit, being of a light fawn colour with a mauve over-check; a very different proposition from Teal's shiny blue serge.

'I didn't know that Police Regulations required you to look like an out-of-work rag and bone man,' he said; and Chief Inspector Teal's complexion was tinged with purple all the way to Hyde Park Corner.

He resented having Inspector Pryke thrust upon him, partly because he resented Inspector Pryke, and partly because the High Fence had been his own individual assignment ever since Johnny Anworth put his knife and fork into that fatal plate of roast beef six weeks ago. For a lieutenant, when necessity called for one, Mr Teal preferred the morose and angular Sergeant Barrow, who had never been known to speak unless he was spoken to, and who then spoke only to utter some cow-like comment to which nobody with anything better to do need have listened. Chief Inspector Teal had none of the theoretical scientific training in criminology with which the new graduates of the Police College were pumped to offensive overflowing, but he had a background of thirty years' hard-won experience which took the intrusion of manicured theorists uneasily; and at the entrance of the small apartment building in which Sunny Jim Fasson had been located he said so.

'I want you to keep quiet and let me do the talking,' was his instruction. 'I know how I'm going to tackle Fasson, and I know how to get what I want out of him.'

Pryke fingered his *MCC* tie.

'Like you've always known how to get what you want out of the Saint?' he drawled.

Mr Teal's lips were tightly compressed as he stumped up the

narrow stairway. His seemingly interminable failure to get anything that he really wanted out of that cool, smiling devil who passed so incongruously under the name of the Saint was a thorn in his side which Inspector Pryke had twisted dexterously before. Whenever Chief Inspector Teal attempted to impress the rising generation of detectives with his superior craftsmanship, that gibe could always be brought up against him, openly or surreptitiously; and Mr Teal was getting so tired of it that it hurt. He wished, viciously, that some of the smart infants who were being pushed up under him could have as much to cope with as he had had in his time.

But Sunny Jim Fasson was quite a different problem from the blue-eyed bantering outlaw who had occupied so much of Mr Teal's time in other days; and he felt a renewal of confidence when he saw Sunny Jim's startled face through the slit of the opening door and wedged his foot expertly in the aperture.

'Don't make a fuss, and nobody's going to hurt you, Sunny,' he said.

Sunny Jim, like Johnny Anworth, was also a philosopher, in his way. He retreated into the tiny bed-sitting-room without dropping the ash from his cigar.

'What's it about this time, Mr Teal?' he inquired, with the *sang-froid* of old experience.

He did not even bother to put on his cultivated American accent; which saved him considerable trouble, for he had been born in the Old Kent Road and had learnt all that he knew of America from the movies.

'It needn't be about some diamond bracelets that were stolen from Peabody's—unless you want it to be,' said Teal, with equal cold-bloodedness.

Sunny Jim raised his eyebrows. The gesture was mechanical.

'I don't know what you mean, Mr Teal.'

'Would you know what I meant,' replied the detective, with impregnable drowsiness, 'if I told you that Peabody has identified your photograph and is quite sure he can identify you; and half the Magnificent Hotel staff are ready to back him up?'

Sunny Jim had no answer to that.

'Mind you,' said Teal, carefully unwrapping a fresh slice of chewing-gum, 'I said that we needn't go into that unless you want to. If you had a little talk with me now, for instance—why, we could settle it all here in this room, and you needn't even come with us to the station. It'd be all over and forgotten—just between ourselves.'

When Sunny Jim Fasson was not wearing the well-trained smile from which he had earned his nickname, his face fell into a system of hard-bitten lines which drew an illuminating picture of shrewd and sharp intelligence. Those lines became visible now. So far as Sunny Jim was concerned, Teal's speech needed no amplification; and Sunny Jim was a man who believed in the comfort and security of Mr James Fasson first, last, and in the middle. If Teal had arrived half an hour later he would have been on his way to Ostend, but as things were he recognised his best alternative health resort.

'I'm not too particular what I talk about with an old friend, Mr Teal,' he said at length.

'Do you sell your stuff to the High Fence, Sunny?' Fasson held his cigar under his nose and sniffed the aroma.

'I believe I did hear of him once,' he admitted cautiously. The appearance of bored sleepiness in Chief Inspector Teal's eyes was always deceptive. In the last few seconds they had made a detailed inventory of the contents of the room, and had observed a torn strip of brown paper beside the waste-basket and a three-inch end of string on the carpet under the table.

'You've already got rid of Peabody's diamond bracelets, haven't you?' he said persuasively; and his somnolent eyes went back to Sunny Jim's face and did not shift from it. 'All I want to know from you is what address you put on the parcel.'

Sunny Jim put his cigar back in his mouth till the end glowed red.

'I did send off a parcel not long ago,' he confessed reminiscently. 'It was addressed to—'

He never said who it was addressed to.

Mr Teal heard the shot behind him, and saw Sunny Jim's hand jerk to his brow and his head jar with the shock of the bullet. The slam of the door followed, as Teal turned round to it in a blank stupor of incredulity. Pryke, who was nearest, had it open again when his superior reached it and Teal barged after him in a kind of incandescent daze, out on to the landing. The sheer fantastic unexpectedness of what had happened had knocked his brain momentarily out of the rhythm of conscious functioning, but he clattered down the stairs on Pryke's heels, and actually overtook him at the door which let them out on to the street.

And having got there, he stopped, with his brain starting work again, overwhelmed by the utter futility of what he was doing.

There was nothing sensational to be seen outside. The road presented the ordinary aspect of a minor thoroughfare in the Shepherd Market area at that time of day. There was an empty car parked on the other side of the road, a man walking by with a brief-bag, two women laden down with parcels puttering in the opposite direction, an errand-boy delivering goods from a tricycle. The commonplace affairs of the district were proceeding uninterrupted, the peace of the neighbourhood was unbroken by so much as a glimpse of any sinister figure with a smoking gun shooting off on the conventional getaway.

Teal's dizzy gaze turned back to his subordinate.

'Did you see him?' he rasped.

'Only his back,' said Pryke helplessly. 'But I haven't the faintest idea which way he went.'

Teal strode across to the errand-boy.

'Did you see a man come rushing out of that building just now?' he barked; and the lad looked at him blankly.

'Wot sort of man, mister?'

'I don't know,' said Teal, with a feeling that he was introducing himself as the most majestic lunatic in creation. 'He'd have been running hell for leather—you must have noticed him—'

The boy shook his head.

'I ain't seen nobody running abaht, not till you come aht yerself, mister. Wot's the matter—'as 'e pinched something?'

Mr Teal did not enlighten him. Breathing heavily, he rejoined Junior Inspector Pryke.

'We'd better get back upstairs and see what's happened,' he said shortly.

But he knew only too well what had happened. The murder of Johnny Anworth had been repeated, in a different guise, under his very nose—and that after he had pleaded so energetically for a chance to guard against it. He did not like to think what ecstatic sarabands of derision must have been dancing themselves silly under the smug exterior of Desmond Pryke. He clumped up the stairs and across the landing again in a dumb paroxysm of futile wrath, and went back into the flat.

And there he halted again, one step inside the room, with his eyes bulging out of their sockets and the last tattered remnants of his traditional pose of sleepiness falling off him like autumn leaves from a tree, staring at what he saw as if he felt that the final vestiges of sanity were reeling away from his overheated mind.

II

The body of Sunny Jim Fasson was no longer there. That was the brain-staggering fact which Chief Inspector Teal had to assimilate. It had simply ceased to exist. For all the immediate evidence which Teal's reddening gaze could pick up to the contrary, Sunny Jim Fasson might never have lived there, might never have been interviewed there, and might never have been shot there. The ultimate abysses of interplanetary space could not have been more innocent of any part of Sunny Jim Fasson than that shabby one room flatlet as Teal saw it then. There could hardly have been much less trace of Sunny Jim if he had never been born.

And instead of that, there was someone else sitting in the chair where the bullet had hit Sunny Jim—a man whose mere recollection was enough to raise Chief Inspector Teal's blood pressure to apoplectic heights, a man whose appearance on that spot, at that precise catastrophic moment, turned what might have been an ordinary baffling mystery into something that made Mr Teal's voice fail him absolutely for several seconds.

'Stand up, Saint,' he got out at last, in a choking gurgle. 'I want you!'

The man peeled himself nonchalantly up from the arm-chair, and managed to convey the impression that he was merely following a course which he had chosen for himself long ago, rather than that he was obeying an order. And Mr Teal glowered at him unblinkingly over every inch of that leisured rise.

To anyone unfamiliar with the dim beginnings and cumulative ramifications of the feud between those two (if anyone so benighted can be imagined to exist in the civilised world) Mr Teal's glower might justifiably have seemed to lack much of the godlike impartiality which ought to smooth the features of a conscientious detective. It was a glower that had no connexion with any detached survey of a situation, any abstract weighing of clues and conundrums. It was, to describe it economically, the kind of glower on which eggs can be fried. It was as calorifically biased and unfriendly as a glower can be.

The Saint didn't seem to notice it. He came upright, a lean, wide-shouldered figure in a light grey suit which had a swashbuckling elegance that nothing Inspector Pryke wore would ever have, and met the detective's torrid glare with cool and quizzical blue eyes.

'Hullo, Claud,' he murmured. 'What are you doing here?'

The detective looked up at him dourly—Teal was not nearly so short as his increasing middle-aged girth made him appear, but he had to look up when the Saint stood beside him.

'I want to know what you're doing here,' he retorted.

'I came to pay a call on Sunny Jim,' said the Saint calmly. 'But he doesn't seem to be here—or did you get here first and knock him off?'

There were times when Mr Teal could exercise an almost superhuman restraint.

'I'm hoping to find out who got here first,' he said grimly. 'Sunny Jim has been murdered.'

The Saint raised one eyebrow.

'It sounds awfully exciting,' he remarked; and his bantering eyes wandered over to Pryke. 'Is this the bloke who did it?'

'This is Junior Inspector Pryke, of C Division,' said Mr Teal formally; and the Saint registered ingenuous surprise.

'Is it really?' he murmured. 'I didn't know they'd put trousers on the Women Police.'

Chief Inspector Teal swallowed hastily; and it is a regrettable fact that a fraction of the inclement ferocity faded momentarily out of his glare. There was no lawful or official reason whatsoever for this tempering of his displeasure, but it was the very first time in his life that he had seen any excuse for the Saint's peculiar sense of humour. He masticated his gum silently for a couple of seconds that gave him time to recover the attitude of mountainous boredom which he was always praying for strength to maintain in the Saint's presence. But his relief was only temporary.

'I suppose you're going to tell me you came to see Fasson just to ask him what he thought about the weather,' he said.

'Certainly not,' said the Saint blandly. 'I wouldn't try to deceive you, Claud. I blew in to see if he knew anything about some diamond bracelets that a bird called Peabody lost this afternoon. I might have pointed out to him that Peabody is very upset about losing those jools. I might have tried to show him the error of his ways, and done my best to persuade him that they ought to be sent back. Or something. But I can't say that I thought of shooting him.'

'How did you know he was shot?' Teal cut in.

'My dear fathead, I don't. I merely said that I didn't think of shooting him. Was he shot?'

Teal hesitated for a moment, studying him with that deceptively bovine gaze.

'Yes, he was shot.'

'When?'

'Just now.'

The bantering blue eyes had an impish twinkle.

'You must have been doing some fast detecting,' said the Saint. 'Or did somebody tell you?'

Mr Teal frowned at him, shifting his gum from tooth to tooth till he got it lodged behind his wisdoms. His sluggish glance travelled once again over that keen sunburned face, handsome as Lucifer and lighted with an indescribable glimmer of devil-may-care mockery; and he wondered if there would ever be any peace for him so long as he was in the employment of the Law and that amazing buccaneer was on the other side.

For Simon Templar was the incalculable outlaw for whom the routines of criminal investigation had no precedents. He belonged to no water-tight classification, followed no rules but his own, fitted into no definite category in the official scheme of things. He was the Saint: a creation of his own, comparable to nothing but himself. From time to time, desperate creatures of that nebulously frontiered stratosphere commonly called 'the Underworld' had gone forth vowing unprintable revenge, and had come back empty-handed—when they came back at all. Many times, Chief Inspector Claud Eustace Teal had thought that all his ambitions would be fulfilled if he could see the Saint safely locked away behind the bars of Larkstone Prison—and yet some of his most spectacular coups could never have been made without the Saint's assistance. And in spite of all the wrath that had been directed on him from these diametrically antagonistic quarters, the Saint had still gone on, a terror to the underworld and a thorn in the side of Scotland Yard, a gay crusader in modern dress who returned from his lawless raids with more booty than any adventurer had ever found before him.

And with all these memories freshened in his mind during that slothful survey, almost against his will, Chief Inspector Teal found himself impotent to believe that the High Fence could be merely another alias of the man before him. It was not psychologically possible. Whatever else could be said about him, the Saint was not a man who sat spinning webs and weaving complex but static mysteries. Everything that he did was active: he would go out to break up the web and take his illicit plunder from the man who wove it, but he wouldn't spin ... And yet there was the evidence of Teal's own flabbergasted senses, there in that room, to be explained away; and Mr Teal had suffered too much at the Saint's hands to feel that there could ever be any comfortable certainty in the wide world when that incorrigible freebooter was around.

He clasped his pudgy hands behind his back and said: 'Sunny Jim was shot in this room, less than five minutes ago. Somebody opened the door and shot him while I was talking to him. He was shot just in time to stop him telling me something I very much wanted to hear. And I want to know what you were doing at that time.'

The Saint smiled rather mildly.

'Is that an invitation or a threat?' he inquired.

'It's whichever you like to make it,' Teal answered grimly. 'Sunny Jim didn't shoot himself, and I'm going to find out who did it.'

'I'm sure you are, Claud,' said the Saint cordially. 'You always do find out these things, with that marvellous brain of yours ... Have you thought of the High Fence?'

Teal nodded.

'I have.'

'What do you know about the High Fence?' demanded Pryke suspiciously.

Simon took out a cigarette-case and looked at him equably.

'This and that. I've been looking for him for some time, you know.'

'What do you want with the High Fence, Saint?' asked Mr Teal.

Simon Templar glanced with unwontedly passionless eyes at the chair where Sunny Jim had stopped talking, and smiled with his lips. He lighted a cigarette.

'The High Fence has killed two men,' he said. 'Wouldn't you like a chance to see him in the dock at the Old Bailey?'

'That isn't all of it,' answered the detective stubbornly. 'You know as well as I do that the High Fence is supposed to keep a lot of the stuff he buys together, and ship it out of the country in big loads. And they say he keeps a lot of cash in hand as well—for buying.'

The glimmer of mockery in the Saint's eyes crisped up into an instant of undiluted wickedness.

'Teal, this is all news to me!'

'You're a liar,' said the detective flatly.

He stared at the Saint with all the necessary symptoms of a return of his unfriendly glower, and added: 'I know what your game is. You know the High Fence; but you don't know what he does with the stuff he's bought, or where he keeps his money. That's all you want to find out before you do anything about putting him in the dock at the Old Bailey on a charge of murder. And when that time comes, you'll buy a new car and pay some more cash into your bank balance. That's all the interest you have in these two men who've been killed.'

'I can't get around to feeling that either of them is an irreparable loss,' Simon admitted candidly. 'But what's all this dramatic lecture leading to?'

'It's leading to this,' said Teal relentlessly. 'There's a law about what you're doing, and it's called being an accessory after the fact.'

Simon aligned both eyebrows. The sheer unblushing impudence of his ingenuousness brought a premonitory tinge of violet into the detective's complexion even before he spoke.

'I suppose you know what you're talking about, Claud,' he drawled. 'But I don't. And if you want to make that speech again in a court of law, they'll want you to produce a certain amount of proof. It's an old legal custom.' Only for the second time in that interview, Simon looked straight at him instead of smiling right through him. 'There's a lot of laws about what you're doing; and they're called slander, and defamation of character, and—'

'I don't care what they're called!'

'But you've got to care,' said the Saint reasonably. 'After all, you're telling me that a bloke's been shot, and that I did it, or I know something about it. Well, let's begin at the beginning. Let's be sure the bloke's dead. Where's his body?'

In spite of certain superficial resemblances, it can be fairly positively stated that Chief Inspector Teal had never, even in some distant incarnation, been a balloon. But if he had been, and the point of a pin had been strategically applied to the most delicate part of his rotundity, it would have had practically the same effect as the Saint's innocently mooted question. Something that had been holding out his chest seemed to deflate, leaving behind it an expanding and exasperating void. He felt as if someone had unscrewed his navel and his stomach had fallen out.

The cigar which had slipped stupidly out of Sunny Jim's mouth when the bullet hit him was lying on the carpet in front of him, tainting the room with an acrid smell of singeing wool. Teal put his foot on it. It was his only concrete assurance that the whole fantastic affair hadn't been a grotesque hallucination—that the overworked brain which had struggled through so many of the Saint's shattering surprises hadn't finally weighed its anchor and gone wallowing off into senile monsoons of delirious delusion. His lips thinned out in an effort of self-control which touched the borders of homicidal fever.

'That's what I want to know,' he said. 'The body was here when I went out. When I came in again it had disappeared—and you were here instead. And I think you know something about it.'

'My dear Claud,' Simon protested, 'what d'you think I am, a sort of amateur body-snatcher?'

'I think you're a—'

Simon raised his hand.

'Hush,' he said, with a nervous glance at Inspector Pryke. 'Not before the lady.'

Teal gulped.

'I think—'

'The trouble is,' said the Saint, 'that you don't. Here you are shooting off your mouth about a body, and nobody knows whether it exists. You wonder whether I could have shot Sunny Jim, when you don't even know whether he's dead. You hint at pinching me for being an accessory after the fact, and you can't produce the fact that I'm supposed to be an accessory to.'

'I can prove—'

'You can't. You can't prove anything, except your own daftness. You're doing that now. You ask me what's happened to Sunny Jim's body, with the idea that I must have done something with it. But if you can't produce this body, how d'you know it ever was a body? How d'you know it didn't get up and walk out while you were away? How d'you know any crime's been committed at all?' The Saint's lean forefinger shot out and tapped the detective peremptorily on the waistcoat, just above his watch-chain. 'You're going to make a prize idiot of yourself again, Claud, if you aren't very careful; and one of these days I shall be very angry with you. I put up with the hell of a lot of persecution from you—'

'Will you stop that?' barked Mr Teal, jerking his tummy hysterically back from the prodding finger.

The Saint smiled.

'I am stopping it, dear old pumpkin,' he pointed out. 'I've just told you that my patience is all wore out. I'm not taking any more. Now you go ahead and think out your move. Do you take a chance on running me in for murdering a bloke that nobody can prove was murdered, and stealing a corpse that nobody can prove is a corpse—or do you phone for your photographers and finger-print fakers and leave me out of it?'

Glowering at him in a supercharged silence that strained against his ribs, Mr Teal thought of all the things he would have liked to do, and realised that he could do none of them. He was tied up in a knot which there was no visible way of unravelling. He had seen similar knots wound round him too often to cherish any illusions on that score—had gorged his spleen too often on the maddeningly confident challenges of that debonaire picaroon to hope that any amount of thought could make this one more digestible.

It was air-tight and water-tight. It was as smooth as the Saint's languid tantalising voice. It located the one unanswerable loophole in the situation and strolled through it with as much room to spare as an ant going through the Arc de Triomphe. It was exactly the sort of thing that the Saint could always be relied upon to do.

The knowledge soaked down into Mr Teal's interior like a dose of molten lead. The ancient duel was embarking upon the umpteenth round of a series which seemed capable of going on into eternity; and the prospect seemed as hopeless as it had always seemed. If Mr Teal had any formulated idea of hell, it was something exactly like that—an endless succession of insoluble riddles that he had to try to solve, while the Saint's impudent forefinger and the Assistant Commissioner's disparaging sniff worked in alternate relays to goad his thoughts away from the last relics of coherence. And there were moments when he wondered if he had already died without knowing, and was already paying for his long-forgotten sins.

'You can go, for the present,' he said smoulderingly. 'I'll find you again when I want you.'

'I'm afraid you will,' said the Saint sadly, and adjusted the brim of his hat to the correct piratical angle. 'Well, I'll be seein' ya, Claud Eustace . . .' He turned his vague, unspeakably mischievous smile on to Junior Inspector Pryke, who had been standing sulkily mute since he was last noticed. 'And you too, Sweet Pea,' he said hopefully.

Chief Inspector Claud Eustace Teal watched his departure with malignant gloom. It was discouragingly reminiscent of too many other Saintly exits that Mr Teal had witnessed, and he had a very apathetic interest in the flashlight photography and finger-print dusting which he had to superintend during the next hour or two.

For those records were made only at the dictation of a system in which Mr Teal was too congenitally rut-sunk to question. There was a fire-escape within easy reach of the bathroom window which had more to tell than any number of photographs of an empty chair from which an unproven corpse had disappeared.

Sunny Jim Fasson had been shot at by somebody who had opened the door of the flatlet while Mr Teal was interrogating him, the same somebody who had found means of silencing Johnny Anworth on the verge of an identically similar squeak; after which Fasson had vanished off the face of the earth. And Teal had a seething conviction that the only living man who knew every secret of what had happened was walking free in the Saint's custom-built shoes.

The Assistant Commissioner was very polite.

'But it has possibly failed to occur to you,' he commented, 'that this is the sort of thing news editors pray for.'

'If you remember, sir,' Pryke put in smugly. 'I was against the idea from the first.'

'Quite,' said the Commissioner. 'Quite.' He was a man who had won his appointment largely on the qualification of a distinguished career of pig-sticking and polo-playing with the Indian Army, and he was inclined to sympathise with the officer whom he regarded as a pukka sahib, like himself. 'But you went with Mr Teal, and you may know why Templar was not at least arrested on suspicion.'

'On suspicion of what?' demanded Teal wildly. 'The worst you could prove is that he abetted Fasson's escape; and that means nothing, because Fasson hadn't even been arrested.'

Pryke nibbled his thumb-nail.

'I believe that if we could account for the Saint, the rest of the mystery would be settled,' he said.

'Mr Teal has been trying to account for the Saint for several years,' the Assistant Commissioner reminded him acrimoniously.

What Mr Teal wanted to say would have reduced Scotland Yard to a small pool of steaming lava.

III

Simon Templar sauntered around the corners of a couple of blocks, and presently waited by the kerb while a big grey saloon cruised slowly up towards him. As it came level, he stepped neatly on to the running-board, opened the nearest door, and sank into the seat beside the driver. As if the upholstery on which he deposited his weight had had some direct connexion with the accelerator, the car picked up speed again and shot away into the traffic with its engine purring so smoothly that the leap of the speedometer needle seemed an absurd exaggeration.

With her small deft hands on the steering-wheel nosing a way through the traffic stream where no one else but the Saint himself would have seen a way visible, Patricia Holm took her eyes momentarily from the road to glance at him helplessly.

'What on earth,' she inquired, 'are we playing at?'

The Saint chuckled.

'Is the game puzzling you, old darling?'

'It's doing its best.' She took his cigarette away from between his fingers while she thrust the murmuring grey car under the snout of a speeding lorry with the other hand. 'You come down this way to see Fasson about some diamonds. You and Hoppy go in to see him. After a while Hoppy comes out with a body; and a long time after that you come out yourself, looking as if you'd just heard the funniest story of your life. Naturally I'm beginning to wonder what we're playing at.'

Simon took out his cigarette-case and replaced his stolen smoke.

'I suppose you aren't so wide of the mark, with the funny story angle,' he admitted. 'But I thought Hoppy would have put you on the trail.'

He slewed round to cock an eyebrow at the passenger who rode in the back seat; but the passenger only gazed back at him with troubled blankness and said. 'I dunno what de game is, neider, boss.'

Hoppy Uniatz had never been really beautiful, even as a child, and the various contacts which his face had had with blunt instruments since then had not improved it. But it has sometimes been known for such faces to be lighted with a radiance of spirituality and intellect in which their battered irregularity of contour is easily forgotten.

The physiognomy of Mr Uniatz was illuminated by no such light. Reluctant as Simon Templar always was to disparage such a faithful friend, he could never honestly claim for Mr Uniatz any of those intellectual qualities which might have redeemed his other failings. A man of almost miraculous agility on the draw, of simple and unquestioning loyalties, of heroic appetite, and of a tank-like capacity for absorbing incredible quantities of every conceivable blend of alcohol—yes, Mr Uniatz possessed all those virtues. But a strenuous pursuit of most of the minor rackets of the Bowery had never left him time to develop the higher faculties of that curious organisation of reactions which can only apologetically be called his brain. Simon Templar perceived that Mr Uniatz could not have enlightened anybody. He was in painful search of enlightenment himself.

Simon dropped an arm over the back of the seat and hauled up another hitherto invisible passenger, on whom Mr Uniatz had been thoughtlessly resting his feet.

'This is Sunny Jim, Pat,' he explained.

'Hoppy did manage to tell me that much,' said Patricia Holm with great patience. 'But did you really have to bring him away?'

'Not really,' said the Saint candidly, allowing the passenger to drop back again on to the floor. 'But it struck me as being quite a good idea. You see, Sunny Jim is supposed to be dead.'

'How do you know he isn't?'

Simon grinned.

'There might be some argument about it,' he conceded. 'At any rate, he's among the Saints.'

'But what was it all about?'

The Saint lighted his cigarette and stretched himself out.

'Well, it was this way. Hoppy and I blew up the fire-escape, as arranged, and went in through the bathroom window. When we got inside, what should we hear but the voice of good old Claud Eustace Teal, holding converse with Sunny Jim. Apparently Claud was just on the point of getting a squeak out of him, and I was just getting down to the keyhole to take a look at the séance and hear what Sunny had to say, when a gun went off and broke up the party. As far as I've been able to make out, somebody opened the front door and took a pot at Sunny Jim at the crucial moment, and Teal went chasing the assassin down the stairs, along with a perfectly twee little policebody from Eton that he had with him.'

Simon drew at his cigarette with a reminiscent smile, while the grey car whirled around Piccadilly Circus and plunged down the Haymarket.

'Anyway, Hoppy and I beetled in while they were away, and took a gander at Sunny Jim. And as a matter of fact, he isn't dead; though he's had the narrowest shave that any man ever had, and his head's going to ring carillons when he wakes up. He's been creased as neatly as I've ever seen it done—the bullet just parted his hair in a new place and knocked him out, but his skull hasn't any holes in it. That's when I had my brilliant idea.'

'I was hoping we'd get to that,' said the girl.

'But haven't you seen it already?' Simon demanded. 'Look at what I've told you. Here's Sunny Jim preparing to squeal, and somebody tries to rub him out. Why? Squealers don't get bumped off, not in this country, just because they may have a little tit-bit to give away. Sunny Jim must have known something worth knowing; and there he was, sitting in his chair, out to the world, and nobody to get in our way. The bumper-offer can't be sure what's happened to him, and Claud Eustace is probably quite sure he's dead. But nobody knows . . . Isn't it all pretty obvious?'

'It's getting clearer.'

'Of course it is! I tell Hoppy to grab the body and hustle it down the fire-escape, out to this car, and pick me up later. And I wait for Claud Eustace and his boy-friend. We exchange the compliments of the season, and have lots of fun and games together.

And then I walk out. As soon as the next editions are on the streets, the bumper-offer is going to know that his body disappeared while I was around, and he's going to work himself into seven different kinds of cold sweat wondering whether it is a body. He may guess that it isn't, and itch to bump me off for what I may have found out from it; but he can't do that because if I got killed he'd never know what had happened to the body and where it might turn up next. Doesn't that make you see the joke?'

Patricia nodded slowly.

'But who,' she said, 'was the bumper-offer?'

'Who else could it be,' asked the Saint, 'but our old friend that all the excitement and bubble is about—the High Fence?'

There were adequate grounds for the outbreak of official excitement and bubble which had been provoked by the man who was known only by that unusual name.

A fence, in the argot, is nothing to do with steeplechasing or an enclosure containing sheep. He is the receiver of stolen goods, the capitalist of crime, and incidentally the middle-man but for whose functioning larceny in most of its forms would soon die a natural death. He runs less risk than any of the actual stealers, and makes much bigger profits. And very often he takes his cut both ways, making his profit on the receipt of stolen goods and betraying the stealers to a friendly detective at the same time.

The fence is a member of an unchartered union, the only code of which is to pay as little for a purchase as the vendor can be persuaded to accept.

Seven or eight months ago, the invisible tentacles of the CID, which spread wider and more delicately than many of its critics would believe, touched on the rumour of a man who violated that rule. He bought nothing but metals and precious stones, and paid twice as much for them as any other receiver in London was offering. By contenting himself with a hundred per cent profit instead of three hundred per cent he could well afford to do it; but it is a curious fact that no other receiver before him has thought of such a scandalously unethical expedient. And through the strange subterranean channels in which such gossip circulates, the word went round that he was 'good'.

Because of the prices he paid, they called him the High Fence; but nobody knew anything more about him. He had no shop where he conducted his business. Anything that was offered to him for sale had to be sent through the post, to an accommodation address which was changed every week. The address was passed round the limited circle of his clients by word of mouth, and it was impossible to find out who first put it into circulation. Every client had always 'heard about it' from another—the trail turned inevitably into a hopeless merry-go-round. Nor was the circle of initiates unrestricted. It was a jealously closed ring of talent which the High Fence picked for himself; and queer things were rumoured to have happened to those who had ventured to spread the good news among their friends without permission. To those who were tempted by circumstances to talk to the CID, even queerer things could happen—as we have shown.

The High Fence might never have encountered a serious setback, if there had not been one outlaw in England for whom queer happenings had no terrors, and to whom the scent of booty was the supreme perfume in the breath of life.

'I'm afraid Claud Eustace has a depressingly cynical idea of what I'm up to,' said the Saint. 'He thinks I know who the High Fence is—in which he's flattering me too much, and I wish he wasn't. And he thinks that all I'm wanting is to find out where this bird keeps his boodle and his cash, so that I can take it off him before he gets pinched.'

'In which he's perfectly right.'

The Saint sighed.

'I don't know where you get these ideas from,' he said in a pained voice. 'By the way, are you going anywhere in particular, or are we just sightseeing?'

'I'm waiting for you to tell me.'

'Let's go to Abbot's Yard—it's about the only hide-out we have left that isn't in Teal's address-book. And I don't think Sunny Jim is going to be too keen on seeing callers for a while.'

He relaxed at full length, with his eyes half closed against the smoke curling past them from his cigarette, while she circled Sloane Square and headed west along the King's Road. The soft waves of her fair golden head rippled in the gentle stir of air that came through the windows; her face was as calmly beautiful as if she had been driving them on nothing more innocuous than the commonplace sightseeing tour which he had mentioned. Perhaps she was only calm because even the most adventurous girl, after some years of partnership with such a man, must achieve permanent nonchalance or perish of nervous exhaustion; but one never knew . . . And in the back of the car, Mr Uniatz and Mr Fasson were both, in their respective ways, silently unconscious.

The car threaded its way more slowly through the clotted congestion of trucks, omnibuses, vans, and drays with which the King's Road is permanently constipated, and turned off abruptly into a narrow side street composed of cottage hovels with freshly painted and utterly dilapidated fronts in approximately equal proportions. It was one of those Chelsea backwaters which are undergoing a gloomy degradation from honest slumdom to synthetic Bohemianism, and the external symptoms of its decay gave it an air of almost pathetic indecision, like a suburban bank manager on a spree in the high spots, who is trying to make up his mind whether to be thoroughly folksy or very dignified, but who is quite certain that he is as sober and important as any of his co-revellers. But in spite of this uninviting aspect, it contained a comfortable studio which the Saint had found useful before; and Simon roused himself cheerfully to open the door beside him as the car stopped.

'I think it's a case for the wheel-chair and blanket,' he said, after a judicial survey of Sunny Jim.

The transportation of an unconscious captive across a London pavement is not quite such an easy and automatic affair as the credulous reader of fiction may have been deluded to believe; but Simon Templar had had such problems to solve before. On one of the rare occasions on which Mr Uniatz did not find it necessary to delay the proceedings with unnecessary questions, he hopped intelligently out of the car and opened the door of the studio with a key which the Saint threw at him. After a brief absence, he returned with an invalid chair. Simon took the folded blanket from the seat, and between them they wrapped the limp figure of Sunny Jim Fasson tenderly up in it—so tenderly that there was not enough of him left protruding for any stray passerby to recognise. In this woolly cocoon they carried him to the chair, and in the chair wheeled him up the steps and into the house, with all the hushed solicitude of two expectant nephews handling a rich and moribund uncle. And, really, that was all about it.

'There is beer in the pantry,' said the Saint, subsiding into a chair in the studio. 'But don't let Hoppy see it, or I never shall. Hoppy, you get a sponge of cold water and see if you can bring the patient round.'

'He does wake up, once,' said Mr Uniatz reminiscently. 'In de car. But I club him wit' de end of my Betsy and he goes to sleep again.'

Simon gazed after him resignedly, and sipped the glass of Carlsberg which Patricia brought to him. A sense of tact and diplomacy could well be added to the other virtues in which Mr Uniatz was so unfortunately deficient. Hoping to extract information from a man by presenting oneself to him as his saviour and honorary guardian angel, one endeavours to calm the aching brain. One tends the wounds. One murmurs consolation and soothing comfort. One does not, intelligently, greet him on his first return to consciousness by clubbing him with the blunt end of a Betsy. It rather ruled out the potentialities of guile and cunning; but the Saint was equally prepared for the alternative.

He finished his cigarette at leisure while Mr Uniatz applied his belated ministrations; and presently an inaugural groan from the invalid chair brought him up to take over the management of the interview.

'Welcome, stranger,' he said genially.

IV

Sunny Jim Fasson did not seem happy. It is not over-stimulating for any man with less solid bone in his head than a Mr Uniatz to first have his skull grazed by a bullet, and then at the first sign of recovery from that ordeal to be slugged over the ear with a gun-butt; and certainly much of the sunshine from which Sunny Jim had once taken his nickname was missing from his countenance. With the damp traces of Hoppy's first-aid practice trickling down his nose and chin, he looked more like a picture of November Day than one of Hail, Smiling Morn.

It was perhaps discouraging that the first person he saw when he blinked open his eyes was Hoppy Uniatz. He stared at him hazily for a moment, while his memory worked painfully back to its last association with that homely face; and then, remembering all, he half rose from the chair and lashed out with his fist. That also was discouraging, for Mr Uniatz had won his scars in a vocation where the various arts of violence are systematised to the ultimate degree: he hopped aside from the blow with an agility that gave an unexpected meaning to his name, and in another split second he had caught Sunny Jim's wrist and twisted it firmly up behind his back.

He looked round at the Saint with a beam of justifiable pride, like a puppy that has performed its latest trick. If he had had a tail, he would have wagged it.

'OK, boss?' he queried. 'Or do I give him de heat?'

'That remains to be seen,' said the Saint imperturbably. He picked up the sponge and weighed it meditatively in his hand. 'Is your brain working again, Sunny, or would you like another refresher?'

Fasson glowered at him sullenly, with a hint of fear in his eyes.

'What do you want?' he snarled.

'Personally, I only want a little talk.' Simon weighed the sponge again, and dropped it back in the basin. 'But Hoppy seems to have other ideas. By the way, have you met Hoppy? This is Mr Uniatz, Jim—a one hundred per cent American from Poland.'

'I know him,' said Fasson viciously. 'He hit me over the head with his gun.'

'So he tells me,' agreed the Saint, with some regret. 'Otherwise this little chat of ours might have been much more amicable. But he's quite a tough guy in his way, is Hoppy; and he's got a kind of natural habit of hitting people with his gun—either with one end or the other. Do you know what he means when he talks about giving you the heat?'

Sunny Jim did not answer. Studying that suspicious surly face from which all the artificial sunshine had been removed, Simon realised that the friendly conversazione which he had had in mind at the beginning would have wanted a lot of organising, even without Hoppy's intervening indiscretion.

'Well, he might mean one of two things, Sunny. He might mean taking you for a ride—ferrying you out to some nice secluded spot and dropping you in a ditch with a tummy-full of liver pills. Or he might mean just making himself sort of unpleasant—twisting your arm off, or burning your feet, or some jolly little romp like that. I never know, with Hoppy. He gets such fascinating ideas. Only the other day, he got hold of a fellow he didn't care for and tied him out on an iron bedstead and burnt candles under the springs—the bloke was awfully annoyed about it.'

'Who are you?' rasped Fasson shakily.

The Saint smiled.

'Templar is the name, dear old bird. Simon Templar. Of course, there are all sorts of funny rumours about my having another name—people seem to think I'm some sort of desperado called . . . let me see, what is it?'

The fear in Sunny Jim's eyes brightened into a sudden spark of panic.

'I know who you are,' he said. 'You're the Saint!'

Simon raised his eyebrows innocently.

'The very name I was trying to remember. People think—'

'You're the High Fence!'

Simon shook his head.

'Oh, no. You're wrong about that.'

'You're the swine who tried to shoot me just now.'

'Wrong again, brother. When I try to shoot people, they don't usually have a chance to be rude to me afterwards. But don't let's talk about unpleasant things like that.' The Saint flipped out his cigarette-case and put a smoke between his lips. 'Let's be friendly as long as we can. I didn't shoot you, but I happened into your place just after the shooting. I sort of felt that you couldn't be feeling too happy about the way things were going, so I shifted you out of there. But I still think we ought to have a talk.'

Fasson's shifty eyes travelled round the room, and came back to the Saint's face. He answered through his teeth.

'I can't tell you anything.'

'Perhaps you haven't quite recovered yet,' said the Saint persuasively. 'After all, you were going to tell Chief Inspector Teal something. By the way, have you met Mr Uniatz? Only the other day—'

'I don't know anything!'

Hoppy Uniatz shuffled his feet. It is improbable that more than two consecutive words of the conversation which has just been recorded had percolated through the protective layers of ivory that encased his brain; but he had a nebulous idea that time was being wasted, and he could not see why.

'Do I give him de heat, boss?' he inquired hopefully.

Simon inhaled thoughtfully; and Mr Uniatz, taking silence for an answer, strengthened his grip. Fasson's face twisted and turned pale.

'Wait a minute!' he gasped shrilly. 'You're breaking my arm!'

'That's too bad,' said the Saint concernedly. 'What does it feel like?'

'You can't do this to me!' shrieked Sunny Jim. 'He'd kill me! You know what happened just now—'

'I know,' said the Saint coolly. 'But there are lots of different ways of dying. Hoppy knows no end of exciting ones, and I've tried to warn you about him. I don't really want to have to let him go ahead with what he's wanting to do, instead of just playing at it as he is now; but if you've absolutely made up your mind . . .'

Sunny Jim gulped. The sharp agony in his shoulder, where Hoppy Uniatz 's powerful leverage was exerting itself, made the other unpleasant possibilities which the Saint had hinted at seem frightfully close at hand; but he could not find a shadow of pity or remorse in the clear blue eyes that were studying him with the dispassionate curiosity of an entomologist watching the wriggling of a captured insect.

'Do you want me to be murdered?' he sobbed.

'I shouldn't weep at your funeral,' Simon confessed cold-bloodedly. 'But I shouldn't look at things so pessimistically, if I were you. We could probably look after you for a bit, if you told us anything worth knowing—we might even get you out of the country and send you away for a holiday in the South of France until the excitement's all over. But you've got to spill what you know first, and I'm waiting for it to dawn on you that you'll either talk voluntarily or else we'll put you through the mangle and wring it out of you.'

His voice was casual and almost kindly; but there was something so tireless and inflexible behind it that Sunny Jim shivered. He was no hot-house flower himself; but in the circles where he moved there were stories about the Saint, brought in by men who had met that amazing buccaneer to their misfortune—legends that told of a slim bantering outlaw whose smile was more deadly than any other man's anger, who faced death with a jest and sent men into eternity with his flippant farewell ringing in their ears . . . The pain in his shoulder sharpened under Hoppy's impatient hands, and he saw that the Saint's dark lawless face was quite impassive, with the trace of an old smile lingering absentmindedly on the reckless lips . . .

'Damn you!' he whimpered. 'I'll talk . . . But you've got to let me go.'

'Tell me something first.'

Fasson's breath came in a grating sigh.

'The Kosy Korner—in Holborn—'

Simon blew a couple of smoke-rings, and nodded to Mr Uniatz. 'OK, Hoppy,' he said. 'Give him a rest.'

Hoppy Uniatz released his grip, and wiped his palms down his trousers. In so far as his gargoyle features were capable of expressing such an emotion, he looked shocked. As one who had himself kept an iron jaw under everything that could be handed to him in the back rooms of more than one station house in his own country, the spectacle of a guy who came apart under a mere preliminary treatment filled him with the same half-incredulous disgust that an English gentleman feels on meeting a cad who is not interested in cricket.

'I guess dese Limeys can't take it, boss,' he said, groping through genuine puzzlement to the only possible conclusion.

Sunny Jim glared at him in vengeful silence. His face was white with pain, and his shoulder really felt as if it had been dislocated. He rubbed it tenderly, while Simon recovered his beer and sat on the edge of the table.

'Well?' Simon prompted him gently.

'I don't know anything much. I've told you—'

'Have you traded with the High Fence before?'

'Yes.' Sunny Jim sat hunched in his chair, shrugging his shoulder gingerly in an occasional effort to reassure himself that the joints were still articulating. The words dragged reluctantly through his mouth. 'That's how I know. I wanted to know who the High Fence was. I sent him some stuff once, and waited outside the address to see who picked it up. I saw who took it. I started to tail him, but then I got picked up by a split, and I lost him while we were talking.'

'But?'

'I saw him again the next day, by accident. In this restaurant.'

'The Kosy Korner?'

Fasson nodded, and licked his lips.

'Can I have a drink?' he asked hoarsely.

The Saint made a sign to Hoppy, who abandoned his futile attempt to drain non-existent dregs out of the bottle from which Simon had refilled his glass, and left the room. The Saint's cool blue eyes did not leave Sunny Jim's face.

'And what happened there?'

Fasson got out of his chair and limped around the table, rubbing his head dazedly.

'This fellow shoved the packet in the pocket of an overcoat that was hanging on the rail—'

At that moment he was beside the empty bottle which Mr Uniatz had put down; and for once Simon Templar's understanding was a fraction of a second slow. He did not clearly comprehend what was happening until the neck of the bottle was clutched in Sunny Jim's fist, swinging up and spinning away from the hand with vicious speed.

With an instinct that was swifter than any reasoned understanding, he ducked his head and felt the cold graze of the glass stroking past his ear before it splintered on the wall behind him with an explosive smash; but that automatic movement of self-preservation lost him a vital second of time. He rolled off the table and leapt for the door, only to have it slammed in his face; and when he had wrenched it open again Sunny Jim's footsteps were clattering wildly down the second flight of stairs.

Sunny Jim Fasson tore out into the narrow street and started to run down towards the bright lights of the main thoroughfare. He didn't know exactly where he was going, but he knew that his one broad object was to remove himself as quickly as possible from the city where so many deadly things had begun to happen in one evening. Chance had given him one infinitesimal spark of knowledge that he should not have possessed, normal psychology had tempted him to use it in the purchase of his freedom when Chief Inspector Teal had called; but he had not thought of the retribution. Of what had happened since that brain-dulling bullet grazed across his head he preferred not to think; but he had a foggy idea that whichever way he turned in that perilous tangle would lead him into new dangers. He had had one warning that day. To be killed for squealing, to be tortured and perhaps killed for not squealing—he saw nothing but trouble in every prospect that was offered to him, except the one primitive remedy of frantic flight. He stumbled into the King's Road with his chest heaving, and hesitated on the corner in a moment's ghastly indecision . . . A motor-cycle with a particularly noisy exhaust had started up behind him, but he did not think to look round. It seemed to backfire twice in quick succession; and a tearing shattering agony beside which Hoppy Uniatz's third degree was a fleabite crashed into his back and sent him sprawling blindly forward into the gutter . . .

Simon Templar stood in the half-open doorway and saw the motor-cycle whip round the corner and vanish with its engine roaring. He was aware that Hoppy Uniatz was breathing heavily down his neck, making strange grunting noises in an ecstasy of impatience to get past him.

'Lemme go after him an' give him de woiks, boss,' he was pleading. 'I'll get him, sure.'

The Saint's fingers were still curled over the butt of his own gun, which he had not had time to draw.

'You're too late, Hoppy,' he said quietly. 'He's got the works.'

He stepped back into the hall and moved aside to let Mr Uniatz look out. A small crowd was gathering round the spread-eagled shape on the corner, and the wail of a police whistle drifted faintly over the rumble of untroubled traffic. Simon closed the door again.

'So ya had him on de spot,' said Mr Uniatz, with proper admiration. 'Chees, boss, you got it all on de top storey. Howja know he was gonna take a powder?'

'I didn't,' said the Saint evenly, and went back up the stairs to Patricia.

He knew of nobody who would mourn the passing of Sunny Jim for long, and his own regret for the untimely accident was as sincere as anyone's.

'We'll be moving, kid,' he said. 'Sunny Jim has clocked out.'

'Did you shoot him?'

He shook his head.

'That was the mistake Hoppy made. But I hadn't any reason to. There was a bloke waiting outside on a motor-bike, and he got him—it may have been the High Fence himself. I thought this address was our own secret, but somebody else seems to have got on to it. So we'll move on.' He lighted another cigarette and trickled an airy feather of smoke through his lips, while Hoppy came plodding up to join them; and she saw that his blue eyes were as bright and cold as steel. 'We've lost our insurance policy, old dear. But there may be something better than an insurance policy at the Kosy Korner; and I'm going to find out what it is if I eat there till I'm poisoned!'

V

Of the millions of people who read of the vanishing and double murder of Sunny Jim Fasson at their breakfast-tables the next morning—the ingredients of the case were sensational enough to give it a place on the front page of every newspaper that had a front page—a certain Mr Clive Enderby was not the least perturbed.

Nobody who saw him going to his office that morning would have thought it. Nobody who looked at him with a cynical eye would have suspected him of ever being perturbed about anything. Nobody would have suspected him of thinking about anything. Pottering down the steps of his old-fashioned apartment in Ladbroke Grove, he looked like a typical middle-aged British businessman.

He was rather thin and long-faced, a little stooped about the shoulders, a little flat about the feet, a little under-exercised about the stomach. These things were not positive characteristics, but rather vague and diffident tendencies: to have been positive about anything would have been bad form, a vulgar demonstration in which only temperamental foreigners (a subhuman species) indulged. He wore a respectable bowler hat, and although it was clear and warm, a dark overcoat and brown kid gloves, because the calendar had not yet announced the official advent of summer. He rode to Holborn Circus on a bus, ingesting his current opinions on every subject under the sun from the Morning Post. No one would have believed that under the crown of that respectable and unemphatic derby he held the key to a riddle that was working Scotland Yard into a lather of exasperation.

From Holborn Circus he walked to Hatton Garden. His office was on the third floor of a sombre building just off that most un-horticultural preserve, where the greatest jewel business in the world is conducted by nondescript men at street corners and over the tables of adjacent cafés and public houses. It consisted of no more than a couple of shabby unpretentious rooms, but a surprising volume of trade in precious stones passed through it. For three hours Mr Enderby was fully occupied, in his slow-moving way, poring over an accumulation of letters and cables from all parts of the world, and dictating stodgy replies to his unattractive secretary, who could have coped efficiently with two hundred and fifty words a minute, but in Mr Enderby's employment had never been strained to a higher average than ten.

At a quarter past twelve he had a telephone call.

'Where are you lunching?' asked the voice.

Mr Enderby showed no surprise or puzzlement at being bluntly addressed with such a question by a caller who did not even announce his identity.

'I thought of going to the Kosy Korner again,' he said primly.

He had a voice rather like an apologetic frog.

'That'll do,' said the receiver, after a moment's thought; and a click terminated the conversation without further ceremony.

Mr Enderby put down the telephone and ponderously finished dictating the letter in which he had been interrupted. He got up, put on his bowler hat and his superfluous overcoat, and went out. On his way through Hatton Garden he stopped and bought two stones from an acquaintance on the pavement, wrapping them in bits of tissue-paper and tucking them away in his waistcoat pocket.

The Kosy Korner is one of those glorified tea-rooms run by impoverished dowagers of stupendous refinement with which the central areas of London are infested. At the time when Mr Enderby arrived there, it was already well filled with an assortment of business men, clerks, stenographers, and shop assistants, all apparently yearning after a spot of Kosiness to stimulate their digestion of that exquisite roast beef and boiled cabbage which has made English cooking famous among gourmets the world over. Mr Enderby filtered through the mob to a groaning coat-rack already laden with the outer garments of other customers, where he parked his bowler hat and overcoat. He sat in a vacant chair and ate his meal as if it were a necessary evil, a dull routine business of stoking his interior with the essential fuel for continued functioning, reading the Morning Post between mouthfuls and paying no attention to anyone else in the place. He washed the repast down with a cup of tea, folded his paper, paid his bill, pushed two coppers under the plate, and got up. He took down his hat from the rack and sorted out his overcoat. There was a small parcel in one side pocket, as he felt when he fished out his gloves, which had not been there when he hung up the coat; but even this did not make him register any surprise. He did not even take it out to see what it was.

Back in his office, Mr Enderby spoke to his secretary.

'I had a large order at lunch for some stones to go to America,' he said. 'They will have to catch the *Oceanic* tomorrow. Will you ring up the insurance company and make the usual arrangements?'

While she was at the telephone, he broke open the parcel from his overcoat pocket and spilled a small handful of diamonds on to his blotter. He looked at them for a moment, and then turned to the safe behind his desk. It was a comparatively new one of the very latest design, a huge gleaming hulk of steel which would have seemed more at home in a bank vault than in that dingy room. He set the two combinations, turned a key in the lock, and swung back the massive door. There was nothing on the shelves but a couple of cheap cardboard boxes. He took them out and tipped their contents on to the blotter also, submerging the first sprinkle of diamonds which he had put down. A solid heaped cone of glittering wealth, diamonds, emeralds, sapphires, and rubies, iridescent with all the colours of the rainbow, winked up at him.

'That will be all right, Mr Enderby,' said his secretary. 'They're sending a man round right away.'

Mr Enderby nodded, and dragged his eyes away from the pile of jewels to glance at the cheap tin clock on the mantelpiece. He was not, as we have seen, very interested in food; but for more years than he could remember he had had a passionate interest in drink. And the hour had not yet struck when such Satanic temptations are officially removed from a nation which would otherwise be certain to spend all its afternoons in drunken debauchery.

'I must leave you to pack them up and attend to the formalities, Miss Weagle,' he said. 'I have—er—another appointment.'

Miss Weagle's stoat-like face did not move a single impolite muscle, although she had listened to a similar ritual every working day for the past five years, and knew perfectly well where Mr Enderby's appointment would be kept. She was not even surprised that he should leave such a collection of gems in her care, for the casualness with which diamond traders handle huge fortunes in stones is only incredible to the layman.

'Very well, Mr Enderby. What is the value of the shipment?'

'Twenty-seven thousand six hundred and fifty pounds,' replied Mr Enderby, after an almost imperceptible deliberation; and he knew his business so well that the most expert and laborious valuation could not have disputed his snap assessment by more than a five-pound note.

He put on his bowler hat and overcoat again, and paddled thirstily out to the streets, mumbling an apology to the red-faced walrus-moustached man whom he had to squeeze past at the top of the narrow stairs; and the walrus-moustached man gazed after him with thoughtful blue eyes which would have seemed incongruously keen and clear if Mr Enderby had noticed them.

The Saint went back across the landing as Mr Enderby's footsteps died away, and knocked on the door of the office.

'I'm from the insurance company,' he said, when Miss Weagle had let him in.

'About the jewels?'

'Yes.'

With his walrus moustache and air of disillusioned melancholy, he reminded Miss Weagle of her mother.

'You've been quick,' she said, making conversation when she ought to have been making love.

'I was out on a job, and I had to ring up the office from just round the corner, so they told me to come along,' Simon explained, wiping his whiskers on his sleeve. He had spent three hours putting on that ragged growth, and every hair was so carefully planted that its falsehood could not have been detected at much closer quarters than he was ever likely to get to with Miss Weagle. He glanced at the little heap of gems, which Miss Weagle had been packing into another cardboard box lined with cotton-wool, 'Are these them?' he asked.

Miss Weagle admitted coyly that those were them. Simon surveyed them disinterestedly, scratching his chin.

'If you'll just finish packing them up, miss,' he said, 'I'll take 'em along now.'

'Take them along?' she repeated in surprise.

'Yes, miss. It's a new rule. Everything of this kind that we cover has to be examined and sealed in our office, and sent off from there. It's on account of all these insurance frauds they've been having lately.'

The illicit passion which Miss Weagle seemed to have been conceiving for him appeared to wane.

'Mr Enderby has been dealing with your firm for a long time,' she began with some asperity.

'I know, miss; but the firm can't make one rule for one customer and another for another. It's just a formality as far as you're concerned, but them's my orders. I'm a new man in this district, and I can't afford to take a chance on my own responsibility. I'll give you a receipt for 'em, and they're covered from the moment they leave your hands.'

He sat down at the desk and wrote out the receipt on a blank sheet of paper, licking his pencil between every word. The Saint was an incomparable artist in characterisation at any time, but he had rarely practised his art under such a steady tension as he did then, for he had no means of knowing how soon the real insurance company's agent would arrive, or how long Mr Enderby's appointment would keep him. But he completed the performance without a trace of hurry, and watched Miss Weagle tucking a layer of tissue over the last row of jewels.

'The value is twenty-seven thousand six hundred and fifty pounds,' she said coldly.

'I'll make a note of it, miss,' said the Saint, and did so.

She finished packing the box, and he picked it up. He still had to get away with it.

'You doing anything particular next Saturday?' he asked, gazing at her with a hint of wistfulness.

'The idea?' said Miss Weagle haughtily.

'Do you like Greta Garbo?'

This was different.

'Oh,' said Miss Weagle.

She wriggled. Simon had rarely witnessed such a revolting spectacle.

'Meet me at Piccadilly Circus at half-past one,' he said.

'All right.'

Simon stuffed the box into one of the pockets of his sober and unimaginative black suit, and went to the door. From the door, he blew a juicy kiss through the fringe of fungus which overhung his mouth, and departed with a wink that left her giggling kittenishly—and he was out of the building before she even looked at the receipt he had left behind, and discovered that his signature was undecipherable and there was no insurance company whatever mentioned on it . . .

It was not by any means the most brilliant and dashing robbery that the Saint had ever committed, but it had a pure outrageous perfection of coincidence that atoned for all its shortcomings in the way of gore. And he knew, without the slightest diminution of the scape-grace beatitude that was performing a hilarious massage over his insides, that nothing on earth could have been more scientifically calculated to fan up the flames of vengeance on every side of him than what he had just done.

What he may not have foreseen was the speed with which the inevitable vengeance would move towards him.

Still wearing his deep-sea moustache and melancholy exterior, he walked west to New Oxford Street and entered a business stationer's. He bought a roll of gummed paper tape, with which he made a secure parcel of Mr Enderby's brown cardboard box, and a penny label which he addressed to Joshua Pond, Esq., Poste Restante, Harwich. Then he went to the nearest post office and entrusted twenty-seven thousand six hundred and fifty pounds to the care of Her Majesty's mails.

Two hours later he crossed Piccadilly from the Green Park underground station, and a vision of slim fair-haired loveliness turned round from a shop window as he swung in towards her.

'Were you waiting for somebody?' he asked gravely. Her eyes, as blue as his own, smiled at him uncertainly.

'I was waiting for a bold bad brigand called the Saint, who doesn't know how to keep out of trouble. Have you seen him?'

'I believe I saw somebody like him sipping a glass of warm

milk at a meeting of the World Federation for Encouraging Kindness to Cockroaches,' he said solemnly. 'Good-looking fellow with a halo. Is that the guy?'

'What else was he doing?' The Saint laughed.

'He was risking the ruin of his digestion with some of Ye Fine Olde Englishe Cookinge which is more deadly than bullets even if it doesn't taste much different,' he said. 'But it may have been worth it. There was a parcel shoved into a bloke's overcoat pocket some time when I was sweating through my second pound of waterlogged cabbage, just like Sunny Jim said it would be, and I trailed the happy recipient to his lair. I suppose I was rather lucky to be listening outside his door just when he was telling his secretary to get an insurance hound over to inspect the boodle—By the way, have you ever seen a woman with a face like a stoat and George Robey eyebrows wriggling seductively? This secretary—'

'Do you mean you—'

'That's just what I do mean, old darling. I toddled straight into the office when this bloke went out, and introduced myself as the insurance hound summoned as aforesaid in Chapter One. And I got out of Hatton Garden with a packet of boodle valued at twenty-seven thousand six hundred and fifty quid, which ought to keep the wolf from the door for another day or two.' The glint of changeless mischief in his eyes was its own infinite elaboration of the theme. 'But it'll bring a lot of other wolves around that'll want rather more getting rid of; and I expect we can look forward to fun and games.'

She nodded.

'They've started,' she said soberly. 'There's a reception committee waiting for you.'

He was quite still for a moment; but the edge of humour in his gaze was altered only to become keener and more subtly dangerous.

'How many?'

'One.'

His brows sloped up in a hair-line of devil-may-care delight that she knew only too well—a contour of impenitent Saintliness that had made trouble-hunting its profession too long to be disturbed when the trouble came unasked.

'Not poor old Claud Eustace again?' he said.

'No. It's that new fellow—the Trenchard product. I've been waiting here three-quarters of an hour to catch you as you came along and tell you. Sam Outrell gave me the wire.'

## VI

The Saint was unperturbed. He had removed the walrus moustache which had whiffled so realistically before Miss Weagle, and with it the roseage complexion and melancholy aspect on which it had bloomed with such lifelike aptness. The costume which he had worn on that occasion had also been put away, in the well-stocked wardrobe of another pied-à-terre which he rented under another of his multitudinous aliases for precisely those skilful changes of identity. He had left the plodding inconspicuous gait of his character in the same place. In a light grey suit which looked as if it had only that morning been unpacked from the tailor's box, and a soft hat canted impudently over one eye, he had a debonair and disreputable elegance which made the deputation of welcome settle into clammily hostile attention.

'I was waiting for you,' said Junior Inspector Pryke damply.

'No one would have thought it,' said the Saint, with a casual smile. 'Do I look like your fairy godmother?' Pryke was not amused.

'Shall we go up to your rooms?' he suggested; and Simon's gaze rested on him blandly.

'What for, Desmond?' He leaned one elbow on the desk at his side, and brought the wooden-faced janitor into the party with a shift of his lazy smile. 'You can't shock Sam Outrell—he knew me before you ever did. And Miss Holm is quite broadminded, too. By the way, have you met Miss Holm? Pat, this is Miss Desdemona Pryke, the Pride of the YWCA—'

'I'd rather see you alone, if you don't mind,' said the detective.

He was beginning to go a trifle white about the mouth; and Simon's eyes marked the symptom with a wicked glitter of unhallowed mischief. It was a glitter that Mr Teal would have recognised only too easily, if he had been there to see it; but for once that long-suffering waist-line of the Law was not its victim.

'What for?' Simon repeated, with a puzzled politeness that was about as cosy and reliable as a tent on the edge of a drifting iceberg. 'If you've got anything to say to me that this audience can't hear, I'm afraid you're shinning up the wrong leg. I'm not that sort of a girl.'

'I know perfectly well what I want to say,' retorted Pryke chalkily.

'Then I hope you'll say it,' murmured the Saint properly. 'Come along, now, Desmond—let's get it over with. Make a clean breast of it—as the bishop said to the actress. Unmask the Public School Soul. What's the matter?'

Pryke's hands clenched spasmodically at his sides.

'Do you know a man called Enderby?'

'Never heard of him,' said the Saint unblushingly. 'What does he do—bore the holes in spaghetti, or something?'

'At about ten minutes to three this afternoon,' said Pryke, with his studiously smooth University accent burring jaggedly at the edges, 'a man entered his office, falsely representing himself to be an agent of the Southshire Insurance Company, and took away about twenty-seven thousand pounds' worth of precious stones.'

Simon raised his eyebrows.

'It sounds like a tough afternoon for Comrade Enderby,' he remarked. 'But why come and tell me? D'you mean you want me to try and help you recover these jools?'

The Antarctic effrontery of his innocence would have left nothing visible in a thermometer but a shrunken globule of congealed quicksilver. It was a demonstration of absolute vacuum in the space used by the normal citizen for storing his conscience that left its audience momentarily speechless. Taking his first ration of that brass-necked Saintliness which had greyed so many of the hairs in Chief Inspector Teal's dwindling crop, Desmond Pryke turned from white to pink, and then back to white again.

'I want to know what you were doing at that time,' he said.

'Me?' Simon took out his cigarette-case. 'I was at the Plaza, watching a Mickey Mouse. But what on earth has that got to do with poor old Enderby and his jools?'

Suddenly the detective's hand shot out and grabbed him by the wrist.

'That's what you've got to do with it. That scar on your forearm. Miss Weagle—Mr Enderby's secretary—saw it on this fake insurance agent's arm when he picked up the parcel of stones. It was part of the description she gave us!'

Simon looked down at his wrist in silence for a moment, the cigarette he had chosen poised forgotten in mid-air, gazing at the tail of the furrowed scar that showed beyond the edge of his cuff. It was a souvenir he carried from quite a different adventure, and he had usually remembered to keep it covered when he was disguised. He realised that he had under-estimated both the eyesight of Miss Weagle and the resourcefulness of Junior Inspector Pryke; but when he raised his eyes again they were still bantering and untroubled.

'Yes, I've got a scar there—but I expect lots of other people have, too. What else did this Weagle dame say in her description?'

'Nothing that couldn't be covered by a good disguise,' said Pryke, with a new note of triumph in his voice. 'Now are you coming along quietly?'

'Certainly not,' said the Saint.

The detective's eyes narrowed.

'Do you know what happens if you resist a police officer?'

'Surely,' said the Saint, supple and lazy. 'The police officer gets a thick ear.'

Pryke let go his wrist, and shoved his hands into his pockets.

'Do you want me to have you taken away by force?' he asked.

'I shouldn't want you to try anything so silly, Desmond,' said the Saint. He put the cigarette between his lips and struck a match with a flick of his thumb-nail, without looking at it. 'The squad hasn't been hatched yet that could take me away by force without a good deal of commotion; and you know it. You'd get more publicity than a Hollywood divorce—or is that what you're wanting?'

'I'm simply carrying out my orders—'

'Whose orders?'

'That's none of your business,' Pryke got out through his teeth.

'I think it is,' said the Saint mildly. 'After all, I'm the blushing victim of this persecution. Besides, Desmond, I don't believe you. I think you're misguided. You're behind the times. How long have you been here waiting for me?'

'I'm not here to be cross-examined by you,' spluttered the detective furiously.

'I'm not cross-examining you, Desmond. I'm trying to lead you into the paths of reason. But you don't have to answer that one if it hurts. How long has this petunia-blossom been here, Sam?'

The janitor glanced mechanically at the clock.

'Since about four o'clock, sir.'

'Has it received any message—a telephone call, or anything like that?'

'No, sir.'

'Nobody's come in and spoken to it?'

'No, sir.'

'In fact, it's just been sitting around here all on its ownsome, like the last rose of summer—'

Junior Inspector Pryke thrust himself up between them, along the desk, till his chest was almost touching the Saint's. His hands were thrust into his pockets so savagely that the coat was stretched down in long creases from his shoulders.

'Will you be quiet?' he blazed quiveringly. 'I've stood as much as I can—'

'As the bishop said to the actress.'

'Are you coming along with me,' fumed the detective, 'or am I going to have you dragged out?'

Simon shook his head.

'You miss the idea, Desmond.' He tapped the other firmly on the lower chest with his forefinger, and raised his eyebrows. 'Hullo,' he remarked, 'your stomach hasn't got nearly so much bounce in it as dear old Teal's.'

'Never mind my stomach!' Pryke almost screamed.

'I don't mind it,' said the Saint generously. 'I admit I haven't seen it in all its naked loveliness; but in its veiled state, at this distance, there seems to be nothing offensive about it.'

The noise that Pryke made can only be likened to that of a kettle coming to the boil.

'I'll hear that another time,' he said. 'Simon Templar, I am taking you into custody—'

'But I'm trying to show you that that's exactly what you mustn't do, Desmond,' said the Saint patiently. 'It would be fatal. Here you are, a rising young officer on the threshold of your career, trying to pull a flivver that'll set you back four years' seniority. I can't let you do it. Why don't you curb the excessive zeal, Rosebud, and listen to reason? I can tell you exactly what's happened.'

'I can tell you exactly what's going to happen—'

'It was like this,' continued the Saint, as if the interruption not merely fell on deaf ears, but had failed miserably in its effort to occur at all. 'This guy Enderby was robbed, as you say. Or he thought he was. Or, still more exactly, his secretary thought he was. A bloke calling himself an insurance agent blew into the office, and breezed out again with a parcel of jools. On account of various complications, the secretary was led to believe that this insurance agent was a fake, and the jools had been pinched. Filled with the same misguided zeal that's pulling the buttons of that horrible waistcoat of yours, Desmond, she called the police. Hearing of this, you came puffing round to see me, with your waistcoat bursting with pride and your brain addled with all the uncomplimentary fairy-tales that Claud Eustace Teal has told you about me.'

'Who said so?'

'I did. It's a sort of clairvoyant gift of mine. But you must listen to the rest of it. You come blowing round here, and wait for me from four o'clock onwards. Pepped up with the idea of scoring a solo triumph, you haven't said anything to anyone about your scheme. Consequently, you don't know what's happened since you left headquarters. 'Which is this. Shortly after the secretary female called for the police, Comrade Enderby himself returned to the office, the shemozzle was explained to him, he explained the shemozzle, and the long and the short of it was that the insurance agent was found to be perfectly genuine, the whole misunderstanding was cleared up, the whole false alarm exposed; and it was discovered that there was nothing to arrest anybody for—least of all me.'

'What makes you think that?'

Simon took in a lungful of tobacco smoke, and inhaled through his nose with a slight smile. What made him think that? It was obvious. It was the fundamental formula on which fifty per cent of his reputation had been built up.

A man was robbed. Ninety-eight times out of a hundred, the fact was never published at all. But if ever, through some misguided agent, or during a spasm of temporary but understandable insanity on the part of the victim himself, the fact happened to be published, that same victim, as soon as he discovered the accident or came to his senses, was the first and most energetic on the field to explain away the problem with which Scotland Yard had been faced—for the simple reason that there would be things much harder to explain away if the robber were ever detected.

And the bereavement of Mr Enderby was so perfectly on all fours with the formula that, with the horns of the dilemma touched in, it would have looked like a purple cow. There was no answer to it. So Mr Enderby had been robbed of some jewels? Well, could he give a description of the jewels, so that if they were recovered . . . How did the Saint know? He smiled, with unusual tolerance.

'Just the same old clairvoyant gift—working overtime for your special benefit, Desmond. But I'll back it for anything you like to bet—even including that perfectly repulsive shirt you're wearing. If you only got wise to yourself, you'd find that nobody wanted me arrested any more; and it'd save both of us no end of trouble. Now, why don't you get on the phone to Headquarters, and bring yourself up to date? Let me do it for you; and then you can save your two-pence to buy yourself a bar of milk chocolate on the way home . . .'

He picked up the telephone on the porter's desk, and pushed his forefinger persuasively into the initial V of the Victoria exchange. It was all ancient history to the Saint, an old game which had become almost stereotyped from many playings, even if with this new victim it had the semblance of a new twist to it. It hadn't seriously occurred to him that the routine could be very different.

And then something hard and compact jabbed into his chest, and his eyes shifted over with genuine surprise from the telephone dial. There was a nickel-plated little automatic in Junior Inspector Pryke's hand—the sort of footling lady-like weapon, Simon couldn't help reflecting, which a man with that taste in clothes must inevitably have affected, but none the less capable of unpleasant damage at contact range. His gaze roamed up to the detective's flaming eyes with a flicker of pained protest that for once was wholly spontaneous and tinged with a glitter of urgent curiosity.

'Put that telephone down,' said Pryke sizzlingly.

Simon put the telephone down. There was something in the other's rabid glare which told him that disobedience might easily make Pryke do something foolish—of which the Saint had no desire to suffer the physical effects.

'My dear old daffodil,' he murmured, 'have you stopped to think that that dinky little pop-gun—'

'Never mind what I think,' rasped the detective, whose range of repartee seemed to make up in venom what it lacked in variety. 'If there's any truth in what you're saying, we can verify it when we get you to the station. But you aren't going to run away until it has been verified. Come along!'

His finger was twitching over the trigger; and the Saint sighed.

He felt rather sorry for Junior Inspector Pryke. While he disliked the man's face, and his voice, and his clothes, and almost everything else about him, he had not actually plumbed such implacable depths of hatred as to wish him to turn himself into a horrible example which would be held up for the disgusted inspection of students of the Police College for the next decade.

But it seemed as if this was the only ambition Desmond Pryke had to fulfil, and he had left no stone unturned in his efforts to achieve it. From permitting himself to be lured into an argument on comparative gastrometry to that final howler of pulling a gun to enforce an ordinary arrest, Junior Inspector Pryke had run doggedly through the complete catalogue of *Things A Young Policeman Should Not Do*; but it was not Simon Templar's fault.

The Saint shrugged.

'OK, Desmond,' he murmured. 'If that's the way you feel about it, I can't stop you. I've done my best. But don't come around asking me for a pension when they drum you out of the Force.'

He put on his hat, and pulled the brim out to the perfect piratical tilt. There was not a shadow of misgiving in the smile that he gave Patricia, and he saw no reason for there to be a shadow.

'Be seein' ya, keed,' he said. 'Don't worry—I'll be back for dinner. But I'm afraid Desdemona is going to have a pain in her little tum-tum before then.'

He sauntered out unhurriedly into Stratton Street, and himself hailed the nearest taxi. Pryke put away his gun and climbed in after him. The cab turned into Piccadilly with a burden of internal silence that was almost broken by the exuberance of its own one-sided rancour.

Simon's nostrils detected a curious sweet scent in the air he was breathing. Ever the genial optimist, he tried to thaw out the polar obmutescence with a fresh turn of pleasant gossip.

'That perfume you're using, Desmond,' he said. 'I don't think

I've come across it before. What's it called—Pansy's Promise? Or is it *Quelques Tantes?*'

'You wait till we get to the station,' said the detective, with sweltering monotony. 'Perhaps you won't feel so funny then.'

'Perhaps I won't,' Simon agreed languidly. 'And perhaps you won't look so funny.'

He yawned. The cab, with all its windows tightly closed, was warm and stuffy; and the conversational limitations of Inspector Pryke were also conducive to slumber.

The Saint closed his eyes. He felt limp and bored and his brain was starting to wander in a most remarkable and disjointed manner. It was all rather voluptuous and dreamy, like sinking away in some Elysian hop-joint . . . Suddenly he felt faintly sick.

He sat up, with a tremendous effort. A message was trying to get through to his brain, but it seemed to be muffled in layer after layer of cotton-wool. His chest was labouring, and he could feel his heart pounding at crazy speed. The face of Junior Inspector Pryke stared back at him through a kind of violet haze. Pryke's chest was heaving also, and his mouth was open: it crossed the Saint's mind that he looked like an agitated fish . . . Then everything within his blurring vision whirled round like a top, and the blood roared in his ears like a thousand waterfalls. The message that had been trying to break through to him flashed in at last, and he made a convulsive lunge towards the window behind the driver's impassive back; but he never reached it. It seemed as if the bottom fell out of the world, and he went plunging down through fold after fold of numbing silence, down and down through cold green clouds of that curious perfume into an infinity of utter nothingness . . .

VII

There was a decanter and three sherry-glasses on the table; and one of the glasses was untouched. They had been set out there more than an hour ago; and the decanter was nearly empty.

Patricia Holm wandered restlessly about the living-room. Her face was quiet and untroubled, but she couldn't relax and sit down. The dark had come down; and the view of the Green Park from the tall windows was hidden by a grey-blue veil in which the yellow specks of the street lamps shone brighter than the stars, and the lights of cars travelling up and down the Mall gleamed like flocks of dawdling comets. She drew the curtains, for something to do, and stole her thirty-seventh glance at the clock. It was a couple of minutes after nine.

'What's happened to him?' she said.

Mr Uniatz shook his head. He stretched out a spade-shaped hand for the decanter, and completed his solo conquest of its contents.

'I dunno,' he said feebly. 'Maybe he couldn't shake de diddo. Dey come dat way, sometimes.'

'He's been arrested before,' she said. 'It's never kept him as long as this. If anything had gone wrong, he ought to have got word through to us somehow.'

Mr Uniatz chewed desperately at his poisonous cigar. He wanted to be helpful. As we have already explained, he was not naturally hot on the higher flights of the intellect; but on such an occasion as this he was not the man to shirk his obligations. The deep creases in his rudimentary forehead bore their own witness to the torture he was enduring from these unaccustomed stresses on his brain.

'Maybe he's on his way, right now,' he hazarded encouragingly.

Patricia threw herself into a chair. It was another restless movement, rather than an attempt to rest.

'That's not enough, Hoppy.' She was thinking aloud, mechanically, more for the anaesthetic effect of actual speech than with any hope of coaxing something useful out of her companion. 'If anything's gone wrong, we've got to be ready for it. We've got to pick up our own cue. He'd expect us to find the answer. Suppose he isn't on his way—what has he done?'

'He's got de ice,' said Mr Uniatz, vaguely.

'I don't know whether he's got it now. Probably he parked it somewhere on his way here. That's what he'd have done if he was expecting trouble. Sometimes he simply puts things in the mail— sends them to a hotel or a poste restante somewhere, and picks them up later on when it's all clear. Usually they aren't even addressed to his own name.'

Hoppy frowned.

'But if dey ain't addressed to his own name,' he said, 'how does he pick dem up?'

'Well, when he goes to pick them up, he gives the name that they were addressed to,' explained Patricia kindly.

Mr Uniatz nodded. He had always been lost in admiration of the Saint's intellectual gifts, and this solution was only one more justification of his faith. Obviously a guy who could work out things like that in his own head had got what it takes.

'But this time we don't know where he's sent them, or what name he addressed them to,' she said.

The tentative expression of pleased complacency faded away from Hoppy's face, and the flutings of honest effort crowded themselves once more into the restricted space between his eyebrows and his hair. He was too loyal to give way to the feeling that this was an unnecessary complication, invented simply to make things more difficult for him; but he wished people wouldn't ask him to tackle problems like that. Reaching again for the decanter and finding it empty, he glowered at it plaintively, like a trusted friend who had done him a gratuitous injury.

'So what?' he said, passing the buck with an air of profound reluctance.

'I must know what's happened to him,' said Patricia steadily.

She got up and lighted a cigarette. Twice more she paced out the length of the room with her supple boyish stride; and then with a sudden resolution she slipped into the chair by the telephone, and dialled Teal's private number.

He was at home. In a few moments his drowsy voice came over the wire.

'Who's that?'

'This is Patricia Holm.' Her voice was as cool and careless as the Saint's own. 'Haven't you finished with Simon yet? We're waiting for him to join us for dinner, and I'm getting hungry and Hoppy is getting away with all the sherry.'

'I don't know what you mean,' he answered suspiciously.

'You ought to know, Claud.'

He didn't seem to know. She explained. He was silent for so long that she thought she had been cut off; and then his suspicious perplexity came through again in the same lethargic monotone.

'I'll ring you again in a few minutes,' he said.

She sat on at the table, smoking her cigarette without enjoyment, playing a noiseless tattoo with her fingertips on the smooth green bakelite of the instrument. Over on the other side of the room, Hoppy Uniatz discovered the untouched glass which had been reserved for the Saint, and drew it cautiously towards him.

In five minutes the telephone bell rang.

'They don't know anything about it at Scotland Yard or Market Street,' Teal informed her. 'And it's the first I've heard of it myself. Is this another of your family jokes, or what?'

'I'm not joking,' said Patricia, and there was a sudden chill in her eyes which would have made the statement superfluous if Teal could have seen her. 'Pryke took him away about half past five. It was a perfectly ridiculous charge, but he wouldn't listen to reason. It couldn't possibly have kept the Saint as long as this.'

The wire was silent again for a second or two. She could visualise the detective sucking his chewing-gum more plainly than television could have shown him.

'I'll come round and see you,' he said.

He was there inside the quarter-hour, with his round harvest-moon face stodgy and disinterested under his shabby pot hat, chewing the same tasteless cud of chicle and listening to the story again. The repetition added nothing to the sum of his knowledge, except that there was no joke involved. When he had heard it through and asked his questions, he called Scotland Yard and Market Street police station again, only to have his inquiries answered by the same blank negatives. Junior Inspector Pryke, apparently, had left Market Street at about a quarter to four, without saying where he was going; and nothing had been heard of him since. Certainly he had not reported in with an arrest anywhere in the Metropolitan area.

Only one thing required no explanation; and he knew that Patricia Holm knew it, by this time, as well as he knew it himself—although her recital had carefully told him nothing more than Simon Templar himself would have done.

'The Saint was after the High Fence,' he said bluntly. 'He robbed Enderby this afternoon. I know it, and you know it, even if it is quite true that Enderby got on to us shortly after the alarm and swore it was all a mistake. Therefore it's obvious that Enderby is something to do with the High Fence. Maybe we can't prove it; but the High Fence knows his own men. It doesn't take much more to work out what happened.'

'I think you're jumping to a lot of conclusions,' said Patricia, with Saintly sweetness, and did not deceive him for an instant.

'Perhaps I am,' he said stolidly. 'But I know what I'd have done if I'd been the High Fence. I'd have heard what had happened as soon as Scotland Yard did; and I'd have watched this place. I'd have seen Pryke come in; and even that mightn't have stopped me . . . They left here in a taxi, did they? Well, you ought to be able to work it out as well as I can.'

'You mean de High Fence puts de arm on him?' asked Mr Uniatz, translating innuendo into an idiom that he could understand.

Teal looked round at him with heavy-lidded eyes in which the perpetual boredom was as flimsy a sham as anyone was likely to see it.

'If you know the answers, I expect you'll go to work on them,' he said, with a stony significance of which he would have been the first to disclaim all knowledge. 'I've got my own job to do. If one of you keeps in touch with this address, I'll let you know if I find out anything.'

He left a roomful of equally stony silence behind him, and went out to take a taxi to Scotland Yard.

The High Fence had got the Saint and Junior Inspector Pryke—he had no doubts about that. He knew, although he could never prove it, that his analysis of the situation had been as mathematically accurate as any jig-saw he would ever put together could hope to be. And it was easier to put together than most problems. He would have been happier if his own course of action had been no less clearly indicated; and it disturbed him more than he would have cared to admit to realise that he was far more concerned about the fate of the Saint than he was about the fate of his own smug subordinate.

This secondary concern, however, was settled shortly after ten o'clock, when a police constable observed a pair of feet protruding from a bush on the edge of Wimbledon Common, and used the feet to haul out the body of a man. In the first flush of instinctive optimism, the policeman thought that the body was dead, and pictured himself (with photograph and biographical note) in the headlines of a sensational murder mystery; but closer investigation showed it to be alive, and with medical assistance it was quite easily resuscitated into a healthily profane Junior Inspector of unmistakable Trenchard parentage.

'So the High Fence didn't kill you,' said Mr Teal malignantly, when a police car had brought the salvage to Scotland Yard.

'I thought you'd be pleased,' retorted Pryke pettishly.

He had a sick headache from the gas which had been pumped into the cab, and he was on the defensive for trouble. Mr Teal did not disappoint him.

'Who told you to arrest the Saint?' he inquired mucilaginously, when Pryke had given his account of the affair.

'I didn't know I had to be told. I heard of the robbery at Enderby's, and there were grounds for believing that the Saint had a hand in it—'

'You know that Enderby has denied that there ever was a robbery, and said it was entirely a misunderstanding?'

'Has he? That's what the Saint told me, but I didn't believe him. I knew nothing about it. I went out as soon as I received the first information, and waited for him at his flat.'

'And you had to use a gun to arrest him.'

Pryke flushed. He had thought it wiser to say nothing about that.

'He refused to come with me,' he said sulkily. 'I had to do something, and I didn't want to make a scene.'

'It would have made the biggest scene you're ever likely to be in, if you had got him to the station and that gun had been mentioned in the police court,' Teal said caustically. 'As it is, you'll be on the carpet first thing in the morning. Or will you tell the Assistant Commissioner that all this was my idea, too?'

Pryke scowled, and said nothing.

'Anyhow,' Teal wound up, 'the Saint has got to be found now. After your performance, he's technically an escaped prisoner. Since it was your arrest, you'd better do something about it.'

'What do you suggest?' asked Pryke, with treacherous humility.

Teal, having no answer, glared at him. Everything that could be prescribed for such an emergency had been done already—every alarm issued, every feeler put out, every net spread. If he could have thought of anything more, Chief Inspector Teal would have done it himself. But there was nothing to guide him: even what had been done was a mere firing of routine shots in the dark. The taxi had disappeared, and no one had even noticed its number. Beyond any doubt, the man who had ordered its movements was the same man who had killed Johnny Anworth and Sunny Jim Fasson—who, unless something were done quickly, would be just as likely to kill Simon Templar. A man knew too much, and he died: the logical sequence was quite clearly established, but Teal found no pleasure in following it to its conclusion.

'Since you're so damned independent of orders and regulations,' he said, with excessive violence, 'you might pay some attention to this man Enderby. I know he swears that the whole thing was a mistake, but I've heard of plenty of those mistakes before. There's no evidence and nothing we can charge him with, but if those stones that were stolen weren't stolen property already, I'll eat my hat. And if Enderby isn't hand in glove with the High Fence, even if he isn't the High Fence himself, I'll eat yours as well.'

Pryke shook his head.

'I don't know that I agree. Fasson was shot as he was running out of Abbot's Yard, and when we made a house-to-house inquiry we found out that Templar had a place there under one of his aliases—'

'Well, what about it? I've never believed that the Saint didn't have something to do with it. I don't believe he killed Fasson; but I do believe that he got the body away from the flat where Fasson was shot, and that Fasson wasn't dead. I believe that he made Fasson talk; and that Fasson wasn't really killed until either the Saint let him go, or he ran away. I think Fasson told him something that made him go after Enderby, and—'

Pryke shook his head again, with an increase of confidence and patronising self-satisfaction that made Teal stop short with his gorge rising under the leaven of undutiful thoughts of murder.

'I think you're wrong,' he said.

'Oh, I am, am I?' said Mr Teal malevolently. 'Well, what's the right answer?'

The smug shaking of Junior Inspector Pryke's head continued until Teal could have kicked him.

'I have a theory of my own,' he said, 'which I'd like to work on—unless you've got something definite that you want me to do.'

'You go ahead and work on it,' replied Teal blisteringly. 'When I want something definite done, I shan't ask you. In another minute you'll be telling me that the Assistant Commissioner is the High Fence.'

The other stood up, smoothing down the points of his waistcoat. In spite of the situation for which he was responsible, his uncrushable superciliousness was reviving outwardly untouched; but Teal saw that underneath it he was hot and simmering.

'That wouldn't be so wild as some of your guesses,' he said mysteriously. 'I'd like to get the Saint—if anyone can be made a Chief Inspector for failing to catch him, they'd have to make a Superintendent of anyone who did it.'

'Make you a Superintendent?' jeered Teal. 'With a name like yours?'

'It's a very good name,' said his junior tartly. 'There was a Pryke at the Battle of Hastings.'

'I'll bet he was a damn good cook,' snarled Mr Teal.


## VIII

For Simon Templar there was an indefinite period of trackless oblivion, from which he was roused now and again to dream curious dim dreams. Once the movement of the cab stopped, and he heard voices; then a door slammed, and he sank back into the dark before his impression had more than touched the fringe of consciousness. Once he seemed to be carried over a gravel path: he heard the scrunch of stones, and felt the grip of the hands that were holding him up, but there was no power of movement in his limbs. It was too much trouble to open his eyes, and he fell asleep again almost immediately. Between those momentary stirrings of awareness, which were so dull and nebulous that they did not even stimulate a desire to amplify them, stretched a colourless void of languorous insensibility in which time had no landmarks.

Then there was the feeling of a hard chair under him, a constriction of cords about his wrists and ankles, and a needle that stabbed his forearm. His eyelids felt weighted down almost beyond his power to lift, but when he dragged them up once he could see nothing. He wondered vaguely whether the room was in darkness, or whether he was blind but he was too apathetic to dwell earnestly on a choice between the alternatives. There was a man who talked softly out of the blackness, in a voice that sounded hazily familiar, asking him a lot of questions. He had an idea that he answered them, without conscious volition and equally without opposition from his will. Afterwards, he could never remember what he said.

Presently the interval of half-consciousness seemed to merge back without a borderline into the limitless background of sleep.

When he woke up again his head ached slightly with a kind of empty dizziness, and his stomach felt as if it had been turned inside out and spun round on a flywheel till it was raw and tender. It was an effort to open his eyes, but not such a hopeless and unimportant feat as it had seemed before. Once open, he had more difficulty at first in focusing them. He had an impression of bare grey boards, and his own feet tied together with strands of new rope. The atmosphere was warm and close, and smelt nauseatingly of paint and oil. There was a thrumming vibration under him, coupled with a separate and distinct swaying movement: after a while he picked an irregular splash and gurgle of water out of the background of sound, and induced his eyes to coordinate on a dark circular window framed in tarnished brass.

'So you're waking up for a last look round, are you?' growled a voice somewhere to his left.

Simon nodded. Shifting his gaze gingerly about, he made out more details. There was an unshaded electric bulb socketed into the low ceiling which gave a harsh but sufficient light. He was in the cabin of a boat—a small craft, by the look and motion of it, either a canal tug or a scrap-heap motor cruiser. From the rows of orderly lights that drifted past the portholes on both sides of the cabin, he deduced that they were running down the Thames.

The man who had spoken sat on an old canvas sack spread out on the bare springs of a bunk, He was a thick-set prognathous individual with thin reddish hair and a twisted mouth, most unnautically clad in a striped suit, a check cap, and canary-yellow shoes.

'Where are we off to?' Simon asked.

The man chuckled.

'You're going to have a look at some fishes. I don't know whether they'll like you, but they'll be able to go on lookin' at you till they get used to it.'

'Is that the High Fence's joke?' inquired Simon sardonically.

'It's the High Fence you're talkin' to.'

The Saint regarded him contemptuously.

'Your name is Quincey. I believe I could give you a list of all your convictions. Let me see. Two for robbery with violence, one for carrying firearms without a licence, one for attempted—'

'All right,' said Quincey good-humouredly. 'I know 'em all myself. But the High Fence and me are like that.' He locked his thick fingers together symbolically. 'We're more or less the same thing. He wouldn't be able to do much without me.'

'He mightn't have been able to get Sunny Jim murdered,' Simon agreed thoughtfully.

'Yes, I did that. It was pretty neat. I was supposed to be waitin' for both of you, but when Fasson came out an' ran down to King's Road, I was frightened of losin' him, so I had to go without you. Yes, I was ridin' the motor-bike. They can't prove it, but I don't mind tellin' you, because you'll never tell anyone else. I killed Sunny Jim—the rat! An' now I'm goin' to feed the great Simon Templar to the fishes. I know a lot of fellers who'd give their right hands to be in my place.'

Simon acknowledged the truth of that. The list of men who would have paid drastically for the privilege of using him for ground-bait in the deepest and hungriest stretch of water at their disposal could have been conveniently added up in round dozens. But his brain was still far from clear, and for the moment he could not see the High Fence's object in sending him to that attractive fate so quickly.

'If you feed me to the fishes, you feed them twenty-seven thousand six hundred and fifty pounds' worth of stones as well— did you know that, brother?' he asked.

Quincey grinned.

'Oh, no, we don't. We know where those are. They're at the

Harwich Post Office, addressed to Mr Joshua Pond. You told us all about that. The High Fence has gone to Harwich to be Mr Pond.'

The Saint's eyes hardened into chips of flint. For an instant of actual physical paralysis, he felt exactly as if he had been kicked in the middle. The terse, accurate, effortless, unhesitating throwing back at him of an arrangement which he had not even told Patricia, as if his brain had been flung open and the very words read out of it, had a staggering calamitousness like nothing he had ever experienced before. It had an unearthly, inescapable completeness that blasted the foundations from under any thought of bluff, and left him staring at something that looked like a supernatural intervention of Doom itself.

His memory struggled muzzily back over the features of his broken dream. The taxi—he had taken it off the kerb right outside his door, without a thought. Ordinarily he would never have done such a thing; but the very positive presence of trouble in the shape of Junior Inspector Pryke had given him a temporary blind spot to the fact that trouble in another shape could still be waiting for him—and might logically be expected to wait in much the same place.

The sickly sweet perfume which he had accused Pryke of using. Pryke's agitated face, gulping like a fish; and the labour of his own breathing. Gas, of course—pumped into the closed cab by some mechanism under the control of the driver, and quick enough in its action to put them out before they were sufficiently alarmed to break a window. Then the scrunch of gravel, and the grip of hands carrying him. He had been taken somewhere. Probably Pryke had been dumped out somewhere on the route. Unlike Mr Teal, Simon hoped he had not been killed—he would have looked forward to experimenting with further variations on that form of badinage to which Desmond was so alluringly sensitive.

The prick of the needle, and the soft voice that asked him questions out of the darkness. Questions that he couldn't remember, that dragged equally forgotten answers out of a drugged sub-consciousness that was too stupefied to lie . . . Understanding came to him out of that fuddled recollection with stunning clarity. There was nothing supernatural about it—only unexpected erudition and refinement. So much neater and surer than the old-fashioned and conventional systems of torture, which, even when they unlocked a man's mouth, gave no guarantee that he spoke the truth . . . He could even identify the drug that must have been used.

'Scopolamine?' he said, without any indication on his face of the shocks he had taken to reach that conclusion.

Quincey scratched the back of his ear.

'I think that's the name. The High Fence thought of it. That's what we are—scientific.'

Simon glanced steadily at the opposite porthole. Something like a solid black screen cut off the procession of embankment lights, briefly, and slid by. It told him that they had not yet passed under all the bridges; but he found it impossible to identify their whereabouts any more particularly. Seen from the unfamiliar viewpoint of the water, the passing lights formed themselves into no patterns which he could positively recognise; and an occasional glimpse of a neon sign, high up on a building, was no more illuminating, except on the superlative merits of Bovril or Guinness. Somewhere below London Bridge, down past the Pool, probably, he would be dropped quietly over the side. There was a queer quiet inevitability about it, a dispassionate scientific precision, which seemed an incongruous end for such a stormy and impetuous life.

'May I have a cigarette?' he asked.

Quincey hesitated for a moment, and then took out a packet of Player's. He put one between the Saint's lips and lighted it for him, and then returned watchfully to his seat on the bunk.

'Thanks,' said the Saint.

His wrists were bound together in front of him, so that he was able to use one hand on the cigarette. He was also able to make an inconspicuous test of the efficiency of the knotting, it was well done; and the new cord would swell up tighter as soon as it got wet.

He got a view of his wrist-watch, and saw that it was a quarter-past ten.

'What day is this?' he said.

'The same day as it's been all the time,' answered Quincey. 'You didn't think we'd keep you under for a week, did you? The sooner you're out of the way, the better. You've given us too much trouble already.'

So it was less than five hours since he had gone to sleep in the taxi. Simon got a perspective on his dream. At that rate, there was a sound chance that the High Fence couldn't have got him to wherever he had been taken, drugged and questioned him, and caught a train out of London in time to reach Harwich before the post-office closed. Therefore he might not be able to collect the package from the poste restante before morning. And if the Saint escaped . . .

Simon realised that he was building some beautiful castles in the air. A dog thrown into the river with a brick tied round its neck would have more or less the same chance of escape as he was offered.

And yet . . . there was a dim preposterous hope struggling in his mind that a miracle might happen—or had happened. Where had he felt the stab of that hypnotic needle? He felt sure that it had been in his right forearm; and there was a vague sort of ache in the same place to confirm the uncertain memory. In that case, was there any reason why his left forearm must have been touched? It was a wildly fantastic hope, an improbable possibility. And yet . . . such unlikely things had happened before, and their not wholly improbable possibility was part of the inspiration behind the more unconventional items of his armoury. It might seem incredible that anyone who knew anything of him could fail to credit him with having something up his sleeve in any emergency; and yet . . . Smoking his cigarette in long tranquil inhalations, he contrived to press his left forearm unobtrusively against his thigh; and what he felt put the dawn of a grim and farfetched buoyancy into his heart.

Quincey got up and pressed his face against one of the portholes. 'It's about time for you to be goin',' he said unemotionally.

He hauled out a heavy iron weight from under the bunk, and bent a short length of rope to a ring set in it. The other end of the rope he knotted to the cords that bound the Saint's ankles. Then he tore a strip of canvas from the sack which he had been sitting on, and stood waiting with it.

'Finish that cigarette,' he said.

Simon drew a last leisured puff, and dropped it on the floor. He looked Quincey in the eyes.

'I hope you'll ask for fish for your last breakfast, on the day they hang you for this,' he said.

'I'll do that for you,' said Quincey, knotting the canvas across his mouth in a rough but effective gag. 'When they hang me. Stand up.'

He pulled the Saint across his shoulder in a fireman's lift, picking up the weight in his left hand, and moved slowly across to the narrow steep companion which led up from the cabin. Mounting the steps awkwardly under his burden, he lifted the hatch with his head and climbed up till he could roll the Saint off on to the deck.

The craft was a small and shabby single-cabin motor boat. A man muffled up in a dark overcoat, with a peaked cap pulled down over his eyes until it almost met the top of his turned-up collar, who was apparently the only other member of the crew, stood at the wheel beside the hatch; but he did not look round. Simon wondered if it was Mr Enderby. The numbers of the gang who actually worked in direct contact with the High Fence would certainly be kept down to the irreducible minimum consistent with adequate functioning, and it might well be that by this time he knew all of them. It was not a racket which called for a large staff given the original idea and the ingenious leader. His one regret was that he had not been able to make the acquaintance of that elusive quantity: it seemed a ridiculously commonplace problem to take out unanswered into eternity, after solving so many mysteries.

Quincey stepped out over him, picked up the weight again, and rolled him like a barrel towards the stern. As he turned over, the Saint saw the rusty counter of a tramp moored in midstream swing by over his head, punctured with an occasional yellow-lighted port. Over on the Surrey side, a freighter was discharging cargo in a floodlit splash of garish flarelight. He heard the rattle and clank of the tackle, the chuffing of steam winches, the intermittent rise of voices across the water. A tug hooted mournfully, feeling its way across the stream.

He lay on the very edge of the counter, with the wake churning and hissing under his side. Quincey bent over him.

'So long, Saint,' he said, without vindictiveness; and pushed outwards.


IX

Simon stocked his lungs to the last cubic millimetre of their capacity, and tensed his muscles involuntarily as he went down. He had a last flash of Quincey's tough freckled face peering after him; and then the black waters closed over his head.

The iron weight jerked at his ankles, and he went rolling over and upright into the cold crushing darkness.

Even as he struck the water he was wrenching his wrists round to seize the uttermost fraction of slack from the cords that bound them. The horror of that helpless plunging down to death, roped hand and foot and ballasted with fifty pounds of iron, was a nightmare that he remembered for the rest of his life; but it is a curious fact that while it lasted his mind was uncannily insulated from it. Perhaps he knew that to have let himself realise it fully, to have allowed his thoughts to dwell for any length of time on the stark hopelessness of his position, would have led inevitably to panic.

His mind held with a terrible intensity of concentration on nothing but the essentials of what he had to do. With his hands twisted round till the cords cut into his flesh, he could get the fingers of his right hands a little way up his left sleeve; and under their tips he could feel the carved shape of something that lay just above his left wrist. That was the one slender link that he had with life, the unconventional item of his armoury which the search that must have been made of his clothes had miraculously overlooked: the thin sharp ivory-hilted knife which he carried in a sheath strapped to his forearm, which had saved him from certain death before and might save him once again. Somehow, slowly, clumsily, with infinite patience and agonising caution, he had to work it out and get it in his hand—moving it in split shavings of an inch, lest it should come loose too quickly and slip out of his grasp to lose itself in the black mud of the river bed, and yet not taking so long to shift it that his fingers would go numb and out of control from the cutting off of the circulation by the tightening ropes. His flesh crawled in the grip of that frightful restraint, and his forehead prickled as if the sweat was trying to break out on it even under the cold clutch of the water that was pressing in at his eardrums. He could feel his heart thudding hollowly in the aching tension of his chest, and a deadly blackness seemed to be swelling up in his brain and trying to overwhelm him in a burst of merciful unconsciousness: every nerve in his body shrieked its protest against the inhuman discipline, cried out for release, for action, for the frantic futile struggle that would anaesthetise the anguish just as surely as it would hasten on the end—for any relief and outlet, however suicidal, that would liberate them from the frightful tyranny of his will.

Perhaps it lasted for three minutes, from beginning to end, that nightmare eternity in which he was anchored to the bottom of the Thames, juggling finickily for life itself. If he had not been a trained underwater swimmer, he could never have survived it at all. There was a time when the impulse to let out his precious breath in a sob of sheer despair was almost more than flesh and blood could resist; but his self-control was like iron.

He won out, somehow. Trickling the air from his lungs in jealously niggard rations that were just sufficient to ease the strain on his chest, he worked the hilt of the knife up with his finger and thumb until he could get another finger on it . . . and another . . . and another . . . until the full haft was clutched in a hand which by that time had practically gone dead. But he was just able to hold it. He forced himself down, bending his knees and reaching forward, until his numbed fingers could feel the taut roughness of the rope by which he was held down to the weight. And then, giving way for the first time in that ghastly ordeal, he slashed at it wildly—slashed again and again, even when his knife met no resistance and he felt himself leaping up through the reluctant waters to the blessed air above . . .

For a long while he lay floating on the stream, with only his face above the surface, balancing himself with slight movements of his legs and arms, sawing in an ecstasy of leisure through the other ropes on his wrists and ankles, and drinking in the unforgettable glory of the night. Afterwards, he could never remember those moments clearly: they were a space out of his life that was cut off from everything in the past and everything in the future, when he thought of inconsequential things with an incomparably vivid rapture, and saw commonplace things with an exquisite sensuous delight that could not have been put into words. He couldn't even recollect how long it lasted, that voluptuous realisation of the act of living; he only knew that at the end of it he saw the black bulk of a ship looming up towards him with a tiny white crest at her bows, and had to start swimming to save himself from being run down. Somehow the swim brought him close to the north bank of the river, and he cruised idly upstream until he found a flight of stone steps leading up into a narrow alley between two buildings. The alley led into a narrow dingy street, and somewhere along the street he found a taxi which, in an unlikely spot like that, could only have been planted there for his especial service by a guardian angel with a most commendable sense of responsibility.

The driver peered at him keenly in the light of the melancholy street lamp under which the cab was parked.

'You're wet,' he said at last, with the same pride of discovery that must have throbbed in Charles Darwin's breast when he gave the fruit of his researches to the world.

'You know, George, I believe you've hit it,' said the Saint, in a whisper of admiring awe in which the old unconquerable mockery was beginning to lift itself again. 'I thought something was wrong, but I couldn't make out what it was. Do you think I can have been in some water?'

The driver frowned at him suspiciously. 'Are you drunk?' he asked, with disarming frankness; and the Saint shook his head.

'Not yet—but I have a feeling that with very little encouragement I could be. I want to go to Cornwall House, Piccadilly; and I'll pay for any damage I do to your lovely cushions.'

Probably it was the tone and manner of what the chauffeur would have described as a toff which dissolved suspicion away into a tolerant appreciation of aristocratic eccentricity, and induced him to accept the fare. At any rate, he accepted it, and even went so far as to oblige Simon with a cigarette.

Lounging back in a corner with the smoke sinking luxuriously into his lungs, the Saint felt his spirits rising with the speed of an irresponsible rocket. The ordeal he had been through, the shadow of death and the strange supreme joy of life after it, slipped back into the annals of memory. To the High Fence, he was dead: he had been dropped off a boat into the lower waters of the Thames with a lump of iron tied to his feet—swallowed up in the bottom ooze and slime of the river, where any secret might well be safe. Both as a proven interferer and a potentially greater menace, he had been removed. But before being drowned, he had given up his secret. He had told exactly what he had done with the parcel of precious stones of which Mr Clive Enderby had been bereaved— and the High Fence was going to Harwich to take the name of

Joshua Pond in vain . . . And Simon Templar had an increasingly blissful idea that he was going to be there to witness the performance.

As the cab drew up before Cornwall House he saw a girl and a man coming out, and decanted himself on to the pavement before the taxi had properly reached a standstill.

'Are you looking for some fun, souls?' he murmured. 'Because if so, I could use you.'

Patricia Holm stared at him for a moment in breathless silence; and then, with an incoherent little cry, she threw herself into his arms . . .

Mr Uniatz swallowed, and touched the Saint with stubby fingers, as if he were something fragile.

'Howja get wet, boss?' he asked.

Simon grinned, and indicated the interested taxi-driver with a movement of his head.

'George here thinks I must have been in some water,' he said. 'Give him a quid for the inspiration, will you?—I only had a fiver on me when I went out, but they pinched it.'

He led Patricia back into the building with a damp arm round her shoulders, while Hoppy paid off the taxi and rejoined them in the foyer. They rode up in the lift in an enforced silence; but Patricia was shaking him by the arm as soon as the door of the apartment had closed behind them.

'Where have you been, boy? What's happened?'

'Were you worried?'

'You know that.'

He kissed her.

'I guess you must have been. Where were you off to?'

'We were going to call on Enderby.' She was still holding herself in the curve of his arm, wet as he was. 'It was the only line we had—what you told me outside here, before Pryke took you off.'

'I could of made him talk, boss,' said Mr Uniatz, in a tone of pardonable disappointment. 'After I'd got t'ru wit' him—'

The Saint smiled.

'I suppose he'd've been lucky to be able to talk. Well, the scheme might still be a good one . . .' He toyed with the idea for a thoughtful moment; and then he shook his head. 'But—no we don't need it now. And there may be something much more useful for you to do. Get me a drink, Pat, if Hoppy's left anything, and I'll tell you.'

Half an hour in his sodden clothes had left him chilled and shivery, but a steep tot of whisky would soon put that right. He lay submerged in a hot bath, with the glass balanced on the edge, and told them the story of his adventures through the open door. It was a tale that made Patricia bite her lips towards the end; but for him it was all in the past. When he came through into the living-room again, cheerful and glowing from the massage of a rough towel, with his hair sleekly brushed again and a woolly bath-robe slung round him, lighting a cigarette with steady hands and the old irrepressible laughter on his lips, it was difficult to imagine that barely an hour ago he had fought one of his most terrific fights with death.

'So here we are,' he said, with the blue lights crisp and dancing in his eyes. 'We don't know who the High Fence is; but we know where he's going, and we know the password he's going to give. It's rather quiet and logical; but we've got him. Just because he's made that one natural mistake. If I were swinging at the bottom of the Pool, as he thinks I am, there wouldn't be a snag in his life. He'd just go to Harwich and recover his boodle; and that would be the end of a spot of very satisfactorily settled bother. But he's going to have a surprise.'

'Can we come with you?' said Patricia.

The Saint shook his head.

'I'd like you to. But I can't be everywhere at once, and I shall want someone in London. You mayn't have realised it, but we still have our own bills to pay. The swine knocked a fiver off me when they took me for that ride, and I want it back. Teal's going to achieve his ambition and lag the High Fence, and that parcel of jools that's going to give the High Fence away is evidence now;

but we've got our Old Age Pensions to think about. Anyone who wants to amuse himself by pumping me up with gas and dope and heaving me into the river has got to pay for his fun. And that's where you two come in.'

He told them of what was in his mind, in terse sparkling sentences, while he dressed. His brain was working at high pressure by that time, throwing ideas together with his own incomparable audacity, building a plan out of a situation that had not yet come to pass, leaving them almost out of breath behind the whirlwind pace of his imagination. And yet, despite the breakneck pace at which he had swept his strategy together, he had no misgivings about it afterwards—not even while he drove his great thundering car recklessly through the night to Harwich, or when he stood outside the post office in the early morning waiting for the doors to open.

It should be all right . . . About some things he had a feeling of sublime confidence, a sense of joyous inevitability, that amounted to actual foreknowledge; and he had the same feeling that morning. These things were ordained: they were the reward of adventure, the deserved corollaries of battle, murder, and—a slight smile touched his lips—the shadow of sudden death. But with all this assurance of foreknowledge, there was still a ghostly pulse of nervous excitement flickering through his spinal cells when the doors opened to let him in—a tingle of deep delight in the infinitely varied twists of the game which he loved beyond anything else in life.

He went up to the counter and propped his elbows on the flat of the telegraph section. He wanted to send a cable to Umpopo in British Bechuanaland; but before he sent it he wanted to know all about the comparative merits of the various word rates. He was prepared, according to the inducements offered, to consider the relative attractions of Night Letters, Week-end Letters, or Deferreds; and he wanted to know everything there was to know about each. Naturally, this took time. The official behind the grille, although he claimed a sketchy familiarity with the whereabouts of British Bechuanaland, had never heard of Umpopo; which is not surprising, because the Saint had never heard of it either before he set out to invent a difficult place to want to send a cable to. But with that indomitable zeal which is the most striking characteristic of post-office officials, he applied himself diligently to the necessary research, while Simon Templar lighted another cigarette and waited patiently for results.

He was wearing a brown tweed cap of a pattern which would never ordinarily have appealed to him, and a pair of tortoise-shell glasses and a black military moustache completed the job of disguising him sufficiently to be overlooked on a casual glance even by anyone who knew him. As the last man on earth whom the High Fence would be expecting to meet, he was as well hidden as if he had been buried under the floor . . . The official behind the counter, meanwhile, was getting buried deeper and deeper under a growing mound of reference books.

'I can't seem to find anything about Umpopo,' he complained peevishly, from behind his unhelpful barricade. 'Are you sure there is a telegraph office there?'

'Oh, yes,' said the Saint blandly. 'At least,' he added, 'there's one at Mbungi, which is only half a mile away.'

The clerk went back through his books in a silence too frightful to describe; and the Saint put his cigarette back between his lips, and then suddenly remained very still.

Another early customer had entered the office. Simon heard his footsteps crossing the floor and passing behind him, but he did not look round at once. The footsteps travelled along to the poste restante section, a couple of yards away, and stopped there.

'Have you anything for Pond?'

The soft voice came clearly to Simon's ears, and he lifted his eyes sidelong. The man was leaning on the counter, like himself, so that his back was half turned; but the Saint's heart stopped beating for a moment.

'What is the first name?' asked the clerk, clearing out the contents of one of the pigeon-holes behind him.

'Joshua.'

Rather slowly and dreamily, the Saint hitched himself up off his elbow and straightened up. Behind his heaped breakwater of reference books, the steaming telegraph official was muttering something profane and plaintive; but the Saint never heard it. He saw the cardboard box which he had posted pushed over to its claimant, and moved along the counter without a sound. His hand fell on the man's shoulder.

'Would you like to see a good-looking ghost?' he drawled, with a throb of uncontrollable beatitude in his voice.

The man spun round with a kind of gasp that was almost a sob. It was Junior Inspector Desmond Pryke.

X

The writer, whose positively Spartan economy of verbiage must often have been noted and admired by every cultured student, recoils instinctively from the temptation to embellish the scene with a well-chosen anthology of those apt descriptive adjectives with which his vocabulary is so richly stocked. The pallor of flabbergasted faces, the glinting of wild eyes, the beading of cold perspirations, the trembling of hands, the tingling of spines, the sinking of stomachs, the coming and going of breath in little short pants—all those facile clichés which might lure less ruggedly disciplined scribes into the pitfall of endeavouring to make every facet of the situation transparent to the most nitwitted reader— none of these things, on this occasion at least, have sufficient enticement to seduce him. His readers, he assures himself, are not nitwits: they are highly gifted and intelligent citizens of phenomenal perspicacity and acceleration on the uptake. The situation, he feels, stated even in the baldest terms, could hide none of its facets from them.

It hid none of them from Simon Templar, or from Junior Inspector Pryke. But Simon Templar was the first to speak again.

'What are you doing here, Desmond?' he asked gently.

Pryke licked his lips, without answering. And then the question was repeated, but Simon Templar did not repeat it.

Chief Inspector Teal stepped out from behind a screen which cut off the Savings Bank section of the counter, and repeated it. His hands were in the pockets of his unnecessary raincoat, and his movement had the same suggestion of weary and reluctant effort that his movements always had; but there was something in the set of his rounded plump jaw and the narrowness of his sleepy-lidded eyes which explained beyond any need of words that he had watched the whole brief incident from beginning to end, and had missed none of the reactions which a police officer on legitimate business need not have shown.

'Yes—what are you doing?' he said.

Pryke's head jerked round again, and his face went another shade greyer. For a further interval of thrumming seconds he seemed to be struggling to find his voice; and the Saint smiled.

'I told you the High Fence would be here to collect his boodle, Claud,' he said; and looked at Pryke again. 'Quincey told me,' he said.

'I don't know what you're talking about.' Pryke had got some kind of control over his throat, but there was a quiver in his breathing which made odd little breaks in the sentence. 'I heard that there were some stolen jewels here—'

'Who from?' Teal asked quietly.

'From a man I found on the theory I was working on. You told me I could—'

'What was his name?'

'That's a long story,' said Pryke hoarsely. 'I met him . . .'

Probably he knew that the game was over—that the bluff was hopeless except as a play for time. The attack was too overwhelming. Watching him with smiling lips and bleak blue eyes, the Saint knew that there wasn't a man living who could have warded it off—whose brain, under the shock, could yet have moved fast enough to concoct a story, instantaneously and without reflection, that would have stood the light of remorseless investigation which must have been directed into it.

'I met him last night,' said Pryke. 'I suppose you have some reason—'

Simon nodded.

'We have,' he said gently. 'We came here to play the grand old parliamentary game of Sitting on the Fence; and it looks as if you are what might be called the sittee.'

'You're crazy,' said Pryke harshly.

His hand was sliding towards his hip, in a casual movement that should have been merely the conventional search for a cigarette-case; and Simon saw it a fraction of a second late.

He saw the flash of the nickel-plated gun, and the shot blasted his eardrums as he flung himself aside. Pryke swerved frantically, hesitated an instant, and turned his automatic on the broad target of Chief Inspector Teal; but before he could touch the trigger again the Saint's legs had swung round in a flailing scissor-sweep that found its marks faultlessly on knee-joint and ankle-bone. Pryke cursed and went down, clean and flat as a dead fish, with a smack that squeezed half the breath out of his body; and the Saint rolled over and held him in an ankle lock while the local men who had been posted outside poured in through the doors.

And that was approximately that.

The Saint continued to lie prostrate on the floor after Pryke had been handcuffed and taken away, letting the profound contentment of the day sink into his soul and make itself gorgeously at home. Misunderstanding his stillness, Mr Teal bent over him with a shadow of alarm on his pink face.

'Are you hurt?' he asked gruffly; and the Saint chuckled.

'Only in my pride.' He reached out and retrieved his cigarette, which had parted company with him during the scuffle, and blew the dust off it before replacing it in his mouth. 'I'm getting a worm's-eye view of life—you might call it an act of penance. If I'd had to make a list of all the people who I didn't think would ever turn out to be the High Fence, your Queen of the May would have been first on the roll. Well, I suppose life has these surprises

. . . But it all fits in. Being on duty at Market Street, he wouldn't have had any trouble in poisoning Johnny Anworth's horseradish; but I'm not quite sure how he got Sunny Jim—'

'I am,' said Teal grimly. 'He was standing a little behind me when I was talking to Fasson—between me and the door. He could have shot Fasson from his pocket and slammed the door before I could look round, without taking a tremendous risk . . . After all, there was no reason for anyone to suspect him. He put it over on all of us.' Teal fingered a slip of chewing-gum out of his pocket and unwrapped it sourly, for he also had his pride. 'I suppose it was you who took Sunny Jim away,' he said suddenly.

Simon grinned.

'Teal! Will you always think these unkind thoughts about me?'

The detective sighed. He picked up the evidential package from the counter, opened it, glanced at the gleaming layers of gems, and stuffed it firmly into his pocket. No one knew better than himself what unkind thoughts he would always have to think. But in this case at least the Saint had done him a service, and the accounts seemed to be all square—which was an almost epoch-making denouement. 'What are you getting out of this?' he inquired suspiciously.

The Saint rose to his feet with a smile, and brushed his clothes.

'Virtue,' he said piously, 'is its own reward. Shall we go and look for some breakfast, or must you get on with your job?'

Mr Teal shook his head.

'I must get back to London—there are one or two things to clear up. Pryke's flat will have to be searched. There's still a lot of stolen property to be recovered, and I shouldn't be surprised to find it there—he must have felt so confident of never being suspected that he wouldn't bother about a secret headquarters. Then we shall have to pull in Quincey and Enderby, but I don't expect they'll give us much trouble now.' The detective buttoned his coat, and his drowsy eyes went over the Saint's smiling face with the perpetual haze of unassuageable doubt still lingering in them. 'I suppose I shall be seeing you again,' he said.

'I suppose you will,' said the Saint, and watched Teal's stolid portly figure lumbering out into the street before he turned into the nearest telephone booth. He agreed with Mr Teal that Pryke had probably been confident enough to use his own apartment as his headquarters. But Patricia Holm and Hoppy Uniatz were already in London, whereas Mr Teal had to get there; and Simon Templar had his own unorthodox interpretation of the rewards of virtue.

I

The visitors who came to see the Saint uninvited were not only members of the CID. In several years of spectacular outlawry, Simon Templar had acquired a reputation which was known wherever newspapers were read.

'There must be something about me that excites the storytelling instinct in people,' he complained once to Patricia Holm, who should have known better than anyone how seriously to take his complaint. 'Four out of every five have it, and their best friends won't tell 'em.'

Most of the legends that circulated about him were fabulously garbled, but the fundamental principles were fairly accurate. As a result, he had an ever-growing public which seemed to regard him as something between a benevolent if slightly weak-minded uncle and a miracle-working odd-job man. They ranged from burglars who thought that his skill might be enlisted in their enterprises for a percentage of the proceeds, to majestic dowagers who thought that he might be instrumental in tracing a long-lost Pekinese; from shop girls in search of romance to confidence men in search of a likely buyer of a gold brick. Sometimes they were interesting, sometimes they were pathetic; mostly they were merely tiresome. But on rare occasions they brought the Saint in touch with those queer happenings and dark corners in other people's lives from which many of his adventures began, and for that reason there were very few of them whom he refused to see.

There was one lady in particular whom he always forced himself to remember whenever he was tempted to dodge one of these callers, for she was quite definitely the least probable herald of adventure who ever crossed his path. He was, as a matter of fact, just ready to go out one morning when Sam Outrell telephoned up to announce her.

'Your Jersey 'as come back from the cleaners, sir,' was his cryptic postscript to the information.

Sam Outrell had been raised on a farm, many years before he came to be head porter in the apartment building on Piccadilly where the Saint lived, and incidentally one of Simon's loyalest watch-dogs; and the subterfuges by which he managed to convey a rough description of visitors who were standing at his elbow were often most abstrusely bucolic. Simon could still remember the occasion when he had been suffering tireless persecution from a stout Society dame who was trying to manufacture divorce evidence against her doddering spouse, on which Sam had told him that 'Your silk purse has turned up, sir,' and had explained later that he meant to convey that 'The old sow's 'ere.'

'I'll have a look at it,' said the Saint, after a brief hesitation.

Viewing Mrs Florence Ellshaw for the first time, when he opened the door to her, Simon could not deny that Sam Outrell had an excuse for his veiled vulgarity. She was certainly very bovine in build, with stringy mouse-coloured hair and a remarkable torso— the Saint didn't dislike her, but he did not feel that Life would have been incomplete if she had never discovered his address.

'It's about me 'usband, sir,' said Mrs Ellshaw, putting the matter in what must have looked to her like a nutshell.

'What is about your husband?' asked the Saint politely.

'I seen 'im,' declared Mrs Ellshaw emphatically. 'I seen 'im last night, plain as I can see you, I did, 'im wot left me a year ago wivout a word, after all I done for 'im, me that never gave 'im a cross word even when 'e came 'ome late an' left all 'is money at the local, as large as life 'e was, an' me workin' me fingers to the bone to feed 'is children, six of 'em wot wouldn't 'ave a rag to their backs if it weren't for me brother Bert as 'as a job in a garridge, with three of his own to look after and his wife an invalid, she often cries all night, it's pitiful—'

Simon perceived that to let Mrs Ellshaw tell her story in her own way would have required a lifetime's devotion.

'What do you want me to do?' he interrupted.

'Well, sir, I seen 'im last night, after 'im leaving me wivout a word, 'e might 'ave bin dead for all I was to know, after all I done for 'im, as I says to 'im only the day before 'e went, I says "Ellshaw," I says, "I'm the best wife you're ever likely to 'ave, an' I defy you to say anythink else," I says, an' me workin' me fingers to the bone, with varicose veins as 'urts me somethink terrible sometimes, I 'as to go an' sit down for an hour, this was in Duchess Place—'

'What was in Duchess Place?' asked the Saint weakly.

'Why, where I sore 'im,' said Mrs Ellshaw, ''im wot left me wivout a word—'

'After all you done for him—'

'An' me doing for gentlemen around 'ere all these months to feed 'is children, wiv me pore legs achin' an 'e turns an' runs away when 'e sees me as if I 'adn't bin the best wife a man ever 'ad, an' never a cross word between us all these years.'

The Saint found it hard to believe that Mrs Ellshaw had reached an intentional full stop, and concluded that she had merely paused for breath. He took a mean advantage of her momentary incapacity.

'Didn't you run after him?' he put in.

'That I did, sir, wiv me pore legs near to bursting after me being on them all day, an' 'e runs into an 'ouse an' slams the door, an' I gets there after 'im an' rings the bell an' nobody answers, though I waits there 'arf an hour if I waited a minnit, ringin' the bell, an' me sufferin' with palpitations wot always come over me if I run, the doctor tole me I mustn't run about, an' nobody answers till I says to meself, "All right, Ellshaw," I says, "I'll be smarter'n you are," I says, an' I goes back to the 'ouse this morning, not 'arf an hour ago it wasn't, an' rings the bell again like it might be a tradesman delivering something, an' 'e opens the door, an' when 'e seen me 'e gets all angry, as if I 'adn't bin the best wife ever a man 'ad—'

'And never a cross word between you all these years—'

'"Yer daft cow," 'e says, "can't yer see yer spoilin' everythin'?" "Never you mind wot I'm spoiling," I says, "even if it is some scarlet 'ussy yer livin' with in that 'ouse, you gigolo," I says, "leaving me wivout a word after all I done for you," I says; and 'e says to me, "'Ere's some money, if that's wot yer after, an' you can 'ave some more any time you want it, so now will you be quiet an' get out of 'ere or else you'll lose me me job, that's wot you'll do, if anybody sees you 'ere," 'e says, an' 'e shoves some money into me 'and an' slams the door again, so I come straight round 'ere to see you, sir.'

'What for?' asked the Saint feebly.

He felt that he was only inviting a fresh cataract of unpunctuated confidences, but he could think of no other question that seemed so entirely apt.

Mrs Ellshaw, however, did not launch out into another long-distance paragraph. She thrust one of her beefy paws into the fleshy canyon that ran down from her breastbone into the kindly concealment of her clothing, and dragged out what looked at first like a crumpled roll of white paper.

'That's wot for,' she said, thrusting the catch towards him.

Simon took it and flattened it out. It was three new five-pound notes clumsily crushed together; and for the first time in that interview he was genuinely interested.

'Is that what he gave you?'

'That's wot he gave me, exactly as 'e put it in me 'and, an' there's somethink dirty about it, you mark my words.'

'What sort of job was your husband in before he—er—left you?' Simon inquired.

''E never 'ad no regular job,' said Mrs Ellshaw candidly. 'Sometimes 'e made a book—you know, sir, that street betting wot's supposed to be illegal. Sometimes 'e used to go to race meetings, but I don't know wot 'e did there, but I know 'e never 'ad fifteen pounds in 'is life that 'e came by honestly, that I know, and I wouldn't let 'im be dishonest, it ain't worth it, with so many coppers about, and 'im a married man wiv six children—'

'What's the address where you saw him?'

'It's in Duchess Place, sir, wot's more like a mews, and the 'ouse is number six, sir, that's wot it is, it's next door to two young gennelmen as I do for, such nice gennelmen they are too, always askin' about me legs—'

The Saint stood up. He was interested, but he had no intention of resuming a study of Mrs Ellshaw's varicose veins.

'I don't know whether I can do anything for you, but I'll see what I can find out—you might like to let me change these fivers for you,' he added. 'Pound notes will be easier for you to manage, and these may help me.'

He put the three banknotes away in a drawer, and saw the last of Mrs Ellshaw with some relief. Her troubles were not so utterly commonplace as he had expected them to turn out when she started talking, and some of the brightest episodes in his career had had the most unpromising beginnings, but there was nothing in the recital he had just listened to which struck him as giving it any special urgency. Even when the whole story was an open book to him, the Saint could not feel that he was to blame for failing to foresee the consequences of Mrs Ellshaw's visit.

He was occupied at that time with quite a different proposition— the Saint was nearly always occupied with something or other, for his ideas of good living were put together on a shamelessly plutocratic scale, and all his expenses were paid out of the proceeds of his raids on those whom he knew as the Ungodly. In this case it was a man of no permanent importance who claimed to be the owner of a mining concession in Brazil. There were always one or two men of that kind on the Saint's visiting list—they were the providential pot-boilers of his profession, and he would have considered it a crime to let them pass him by, but only a very limited number of them have been found worthy of commemoration in these chronicles. He walked home from the conclusion of this casual episode at two o'clock in the morning, and might have died before dawn if Sam Outrell had been less conscientious.

'The men have been to fix your extension telephone,' was the message passed on to him by the night porter; and the Saint, who had not ordered an extension telephone at all, was silently thoughtful in the lift that whisked him up to his floor.

He walked down the corridor, as soundless as a prowling cat on the thick carpet, past the entrance of his own suite to another door at the very end of the passage. There was a key on his chain to unlock it; and he stepped out on to the fire-escape and lighted a cigarette under the stars.

From the handrail of the grating where he stood, it was an easy swing to his bathroom window, which was open. He passed across the sill like a shadow and went from room to room with a gun in his hand, searching the darkness with supersensitive faculties for anything that might be waiting to catch him unawares. Everything was quiet; but he touched pieces of furniture, and knew that they had been moved. The drawers of his desk were open, and his foot rustled against a sheaf of papers carelessly thrown down on the floor. Without touching a light switch he knew that the place had been effectively ransacked; but he came to the hall without finding a trace of any more actively unfriendly welcome.

It was not until he switched on the hall light that he saw what his fate ought to have been.

There was a cheap fibre attaché-case standing close to the entrance—if he had moved another step to one side he would have kicked it. Two thin insulated wires ran from it to the door and terminated in a pair of bright metal contacts like a burglar alarm, one of them screwed to the frame and the other to the door itself. If he had entered in the normal way, they would have completed the circuit directly the door began to open; and he had no doubt what the sequel would have been.

An ingenious mixture of an electrical detonator, a couple of pounds of gelignite, and an assortment of old scrap-iron, was indicated inside that shabby case; but the Saint did not attempt to make certain of it, because it was not beyond the bounds of possibility that some such eccentric entrance as he had made could have been foreseen, and a second detonator provided to act on anyone who opened the valise to investigate it. He disconnected the wires, and drove out to Hammersmith Bridge with the souvenir, very cautiously, as soon as he could fetch his car from the garage, and lowered his potential decease on a string to the bottom of the Thames.

So far as he could tell, only the three five-pound notes which he had put away in his desk had been taken. It was this fact which made him realise that the search of his rooms had not been a merely mechanical preliminary to the planting of a booby-trap by one of the many persons who had reason to desire his funeral. But it was not until the next morning that he realised how very important the disappearance of Mr Ellshaw must be, when he learned how Mrs Ellshaw had left her troublesome veins behind her for all time.

II

The body was taken out of the Thames just below London Bridge by the river police. There were no marks of violence beyond a slight bruise on the forehead which might have been caused by contact with the piers of one of the upper bridges. Death was due to drowning.

'It's as obvious as any suicide can be,' said Chief Inspector Claud Eustace Teal. 'Apparently the woman's husband left her about a year ago, and she had to work like a slave to keep the children. Her neighbours say she was very excited the night before, talking incoherently about having seen her husband and him having refused to recognise her. If that was true, it provides a motive; if it wasn't, it covers "unsound mind".'

The Saint lounged back in his chair and crossed his feet on a sheaf of reports on Mr Teal's sacred desk.

'As a matter of fact, it was true,' he said. 'But it doesn't provide a motive—it destroys it.'

If anybody else had made such a statement Mr Teal would have jeered at him, more or less politely according to the intruder's social standing; but he had been sitting at that desk for too many years to jeer spontaneously at anything the Saint said. He shuffled his chewing-gum to the back of his mouth and gazed across the Saint's vandal shoes with sporously clouded eyes.

'How do you know?'

'Because she came to see me yesterday morning with the same story, and I'd promised to see what I could do for her.'

'You think it was murder?' asked Teal, with cherubic impassivity.

Simon shrugged.

'I'd promised to look into it,' he repeated. 'In fact, she had a date to come and see me again on Friday evening and hear if I'd managed to find out anything. If she had enough faith in me to bring me her troubles in the first place, I don't see her diving into the river before she knew the verdict.'

Teal brought his spearmint back into action, and worked on it for a few seconds in silence. He looked as if he were on the point of falling asleep.

'Did she say anything to make you think she might be murdered?'

'Nothing that I understood. But I feel kind of responsible. She was killed after she'd been to see me, and it's always on the cards that she was killed because of it. There was something fishy about her story, anyhow, and people in fishy rackets will do plenty to keep me out of 'em . . . I was nearly murdered myself last night.'

'Nearly?' said Mr Teal.

He seemed disappointed.

'I'm afraid so,' said the Saint cheerfully. 'Give me something to drink and find out for yourself whether I'm a ghost.'

'Do you think it was because of something Mrs Ellshaw told you?'

'I'm damned if I know, Claud. But somebody put down all the makings of a Guy Fawkes picnic in Cornwall House last night, and I shouldn't be talking to you now if I hadn't been born careful as well as lucky—there's something about the way I insist on keeping on living which must be frightfully discouraging to a lot of blokes, but I wouldn't believe for a moment that you were one of them.'

Chief Inspector Teal chewed his way through another silence. He knew that the Saint had called on him to extract information, not to give it. Simon Templar gave nothing away, where Scotland Yard was at the receiving end. A Commissioner's post-mortem on the remains of a recent sensational case in which the Saint had played a leading and eventually helpful part had been held not long ago: it had, however, included some unanswerable questions about the fate of a large quantity of stolen property which the police had expected to recover when they laid the High Fence by the heels, and Mr Teal was still smarting from some of the things which had been said. He had been wielding his unavailing bludgeon in the endless duel between Scotland Yard and that amazing outlaw too long to believe that the Saint would ever consult him with no other motive than a Boy Scout ambition to do him a good turn. Every assistance that Simon Templar had ever given the Metropolitan Police had had its own particular string tied to it, but in Teal's job he had to take the strings with the favours. The favours had helped to put paid to the accounts of many elusive felons; the strings accounted for many of the silver threads among Mr Teal's dwindling fleece of gold, and seemed likely to account for many more.

'If you think Mrs Ellshaw was murdered, that's your affair,' he said at last. 'We haven't any reason to suspect it—yet. Or do you want to give us any?'

Simon thought for a moment, and said: 'Do you know anything about the missing husband?'

'As a matter of fact, we did use to know him. He was about the worst card-sharp we ever had on our records. He used to work the race trains, usually—he always picked on someone who'd had too much to drink, and even then he was so clumsy that he'd have been lagged a dozen times if the mugs he found hadn't been too drunk to remember what he looked like. Does that fit in with your theory?' Teal asked, with the disarming casualness of a gambolling buffalo.

The Saint smiled.

'I have no theory, Claud. That's what I'm looking for. When I've got one, we might have another chat.'

There was nothing more to be got out of him; and the detective saw him go with an exasperated frown creasing down over his sleepy blue eyes.

As a matter of fact, the Saint had been perfectly straightforward—chiefly because he had nothing to conceal. He had no theory, but he was certainly looking for one. The only thing he had kept back was the address where Mrs Ellshaw had seen her mysterious husband. It was the only information he had from which to start his inquiries; and Mr Teal remembered that he had forgotten to ask for it five minutes after the Saint had left.

It was not much consolation for him to realise that the Saint would never have given him the information even if he had asked for it. Simon Templar's idea of criminal investigation never included any premature intrusions by the Department provided by London's ratepayers for the purpose, and he had his own methods of which that admirable body had never approved.

He went out of Scotland Yard and walked round to Parliament Square with a strange sensation going through him as if a couple of dozen fleas in hobnailed boots were playing hopscotch up and down his spine. The sensation was purely psychic, for his nerves were as cold as ice, as he knew by the steadiness of his hand when he stopped to light a cigarette at the corner of Whitehall; but he recognised the feeling. It was the supernatural, almost clairvoyant tingle that rippled through his consciousness when intuition leapt ahead of logic—an uncanny positive prescience for which logic could only trump up weak and fumbling reasons. He knew that Adventure had opened her arms to him again—that something had happened, or was happening, that was bound to bring him once more into the perilous twisted trails in which he was most at home—that because a garrulous charwoman had taken it into her head to bring him her troubles, there must be fun and games and boodle waiting for him again under the shadow of sudden death. That was his life, and it seemed as if it always would be.

He had nothing much to go on, but that could be rectified. The Saint had a superb simplicity of outlook in these matters. A taxi came cruising by, and stopped when he put up his hand.

'Take me to Duchess Place,' he said. 'It's just at the back of Curzon Street. Know it?'

The driver said that he knew it. Simon relaxed in a corner and propped up his feet on the spare seat diagonally opposite, while the cab turned up Birdcage Walk and wriggled through the Green Park towards Hyde Park Corner. Once he roused himself to test the mechanism of the automatic in his hip pocket; once again to loosen the thin-bladed knife in its sheath under his left sleeve. Neither of those weapons was part of the conventional outfit which anyone so impeccably dressed as he was would have been expected to wear, but for many years the Saint had placed caution so far before convention that convention was out of sight.

He paid off his taxi at the corner of Duchess Place and walked up towards number six. It was one of a row of those dingy unimaginative brick houses, with rusty iron railings and shabbily painted windows, which would be instantly ranked as cheap tenement cottages by any stranger who had not heard of the magic properties of the word 'Mayfair'. Simon went up the steps and rang the tarnished brass bell without hesitation—he hadn't the faintest notion how he would continue when the door was opened, if it was opened, but he had gone into and emerged from a great deal of trouble with the same blithe willingness to let circumstances provide for him.

The door opened in a few moments; and circumstances proceeded to provide for him so completely and surprisingly that he was ready for some unpleasantness.

The man who looked out of the door was rather small and wiry, with thin grey hair and a sallow bird-like Cockney face on which the reddish tint of his nose stood out so unexpectedly that it looked at first sight like one of those ageless carnival novelties which give so much harmless pleasure to adult infants engaged in the laborious business of having a good time. With his threadbare and baggy trousers, and his pink shirt fastened together with a stud at the neck but virginally innocent of collar or tie, he looked like the very last sort of man who ought to be answering a doorbell in that expensive slum.

'I want to see Mr Ellshaw,' said the Saint, with sublime directness; and knew at once that he was talking to the man he wanted.

His first surprise was when this was admitted.

'I'm Ellshaw,' said the man at once. 'You're Mr Templar, ain't yer?'

The Saint drew at his cigarette with a certain added thoughtfulness. He never forgot a face; and he was sure that this little bird with the carmine beak could not have slipped out of his mind very easily if their paths had ever crossed before. But he acknowledged the identification with outwardly unaltered amiability.

'How did you know that, Archibald?'

'I was just comin' round to see yer, guv'nor.' The little man opened the door wider, and stepped back invitingly. 'Would yer like ter step inside fer a minute?—I've got somefink to tell yer.'

The Saint stepped inside. He put his hands in his pockets as he crossed the threshold, and one of them rested on the butt of his gun.

Ellshaw led him through the uncarpeted hall to the nearest door, which brought them into the front ground-floor room. There was hardly any furniture in it—a piece of cheap hair carpet, a painted deal table carrying a bottle and glasses and the scars of cigarette-ends, and a couple of ancient arm-chairs with soiled chintz covers, would have formed a practically complete inventory. There were grimy lace curtains nailed up on the windows at the street end, and a door communicating with the back room at the other. From the oak parquet floor, the tinted ceiling and tasteful electric-light fittings, it was obvious that the room had once been lived in by someone of a definite class, but everything in it at that moment spoke loudly of the shoddiest stock of the second-hand sale-room.

'Sit down, guv'nor,' said Ellshaw, moving over to the chair nearer the window and leaving Simon no choice about the other. ''Ow abaht a drink?'

'No, thanks,' said the Saint, with a faint smile. 'What is it you were so anxious to tell me?'

Ellshaw settled himself in his chair and lighted a drooping fag.

'Well, guv'nor, it's abaht me ole woman. I left 'er a year ago. Between you an' I, she 'ad a lot of bad points, not that I want to speak evil of the dead—oh, yes, I know 'ow she committed suicide,' he said, answering the slight lift of the Saint's eyebrows. 'I sore it in the pypers this mornin'. But she 'ad 'er faults. She couldn't never keep 'er mouf shut. Wot could I do? The rozzers was lookin' for me on account of some bloke that 'ad a grudge against me an' tried ter frame me up, an' I knew if she'd knowed where I'd gorn she couldn't 'ave 'elped blabbin' it all over the plyce.'

Simon was beginning to understand that he was listening to a speech in which the little Cockney had been carefully rehearsed— there was an artificial fluency about the way the sentences rattled off the other's tongue which gave him his first subtle warning. But he lay back in his chair and crossed his legs without any sign of the urgent questions that were racing through his mind.

'What was the matter?' he asked.

'Well, guv'nor, between you an' I, seein' as you understands these things, I used ter do a bit of work on the rice trains. Nothink dishonest, see—just a little gamble wiv the cards sometimes. Well, one dye a toff got narsty an' said I was cheatin', an' we 'ad a sort of mix-up, and my pal wot I was workin' wiv, 'e gets up an' slugs this toff wiv a cosh an' kills 'im. It wasn't my fault, but the flatties think I done it, an' they want me for murder.'

'That's interesting,' said the Saint gently. 'I was talking to Chief Inspector Teal only a little while ago about you, and he didn't tell me you were wanted.'

Ellshaw was only disconcerted for a moment.

'I don't spect 'e would've told yer, knowin' wot you are,

guv'nor—if you'll ixcuse me syin' so. But that's Gawd's troof as sure as I'm sittin' 'ere; an' I wanted to come an' see yer—'

Simon was watching his eyes, and saw them wavering to some point behind his shoulder. He saw Ellshaw's face twitch into a sudden tension, and remembered the communicating door behind him in the same instant. With a lightning command of perfectly supple muscles he threw himself sideways over the arm of the chair, and felt something swish past his head and thud solidly into the upholstery, beating out a puff of grey dust.

In a flash he was on his feet again, in time to see the back of a man ducking through the door. His gun was out in his hand, and his brain was weighing out pros and cons with cool deliberation even while his finger tightened on the trigger. The cons had it— it was no use shooting unless he aimed to hit his target, and at that embryonic stage of the developments a hospital capture would be more of a liability than an asset. He dropped the automatic back in his pocket and jumped for the door empty- handed. It slammed in his face as he reached it, and a bottle wildly thrown from behind smashed itself on the wall a foot from his head. Calmly ignoring the latter interruption, Simon stepped back and put his heel on the lock with his weight behind it. The door, which had never been built to withstand that kind of treatment, surrendered unconditionally, and he went through into a chamber barely furnished as a bedroom. There was nobody under the bed or in the wardrobe; but there was another door at the side, and this also was locked. Simon treated it exactly as he had treated the first, and found himself back in the hall—just at the moment when the front door banged.

Ellshaw himself had vanished from the front room when he reached it; and the Saint leaned against the wreckage of the communicating door and lighted a fresh cigarette with a slow philosophical grin for his own ridiculous easiness.

As soon as they learned that the bomb had failed to take effect, of course, they were expecting him to follow up the clue which Mrs Ellshaw must have given him. Probably she had been followed from Duchess Place the previous morning, and it would not have been difficult for them to find out whom she went to see. The rest was inevitable; and the only puzzle in his mind was why the attempt had not been made to do something more conclusive than stunning him with a rubber truncheon while he sat in that chair with his back to the door.

But who were 'they'? He searched the house from attic to basement in the hope of finding an answer, but he went through nothing more enlightening than a succession of empty rooms. Inquiries about the property at neighbouring estate agents might lead on to a clue, but there was none on the premises. The two ground-floor rooms were the only ones furnished—apparently Ellshaw had been living there for some time, but there was no evidence to show whether this was with or without the consent and knowledge of the landlord.

Simon went out into the street rather circumspectly, but no second attack was made on him. He walked back to Cornwall House to let Patricia Holm know what was happening, and found a message waiting for him.

'Claud Eustace Teal rang up—he wants you to get in touch with him at once,' she said, and gazed at him accusingly. 'Are you in trouble again, old idiot?'

He ruffled her fair hair.

'After a fashion I am, darling,' he confessed. 'But it isn't with Claud—not yet. What the racket is I don't know, but they've tried to get me twice in the last twelve hours, which is good going.'

'Who are they?'

'That's the question I've been asking myself all day. They're just "person or persons unknown" at present; but I feel that we shall get to know each other better before long. And that ought to be amusing. Let's see what Claud Eustace is worrying about.'

He picked up the telephone and dialled Scotland Yard. Instructions must have been left with the switchboard operator, for he had scarcely given his name when he heard Teal's sleepy voice.

'Were you serious about getting a bomb last night, Templar?'

'Mr Templar to you, Claud,' said the Saint genially. 'All the same, I was serious.'

'Can you describe the bomb again?'

'It was built into a small fibre attaché-case—I didn't take it apart to inspect the works, but it was built to fire electrically when the door was opened.'

'You haven't got it there, I suppose?'

Simon smiled.

'Sure—I wouldn't feel comfortable without it. I keep it on the stove and practise tap-dancing on it. Where's your imagination?'

Teal did not answer at once.

'A bomb that sounds like exactly the same thing was found in Lord Ripwell's house at Shepperton today,' he said at last. 'I'd like to come round and see you, if you can wait a few minutes for me.'

III

The detective arrived in less than a quarter of an hour, but not before Simon had sent out for a packet of spearmint for him. Teal glanced at the pink oblong of waxed paper sitting up sedately in the middle of the table, and reached out for it with a perfectly straight face.

'Ripwell—isn't he the shipping millionaire?' said the Saint.

Teal nodded.

'It's very nearly a miracle that he isn't "the late" shipping millionaire,' he said.

Simon lighted a cigarette.

'Did you come here to tell me about it or to ask me questions?'

'You might as well know what happened,' said the detective, unwrapping a wafer of his only vice with slothful care. 'Ripwell intended to go down to his river house this evening for a long weekend, but during the morning he found that he wanted a reference book which he had left down there on his last visit. He sent his chauffeur down for it, but when the man got there he found that he'd forgotten to take the key. Rather than go back, he managed to get in through a window, and when he came to let himself out again he found the bomb. It was fixed just inside the front door, and would have been bound to get the first person who opened it, which would probably have been Ripwell himself— apparently he doesn't care much about servants when he uses the cottage. That's about all there is to tell you, except that the description I have of the bomb from the local constabulary sounded very much like the one you spoke of to me, and there may be some reason to think that they were both planted by the same person.'

'And even on the same day,' said the Saint.

'That's quite possible. Ripwell's secretary went down to the house the day before for some papers, and everything was quite in order then.'

The Saint blew three perfect smoke-rings and let them drift up to the ceiling.

'It all sounds very exciting,' he murmured.

'It sounds as if you may have been right about Mrs Ellshaw, if all you told me was true,' said Teal grimly. 'By the way, where was it she saw her husband?'

Simon laughed softly.

'Claud, that "by the way" of yours is almost a classic. But I wouldn't dream of keeping a secret from you. She saw him at number six, Duchess Place, just round a couple of corners from here. I know he was there, because I saw him myself a little while ago. But you won't find him if you go round now.'

'How do you know that?'

'Because he's pulled his freight—he and another guy who tried to blip me over the head.'

Teal chewed out his gum into a preoccupied assortment of patterns, gazing at him stolidly.

'Is that all you mean to tell me?'

Simon cocked an abstracted eyebrow at him.

'Meaning?'

'If an attempt was made to murder you, there must be a reason for it. You may have made yourself dangerous to this man, or this gang, in some way, and they want to get rid of you. Why not let us give you a hand for once?'

Pride would not let Mr Teal say any more; but Simon saw the blunt sincerity in the globular pink face, and knew that the detective was not merely putting on a routine blarney.

'Are you getting sentimental in your old age, Claud?' he protested, in a strain of mockery that was kinder than usual.

'I'm only doing my job.' Teal made the admission grudgingly, as if he was afraid of betraying an official secret. 'I know you sometimes get on to things before we hear of them, and I thought you might like to work in with us for a change.'

Simon looked at him soberly. He understood the implications of everything that Teal had left unsaid, the unmentioned vials of acid comment which must have been decanted on that round lethargic head as a result of their last contest; and he sympathised. There had never been any malice behind the ebullitions of Teal-baiting which enlivened so many chapters of his scapegrace career.

He hooked one leg over the arm of his chair.

'I'd like to help you—if you helped me,' he said seriously. 'But I've damned little to offer.'

He hesitated for a moment, and then ran briefly over the events which had made up the entertainment in Duchess Place.

'I don't suppose that's much more use to you than it is to me,' he ended up. 'My part of it hangs together, but I don't know what it hangs on. Mrs Ellshaw was killed because she'd seen her husband, and I was offered the pineapple because I knew she'd seen him. The only thing I don't quite understand is why they didn't try to kill me when they had me in Duchess Place; but maybe they didn't want to hurry it. Anyway, one gathers that Ellshaw is a kind of unhealthy guy to see—I wonder if Ripwell saw him?'

'I haven't seen Ripwell myself yet,' said Teal. 'He's gone down to Shepperton to look at things for himself, and I shall have to go down tonight and have a talk with him. But I thought I'd better see you first.'

The Saint fixed him with clear and speculative blue eyes for a few seconds, and then he drawled: 'I could run you down in the car.'

Somehow or other, that was what happened; Mr Teal was never quite sure why. He assured himself that he had never contemplated such a possibility when he set out to interview the Saint.

In any case on which he was engaged, he insisted to this sympathetic internal Yes-man, the last thing he wanted was to have Simon Templar messing about and getting in his way. He winced to think of the remarks the Assistant Commissioner would make if he knew about it. He told himself that his only reason for accepting the Saint's offer was to have both his witnesses at hand for an easier comparison of clues; and he allowed himself to be hurled down to Shepperton in the Saint's hundred-mile-an-hour road menace with his qualms considerably soothed by the adequacy of this ingenious excuse.

They found his lordship pottering unconcernedly in his garden—a tall spare vigorous man with white hair and a white moustache. He had an unassuming manner and a friendly smile that were leagues apart from the conventional idea of a big business man.

'Chief Inspector Teal? I'm pleased to meet you. About that bomb, I suppose—a ridiculous affair. Some poor devil as mad as a hatter about capitalists or something, I expect. Well, it didn't do me any harm. Is this your assistant?'

His pleasant grey eyes were glancing over the Saint; Teal performed the necessary introduction with some trepidation.

'This is Mr Templar, your lordship. I only brought him with me because—'

'Templar?' The grey eyes twinkled. 'Not the great Simon Templar, surely?'

'Yes, sir,' said Teal uncomfortably. 'This is the Saint. But—'

He stopped, with his mouth open and his eyes starting to protrude, blinking speechlessly at one of the most astounding spectacles of his life. Lord Ripwell had got hold of the Saint's hand, and was pumping it up and down and beaming all over his face with spontaneous warmth that was quite different from the cheerful courtesy with which he had greeted Mr Teal himself.

'The Saint? Bless my soul! What a coincidence! I think I've read about everything you've ever done, but I never thought I should meet you. So you really do exist. That's splendid. My dear fellow—'

Mr Teal cleared his throat hoarsely.

'I was trying to explain to your lordship that—'

'Remember the way you put it over on Rayt Marius twice running?' chortled his lordship, continuing to pump the Saint's hand. 'I think that was about the best thing you've ever done. And the way you got Hugo Campard, with that South American revolution? I never had any use for that man—knew him too well myself.'

'I brought him down,' said Mr Teal, somewhat hysterically, 'because he had the same—'

'And the way you blew up Francis Lemuel?' burbled Lord Ripwell. 'Now, that was a really good job of bombing. You'll have to let me into the secret of how you did that before you leave here. I say, I'll bet Chief Inspector Teal would like to know. Wouldn't he? You must have led him a beautiful dance.'

Mr Teal felt that he was gazing at something that Could Not Possibly Happen. The earth was reeling across his eyes like a fantastic roundabout. He would have been incapable of further agonies of dizzy incredulity if Lord Ripwell had suddenly gone down on all fours behind a bush and tried to growl like a bear.

The effort which he had to exert to get a grip on the situation must have cost him two years of life.

'I brought the Saint down, your lordship, because he seemed to have some kind of knowledge of the matter, and I thought—'

'Quite,' drivelled his lordship. 'Quite. Quite right. Now I know that everything's in good hands. If anybody knows how to solve the mystery, it's Mr Templar. He's got more brains than the whole of Scotland Yard put together. I say, Templar, you showed them how to do their own job in that Jill Trelawney case, didn't you? And you had them guessing properly when Renway—that Treasury fellow—you know—'

Chief Inspector Teal suppressed an almost uncontrollable shudder. Lord Ripwell was actually digging Simon Templar in the ribs.

It was some time before Mr Teal was able to take command again, and even then it was a much less positive sort of command than he had intended to maintain.

'Have you ever come across a man named Ellshaw?' he asked, when he could persuade Lord Ripwell to pay any attention to him.

'Ellshaw? Ellshaw? Never heard of him. No. What is he?'

'He is a rather bad cardsharper, your lordship.'

'I don't play cards. No. I don't know him. Why?'

'There is some reason to believe that he may be connected with these bombing attempts. Did you ever by any chance meet his wife—Mrs Florence Ellshaw? She was a sort of charwoman.'

Ripwell shook his head.

'I don't think I've ever employed any sort of charwoman.' He looked up and raised his voice. 'Hey, Martin, have we ever had a charwoman called Mrs Ellshaw?'

'No, sir,' answered the youngish man who was coming across the lawn from the house, as he joined them. 'At least, not in my time.'

Ripwell introduced them.

'This is Mr Irelock—my secretary. He's been looking after me for five years, and he knows as much as I do.'

'I'm sure that we've never employed anyone of that name,' said Martin Irelock. To describe him in a sentence, he looked like a grown-up and rather serious-minded Kewpie with hornrimmed glasses fixed across the bridge of his nose as firmly as if they had grown there. 'Do you think he has something to do with this business, Inspector?'

'It's just a theory, but it's the only one we have at present,' said Mr Teal.

He summarised Simon Templar's knowledge of the mystery for them. Lord Ripwell was interested in this. He slapped the Saint on the back.

'Damn good,' he applauded. 'But why ever didn't you shoot the man when you had the chance? Then everything would have been cleared up.'

'Claud Eustace doesn't like me shooting people,' said the Saint mildly, at which Lord Ripwell guffawed in a manner which removed the last shadow of doubt from Teal's mind that at least one member of the peerage was in an advanced and malignant stage of senile decay.

Teal almost strangled himself.

'Apparently both the bombs were planted on the same day,' he said, trying to lead the conversation back into the correct vein with all the official dignity of which he was capable. 'I understand that your secretary—'

'That's right,' agreed Irelock. 'I had to come down here the day before yesterday, and there was no bomb here then.'

'What time did you leave?'

'Just after six—I caught the six-twenty back to town.'

'So the bomb must have been placed here at some time between six o'clock on Wednesday and the time the chauffeur found it this morning.' Teal's baby-blue eyes, throttled down again to a somewhat strained drowsiness, were scanning the house and garden. The grounds were only about three-quarters of an acre in extent, bordered by the road on one side and the river on another, and separated from its neighbours by well-grown cypress hedges on the other two boundaries. In such a comparatively quiet situation, it might not be difficult to hear of anyone who had been seen loitering about the vicinity. 'The local police may have learnt something more by this time, of course,' he said.

'We'll get the Inspector to come round after dinner,' said Ripwell affably. 'You'll stay, of course.'

Teal chewed for a while, pursing his lips.

'I'd rather take your lordship back to London with me,' he said; and Ripwell frowned puzzledly.

'What on earth for?'

'Both the bombing attempts failed, but these people seem pretty determined. They made a second attempt to get Templar a few hours after the first. There's every chance that they may make a second attempt to get you; and it's easier to look after a man in London.'

If it is possible for a man to snort good-humouredly, Lord Ripwell achieved the feat.

'Stuff and nonsense, Inspector,' he said. 'I came down here for a rest and some fresh air, and I'm not going to run away just because of a thing like this. I don't expect we'll hear any more about it; but if we do, I'm in good hands. Anybody who tries to kill me while the Saint's here will be biting off a bit more than he can chew—eh? What d'you say, Templar?'

'I was trying to explain to your lordship,' said Teal thickly, 'that I only brought Templar down to compare his story with yours. He has no official standing whatever, and as far as I am concerned he can go home—'

'Eh? What? Go home?' said Lord Ripwell, who had suddenly become very obtuse or very determined. 'Don't be silly. I'm sure he doesn't want to go home. He likes this sort of thing. It isn't troubling him at all. And I want to talk to him about some of his exploits—I've wanted to for years. I like him. Wish my son was half the man he is.' His lordship gurgled, with what Mr Teal, from his prejudiced viewpoint, considered to be positively doddering glee. 'You don't want to go home, do you, Templar?'

Simon tapped out a cigarette on his case, and smiled. It was certainly rather a gorgeous situation. His gaze flickered wickedly over Claud Eustace Teal's reddening face.

'All the excitement seems to go on around Lord Ripwell and me,' he murmured. 'With both of us here together under the same roof, we could look forward to a gay week-end. I think it would be a grand idea to stay.'

IV

'Well, what d'you make of it, Templar?' asked Ripwell, when they were scattered about the living-room around a bottle of excellent dry sherry.

Simon shrugged.

'Up to the present, nothing at all. All of you know as much as I do. There seems to be some kind of move afoot to discourage people from seeing Ellshaw; but I've taken a gander at him myself, and I didn't notice anything about him that anyone would be crazy to see. All the same, there must be something big behind it—you don't get three murders planned for the same day because somebody wants to keep the name of his tailor secret.'

'Do you think you could ever have known Ellshaw under another name, your lordship?' asked Teal. 'Can you think of anyone who might have a bad enough grievance against you to want to blow you up?'

'I haven't an enemy in the world,' said Lord Ripwell; and, looking at his clean pleasant face and friendly eyes, the statement was easy to believe.

The Saint grinned slowly, and reached out to refill his glass.

'I have plenty,' he remarked. 'But if you haven't any, it disposes of that motive. Anyway, it's my experience that your enemies won't take nearly as many risks to kill you as the blokes who just think you might stand in their way. Revenge may be sweet, but boodle buys a hell of a lot more cigars.'

'Are we to consider ourselves in a state of siege?' inquired Irelock somewhat ironically.

'Not unless it amuses you,' answered the Saint coolly. 'But I don't think anyone in this gathering who wants to live to a great age ought to be too casual about standing in front of windows or wandering around the garden after dark. The Ellshaw-hiding outfit keeps moving pretty quickly, by the looks of things, and they have enterprising ideas.'

Ripwell looked almost hopeful.

'I suppose you've got a gun, Inspector?'

Mr Teal moved his head in a slow negative gesture, with his jaws working phlegmatically.

'No, I'm not armed,' he said tolerantly; and his gaze shifted deliberately on to the Saint, as if estimating the degree of certainty with which he could pick out one man who was.

'I think we have a revolver somewhere,' said Irelock.

'By George, so we have!' exclaimed Ripwell. 'See if you can find it, Martin.'

'There isn't any ammunition,' said Irelock cynically.

His lordship's face fell momentarily. Then he recovered buoyantly.

'We'll have to get some—I've got a licence for it. Never thought I should want it, but this is absolutely the time. Where can I get some cartridges? What d'you say, Inspector? With all this business going on, I'm entitled to have a gun in self-defence, what?'

Mr Teal had the typical English police officer's distaste for firearms, but he had no authority to show his disapproval.

'Certainly, if you have a licence, you're entitled to it,' he replied unenthusiastically. 'The local police may be able to lend you a few rounds of ammunition.'

There was another arrival before dinner in the shape of Lord Ripwell's son, the Honourable Kenneth Nulland, who drove up in a very small and very noisy sports car. Irelock went out to meet him and brought him in—he was a young man with fair wavy hair and a face rather like a bright young cod, and he was very agitated. He shook hands limply.

'Haven't you solved the mystery yet? It's no good asking me to help you. I think it was the jolly old Communists, or the Fascists, or something. Anyhow, I hope they don't try anything more while I'm here—I can only just stay to dinner.'

'I thought you were coming down for the week-end,' said his father slowly.

'Sorry, Pop. Old Jumbo Ferris rang up and asked me to go to a party—he's having a jolly old beano down at his place in Hampshire.'

'Did you have to accept? Cicely's coming over tomorrow.'

Nulland shook his head. He grabbed a drink and hung himself over a chair, rather like a languid eel in plus fours.

'Sorry, Pop. But she won't miss me.'

'I don't blame her,' said Ripwell, with devastating candour. He turned to Teal and the Saint. 'Cicely Holland's a sort of protégée of mine. Works in my office. Daughter of a pal of mine when I was young. Never made any money, but he was a pal till he died. Damned fine girl. I wish Kenneth was fit to marry her. She won't look at him as he is, and I wouldn't either.'

Kenneth Nulland grinned weakly.

'Pop thinks I'm a jolly old prodigal son,' he explained.

The explanation was scarcely necessary. Simon sensed the bitter disappointment behind Lord Ripwell's vigorous frankness, and, for his own comfort, led the conversation away into a less personal channel. But while he went on casually talking he studied Lord Ripwell's heir-presumptive more closely, and realised that Nulland was simultaneously studying him. The youngster was a mass of undisciplined nerves under his flaccid posturing, and the inane clichés which made up ninety per cent of his dialogue came pattering out so noisily at the slightest lull in the general talk that Simon wondered why he was so afraid of silence.

Teal noticed it too.

'What do you think?' he asked the Saint.

They were alone together for a moment after dinner—Lord Ripwell was telephoning the local Inspector, and Nulland had taken Martin Irelock out to admire some new gadget he had had fitted to his car.

'He's frightened,' said the Saint carefully. 'But I don't know that it would take much to frighten him. Maybe he doesn't want to be blown up.'

Mr Teal sucked at his after-dinner ration of spearmint. He was letting himself become temporarily resigned to the irregularity of his position. After all, there was nothing else that he could do about it. The house was Lord Ripwell's, and the case was more or less Lord Ripwell's: if Lord Ripwell wanted the Saint to stay with him, that was Lord Ripwell's business and nobody else's. Even the Assistant Commissioner, Teal tried to tell himself with more confidence than he actually felt, could have found no flaw in the transparent logic of the argument. Therefore, proceeded Chief Inspector Teal, brilliantly scoring all the points in this pleasant imaginary debate with the spectre of his superior officer, since the Saint had to be accepted, it was simply an obvious stroke of masterly and unscrupulous cunning to pick his brains for any help they could be induced to yield.

'That fellow has something on his mind,' said the detective, astutely pursuing this Machiavellian plan.

'If you could call it a mind,' said the Saint, docilely surrendering the fruits of his cerebration.

Teal screwed up a scrap of pink paper in his pudgy fingers.

'I suppose he'd come into all Ripwell's money, if a bomb went off as it was meant to.'

'Don't forget he'd come into all Mrs Ellshaw's money as well—and mine,' said the Saint, with the utmost kindness. 'And I'll bet he'd need it all. There's a beautiful motive in that, waiting for some bright detective to dig it out, Claud. I expect Ripwell gives him a perfectly miserly allowance, don't you? Ripwell strikes one as that sort of man.'

Mr Teal's mouth tightened—he was an amiable man in most ways, but he had a train of memories behind him which were apt to start a quite unreasonably truculent inflammation in his stout bosom when the Saint smiled at him so compassionately and said things which made him feel that his legs were being playfully lengthened. He might even have responded with fatal rudeness, if he had had time to compose a sufficiently crushing retort; but Lord Ripwell joined them again before this devastating gem of repartee was polished to his mordant satisfaction.

'Inspector Oldwood will be over in ten minutes,' said his lordship. 'He's bringing some ammunition for my gun—I wish I knew where the damned thing was.' He went to the French window that opened on to the garden at the side, and peered out. 'Hey, Martin!'

It was nearly dark outside, and the air had turned cool directly the sun went down. Simon Templar, lighting one of Lord Ripwell's cigars by the mantelpiece, wondered if that seasonable evening chill was enough to account for the way Kenneth Nulland seemed to be shivering when he came in behind the secretary.

'Martin, where is that damned revolver? I haven't seen it for months.'

'I think it's in the loft,' said Irelock. 'Shall I have a look for it tomorrow?'

'Tomorrow?' repeated Ripwell, screwing up his face like a disappointed schoolboy. 'Eh? What? I want it now. Suppose this gang comes back tonight? Nonsense. What's the matter with looking for it now?'

'Right-ho,' said Irelock peaceably. 'I'll look for it now.'

'Right-jolly-old-ho,' echoed Nulland, peeling himself off the edge of the table in his undulating boneless way. 'And I must be tootling along. Cheerio, Pop. Sorry I can't stay longer, but jolly old Jumbo Ferris is always complaining about me being late for his parties. Toodle-oo, Martin—'

Mr Teal cleared his throat.

'Just a minute, Mr Nulland,' he said. 'There are one or two small questions you might be able to help us with before you go.'

The young man's restless eyes travelled about the room.

'What are they? I don't know anything.'

'Have you ever met a man named—'

'Look!'

It was Irelock's voice, sharp and unnatural. Wheeling round to look at him, the Saint saw that his face was tense and startled, his weak eyes in their tortoise-shell frames staring rigidly at the window.

'What is it?' snapped Teal.

'A man looked in—just now—with a mask on his face. I saw him—'

Teal put his gum away in the side of his mouth and waded towards the casement with surprising speed for a man of his flabby dimensions, but Simon was even quicker. His hand dropped on the detective's shoulder.

'Wait for it, Claud! You may be just ballast at Scotland Yard, but you're the light of my life—and I'd hate you to go out too soon. Switch off those lights, somebody!'

It was Lord Ripwell who carried out the order, and the Saint's voice went on speaking in the dark.

'OK, souls. Now you can get on with it. But try to remember what I told you about standing in front of lighted windows—and watch your step outside. Will someone show me the way to the back door?'

'I will,' barked Ripwell eagerly.

He grabbed Simon by the arm and hustled him into the hall. Irelock called out: 'Shall Ken and I take the front?'

'Do that,' said the Saint, and slipped out his automatic as he followed Ripwell into the kitchen.

'I wish I knew where that damned revolver of mine was,' said his lordship plaintively, as he shot back the bolt of the trades door.

The Saint smiled.

'Since you haven't got it, you'd better let me go first. And put down that cigar—it's a swell target.'

He slipped out into the cool darkness, thumbing down the safety catch of his gun with an absurd feeling of unreality. The night was moonless, and the sky was a film of deep grey, only a shade lighter than the dull black of the earth and the trees. A stir of the air that was too soft even to be called a breeze brought the mingled scents of the river and damp grasses to his nostrils: everything was so suddenly quiet and peacefully commonplace after the boisterous confusion of their dispersal that he almost put his gun away again and laughed at himself. Such things did not happen. And yet—he would have liked to know why Kenneth Nulland was afraid, and what his reaction to the name of Ellshaw would have been . . .

Crack!

The shot crashed out from the front of the house, and a shout followed it. He heard the roar of an engine, and all the feeling of unreality vanished. As he raced up the strip of turf under the shadow of the wall he heard a shrill cry for help, in what sounded like Kenneth Nulland's voice.

Crack!

A tongue of flame split the blackness ahead, and he heard Lord Ripwell gasp at his heels. He whipped up his gun and fired at the flash—there was no danger of mistaken identity there, for on the analysis they had held a short while ago he was the only one of the party who was armed. Therefore the other gun belonged to one of the raiding party—however many of them there were. It spoke again, and the thunder of his second shot rang out on the reverberations of the first, but it was blind shooting with a hundred chances to one against a hit.

Someone ran over the grass and plunged through the cupressus hedge into the road, and the car's engine roared louder. Simon tore recklessly in pursuit, and came out into the gravelled lane as the flaring headlights leapt towards him. A man lurched out of the darkness and struck at him, catching him on the shoulder; and the Saint spun round and caught the striking wrist. The forefinger of his other hand took up the resistance of the trigger.

'Are you ready to die?' he said softly.

'Oh, Lord!' ejaculated Martin Irelock.

Simon let him go, and turned round again as the red tail light of the car whirled round the near corner.

'Hell!' He dropped the gun in his pocket. 'Maybe I can catch them with my car.'

He ran over the drive and leapt into the seat of the Hirondel. There was not a sound when he pressed the starter button, and he slid his hand along under the dash and felt wires trailing loose. It would take precious minutes to get out a light and re-connect them, and by that time the chase would be hopeless. With a sigh he opened the door and stepped down again; and then a match flared some distance away, and he heard Teal's voice.

'Give me a hand, someone.'

He went back to the corner of the house; and saw that the man who lay on the ground, with Teal bending over him, was Lord Ripwell.

V

The match flickered out, and Teal struck another. Ripwell's eyes were open, and he was breathing painfully.

'Don't bother about me—I'm not hurt. Just a scratch. I'll—be all right. Did you get—any—of those villains?'

'I'm afraid not,' said the Saint grimly.

They picked him up and carried him into the house. The bullet had passed through his chest just below the right shoulder—there was an ugly exit wound which had smashed his shoulder-blade, but the internal injuries were probably clean.

'I forgot to—put down—the cigar,' he said with a twisted mouth, when they had settled him on his bed.

The Saint understood. Ripwell had been running just behind him and a little to one side when the first shot that he saw was fired. Simon realised now that he had heard him gasp when the bullet struck, but in the excitement of the moment he had not recognised the sound.

'Where's the nearest doctor?' asked Teal, turning to Irelock.

It was only then, when they were all gathered in the same room, that Simon realised that they were still one short of their number.

'Where's Ke—'

He started the question without thinking, and could have bitten his tongue the next moment; but he broke off too late. Ripwell struggled up on his elbow and stared from face to face, finishing the name for him in his clear commanding voice.

'Kenneth! Where's Kenneth?'

There was an answer in Irelock's pale strained features, at least enough answer for the Saint to read, even before the secretary began to stammer: 'He's—he's gone—'

'Gone to see if he can catch Inspector Oldwood on his way

here, hasn't he?' Simon caught him up in an instant, with cold blue eyes cutting off the truth with a flash of steel. 'We'd better go and grab this doctor, and we may meet them.'

He dragged Irelock out of the room and ran him down the stairs. In the hall he faced him, taking out a cigarette and straightening it between steady brown fingers.

'What has happened to Kenneth?' he asked.

'They got him.' Irelock was trembling slightly, and his grown-up Kewpie face looked older and tensely hard. 'We opened the front door, and somebody fired at us. Got me in the arm—only a graze.' He pulled up his sleeve to show a raw straight furrow scored at an angle across his wrist. 'I ran out and got hit in the stomach—not with a bullet this time, but it almost laid me out. I heard Ken yell for help, and then I heard people running away. I ran after them, and then I caught you. You remember. But they must have got Ken.'

Simon flicked his thumb over his lighter, and drew his cigarette red in the flame.

'I only heard one shot before they started potting at me. Have you got a torch?'

They went out and searched the garden with an electric flashlight which Irelock produced from the kitchen. Inspector Oldwood arrived and challenged them while they were doing it, but relaxed when he recognised Ripwell's secretary. He had come from the opposite direction to that which the escaping car had taken, and he had seen no one on the road near the cottage. Certainly he had not seen Nulland.

One or two startled villagers and a handful of young people from adjacent bungalows, attracted by the noise and the shooting, were revealed at the gate in the fringe of the torchlight; and Oldwood pressed them into the search while Irelock went back into the house to telephone for a doctor. There was not a great deal of ground to cover, and two of the holiday bungalow party had torches. In twenty minutes the last of the searchers had drifted back to the front drive.

'Perhaps he went for help,' said Oldwood, who had not had

time to learn more than the vaguest rudiments of the story.

'I don't think so,' said the Saint.

He noticed something else, in the reflected glow of the hovering ovals of torchlight, and swept his own light over the drive again. The Hirondel showed up its gleaming lines of burnished metal, exactly where he had left it when he first drove in; but it was the only car there. Of Kenneth Nulland's noisy little roadster there was no trace but the tyre tracks in the gravel.

Simon whistled softly.

'In his own car, too, by God! That's hot stuff—or is it?'

He saw something else, which had been overlooked in the first search—a small dark shadow on the ground close to the place where Nulland's car had stood—and went over to it. It was a red silk handkerchief, and when he picked it up he felt that it was wet and sticky.

'We'd better see how badly Ripwell's hurt,' he said.

The doctor had arrived while the search was going on, stopping his car outside the gates, but he was still busy upstairs when Teal came down and joined them.

'He ought to pull through,' was Teal's unofficial report. 'He's stopped a nasty packet, but the doctor says his constitution is as sound as a bell. What's this about Nulland?'

'What's this about, anyhow?' asked Oldwood more comprehensively.

He was a red-faced grizzled man who looked more like a rather hard-bitten farmer than anything else, with an air of quiet self-contained confidence which was not to be flustered even by such sensational events as he had walked into. When his knowledge had been brought up to date he was still quiet and deliberate, stuffing his pipe with square unhurried fingers.

'I haven't anything for you,' he said at the end. 'I haven't been able to trace any suspicious characters hanging around here yet, but I'm still making inquiries.'

'I wonder whether Nulland was kidnapped, or if he ran away,' said Teal stolidly.

'The evidence doesn't show that he ran away,' said the Saint.

He produced the silk handkerchief which he had picked up in the drive. There was an embroidered 'K' in one corner, and the wet stickiness on it was blood.

Teal studied the relic and passed it over to the local man, who put it away in an envelope.

'What are the roads like around here, Oldwood? We can try to stop that car.'

'They can't have gone Chertsey way,' said Oldwood, striking a match. 'Because that's the way I came from. They may have gone almost anywhere else. There's a road to Staines, another to Sunbury, and another to Walton—and half a dozen different routes they could take from any of those places.'

'Added to which,' murmured the Saint, 'there must be at least fifty other baby sports cars exactly like his wandering about Surrey tonight.'

'It'll have to be tried,' said Teal doggedly. 'Do you know the number, Mr Irelock?'

The secretary hadn't noticed it. Apparently Nulland changed his cars at an average rate of about once a month, except when one of his frequent accidents compelled an even quicker change, and it was almost beyond anyone's power to keep track of the numbers. The instructions that Teal telephoned out were hardly more than a hopeless routine, and all of them knew it.

He had just finished when the doctor came downstairs to confirm the preliminary bulletin.

'He's fairly comfortable now, but he'll want looking after for the next couple of days—I don't think there's any need to move him to the hospital. I'll send a nurse along tonight if I can get hold of one—otherwise I'll bring her over with me tomorrow morning.'

'I suppose you didn't find a bullet,' said Teal.

The doctor shook his head.

'It went right through him. From the look of the wound I should say it must have been fired from a fairly large-calibre gun.'

'That reminds me,' said Oldwood, searching his jacket pockets, 'I brought over those cartridges that he asked for. You may as well have them, but I don't know that they're much use now.'

'They may be useful,' said Irelock. 'We'd better keep some sort of guard while all this is going on.'

'I'll send a man over as soon as I get back to the station,' said Oldwood, and stood up. 'You might give me a lift, Doctor, if it isn't taking you out of your way. There's nothing more we can do tonight.'

Irelock saw them out, and then went back up the stairs to look in on Ripwell; and the Saint lighted another cigarette and stretched out his legs under the table. There was a train of thought shunting about in the half-intuitive sidings of his mind, backing and puffing tentatively, feeling its way breathlessly over a maze of lines with only one dim signal to guide it; but something about the way it was moving sent that weird sixth-sense tingle coursing again over his thoracic vertebrae. Teal trudged about over a minute area of carpet with his jaw oscillating rhythmically, and his sleepy eyes kept returning to the inscrutable immobility of the Saint's brown face.

'Well, what do you make of it now?' he said at last.

Simon came far enough out of his trance to put his smouldering cigarette back between his lips.

'I think it was magnificently staged,' he said.

'How do you mean—magnificently? To try something like this only an hour or two after we get here, and make a success of it—'

'I like the organisation,' said the Saint dreamily. 'Think it over, Claud. A bloke pushes his face against the window, and there's a first-class scare. The gathering breaks up and goes dashing out in the dark through three separate doors. There are five of us milling around in all directions, and yet it only takes a few seconds to sort out the right people and make a job of it. The bullet that hit Ripwell may have been meant for either him or me, but we were the two who got the bombs to begin with. Young Nulland is snatched off—a member of the same family—but nobody seems to have tried to grab Irelock when he was knocked out. And nobody tries to damage that beautiful stomach of yours.'

'That may only be because they didn't have time.'

'Or else because you don't know enough to be dangerous.'

Mr Teal scowled.

'Nulland's car was only a two-seater, wasn't it?' He stared at the curtained windows, working at the problem in his own slow methodical way. 'We ought to have tried the river . . . These people are clever.'

'How many have you counted up to?'

'Ellshaw's the only one we know personally, but you saw another man in Duchess Place when you went there. I don't know how many more there are, but Ellshaw couldn't do it all alone. I know that man, and I'd swear he wasn't a killer.'

The door opened and Irelock returned, bringing a bottle and glasses on a tray.

'What are the four motives that might make anyone a killer?' asked the Saint.

Teal's heavy lids settled more wearily over his eyes.

'Revenge? Nobody whom he's attacking ever seems to have met him before, except his wife. Jealousy?'

'Of what?'

'The fear of being found out?' suggested Irelock.

'We haven't anything against him,' answered the detective. 'And I don't know how to believe that he's done anything before that would be big enough to give him such a guilty conscience. He's the type that makes the usual whine about persecution when he's caught, but he always goes quietly.'

Simon nodded.

'So that only leaves the best motive of all. Money. Big money.'

'Extortion?' queried Teal sceptically.

'It has been done,' said the Saint mildly. 'But it doesn't meet all the facts this time. What's he going to extort from Mrs Ellshaw and me? And how can we know anything that might spoil the racket before Nulland's even been kidnapped—much less before anyone's put in the bill for ransom? And how the hell could you get a ransom out of Lord Ripwell if he was dead? Don't forget that he was on the bumping-off list before tonight.'

Chief Inspector Teal breathed audibly.

'Well, if you've got a theory of your own, I'd like to hear it. All you've done yet is to make it more complicated.'

'On the contrary,' said the Saint, with that intangible intuitive train of thought still shuffling through the untracked subconscious labyrinths of his imagination, 'I think it's getting simpler.'

'You've got a theory?' Irelock pressed him eagerly.

The Saint smiled.

'For the first time since all the excitement started, I've got more than a theory,' he answered softly. 'I've got a fact.'

'What is it?' demanded Teal, too quickly; and the Saint grinned gently, and got up with a swing of his long legs.

'You'd like to know, wouldn't you? Well, how do you know you don't?'

Mr Teal swallowed the last faint scrap of flavour out of his gum, and blinked at him.

'How do I know—'

'How do you know you don't? Because you do.' Simon Templar flattened the stump of his cigarette in an ashtray, and laughed at him soundlessly. He put his hand on Teal's cushy shoulder. 'It's all there waiting for you, Claud, if you figure it out. Think back a bit, and work on it. Who's supposed to be the detective here—you or me?'

'Do you mean you know who's responsible?' asked Irelock.

The Saint turned his head.

'Not yet. Not positively. I've just got a few ideas walking around in my mind. One or two of 'em have got together for a chat, and when they've all met up I think they're going to tell me something. I'd like to see how his lordship's getting on.'

He went upstairs and let himself quietly into the bedroom. Ripwell was smoking a cigar and reading a book, and he looked up with a steady smile that overcame the pallor of his face.

'Looks as if I'm pretty hard to kill, what? You were splendid—wish we'd caught one of those blighters. Why the devil didn't I have that damned revolver? I might have bagged one myself.'

'Inspector Oldwood brought over some ammunition for you,' said the Saint. I'll see that you have it before we turn in. It's a comforting thing to have under your pillow.'

'Damned comforting,' agreed his lordship. 'I don't mind telling you I'm glad to have you in the house—you won't be leaving yet, will you?'

'Not for a while.'

Lord Ripwell grunted cheerfully.

'That's good. They got Kenneth, didn't they? Oh, yes, I know—I dragged it out of Martin just now. Decent of you to try and keep it from me, but I'd rather know. I can stand a good deal. Wish Kenneth could. Still, an experience like that may wake him up a bit. What d'you think they'll do to him?'

'I don't know. But somehow I don't think it'll be anything—fatal.'

Ripwell nodded.

'Neither do I. If they'd wanted to—do that . . . they needn't have taken him away. I'm glad you think so too, though. I wouldn't like to feel I was hoodwinking myself. Somebody'd better ring up that chap Ferris and tell him Ken won't be coming down.'

'Do you know the number?'

'Never did know it. Ring up his flat in London and see if you can get it from there. The least we can do is to save Kenneth from getting in trouble for being late again. You'll find a directory under that table. Address in Duchess Place somewhere, I think.'

'What?'

The question was slapped out of the Saint with such spontaneous startlement that Ripwell dropped his cigar and scorched the sheet.

'Eh? What? What's the matter?'

'Did you say Duchess Place?'

Ripwell picked up his cigar and dusted off the debris of ash from the bedclothes.

'I think that's right. Kenneth has talked about it. Why?'

Simon did not answer. He sprang up and dived under the extension telephone table by the bedside for the directory. He could hear Mrs Florence Ellshaw's unmusical voice rasping in his ear as clearly as if her ghost had been standing beside him, repeating the fragments of her long-winded and meandering story: '. . . in Duchess Place, sir . . . number six . . . next door to two young gennelmen as I do for, such nice young gennelmen . . .'

'Does he share this flat with another fellow?' Simon jerked out, whipping over the pages.

Lord Ripwell raised his eyebrows foggily.

'I believe he does. Don't know who it is, though. How did you know?'

The Saint didn't answer that one, either. He had found his place in the directory and ran down the list of Ferrises until he came to one whose address was in Duchess Place—at number eight, Duchess Place. And he was staring at the entry with a queer short-winded feeling sinking into his solar plexus and an electric buck-and-wing careering over his ganglions in a style that eclipsed everything else of its kind hitherto. It was several seconds before he spoke at all.

'Holy smoke,' he breathed. 'Jolly Old Jumbo!'

VI

'What's the matter?' repeated Lord Ripwell, with pardonable blankness.

'Nothing,' said the Saint absently. 'It's just some more of the pieces falling into place. Wait a minute.'

He jumped up and began to pace quickly up and down the room, slamming the directory shut and chucking it back under the table. The train of thought was moving faster, dashing hectically up and down over its maze of sidings faster than he was covering the floor. His tanned keen face was cut into bronze lines of intense thought, with his sea-blue eyes blazing vividly against the sunburned background. He wheeled round with his fist smashing impetuously into his palm.

'It's getting together . . . To kill Mrs Ellshaw just because she'd come to see me wasn't such a good motive. I was flattering myself a bit. But she'd always have to talk—to someone. Suppose it was the two young gennelmen that she did for? That's the sort of coincidence that happens. When Ellshaw had to disappear, who could have foreseen that his wife might go to work for someone who knew the bloke who . . . Wait for it again . . . Yes, they knew Kenneth. And Kenneth never said whether he'd heard of Ellshaw— never had a chance to . . . My God, I'd forgotten that piece of organisation!'

Ripwell's pleasant face was hardening uncertainly.

'What are you driving at? If you're suggesting that Kenneth is a murderer—'

'Murder?' The Saint came up with a start, half dazed, out of the trance in which he had been letting his thoughts race on aloud, without making any effort to dictate their destination. 'I never said that. But—God, am I getting this untied?'

'I don't know what you mean,' persisted Ripwell hoarsely.

Simon swung back to the bed and dropped his hands on the old man's shoulders.

'Don't worry,' he said gently. 'I'm sorry—I didn't mean to scare you. Even now. I'm not quite sure what I do mean. But I'll look after things. And I'll be right back.'

He pressed Ripwell quietly back on the pillows and went out quickly, making for the stairs with an exuberant stride that almost bowled Martin Irelock off the landing.

'What's the excitement?' demanded the secretary.

'I've got some more ideas.' Simon kept hold of the arm which he had clutched to save Irelock from taking the worst of the spill. 'Are you busy?'

'No—I was just making sure that your room's all right.'

'Then come downstairs again. I want to talk to you.'

He did not release the arm until they were downstairs in the living-room. The French casement was ajar, the half-drawn curtains stirring in the draught. Simon took out his cigarette-case.

'Where's Teal?'

'I don't know. Oldwood's man just arrived—I expect he's showing him round.'

The Saint put a cigarette between his lips and took a match from the ash-stand, stroking it alight with his thumb-nail.

'I've remembered something that may interest you,' he said. 'An interesting scientific fact. If you have a sample of fresh blood, it's possible to analyse its type and get an exact mathematical ratio of probabilities that it came from some particular person.'

Irelock blinked.

'Is it really? That's interesting.'

'I said it was interesting. How does it appeal to you?'

The secretary picked up the whisky decanter mechanically, and poured splashes into the three glasses on the tray. All the splashes did not go into the glasses.

'I don't know—why should it appeal to me particularly?'

'Because,' answered the Saint deliberately, 'I've an idea that if I asked Teal to have the blood on Ken's handkerchief analysed, and then we took a sample of your blood from that graze on your arm, we'd find that the odds were that it was your blood!'

'What do you—'

'What do I mean? I'm always hearing that question. I mean that I told you and Teal just now that I'd got a fact, and this is it. There was only one shot fired in the front of the house. It scratched your wrist—low down. This handkerchief was in Kenneth's breast pocket. I noticed it. While it's possible that you may have gone out of the door with your hands shoulder high, it's damned unlikely; and therefore I didn't quite see how a bullet that passed you about the level of your hips could have hit Ken in the chest, unless the warrior who fired it was lying at your feet—which again is unlikely.'

Irelock's knuckles showed white where he gripped his glass, and for a second or two he made no reply. Then, with an imperceptible shrug, he looked back at the Saint, tight-lipped.

'All right,' he said, with a nod of grim resignation. 'You've seen through it. I'm afraid I should make a rotten criminal. It was my blood.'

'How come?'

Irelock grimaced ruefully.

'Teal suspected it.'

'You mean to tell me that Ken ran away?'

'Yes.'

Simon drew smoke from his cigarette and trickled it through his nostrils.

'Go on.'

'That's about all I know. I don't know why. I could see a silhouette of the car against the headlights when they were switched on, and there was only one man in it. I found the handkerchief while I was pretending to help you to look for him, and I wiped it on my arm and dropped it back on the drive. I suppose it was a silly thing to do, but the only thing I could think of was how to try and cover him up—to make it look as if he hadn't run away.'

There was no doubt that he was speaking the truth, but Simon drove on at him relentlessly.

'Why should you think he wanted covering up?'

'Why else should he want to run away? Besides, you must have seen that there was something on his mind all the evening—I saw you looking at him. I don't know what it was. But he's always been wild. I've tried to help him. Lord Ripwell would probably have disinherited him more than once if I hadn't been able to get him out of some of his scrapes.'

'Such as?'

'Oh, the usual wild things that a fellow like that does. He gambles. And he drinks too much.'

'Gets obstreperous when he's tight, does he?'

'Yes. You wouldn't think it of him, but he does. When he's

drunk he'd pick a fight with anybody, but when he's sober he'd run away from a mouse.'

'Could he have killed anyone when he was drunk?' Irelock stared at him with horror.

'Good Lord!—you don't think that?'

'I don't know what I think,' said the Saint impatiently. 'I'm just trying to sort things out. Ripwell hasn't disinherited him yet, has he? Well, who'd make the biggest profit out of Ripwell's death? . . . But even that hasn't anything to do with the rest of it. There are two mysteries tangled up, and I'm trying to make them tie. The hell with it!'

He picked up a glass and subsided with it into a chair, frowning savagely. Odd loose ends out of the tangle kept on linking up and matching, tantalising him with a deceptive hope that the rest of the pattern was just about to follow on and fall neatly into place; but at the climax there was always one clashing colour, some shape or other that did not fit. Somewhere in the web there must be a thin tortuous thread that would hold it all together, but the thread was always dancing just beyond his grasp.

'If—if you're not quite sure,' Irelock was saying hesitantly, 'have you got to say anything to Teal? I mean, unless Lord Ripwell—unless everybody's got to know that Kenneth funked . . .'

He broke off at the sound of a footstep on the path outside, but his bright eyes continued the appeal. Simon moved his head non-committally, but he had no immediate intention of making Chief Inspector Teal a free gift of the wear and tear on his own valuable grey matter.

'I've posted the constable outside, under the bedroom window,' said the detective, and looked at the glass which Irelock was offering him. 'No, thank you—fat men didn't ought to drink. It's bad for the heart. The doctor hasn't been able to get hold of a nurse yet, so we'd better take it in turns to sit up.'

Irelock nodded, and took the first sip at his highball.

'I don't mind taking the—'

His voice wrenched into a ghastly retching sound, and they

stared at him in momentary paralysis. And then, as Simon started to his feet, he lurched forward and knocked the glass spinning out of the Saint's hand with a convulsive sweep of his arm.

'For God's sake!' he gasped. 'Don't drink . . . Poison!'

### VII

Simon sprang forward and caught him before Teal's lumbering movement in the same direction had more than started, but Irelock flung him off with demented energy and went staggering to the window. They heard him vomiting painfully outside.

'Get on the phone for a doctor,' snapped the Saint, as he dashed after him.

Irelock reeled into his arms in the darkness.

'Get me back,' he panted huskily. 'Maybe—all right . . . Get . . . mustard and water—'

Simon brought him back into the room and laid him down on the sofa—he was curiously black about the eyes and the perspiration was streaming off him. Teal came in with the emetic almost at once, having gone out and found it on his own initiative; and there was a further period of unpleasantness . . .

'All right—thanks.'

Irelock lay back at last with a groan. His breathing was still laboured, but the spasmic twitching of his limbs was reduced to a faint trembling.

'I'm feeling—better . . . Think we—got rid of it—in time . . . That would have been—another mystery—for you!'

To Simon Templar there was no mystery. His glance flashed from the whisky decanter to the still open French door through which Teal had come in, and he looked up to find Mr Teal's somnolent eyes following the same route. His gaze crystallised thoughtfully.

'While you were outside posting your cop under the window, Claud Eustace! Is that organisation and is that nerve, or what is it?'

He took up the untouched glass which Mr Teal had declined, and moistened his mouth from it, holding the liquid only for a moment. There was a distinctive sweet oily taste in it which might have passed unnoticed under the sharper bite of the spirit unless he had been looking for it, and he retained a definition of the savour in his memory after he had spat out the sip.

Teal's eyes were wide open.

'Then they still can't be far away,' he said.

The Saint's lips stirred in an infinitesimal reckless smile.

'One day you'll be a detective after all, Claud,' he murmured. Teal was starting to move ponderously towards the window, but Simon passed him with his long easy stride and stopped him. 'But I'm afraid you'll never be a night hunter. Let me go out.'

'What can you do?' asked Teal suspiciously.

'I can't arrest him,' Simon admitted. 'But I can be a good dog and bring you the bone. We missed a trick last time—crashing out like a mob of blasted red-faced fox-hunting squires after a poacher. You wouldn't catch anyone but a damn fool that way, on a dark night like this. But I know the game. I'll go out and be as invisible as a worm, and if anyone steps inside these grounds again I'll get him. And I think somebody will be coming!'

The detective hesitated. His memories of the Assistant Commissioner floated bogeyly across his imagination; the memory of all the deceptions he had suffered from the Saint narrowed his eyes. But he knew as well as anyone what amazing things Simon Templar could do in the dark, and he knew his own limitations.

'If you do catch anyone, will you promise to bring him in?'

'He's yours,' said the Saint tersely; but he made a mental reservation about the exact time at which that transfer of property would come into effect.

He went out alone, dissolving noiselessly into the night like a wandering shadow. From the blackness outside the window he watched Teal using the telephone, and presently saw the lights of a car drive up and stop outside the gate. The doctor walked up the short drive and was challenged on his way by the police guard; and Simon took that opportunity of introducing himself.

'This is a funny business, sir, isn't it?' said the constable, when the doctor had gone on into the house.

He was a middle-aged beefy man who kept shaking himself down uncomfortably in his plain clothes, as if he had been wearing a uniform too long to feel thoroughly at home in any other garb. He would probably continue to wear a uniform for the rest of his life, but it was no less probable that he was quite contented with the prospect.

Simon strolled back with him to his post, and gave him a cigarette. He did not expect the man he was waiting for to enter the grounds for a little while.

'Kidnapped 'is lordship's son, too, didn't they?' said the policeman. 'Now, why should they want to do that?'

The question was put more or less in rhetorical appeal to some unspecified oracle, rather than as one demanding a direct answer; and the Saint did not immediately attempt to answer it.

'I suppose you know Lord Ripwell fairly well,' he said, striking a match.

'Well, so-and-so,' said the constable, puffing. 'Must be about five year now, sir—ever since 'e bought the house.'

'I shouldn't think he'd be an easy man to extort money from.'

'I wouldn't like to be the man to try it. Mind you, 'is lordship's known to be a generous gentleman—do anything for a fellow oo's out of luck, if he's asked properly. But not the kind you could force anything out of. No, sir. Why, I remember in my time what 'appened to a chap oo tried to blackmail 'im.'

The stillness of the Saint's eyes could not be seen in the dark.

'Somebody tried to blackmail him once, did they?' he said quietly.

'Yes, sir. It wasn't nothing much they 'ad to blackmail 'im with, but you can see for yourself 'is lordship must've been quite a lad in 'is time, and some people are that narrow-minded they don't expect a man to be even 'uman.' There was a sympathetic note in the constable's voice which hinted that he himself could modestly claim, in his own time, to have been Quite A Lad. 'Anyway, all 'is lordship did was to get the Inspector up and 'ave him listen to some of this talk. And then, when he could 'ave 'ad the fellow sent to prison, he wouldn't even prosecute 'im.'

'No?'

'Wouldn't even make a charge. "I don't want to be vindictive," he says. "The silly ass 'as had a good fright," he says, "and now you let him go. You can see he's just some down-and-out idiot oo thought 'e could make some easy money." And in the end I believe 'e gave the chap 'is fare back to London.'

'Who was this fellow?' Simon asked.

'I dunno. Said 'is name was Smith, like most of 'em do when they're first caught. We never had no chance to find out oo he really was, on account of 'is lordship not prosecuting 'im, but 'e did look pretty down and out. Seedy little chap with a great red nose on 'im like a stop light.'

The doctor came out and returned to his car—Simon heard his parting conversation with Teal at the door, and gathered that Martin Irelock was in no danger. The hum of the car died away; and Simon gave the talkative guard another cigarette and faded back into the dark to resume his own prowling.

His brain was becoming congested with new things to think about. So an attempt had been made to extort money from Ripwell. He was confirmed in his own estimate of the prospects of the hopeful extorter, but apparently the aspirant himself had required to be convinced by experience. There was something about the anecdote as he felt it which gave him a distinct impression of a trial balloon. Someone had wanted first-hand knowledge of Lord Ripwell's reaction to such an attempt; and the constable's brief description of the aspiring blackmailer had one prominent feature in common with the elusive Mr Ellshaw. Curiously enough, in spite of the increased congestion of ideas, the Saint felt that the mystery was gradually becoming less mysterious . . .

He moved round the house as soundlessly as a hunting cat. As

Chief Inspector Teal knew and admitted, queer things, almost incredible things, happened to Simon Templar when he got out in the dark—things which would never have been believed by the uninitiated observer who had only seen him in his sophisticated moods. He could leave his immaculately dressed, languidly bantering sophistication behind him in a room, and go out to become an integral part of the wild. He could go out and move through the night with the supple smoothness of a panther, without rustling a blade of grass under his feet, merging himself into minute scraps of shadow like a jungle animal, feeling his way uncannily between invisible obstructions, using strange faculties of scent and hearing with such weird certainty that those who knew him best, when they thought about it, sometimes wondered if the roots of all his amazing outlawry might not be found threading down into the deeps of this queer primitive instinct.

No living man could have seen or heard him as he passed on his silent tour, summarising the square lights of windows in the black cube of the house. Lord Ripwell's lighted window, under which the police guard stood, was on one side. A bulb burned faintly in the hall, at the front, facing closely on to the road. The dully luminous colour of curtains on the other side marked the living-room which he had left not long ago. At the back of the house, where the Thames margined the grounds, he could see one red-shaded lamp in an upstairs window—presumably that was Irelock's room, for he had gathered that the only domestic servant employed at the cottage was a daily woman who had gone home immediately after dinner. Chief Inspector Teal must have been keeping watch downstairs with a dwindling supply of spearmint; and Simon wondered whether he had been jarred far enough out of his principles to take over Lord Ripwell's revolver and the ammunition, to wait with him for the sudden death that would surely stalk through that place again before morning.

He came down to the water's edge and sat with his back to a tree, as motionless as if he had been one of its own roots. Surely, he knew, the death would come; but whether it would successfully claim a victim depended largely upon him. There was a smooth speed about every move of the case which appealed to him: it was cut and thrust, parry and riposte—a series of lightning adjustments and counter-moves which he could appreciate for its intrinsic qualities even while he was still fumbling for the connecting link that held it all together. The poison which had found its way into the whisky less than an hour ago belonged to the same scheme of things. He could recall its peculiar sweet oily taste on his tongue, and he thought he knew what it was. The symptoms which Martin Irelock had shown corroborated it. Very few men would have known that it was poisonous at all. How should an illiterate little race-train rat like Ellshaw have known it?

A mosquito zoomed into his ear with a vicious ping, and one of his thighs began to itch; but still he did not move. At other times in his life he had lain out like that, immobile as a carved outcrop of rock, combing the dark with keyed-up senses as delicate as those of any savage, when the first man whose nerves had cracked under the unearthly strain would have paid for the microscopic easing of a cramped muscle with his life. That utter relaxation of every expectant sinew, the super-sensitive isolation of every faculty from all disturbances except those which he was waiting for, had become so automatic that he used no conscious effort to achieve it. And in that way, without even turning his head, he became aware of the black ghost of a canoe that was drifting soundlessly down the stream towards the place where he sat.

Still he did not move. A nightingale started to tune up in the branches over his head, and a frail wisp of cloud floated idly across the hazy stars which were the only light in the darkness. The canoe was only a dim black brush-stroke on the grey gloom, but he saw that there was only one man in it, and saw the ripple of tarnished-silver water as the unknown dipped his paddle and turned the craft in towards the bank. It seemed unlikely that any ordinary man would be cruising down the river at that hour alone, revelling in a dreamy romance with himself, and the Saint had an idea that the man who was coming towards him was not altogether ordinary. Unless a dead man creeping down the Thames in a canoe at midnight could be called ordinary.

The canoe slid under the bank, momentarily out of sight; but the Saint's ears carried on the picture of what was happening. He heard the soft rustle of grasses as the side scraped the shore, the plip-plop of tiny drops of water as the wet paddle was lifted inboard, the faint grate of the wood as it was laid down. He sat on under his tree without a stir in his graven stillness, building sound upon sound into a construction of every movement that was as vividly clear to him as if he had watched it in broad daylight. He heard the scuff of a leather shoe-sole on the wood, quite different from the dull grate of the paddle; the rustle of creased clothing; the whisper of turf pressed underfoot. Then a soundless pause. He sensed that the man who had disembarked was probing the night clumsily, looking for some sign or signal, hesitating over his next move. Then he heard the frush of trodden grass again, and a sifflation of suppressed breathing that would have been quite inaudible to any hearing less uncannily acute than his.

A shadow loomed up against the stygian tarnish of the water, half the height of a man, and remained still. The prowler was sitting on the bank, waiting for something which Simon could not divine. There was a longer and more complicated rustling, a tentative scratch and an astonishingly loud sizzle of flame; and the man's head and shoulders leapt up out of the dark for an instant in startlingly crisp silhouette against the glow of a match cupped in his hands.

The Saint moved for the first time. He rolled up silently and smoothly on to his feet, straightening his knees gradually until he came upright. The pulsing of his heart had settled down to a steady acceleration that did nothing to disturb the feline flow of any of his movements. It was only a level beat of excitement in his veins, a throbbing eagerness to complete his acquaintance with that elusive man around whose fanatical seclusion centred so much violence and sudden death.

Simon came up behind him very quietly. The man never knew he was coming, had no warning of danger before two sets of steel fingers closed on his throat. And when it was too late for him to do anything useful. He was not very strong, and he was almost paralysed with the heart-stopping horror of that silent attack out of the dark. The cry that burst involuntarily from his lungs was crushed by the choking grip of his neck before it could come to sound in his mouth, and a heavy knee settled snugly into the small of his back and pinned him helplessly to the ground in spite of all his frantic struggles. It was all over very quickly.

The Saint felt him go limp, and cautiously relaxed the pressure of his hands. Then he slipped his arms under the man's unconscious body and lifted him up. The whole encounter had made very little noise; and Simon was no less attentive to silence than he had been before, while he carried the man down the bank and laid him out in the canoe. A couple of deft sweeps of the paddle sent the craft skimming out into the stream; but the Saint kept it moving until a bend in the river hid the lights of the house before he struck a match and inspected the face of his capture.

It was Ellshaw.

## VIII

'Now you are going to talk, brother,' said the Saint. He sat facing his trophy over another flickering match, giving the other every facility to recognise him before the light went out. Ellshaw's face was wet with the river water that had been slopped over him to help him back to unhappy consciousness; but there was something else on his face besides water—a pale clammy fright that made his oversized red nose stand out like a full-blown rose against the blanched sickliness of his cheeks.

The match spun from the Saint's fingers into the water with an expiring hiss, dropping the curtain of blackness between them again; and the Cockney's adenoidal voice croaked hysterically through the curtain.

'I can't tell yer nothing, guv'nor—strike me dead if I can!'

'I shouldn't dream of striking you dead if you can,' said the Saint kindly. 'But if you can't . . . well, I really shouldn't know what to do with you. I couldn't just let you run away, because then you might begin to think you'd scored off me and get a swollen head, which would be very bad for you. I couldn't adopt you as a pet and take you around with me on a lead, because I don't like your face so much. I couldn't put you in a cage and send you to the Zoo, because the other monkeys might object. And so the question would arise, brother, how would one get rid of you? And of course it would always be so easy to get hold of your skinny neck again for a while, and hold you under water while you blew bubbles.'

'Yer wouldn't dare!' panted Ellshaw.

'No?' The Saint's voice was just an infinitely gentle challenge lilting out of the darkness. 'Did you get a good look at me when I struck that match, by any chance? You knew me well enough when I dropped in to see you in Duchess Place. And you talked as if you'd heard all about me, too. Did somebody ever tell you there was anything I didn't dare?'

He could hear the racking harshness of the man's breathing.

'Yer wouldn't dare,' Ellshaw repeated as if he was only trying to convince himself. 'That—that 'ud be murder!'

'Yeah?' drawled the Saint. 'I'm not so sure. You tell me the answer, brother, out of that vast general-knowledge fund of yours—is it legally possible to kill a man who's already dead? Because you are dead, aren't you? You were murdered nearly a year ago.'

It was a shot literally in the dark, but the sharp catch of the other's breath was as clear an answer to him as if he had had a searchlight focused down the boat. His thumb-nail gritted across another match, and the flame cut the pitiless buccaneering line of his face out of the gloom for as long as it took him to light a cigarette. And then there was only the red tip of the cigarette glowing in the intensified dark, and his voice coming from behind it: 'So how on earth could I murder you again, brother? I could only make you stay dead, and I don't think anybody's ever laid down the law about a crime like that.'

'I don't know nothing,' persisted Ellshaw hoarsely. 'Honest I don't.'

'Honest you do,' said the Saint persuasively. 'But I didn't even ask for your opinion. Just you come through with what's on your mind, and I'll let you know whether I think it was worth knowing.'

Ellshaw did not answer at once; and Simon went on quite calmly, with a matter-of-fact detachment that was more deadly than any bullying bluster: 'Don't kid yourself, sonny. If I had to toast your feet over a hot fire to make you talk, it wouldn't be the first toasting party I'd been out on. If I ever felt like wiping you off the face of the earth, I'd do it and never have a sleepless night on account of it. But just for this one occasion, I'm liable to be as good as you'll let me. When I came out here to catch a man, I told Chief Inspector Teal I'd bring him back with me, and I'd just as soon bring him back alive. What Teal will do to you when he gets you depends a whole lot on how you open your mouth first. Get wise to the spot you're sitting in, Ellshaw. It isn't everybody's idea of a good time to get himself hanged; but nobody who did a good job of King's Evidence has ever been strung up yet.'

'They couldn't do it,' said Ellshaw sobbingly. 'They couldn't 'ang me. I ain't done nothing—'

'What about your wife?' said the Saint ruthlessly.

'She's all right, guv'nor. I swear she is. Nobody's done 'er no 'arm. I can tell you all abaht that.'

'Tell me.'

'Well, guv'nor, it was like this. When she spotted me in Duchess Plyce, an' I 'ad to get rid of 'er, we thought afterwards she might go blabbin' abaht 'aving seed me, so we 'ad to keep 'er quiet, see? But she ain't dead. She just got took off to some other place an' kep' there so she couldn't talk. We couldn't 'ave people lookin' for 'er, though, an' kickin' up a fuss; so we 'ad to give out she was dead, see?'

'Did you have to get the police to fish her dead body out of the Thames as well—just to make it more convincing?' asked the Saint coldly.

He was not quite sure what answer he expected—certainly he had not looked at the question as a vital thrust in the argument.

The reaction which it obtained startled him, and he was surprised to find that he could still be startled.

For some seconds Ellshaw did not speak at all; and then his voice was shockingly different from the defiant whine in which he had been talking before.

'Go on,' he said huskily. 'Yer can't tike me in wiv a yarn like that.'

'My dear sap,' said the Saint slowly, 'I don't want to take you in with any yarn. I'm only telling you. Your wife's body was taken out of the river last night. It was supposed to be suicide at first, but now they're pretty sure it was murder.'

There was another silence at the opposite end of the canoe; and Simon Templar drew his cigarette to an instant's bright gleam of red in which the lines of his mouth could be seen as intent and inexorable as a stone mask, and went on without a change in the purring level of his voice.

'If you keep your mouth shut I wouldn't give you a bad penny for your chance. You can put a lot of things over on a jury, but somehow or other they never take a great shine to a fellow who kills his own wife. Of course, they say hanging isn't such a bad death . . .'

Ellshaw was making queer noises in his throat, as if he was struggling to do something with his voice.

'Oh Gawd!'

His feet shuffled on the bottom. His breath was whistling through his teeth with a weird harshness that chilled something dormant in the Saint's heart.

'You ain't tryin' to scare me, are yer? Yer just tellin' me the tile to make me talk. She ain't—dead?'

'I'm afraid she is.'

Ellshaw gulped.

'My Gawd . . .' His voice went shrill. 'The dirty lyin' swine! The rat! He told me—'

There was a sound as if he flopped over athwart. In another moment he was sprawled across the Saint's feet, clutching aimlessly at Simon with crazy shaking hands.

'I didn't do it,' he blubbered. 'I swear I didn't! I didn't wish 'er dead. I believed wot I told yer. I thought she was just 'idden away somewhere, like I was. I ain't never murdered nobody!'

'Didn't you know that Lord Ripwell was to be murdered?' said the Saint relentlessly. 'Didn't you know that I was to be murdered?'

'Yes, I did!' shouted the other wildly. 'But I wouldn't 'ave murdered Florrie. I wouldn't 'ave stood for killin' me own missus. That filthy double-crossin'—'

Simon gripped him by the shoulders.

'Will you squeal, Ellshaw?'

He could feel the man's stupefied eyes straining to find him in the darkness.

'Yes, I'll squeal. My Gawd, I'll squeal!'

'You're a bright boy after all,' said the Saint.

He pushed the demented man away and took up his paddle again. Driving the canoe back up the stream with cool steady strokes, he felt a great ease of triumph. It was the same quiet thrill that a chess-player must feel on mastering an intricate problem. He realised with a touch of humour that it was one of the very few episodes in which success could not conceivably bring him one pennyworth of boodle; but it made no difference to his satisfaction. He had taken one of his impulsively wholehearted likings to Lord Ripwell.

The red light in the back upper window swam into view again past a clump of trees, and he turned the canoe into the bank and drove the paddle-blade into the shallow river bed to hold it. Ellshaw was still moaning and muttering incoherently; and, for his own sake, Simon hauled him up out of the canoe and shook him vigorously.

'Snap out of it, brother. This is your chance to get even—and shift yourself off the high jump at the same time.'

'I'm going to squeal,' repeated Ellshaw dazedly.

The Saint kept hold of him.

'OK. Then come up to the house and let Teal listen to it.'

He rushed the trembling man over the rough lawn and up the side of the house to the French window of the living-room. There was an exclamation somewhere in the middle distance, and heavy feet pounded after him. The beam of a bullseye lantern picked him up.

'Oh, it's you, sir,' said the police guard, illuminatingly. 'I thought—Gosh, what have you got there?'

'A tandem bicycle,' said the Saint shortly. 'Get back to your post.'

Teal, startled by the noise, was on his feet when he thrust his prize into the room. The detective's jaw hung open, and for a second or two he stopped chewing.

'Good Lord—is that—'

'Yes, it is, Claud. A new gadget for punching holes in Cellophane. If I could go on thinking up questions like that, I might be a policeman myself. Which God forbid. Don't you know your boyfriend?'

For once in his life Chief Inspector Teal was incapable of being offended.

'Ellshaw! Was he outside?'

'No, he was baked into the middle of a sausage-roll in the pantry perfectly disguised as a new genius from Scotland Yard.'

'How did you know he'd be there?'

'Oh, my God!' Simon pushed the harvest of his brain work into a chair like a sack of beans, and subsided against the table. 'Have I got to do everything for you? All right. It was only this morning that I crashed into Duchess Place. I ought to have been killed last night. Since that failed, they hoped to get me this morning when I went nosing around. When that fell through, they had to make a quick getaway. I assumed that they were so far from expecting trouble that they hadn't got a spare bolt-hole waiting to move into. Therefore they had to do something temporary. The Grand Panjandrum couldn't have been a Grand Panjandrum at all if he hadn't known that Ellshaw was a bit of a dim bulb. Therefore he wouldn't want to risk letting him far out of his reach. He knew he was coming down here this afternoon, so naturally he'd park Ellshaw somewhere locally where he could get in touch with him, while he figured out what they were going to do next. Having made up his mind, he'd have to tell Ellshaw. Therefore Ellshaw would have to come to him for instructions—it would probably be easier than him going to see Ellshaw, and at the time he'd think it was just as safe. Therefore Ellshaw had to come here. Therefore he probably had to come here soon. Therefore he'd probably come tonight. And even if he didn't, I couldn't do any harm by waiting. Therefore I waited. QED. Or do you want a dictionary to help you out with the two-syllable words?'

Teal swallowed.

'Then he was—'

His eyes travelled to a carefully corked bottle on a side table. Simon knew at once that it must be a sample of whisky corked for analysis, and smiled faintly.

'You needn't bother with that,' he said. 'I can tell you what's in it. It's nitroglycerine . . . as used in making the best bombs. If Irelock hasn't coughed it all up you could drop him down the stairs and blow up the house; but it's a deadly enough poison without that. No, I don't think Ellshaw did it. He wouldn't have known. But the man who made our two bombs might have.'

'Then do you mean it isn't Ellshaw—'

'Of course not. It's much too big for him. There he is. Look at him. There's the guy that all the commotion's about—the great million-pound mystery that people had to be killed to keep. But he isn't the brains. He couldn't do anything at all. He's dead!'

Mr Teal blinked, staring at the red-nosed snivelling man who lay sprawling hot-eyed in a chair where Simon had thrown him. He looked alive. The low-pitched gasping noises that broke through his lips sounded alive.

'How is he dead?' Teal asked stupidly.

'Because he's been murdered. And don't forget something else. He's King's Evidence—I promised him that, and you haven't a case to go to a jury without him.'

The detective hesitated.

'But if he had anything to do with murdering his wife—'

'He didn't. I believe that, and so will you. He was double-crossed. After his wife had seen him, he was told she'd got to disappear in case she shot her mouth. He thought she was just going to be kept somewhere in hiding, like he was. He'll tell you all about it. The Grand Panjandrum knew he'd never stand for killing his wife, so that was the story. And that's why he's going to squeal. You are going to squeal, aren't you, Ellshaw?'

The man licked his lips.

'Yes, I'll talk. I'll tell everythink I know.' His voice had gone back to its normal level, but it was coarse and raspy with the blind vindictiveness of the passion that was sweating down inside him. 'But I didn't kill Florrie. Nobody 'ad to kill 'er. I didn't know nothink about it. I'll tell yer.'

The Saint lighted a cigarette and drew the smoke down into his lungs.

'There you are, Claud,' he murmured. 'Your case is all laid out for you. Shall I start the story or shall Ellshaw?'

Teal nodded.

'I think we'd better wait a moment before we begin,' he said. 'Our police methods are useful sometimes. We've got young Nulland.'

'You have?'

'Yes.' Mr Teal was beginning to recover some of his habitual bored smugness. 'He was held up with a puncture just outside Sunningdale, and a motor-cycle patrol spotted him—I had a phone call while the doctor was here last. He's being sent back under guard—they ought to arrive any minute now.'

Simon raised his eyebrows.

'So you know that he wasn't kidnapped after all?'

'It doesn't look like it,' replied the detective stolidly. 'Anyhow, there was nobody with him, when he was found, and he hadn't any convincing story to tell. We'll soon know, when he gets here.'

The Saint let go a trickle of smoke; but before he could speak again a car hummed slowly up the road and stopped opposite the house. He sat up, with the careless lights wakening in his blue eyes, and listened to the tread of footsteps coming up the drive.

'Didn't I tell you we were going to have fun?' he remarked. 'I think your police are wonderful.'

Mr Teal looked at him for a moment, and then went out to open the front door.

Simon's glance followed him, and then turned back to the man who sat quivering in the arm-chair. He swung his legs off the table.

'You're the exhibit, aren't you?' he said softly.

He turned the chair round so that Ellshaw faced the door and must be the first person whom the returning prodigal would see when he entered the room. Then he went back to his perch on the table and went on with his cigarette. Outwardly he was quite calm; and yet he was waiting for a moment which in its own way was the tensest climax of the adventure. Out of the twisted tangled threads, in breathless pauses between the shuttling of move and counter-move and unexpected revelation, he had at last built up a pattern and a theory. All the threads were in place; and it only wanted that last flash of the shuttle to bind them all irrefragably together—or tangle the web once more and set him back to the place where he began.

Inspector Oldwood came first; then the Honourable Kenneth Nulland; last of all came Teal, completing the party and closing the door behind him. Presumably the guard who had brought Nulland over from Sunningdale had been dismissed, or told to wait outside.

Simon did not so much as glance at the two detectives. His eyes were fixed on the pale fish-like face of Lord Ripwell's son and heir.

He saw the face turn whiter, and saw the convulsive twitch of the young man's hands and the sudden glazing of his eyes. Nulland's lips moved voicelessly once or twice before any sound came.

'Oh, God,' he said; and went down without another word in a dead faint.

Simon Templar drew a deep breath. 'Now I can tell you a story,' he said.


IX

Nulland sat on the sofa after they had brought him round. He sat staring at Ellshaw as if his brain was still incredulously trying to absorb the evidence of his eyes; and Ellshaw stared back at him with dry lips and stony eyes.

'I think this all began more than a year ago,' said the Saint.

Chief Inspector Teal searched for a fresh wafer of chewing-gum and unwrapped it. It was significant that at this time he made no attempt to assert his own authority to take charge of the proceedings; and, after one curious glance at him, Inspector Oldwood pulled out his pipe and found his way to a chair without interrupting.

'The idea, of course, was to get hold of Ripwell's money,' Simon went on, lighting a cigarette. 'Probably any other millionaire's money would have done just as well, but Ripwell was the obvious victim close at hand. The question was how to do it. Ordinary swindling could be ruled out: Ripwell was much too keen a business man to let himself be diddled out of anything more than paltry sums. That left, on the face of it, one other chance—extortion. Well, that was tried, in a tentative sort of way. Ellshaw came here with some minor secret out of Ripwell's past, and the result was just about what one would expect. Ripwell laid a trap for him, gave him a good scare, as he thought, and then didn't bother to prosecute him.'

'How on earth did you know that?' asked Oldwood, with some surprise.

'From your cop outside—I was having a chat with him, and it just happened to come out. But I recognised Ellshaw from the description of this attempted blackmailer, which you probably couldn't have done, and that made a lot of difference. But even so, it was only incidental evidence. It just clinched an explanation of why the blackmail had to be tackled afresh in a more roundabout way. I don't think Ellshaw's little effort was ever meant to succeed. It was meant to give a direct line on the way Ripwell could be expected to react to a bigger proposition, and it washed him out pretty completely. So that was when the real plot started.'

'You mean, to murder Lord Ripwell?' said Teal hesitantly.

'Yes. Of course, wilful murder was a much bigger proposition; but it had to be faced. And it was about the only solution. If Ripwell's money couldn't be extorted out of him, it could still be inherited. I'll give our friend all the credit for looking at it cold-bloodedly, facing the facts, seeing the answer, and making the best possible use of the bare material at his disposal. Take a look at Nulland for yourselves—weak, vain, rather stupid, a gambler, capable of extraordinary viciousness when he's in liquor—'

Mr Teal's cherubic pink face seemed to go a shade less rubicund.

'But—good God!' he said. 'To murder his own father—'

Simon looked at him oddly.

'You know, Claud, there are times when I ask myself whether anyone could possibly be so dumb as you try to make yourself out,' he remarked compassionately. 'All I'm doing is to tell you the facts about Nulland's character as I had them from Martin Irelock,' and he ought to know what he's talking about. He does know, too, and he could prove it. Naturally he wouldn't think of doing it; and I'm not too prejudiced, and I've got Ellshaw for a witness. Irelock wants to cover up Nulland. That's why he put down that fake bloodstained handkerchief tonight, to make it look more positively like kidnapping—and I'm ready to bet that he actually told Kenneth to run away in the first place—because he could see that Nulland was shaking in his boots at the idea of being surrounded with detectives, even a wretched imitation of a detective like you, Claud. Irelock knew that Nulland couldn't get through the rest of the evening, let alone the week-end, without getting caught out; and he was ready to go to any lengths to save him. He's been setting himself up as a shield all along. Anywhere between last week and a year ago, when Nulland thought he'd killed Ellshaw, Irelock played guardian angel.'

'Do you mean Irelock was in it with him?' stammered Mr Teal blankly.

The Saint's lips twitched helplessly; but he held back the scathing retort which they were shaping automatically. His keen ears had caught an infinitesimal sound outside the room, and in one amazing soundless moment he had hitched himself off the table and crossed over to the door. He turned the handle and whipped it open, and his long arm shot out and caught Martin Irelock as the secretary was turning away.

'Come in,' said the Saint's gentlest voice. 'Come in and help me finish my story.'

Irelock came in because he had to. With the Saint's iron grip on his arm, he had no option. He was in his pyjamas and a thick camel-hair dressing-gown, and his unnaturally old doll-like face was even greyer than it had been when he had swallowed his recent glassful of whisky and nitroglycerine. Simon closed the door again and stayed with his back to it.

'What's the matter?' demanded Irelock, in a strangely weak voice. 'I heard somebody arrive—'

'Lots of people have been arriving, dear old fruit,' said the Saint heartily. 'In fact, the whole cast is more or less assembled. We were only waiting for you to complete the party. And now I want you to tell all these nice kind policemen how you set out to get hold of Ripwell's millions.'

'I don't know what you're talking about,' said Irelock throatily.

'No?' The Saint's voice returned to gentleness. 'Well, you've got a lot of good precedents for that remark. I think nearly all the best murderers have said it. But this time we know too many of the answers. In fact, I think I could almost finish the job without any help from you. We all know how, when you first got the idea of making yourself rich, you tried Ripwell on blackmail—through Ellshaw here. And we were just starting to reconstruct your next move. We've seen how you must have figured out that if you couldn't get anything out of Ripwell, it'd be a damned sight easier to get it out of his son. We've got a good idea of how you set about it. Using Ellshaw again, you must have engineered Kenneth into a gamble with him. You knew Kenneth's weaknesses. You fed him plenty of drink at the same time. Ellshaw is such a damn bad cardsharper that people see through him even when they are tight, as Teal told me. Kenneth saw through him. There was a quarrel, then a fight. Ellshaw got laid out—as you'd planned. And then you sobered Kenneth up and told him Ellshaw was dead. You said you'd find a way to get rid of the body and cover up the evidence, and later you told him you'd done it. And from that moment he was in your power to do what you liked with—while you were making him believe, all the time, that you were his best friend. All you had to do was to hide your partner—Ellshaw—away, while you got rid of Ripwell; and then, after Kenneth had inherited the money, everything was set for you to start putting on the screw.'

'That's right, guv'nor,' Ellshaw broke in savagely. 'That's wot 'e told me. An' I shammed dead, an' everything. And then the dirty double-crossin' swine—'

'The man's raving,' said Irelock unsteadily.

'Nuts,' said the Saint crisply. 'You're through, and you know it. Kenneth's here to tell the world how you kidded him you were saving him from the gallows. Ellshaw's here to tell us that that's the plot as you put it up to him. And Ellshaw's here as well to tell us how you double-crossed him by killing his wife!'

Ellshaw was coming up out of his chair with a red flame in his eyes. His fingers were curled and rigid like claws.

'Yes, that's wot you did,' he snarled. 'You told me she wouldn't come to no 'arm—you swore you was only goin' to 'ide 'er away somewhere. And you killed 'er! You murdered my wife. You told me a lot of lies. You knew I wouldn't've let yer do it if I'd known.

And you were goin' to keep me workin' in with you, 'elpin' yer to mike money an' playin' all yer dirty games, when all the time you'd got Florrie's blood on yer 'ands. My Gawd, if 'anging isn't too good for yer—'

His voice went into a sort of shriek. Oldwood, who was nearest, wrapped powerful arms round him and held him back.

'That's the swine as did it!' screamed Ellshaw. ''E told me wot 'e was up to, 'ow 'e was goin' to kill Lord Ripwell an' then put the black on 'is son fer 'aving killed me in a fight. I know all about it! An' I can tell yer 'ow 'e meant to kill Mr Templar in Duchess Place—'

'Take it easy,' said Oldwood, struggling with him.

Teal thrust himself forward at last, a massive figure of belated officialdom coming into its egregious own. He looked at Nulland.

'Is that true?'

The young man swallowed.

'Yes,' he said in a low voice. 'At least, the part about me is.'

'You ran away tonight because you thought we were after you?'

The other nodded without speaking; and Teal turned back to Irelock.

'Have you got any answer to make?'

Irelock stood silent, looking from face to face. His mouth tightened, making his Kewpie face seem even more grotesquely grown up, but he did not open it to reply. The detective waited; then he shrugged.

'Very well. I shall have to take you into custody, of course. I had to warn you that anything you say may be taken down and used in evidence against you.'

For the first time since he had come into the room, Irelock met his eyes. He even smiled slightly.

'That's hardly necessary, Inspector,' he said. 'You seem to have plenty of evidence already. I think I can flatter myself that it took a clever man to catch me.' His gaze wandered significantly over to the Saint. 'When did you first—suspect me?'

'When you saw a face at the window,' Simon told him, 'and

the party broke up at a very psychological moment. I hadn't anything definite even then; but I began to wonder.'

Irelock nodded. 'That was bad luck, of course,' he said matter-of-factly. 'But I had to do something to stop Kenneth finding out that Ellshaw had been seen alive. Then, after I'd started a scare, I thought I might as well go on with it. If I'd been lucky, I might have got you and Ripwell in the garden—as it was, you nearly got me.' He touched his forearm, where the bullet had grazed him. 'But it made my story more circumstantial. It was only afterwards that I realised that Kenneth might be suspected, and I had to try and manufacture some evidence in his favour.'

'Why did you drink your own poison?'

'Partly because Teal wouldn't drink, and by that time I knew I'd got to get rid of both of you together. Partly because you'd just been saying things which showed me that you were fairly hot on my trail—I didn't know what you might have said to Teal already. It was the only time I lost my nerve. I tried to turn the idea into a way of throwing you off the scent again.'

'Do you realise the meaning of all you're saying?' asked Teal grimly.

Irelock sighed.

'Oh, yes. Quite well. But there doesn't seem to be much point in giving you any more trouble. After all, you've got other witnesses. You ought not to have Ellshaw; but that's another piece of bad luck. I told him that if he saw a red light in my window he was to keep away, but apparently he didn't keep away far enough.'

'One more question,' said the Saint. 'Why didn't you kill me in Duchess Place?'

'Because I hadn't got a gun,' answered Irelock simply. 'I never set out to go in for that sort of crime—not till it was thrust on me. I notice that murderers in books always have guns, but they aren't really easy for the amateur to get hold of. I should have got rid of you like I got rid of Mrs Ellshaw—knocked you out and sunk you in the river while you were unconscious. It was only when things began to happen down here that I got hold of Ripwell's old revolver. And of course he did have some ammunition; but he'd forgotten it.'

'Have you still got this gun?' Teal asked quickly.

Irelock's lips moved in a wan smile, and he put his right hand into the breast of his dressing-gown. Three of them at least caught the sudden cunning shift of his eyes, and realised too late what was coming—it was queer, Simon reflected afterwards, how completely they had been taken in by his implied surrender, when every one of them should have known that the murderers who make a full and calm confession at the moment when they are unmasked are as rare as fresh pineapples in Lapland.

What Ellshaw knew, or what he guessed, none of them ever discovered. It is only on record that he was the first of them to move, the only one to get up and go straight for Irelock. Twice the room rocked to the crash of the heavy gun, and Ellshaw staggered at the impact of each shot; but he held on his course. He must have been dead on his feet; but in some uncanny way he caught Irelock at the door and fell on his arm, dragging the revolver down so that it could only aim at the floor. It took two men to unlock the clutch of his fingers on Irelock's wrist; and the bruises of that dying grip were still stamped on the other's flesh a fortnight later, when he stepped down from the dock to wait for the answer to the greatest mystery of all.

# THE MIRACLE TEA PARTY

I

This story starts with four wild coincidences; so we may as well admit them at once and get it over with, and then there will be no more argument. The chronicler makes no apologies for them. A lot of much more far-fetched coincidences have been allowed to happen without protest in the history of the world, and all that can be done about it is to relate them exactly as they took place. And if it should be objected that these particular coincidences led to the downfall of sundry criminals who might otherwise never have been detected, it must be pointed out that at least half the convicts at present taking a cure in the cooler were caught that way.

Chief Inspector Claud Eustace Teal sat in a tea shoppe that was not much more than a powerful stone's throw from Scotland Yard. Dispassionately considered, it was quite a suitable target for stone-throwing, being one of those dens of ghastly chintz-curtained cheerfulness which stand as grisly omens of what the English-speaking races can expect from a few more generations of purity and hygiene; but Mr Teal held it in a sort of affection born of habit.

He had finished his tea, and he sat glancing over a newspaper. And in order that there may be positively no deception about this, it must be admitted at once that not even the most enthusiastic advocate of temperance would have chosen him as an advertisement of the place that he was in. Mr Teal, in fact, who even at his best suffered from certain physical disadvantages which made it permanently impossible for him to model for a statue of Dancing Spring, was at that moment not even in the running for a picture of Mellow Autumn. His round pink face had a distinctly muddy tinge under its roseate bloom; the champing of his jaws on the inevitable wodge of spearmint was visibly listless; and his china-blue eyes contained an expression of joyless but stoical endurance. He looked, to speak with complete candour, rather like a discontented cow with a toothache.

After a while he put the newspaper aside and simply sat, gazing mournfully into space. It was a Sunday afternoon, and at that rather late hour he had the place to himself, except for a vacant-faced waitress who sat in a corner knitting some garment in a peculiarly dreadful shade of mustard yellow. A small radio on the mantelpiece, strategically placed between a vase of artificial flowers and a bowl of wax fruit, was emitting strains of that singularly lugubrious and eviscerated music which supplies the theme song of modern romance. Mr Teal appeared to be enduring that infliction in the same spirit as Job might have endured the development of his sixty-second boil. He looked as if he was only waiting for someone to come along and relieve him of the cares of the Universe.

Someone did come along, but not with that intention. The crash of the door opening made Mr Teal's overwrought nerves wince; and when he saw who it was he closed his eyes for a moment in sheer agony. For although Mr William Kennedy was easily the most popular of the Assistant Commissioners, his vast and jovial personality was approximately the last thing that a man in Mr Teal's condition is able to appreciate.

'Hullo, laddie!' he roared, in a voice that boomed through the room like a gale. 'What's the matter? You look like a cold poached egg left over from yesterday's breakfast. What are you doing— thinking about the Saint?'

Mr Teal started as if an electric current had been applied to his posterior. He had expected the worst, but this was worse than that. If anything could have been said to fill his cup of suffering to the brim, that something had been said. Mr Teal now looked as if there was nothing left except for him to find some suitably awful spot in which to die.

Scientists, whose restless researches leave no phenomenon unprobed, have discovered that certain persons are subject to quite disproportionately grievous reactions from stimuli which to other persons are entirely innocuous. These inordinate sensitivities are known as allergies. Some people are allergic to oysters, others to onions; others need only eat a strawberry to be attacked by violent pains and break out in a rash.

Chief Inspector Teal was allergic to the Saint. But it must be admitted that this was an acquired rather than a congenital allergy. It is true that Mr Teal, on account of his profession, was theoretically required to be allergic to every kind of law-breaker; but there was nothing in his implied contract with the State which required him to be pierced by such excruciating pains or to break out in such a vivid erythema as he was apt to do whenever he heard the name or nickname of that incorrigible outlaw who had been christened Simon Templar.

But the Saint was the kind of outlaw that no officer of the Law can ever have had to cope with since the Sheriff of Nottingham was pestered into apoplexy by the Robin Hood of those more limited days. There was no precedent in modern times for anything like him; and Mr Teal was convinced that it could only be taken as evidence of the deliberate maliciousness of Fate that out of all the other police officers who might have been chosen for the experiment the lot had fallen upon him. For there was no doubt at all in his mind that all the griefs and woes which had been visited upon him in recent years could be directly attributed to that amazing buccaneer whose unlawful excursions against evil doers had made criminal history, and yet whose legal conviction and punishment was beginning to seem as hopelessly improbable an event as the capture of a genuine and indisputable sea-serpent. Kennedy was not being deliberately cruel. It was simply his uninhibited proclamation of what was an almost automatic association of ideas to anyone who knew anything at all about Teal's professional life: that whenever Mr Teal looked as if he was in acute agony he was undergoing a spell of Saint trouble. The fact that Mr Teal, as it happened, had not been thinking about the Saint at all when Kennedy came in only gave the reminder a deeper power to wound.

'No, sir,' said Mr Teal, with the flimsiest quality of restraint. 'I was not thinking about the Saint. I haven't seen him for weeks; I don't know what he's doing; and what's more, I don't care.'

Kennedy raised his eyebrows.

'Sorry, laddie. I thought from your appearance—'

'What's wrong with my blasted appearance?' snarled the detective, with a reckless disregard for discipline of which in normal times he would never have been capable; but Kennedy had no great respect for trivial formalities.

'Blasted is right,' he agreed readily. 'You look like something the lightning had started out to strike and then given up as a work of supererogation. What is it, then? Have you been getting hell for falling down on that espionage business?'

Mr Teal was able to ignore that. It was true that he had made very little headway with the case referred to, but that was not worrying him unduly. When official secrets spring a leak, it is usually a slow job to trace the leakage to its source, and Teal was too old a hand to let himself be disturbed by the slowness of it.

His trouble was far more intimate and personal; and the time has now come when it must be revealed.

Mr Teal was suffering from indigestion.

It was a complaint that had first intruded itself on his consciousness some weeks ago; since when its symptoms had become steadily more severe and regular, until by this time he had come to regard a stomach-ache as the practically inevitable sequel to any meal he ate. Since Mr Teal's tummy constituted a very large proportion of Mr Teal, his sufferings were considerable. They made him pessimistic and depressed, and more than usually morose. His working days had become long hours of discomfort and misery, and it seemed an eternity since he had spent a really restful and dreamless night. Even now, after having forgone his Sunday dinner in penitence for the price he had had to pay for bacon and eggs at breakfast, the cream bun to whose succulent temptation he had not long ago succumbed was already beginning to give him the unhappily familiar sensation of having swallowed a live and singularly vicious crab. And this was the mortal dolour in addition to which he had had to receive a superfluous reminder of the Saint.

The waitress at last succeeded in gaining audience.

'Yes,' boomed Kennedy. 'Tea. Strong tea. And about half a ton of hot buttered crumpets.'

Mr Teal closed his eyes again as another excruciating cramp curled through him.

In his darkened loneliness he became aware that the music had been interrupted and the radio was talking.

'. . . and this amazing tea is not only guaranteed to relieve indigestion immediately, but to effect a complete and permanent cure,' said a clear young voice with a beautiful Oxford accent. 'Every day we are receiving fresh testimonials—'

'My God,' said Teal with a shudder, 'where is that Eric-or-Little-by-Little drivelling from?'

'Radio Calvados,' answered Kennedy. 'One of the new continental stations. They go to work every Sunday. I suppose we shall have to put up with it as long as the B.B.C. refuses to produce anything but string quartets and instructive talks on Sundays.'

'Miracle Tea,' said Eric, continuing little by little. 'Remember that name. Miracle Tea. Obtainable from all high-class chemists, or direct by post from the Miracle Tea Company, 909, Victoria Street, London. Buy some Miracle Tea tonight! . . . And now we shall conclude this programme with our signature song—Tea for You.'

Mr Teal held on to his stomach as the anguishing parody proceeded to rend the air.

'Miracle Tea!' he rasped savagely. 'What'll they think of next? As if tea could cure indigestion! Pah!'

The way he said 'Pah!' almost blew his front teeth out; and Kennedy glanced at him discerningly.

'Oh, so that's the trouble, is it? The mystery is solved.'

'I didn't say—'

Kennedy grinned at him.

The door of the tea shoppe opened again, to admit Inspector Peters, Kennedy's chief assistant.

'Sorry I was so long, sir,' he apologised, taking the vacant chair at their table. 'The man was out—'

'Never mind that,' said Kennedy. 'Teal's got indigestion.'

'You can fix that with a bit of bicarb,' said Peters helpfully.

'So long as it isn't something more serious,' said Kennedy, reaching for the freshly arrived plate of hot buttered crumpets with a hand like a leg of mutton and the air of massive confidence which can only be achieved by a man of herculean physique who knows that his interior would never dare to give him any backchat. 'I've been noticing his face lately. I must say I've been worried about it, but I didn't like to mention it before he brought it up.'

'You mean the twitching?' asked Peters.

'Not so much the twitching as the jaundiced colour. It looks bad to me.'

'Damn it,' began Teal explosively.

'Acid,' pronounced Kennedy, engulfing crumpets. 'That's generally the beginning of the trouble. Too much acid swilling around the lining of your stomach, and where are you? In next to no time you're a walking mass of gastric ulcers. You know what happens when a gastric ulcer eats into a blood-vessel?'

'You bleed to death?' asked Peters interestedly.

'Like a shot,' said Kennedy, apparently unaware of the fact that Teal was starting to simmer and splutter like a pan full of hot grease. 'It's even worse when the ulcer makes a whacking great hole in the wall of the stomach and your dinner falls through into the abdominal cavity . . .'

Mr Teal clung to his chair and wished that he had been born deaf.

It was no consolation at all to him to recall that it had actually been the Saint himself who had started the fashion of making familiar and even disgusting comments on the shape and dimensions of the stomach under discussion, a fashion which Mr Teal's own colleagues, to their eternal disgrace, had been surprisingly quick to adopt. And now that it had been revealed that his recent irritability had been caused by acute indigestion, the joke would take a new lease of life. It is a curious but undeniable fact that a man may have a headache or a toothache or an earache and receive nothing but sympathy from those about him; but let his stomach ache and all he can expect is facetiousness of the most callous and offensive kind. Mr Teal's stomach was a magnificently well-developed organ, measuring more inches from east to west than he cared to calculate, and he was perhaps excessively sensitive about it; but in its present condition the most faintly flippant reference to it was exquisite torment.

He stood up.

'Will you excuse me, sir?' he said, with as much dignity as he could muster. 'I've got a job to do this evening.'

'Don't forget to buy some Miracle Tea on your way home,' was Kennedy's farewell.

Mr Teal walked up Victoria Street in the direction of his modest lodgings. He had no job to do at all; but it would have been physically impossible for him to have stomached another minute of the conversation he had left behind him. He walked, because he had not far to go, and the exercise helped to distract his thoughts from the feeling that his intestines were being gnawed by a colony of hungry rats. Not that the distraction was by any means complete: the rats continued their remorseless depredations. But he was able to give them only half his attention instead of the whole of it.

In the circumstances it was perhaps natural that the broadcast which had been added to his current griefs should remain vaguely present in the background of his mind. The address given had been in Victoria Street. And therefore it was perhaps not such a wild coincidence after all that he should presently have found himself gazing at a large showcard in the window of a chemist's shop which he must have been passing practically every day for the last two months.

Indigestion?
Try
Miracle Tea
3/6 a packet

Mr Teal was not even averagely gullible; but a man in his state of mind is not fully responsible for his actions. The tribulations of the last few weeks had reduced him to a state of desperation in which he would have tried a dose of prussic acid if it had been recommended with sufficient promises of alleviating his distress.

With a furtive glance around him, as if he was afraid of being caught in a disreputable act, he entered the shop and approached the counter, behind which stood a shifty-eyed young man in a soiled white coat.

'A packet of Miracle Tea,' said Mr Teal, lowering his voice to a mumble, although the shop was empty, as though he had been asking for some unmentionable merchandise.

He planked down a half-crown with unconvincing defiance.

The assistant hesitated for a moment, turned, and took an oblong yellow packet from a shelf behind him. He hesitated again, still holding it as if he was reluctant to part with it.

'Yes, sir?' he said suggestively.

'What d'you mean—"yes, sir?"' blared Mr Teal with the belligerence of increasing embarrassment.

'Isn't there something else, sir?'

'No, there isn't anything else!' retorted the detective, whose sole remaining ambition was to get out of the place as quickly as possible with his guilty purchase. 'Give me that stuff and take your money.'

He reached over and fairly snatched the yellow packet out of the young man's hand, stuffed it into his pocket, and lumbered out as if he were trying to catch a train. He was in such a hurry that he almost bowled over another customer who was just entering the shop—and this customer, for some reason, quickly averted his face.

Mr Teal was too flustered even to notice him. He went plodding more rapidly than usual on his homeward way, feeling as if his face was a bright crimson which would announce his shame to any passer-by, and never dreaming that Destiny had already grasped him firmly by the scruff of the neck.

Five minutes later he was trudging through a narrow side street within a couple of blocks of his apartment. The comatose dusk of Sunday evening lay over it like a shroud: not a single other human creature was in sight, and the only sound apart from the solid tread of his own regulation boots was a patter of hurried footsteps coming up behind him. There was nothing in that to make him turn his head ... The footsteps caught up until they were almost on his heels; and then something hit him a terrific blow on the side of the head and everything dissolved into black darkness.

II

Simon Templar's views on the subject of Chief Inspector Teal, unlike Chief Inspector Teal's views on the subject of the Saint, were apt to fluctuate between very contradictory extremes. There were times when he felt that life would lose half its savour if he were deprived of the perpetual joy of dodging Teal's constant frantic efforts to put him behind bars; but there were other times when he felt that his life would be a lot less strenuous if Teal's cardinal ambition had been a little less tenacious. There had been times when he had felt sincere remorse for the more bitter humiliations which he had sometimes been compelled to inflict on Mr Teal, even though these times had been the only alternatives to his own defeat in their endless duel; there had been other times when he could have derived much satisfaction from beating Teal over the head with a heavy bar of iron with large knobs on the end.

One thing which the Saint was certain about, however, was that his own occasional urges to assault the detective's cranium with a blunt instrument did not mean that he was at any time prepared to permit any common or garden thug to take the same liberties with that long-suffering dome.

This was the last of the coincidences of which due warning has already been given—that Simon Templar's long sleek Hirondel chanced to be taking a short cut through the back streets of the district at that fateful hour, and whirled round a corner into the one street where it was most needed at the precise moment when Teal's ample body was spreading itself over the pavement as flat as a body of that architecture can conveniently be spread without the aid of a steam-roller.

The Saint's foot on the accelerator gave the great car a last burst in the direction of the spot where these exciting things were happening, and then he stood on the brakes. The thug who had committed the assault was already bending over Teal's prostrate form when the screech of skidding tyres made him stop and look up in startled fear. For a split second he hesitated, as if considering whether to stand his ground and give battle; but something about the sinewy breadth of the Saint's shoulders and the athletic and purposeful speed with which the Saint's tall frame catapulted itself out of the still sliding car must have discouraged him. A profound antipathy to the whole scene and everyone in it appeared to overwhelm him; and he turned and began to depart from it like a stone out of a sling.

The Saint started after him. At that moment the Saint had no idea that the object of his timely rescue was Chief Inspector Teal in person; it was simply that the sight of one bloke hitting another bloke with a length of gaspipe was a spectacle which inevitably impelled him to join in the festivities with the least possible delay. But as he started in pursuit he caught his first glimpse of the fallen victim's face, and the surprise checked his stride as if he had run into a wall. He paused involuntarily to confirm the identification; and that brief delay lost him any chance he might have had of making a capture. The thug was already covering the ground with quite remarkable velocity, and the extra start he had gained from the Saint's hesitation had given him a lead which even Simon Templar's long legs doubted their ability to make up. Simon gave up the idea with a regretful sigh, and stooped to find out how much damage had been sustained by his favourite enemy.

It only took him a moment to assure himself that his existence was unlikely to be rendered permanently uneventful by the premature removal of its most pungent spice; but nevertheless there was also no doubt that Teal was temporarily in the land of dreams, and that it would do the Saint himself no good to be found standing over his sleeping body. On the other hand, to leave Mr Teal to finish his sleep in peace on the sidewalk was something which no self-respecting buccaneer could do. The actual commotion from which the situation had evolved had been practically negligible. Not a window had been flung up; not a door had been opened. The street remained sunken in its twilight torpor, and once again there was no other living soul in sight.

The Saint shrugged. There seemed to be only one thing to do, so he did it. With a certain amount of effort, he picked up Mr Teal's weighty person and heaved it into the car, dumped Teal's mackintosh and hat on top of him, picked up an oblong yellow package which had fallen out of his pocket and slung that in as well, got into the driving seat himself, and drove away.

That Simon's diagnosis had been accurate was proved by the fact that Teal was beginning to groan and blink his eyes when the Hirondel pulled up at his front door. The Saint lighted a cigarette and looked at him reproachfully.

'I'm ashamed of you,' he said. 'An old man of your age, letting yourself be picked up in the gutter like that. And not even during licensing hours, either. Where did you get the embalming fluid?'

'So it was you, was it?' Teal muttered thickly.

'I beg your pardon?'

'What the hell was the idea?' demanded Teal, with a growing indignation which left no doubt of his recovery.

'The idea of what?'

'Creeping up behind me and knocking me on the head! If you think I'm going to let you get away with that—

'Claud,' said the Saint, 'do I understand that you're accusing me again?'

'Oh, no!' Teal had his eyes wide open now, and they were red with wrath. The edge of his sarcasm was as silky and delicate as the blade of a cross-cut saw. 'It was two other people. They fell out of the sky with parachutes—'

The Saint sighed.

'I don't want to interrupt you. But can this great brain of yours see any particular reason why I should cosh you today? We haven't seen each other for ages, and so far as I know you haven't been doing anything to make me angry. And even if you had, and I thought it would be good for you to be bopped over the bean, do you think I'd take the trouble to bring you home afterwards? And even if I brought you home afterwards, do you think I'd let you wake up while I was still around, instead of bopping you again and leaving you to wake up without knowing I'd been anywhere near you? I am a very modest man, Claud,' said the Saint untruthfully, 'but there are some aspersions on my intelligence which cut me to the quick, and you always seem to be the guy who thinks of them.'

Mr Teal rubbed his head.

'Well, what did happen?' he demanded grudgingly.

'I don't really know. When I shot over the horizon, there was some guy in the act of belting you over the lid with a handy piece of lead pipe. I thought of asking him to stop and talk it over, but he ran too fast. So I just loaded you into the old jalopy and brought you home. Of course, if you really wanted to go on dozing in the gutter I can take you back.'

The detective looked about him. His aching skull was clearing a little, enough at least for him to be able to see that this latest misfortune was something which, for once, might not be chargeable to the Saint's account. This realisation did not actually improve his temper.

'Have you any idea who it was?'

'That's a large order, isn't it? If you're as charming to all your other clients as you usually are to me, I should say that London must be crawling with birds who'd pay large sums of money for the fun of whacking you on the roof with a lump of iron.'

'Well, what did this one look like?' snarled Teal impatiently.

'I'm blowed if I could draw his picture, Claud. The light was pretty bad, and he didn't stay very long. Medium height, ordinary build, thin face—nothing definite enough to help you much, I'm afraid.'

Teal grunted.

Presently he said: 'Thanks, anyway.'

He said it as if he hated to say it, which he did. Being under any obligation to the Saint hurt him almost as much as his indigestion. Promptly he wished that he hadn't thought of that comparison. His stomach, reviving from a too fleeting anaesthesia, reminded him that it was still his most constant companion. And now he had a sore and splitting head as well. He realised that he felt about as unhappy as a man can feel.

He opened the door of the car, and took hold of his raincoat and bowler hat.

'G'night,' he said.

'Good night,' said the Saint cheerfully. 'You know where I live, any time you decide you want a bodyguard.'

Mr Teal did not deign to reply. He crossed the sidewalk rather unsteadily, mounted the steps of the house, and let himself in without looking back. The door closed again behind him.

Simon chuckled as he let in the clutch and drove on towards the appointment to which he had been on his way. The episode which had just taken place would make a mildly amusing story to tell: aside from that obvious face value, he didn't give it a second thought. There was no reason why he should. There must have been enough hoodlums in the Metropolis with long-cherished dreams of vengeance against Mr Teal, aside from ordinary casual footpads, to account for the sprinting beater-up who had made such an agile getaway: the only entertaining angle was that Coincidence should have chosen the Saint himself, of all possible people, to be the rescuer.

That was as much as the Saint's powers of clairvoyance were worth on that occasion.

Two hours later, when he had parked the Hirondel in the garage at Cornwall House, his foot kicked something out of the door as he got out. It was the yellow packet that had slipped out of Teal's pocket, which had fallen on to the floor and been left there forgotten by both men.

Simon picked it up; and when he saw the label he sighed, and then grinned again. So that was a new depth to which Mr Teal had sunk; and the revelation of the detective's dyspepsia would provide a little extra piquancy to their next encounter in badinage . . .

He went on reading the exaggerated claims made for Miracle Tea on the wrapper as he rode up in the elevator to his apartment. And as he read on, a new idea came to him, an idea which could only have found a welcome in such a scapegrace sense of mischief as the Saint's. The product was called Miracle Tea, and there seemed to be no reason why it should not be endowed with miraculous properties before being returned to its owner. Chief Inspector Teal would surely be disappointed if it failed to perform miracles. And that could so easily be arranged. The admixture of a quantity of crushed senna pods, together with a certain amount of powdered calomel—the indicated specific in all cases of concussion . . .

In his own living-room, the Saint proceeded to open the packet with great care, in such a way that it could be sealed again and bear no trace of having been tampered with.

Inside, there seemed to be a second paper wrapping. He took hold of one corner of it and pulled experimentally. A complete crumpled piece of paper came out in his fingers. Below that, there was another crumpled white pad. And after that, another. It went on until the whole package was empty, and the table on which he was working was covered with those creased white scraps. But no tea came to light. He picked up one of the pieces of paper and cautiously unfolded it, in case it should be the container of an individual dose. And then suddenly he sat quite still, while his blue eyes froze into narrowed pools of electrified ice as he realised what he was looking at.

It was a Bank of England note for fifty pounds.

### III

'Miracle Tea,' said the Saint reverently, 'is a good name for it.'

There were thirty of those notes—a total of fifteen hundred pounds in unquestionably genuine cash, legal tender and ripe for immediate circulation.

There was a light step behind him, and Patricia Holm's hand fell on his shoulder.

'I didn't know you'd come in, boy,' she said; and then she didn't go on. He felt her standing unnaturally still. After some seconds she said: 'What have you been doing—breaking into the baby's money-box?'

'Getting ready to write some letters,' he said. 'How do you like the new notepaper?'

She pulled him round to face her.

'Come on,' she said. 'I like to know when you're going to be arrested. What's the charge going to be this time—burgling a bank?' He smiled at her.

She was easy to smile at. Hair like ripe corn in the sun, a skin like rose-petals, blue eyes that could be as wicked as his own, the figure of a young nymph, and something else that could not have been captured in any picture, something in her that laughed with him in all his misdeeds.

'Tea-drinking is the charge,' he said. 'I've signed the pledge, and henceforward this will be my only beverage.'

She raised her fist.

'I'll push your face in.'

'But it's true.'

He handed her the packet from which the money had come. She sat on the table and studied every side of it. And after that she was only more helplessly perplexed.

'Go on,' she said.

He told her the story exactly as it had happened.

'And now you know just as much as I do,' he concluded. 'I haven't even had time to do any thinking on it. Maybe we needn't bother. We shall wake up soon, and everything will be quite all right.'

She put the box down again and looked at one of the notes.

'Are they real?'

'There isn't a doubt of it.'

'Maybe you've got away with Teal's life savings.'

'Maybe. But he has got a bank account. And can you really see Claud Eustace hoarding his worldly wealth in packets of patent tea?'

'Then it must be evidence in some case he's working on.'

'It could be. But again, why keep it in this box?' Simon turned the yellow packet over in his supple hands. 'It was perfectly sealed before I opened it. It looked as if it had never been touched. Why should he go to all that trouble? And suppose it was evidence just as it stood, how did he know what the evidence was without opening it? If he didn't know, he'd surely have opened it on the spot, in front of witnesses. And if he did know, he had no business to take it home. Besides, if he did know that he was carrying dangerous evidence, he wouldn't have had to think twice about what motive there might be for slugging him on his way home; but he didn't seem to have the slightest idea what it was all about.'

Patricia frowned.

'Could he be taking graft? This might be a way of slipping him the money.'

Simon thought that over for a while; but in the end he shook his head.

'We've said a lot of rude things about Claud Eustace in our

time, but I don't think even we could ever have said that seriously. He may be a nuisance, but he's so honest that it runs out of his ears. And still again, he'd have known what he was carrying, and known what anybody who slugged him might have been after, and the first thing he did when he woke up would have been to see if he'd still got the dough. But he didn't. He didn't even feel in his pockets.'

'But wasn't he knocked silly?'

'Not that silly.'

'Perhaps he was quite sure what had happened, and didn't want to give himself away.'

'With me sitting beside him? If he'd even thought he'd lost something valuable, it wouldn't have been quite so easy for me to convince him that I wasn't the warrior with the gaspipe. He could have arrested me himself and searched me on the spot without necessarily giving anything away.'

The girl shrugged despairingly. 'All right. So you think of something.' The Saint lighted a cigarette.

'I suppose I'm barmy, but there's only one thing I can think of. Claud Eustace didn't have the foggiest idea what was in the packet. He had a pain in his tum-tum, and he just bought it for medicine on the way home. It was meant to be handed to someone else, and the fellow in the shop got mixed up. As soon as Teal's gone out with it, the right man comes in, and there is a good deal of commotion. Somebody realises what's happened, and goes dashing after Teal to get the packet back. He bends his blunt instrument over Teal's head, and is just about to frisk him when I arrive and spoil everything, and he has to lam. I take Teal home, and Teal has something else to think about besides his tummy-ache, so he forgets all about his Miracle Tea, and I win it. And is it something to win!'

The Saint's eyes were kindling with an impish excitement that had no direct connection with the windfall that had just dropped into his lap. Patricia did not need him to say any more to tell her what was going on in his mind. To the Saint, any puzzle was a potential adventure; and the Saint on the trail of adventure was a man transformed, a dynamic focus of ageless and superhuman forces against which no ordinary mortal could argue. She had known him so well for so many years, had known so long that he was beyond her power to change, even if she had wished to change him.

She said slowly: 'But what is the racket?'

'That would be worth knowing,' he said; and he had no need to say that he intended to know. He leaned back ecstatically. 'But just think of it, darling! If we could only see the uproar and agitation that must be going on at this minute in the place where this tea came from . . .'

As a matter of record, the quality of the uproar and the agitation in the shop where Mr Teal had made his purchase would not have disappointed him at all; although in fact it had preceded this conversation by some time.

Mr Henry Osbett, registered proprietor of the drug store at 909, Victoria Street, which was also the registered premises of the Miracle Tea Company, was normally a man of quite distinguished and even haughty aspect, being not only tall and erect, but also equipped with a pair of long and gracefully curved moustaches which stuck out on either side of his face like the wings of a soaring gull, which gave him a rather old-fashioned military air in spite of his horn-rimmed glasses. Under the stress of emotion, however, his dignity was visibly frayed. He listened to his shifty-eyed assistant's explanations with fuming impatience.

'How was I to know?' the young man was protesting. 'He came at exactly the right time, and I've never seen Nancock before. I didn't mean to give him the packet without the password, but he snatched it right out of my hand and rushed off.'

'Excuses!' snarled the chemist, absent-mindedly grabbing handfuls of his whiskers and tying them in knots. 'Why, if you'd even known who he was—'

'I didn't know—not until Nancock told me. How could I know?'

'At least you could have got the package back.'

The other swallowed.

'I'd only have got myself caught,' he said sullenly. 'That chap who jumped out of the car was twice my size. He'd've killed me!'

Mr Osbett stopped maltreating his moustache and looked at him for a long moment in curiously contrasting immobility.

'That might have saved someone else the trouble,' he said; and the tone in which he said it made the young man's face turn grey.

Osbett's cold stare lasted for a moment longer; and then he took a fresh grip on his whiskers and turned and scuttled through to the back of the shop. One might almost have thought that he had gone off in the full flush of enthusiasm to fetch an axe.

Beyond the dispensing room there was a dark staircase. As he mounted the stairs his gait and carriage changed in subtle ways until it was as if a different man had entered his clothes. On the upper landing his movements were measured and deliberate. He opened a door and went into a rather shabby and nondescript room which served as his private office. There were two or three old-fashioned filing cabinets, a littered desk with the polish worn off at the edges, a dingy carpet, and a couple of junk-store chairs. Mr Osbett sat down at the desk and opened a packet of cheap cigarettes.

He was a very worried man, and with good reason; but he no longer looked flustered. He had, at that moment, a very cold-blooded idea of his position. He was convinced that Teal's getaway with the packet of Miracle Tea had been neither premeditated nor intentional—otherwise there would have been further developments before this. It had simply been one of those fantastic accidents which lie in wait for the most careful conspiracies. That was a certain consolation; but not much. As soon as the contents of the packet were opened there would be questions to answer; and while it was quite certain that nothing criminal could be proved from any answers he cared to give, it would still make him the object of an amount of suspicious attention which might easily lead to disaster later. There remained the chance that Teal might not decide to actually take a dose of Miracle Tea for some hours yet, and it was a chance that had to be seized quickly.

After another moment's intensive consideration, Mr Osbett picked up the telephone.

## IV

Simon Templar had been out and come in again after a visit to the nearest chemist. Now he was industriously stirring an interesting mixture in a large basin borrowed from the kitchen. Patricia Holm sat in an armchair and watched him despairingly.

'Did you ever hear a proverb about little things pleasing little minds?' she said.

Unabashed, the Saint put down his spoon and admired his handiwork. To any but the most minute examination, it looked exactly like a high-grade small-leaf tea. And some of it was. The other ingredients were hardly less ordinary, except in that particular combination.

'Did you ever hear another proverb about a prophet in his own country?' he answered. 'If you had a little more reverence for my mind, you'd see that it was nearly double its normal size. Don't you get the idea?'

'Not yet.'

'This is what I originally meant to do. Maybe it wasn't such a huge idea then; although if I could get enough little ideas that handed me fifteen hundred quid a time I wouldn't worry so much about passing up the big stuff. But still that was just good clean fun. Now it's more than that. If I'm right, and Teal still doesn't know what he had in his pocket this afternoon, we don't want him to even start thinking about it. Therefore I just want to return him his Miracle Tea, and I'll be sure he won't give it another thought. But I never had any Miracle Tea. Therefore I've got to concoct a passable substitute. I don't know the original formula; but if this recipe doesn't live up to the name, I'll drink a gallon of it.'

'Of course,' she said, 'you couldn't just go out and buy another packet to give him.'

Simon gazed at her in stunned admiration.

'Could you believe that I never thought of that?'

'No,' said Patricia.

'Maybe you're right,' said the Saint ruefully.

He gave the basin another stir, and shrugged.

'Anyway,' he said, 'it'd be a pity to waste all this work, and the chance of a lifetime as well.'

He sat down at the table and cheerfully proceeded to pack his own remarkable version of Miracle Tea into the original carton. Having stuffed it full, he replaced the seals and wrappings with as much care as he had removed them; and when he had finished there was not a trace to show that the package had ever been tampered with.

'What will you do if he dies?' asked the girl.

'Send a wreath of tea roses to his funeral,' said the Saint. He put down the completed packet after he had inspected it closely from every angle, and moved himself over to a more comfortable lounging site on the settee. His eyes were alert and hot with a gathering zest of devilment. 'Now we go into the second half of this brilliant conspiracy.'

'What does that mean?'

'Finding out where Claud Eustace buys fifteen hundred quid for half a dollar. Just think, sweetheart—we can go shopping once a week and keep ourselves in caviar without ever doing another stroke of work!'

He reached for the telephone and set it on his lap while he dialled Teal's private number with a swift and dancing forefinger. The telephone, he knew, was beside Teal's bed; and the promptness with which his ring was answered established the detective's location with quite miraculous certainty.

'I hope,' said the Saint, with instantaneous politeness, 'that I haven't interrupted you in the middle of any important business, Claud.'

The receiver did not actually explode in his ear. It was a soundly constructed instrument, designed to resist spontaneous detonation. It did, however, appear to feel some strain in reproducing the cracked-foghorn cadence in which the answering voice said: 'Who's that?'

'And how,' said the Saint, 'is the little tum-tum tonight?'

Mr Teal did not repeat his question. He had no need to. There was only one voice in the whole world which was capable of inquiring after his stomach with the exact inflexion which was required to make that hypersensitive organ curl up into tight knots that sent red and yellow flashes squirting across his eyeballs.

Mr Teal did not groan aloud; but a mute organic groan swept through him like a cramp from his fingertips to his toes.

It is true that he was in bed, and it is also true that he had been interrupted in the middle of some important business; but that important business had been simply and exclusively concerned with trying to drown his multitudinous woes in sleep. For a man in the full bloom of health to be smitten over the nob with a blunt instrument is usually a somewhat trying experience; but for a man in Mr Teal's dyspeptic condition to be thus beaned is ultimate disaster. Mr Teal now had two fearful pains rivalling for his attention, which he had been trying to give to neither. The only way of evading this responsibility which he had been able to think of had been to go to bed and go to sleep, which is what he had set out to do as soon as the Saint had left him at his door; but sleep had steadfastly eluded him until barely five minutes before the telephone bell had blared its recall to conscious suffering into his anguished ear. And when he became aware that the emotions which he had been caused by that recall had been wrung out of him for no better object than to answer some Saintly badinage about his abdomen, his throat closed up so that it was an effort for him to breathe.

'Is that all you want to know?' he got out in a strangled squawk. 'Because if so—'

'But it bothers me, Claud. You know how I love your tummy. It would break my heart if anything went wrong with it.'

'Who told you anything was wrong with it?'

'Only my famous deductive genius. Or do you mean to tell me you drink Miracle Tea because you like it?'

There was a pause. With the aid of television, Mr Teal could have been seen to wriggle. The belligerent blare crumpled out of his voice.

'Oh,' he said weakly. 'What miracle tea?'

'The stuff you had in your pocket this afternoon. I threw it into the car with your other things when I picked you up, but we forgot it when you got out. I've just found it. Guaranteed to cure indigestion, colic, flatulence, constipation, venomous bile, spots before the eyes ... I didn't know you had so many troubles, Claud.'

'I haven't!' Teal roared defiantly. His stomach promptly performed two complicated and unprecedented evolutions and made a liar of him. He winced, and floundered. 'I—I just happened to hear it advertised on the radio, and then I saw another advertisement in a shop window on the way home, so I thought I'd try some. I—I haven't been feeling very fit lately—'

'Then I certainly think you ought to try something,' said the Saint charitably. 'I'll beetle over with your poison right away; and if I can help out with a spot of massage, you only have to say the word.'

Mr Teal closed his eyes. Of all the things he could think of which might aggravate his miseries, a visit from the Saint at that time was the worst.

'Thanks,' he said with frantic earnestness, 'but all I want now is to get some sleep. Bring it over some other time, Saint.'

Simon reached thoughtfully for a cigarette.

'Just as you like, Claud. Shall we say the May Fair tomorrow, at four o'clock?'

'You could send it round,' Teal said desperately. 'Or just throw it away, I can get some more. If it's any bother—'

'No bother at all, dear old collywobble. Let's call it a date. Tomorrow at four—and we'll have a cup of tea together . . .'

The Saint laid the telephone gently back on its bracket and replaced it on the table beside him. His thumb flicked over the wheel of his lighter; and the tip of his cigarette kindled to a glow that matched the brightening gleam of certainty in his blue eyes.

He had obtained all the information he wanted without pressing a single conspicuous question. Mr Teal had bought his Miracle Tea on the way home—and Simon knew that Mr Teal's way home, across Parliament Square and up Victoria Street, was so rigidly established by years of unconscious habit that a blind man could almost have followed it by tracing the groove which the detective's regulation boots must by that time have worn along the pavement. Even if there were more than one chemist's along that short trail with a Miracle Tea advertisement in the window, the process of elimination could not take long . . .

Patricia was watching him. She said: 'So what?'

'So we were right,' said the Saint; and his voice was lilting with incorrigible magic. 'Claud doesn't give a damn about his tea. It doesn't mean a thing in his young life. He doesn't care if he never sees it again. He just bought it by a fluke, and he doesn't even know what sort of a fluke it was.'

'Are you sure?' asked Patricia cautiously. 'If he just doesn't want you to suspect anything—'

The Saint shook his head.

'I know all Claud's voices much too well. If he'd tried to get away with anything like that, I should have heard it. And why should he try? I offered to bring it round at once, and he could have just said nothing and let me bring it. Why should he take any risk at all of something going wrong when he could have had the package back in half an hour. Teal may look dumb sometimes, but you can't see him being so dumb as that.' Simon stood up, and his smile was irresistibly expectant. 'Come out into the wide world with me, darling, and let's look for this shop where they sell miracles!'

His energy carried her off like a tide-race; the deep purr of the Hirondel as he drove it at fantastic speed to Parliament Square was in tune with his mood. Why it should have happened again, like this, he didn't know; but it might as well have been this way as any other. Whatever the way, it had been bound to happen. Destiny could never leave him alone for long, and it must have been at least a week since anything exciting had happened to him. But now that would all be put right, and there would be trouble and adventure and mystery again, and with a little luck some boodle at the end; that was all that mattered. Somewhere in this delirious business of Miracle Tea and Bank of England notes there must be crime and dark conspiracies and all manner of mischief—he couldn't surmise yet what kind of racket could subsist on trading handfuls of banknotes for half-crowns, but it was even harder to imagine anything like that in a line of legitimate business, so some racket or other it must be, and new rackets could never be altogether dull.

He parked the car illegally on the corner of Victoria Street, and got out.

'Let's walk,' he said.

He took Patricia's arm and strolled with her up the street; and as they went he burbled exuberantly.

'Maybe it's an eccentric millionaire who suffered from acute dyspepsia all his life, and in his will he directed that all his fortune was to be distributed among other sufferers, because he knew that there really wasn't any cure at all, but at least the money would be some consolation. So without any publicity his executors had the dough wrapped up in packets labelled as an indigestion cure, feeling pretty sure that nobody who didn't have indigestion would buy it, and thereby saving themselves the trouble of sorting through a lot of applicants with bogus belly-aches . . . Or maybe it's some guy who has made all the money in the world out of defrauding the poor nitwitted public with various patent medicines, whose conscience has pricked him in his old age so that he is trying to fix himself up for the Hereafter by making restitution, and the most appropriate way he can think of to do that is to distribute the geetus in the shape of another patent medicine, figuring that that is the way it's most likely to fall into the same hands that it originally came from . . . Or maybe—'

'Or maybe,' said Patricia, 'this is the place you're looking for.'

Simon stopped walking and looked at it.

There was a showcard in the centre of the window—the same card, as a matter of fact, which Mr Teal had seen. But the Saint was taking no chances.

'Let's make sure,' he said.

He led her the rest of the way up the street for a block beyond the turning where Mr Teal would have branched off on the most direct route to his lodgings, and back down the opposite side; but no other drug-store window revealed a similar sign.

Simon stood on the other side of the road again, and gazed across at the brightly lighted window which they had first looked at. He read the name 'Henry Osbett & Co.' across the front of the shop.

He let go Patricia's arm.

'Toddle over, darling,' he said, 'and buy me a packet of Miracle Tea.'

'What happens if I get shot?' she asked suspiciously.

'I shall hear the bang,' he said, 'and phone for an ambulance.'

Two minutes later she rejoined him with a small neat parcel in her hand. He fell in beside her as she came across the road, and turned in the direction of the lower end of the street, where he had left the car.

'How was Comrade Osbett?' he murmured. 'Still keeping up with the world?'

'He looked all right, if he was the fellow who served me.' She passed him the packet she was carrying. 'Now do you mind telling me what good this is supposed to do?'

'We must listen to one of their broadcasts and find out. According to the wrapper, it disperses bile—'

She reached across to his hip pocket, and he laughed.

'OK, darling. Don't waste any bullets—we may need them. I

just wanted to find out if there were any curious features about buying Miracle Tea, and I didn't want to go in myself because I'm liable to want to go in again without being noticed too much.'

'I didn't see anything curious,' she said. 'I just asked for it, and he wrapped it up and gave it to me.'

'No questions or stalling?'

'No. It was just like buying a toothbrush or anything else.'

'Didn't he seem to be at all interested in who was buying it?'

'Not a bit.'

He held the package to his ear, shook it, and crunched it speculatively.

'We'll have a drink somewhere and see if we've won anything,' he said.

At a secluded corner table in the Florida, a while later, he opened the packet, with the same care to preserve the seals and wrappings as he had given to the first consignment, and tipped out the contents on to a plate. The contents, to any ordinary examination, consisted of nothing but tea—and, by the smell and feel of it, not very good tea either.

The Saint sighed, and called a waiter to remove the mess.

'It looks as if we were wrong about that eccentric millionaire,' he said. 'Or else the supply of do-re-mi has run out ... Well, I suppose we shall just have to go to work again.' He folded the container and stowed it carefully away in his pocket; and if he was disappointed he was able to conceal his grief. A glimmer of reckless optimism curled the corners of his mouth. 'You know, darling, I have a hunch that some interesting things are going to happen before this time tomorrow night.'

He was a better prophet than he knew, and it took only a few hours to prove it.


V


Simon Templar slept like a child. A thunderstorm bursting over his roof would not have woken him; a herd of wild elephants stampeding past his bed would scarcely have made him stir; but one kind of noise that other ears might not have heard at all even in full wakefulness brought him back instantaneously to life with every faculty sharpened and on tiptoe.

He awoke in a breathless flash, like a watchdog, without the slightest perceptible alteration in his rate of breathing or any sudden movement. Anyone standing over him would not have even sensed the change that had taken place. But his eyes were half open, and his wits were skidding back over his last split second of sleep like the recoil of taut elastic, searching for a definition of the sound that had roused him.

The luminous face of a clock across the room told him that he had slept less than two hours. And the thinly phosphorescent hands hadn't moved on enough for the naked eye to see when he knew why he was awake.

In the adjoining living-room, something human had moved.

Simon drew down the automatic from under his pillow and slid out of bed like a phantom. He left the communicating door alone, and sidled noiselessly through the other door which led out into the hall. The front door was open just enough to split the darkness with a knife-edge of illumination from the lights on the landing outside: he eased over to it like a cat, slipped his fingers through the gap, and felt the burred edges of the hole which had been drilled through the outside of the frame so that the catch of the spring lock could be pushed back.

A light blinked beyond the open door of the living-room. The Saint came to the entrance and looked in. Silhouetted against the subdued glow of an electric torch he saw the shape of a man standing by the table with his back to the door, and his bare feet padded over the carpet without a breath of sound until they were almost under the intruder's heels. He leaned over until his lips were barely a couple of inches from the visitor's right ear.

'Boo,' said the Saint.

It was perhaps fortunate for the intruder that he had a strong heart, for if he had had the slightest cardiac weakness the nervous shock which spun him round would have probably popped it like a balloon. As it was, an involuntary yammer of sheer primitive fright dribbled out of his throat before he lashed out blindly in no less instinctive self-defence.

Simon had anticipated that. He was crouching almost to his knees by that time, and his left arm snaked around the lower part of the man's legs simultaneously with a quick thrust of his shoulder against the other's thighs.

The burglar went over backwards with a violent thud; and as most of his breath jolted out of him he freighted it with a selection of picturesque expletives which opened up new vistas of biologic theory. One hand, swinging up in a vicious arc, was caught clearly in the beam of the fallen flashlight, and it was not empty.

'I think,' said the Saint, 'we can do without the persuader.'

He jabbed the muzzle of his gun very hard into the place where his guest's ribs forked, and heard a satisfactory gasp of pain in response. His left hand caught the other's wrist as it descended, twisted with all the skill of a manipulative surgeon, and let go again to grab the life-preserver as it dropped out of the man's numbed fingers.

'You mustn't hit people with things like this,' he said reprovingly. 'It hurts . . . Doesn't it?'

The intruder, with jagged stars shooting through his head, did not offer an opinion; but his squirming lost nearly all of its early vigour. The Saint sat on him easily, and made sure that there were no other weapons on his person before he stood up again. The main lights clicked on with a sudden dazzling brightness. Patricia Holm stood in the doorway, the lines of her figure draping exquisite contours into the folds of a filmy négligé, her fair hair tousled with sleep and hazy startlement in her blue eyes.

'I'm sorry,' she said. 'I didn't know you had company.'

'That's all right,' said the Saint. 'We're keeping open house.'

He lounged back to rest the base of his spine against the edge of the table and inspected the caller in more detail. He saw a short-legged barrel-chested individual with a thatch of carroty hair, a wide coarse-lipped mouth, and a livid scar running from one side of a flattened nose to near the lobe of a misshapen ear; and recognition dawned in his gaze.

He waved his gun in a genial gesture.

'You remember our old pal and playmate, Red McGuire?' he murmured. 'Just back from a holiday at Parkhurst after his last job of robbery with violence. Somebody told him about all those jewels we keep around, and he couldn't wait to drop in and see them. Why didn't you ring the bell, Red, and save yourself the trouble of carving up our door?'

McGuire sat on the floor and tenderly rubbed his head.

'OK,' he growled, 'I can do without the funny stuff. Go on an' call the cops.'

Simon considered the suggestion. It seemed a very logical procedure. But it left an unfinished edge of puzzlement still in his mind.

There was something about finding himself the victim of an ordinary burglary that didn't quite ring bells. He knew well enough that his reputation was enough to make any ordinary burglar steer as far away from him as the landscape would allow. And serious burglars didn't break into any dwelling chosen at random and hope for the best, without even knowing the identity of the occupant—certainly not burglars with the professional status of Red McGuire. Therefore . . .

His eyes drained detail from the scene with fine-drawn intentness. Nothing seemed to have been touched. Perhaps he had arrived too quickly for that. Everything was as he had left it when he went to bed. Except—The emptied packet of Miracle Tea which Patricia had bought for him that evening was still in his coat pocket. The packet which he had refilled for Teal's personal consumption was still on the table . . . Or was it?

For on the floor, a yard from where Red McGuire had fallen, lay another identical packet of Miracle Tea.

Simon absorbed the jar of realisation without batting an eyelid.

But a slowly increasing joy crept into the casual radiance of his smile.

'Why ask me to be so unfriendly, Red?' he drawled. 'After all, what's a packet of tea between friends?'

If he needed any confirmation of his surmise, he had it in the way Red McGuire's small green eyes circled the room and froze on the yellow carton beside him before they switched furtively back to the Saint's face. 'Wot tea?' McGuire mumbled sullenly.

'Miracle Tea,' said the Saint gently. 'The juice that pours balm into the twinging tripes. That's what you came here for tonight, Red. You came here to swipe my beautiful packet of gut-grease and leave some phony imitation behind instead!'

McGuire glowered at him stubbornly. 'I dunno wot yer talkin' abaht.'

'Don't you?' said the Saint, and his smile had become almost affectionate. 'Then you're going to find the next half-hour tremendously instructive.'

He straightened up and reached over for a steel chair that stood close to him, and slid it across in the direction of his guest.

'Don't you find the floor rather hard?' he said. 'Take a pew and make yourself happy, because it looks as if we may be in for a longish talk.'

A wave of his gun added a certain amount of emphasis to the invitation, and there was a crispness in his eyes that carried even more emphasis than the gun.

McGuire hauled himself up hesitantly and perched on the edge of the chair. And the Saint beamed at him.

'Now if you'll look in the top drawer of the desk, Pat—I think there's quite a collection of handcuffs there. About three pairs ought to be enough. One for each of his ankles, and one to fasten his hands behind him.'

McGuire shifted where he sat.

'Wot's the idea?' he demanded uneasily.

'Just doing everything we can to make you feel at home,' answered the Saint breezily. 'Would you mind putting your hands behind you so that the lady can fix you up? . . . Thanks ever so much . . . Now if you'll just move your feet back up against the legs of the chair—'

Rebellious rage boiled behind the other's sulky scowl, a rage that had its roots in a formless but intensifying fear. But the Saint's steady hand held the conclusive argument, and he kept that argument accurately aligned on McGuire's wishbone until the last cuff had been locked in place and the strong-arm expert was shackled to the steel chair-frame as solidly as if he had been riveted on to it.

Then Simon put down his automatic and languidly flipped open the cigarette-box.

'I hate to do this to you,' he said conversationally, 'but we've really got to do something about that memory of yours. Or have you changed your mind about answering a few questions?'

McGuire glared at him without replying.

Simon touched a match to his cigarette and glanced at Patricia through a placid trail of smoke.

'Can I trouble you some more, darling? If you wouldn't mind plugging in that old electric curling-iron of yours—'

McGuire's eyes jerked, and the handcuffs clinked as he strained suddenly against them.

'Go on, why don't yer call the cops?' he blurted hoarsely. 'You can't do anything to me!'

The Saint strolled over to him.

'Just who do you think is going to stop me?' he asked kindly.

He slipped his hands down inside McGuire's collar, one on each side of the neck, and ripped his shirt open clear to the waist with one swift wrench that sprang the buttons pinging across the room like bullets.

'Get it good and hot, darling,' he said over his shoulder, 'and we'll see how dear old Red likes the hair on his chest waved.'

## VI

Red McGuire stared up at the Saint's gentle smile and ice-cold eyes, and the breath stopped in his throat. He was by no means a timorous man, but he knew when to be afraid—or thought he did.

'You ain't given me a chance, guv'nor,' he whined. 'Why don't yer arsk me somethink I can answer? I don't want to give no trouble.'

Simon turned away from him to flash a grin at Patricia—a grin that McGuire was never meant to see.

'Go ahead and get the iron, sweetheart,' he said, with blood-curdling distinctness, and winked at her. 'Just in case dear old Red changes his mind.'

Then the wink and the grin vanished together as he whipped round on his prisoner.

'All right,' he snapped. 'Tell me all you know about Miracle Tea!'

'I dunno anythink about it, so help me, guv'nor. I never heard of it before tonight. All I know is I was told to come here wiv a packet, an' if I found another packet here I was to swop them over an' bring your packet back. That's all I know about it, strike me dead if it ain't.'

'I shall probably strike you dead if it is,' said the Saint coldly. 'D'you mean to tell me that Comrade Osbett didn't say any more than that?'

'Who's that?'

'I said Osbett. You know who I'm talking about.'

'I never heard of 'im.'

Simon moved towards him with one fist drawn back.

'That's Gawd's own truth!' shouted McGuire desperately. 'I said I'd tell yer anythink I could, didn't I? It ain't my fault if I don't know everythink—'

'Then who was it told you to come here and play tea-parties?'

'I dunno . . . Listen!' begged McGuire frantically. 'This is a squeal, ain't it? Well, why won't yer believe me? I tell yer, I don't know. It was someone who met me when I come out of stir. I dunno wot his name is, an' in this business yer don't arsk questions. He ses to me, would I like fifty quid a week to do any dirty work there is going, more or less. I ses, for fifty quid a week I'll do anything he can think of. So he gives me twenty quid on account, an' tells me to go anywhere where there's a telephone an' just sit there beside it until he calls me. So tonight he rings up—'

'And you never knew who he was?'

'Never in me life, strike me dead—'

'How do you get the rest of your money?'

'He just makes a date to meet me somewhere an' hands it over.'

'And you don't even know where he lives?'

'So help me, I don't. All I got is a phone number where I can ring him.'

'What is this number?'

'Berkeley 3100.'

Simon studied him calculatingly. The story had at least a possibility of truth, and the way McGuire told it it sounded convincing. But the Saint didn't let any premature camaraderie soften his implacably dissecting gaze.

He said: 'What sort of a guy is he?'

'A tall thin foreign-looking bloke wiv a black beard.'

It still sounded possible. Whatever Mr Osbett's normal appearance might be, and whatever kind of racket he might be in, he might easily be anxious not to have his identity known by such dubiously efficient subordinates as Red McGuire.

'And exactly how,' said the Saint, 'did your foreign-looking bloke know that I had any miracles in the house?'

'I dunno—'

Patricia Holm came back into the room with a curling-iron that glowed dull red.

Simon turned and reached for it.

'You're just in time, darling,' he murmured. 'Comrade McGuire's memory is going back on him again.'

Comrade McGuire gaped at the hot iron, and licked his lips.

'I found that out meself, guv'nor,' he said hurriedly. 'I was goin' to tell yer—'

'How did you find out?'

'I heard somethink on the telephone.'

The Saint's eyes narrowed.

'Where?'

'In the fust house I went to—somewhere near Victoria Station. That was where I was told to go fust an' swop over the tea. I got in all right, but the bloke was there in the bedroom. I could hear 'im tossing about in bed. I was standin' outside the door, wondering if I should jump in an' cosh him, when the telephone rang. I listened to wot he said, an' all of a sudding I guessed it was about some tea, an' then once he called you "Saint," an' I knew who he must be talkin' to. So I got out again an' phoned the guv'nor an' told him about it; an' he ses, go ahead an' do the same thing here.'

Simon thought back over his conversation with Mr Teal; and belief grew upon him. No liar could have invented that story, for it hung on the fact of a telephone call which nobody else besides Teal and Patricia and himself could have known about.

He could see how the mind of Mr Osbett would have worked on it. Mr Osbett would already know that someone had interrupted the attempt to recover the package of tea from Chief Inspector Teal on his way home, that that someone had arrived in a car, and that he had presumably driven Teal the rest of the way after the rescue. If someone was phoning Teal later about a packet of tea, the remainder of the sequence of accidents would only have taken a moment to reconstruct ... And when the Saint thought about it, he would have given a fair percentage of his fifteen hundred pounds for a glimpse of Mr Osbett's face when he learned into what new hands the packet of tea had fallen.

He still looked at Red McGuire.

'How would you like to split this packet of tea with me?' he asked casually. McGuire blinked at him.

'Blimey, guv'nor, wot would I do wiv arf a packet of tea?'

Simon did not try to enlighten him. The answer was enough

to consolidate the conclusion he had already reached. Red McGuire really didn't know what it was all about—that was also becoming credible. After all, any intelligent employer would know that Red McGuire was not a man who could be safely led into temptation.

The Saint had something else to think about. His own brief introductory anonymity was over, and henceforward all the attentions of the ungodly would be lavished on himself—while he was still without one single solid target to shoot back at.

He sank into a chair and blew the rest of his cigarette into a meditative chain of smoke-rings; and then he crushed the butt into an ashtray and looked at McGuire again.

'What happens to your fifty-quid-a-week job if you go back to stir, Red?' he inquired deliberately.

The thug chewed his teeth.

'I s'pose it's all over with, guv'nor.'

'How would you like to phone your boss now—for me?'

Fear swelled in McGuire's eyes again as the Saint's meaning wore its way relentlessly into his understanding. His mouth opened once or twice without producing any sound.

'Yer carn't arsk me to do that!' he got out at last. 'If he knew I'd double-crorst 'im—he said—'

Simon rose with a shrug.

'Just as you like,' he said carelessly. 'But one of us is going to use the telephone, and I don't care which it is. If I ring up Vine Street and tell 'em to come over and fetch you away, I should think you'd get about ten years, with a record like yours. Still, they say it's a healthy life, with no worries—'

'Wait a minute,' McGuire said chokily. 'What do you do if I make this call?'

'I'll give you a hundred quid in cash; and I'll guarantee that when I'm through with your boss he won't be able to do any of those things he promised.'

McGuire was no mathematician, but he could do simple arithmetic. He gulped something out of his throat.

'OK,' he grunted. 'It's a bet.'

Simon summed him up for a moment longer, and then hauled his chair over to within reach of the table where the telephone stood. He picked up the receiver and prodded his forefinger into the first perforation of the dial.

'All you're going to do,' he said, as he went on spelling out BER 3100, 'is to tell the big bearded chief that you've been through this place with a fine comb, and the only tea-leaf in it is yourself. Do you get it? No Saint, no tea—no soap . . . And I don't want to frighten you or anything like that, Red, but I just want you to remember that if you try to say any more than that, I've still got you here, and we can easily warm up the curling-tongs again.'

'Don't yer think I know wot's good for me?' retorted the other sourly.

The Saint nodded warily, and heard the ring of the call in the receiver. It was answered almost at once, in a sharp cultured voice with a slight foreign intonation.

'Yes? Who is that?'

Simon put the mouthpiece to McGuire's lips.

'McGuire calling,' said the burglar thickly.

'Well?'

'No luck, guv'nor. It ain't here. The Saint's out, so I had plenty of time. I couldn't've helped findin' it if it'd been here.'

There was a long pause.

'All right,' said the voice curtly. 'Go home and wait for further orders. I'll call you tomorrow.'

The line went down with a click.

'And I wouldn't mind betting,' said the Saint, as he put the receiver back, 'that that's the easiest hundred quid you ever earned.'

McGuire tugged impatiently at his manacles.

'Well, yer got wot yer wanted, didn't yer?' he snarled. 'Come on an' take orf these ruddy bracelets an' let me go.'

The Saint shook his head.

'Not quite so fast, brother,' he said. 'You might think of calling up your boss again and having another chat with him before you went to bed, and I'd hate him to get worried at this hour of the night. You stay right where you are and get some of that beauty sleep which you need so badly, because after what I'm going to do tomorrow your boss may be looking for you with a gun!'

### VII

Early rising had never been one of the Saint's favourite virtues, but there were times when business looked more important than leisure. It was eleven o'clock the next morning—an hour at which he was usually beginning to think drowsily about breakfast—when he sauntered into the apothecarium of Mr Henry Osbett.

In honour of the occasion, he had put on his newest and most beautiful suit, a creation in pearl-grey fresco over which his tailor had shed tears of ecstasy in the fitting-room; his piratically tilted hat was unbelievably spotless; his tie would have humbled the gaudiest hues of dawn. He had also put on, at less expense, a vacuous expression and an inanely chirpy grin that completed the job of typing him to the point where his uncle, the gouty duke, loomed almost visibly in his background.

The shifty-eyed young assistant who came to the counter might have been pardoned for keeling over backwards at the spectacle; but he only recoiled half a step and uttered a perfunctory 'Yes, sir?'

He looked nervous and preoccupied. Simon wondered whether this nervousness and preoccupation might have had some connection with a stout and agitated-looking man who had entered the shop a few yards ahead of the Saint himself. Simon's brightly vacant eyes took in the essential items of the topography without appearing to notice anything—the counter with its showcases and displays of patent pills and liver salts, the glazed compartment at one end where presumably prescriptions were dispensed, the dark doorway at the other end which must have led to the intimate fastnesses of the establishment. Nowhere was the stout man visible; therefore, unless he had dissolved into thin air, or disguised himself as a bottle of bunion cure, he must have passed through that one doorway ... The prospects began to look even more promising than the Saint had expected ...

'This jolly old tea, old boy,' bleated the Saint, producing a package from his pocket. 'A friend of mine—chappie named Teal, y'know, great detective and all that sort of thing—bought it off you last night and then decided he wouldn't risk taking it. He was goin' to throw it down the drain; but I said to him, "Why waste a perfectly good half-dollar, what?" I said. "I'll bet they'll change it for a cake of soap, or something," I said. "I'll take it in and change it myself," I told him. That's right, isn't it? You will change it, won't you?'

The shifty-eyed youth was a bad actor. His face had gone white, then red, and finally compromised by remaining blotchy. He gaped at the packet as if he was really starting to believe that there were miracles in Miracle Tea.

'We—we should be glad to change it for you, sir,' he gibbered.

'Fine!' chortled the Saint. 'That's just what I told jolly old Teal. You take the tea, and give me a nice box of soap. I expect Teal can use that, but I'm dashed if I know what he could do with tea—'

He was talking to a vanishing audience. The youth, with a spluttered 'Excuse me, sir,' had grabbed the package off the counter and was already making a dive for the doorway at the far end; and the imbecile grin melted out of the Saint's face like a wax mould from a casting of hot bronze.

One skeleton instant after the assistant had disappeared, he was over the counter with the swift silence of a cat.

But even if he had made any noise, it is doubtful whether the other would have noticed it. The shifty-eyed youth was so drunk with excitement that his brain had for the time being practically ceased to function. If it hadn't he might have stopped to wonder why Mr Teal should have handed the tea to a third party; or why the third party, being so obviously a member of the idle rich, should have even bothered about exchanging it for a box of soap.

He might have asked himself a great many inconvenient questions; but he didn't. Perhaps the peculiarly fatuous and guileless character which the Saint had adopted for the interview had something to do with that egregious oversight—at least, that was what Simon Templar had hoped for . . . And it is at least certain that the young man went blundering up the stairs without a backward glance, while the Saint glided like a ghost into the gloomy passage-way at the foot of the stairs . . .

In the dingy upper room which was the young man's destination, Mr Osbett was entertaining the stout and agitated man. That is to say, he was talking to him. The agitated man did not look very entertained.

'It's no good cursing me, Nancock,' Osbett was saying, in his flustered old-maidish way. 'If you'd been on time last night—'

'I was on time!' yelped the perspiring Mr Nancock. 'It was that young idiot's fault for handing the package over without the password—and to Teal, of all people. I tell you, I've been through hell! Waiting for something to happen every minute—waiting, waiting . . . It isn't even safe for me to be here now—'

'That's true,' said Osbett, with one of his curiously abrupt transformations to deadly coldness. 'Who told you to come here?'

'I came here because I want my money!' bawled the other hysterically. 'What do you think I've done your dirty work for? Do you think I'd have taken a risk like this if I didn't need the money? Is it my fault if your fool of an assistant gives the money to the wrong man? I don't care a damn for your penny-dreadful precautions, and all this nonsense about signs and countersigns and keeping out of sight. What good has that done this time? I tell you, if I think you're trying to cheat me—'

'Cheat you?' repeated the chemist softly. The idea seemed to interest him. 'Now, I wonder why you should be the first to think of that?'

There was a quality of menace in his voice which the stout man did not seem to hear. His mouth opened for a fresh outburst; but the outburst never came. The first word was on his lips when the door opened and the shifty-eyed youth burst in without the formality of a knock.

'It's Teal's—packet!' he panted out. 'A man just came in and said he wanted to change it! He said—Teal gave it to him. It hasn't been opened!'

Nancock jumped up like a startled pig, with his mouth still open where the interruption had caught it. An inarticulate yelp was the only sound that came out of it.

Osbett got up more slowly.

'What sort of man?' he snapped, and his voice was hard and suspicious.

The youth wagged his hands vaguely.

'A silly-ass sort of fellow—Burlington Bertie kind of chap—I didn't notice him particularly—'

'Well, go back and notice him now!' Mr Osbett was flapping ditherily again. 'Keep him talking. Make some excuse, but keep him there till I can have a look at him.'

The assistant darted out again and went pelting down the stairs— so precipitately that he never noticed the shadow that faded beyond the doorway of the stock-room on the opposite side of the landing.

Osbett had seized the packet of tea and was feeling it eagerly. The suspicious look was still in his eyes, but his hands were shaking with excitement.

'It feels like it!' he muttered. 'There's something funny about this—'

'Funny!' squeaked Nancock shrilly. 'It's my money, isn't it? Give it to me and let me get out of here!'

'It will be lucky for you if it is your money,' Osbett said thinly. 'Better let me make sure.' He ripped open the package. There was no tea in it—only crumpled pieces of thin white paper. 'Yes, this is it. But why . . . My God!'

The oath crawled through his lips in a tremulous whisper. He looked as if he had opened the package and found a snake in his hands. Nancock, staring at him, saw that his face had turned into a blank grey mask in which the eyes bulged like marbles.

Osbett spread out the piece of paper which he had opened. It was not a banknote. It was simply a piece of perforated tissue on which had been stamped in red the drawing of a quaint little figure with straight lines for body and legs and arms and an elliptical halo slanted over his round featureless head . . . Osbett tore open the other papers with suddenly savage hands. Every one of them was the same, stamped with the same symbolic figure . . .

'The Saint!' he whispered.

Nancock goggled stupidly at the scattered drawings.

'I—I don't understand,' he faltered, and he was white at the lips.

Osbett looked up at him.

'Then you'd better start thinking!' he rasped, and his eyes had gone flat and emotionless again. 'The Saint sent this, and if he knows about the money—'

'Not "sent", dear old Whiskers, not "sent",' a coolly mocking voice corrected him from the doorway. 'I brought it along myself, just for the pleasure of seeing your happy faces.'

The Saint stood leaning against the jamb of the door, smiling and debonair.

## VIII

The two men stood and gawped at him as if he had been a visitor from Mars. A gamut of emotions that must have strained their endocrine glands to bursting point skittered over their faces like foam over a waterfall. They looked as if they had been simultaneously goosed with high-voltage wires and slugged in the solar plexus with invisible sledge-hammers. Simon had to admit that there was some excuse for them. In fact, he had himself intentionally provided the excuse. There were certain reactions which only the ungodly could perform in their full richness that never failed to give him the same exquisite and fundamental joy that the flight and impact of a well-aimed custard pie gives to a movie audience; and for some seconds he was regaled with as ripe and rounded an exhibition of its kind as the hungriest heart could desire.

The Saint propped himself a little more comfortably against his backrest, and flicked a tiny bombshell of ash from his cigarette.

'I hope you don't mind my asking myself in like this,' he remarked engagingly. 'But I thought we ought to get together on this tea business. Maybe I could give you some new ideas. I was mixing a few odds and ends together myself yesterday—'

Credit must be given to Mr Osbett for making the first recovery. He was light-years ahead of Nancock, who stood as if his feet had sunk into the floor above the ankles, looking as though his lower jaw had dislocated itself at its fullest stretch. In one sheeting flash of dazzling clarity it dawned upon him that the man who stood there was unarmed—that the Saint's hands were empty except for a cigarette. His mouth shut tight under the spreading plumes of his moustache as he made a lightning grab towards the inside of his coat.

'Really!' protested the Saint. 'Weren't you ever taught not to scratch yourself in public?'

Osbett had just time to blink—once. And then he felt as if a cyclone had hit him. His fingers had not even closed on the butt of the automatic in his shoulder holster when he found himself full in the path of what seemed like a ton of incarnate dynamite moving with the speed of an express train. Something like a chunk of teak zoomed out of the cyclone and collided with his jaw: as if from a great distance, he heard it make a noise like a plank snapping in half. Then his head seemed to split open and let in a gash of light through which his brain sank down into cottony darkness.

The rest of him cannoned soggily into Nancock, bounded sideways, and cascaded over a chair. Osbett and the chair crashed to the floor together; and the stout man reeled drunkenly.

'Here,' he began.

Perhaps he did not mean the word as an invitation, but it appeared to have that effect. Something possessed of staggering velocity and hardness accepted the suggestion and moved into his stomach. The stout man said 'Oof!' and folded over like a jack-knife. This put his chin in line with another projectile that seemed to be travelling up from the floor. His teeth clicked together and he lay down quite slowly, like a collapsing concertina.

Simon Templar straightened his tie and picked up the cigarette which he had dropped when the fun started. It had not even had time to scorch the carpet.

He surveyed the scene with a certain shadow of regret. That was the worst of having to work quickly—it merely whetted the appetite for exercise, and then left nothing for it to expend itself on. However, it was doubtful whether Osbett and Nancock could ever have provided a satisfactory workout, even with plenty of time to develop it . . . The Saint relieved Osbett of his gun, felt Nancock's pockets for a weapon and found nothing, and then rose quickly as a scutter of footsteps on the stairs reminded him that he still had one more chance to practise his favourite uppercut. He leaped behind the door as the shifty-eyed assistant tumbled in.

The assistant was blurting out his news as he came.

'Hey, the fellow's disappeared—'

Simon toed the door away from between them and grinned at him.

'Where do you think he went to?' he inquired interestedly.

His fist jolted up under the youth's jaw, and the assistant sat down and unrolled himself backwards and lay still.

The Saint massaged his knuckles contentedly, and pulled a large roll of adhesive tape from his pocket. He used it to fasten the three sleeping beauties' hands and feet together, and had enough left to fasten over their mouths in a way that would gravely handicap any loquacity to which they might be moved when they woke up.

Not that they were showing any signs of waking up for some time to come, which was another disadvantage attached to the effectiveness of that sizzling uppercut. By all the symptoms, it would be quite a while before they were in any condition to start a conversation. It was an obstacle to further developments which Simon had not previously considered, and he scratched his head over it in a moment of indecision. As a matter of fact, he had not given much previous consideration to anything beyond that brief and temporarily conclusive scuffle—he never made any definite plans on such occasions, but he had an infinite faith in impromptu action and the bountiful inspirations of Providence. Meanwhile, no harm would probably be done by making a quick and comprehensive search of the premises, or—

In the stillness of his meditation and the surrounding atmosphere of sleep, an assortment of sounds penetrated to his ears from the regions downstairs. There was some forced and pointed coughing, an impatient shuffling of feet, and the tapping of a coin on plate glass. More business had apparently arrived, and was getting restive.

A faintly thoughtful tilt edged itself into his eyebrows.

He glanced round the room, and saw a slightly grubby white coat hanging behind the door. In a moment he had slipped into it and was buttoning it as he skated down the stairs.

The customer was a fat and frowsy woman in a bad temper.

'Tike yer time, dontcher?' she said scathingly. 'Think I've got all die ter wiste, young man? You're new here, aintcher? Where's Mr Osbett?'

'Some people, madam, prefer to call me fresh,' replied the Saint courteously. 'Mr Osbett is asleep at the moment, but you may confide in me with perfect confidence.'

'Confide in yer?' retorted the lady indignantly. 'None o' your sauce, young feller! I want three pennyworth of lickerish an' chlorodeen lozenges, an' that's all. Young Alf's corf is awful bad agin this morning.'

'That's too bad,' said the Saint, giving the shelves a quick once-over, and feeling somewhat helpless. 'Just a minute, auntie—I'm still finding my way around.'

'Fresh,' said the lady tartly, 'is right.'

Liquorice and chlorodyne lozenges were fairly easy. The Saint found a large bottle of them after a short search, and proceeded to tip half of it into a paper bag.

''Ere, I don't want all that,' yelped the woman. 'Three pennyworth, I said!'

Simon pushed the bag over the counter.

'As an old and valued customer, please accept the extra quantity with Mr Osbett's compliments,' he said generously. 'Threepence is the price to you, madam, and a bottle of cough mixture thrown in. Oh, yes, and you'd better give young Alf some cod-liver oil—'

He piled merchandise towards her until she grabbed up as much as she could carry and palpitated nervously out into the street. Simon grinned to himself and hoped he had not overdone it. If the news of his sensational bargain sale spread around the district, he would have his hands full.

During the lull that followed he tried to take a survey of the stock. He would be safe enough with proprietary goods, but if anyone asked for some more complicated medicine he would have to be careful. He had no grudge to work off against the neighbourhood at large; which was almost a pity.

The next customer required nothing more difficult than aspirin, and left the shop in a kind of daze when the Saint insisted on supplying a bottle of a hundred tablets for the modest price of twopence.

Simon took a trip upstairs and found that his three prizes had still failed to progress beyond the stage of half-conscious moanings and a spasmodic twitching of the lower limbs. He returned downstairs to attend to a small snotty-nosed urchin who was asking for a shilling tin of baby food. Simon blandly handed her the largest size he could see, and told her that Mr Osbett was making special reductions that morning.

'Coo!' said the small child, and added a bag of pear-drops to the order.

Simon poured out a pound of them—'No charge for that, Delilah—Mr Osbett is giving pear-drops away for an advertisement'—and the small child sprinted out as if it was afraid of waking up before it got home.

The Saint lighted another cigarette and waited thoughtfully. Supplying everybody who came in with astounding quantities of Mr Osbett's goods at cut-throat prices was amusing enough, admittedly, but it was not getting him anywhere. And yet a hunch that was growing larger every minute kept him standing behind the counter.

Maybe it wasn't such a waste of time—The package of Miracle Tea in which he had found fifteen hundred testimonials to the lavish beneficence of his guardian angel had come from that shop; presumably it had been intended for some special customer; presumably also it was not the only eccentric transaction that had taken place there, and there was no reason why it should be the last. Maybe no other miracles of the same kind were timed to take place that day; and yet . . .

Mr Osbett's boxes of extra special toilet soap, usually priced at seven and sixpence, were reduced for the benefit of a charming young damsel to a shilling each. The charming damsel was so impressed that she tentatively inquired the price of a handsome bottle of bath salts.

'What, this?' said the Saint, taking the flagon down and wrapping it up. 'As a special bargain this morning, sweetheart, we're letting it go for sixpence.'

It went for sixpence, quickly. The Saint handed over her change without encouraging further orders—as a matter of fact, he was rather anxious to get rid of the damsel, in spite of her charm and obvious inclination to be friendly, for a man with a thin weasel face under a dirty tweed cap already overdue for the dustbin had come in, and was earnestly inspecting a showcase full of safety razors and other articles which are less widely advertised. Quite obviously the man was not anxious to draw attention to himself while there was another customer in the shop; and while there was at least one perfectly commonplace explanation for that kind of bashfulness, the Saint felt a spectral tingle of expectation slide over his scalp as the girl went out and Weasel Face angled over to the counter.

'I haven't seen you before,' he stated.

His manner was flatly casual, but his small beady eyes flitted over Simon's face like flies hovering.

'Then you should be enjoying the view,' said the Saint affably. 'What can I sell you today, comrade? Hot water bottles? Shaving cream? Toothpaste? We have a special bargain line of castor oil—'

'Where's Ossy?'

'Dear old Ossy is lying down for a while—I think he's got a headache, or something. But don't let that stop you. Have you tried some of our Passion Flower lipstick, guaranteed to seduce at the first application?'

The man's eyes circled around again. He pushed out a crumpled envelope.

'Give Ossy my prescription, and don't talk so much.'

'Just a minute,' said the Saint.

He took the envelope back towards the staircase and slit it open. One glance even in the dim light that penetrated there was enough to show him that whatever else the thin sheet of paper it contained might mean, it was not a prescription that any ordinary pharmacist could have filled.

He stuffed the sheet into his pocket and came back.

'Will you call again at six o'clock?' he said, and his flippancy was no longer obtrusive. 'I'll have it ready for you then.'

'Awright.'

The beady eyes sidled over him once more, a trifle puzzledly, and the man went out.

Simon took the paper back into the dispensing room and spread it out under a good light. It was a scale plan of a building, with every detail plainly marked even to the positions of the larger pieces of furniture, and provided in addition with a closely-written fringe of marginal notes which to the Saint's professional scrutiny provided every item of information that a careful burglar could have asked for; and the first fascinating but still incomplete comprehension of Mr Osbett's extraordinary business began to reveal itself to him as he studied it.

IX

The simple beauty of the system made his pulses skip. Plans like that could be passed over in the guise of prescriptions; boodle, cash payments for services rendered, or almost anything else, could be handed over the counter enclosed in tubes of cold cream or packets of Miracle Tea; and it could all be done openly and with impunity even while other genuine customers were in the shop waiting to be served. Even if the man who did it were suspected and under surveillance, the same transactions could take place countless times under the very eyes of a watcher, and be dismissed as an entirely unimportant feature of the suspect's daily activities. Short of deliberate betrayal, it left no loophole through which Osbett himself could be involved at all—and even that risk, with a little ingenuity, could probably be manipulated so as to leave someone like the shifty-eyed young assistant to hold the baby. It was foolproof and puncture-proof—except against such an unforeseen train of accidents as had delivered one fatal package of Miracle Tea into Chief Inspector Teal's unwitting paws, and tumbled it from his pocket into Simon Templar's car.

The one vast and monumental question mark that was left was wrapped all the way round the mystery of what was the motive focus of the whole machinery.

A highly organised and up-to-date gang of thieves, directed by a Master Mind and operating with the efficiency of a big business? The answer seemed trite but possible. And yet . . .

All the goods he could see round him were probably as genuine as patent slimming salts and mouth washes can be—any special packages would certainly be kept aside. And there was nothing noticeably out of place at that time. He examined the cash register. It contained nothing but a small amount of money, which he transferred to a hospital collecting box on the counter. The ancient notes and invoices and prescriptions speared on to hook files in the dispensing compartment were obviously innocuous—nothing incriminating was likely to be left lying about there.

The first brisk spell of trade seemed to have fallen off, and no one else had entered the shop since the visit of Weasel Face. Simon went back upstairs, and investigated the room into which he had dodged when he followed the shifty-eyed youth up the stairs. He remembered it as having had the air of a store-room of some kind, and he was right. It contained various large jars, packing-cases, and cardboard cartons labelled with assorted names and cryptic signs, some of them prosaically familiar, stacked about in not particularly methodical piles. But the whole rear half of the room, in contrasting orderliness, was stacked from floor to ceiling with mounds of small yellow packages that he could recognise at a glance.

He looked around again, and on one wall he found in a cheap frame the official certificate which announced to all whom it might concern that Mr Henry Osbett had dutifully complied with the Law and registered the fact that he was trading under the business name of The Miracle Tea Company.

'Well, well, well,' said the Saint dreamily. 'What a small world it is after all . . .'

He fished out his cigarette-case and smoked part of the way through a cigarette while he stood gazing abstractedly over the unilluminating contents of the room, and his brain was a whirlpool of new and startling questions.

Then he pulled himself together and went back to the office.

The three men he had left there were all awake again by then and squirming ineffectually. Simon shook his head at them.

'Relax, boys,' he said soothingly. 'You're only wearing yourselves out. And think what a mess you're making of your clothes.'

Their swollen eyes glared at him mutely with three individual renderings of hate and malevolence intensified by different degrees of fear; but if the Saint had been susceptible to the cremating power of the human eye he would have been a walking cinder many years ago.

Calmly he proceeded to empty their pockets and examine every scrap of paper he found on them; but except for a driving licence which gave him Mr Nancock's name and address in Croydon he was no wiser when he had finished.

After that he turned his attention to the filing cabinet; but as far as a lengthy search could tell it contained nothing but a conventional collection of correspondence on harmless matters concerned with the legitimate business of the shop and the marketing of Miracle Tea. He sat down in Mr Osbett's swivel chair and went systematically through the drawers of the desk, but they also provided him with no enlightenment. The net result of his labours was a magnificent and symmetrically rounded zero.

The Saint's face showed no hint of his disappointment. He sat for a few seconds longer, tilting himself gently back and forth; and then he stood up.

'It's a pity you don't keep more money on the premises, Henry,' he remarked. 'You could have saved yourself a stamp.'

He picked up a paper-knife from the desk and tested the blade with his thumb. It was sharp enough. The eyes of the bound men dilated as they watched him.

The Saint smiled.

'From the way you were talking when I first came in, it looks as if you know my business,' he said. 'And I hope you've realised by this time that I know yours. It isn't a very nice business; but that's something for you to worry about. All I'm concerned with is to make sure that you pay the proper luxury tax to the right person, which happens to be me. So will you attend to it as soon as possible, Henry? I should think about ten thousand pounds will do for a first instalment. I shall expect it in one-pound notes, delivered by messenger before two-thirty p.m. tomorrow. And it had better not be late.' The Saint's blue eyes were as friendly as frozen vitriol. 'Because if it is, Chief Inspector Teal will be calling here again—and next time it won't be an accident . . . Meanwhile'—

the knife spun from his hands like a whirling white flame, and the three men flinched wildly as the point buried itself with a thud in the small space of carpet centrally between them—'if one of you gets to work with that, you ought to be up and about again in a few minutes. Goodbye, girls; and help yourself to some sal volatile when you get downstairs.'

It was nearing one o'clock by his watch when he reached the street; and Patricia was ordering herself a second Martini when he strolled into the cocktail room at Quaglino's.

She leaned back and closed her eyes.

'I know,' she said. 'Teal and the Flying Squad are about two blocks behind you. I can tell by the smug look on your face.'

'For once in your life you're wrong,' he said as he lowered himself into a chair. 'They're so far behind that if Einstein is right they ought to have been here an hour ago.'

Over lunch he gave her an account of his morning.

'But what is it all about?' she said.

He frowned.

'I just wish I knew, darling. But it's something bigger than burglary—you can take bets on that. If Henry Osbett is the Miracle Teapot in person, the plot is getting so thick you could float rocks on it. If I haven't got mixed on what Claud Eustace told me last night, they run a radio programme, and that costs plenty of dough and trouble. No gang of burglars would bother to go as far as that, even to keep up appearances. Therefore this is some racket in which the dough flows like water; and I wish I could think what that could be. And it's run by experts. In the whole of that shop there wasn't a single clue. I'll swear that Claud Eustace himself could put it through a sieve and not find anything . . . I was just bluffing Henry, of course, but I think I made a good job of it.'

'You don't think he'll pay, do you?'

'Stranger things have happened,' said the Saint hopefully. 'But if you put it like that—no. That was just bait. There wasn't anything else useful that I could do. If I'd had them somewhere else I might have beaten it out of them, but I couldn't do it there, and I couldn't put them in a bag and bring them home with me. Anyhow, this may be a better way. It means that the next move is up to the ungodly, and they've got to make it fast. And that may give us our break.'

'Of course it may,' she agreed politely. 'By the way, where did you tell me once you wanted to be buried?'

He chuckled.

'Under the foundation stone of a brewery,' he said. 'But don't worry. I'm going to take a lot of care of myself.'

His idea of taking care of himself for that afternoon was to drive the Hirondel down to the factory at an average speed of about sixty miles an hour to discuss the installation of a new type of supercharger designed to make the engine several degrees more lethal than it was already, and afterwards to drive back to London at a slightly higher speed in order to be punctual for his appointment with Mr Teal. Considering that ride in retrospect, he sometimes wondered whether he would have any chance of claiming that the astounding quality of care which it showed could be credited entirely to his own inspired forethought.

It was on the stroke of four when he sailed into the May Fair and espied the plump and unromantic shape of Chief Inspector Teal dumped into a pink brocade armchair and looking rather like a bailiff in a boudoir.

Teal got up as the Saint breezed towards him; and something in the way he straightened and stood there almost checked Simon in the middle of a stride. Simon forced himself to keep coming without a flaw in the smooth surface of his outward tranquillity; but a sixth sense was rocketing red danger signals through his brain even before he heard the detective's unnaturally hard gritty voice.

'I've been waiting for you, Saint!'

'Then you must have been early, Claud,' said the Saint. His smile was amiable and unruffled, but there was an outlaw's watchfulness at the back of his bantering eyes. 'Is that any excuse for the basilisk leer? Anyone would think you'd eaten something—'

'I don't want to hear any more of that,' Teal said crunchily. 'You know damned well why I'm waiting for you. Do you know what this is?'

He flourished a piece of paper in Simon's face.

The Saint raised his eyebrows.

'Not another of those jolly old warrants?' he murmured. 'You must be getting quite a collection of them.'

'I'm not going to need to collect any more,' Teal said grimly. 'You went too far when you left your mark on the dead man you threw out of your car in Richmond Park this afternoon. I'm taking you into custody on a charge of wilful murder!'

X

Simon took Mr Teal by the arm and led him back to a seat. He was probably the only man in the world who could have got away with such a thing, but he did it without the faintest sign of effort. He switched on about fifty thousand watts of his personality, and Mr Teal was sitting down beside him before he recovered from it.

'Damn it, Templar, what the hell do you think you're doing?' he exploded wrathfully. 'You're under arrest!'

'All right, I'm under arrest,' said the Saint accommodatingly, as he stretched out his long legs. 'So what?'

'I'm taking you into custody—'

'You said that before. But why the hurry? It isn't early closing day at Vine Street, is it? Let's have our tea first, and you can tell me all about this bird I'm supposed to have moidered. You say he was thrown out of a car—'

'Your Hirondel!'

'But why mine? After all, there are others. I don't use enough of them to keep the factory going by myself.'

The detective's jaws clamped on his chewing gum.

'You can say all that to the magistrate in the morning,' he retorted dourly. 'It isn't my job to listen to you. It's my job to take you to the nearest police station and leave you there, and that's what I'm going to do. I've got a car and a couple of men at each of the entrances, so you'd better not give any trouble. I had an idea you'd be here at four o'clock—'

'So I spend the afternoon moidering people and chucking them out of cars, and then rush off to meet you so you needn't even have the trouble of looking for me; I even use my own famous Hirondel so that any cop can identify it, and put my trademark on the deceased to make everything easy for the prosecution. You know, Claud,' said the Saint pensively, 'there are times when I wonder whether I'm quite sane.'

Teal's baby blue eyes clung to him balefully.

'Go on,' he grated. 'Let's hear the new alibi. It'll give me plenty of time to get it torn down before you come up for trial!'

'Give me a chance,' Simon protested. 'I don't even know what time I'm supposed to have been doing all these exciting things.'

'You know perfectly well—'

'Never mind. You tell me, and let's see if we agree. What time did I sling this stiff out of my car?'

'A few minutes after three—and he was only killed a few minutes before that.'

The Saint opened his cigarette-case.

'That rather tears it,' he said slowly; and Teal's eyes kindled with triumph.

'So you weren't quite so smart—'

'Oh, no,' said the Saint diffidently. 'I was just thinking of it from your point of view. You see, just at that time I was at the Hirondel factory at Staines, talking about a new blower that I'm thinking of having glued on to the old buzz-wagon. We had quite a conference over it. There was the works manager, and the service manager, and the shop foreman, and a couple of mechanics thrown in, so far as I remember. Of course, everybody knows that the whole staff down there is in my pay, but the only thing I'm worried about is whether you'll be able to make a jury believe it.'

A queerly childish contraction warped itself across Mr Teal's rubicund features. He looked as if he had been suddenly seized with an acute pain below the belt, and was about to burst into tears.

Both of these diagnoses contained an element of truth. But they were far from telling the whole story.

The whole story went too far to be compressed into a space less than volumes. It went far back into the days when Mr Teal had been a competent and contented and commonplace detective, adequately doing a job in which miracles did not happen and the natural laws of the universe were respected and cast-iron cases were not being perennially disintegrated under his nose by a bland and tantalising buccaneer whose elusiveness had almost started to convince him of the reality of black magic. It coiled through an infinite history of incredible disasters and hairbreadth frustrations that would have wrung the withers of anything softer than a marble statue. It belonged to the hysterical saga of his whole hopeless duel with the Saint.

Mr Teal did not burst into tears. Nor, on this one unprecedented occasion, did he choke over his gum while a flush of apoplectic fury boiled into his round face. Perhaps there were no more such reactions left in him; or perhaps on this one occasion an inescapable foreboding of the uselessness of it all strangled the spasm before it could mature and gave him the supernatural strength to stifle his emotions under the pose of stolid somnolence that he could so rarely preserve against the Saint's fiendishly shrewd attack. But however he achieved the feat, he managed to sit quite still while his hot resentful eyes bored into the Saint's smiling face for a time before he struggled slothfully to his feet.

'Wait a minute,' he said thickly.

He went over and spoke to a tall cadaverous man who was hovering in the background. Then he came back and sat down again.

Simon trickled an impudent streamer of smoke towards him.

'If I were a sensitive man I should be offended, Claud. Do you have to be quite so obvious about it when you send Sergeant Barrow to find out whether I'm telling you the truth? It isn't good manners, comrade. It savours of distrust.'

Mr Teal said nothing. He sat champing soporifically, staring steadfastly at the polished toes of his regulation boots, until Sergeant Barrow returned.

Teal got up and spoke to him at a little distance; and when he rejoined the Saint the drowsiness was turgid and treacle-thick on his pink full-moon face.

'All right,' he bit out in a cracked voice, through lips that were stiff and clumsy with the bitterness of defeat. 'Now suppose you tell me how you did it.'

'But I didn't do it, Claud,' said the Saint, with a seriousness that edged through his veneer of nonchalance. 'I'm as keen as you are to get a line on this low criminal who takes my trademark in vain. Who was the bloke they picked up this afternoon?'

For some reason which was beyond his understanding, the detective stopped short on the brink of a sarcastic comeback.

'He was an Admiralty draughtsman by the name of Nancock,' he said; and the gauzy derision in the Saint's glance faded out abruptly as he realised that in that simple answer he had been given the secret of Mr Osbett's remarkable chemistry.

XI

It was as if a distorting mirror had been suddenly flattened out, so that it reflected a complete picture with brilliant and lifelike accuracy. The figures in it moved like marionettes.

Simon even knew why Nancock had died. He himself, ironically for Teal's disappointment, had sealed the fat man's death-warrant without knowing it. Nancock was the man for whom the fifteen-hundred-pound packet of Miracle Tea had been intended; Nancock had been making a fuss at the shop when the Saint arrived. The fuss was due to nothing but Nancock's fright and greed, but to suspicious eyes it might just as well have looked like the overdone attempt of a guilty conscience to establish its own innocence.

Nancock's money had passed into the Saint's hands, the Saint had got into the shop on the pretext of bringing the same package back, and the Saint had said: 'I know all about your business.' Simon could hear his own voice saying it. Osbett had made from that the one obvious deduction. Nancock had been a dead man when the Saint left the shop.

And to dump the body out of a Hirondel, with a Saint drawing pinned to it, was a no less obvious reply. Probably they had used one of his own authentic drawings, which had still been lying on the desk when he left them. He might have been doing any one of a dozen things that afternoon which would have left him without an alibi.

He had told Patricia that the next move was up to the ungodly, and it had come faster than he had expected. But it had also fulfilled all his other hopes.

'Claud,' he said softly, 'how would you like to make the haul of a lifetime?'

Teal sat and looked at him.

'I'll trade it,' said the Saint, 'for something that'll hardly give you any trouble at all. I was thinking of asking you to do it for me anyhow, in return for saving your life last night. There are certain reasons why I want to know the address where they have a telephone number Berkeley 3100. I can't get the information from the telephone company myself, but you can. I'll write it down for you.' He scribbled the figures on a piece of paper. 'Let me know where that number lives, and I'll give you your murderer and a lot more.'

Teal blinked suspiciously at the memorandum.

'What's this got to do with it?' he demanded.

'Nothing at all,' said the Saint untruthfully. 'So don't waste your time sleuthing around the place and trying to pick up clues. It's just some private business of my own. Is it a sale?'

The detective's eyes hardened.

'Then you do know something about all this!'

'Maybe I'm just guessing. I'll be able to tell you later. For once in your life, will you let me do you a good turn without trying to argue me out of it?'

Mr Teal fought with himself. And for no reason that he could afterwards justify to himself, he said grudgingly: 'All right. Where shall I find you?'

'I'll stay home till I hear from you.' Simon stood up, and suddenly remembered for the first time why he was there at all. He pulled a yellow package out of his pocket and dropped it in the detective's lap. 'Oh, yes. And don't forget to take some of this belly balm as soon as you get the chance. It may help you to get back that sweet disposition you used to have, and stop you being so ready to think unkind thoughts about me.'

On the way home he had a few qualms about the ultimate wisdom of that parting gesture, but his brain was too busy to dwell on them. The final patterns of the adventure were swinging into place with the regimented precision that always seemed to come to his episodes after the most chaotic beginnings, and the rhythm of it was like wine in his blood.

He had made Teal drive slowly past Cornwall House with him in a police car, in case there were any watchers waiting to see whether the attempt to saddle him with Nancock's murder would be successful. From Cannon Row police station, which is also a rear exit from Scotland Yard, he took a taxi back to his apartment, and stopped at a newsagent's on the way to buy a copy of a certain periodical in which he had hitherto taken little interest. By the time he got home it had given him the information he wanted.

Sam Outrell, the janitor, came out from behind the desk as he entered the lobby.

'Those men was here, sir, about two hours ago, like you said they would be,' he reported. 'Said you'd sent 'em to measure the winders for some new curtains. I let 'em in like you told me, an' they went through all the rooms.'

'Thanks a lot, Sam,' said the Saint, and rode up in the lift with another piece of his mosaic settled neatly into place.

He came into the living-room like a ray of sunshine and spun his hat over Patricia's head into a corner.

'Miracle Tea is on the air in about ten minutes,' he said, 'with a programme of chamber music. Could anything be more appropriate?' Patricia looked up from her book.

'I suppose you've heard about our curtain measurers?'

'Sam Outrell told me. Do I get my diploma in advanced prophetics? After the party I had this morning, I knew it wouldn't be long before someone wanted to know what had happened to Comrade McGuire. Did you get him to Weybridge in good condition?'

'He didn't seem to like being locked in the trunk of the Daimler very much.'

The Saint grinned, and sat down at the desk to dismantle his automatic. He opened a drawer and fished out brushes and rags and cleaning oil.

'Well, I'm sure he preferred it to being nailed up in a coffin,' he said callously. 'And he's safe enough there with Orace on guard. They won't find him in the secret room, even if they do think of looking down there ... Be a darling and start tuning in Radio Calvados, will you?'

For a short while she was busy with the dials of the radiogram; and then she came back and watched him in silence while he went over his gun with the loving care of a man who knew how much might hang on the light touch of a trigger.

'Something else has happened,' she said at last. 'And you're holding out on me.'

Simon squinted complacently up a barrel like burnished silver, and snapped the sliding jacket back into place. There was a dynamic exuberance in his repose that no artist could have captured, an aura of resilient swiftness poised on a knife-edge of balance that sent queer little feathery ripples up her spine.

'A lot more is going to happen,' he said. 'And then I'll tell you what a genius I am.'

She would have made some reply; but suddenly he fell into utter stillness with a quick lift of his hand.

Out of the radio, which had been briefly silent, floated the opening bars of the Spring Song. And his watch told him that it was the start of the Miracle Tea Company's contribution to the load that the twentieth-century ether has to bear.

Shortly the music faded to form a background for a delicate Oxford accent informing the world that this melody fairly portrayed the sensations of a sufferer from indigestion after drinking a nice big cup of Miracle Tea. There followed an unusually nauseating dissertation on the manifold virtues of the product, and then a screeching slaughter of the Grand March from Tannhauser played by the same string quartet. Patricia got up pallidly and poured herself out a drink.

'I suppose we do have to listen to this?' she said.

'Wait,' said the Saint.

The rendition came to its awful end, and the voice of Miracle Tea polluted the air once again.

'Before we continue our melody programme, we should like to read you a few extracts from our file of unsolicited letters from sufferers who have tried Miracle Tea. Tonight we are choosing letters one thousand and six, one thousand and fourteen, and one thousand and twenty-seven . . .'

The unsolicited letters were read with frightful enthusiasm, and the Saint listened with such intentness that he was obviously paying no attention to the transparently bogus effusions. He sat with the gun turning gently in his hands and a blindingly beatific smile creeping by hesitant degrees into the lines of his chiselled fighting mouth, so that the girl looked at him in uncomprehending wonderment.

'. . . And there, ladies and gentlemen, you have the opinions of the writers whose letters are numbered one thousand and six, one thousand and fourteen, and one thousand and twenty-seven in our files,' said the voice of the announcer, speaking with tedious deliberation. 'These good people cured themselves by drinking Miracle Tea. Let me urge you to buy Miracle Tea—tonight. Buy Miracle Tea! . . . And now the string quartet will play Drink to Me Only—'

There were two more short numbers and the broadcast was over. Simon switched off the radio as the next advertiser plunged into his act.

'Well,' said Patricia mutinously, 'are you going to talk?'

'You heard as much as I did.'

'I didn't hear anything worth listening to.'

'Nor did I. That's the whole point. There wasn't anything worth listening to. I was looking for an elaborate code message. An expert like me can smell a code message as far off as a venerable gorgonzola—there's always a certain clumsiness in the phrasing. This was so simple that I nearly missed it.'

Patricia gazed into the depths of her glass.

She said: 'Those numbers—'

He nodded.

'The "thousand" part is just coverage. Six, fourteen, and twenty-seven are the operative words. They have to buy Miracle Tea—tonight. Nothing else in the programme means a thing. But according to that paper I brought in, Miracle Tea broadcasts every night of the week; and that means that any night the Big Shot wants to he can send out a call for the men he wants to come and get their orders or anything else that's waiting for them. It's the last perfect touch of organisation. There's no connecting link that any detective on earth could trace between a broadcast and any particular person who listens to it. It means that even if one of his operatives should be under suspicion, the Big Shot can contact him without the shadow of a chance of transferring suspicion to himself. You could think of hundreds of ways of working a few numbers into an advertising spiel, and I'll bet they have a new one every time.'

She looked at him steadily.

'But you still haven't told me what—'

The telephone rang before he could answer.

Simon picked it up.

'Metropolitan Police Maternity Home,' he said.

'Teal speaking,' said a familiar voice with an unnecessarily pugnacious rasp in it. 'I've got the information you asked for about that phone number. The subscriber is Baron Inescu, 16, North Ashley Street, Berkeley Square. Now what was that information you were going to give me in return?'

The Saint unpuckered his lips from a long inaudible whistle.

'OK, Claud,' he said, and the words lilted. 'I guess you've earned it. You can start right now. Rush one of your squads to Osbett's Drug Store, 909, Victoria Street—the place where you bought your Miracle Tea. Three other guys will be there shopping for Miracle Tea at any moment from now on. I can't give you any description of them, but there's one sure way to pick them out. Have one of your men go up to everyone who comes out of the shop and say: 'Are you six, fourteen, or twenty-seven?' If the guy jumps halfway out of his skin, he's one of the birds you want. And see that you get his Miracle Tea as well!'

'Miracle Tea!' sizzled the detective, with such searing savagery that the Saint's ribs suddenly ached with awful intuition. 'I wish—' He stopped. Then he said: 'What's this about Miracle Tea? Are you trying to be funny?'

'I was never so serious in my life, Claud. Get those three guys, and get their packets of Miracle Tea. You'll find something interesting in them.'

Teal's silence reeked of tormented indecision.

'If I thought—'

'But you never have, Claud. Don't spoil your record now. Just send that squad out and tell 'em to hustle. You stay by the telephone, and I ought to be able to call you within an hour to collect the Big Shot.'

'But you haven't told me—' Again Teal's voice wailed off abruptly. Something like a stifled groan squeezed into the gap. He spoke again in a fevered gabble. 'All right all right I'll do it, I can't stop now to argue but God help you—'

The connection clicked off even quicker than the sentence could finish.

Simon fitted his automatic into the spring clip holster under his coat, and stood up with a slow smile of ineffable impishness creeping up to his eyes.

XII

16, North Ashley Street stood in the middle of one of those rows of crowded but discreetly opulent dwellings which provide the less squalid aspect of certain parts of Mayfair. Lights could be seen in some of the windows, indicating that someone was at home; but the Saint was not at all troubled about that. It was, in fact, a stroke of luck which he had hoped for.

He stepped up to the front door with the easy aplomb of an invited guest arriving punctually for dinner, and put his finger on the bell. He looked as cool as if he had come straight off the ice, but under the rakish brim of his hat the hell-for-leather mischief still rollicked in his eyes. One hand rested idly between the lapels of his coat, as if he were adjusting his tie . . .

The door opened, exposing a large and overwhelming butler. The Saint's glance weighed him with expert penetration. Butlers are traditionally large and overwhelming, but they are apt to run large in the wrong places. This butler was large in the right places. His shoulders looked as wide as a wardrobe, and his biceps stretched tight wrinkles into the sleeves of his well-cut coat.

'Baron Inescu?' inquired the Saint pleasantly.

'The Baron is not—'

Simon smiled, and pressed the muzzle of his gun a little more firmly into the stomach in front of him.

The butler recoiled, and the Saint stepped after him. He pushed the door shut with his heel.

'Turn round.'

Tensely the butler started to obey. He had not quite finished the movement when Simon lifted his gun and jerked it crisply down again. The barrel made a sharp smacking sound on the back of the butler's bullet head; and the result, from an onlooker's point of view, was quite comical. The butler's legs bowed outwards, and he rolled down on to his face with a kind of resigned reluctance, and lay motionless.

For a second the Saint stood still, listening. But except for that single clear-cut smack there had been no disturbance, and the house remained quiet and peaceful.

Simon's eyes swept round the hall. In a corner close to the front door there was a door which looked as if it belonged to a coat cupboard. It was a coat cupboard. The Saint pocketed his gun for long enough to drag the butler across the marble floor and shove him in. He locked the door on him and took the key—he was a pretty accurate judge of the comparative toughness of gunbarrels and skulls, and he was confident that the butler would not be constituting a vital factor in anybody's life for some time.

He travelled past the other doors on the ground floor like a voyaging wraith, listening at each one of them, but he could hear no signs of life in any of the rooms beyond. From the head of the basement stairs he heard an undisturbed clink of dishes and mutter of voices which reassured him that the rest of the staff were strictly minding their own business.

In another moment he was on his way up the main staircase.

On the first wide landing he knew he was near his destination. Under one door there was a thin streak of light, and as he inched noiselessly up to it he heard the faint syncopated patter of a typewriter. Then the soft burr of a telephone interrupted it.

A voice said: 'Yes . . . Yes.' There was a slight pause; then: 'Vernon? Here is your copy for the special nine o'clock broadcast. Take it down. "Why suffer from indigestion when relief is so cheap? Two cups will make your pains vanish—only two. Four cups will set you on the road to a complete cure—so why not take four? But after sixteen cups you will forget that indigestion ever existed. Think of that. Sixteen cups will make you feel ten years younger. Wouldn't you like to feel ten years younger in a few days? Buy Miracle Tea—tonight!" . . . Have you got that? . . . Splendid. Good night!'

The receiver rattled back. And the latch of the door rattled as Simon Templar closed it behind him.

The man at the desk spun round as if a snake had bitten him.

'Good evening, Baron,' said the Saint.

He stood there smiling, blithe and elegant and indescribably dangerous.

The Baron stared frozenly back at him. He was a tall, clean-shaven man with dark hair greying at the temples, and he wore impeccable evening clothes with the distinction of an ambassador: but he had spoken on the telephone in a voice that was quite strangely out of keeping with his appearance. And the Saint's smile deepened with the joy of final certainty as he held his gun steadily aligned on the pearl stud in the centre of the Baron's snowy shirt-front.

The first leap of fear across the Baron's dark eyes turned into a convincing blaze of anger.

'What is the meaning of this?'

'At a rough guess, I should say about fifteen years—for you,' answered the Saint equably. 'It'll be quite a change from your usual environment, I'm afraid. That is, if I can judge by the pictures I've seen of you in the society papers. Baron Inescu driving off the first tee at St Andrew's—Baron Inescu at the wheel of his yacht at Cowes—Baron Inescu climbing into his new racing monoplane. I'm afraid you'll find the sporting facilities rather limited at Dartmoor, Baron . . . or would you rather I called you—Henry?' The Baron sat very still. 'You know a great deal, Mr Templar.'

'Just about all I need to know, I think. I know you've been running the most efficient espionage organisation that poor old Chief Inspector Teal has had to scratch his head over for a long time. I know that you had everything lined up so well that you might have got away with it for years if it hadn't been for one of those Acts of God that the insurance companies never want to underwrite. I told you I knew all about it this morning, but you didn't believe me. By the way, how does the jaw feel tonight?'

The other watched him unwinkingly. 'I'm afraid I did find it hard to believe you,' he said evenly. 'What else do you know?'

'I know all about your phoney broadcasts. And if it's of any interest to you, there will be a squad of large flat-footed bogey-men waiting for numbers six, fourteen, and twenty-seven when they stop by for their Miracle Tea ... I also know that instead of getting ready to pay me the tax I asked for, you tried to frame me for the murder of Nancock this afternoon. And I resent that, Henry.'

'I apologise,' said the Baron suavely. 'You shall have your money tomorrow—'

The Saint shook his head, and his eyes were glacially blue.

'You had your chance, and you passed it up. I shall help myself to the money.' He saw the other's eyes shift fractionally to the safe in the corner, and laughed softly. 'Give me the keys, Henry.'

The Baron hesitated a moment before he moved.

Then he put his hand slowly into his trouser pocket and pulled out a bunch of keys on a platinum chain. He detached them and threw them on to the desk.

'You have the advantage, Mr Templar,' he said smoothly. 'I give you the keys because you could easily take them yourself if I refused. But you're very foolish. There are only about three thousand pounds in the safe. Why not be sensible and wait till the morning?'

'In the morning you'll be too busy trying to put up a defence at the police court to think about me,' said the Saint coldly.

He moved towards the desk; but he did not pick up the keys at once. His eyes strayed to the sheet of paper in the typewriter; and yet they did it in such a way that the Baron still knew that the first move he made would call shattering death out of the trim unwavering automatic.

Simon read:

In conjunction with Numbers 4, 10, and 16 you will proceed at once to Cheltenham and establish close watch on Sir Roland Hale who is

on holiday there. Within 24 hours you will send report on the method
by which urgent War Office messages—

Simon's eyes returned to the Baron's face.

'What more evidence do you think Chief Inspector Teal will
need?' he said.

'With a name like mine?' came the scornful answer. 'When I
tell them that you held me at the point of a gun while you wrote
that message on my typewriter—'

'I'm sure they'll be very polite,' said the Saint. 'Especially when
they find that yours are the only fingerprints on the keys.'

'If you made me write it under compulsion—'

'And the orders in the packets of Miracle Tea which numbers
six, fourteen, and twenty-seven are going to buy tonight came
from the same machine.'

The Baron moistened his lips.

'Let us talk this over,' he said.

The Saint said: 'You talk.'

He picked up the telephone and dialled 'o'.

He said: 'I want to make a call to France—Radio Calvados.'

The Baron swallowed.

'Wait a minute,' he said desperately. 'I—'

'Incidentally,' said the Saint, 'there'll be a record that you had
a call to Radio Calvados this evening, and probably on lots of
other evenings as well. And I'm sure we shall find that Henry
Osbett moustache of yours somewhere in the house—not to
mention the beard you wore when you were dealing with Red
McGuire. I suppose you needed some thug outside the organisation
in case you wanted to deal drastically with any of the ordinary
members, but you picked the wrong man in Red. He doesn't like
hot curling-irons.'

Inescu's fists clenched until the knuckles were bleached. His
face had gone pale under its light tan. The Saint's call came through.

'Mr Vernon, please,' he said.

He took out his cigarette-case, opened it, and lighted a cigarette with the hand that held his gun, all in some astonishing manner that never allowed the muzzle to wander for an instant from its aim on the Baron's shirt-stud; and then an unmistakable Oxford accent said: 'Hullo?'

'Vernon?' said the Saint, and his voice was so exactly like the voice affected by Mr Henry Osbett that its originator could scarcely believe his ears. 'I've got to make a change in that copy I just gave you. Make it read like this: "They say there is safety in numbers. In that case, you can't go wrong with Miracle Tea. There are many numbers in our files, but they all praise Miracle Tea. Every number has the same message. Why should you be left out? All of you, buy Miracle Tea—tonight!" . . . Have you got it? . . . Good. See that it goes in without fail.'

Simon pressed the spring bracket down with his thumb, still holding the receiver.

The Baron's stare was wide and stupefied.

'You're mad!' he said hoarsely. 'You're throwing away a fortune—'

Simon laughed at him, and lifted the receiver to his ear again. He dialled the number of Scotland Yard.

'Give me Chief Inspector Teal,' he said. 'The Saint calling.'

There was some delay on the switchboard.

The Saint looked at Baron Inescu and said: 'There's one thing you forget, Baron. I like money as much as anybody else, and I use more of it than most people. But that's a side-line. I also deliver justice. When you get to Dartmoor, you'll meet some other men that I've sent there. Ask them about it. And then you in your turn will be able to tell the same story.'

The voice of Chief Inspector Teal blared short-windedly in his ear.

'Yes?'

'Oh, Claud? How's the old tum-tum getting . . . All right, if it's a sore subject; but I wondered . . . Yes, of course I have. Just a minute. Did you get six, fourteen, and twenty-seven?' Simon listened, and the contentment ripened on his face. 'Well, didn't I tell you? And now you can have some more for the bag. At any time after nine o'clock there's going to be a perfect stampede of blokes asking for Miracle Tea, so you can send your squad back for more. They'd better take over the shop and grab everyone who tries to buy Miracle Tea. And while they're doing that I've got the Big Shot waiting for you. Come and get him. The address is— Excuse me.'

The Saint had the telephone in one hand and a gun in the other, and it seemed impossible for him to have done it, but a narrow-bladed ivory-hilted knife stuck quivering in the desk half an inch from the Baron's fingers as they slid towards a concealed bell. And the Saint went on talking as if nothing had happened.

'Sixteen North Ashley Street, Berkeley Square; and the name is Inescu . . . Yes, isn't that a coincidence? But there's all the evidence you'll need to make you happy, so I don't see why you should complain. Come along over and I'll show you.'

'I'll send someone over,' Teal said stiffly. 'And thanks very much.'

Simon frowned a little.

'Why send someone?' he objected. 'I thought—'

'Because I'm busy!' came a tortured howl that nearly shattered the receiver. 'I can't leave the office just now. I—I'll have to send someone.'

The Saint's eyebrows slowly lifted.

'But why?' he persisted.

Eventually Mr Teal told him.

## XIII

Simon Templar sat on the desk in Chief Inspector Teal's office a fortnight later. The police-court proceedings had just been concluded after a remand, and Baron Inescu, alias Henry Osbett, had been committed for trial in company with some three dozen smaller cogs in his machine. The report was in the evening paper which Simon had bought, and he pointed it out to Teal accusingly.

'At least you could have rung me up and thanked me again for making you look like a great detective,' he said.

Mr Teal strip-teased a slice of chewing-gum and fed it into his mouth. 'I'm sorry,' he said. 'I meant to do it, but there was a lot of clearing-up work to do on the case. Anyway, it's out of my hands now, and the Public Prosecutor is pretty satisfied. It's a pity there wasn't enough direct evidence to charge Inescu with the murder of Nancock, but we haven't done badly.'

'You're looking pretty cheerful,' said the Saint.

This was true. Mr Teal's rosy face had a fresh pink glow, and his cherubic blue eyes were clear and bright under his sleepily drooping lids.

'I'm feeling better,' he said. 'You know, that's the thing that really beats me about this case. Inescu could have made a fortune out of Miracle Tea without ever going in for espionage—

The Saint's mouth fell open.

'You don't mean to say—' he ejaculated, and couldn't go on. He said: 'But I thought you were ready to chew the blood out of everyone who had anything to do with Miracle Tea, if you could only have got away from—'

'I know it was rather drastic,' Teal said sheepishly. 'But it did the trick. Do you know, I haven't had a single attack of indigestion since I took that packet; and I even had roast pork for dinner last night!'

Simon Templar drew a long deep breath and closed his eyes. There were times when even he felt that he was standing on holy ground.

# THE AFFAIR OF HOGSBOTHAM

I

'There are times,' remarked Simon Templar, putting down the evening paper and pouring himself a second glass of Tio Pepe, 'when I am on the verge of swearing a great oath never to look at another newspaper as long as I live. Here you have a fascinating world full of all kinds of busy people, being born, falling in love, marrying, dying and being killed, working, starving, fighting, splitting atoms and measuring stars, inventing trick corkscrews and relativity theories, building skyscrapers and suffering hell with toothache. When I buy a newspaper I want to read all about them. I want to know what they're doing and creating and planning and striving for and going to war about—all the exciting vital things that make a picture of a real world and real people's lives. And what do I get?'

'What do you get, Saint?' asked Patricia Holm with a smile.

Simon picked up the newspaper again.

'This is what I get,' he said. 'I get a guy whose name, believe it or not, is Ebenezer Hogsbotham. Comrade Hogsbotham, having been born with a name like that and a face to match it, if you can believe a newspaper picture, has never had a chance in his life to misbehave, and has therefore naturally developed into one of those guys who feel that they have a mission to protect everyone else from misbehaviour. He has therefore been earnestly studying the subject in order to be able to tell other people how to protect themselves from it.

'For several weeks, apparently, he has been frequenting the bawdiest theatres and the nudest night clubs, discovering just how much depravity is being put out to ensnare those people who are not so shiningly immune to contamination as himself; as a result of which he has come out hot and strong for a vigorous censorship of all public entertainment. Since Comrade Hogsbotham has

710

carefully promoted himself to be president of the National Society for the Preservation of Public Morals, he hits the front-page headlines while five hundred human beings who get themselves blown to bits by honourable Japanese bombs are only worth a three-line filler on page eleven. And this is the immortal utterance that he hits them with: "The public has a right to be protected," he says, "from displays of suggestiveness and undress which are disgusting to all right-thinking people." ... "Right-thinking people", of course, only means people who think like Comrade Hogsbotham; but it's one of those crushing and high-sounding phrases that the Hogsbothams of this world seem to have a monopoly on. Will you excuse me while I vomit?'

Patricia fingered the curls in her soft golden hair and considered him guardedly.

'You can't do anything else about it,' she said. 'Even you can't alter that sort of thing, so you might as well save your energy.'

'I suppose so.' The Saint scowled. 'But it's just too hopeless to resign yourself to spending the rest of your life watching nine-tenths of the world's population, who've got more than enough serious things to worry about already, being browbeaten into a superstitious respect for the humbug of a handful of yapping crypt-orchid Hogsbothams. I feel that somebody on the other side of the fence ought to climb over and pin his ears back ... I have a pain in the neck. I should like to do something to demonstrate my unparalleled immorality. I want to go out and burgle a convent; or borrow a guitar and parade in front of Hogsbotham's house, singing obscene songs in a beery voice.'

He took his glass over to the window and stood there looking down over Piccadilly and the Green Park with a faraway dreaminess in his blue eyes that seemed to be playing with all kinds of electric and reprehensible ideas beyond the humdrum view on which they were actually focused; and Patricia Holm watched him with eyes of the same reckless blue but backed by a sober understanding. She had known him too long to dismiss such a mood as lightly as any other woman would have dismissed it. Any other man might have voiced the same grumble without danger of anyone else remembering it beyond the next drink; but when the man who was so fantastically called the Saint uttered that kind of unsaintly thought, his undercurrent of seriousness was apt to be translated into a different sort of headline with a frequency that Patricia needed all her reserves of mental stability to cope with. Some of the Saint's wildest adventures had started from less sinister openings than that, and she measured him now with a premonition that she had not yet heard the last of that random threat. For a whole month he had done nothing illegal, and in his life thirty days of untarnished virtue was a long time. She studied the buccaneering lines of his lean figure, sensed the precariously curbed restlessness under his lounging ease, and knew that even if no exterior adventure crossed his path that month of peace would come to spontaneous disruption . . .

And then he turned back with a smile that did nothing to reassure her.

'Well, we shall see,' he murmured, and glanced at his watch. 'It's time you were on your way to meet that moribund aunt of yours. You can make sure she hasn't changed her will, because we might stir up some excitement by bumping her off.'

She made a face at him and stood up.

'What are you going to do tonight?'

'I called Claud Eustace this morning and made a date to take him out to dinner—maybe he'll know about something exciting that's going on. And it's time we were on our way too. Are you ready, Hoppy?'

The rudimentary assortment of features which constituted the hairless or front elevation of Hoppy Uniatz's head emerged lingeringly from behind the bottle of Caledonian dew with which he had been making another of his indomitable attempts to assuage the chronic aridity of his gullet.

'Sure, boss,' he said agreeably. 'Ain't I always ready? Where do we meet dis dame we gotta bump off?'

The Saint sighed.

'You'll find out,' he said. 'Let's go.'

Mr Uniatz trotted placidly after him. In Mr Uniatz's mind, a delicate organ which he had to be careful not to overwork, there was room for none of the manifestations of philosophical indignation with which Simon Templar was sometimes troubled. By the time it had found space for the ever-present problems of quenching an insatiable thirst and finding a sufficient supply of lawfully bumpable targets to keep the rust from forming in the barrel of his Betsy, it really had room for only one other idea. And that other permanently comforting and omnipresent notion was composed entirely of the faith and devotion with which he clung to the intellectual pre-eminence of the Saint. The Saint, Mr Uniatz had long since realised, with almost religious awe, could Think. To Mr Uniatz, a man whose rare experiments with Thought had always given him a dull pain under the hat, this discovery had simplified life to the point where Paradise itself would have had few advantages to offer, except possibly rivers flowing with Scotch whisky. He simply did what he was told, and everything came out all right. Anything the Saint said was OK with him.

It is a lamentable fact that Chief Inspector Claud Eustace Teal had no such faith to buoy him up. Mr Teal's views were almost diametrically the reverse of those which gave so much consolation to Mr Uniatz. To Mr Teal, the Saint was a perennial harbinger of woe, an everlasting time-bomb planted under his official chair—with the only difference that when ordinary bombs blew up they were at least over and done with, whereas the Saint was a bomb with the supernatural and unfair ability to blow up whenever it wanted to without in any way impairing its capacity for future explosions. He had accepted the Saint's invitation to dinner with an uneasy and actually unjustified suspicion that there was probably a catch in it, as there had been in most of his previous encounters with the Saint; and there was a gleam of something like smugness in his sleepy eyes as he settled more firmly behind his desk at Scotland Yard and shook his head with every conventional symptom of regret.

'I'm sorry, Saint,' he said. 'I ought to have phoned you, but I've been so busy. I'm going to have to ask you to fix another evening. We had a bank hold-up at Staines today, and I've got to go down there and take over.'

Simon's brows began to rise by an infinitesimal hopeful fraction.

'A bank hold-up, Claud? How much did they get away with?'

'About fifteen thousand pounds,' Teal said grudgingly. 'You ought to know. It was in the evening papers.'

'I do seem to remember seeing something about it tucked away somewhere,' Simon said thoughtfully. 'What do you know?'

The detective's mouth closed and tightened up. It was as if he was already regretting having said so much, even though the information was broadcast on the streets for anyone with a spare penny to read. But he had seen that tentatively optimistic flicker of the Saint's mocking eyes too often in the past to ever be able to see it again without a queasy hollow feeling in the pit of his ample stomach. He reacted to it with a brusqueness that sprang from a long train of memories of other occasions when crime had been in the news and boodle in the wind, and Simon Templar had greeted both promises with the same incorrigibly hopeful glimmer of mischief in his eyes, and that warning had presaged one more nightmare chapter in the apparently endless sequence that had made the name of the Saint the most dreaded word in the vocabulary of the underworld and the source of more grey hairs in Chief Inspector Teal's dwindling crop than any one man had a right to inflict on a conscientious officer of the law.

'If I knew all about it I shouldn't have to go to Staines,' he said conclusively. 'I'm sorry, but I can't tell you where to go and pick up the money.'

'Maybe I could run you down,' Simon began temptingly. 'Hoppy and I are all on our own this evening, and we were just looking for something useful to do. My car's outside, and it needs some exercise. Besides, I feel clever tonight. All my genius for sleuthing and deduction—'

'I'm sorry,' Teal repeated. 'There's a police car waiting for me already. I'll have to get along as well as I can without you.' He stood up, and held out his hand. A sensitive man might almost have thought that he was in a hurry to avoid an argument. 'Give me a ring one day next week, will you? I'll be able to tell you all about it then.'

Simon Templar stood on the Embankment outside Scotland Yard and lighted a cigarette with elaborately elegant restraint.

'And that, Hoppy,' he explained, 'is what is technically known as the Bum's Rush.'

He gazed resentfully at the dingy panorama which is the sum total of everything that generations of London architects and County Councils have been able to make out of their river frontages.

'Nobody loves us,' he said gloomily. 'Patricia forsakes us to be a dutiful niece to a palsied aunt, thereby leaving us exposed to every kind of temptation. We try to surround ourselves with holiness by dining with a detective, and he's too busy to keep the date. We offer to help him and array ourselves on the side of law and order, and he gives us the tax-collector's welcome. His evil mind distrusts our immaculate motives. He is so full of suspicion and uncharitableness that he thinks our only idea is to catch up with his bank holder-uppers before he does and relieve them of their loot for our own benefit. He practically throws us out on our ear, and abandons us to any wicked schemes we can cook up. What are we going to do about it?'

'I dunno, boss.' Mr Uniatz shifted from one foot to the other, grimacing with the heroic effort of trying to extract a constructive suggestion from the gummy interior of his skull. He hit upon one at last, with the trepidant amazement of another Newton grasping the law of gravity. 'Maybe we could go some place an' get a drink,' he suggested breathlessly.

Simon grinned at him and took him by the arm.

'For once in your life,' he said, 'I believe you've had an inspiration. Let us go to a pub and drown our sorrows.'

On the way he bought another evening paper and turned wistfully to the story of the bank hold-up; but it gave him very little more than Teal had told him. The bank was a branch of the City & Continental, which handled the accounts of two important factories on the outskirts of the town. That morning the routine consignment of cash in silver and small notes had been brought down from London in a guarded van to meet the weekly payrolls of the two plants; and after it had been placed in the strong-room the van and the guards had departed as usual, although the factory messengers would not call for it until the afternoon. There was no particular secrecy about the arrangements, and the possibility of a hold-up of the bank itself had apparently never been taken seriously. During the lunch hour the local police, acting on an anonymous telephone call, had sent a hurried squad to the bank in time to interrupt the hold-up; but the bandits had shot their way out, wounding two constables in the process; and approximately fifteen thousand pounds' worth of untraceable small change had vanished with them. Their car had been found abandoned only a few blocks from the bank premises, and there the trail ended; and the Saint knew that it was likely to stay ended there for all the clues contained in the printed story. England was a small country, but it contained plenty of room for two unidentified bank robbers to hide in.

Simon refolded the newspaper and dumped it resignedly on the bar; and as he did so it lay in such a way that the headlines summarising the epochal utterance of Mr Ebenezer Hogsbotham stared up at him with a complacent prominence that added insult to injury.

The Saint stared malevolently back at them; and in the mood which circumstances had helped to thrust upon him their effect had an almost fateful inevitability. No other man on earth would have taken them in just that way; but there never had been another man in history so harebrained as the Saint could be when his rebellious instincts boiled over. The idea that was being born to him grew momentarily in depth and richness. He put down his glass, and went to the telephone booth to consult the directory. The action was rather like the mental tossing of a coin. And it came down heads. Mr Hogsbotham was on the telephone. And accordingly, decisively, his address was in the book . . .

The fact seemed to leave no further excuse for hesitation. Simon went back to the bar, and his head sang carols with the blitheness of his own insanity.

'Put that poison away, Hoppy,' he said. 'We're going places.'

Mr Uniatz gulped obediently, and looked up with a contented beam.

'Dijja t'ink of sump'n to do, boss?' he asked eagerly.

The Saint nodded. His smile was extravagantly radiant.

'I did. We're going to burgle the house of Hogsbotham.'

## II

It was one of those lunatic ideas that any inmate of an asylum might have conceived, but only Simon Templar could be relied on to carry solemnly into execution. He didn't waste any more time on pondering over it, or even stop to consider any of its legal aspects. He drove his huge cream and red Hirondel snarling over the roads to Chertsey at an average speed that was a crime in itself, and which would probably have given a nervous breakdown to any passenger less impregnably phlegmatic than Mr Uniatz; but he brought it intact to the end of the trip without any elaborations on his original idea or any attempt to produce them. He was simply on his way to effect an unlawful entry into the domicile of Mr Hogsbotham, and there to do something or other that would annoy Mr Hogsbotham greatly and at the same time relieve his own mood of general annoyance; but what that something would be rested entirely with the inspiration of the moment. The only thing he was sure about was that the inspiration would be forthcoming.

The telephone directory had told him that Mr Hogsbotham lived at Chertsey. It also located Mr Hogsbotham's home on Greenleaf Road, which Simon found to be a narrow turning off Chertsey Lane running towards the river on the far side of the town. He drove the Hirondel into a field a hundred yards beyond the turning and left it under the broad shadow of a clump of elms, and returned to Greenleaf Road on foot. And there the telephone directory's information became vague. Following the ancient custom by which the Englishman strives to preserve the sanctity of his castle from strange visitors by refusing to give it a street number, hiding it instead under a name like 'Mon Repos', 'Sea View', 'The Birches', 'Dunrovin', 'Jusweetu', and other similar whimsies, the demesne of Mr Hogsbotham was apparently known simply as 'The Snuggery'. Which might have conveyed volumes to a postman schooled in tracking self-effacing citizens to their lairs, but wasn't the hell of a lot of help to any layman who was trying to find the place for the first time on a dark night.

Simon had not walked very far down Greenleaf Road when that fact was brought home to him. Greenleaf Road possessed no street lighting to make navigation easier. It was bordered by hedges of varying heights and densities, behind which lighted windows could sometimes be seen and sometimes not. At intervals, the hedges yawned into gaps from which ran well-kept drives and things that looked like cart-tracks in about equal proportions. Some of the openings had gates, and some hadn't. Some of the gates had names painted on them; and on those which had, the paint varied in antiquity from shining newness to a state of weather-beaten decomposition which made any name that had ever been there completely illegible. When the Saint realised that they had already passed at least a dozen anonymous entrances, any one of which might have led to the threshold of Mr Hogsbotham's Snuggery, he stopped walking and spoke eloquently on the subject of town planning for a full minute without raising his voice.

He could have gone on for longer than that, warming to his subject as he developed the theme; but farther down the road the wobbling light of a lone bicycle blinked into view, and he stepped out from the side of the road as it came abreast of them and kept his hat down over his eyes and his face averted from the light while he asked the rider if he knew the home of Hogsbotham.

'Yes, sir, it's the fourth 'ouse on yer right the way yer goin'. Yer carn't miss it,' said the wanderer cheerfully, with a native's slightly patronising simplicity, and rode on.

The Saint paused to light a cigarette, and resumed his stride. The lines of his face dimly illumined in the glow of smouldering tobacco were sharp with half-humorous anticipation.

'Hogsbotham may be in London investigating some more night clubs,' he said. 'But you'd better get a handkerchief tied round your neck so you can pull it up over your dial—just in case. We don't want to be recognised, because it would worry Claud Eustace Teal, and he's busy.'

He was counting the breaks in the hedges as he walked. He counted three, and stopped at the fourth. A gate that could have closed it stood open, and he turned his pocket flashlight on it cautiously. It was one of the weather-beaten kind, and the words that had once been painted on it were practically undecipherable, but they looked vaguely as if they might once have stood for 'The Snuggery'.

Simon killed his torch after that brief glimpse. He dropped his cigarette and trod it out under his foot.

'We seem to have arrived,' he said. 'Try not to make too much noise, Hoppy, because maybe Hogsbotham isn't deaf.'

He drifted on up the drive as if his shoes had been soled with cotton wool. Following behind him, Mr Uniatz's efforts to lighten his tread successfully reduced the total din of their advance to something less than would have been made by a small herd of buffalo; but Simon knew that the average citizen's sense of hearing is mercifully unselective. His own silent movements were more the result of habit than of any conscious care.

The drive curved around a dense mass of laurels, above which the symmetrical spires of cypress silhouetted against the dark sky concealed the house until it loomed suddenly in front of him as if it had risen from the ground. The angles of its roof-line cut a serrated pattern out of the gauzy backcloth of half-hearted stars hung behind it; the rest of the building below that angled line was merely a mass of solid blackness in which one or two knife-edges of yellow light gleaming between drawn curtains seemed to be suspended disjointedly in space. But they came from ground-floor windows, and he concluded that Ebenezer Hogsbotham was at home.

He did not decide that Mr Hogsbotham was not only at home, but at home with visitors, until he nearly walked into a black closed car parked in the driveway. The car's lights were out, and he was so intent on trying to establish the topography of the lighted windows that the dull sheen of its coachwork barely caught his eye in time for him to check himself. He steered Hoppy round it, and wondered what sort of guests a man with the name and temperament of Ebenezer Hogsbotham would be likely to entertain.

And then, inside the house, a radio or gramophone began to play.

It occurred to Simon that he might have been unnecessarily pessimistic in suggesting that Mr Hogsbotham might not be deaf. From the muffled quality of the noise which reached him, it was obvious that the windows of the room in which the instrument was functioning were tightly closed; but even with that obstruction, the volume of sound which boomed out into the night was startling in its quantity. The opus under execution was the 'Ride of the Valkyries', which is admittedly not rated among the most ethereal melodies in the musical pharmacopoeia; but even so, it was being produced with a vim which inside the room itself must have been ear-splitting. It roared out in a stunning *fortissimo* that made the Saint put his heels back on the ground and disdain even to moderate his voice.

'This is easy,' he said. 'We'll just batter the door down and walk in.'

He was not quite as blatant as that, but very nearly. He was careful enough to circle the house to the back door; and whether he would actually have battered it down remained an unanswered question, for he had no need to use any violence on it at all. It opened when he touched the handle, and he stepped in as easily as he had entered the garden.

Perhaps it was at that point that he first realised that the unplanned embryo of his adventure was taking a twist which he had never expected of it. It was difficult to pin down the exact moment of mutation, because it gathered force from a series of shocks that superimposed themselves on him with a speed that made the separate phases of the change seem somewhat blurred. And the first two or three of those shocks chased each other into his consciousness directly that unlatched back door swung inwards under the pressure of his hand.

The very fact that the door opened so easily to his exploring touch may have been one of them; but he could take that in his stride. Many householders were inclined to be absent-minded about the uses of locks and bolts. But the following blows were harder to swallow. The door opened to give him a clear view of the kitchen; and that was when the rapid sequence of impacts began to make an impression on his powers of absorption.

To put it bluntly, which is about the only way anything of that kind could be put, the door opened to give him a full view of what appeared to be quite a personable young woman tied to a chair.

There was a subsidiary shock in the realisation that she appeared to be personable. Without giving any thought to the subject, Simon had never expected Mr Hogsbotham to have a servant who was personable. He had automatically credited him with a housekeeper who had stringy mouse-coloured hair, a long nose inclined to redness, and a forbidding lipless mouth, a harridan in tight-laced corsets whose egregiously obvious virtue would suffice to strangle any gossip about Mr Hogsbotham's bachelor *ménage*— Mr Hogsbotham had to be a bachelor, because it was not plausible that any woman, unless moved by a passion which a man of Mr Hogsbotham's desiccated sanctity could never hope to inspire, would consent to adopt a name like Mrs Hogsbotham.

The girl in the chair appeared to be moderately young,

moderately well-shaped, and moderately inoffensive to look at; although the dishcloth which was knotted across her mouth as a gag made the last quality a little difficult to estimate. Yet she wore a neat housemaid's uniform, and therefore she presumably belonged to Mr Hogsbotham's domestic staff.

That also could be assimilated—with a slightly greater effort. It was her predicament that finally overtaxed his swallowing reflexes. It was possible that there might be some self-abnegating soul in the British Isles who was willing to visit with Mr Hogsbotham; it was possible that Mr Hogsbotham might be deaf; it was possible that he might be careless about locking his back door; it was possible, even, that he might employ a servant who didn't look like the twin sister of a Gorgon; but if he left her tied up and gagged in the kitchen while he entertained his guests with ear-shattering excerpts from Wagner, there was something irregular going on under his sanctimonious roof which Simon Templar wanted to know more about.

He stood staring into the maid's dilated eyes while a galaxy of fantastic queries and surmises skittered across his brain like the grand finale of a firework display. For one long moment he couldn't have moved or spoken if there had been a million-dollar bonus for it.

Mr Uniatz was the one who broke the silence, if any state of affairs that was so numbingly blanketed by the magnified blast of a symphony orchestra could properly be called a silence. He shifted his feet, and his voice grated conspiratorially in the Saint's ear.

'Is dis de old bag, boss?' he inquired with sepulchral *sangfroid*; and the interruption brought Simon's reeling imagination back to earth.

'What old bag?' he demanded blankly.

'De aunt of Patricia's,' said Mr Uniatz, no less blank at even being asked such a question, 'who we are goin' to bump off.'

The Saint took a firmer grip of material things.

'Does she look like an old bag?' he retorted.

Hoppy inspected the exhibit again, dispassionately.

'No,' he admitted. He seemed mystified. Then a solution dawned dazzlingly upon him. 'Maybe she has her face lifted, boss,' he suggested luminously.

'Or maybe she isn't anybody's aunt,' Simon pointed out.

This kind of extravagant speculation was too much for Mr Uniatz. He was unable to gape effectively on account of the handkerchief over his mouth, but the exposed area between the bridge of his nose and the brim of his hat hinted that the rest of his face was gaping.

'And maybe we've run into something,' said the Saint.

The rest of his mind was paying no attention to Hoppy's problems. He was not even taking much notice of the maid's panic-stricken eyes as they widened still further in mute terror at the conversation that was passing over her head. He was listening intently to the music that still racketed stridently in his eardrums, three times louder now that he was inside the house. There had been a time in the history of his multitudinous interests when he had had a spell of devotion to grand opera, and his ears were as analytically sensitive as those of a trained musician. And he was realising, with a melodramatic suddenness that prickled the hairs on the nape of his neck, that the multisonous shrillness of the Ride of the Valkyries had twice been mingled with a brief high-pitched shriek that Wagner had never written into the score.

His fingers closed for an instant on Hoppy's arm.

'Stay here a minute,' he said.

He went on past the trussed housemaid, out of the door on the far side of the kitchen. The screeching fanfares of music battered at him with redoubled savagery as he opened the door and emerged into the cramped over-furnished hall beyond it. Aside from its clutter of fretwork mirror-mountings, spindly umbrella-stands and etceteras, and vapid Victorian chromos, it contained only the lower end of a narrow staircase and three other doors, one of which was the front entrance. Simon had subconsciously observed a serving hatch in the wall on his left as he opened the kitchen door, and on that evidence he automatically attributed the left-hand door in the hallway to the dining-room. He moved towards the right-hand door. And as he reached it the music stopped, in the middle of a bar, as if it had been sheared off with a knife, leaving the whole house stunned with stillness.

The Saint checked on one foot, abruptly conscious even of his breathing in the sudden quiet. He was less than a yard from the door that must have belonged to the living-room. Standing there, he heard the harsh rumble of a thick brutal voice on the other side of the door, dulled in volume but perfectly distinct.

'All right,' it said. 'That's just a sample. Now will you tell us what you did with that dough, or shall we play some more music?'

### III

Simon lowered his spare foot to the carpet, and bent his leg over it until he was down on one knee. From that position he could peer through the keyhole and get a view of part of the room.

Directly across from him, a thin small weasel-faced man stood over a radiogram beside the fireplace. A cigarette dangled limply from the corner of his mouth, and the eyes that squinted through the smoke drifting past his face were beady and emotionless like a snake's. Simon placed the lean cruel face almost instantly in his encyclopaedic mental records of the population of the underworld, and the recognition walloped into his already tottering awareness to register yet another item in the sequence of surprise punches that his phenomenal resilience was trying to stand up to. The weasel-faced man's name was Morris Dolf; and he was certainly no kind of guest for anyone with the reputation of Ebenezer Hogsbotham to entertain.

The Saint's survey slid off him on to the man who sat in front of the fireplace. This was someone whom the Saint did not recognise, and he knew he was not Mr Hogsbotham. He was a man with thin sandy hair and a soft plump face that would have fitted very nicely on somebody's pet rabbit. At the moment it was a very frightened rabbit. The man sat in a stiff-backed chair placed on the hearth-rug, and pieces of clothes-line had been used to keep him there. His arms had been stretched round behind him and tied at the back of the chair so that his shoulders were hunched slightly forward by the strain. His shirt had been ripped open to the waist, so that his chest was bare; and his skin was very white and insipid, as if it had never seen daylight since he was born. It was so white that two irregular patches of inflammation on it stood out like blotches of dull red paint. His lips were trembling, and his eyes bulged in wild orbs of dread.

'I don't know!' he blubbered. 'I tell you, you're making a mistake. I don't know anything about it. I haven't got it. Don't burn me again!'

Morris Dolf might not have heard. He stood leaning boredly against the radiogram and didn't move.

Someone else did. It was a third man, whose back was turned to the door. The back was broad and fitted tightly into his coat, so that the material wrinkled at the armpits, and the neck above it was short and thick and reddish, running quickly into close-cropped wiry back hair. The whole rear view had a hard coarse physical ruthlessness that made it unnecessary to see its owner's face to make an immediate summary of his character. It belonged without a shadow of doubt to the thick brutal voice that Simon had heard first—and equally without doubt, it could not possibly have belonged to Mr Ebenezer Hogsbotham.

The same voice spoke again. It said: 'OK, Verdean. But you're the one who made the mistake. You made it when you thought you'd be smart and try to double-cross us. You made it worse when you tried to turn us in to the cops, so we could take the rap for you and leave you nothing to worry about. Now you're going to wish you hadn't been so damn smart.'

The broad back moved forward and bent towards the fireplace. The gas fire was burning in the grate, although the evening was warm; and all at once the Saint understood why he had heard through the music those screechy ululations which no orchestral instrument could have produced. The man with the broad back straightened up again, and his powerful hand was holding an ordinary kitchen ladle of which the bowl glowed bright crimson.

'You have it just how you like, rat,' he said. 'I don't mind how long you hold out. I'm going to enjoy working on you. We're going to burn your body a bit more for a start, and then we'll take your shoes and socks off and put your feet in the fire and see how you like that. You can scream your head off if you want to, but nobody'll hear you over the gramophone . . . Let's have some more of that loud stuff, Morrie.'

Morris Dolf turned back to the radiogram, without a flicker of expression, and moved the pick-up arm. The 'Ride of the Valkyries' crashed out again with a fearful vigour that would have drowned anything less than the howl of a hurricane; and the broad back shifted towards the man in the chair.

The man in the chair stared in delirious horror from the glowing ladle to the face of the man who held it. His eyes bugged until there were white rims all round the pupils. His quivering lips fluttered into absurd jerky patterns, pouring out frantic pleas and protestations that the music swamped into inaudibility.

Simon Templar removed his eye from the keyhole and loosened the gun under his arm. He had no fanciful ideas about rushing to the rescue of a hapless victim of persecution. In fact, all the more subtle aspects of the victim looked as guilty as hell to him— if not of the actual double-crossing that seemed to be under discussion, at least of plenty of other reprehensible things. No entirely innocent householder would behave in exactly that way if he were being tortured by a couple of invading thugs. And the whole argument as Simon had overheard it smelled ripely with the rich fragrance of dishonour and dissension among thieves. Which was an odour that had perfumed some of the most joyous hours of the Saint's rapscallion life. By all the portents, he was still a puzzlingly long way from getting within kicking distance of the elusive Mr Hogsbotham; but here under his very nose was a proposition that looked no less diverting and a lot more mysterious; and the Saint had a sublimely happy-go-lucky adaptability to the generous vagaries of Fate. He took his gun clear out of the spring harness where he carried it, and opened the door.

He went in without any stealth, which would have been entirely superfluous. The operatic pandemonium would have made his entrance mouse-like if he had ridden in on a capering elephant. He walked almost nonchalantly across the room; and its occupants were so taken up with their own business that he was within a couple of yards of them before any of them noticed that he was there.

Morris Dolf saw him first. His beady eyes swivelled incuriously towards the movement that must have finally caught the fringes of their range of vision, and became petrified into glassy blankness as they fastened on the Saint's tall figure. His jaw dropped so that the cigarette would have fallen out of his mouth if the adhesive dampness of the paper hadn't kept it hanging from his lower lip. He stood as horripilantly still as if a long icy needle had shot up out of the floor and impaled him from sacrum to occiput.

That glazed paralysis lasted for about a breath and a half. And then his right hand whipped towards his pocket.

It was nothing but an involuntary piece of sheer stupidity born out of shock, and the Saint was benevolent enough to treat it that way. He simply lifted the gun in his hand a little, bringing it more prominently into view; and Dolf stopped himself in time.

The man with the beefy neck, in his turn, must have caught some queer impression from Dolf's peculiar movements out of the corner of his eye. He turned and looked at his companion's face, froze for an instant, and then went on turning more quickly, straightening as he did so. He let go the red-hot ladle, and his right hand started to make the same instinctive grab that Dolf had started—and stopped in mid-air for the same reason. His heavy florid features seemed to bunch into knots of strangulated viciousness as he stood glowering numbly at the Saint's masked face.

Simon stepped sideways, towards the blaring radiogram, and lifted the needle off the record. The nerve-rasping bombardment of sound broke off into blissful silence.

'That's better,' he murmured relievedly. 'Now we can all talk to each other without giving ourselves laryngitis. When did you discover this passion for expensive music, Morrie?'

Morris Dolf's eyes blinked once at the jar of being addressed by name, but he seemed to find it hard to work up an enthusiasm for discussing his cultural development. His tongue slid over his dry lips without forming an answering syllable.

Simon turned to the big florid man. Now that he had seen his face, he had identified him as well.

'Judd Kaskin, I believe?' he drawled, with the delicate suavity of an ambassador of the old régime. 'Do you know that you're burning the carpet?'

Kaskin looked at the fallen ladle. He bent and picked it up, rubbing the sole of his shoe over the smouldering patch of rug. Then, as if he suddenly realised that he had done all that in mechanical obedience to a command that the Saint hadn't even troubled to utter directly, he threw it clattering into the fireplace and turned his savage scowl back to the Saint.

'What the hell do you want?' he snarled.

'You know, I was just going to ask you the same question,' Simon remarked mildly. 'It seemed to me that you were feeling your oats a bit, Judd. I suppose you get that way after doing five years on the Moor. But you haven't been out much more than three months, have you? You shouldn't be in such a hurry to go back.'

The big man's eyes gave the same automatic reaction as Dolf's had given to the accuracy of the Saint's information, and hardened again into slits of unyielding suspicion.

'Who the hell are you?' he grated slowly. 'You aren't a cop. Take that rag off your face and let's see who you are.'

'When I'm ready,' said the Saint coolly. 'And then you may wish I hadn't. Just now. I'm asking the questions. What is this double-cross you're trying to find out about from Comrade Verdean?'

There was a silence. Morris Dolf's slight expression was fading out again. His mouth closed, and he readjusted his cigarette. Simon knew that behind that silent hollow-cheeked mask a cunning brain was getting back to work.

Kaskin's face, when he wanted to play tricks with it, could put on a ruddy rough-diamond joviality that was convincing enough to deceive most people who did not know too much about his criminal record. But at this moment he was making no effort to put on his stock disguise. His mouth was buttoned up in an ugly down-turned curve.

'Why don't you find out, if you're so wise?'

'I could do that,' said the Saint.

He moved on the arc of a circle towards Verdean's chair, keeping Dolf and Kaskin covered all the time. His left hand dipped into his coat pocket and took out a penknife. He opened it one-handed, bracing it against his leg, and felt around to cut the cords from Verdean's wrists and ankles without shifting his eyes for an instant from the two men at the other end of his gun.

'We can go on with the concert,' he explained gently. 'And I'm sure Comrade Verdean would enjoy having a turn as Master of Ceremonies. Put the spoon back in the fire, Verdean, and let's see how Comrade Kaskin likes his chops broiled.'

Verdean stood up slowly, and didn't move any farther. His gaze wavered idiotically over the Saint, as if he was too dazed to make up his mind what he ought to do. He pawed at his burned chest and made helpless whimpering noises in his throat, like a sick child.

Kaskin glanced at him for a moment, and slowly brought his eyes back to the Saint again. At the time, Simon thought that it was Verdean's obvious futility that kindled the stiffening belligerent defiance in Kaskin's stare. There was something almost like tentative domination in it.

Kaskin sneered: 'See if he'll do it. He wouldn't have the guts.

And you can't, while you've got to keep that gun on us. I'm not soft enough to fall for that sort of bluff. You picked the wrong show to butt in on, however you got here. You'd better get out again in a hurry before you get hurt. You'd better put that gun away and go home, and forget you ever came here—'

And another voice said: 'Or you can freeze right where you are. Don't try to move, or I'll let you have it.'

The Saint froze.

The voice was very close behind him—too close to take any chances with. He could have flattened Kaskin before it could carry out its threat, but that was as far as he would get. The Saint had a cold-blooded way of estimating his chances in any situation; and he was much too interested in life just then to make that kind of trade. He knew now the real reason for Kaskin's sudden gathering of confidence, and why the big man had talked so fast in a strain that couldn't help centring his attention. Kaskin had taken his opportunity well. Not a muscle of his face had betrayed what he was seeing; and his loud bullying voice had effectively covered any slight noise that the girl might have made as she crept up.

The girl. Yes. Simon Templar's most lasting startlement clung to the fact that the voice behind him unmistakably belonged to a girl.

## IV

'Drop that gun,' she said, 'and be quick about it.'

Simon dropped it. His ears were nicely attuned to the depth of meaning behind a voice, and this voice meant what it said. His automatic plunked on the carpet; and Morris Dolf stooped into the scene and snatched it up. Even then, Dolf said nothing. He propped himself back on the radiogram and kept the gun levelled, watching Simon in silence with sinister lizard eyes. He was one of the least talkative men that Simon had ever seen.

'Keep him covered,' Kaskin said unnecessarily. 'We'll see what he looks like.'

He stepped forward and jerked the handkerchief down from the Saint's face.

And then there was a stillness that prolonged itself through a gamut of emotions which would have looked like the most awful kind of ham acting if they had been faithfully recorded on celluloid. Neither Dolf nor Kaskin had ever met the Saint personally; but his photograph had at various times been published in almost every newspaper on earth, and verbal descriptions of him had circulated through underworld channels so often that they must have worn a private groove for themselves. Admittedly there were still considerable numbers of malefactors to whom the Saint was no more than a dreaded name; but Messrs Dolf and Kaskin were not among them. Recognition came to them slowly, which accounted for the elaborate and long-drawn detail of their changing expressions; but it came with a frightful certainty. Morris Dolf's fleshless visage seemed to grow thinner and meaner, and his fingers twitched hungrily around the butt of Simon's gun. Judd Kaskin's sanguine complexion changed colour for a moment, and then his mouth twisted as though tasting its own venom.

'The Saint!' he said hoarsely.

'I told you you might be sorry,' said the Saint.

He smiled at them pleasantly, as if nothing had happened to disturb his poise since he was holding the only weapon in sight. It was a smile that would have tightened a quality of desperation into the vigilance of certain criminals who knew him better than Dolf and Kaskin did. It was the kind of smile that only touched the Saint's lips when the odds against him were most hopeless— and when all the reckless fighting vitality that had written the chapter headings in his charmed saga of adventure was blithely preparing to thumb its nose at them . . .

Then he turned and looked at the girl.

She was blonde and blue-eyed, with a small face like a very pretty baby doll; but the impression of vapid immaturity was contradicted by her mouth. Her mouth had character—not all of it very good, by conventional standards, but the kind of character that has an upsetting effect on many conventional men. It was a rather large mouth, with a sultry lower lip that seemed to have been fashioned for the express purpose of reviving the maximum amount of the Old Adam in any masculine observer. The rest of her, he noticed, carried out the theme summarised in her mouth. Her light dress moulded itself to her figure with a snugness that vouched for the fragility of her underwear, and the curves that it suggested were stimulating to the worst kind of imagination.

'Angela,' said the Saint genially, 'you're looking very well for your age. I ought to have remembered that Judd always worked with a woman, but I didn't think he'd have one with him on a job like this. I suppose you were sitting in the car outside, and saw me arrive.'

'You know everything, don't you?' Kaskin gibed.

He was recovering from the first shock of finding out whom he had captured; and the return of his self-assurance was an ugly thing.

'Only one thing puzzles me,' said the Saint equably. 'And that is why they sent you to Dartmoor instead of putting you in the Zoo. Or did the R.S.P.C.A. object on behalf of the other animals?'

'You're smart,' Kaskin said lividly. His ugliness had a hint of bluster in it that was born of fear—a fear that the legends about the Saint were capable of inspiring even when he was apparently disarmed and helpless. But the ugliness was no less dangerous for that reason. Perhaps it was more dangerous ... 'You're smart, like Verdean,' Kaskin said. 'Well, you saw what he got. I'm asking the questions again now, and I'll burn you the same way if you don't answer. And I'll burn you twice as much if you make any more funny answers. Now do your talking, smart guy. How did you get here?'

'I flew in,' said the Saint, 'with my little wings.'

Kaskin drew back his fist.

'Wait a minute,' said the girl impatiently. 'He had another man with him.'

Kaskin almost failed to hear her. His face was contorted with the blind rage into which men of his type are fatally easy to tease. His fist had travelled two inches before he stopped it. The girl's meaning worked itself into his intelligence by visibly slow degrees, as if it had to penetrate layers of gum. He turned his head stiffly.

'What's that?'

'There were two of them. I saw them.'

'Then where's the other one?' Kaskin said stupidly.

Simon was asking himself the same question; but he had more data to go on. He had left the kitchen door open, and also left the living-room door open behind him when he came in. The girl had come in through the door without touching it; and she must have entered the house at the front, or she would have met Hoppy before. The chances were, therefore, that Hoppy had heard most of the conversation since the music stopped. But with the living-room door still open, and three of the ungodly in the room facing in different directions, it would be difficult for him to show himself and go into action without increasing the Saint's danger. He must have been standing in the hall by that time, just out of sight around the edge of the doorway, waiting for Simon to make him an opening. At least, Simon hoped he was. He had to gamble on it, for he was never likely to get a better break.

Kaskin swung back on him to repeat the question in a lower key.

'Where's your pal, smart guy?'

'You haven't looked at the window lately, have you?' said the Saint blandly.

At any other time it might not have worked; but this time the ungodly were at a disadvantage because one of their own number had brought up the subject. They had another disadvantage, because they didn't realise until a second later that the room contained more than one window. And their third misfortune was that they all gave way simultaneously to a natural instinct of self-preservation that the Saint's indescribably effortless serenity did everything in its power to encourage. All of them looked different ways at once, while all of them must have assumed that somebody else was continuing to watch the Saint. Which provided a beautiful example of one of those occasions when unanimity is not strength.

Kaskin was nearly between Simon and the girl, and the Saint's swift sidestep perfected the alignment. The Saint's right foot drove at the big man's belt buckle, sent Kaskin staggering back against her. She was caught flat-footed, and started moving too late to dodge him. They collided with a thump; but Kaskin's momentum was too great to be completely absorbed by the impact. They reeled back together, Kaskin's flailing arms nullifying the girl's desperate effort to regain her balance. The small nickelled automatic waved wildly in her hand.

Simon didn't wait to see how the waltz worked out. He had only a matter of split seconds to play with, and they had to be crowded ones. He was pivoting on his left foot, with his right leg still in the air, even as Kaskin started caroming backwards from the kick; and Morris Dolf was a fraction of an instant slow in sorting out the situation. The Saint's left hand grabbed his automatic around the barrel before the trigger could tighten, twisting it sideways out of line: it exploded once, harmlessly, and then the Saint's right fist slammed squarely on the weasel-faced man's thin nose. Morris Dolf's eyes bleared with agony, and his fingers went limp with the stunning pain. Simon wrenched the gun away and reversed the butt swiftly into his right hand.

The Saint spun round. Hoppy's chunky outline loomed in the doorway, his massive automatic questing for a target, a pleased warrior smile splitting the lower half of his face. But Kaskin was finding solid ground under his feet again, and his right hand was struggling with his hip pocket. The girl's nickel-plated toy was coming back to aim. And behind him, the Saint knew that Morris Dolf was getting out another gun. Simon had only taken back the automatic he had lost a short while earlier. Morris Dolf still had his own gun. The Saint felt goose-pimples rising all over him.

'The lights, Hoppy!' he yelled. 'And scram out the front!'

He dived sideways as he spoke; and darkness engulfed the room mercifully as he did it. Cordite barked malignantly out of the blackness, licking hot orange tongues at him from two directions: he heard the hiss and smack of lead, but it did not touch him. And then his dive cannoned him into the man called Verdean.

It was Verdean that he had meant to reach. His instinct had mapped the campaign with a speed and sureness that deliberate logic still had to catch up with. But all the steps were there. The atmosphere of the moment showed no probability of simmering down into that mellow tranquillity in which heart-to-heart talks are exchanged. The Saint very much wanted a heart-to-heart talk with somebody, if only to satisfy a perfectly normal inquisitiveness concerning what all the commotion was about. But since Messrs Dolf and Kaskin had been asking the questions when he arrived, it appeared that Mr Verdean might know more of the answers than they did. Therefore Mr Verdean looked like the prize catch of the evening. Therefore Mr Verdean had to be transported to an atmosphere where heart-to-heart talking might take place. It was as simple as that.

The Saint gripped Verdean by the arm, and said: 'Let's go somewhere else, brother. Your friends are getting rough.'

Verdean took one step the way the Saint steered him, and then he turned into a convincing impersonation of an hysterical eel. He squirmed against the Saint's grasp with the strength of panic, and his free arm whirled frantically in the air. His knuckles hit the Saint's cheek-bone near the eye, sending a shower of sparks across Simon's vision.

Simon might have stopped to reason with him, to persuasively point out the manifest arguments in favour of adjourning to a less hectic neighbourhood; but he had no time. No more shots had been fired, doubtless because it had been borne in upon the ungodly that they stood a two to one chance of doing more damage to each other than to him, but he could hear them blundering in search of him. The Saint raised his gun and brought the barrel down vigorously where he thought Verdean's head ought to be. Mr Verdean's head proved to be in the desired spot; and Simon ducked a shoulder under him and lifted him up as he collapsed.

The actual delay amounted to less than three seconds. The ungodly were still blinded by the dark, but Simon launched himself at the window with the accuracy of a homing pigeon.

He wasted no time fumbling with catches. He hit the centre of it with his shoulder—the shoulder over which Verdean was draped. Verdean, in turn, hit it with his hams; and the fastening was not equal to the combined load. It splintered away with a sharp crack, and the twin casements flew open crashingly. Verdean passed through them into the night, landing in soft earth with a soggy thud; and the Saint went on after him as if he were plunging into a pool. He struck ground with his hands, and rolled over in a fairly graceful somersault as a fourth shot banged out of the room he had just left.

A gorilla paw caught him under the arm and helped him up, and Mr Uniatz's voice croaked anxiously in his ear.

'Ya ain't stopped anyt'ing, boss?'

'No.' Simon grinned in the dark. 'They aren't that good. Grab hold of this bird and see if the car'll start. They probably left the keys in it.'

He had located Mr Verdean lying where he had fallen. Simon raised him by the slack of his coat and slung him into Hoppy's bearlike clutch, and turned back towards the window just as the lights of the living-room went on again behind the disordered curtains.

He crouched in the shadow of a bush with his gun raised, and said in a much more carrying voice: 'I bet I can shoot my initials on the face of the first guy who sticks his nose outside.'

The lights went out a second time; and there was a considerable silence. The house might have been empty of life. Behind him, Simon heard an engine whine into life, drop back to a subdued purr as the starter disconnected. He backed towards the car, his eyes raking the house frontage relentlessly, until he could step on to the running-board.

'OK, Hoppy,' he said.

The black sedan slid forward. Another shot whacked out behind as he opened the door and tumbled into the front seat, but it was yards wide of usefulness. The headlights sprang into brilliance as they lurched through an opening ahead and skidded round in the lane beyond. For the first time in several overcrowded minutes, the Saint had leisure to get out his cigarette-case. The flame of his lighter painted jubilantly mephistophelian highlights on his face.

'Let's pick up our own car,' he said. 'Then we'll take our prize home and find out what we've won.'

He found out sooner than that. He only had to fish out Mr Verdean's wallet to find a half-dozen engraved cards that answered a whole tumult of questions with staggering simplicity. They said:

---

### MR. ROBERT VERDEAN

BRANCH MANAGER
CITY & CONTINENTAL BANK LTD
STAINES

---

V

Patricia Holm put two lumps of sugar in her coffee and stirred it.

'Well, that's your story,' she said coldly. 'So I suppose you're sticking to it. But what were you doing there in the first place?'

'I told you,' said the Saint. 'We were looking for Hogsbotham.'

'Why should you be looking for him?'

'Because he annoyed me. You remember. And we had to do something to pass the evening.'

'You could have gone to a movie.'

'What, and seen a picture about gangsters? You know what a demoralising influence these pictures have. It might have put ideas into my head.'

'Of course,' she said. 'You didn't have any ideas about Hogs-botham.'

'Nothing very definite,' he admitted. 'We might have just wedged his mouth open and poured him full of gin, and then pushed him in the stage door of a leg show, or something like that. Anyway, it didn't come to anything. We got into the wrong house, as you may have gathered. The bloke who told us the way said 'the fourth house,' but it was too dark to see houses. I was counting entrances; but I didn't discover until afterwards that Verdean's place has one of those U-shaped drives, with an in and an out gate, so I counted him twice. Hogsbotham's sty must have been the next house on. Verdean's house is called 'The Shutters', but the paint was so bad that I easily took it for 'The Snuggery'. After I'd made the mistake and got in there, I was more or less a pawn on the chessboard of chance. There was obviously something about Verdean that wanted investigating, and the way things panned out it didn't look healthy to investigate him on the spot. So we just had to bring him away with us.'

'You didn't have to hit him so hard that he'd get concussion and lose his memory.'

Simon rubbed his chin.

'There's certainly something in that, darling. But it was all very difficult. It was too dark for me to see just what I was doing, and I was in rather a rush. However, it does turn out to be a bit of a snag.'

He had discovered the calamity the night before, after he had unloaded Verdean at his country house at Weybridge—he had chosen that secluded lair as a destination partly because it was only about five miles from Chertsey, partly because it had more elaborate facilities for concealing captives than his London apartment. The bank manager had taken an alarmingly long time to recover consciousness; and when he eventually came back to life it was only to vomit and moan unintelligibly. In between retchings, his eyes wandered over his surroundings with a vacant stare into which even the use of his own name and the reminders of the plight from which he had been extricated could not bring a single flicker of response. Simon had dosed him with calomel and sedatives and put him to bed, hoping that he would be back to normal in the morning; but he had awakened in very little better condition, clutching his head painfully and mumbling nothing but listless uncomprehending replies to any question he was asked.

He was still in bed, giving no trouble but serving absolutely no useful purpose as a source of information; and the Saint gazed out of the window at the morning sunlight lancing through the birch and pine glade outside, and frowned ruefully over the consummate irony of the impasse.

'I might have known there'd be something like this waiting for me when you phoned me to come down for breakfast,' said Patricia stoically. 'How soon are you expecting Teal?'

The Saint chuckled.

'He'll probably be sizzling in much sooner than we want him— a tangle like this wouldn't be complete without good old Claud Eustace. But we'll worry about that when it happens. Meanwhile, we've got one consolation. Comrade Verdean seems to be one of those birds who stuff everything in their pockets until the stitches begin to burst. I've been going over his collection of junk again, and it tells quite a story when you put it together.'

Half of the breakfast table was taken up with the potpourri of relics which he had extracted from various parts of the bank manager's clothing, now sorted out into neat piles. Simon waved a spoon at them.

'Look them over for yourself, Pat. Nearest to you, you've got a couple of interesting souvenirs. Hotel bills. One of 'em is where Mr Robert Verdean stayed in a modest semi-boarding-house at Eastbourne for the first ten days of July. The other one follows straight on for the next five days; only it's from a swank sin-palace at Brighton, and covers the sojourn of a Mr and Mrs Jones who seem to have consumed a large amount of champagne during their stay. If you had a low mind like mine, you might begin to jump to a few conclusions about Comrade Verdean's last vacation.'

'I could get ideas.'

'Then the feminine handkerchief—a pretty little sentimental souvenir, but rather compromising.'

Patricia picked it up and sniffed it.

'Night of Sin,' she said with a slight grimace.

'Is that what it's called? I wouldn't know. But I do know that it's the same smell that the blonde floozie brought in with her last night. Her name is Angela Lindsay; and she has quite a reputation in the trade for having made suckers out of a lot of guys who should have been smarter than Comrade Verdean.'

She nodded.

'What about the big stack of letters. Are they love-letters?'

'Not exactly. They're bookmaker's accounts. And the little book on top of them isn't a heart-throb diary—it's a betting diary. The name on all of 'em is Joseph Mackintyre. And you'll remember from an old adventure of ours that Comrade Mackintyre has what you might call an elastic conscience about his bookmaking. The story is all there, figured down to pennies. Verdean seems to have started on the sixth of July, and he went off with a bang. By the middle of the month he must have wondered why he ever bothered to work in a bank. I'm not surprised he had champagne every night at Brighton—it was all free. But the luck started to change after that. He had fewer and fewer winners, and he went on plunging more and more heavily. The last entry in the diary, a fortnight ago, left him nearly five thousand pounds in the red. Your first name doesn't have to be Sherlock to put all those notes together and make a tune.'

Patricia's sweet face was solemn with thought.

'Those two men,' she said. 'Dolf and Kaskin. You knew them. What's their racket?'

'Morrie was one of Snake Ganning's spare-time boys once. He's dangerous. Quite a sadist, in his nasty little way. You could hire him for anything up to murder, at a price; but he really enjoys his work. Kaskin has more brains, though. He's more versatile. Confidence work, the old badger game, living off women, protection rackets—he's had a dab at all of them. He's worked around racetracks quite a bit, too, doping horses and intimidating jockeys and bookmakers and so forth, which makes him an easy link with Mackintyre. His last stretch was for manslaughter. But bank robbery is quite a fancy flight, even for him . . . He must have been getting ideas.'

Patricia's eyes turned slowly towards the morning paper in which the hold-up at Staines still had a place in the headlines.

'You mean you think—'

'I think our guardian angel is still trying to take care of us,' said the Saint; and all the old impenitent mischief that she knew too well was shimmering at the edges of his smile. 'If only we knew a cure for amnesia, I think we could be fifteen thousand pounds richer before bed-time. Add it up for yourself while I take another look at the patient.'

He got up from the table and went through to the study which adjoined the dining-room. It was a rather small, comfortably untidy room, and the greater part of its walls were lined with built-in bookshelves. When he went in, one tier of shelving about two feet wide stood open like a door; beyond it, there appeared to be a narrow passage. The passage was actually a tiny cell, artificially lighted and windowless, but perfectly ventilated through a grating that connected with the air-conditioning system which served the rest of the house. The cell was no more than a broad gap between the solid walls of the rooms on either side of it, so ingeniously squeezed into the architecture of the house that it would have taken a clever surveyor many hours of work with a foot-rule to discover its existence. It had very little more than enough room for the cot in which Verdean lay, and the table and chair at which Hoppy Uniatz was dawdling over his breakfast—if any meal which ended after noon, and was washed down with a bottle of Scotch whisky, could get by with that name.

Simon stood just inside the opening and glanced over the scene.

'Any luck yet?' he asked.

Mr Uniatz shook his head.

'De guy is cuckoo, boss. I even try to give him a drink, an' he don't want it. He t'rows it up like it might be perzon.'

He mentioned this with the weighty reluctance of a psychiatrist adducing the ultimate evidence of dementia praecox.

Simon squeezed his way through and slipped a thermometer into the patient's mouth. He held Verdean's wrist with sensitive fingers.

'Don't you want to get up, Mr Verdean?'

The bank manager gazed at him expressionlessly.

'You don't want to be late at the bank, do you?' said the Saint. 'You might lose your job.'

'What bank?' Verdean asked.

'You know. The one that was robbed.'

'I don't know. Where am I?'

'You're safe now. Kaskin is looking for you, but he won't find you.'

'Kaskin,' Verdean repeated. His face was blank, idiotic. 'Is he someone I know?'

'You remember Angela, don't you?' said the Saint. 'She wants to see you.'

Verdean rolled his head on the pillow.

'I don't know. Who are all these people? I don't want to see anyone. My head's splitting. I want to go to sleep.'

His eyes closed under painfully wrinkled brows.

Simon let his wrist fall. He took out the thermometer, read it, and sidled back to the door. Patricia was standing there.

'No change?' she said; and the Saint shrugged.

'His temperature's practically normal, but his pulse is high. God alone knows how long it may take him to get his memory back. He could stay like this for a week; or it might even be years. You never can tell. . . I'm beginning to think I may have been a bit too hasty with my rescuing-hero act. I ought to have let Kaskin and Dolf work him over a bit longer, and heard what he had to tell them before I butted in.'

Patricia shook her head.

'You know you couldn't have done that.'

'I know.' The Saint made a wryly philosophic face. 'That's the worst of trying to be a buccaneer with a better nature. But it would have saved the hell of a lot of trouble, just the same. As it is, even if he does recover his memory, we're going to have to do something exciting ourselves to make him open up. Now, if we could only swat him. On the head in the opposite direction and knock his memory back again—'

He broke off abruptly, his eyes fixed intently on a corner of the room; but Patricia knew that he was not seeing it. She looked at him with an involuntary tightening in her chest. Her ears had not been quick enough to catch the first swish of tyres on the gravel drive which had cut off what he was saying, but she was able to hear the car outside coming to a stop.

The Saint did not move. He seemed to be waiting, like a watchdog holding its bark while it tried to identify a stray sound that had pricked its ears. In another moment she knew what he had been waiting for.

The unmistakable limping steps of Orace, Simon Templar's oldest and most devoted retainer, came through the hall from the direction of the kitchen and paused outside the study.

'It's that there detective agyne, sir,' he said in a fierce whisper. 'I seen 'im fru the winder. Shall I chuck 'im aht?'

'No, let him in,' said the Saint quietly. 'But give me a couple of seconds first.'

He drew Patricia quickly out of the secret cell, and closed the study door. His lips were flirting with the wraith of a Saintly smile, and only Patricia would have seen the steel in his blue eyes.

'What a prophet you are, darling,' he said.

He swung the open strip of bookcase back into place. It closed silently, on delicately balanced hinges, filling the aperture in the wall without a visible crack. He moved one of the shelves to lock it. Then he closed a drawer of his desk which had been left open, and there was the faint click of another lock taking hold. Only then did he open the door to the hall—and left it open. And with that, a master lock, electrically operated, took control. Even with the knowledge of the other two operations, nothing short of pickaxes and dynamite could open the secret room when the study door was open; and one of the Saint's best bets was that no one who was searching the house would be likely to make a point of shutting it.

He emerged into the hall just as Chief Inspector Teal's official boots stomped wrathfully over the threshold. The detective saw him as soon as he appeared, and the heightened colour in his chubby face flared up with the perilous surge of his blood-pressure. He took a lurching step forward with one quivering forefinger thrust out ahead of him like a spear.

'You, Saint!' he bellowed. 'I want you!'

The Saint smiled at him, carefree and incredibly debonair.

'Why, hullo, Claud, old gumboil,' he murmured genially. 'You seem to be excited about something. Come in and tell me all about it.'

## VI

Simon Templar had never actually been followed into his living-room by an irate mastodon; but if that remarkable experience was ever to befall him in the future, he would have had an excellent standard with which to compare it. The imitation as rendered by Chief Inspector Claud Eustace Teal was an impressive performance, but it seemed to leave the Saint singularly unconcerned. He waved towards one armchair and deposited himself in another, reaching for cigarette-box and ashtray.

'Make yourself at home,' he invited affably. 'Things have been pretty dull lately, as I said last night. What can I do to help you?'

Mr Teal gritted his teeth over a lump of chewing gum with a barbarity which suggested that he found it an inferior substitute for the Saint's jugular vein. Why he should have followed the Saint at all in the first place was a belated question that was doing nothing to improve his temper. He could find no more satisfactory explanation than that the Saint had simply turned and calmly led the way, and he could hardly be expected to go on talking to an empty hall. But in the act of following, he felt that he had already lost a subtle point. It was one of those smoothly infuriating tricks of the Saint to put him at a disadvantage which never failed to lash Mr Teal's unstable temper to the point where he felt as if he were being garrotted with his own collar.

And on this occasion, out of all others, he must control himself. He had no need to get angry. He held all the aces. He had everything that he had prayed for in the long sections of his career that had been consecrated to the heart-breaking task of trying to lay the Saint by the heels. He must not make any mistakes. He must not let himself be baited into any more of those unbelievable indiscretions that had wrecked such opportunities in the past, and that made him sweat all over as soon as he had escaped from the Saint's maddening presence. He told himself so, over and over again, clinging to all the tatters of his self-restraint with the doggedness of a drowning man. He glared at the Saint with an effort of impassivity that made the muscles of his face ache.

'You can help me by taking a trip to the police station with me,' he said. 'Before you go any further, it's my duty to warn you that you're under arrest. And I've got all the evidence I need to keep you there!'

'Of course you have, Claud,' said the Saint soothingly. 'Haven't you had it every time you've arrested me? But now that you've got that off your chest, would it be frightfully tactless if I asked you what I'm supposed to have done?'

'Last night,' Teal said, grinding his words out under fearful compression, 'a Mr Robert Verdean, the manager of the City and Continental Bank's branch at Staines, was visited at his home in Chertsey by two men. They tied up his servant in the kitchen, and went on to find him in the living-room. The maid's description of them makes them sound like the two men who held up the same bank that morning. They went into the living-room and turned on the radio.'

'How very odd,' said the Saint. 'I suppose they were trying to console Comrade Verdean for having his bank robbed. But what has that got to do with me? Or do you think I was one of them?'

'Shortly afterwards,' Teal went on, ignoring the interruption, 'two other men entered the kitchen with handkerchiefs tied over their faces. One of them was about your height and build. The maid heard this one address the other one as "Hoppy."'

Simon nodded perfunctorily.

'Yes,' he said; and then his eyebrows rose. 'My God, Claud, that's funny! Of course, you're thinking—'

'That American gangster who follows you around is called Hoppy, isn't he?'

'If you're referring to Mr Uniatz,' said the Saint stiffly, 'he is sometimes called that. But he hasn't got any copyright in the name.'

The detective took a fresh nutcracker purchase on his gum.

'Perhaps he hasn't. But the tall one went into the living-room. The radio was switched off and on and off again, and then it stayed off. So the maid heard quite a bit of the conversation. She heard people talking about the Saint.'

'That's one of the penalties of fame,' said the Saint sadly. 'People are always talking about me, in the weirdest places. It's quite embarrassing sometimes. But do go on telling me about it.'

Mr Teal's larynx suffered a spasm which interfered momentarily with his power of speech.

'That's all I have to tell you!' he yelped, when he had partially cleared the obstruction. 'I mean that you and that Uniatz creature of yours were the second two men who arrived. After that, according to the maid, there was a lot of shooting, and presently some neighbours arrived and untied her. All the four men who had been there disappeared, and so did Mr Verdean. I want you on suspicion of kidnapping him; and if we don't find him soon there'll probably be a charge of murder as well!'

Simon Templar frowned. His manner was sympathetic rather than disturbed.

'I know how you feel, Claud,' he said commiseratingly. 'Naturally you want to do something about it; and I know you're quite a miracle worker when you get going. But I wish I could figure out how you're going to tie me up with it, when I wasn't anywhere near the place.'

The detective's glare reddened.

'You weren't anywhere near Chertsey, eh? So we've got to break down another of your famous alibis. All right, then. Where were you?'

'I was at home.'

'Whose home?'

'My own. This one.'

'Yeah? And who else knows about it?'

'Not a lot of people,' Simon confessed. 'We were being quiet. You know. One of those restful, old-fashioned, fireside evenings. If it comes to that, I suppose there isn't an army of witnesses. You can't have a quiet restful evening with an army of witnesses cluttering up the place. It's a contradiction in terms. There was just Pat, and Hoppy, and of course good old Orace—'

'Pat and Hoppy and Orace,' jeered the detective. 'Just a quiet restful evening. And that's your alibi—'

'I wouldn't say it was entirely my alibi,' Simon mentioned diffidently. 'After all, there are several other houses in England. And I wouldn't mind betting that in at least half of them, various people were having quiet restful evenings last night. Why don't you go and ask some of them whether they can prove it? Because you know that being a lot less tolerant and forbearing than I am, they'd only tell you to go back to Scotland Yard and sit on a radiator until you'd thawed some of the clotted suet out of your brains. How the hell would you expect anyone to prove he'd spent a quiet evening at home? By bringing in a convocation of bishops for witnesses? In a case like this, it isn't the suspect's job to prove he was home. It's your job to prove he wasn't.'

Chief Inspector Teal should have been warned. The ghosts of so many other episodes like this should have risen up to give him caution. But they didn't. Instead, they egged him on. He leaned forward in a glow of vindictive exultation.

'That's just what I'm going to do,' he said, and his voice grew rich with the lusciousness of his own triumph. 'We aren't always so stupid as you think we are. We found fresh tyre tracks in the drive, and they didn't belong to Verdean's car. We searched every scrap of ground for half a mile to see if we could pick them up again. We found them turning into a field quite close to the end of Greenleaf Road. The car that made 'em was still in the field—it was reported stolen in Windsor early yesterday morning. But there were the tracks of another car in the field, overlapping and underlapping the tracks of the stolen car, so that we know the kidnappers changed to another car for their getaway. I've got casts of those tracks, and I'm going to show that they match the tyres on your car!'

The Saint blinked.

'It would certainly be rather awkward if they did,' he said uneasily. 'I didn't give anybody permission to borrow my car last night, but of course—'

'But of course somebody might have taken it away and brought it back without your knowing it,' Teal said with guttural sarcasm. 'Oh, yes.' His voice suddenly went into a squeak. 'Well, I'm going to be in court and watch the jury laugh themselves sick when you try to tell that story! I'm going to examine your car now, in front of police witnesses, and I'd like them to see your face when I do it!'

It was the detective's turn to march away and leave the Saint to follow. He had a moment of palpitation while he wondered whether the Saint would do it. But as he flung open the front door and crunched into the drive, he heard the Saint's footsteps behind him. The glow of triumph that was in him warmed like a Yule log on a Christmas hearth. The Saint's expression had reverted to blandness quickly enough, but not so quickly that Teal had missed the guilty start which had broken through its smooth surface. He knew, with a blind ecstasy, that at long last the Saint had tripped . . .

He waved imperiously to the two officers in the prowl car outside, and marched on towards the garage. The Saint's Hirondel stood there in its glory, an engineering symphony in cream and red trimmed with chromium, with the more sedate black Daimler in which Patricia had driven down standing beside it; but Teal had no aesthetic admiration for the sight. He stood by like a pink-faced figure of doom while his assistants reverently unwrapped the moulage impressions; and then, like a master chef taking charge at the vital moment in the preparation of a dish for which his underlings had laid the routine foundations, he took the casts in his own hands and proceeded to compare them with the tyres on the Hirondel.

He went all round the Hirondel twice.

He was breathing a trifle laboriously, and his face was redder than before—probably from stooping—when he turned his attention to the Daimler.

He went all round the Daimler twice, too.

Then he straightened up and came slowly back to the Saint. He came back until his face was only a few inches from the Saint's. His capillaries were congested to the point where his complexion had a dark purple hue. He seemed to be having more trouble with his larynx.

'What have you done to those tyres?' he got out in an hysterical blare.

The Saint's eyebrows drew perplexedly together.

'What have I done to them? I don't get you, Claud. Do you mean to say they don't match?'

'You know damn well they don't match! You knew it all the time.' Realisation of the way the Saint had deliberately lured him up to greater heights of optimism, only to make his downfall more hideous when it came, brought something like a sob into the detective's gullet. 'You've changed the tyres!'

Simon looked aggrieved.

'How could I, Claud? You can see for yourself that these tyres are a long way from being new—'

'What have you done with the tyres you had on the car last night?' Teal almost screamed.

'But these are the only tyres I've had on the car for weeks,' Simon protested innocently. 'Why do you always suspect me of such horrible deceits? If my tyres don't match the tracks you found in that field, it just looks to me as if you may have made a mistake about my being there.'

Chief Inspector Teal did a terrible thing. He raised the casts in his hands and hurled them down on the concrete floor so that they shattered into a thousand fragments. He did not actually dance on them, but he looked as if only an effort of self-control that brought him to the brink of an apoplectic stroke stopped him from doing so.

'What have you done with Verdean?' he yelled.

'I haven't done anything with him. Why should I have? I've never even set eyes on the man.'

'I've got a search warrant—'

'Then why don't you search?' demanded the Saint snappily, as though his patience was coming to an end. 'You won't believe anything I tell you, anyhow, so why don't you look for yourself? Go ahead and use your warrant. Tear the house apart. I don't mind. I'll be waiting for you in the living-room when you're ready to eat some of your words.'

He turned on his heel and strolled back to the house.

He sat down in the living-room, lighted a cigarette, and calmly picked up a magazine. He heard the tramp of Teal and his minions entering the front door, without looking up. For an hour he listened to them moving about in various parts of the house, tapping walls and shifting furniture; but he seemed to have no interest beyond the story he was reading. Even when they invaded the living-room itself, he didn't even glance at them. He went on turning the pages as if they made no more difference to his idleness than a trio of inquisitive puppies.

Teal came to the living-room last. Simon knew from the pregnant stillness that presently supervened that the search had come to a

stultifying end, but he continued serenely to finish his page before
he looked up.

'Well,' he said at length, 'have you found him?'

'Where is he?' shouted Teal, with dreadful savagery.

Simon put down the magazine.

'Look here,' he said wearily. 'I've made a lot of allowances for
you, but I give up. What's the use? I tell you I was at home last
night, and you can't prove I wasn't; but just because you want me
to have been out, I must be faking an alibi. You've got casts of the
tyre tracks of a car that was mixed up in some dirty business last
night, and they don't match the tracks of either of my cars; but
just because you think they ought to match, I must have changed
my tyres. I tell you I haven't kidnapped this fellow Verdean, and
you can't find him anywhere in my house; but just because you
think I ought to have kidnapped him, I must have hidden him
somewhere else. Every shred of evidence is against you, and therefore
all the evidence must be wrong. You couldn't possibly be wrong
yourself, because you're the great Chief Inspector Claud Eustace
Teal, who knows everything and always gets his man. All right.
Every bit of proof there is shows that I'm innocent, but I must be
guilty because your theories would be all wet if I wasn't. So why
do we have to waste our time on silly little details like this? Let's
just take me down to the police station and lock me up.'

'That's just what I'm going to do,' Teal raved blindly.

The Saint looked at him for a moment, and stood up.

'Good enough,' he said breezily. 'I'm ready when you are.'

He went to the door and called: 'Pat!' She answered him, and
came down the stairs. He said: 'Darling, Claud Eustace has had
an idea. He's going to lug me off and shove me in the cooler on
a charge of being above suspicion. It's a new system they've
introduced at Scotland Yard, and all the laws are being altered to
suit it. So you'd better call one of our lawyers and see if he knows
what to do about it. Oh, and you might ring up some of the
newspapers while you're on the job—they'll probably want to
interview Claud about his brainwave.'

'Yes, of course,' she said enthusiastically, and went towards the telephone in the study.

Something awful, something terrifying, something freezing and paralysing, damp, chilly, appalling, descended over Chief Inspector Teal like a glacial cascade. With the very edge of the precipice crumbling under his toes, his eyes were opened. The delirium of fury that had swept him along so far coagulated sickeningly within him. Cold, pitiless, inescapable facts hammered their bitter way through into the turmoil of his brain. He was too shocked at the moment even to feel the anguish of despair. His mind shuddered under the impact of a new kind of panic. He took a frantic step forward—a step that was, in its own way, the crossing of a harrowing Rubicon.

'Wait a minute,' he stammered hoarsely.

VII

Fifteen minutes later, Simon Templar stood on the front steps and watched the police car crawl out of the drive with its cargo of incarnate woe. He felt Patricia's fingers slide into his hand, and turned to smile at her.

'So far, so good,' he said thoughtfully. 'But only so far.'

'I thought you were joking, at breakfast,' she said. 'How did he get here so soon?'

He shrugged.

'That wasn't difficult. I suppose he stayed down at Staines last night; and the Chertsey police would have phoned over about the Verdean business first thing this morning, knowing that he was the manager of the bank that had been held up. Claud must have shot off on the scent like a prize greyhound, and I'm afraid I can sympathise with the way he must have felt when he arrived here.'

'Well, we're still alive,' she said hopefully. 'You got rid of him again.'

'Only because his nerves are getting a bit shaky from all the times I've slipped through his fingers, and he's so scared of being made a fool of again that he daren't move now without a cast-iron case, and I was able to pick a few awkward holes in this one. But don't begin thinking we've got rid of him for keeps. He's just gone away now to see if he can stop up the holes again and put some more iron in the evidence, and he's sore enough to work overtime at it. He's going to be three times as dangerous from now on. Worse than that, he's not so dumb that he isn't going to put two and two together about all this commotion around Verdean coming right on top of the robbery. You can bet the Crown Jewels to a showgirl's virtue that he's already figured out that Verdean was mixed up in it in some way. While we're stuck with Verdean, and Verdean is stuck with amnesia.' The Saint closed the front door with sombre finality. 'Which is the hell of a layout from any angle,' he said. 'Tell Orace to bring me a large mug of beer, darling, because I think I am going to have a headache.'

His headache lasted through a lunch which Orace indignantly served even later than he had served breakfast, but it brought forth very little to justify itself. He had gone over the facts at his disposal until he was sick of them, and they fitted together with a complete and sharply-focused deductive picture that Sherlock Holmes himself could not have improved on, without a hiatus or a loose end anywhere—only the picture merely showed a plump rabbit-faced man slinking off with fifteen thousand pounds in a bag, and neglected to show where he went with it. Which was the one detail in which Simon Templar was most urgently interested. He was always on the side of the angels, he told himself, but he had to remember that sanctity had its own overhead to meet.

Verdean showed no improvement in the afternoon. Towards five o'clock the Saint had a flash of inspiration, and put in a long-distance call to a friend in Wolverhampton.

'Dr Turner won't be back till tomorrow morning, and I'm afraid I don't know how to reach him,' said the voice at the other end of the wire; and the flash flickered and died out at the sound. 'But I can give you Dr Young's number—'

'I am not having a baby,' said the Saint coldly, and hung up.

He leaned back in his chair and said, quietly and intensely: 'Goddamn.'

'You should complain,' said Patricia. 'You Mormon.'

She had entered the study from the hall, and closed the door again behind her. The Saint looked up from under mildly interrogative brows.

'I knew you adored me,' he said, 'but you have an original line of endearing epithets. What's the origin of this one?'

'Blonde,' she said, 'and voluptuous in a careful way. Mushy lips and the-old-baloney eyes. I'll bet she wears black lace undies and cuddles like a kitten. She hasn't brought the baby with her, but she's probably got a picture of it.'

The Saint straightened.

'Not Angela?' he ventured breathlessly.

'I'm not so intimate with her,' said Patricia primly. 'But she gave the name of Miss Lindsay. You ought to recognise your own past when it catches up with you.'

Simon stood up slowly. He glanced at the closed section of bookcase, beyond which was the secret room where Hoppy Uniatz was still keeping watch over Mr Verdean and a case of Vat 69; and his eyes were suddenly filled with an unholy peace.

'I do recognise her, darling, now I think about it,' he said. 'This is the one who had the twins.' He gripped her arm, and his smile wavered over her in a flicker of ghostly excitement. 'I ought to have known that she'd catch up with me. And I think this is the break I've been waiting for all day . . .'

He went into the living-room with a new quickness in his step and a new exhilaration sliding along his nerves. Now that this new angle had developed, he was amazed that he had not been expecting it from the beginning. He had considered every other likely eventuality, but not this one; and yet this was the most obvious one of all. Kaskin and Dolf knew who he was, and some of his addresses were to be found in various directories that were at the disposal of anyone who could read: it was not seriously plausible that after the night before they would decide to give up their loot and go away and forget about it, and once they had made up their minds to attempt a comeback it could only have been a matter of time before they looked for him in Weybridge. The only thing he might not have anticipated was that they would send Angela Lindsay in to open the interview. That was a twist which showed a degree of circumspection that made Simon Templar greet her with more than ordinary watchfulness.

'Angela, darling!' he murmured with an air of pleased surprise, 'I never thought I should see you in these rural parts. When did you decide to study bird life in the suburbs?'

'It came over me suddenly, last night,' she said. 'I began to realise that I'd missed something.'

His eyes were quizzically sympathetic.

'You shouldn't be too discouraged. I don't think you missed it by more than a couple of inches.'

'Perhaps not. But a miss is—'

'I know. As good as in the bush.'

'Exactly.'

He smiled at her, and offered the cigarette-box. She took one, and he gave her a light. His movements and his tone of voice were almost glisteningly smooth with exaggerated elegance. He was enjoying his act immensely.

'A drink?' he suggested; but she shook her head.

'It mightn't be very good for me, so I won't risk it. Besides, I want to try and make a good impression.'

He was studying her more critically than he had been able to the night before, and it seemed to him that Patricia's description of her was a little less than absolutely fair. She had one of those modern streamlined figures that look boyish until they are examined closely, when they prove to have the same fundamental curves that grandma used to have. Her mouth and eyes were effective enough even if the effect was deplorable from a moral standpoint. And although it was true that even a comparatively unworldly observer would scarcely have hesitated for a moment over placing her in her correct category, it was also very definitely true that if all the other members of that category had looked like her, Mr Ebenezer Hogsbotham would have found himself burning a very solitary candle in a jubilantly naughty world.

The Saint went on looking at her with amiable amusement at the imaginative vistas opened up by that train of thought. He said: 'You must have made quite an impression on Comrade Verdean. And you drank champagne with him at Brighton.'

She put her cigarette to her lips and drew lightly at it while she gazed at him for a second or two in silence. Her face was perfectly composed, but her eyes were fractionally narrowed.

'I'll give you that one,' she said at length. 'We've been wondering just how much you really knew. Would you care to tell me the rest, or would that be asking too much?'

'Why, of course,' said the Saint obligingly. 'If you're interested. It isn't as if I'd be telling you anything you don't know already.'

He sat down and stretched out his long legs. He looked at the ceiling. He was bluffing, but he felt sure enough of his ground.

'Kaskin and Dolf picked up Verdean on his holiday at Eastbourne,' he said. 'Kaskin can make himself easy to like when he wants to—it's his stock-in-trade. They threw you in for an added attraction. Verdean fell for it all. He was having a swell time with a bunch of good fellows. And you were fairly swooning into his manly arms. It made him feel grand, and a little bit dizzy. He had to live up to it. Kaskin was a sporty gent, and Verdean was ready to show that he was a sporty gent too. They got him to backing horses, and he always backed winners. Money poured into his lap. He felt even grander. It went to his head—where it was meant to go. He left his boarding-house, and pranced off to Brighton with you on a wild and gorgeous jag.'

Simon reached for a cigarette.

'Then, the set-back,' he went on. 'You had expensive tastes, and you expected him to go on being a good fellow and a sporty gent. But that looked easy. There was always money in the gee-gees, with Kaskin's expert assistance. So he thought. Only something went haywire. The certainties didn't win. But the next one would always get it back. Verdean began to plunge. He got wilder and wilder as he lost more and more. And he couldn't stop. He was infatuated with you, scared stiff of losing you. He lost more money than he had of his own. He started embezzling a little, maybe. Anyway, he was in the cart. He owed more money than he could hope to pay. Then Kaskin and Dolf started to get tough. They told him how he could pay off his debt, and make a profit as well. There was plenty of money in the bank every week, and it would be very easy to stage a hold-up and get away with it if he was co-operating. Kaskin and Dolf would do the job and take all the risk, and all he had to do was to give them the layout and make everything easy for them. He'd never be suspected himself, and he'd get his cut afterwards. But if he didn't string along—well, someone might have to tell the head office about him. Verdean knew well enough what happens to bank managers who get into debt, particularly over gambling. He could either play ball or go down the drain. So he said he'd play ball. Am I right?'

'So far. But I hope you aren't going to stop before the important part.'

'All right. Verdean thought some more—by himself. He was sunk, anyhow. He had to rob the bank if he was going to save his own skin. So why shouldn't he keep all the boodle for himself? . . . That's just what he decided to do. The branch is a small one, and nobody would have thought of questioning anything he did. It was easy for him to pack a load of dough into a small valise and take it out with him when he went home to lunch—just before the hold-up was timed to take place. Nobody would have thought of asking him what he had in his bag; and as for the money, well, of course the hold-up men would be blamed for getting away with it. But he didn't want Judd and Morrie on his tail, so he tipped off the police anonymously, meaning for them to be caught, and feeling pretty sure that nobody would believe any accusations they made about him—or at least not until he had plenty of time to hide it . . . There were still a few holes in the idea, but he was too desperate to worry about them. His real tragedy was when Kaskin and Dolf didn't get caught after all, and came after him to ask questions. And naturally that's when we all started to get together.'

'And then?'

The Saint raised his head and looked at her again.

'Maybe I'm very dense,' he said apologetically, 'but isn't that enough?'

'It's almost uncanny. But there's still the most important thing.'

'What would that be?'

'Did you find out what happened to the money?'

The Saint was silent for a moment. He elongated his legs still farther, so that they stretched out over the carpet like a pier; his recumbent body looked as if it were composing itself for sleep. But the eyes that he bent on her were bright and amused and very cheerfully awake.

She said: 'What are you grinning about?'

'I'd just been wondering when it was coming, darling,' he murmured. 'I know that my dazzling beauty brings admiring sightseers from all quarters like moths to a candle, but they usually want something else as well. And it's been very nice to see you and have this little chat, but I was always afraid you were hoping to get something out of it. So this is what it is. Morrie and Judd sent you along to get an answer to that question, so they'd know whether it was safe to bump me off or not. If Verdean is still keeping his mouth shut, they can go ahead and fix me a funeral; but if I've found out where it is I may have even moved it somewhere else by now, and it would be awkward to have me buried before I could tell them where I'd moved it to. Is that all that's worrying you?'

'Not altogether,' she said, without hesitation. 'They didn't have to send me for that. I talked them into letting me come because I told them you'd probably talk to me for longer than you'd talk to them, and anyhow you wouldn't be so likely to punch me on the nose. But I really did it because I wanted to see you myself.'

The flicker that passed over Simon's face was almost imperceptible.

'I hope it's been worth it,' he said flippantly; but he was watching her with a coolly reserved alertness.

'That's what you've got to tell me,' she said. She looked away from him for a moment, stubbed out her cigarette nervously, looked back at him again with difficult frankness. Her hands moved uncertainly. She went on in a rush: 'You see, I know Judd doesn't mean to give me my share. I could trust you. Whatever happens, they're going to give you trouble. I know you can take care of yourself, but I don't suppose you'd mind having it made easier for you. I could be on your side, without them knowing, and I wouldn't want much.'

The Saint blew two smoke-rings with leisured care, placing them side by side like the lenses of a pair of hornrimmed spectacles. They drifted towards the ceiling, enlarging languidly.

His face was inscrutable, but behind that pleasantly non-committal mask he was thinking as quickly as he could.

He might have come to any decision. But before he could say anything there was an interruption.

The door was flung open, and Hoppy Uniatz crashed in.

Mr Uniatz's face was not at all inscrutable. It was as elementarily easy to read as an infant's primer. The ecstatic protrusion of his eyes, the lavish enthusiasm of his breathing, the broad beam that divided his physiognomy into two approximately equal halves, and the roseate glow which suffused his homely countenance, were all reminiscent of the symptoms of bliss that must have illuminated the features of Archimedes at the epochal moment of his life. He looked like a man who had just made the inspirational discovery of the century in his bath.

'It woiked, boss,' he yawped exultantly, 'it woiked! De dough is in Hogsbotham's bedroom!'


VIII

Simon Templar kept still. It cost him an heroic effort, but he did it. He felt as if he were balanced on top of a thin glass flagpole in the middle of an earthquake, but he managed to keep the surface of his nonchalance intact. He kept Angela Lindsay's hands always within the radius of his field of vision, and said rather faintly: 'What woiked?'

Mr Uniatz seemed slightly taken aback.

'Why, de idea you give me dis afternoon, boss,' he explained, as though he saw little need for such childish elucidations. 'You remember, you are saying why can't we sock dis guy de udder way an' knock his memory back. Well, I am t'inkin' about dat, an' it seems okay to me, an' I ain't got nut'n else to do on account of de door is locked an' I finished all de Scotch; so I haul off an' whop him on de toinip wit' de end of my Betsy. Well, he is out for a long time, an' when he comes round he still don't seem to know what it's all about, but he is talkin' about how dis guy Hogsbotham gives him a key to look after de house when he goes away, so he goes in an' parks de lettuce in Hogsbotham's bedroom. It is a swell idea, boss, an' it woiks,' said Mr Uniatz, still marvelling at the genius which had conceived it.

The Saint felt a clutching contraction under his ribs which was not quite like the gastric hollowness of dismay and defensive tension which might reasonably have been there. It was a second or two before he could get a perspective on it; and when he did so, the realisation of what it was made him feel slightly insane.

It was simply a wild desire to collapse into helpless laughter. The whole supernal essence of the situation was so immortally ludicrous that he was temporarily incapable of worrying about the fact that Angela Lindsay was a member of the audience. If she had taken a gun out of her bag and announced that she was going to lock them up while she went back to tell Kaskin and Dolf the glad news, which would have been the most obviously logical thing for her to do, he would probably have been too weak to lift a finger to prevent it.

Perhaps the very fact that she made no move to do so did more than anything else to restore him to sobriety.

The ache in his chest died away, and his brain forced itself to start work again. He knew that she had a gun in her bag—he had looked for it and distinguished the outline of it when he first came into the room to meet her, and that was why he had never let himself completely lose sight of her hands. But her hands only moved to take another cigarette. She smiled at him as if she was sharing the joke, and struck a match.

'Well,' he said dryly, 'it looks like you've got your answer.'

'To one question,' she said. 'You haven't answered the other. What shall I tell Judd?'

Simon studied her for the space of a couple of pulse-beats. In that time, he thought with a swiftness and clarity that was almost clairvoyant. He saw every angle and every prospect and every possible surprise.

He also saw Patricia standing aghast in the doorway behind the gorilla shoulders of Mr Uniatz, and grinned impudently at her.

He stood up, and put out his hand to Angela Lindsay.

'Go back and tell Morrie and Judd that we found out where the dough was last night,' he said. 'Verdean had buried it in a flower-bed. A couple of pals of mine dug it out in the small hours of this morning and took it to London. They're sitting over it with a pair of machine-guns in my apartment at Cornwall House now, and I dare anybody to take it away. That ought to hold 'em ... Then you shake them off as soon as you can, and meet me at the Stag and Hounds opposite Weybridge Common in two hours from now. We'll take you along with us and show you Hogsbotham's nightshirts!'

She faced him steadily, but with a suppressed eagerness that played disturbing tricks with her moist lips.

'You mean that? You'll take me in with you?'

'Just as far as you want to be taken in, kid,' said the Saint.

He escorted her to the front door. There was no car outside, but doubtless Messrs Kaskin and Dolf were waiting for her a little way up the road. He watched her start down the drive, and then he closed the door and turned back.

'You'd look better without the lipstick,' said Patricia judicially.

He thumbed his nose at her and employed his handkerchief.

'Excuse me if I seem slightly scatter-brained,' he remarked. 'But all this is rather sudden. Too many things have happened in the last few minutes. What would you like to do with the change from fifteen thousand quid? There ought to be a few bob left after I've paid for my last lot of shirts and bought a new distillery for Hoppy.'

'Have you fallen right off the edge,' she asked interestedly, 'or what is it?'

'At a rough guess, I should say it was probably What.' The Saint's happy lunacy was too extravagant to cope with. 'But who cares? Why should a little thing like this cause so much commotion? Have you no faith in human nature? The girl's better nature has revived. My pure and holy personality has done its work on her. It never fails. My shining example has made her soul pant for higher things. From now on, she is going to be on the side of the Saints. And she is going to take care of Judd and Morrie. She is going to lead them for us, by the nose, into the soup. Meanwhile, Professor Uniatz has shaken the scientific world to its foundations with his new and startling treatment for cases of concussion. He has whopped Comrade Verdean on the turnip with the end of his Betsy and banged his memory back, and we are going to lay our hands on fifteen thousand smackers before we go to bed tonight. And we are going to find all this boodle in the bedroom of Ebenezer Hogsbotham, of all the superlative places in the world. I ask you, can life hold any more?'

He exploded out of the hall into the study, and went on into the secret room, leaving her staring after him a trifle dazedly.

He was bubbling with blissful idiocy, but his mind was cool. He had already diagnosed the effects of the Uniatz treatment so completely that his visit was really only intended to reassure himself that it had actually worked. He studied Verdean cold-bloodedly. The bank manager's eyes were vacant and unrecognising: he rolled his head monotonously from side to side and kept up a delirious mumble from which the main points of the summary that Hoppy Uniatz had made were absurdly easy to pick out. Over and over again he reiterated the story—how Mr Hogsbotham had asked him as a neighbour to keep an eye on the house during some of his absences, how he had been entrusted with a key which he had never remembered to return, and how when he was wondering what to do with the stolen money he had remembered the key and used it to find what should have been an unsuspectable hiding-place for his booty. He went on talking about it . . .

'He is like dis ever since he wakes up,' Hoppy explained, edging proudly in behind him.

The Saint nodded. He did not feel any pity. Robert Verdean was just another man who had strayed unsuccessfully into the paths of common crime; and even though he had been deliberately led astray, the mess that he was in now was directly traceable to nothing but his own weakness and cupidity. In such matters, Simon Templar saved his sympathy for more promising cases.

'Put his clothes back on him,' he said. 'We'll take him along too. Your operation was miraculous, Hoppy, but the patient is somewhat liable to die, and we don't want to be stuck with his body.'

Patricia was sitting on the study desk when he emerged again, and she looked at him with sober consideration.

'I don't want to bore you with the subject,' she said, 'but are you still sure you haven't gone off your rocker?'

'Perfectly sure,' he said. 'I was never rocking so smoothly in my life.'

'Well, do you happen to remember anyone by the name of Teal?'

He took her arm and chuckled.

'No, I haven't forgotten. But I don't think he'll be ready for this. He may have ideas about keeping an eye on me, but he won't be watching for Verdean. Not here, anyway. Hell, he's just searched the house from top to bottom and convinced himself that we haven't got Verdean here, however much he may be wondering what else we've done with him. And it's getting dark already. By the time we're ready to go, it'll be easy. There may be a patrol car or a motor-cycle cop waiting down the road to get on our tail if we go out, but that'll be all. We'll drive around the country a bit first and lose them. And then we will go into this matter of our old age pensions.'

She might have been going to say some more. But she didn't. Her mouth closed again, and a little hopeless grimace that was almost a smile at the same time passed over her lips. Her blue eyes summed up a story that it has already taken all the volumes of the Saint Saga to tell in words. And she kissed him.

'All right, skipper,' she said quietly. 'I must be as crazy as you are, or I shouldn't be here. We'll do that.'

He shook his head, holding her.

'So we shall. But not you.'

'But—'

'I'm sorry, darling. I was talking about two other guys. You're going to stay out of it, because we're going to need you on the outside. Now, in a few minutes I'm going to call Peter, and then I'm going to try and locate Claud Eustace; and if I can get hold of both of them in time the campaign will proceed as follows . . .'

He told it in quick clean-cut detail, so easily and lucidly that it seemed to be put together with no more effort than it took to understand and remember it. But that was only one of the tricks that sometimes made the Saint's triumphs seem deceptively facile. Behind that apparently random improvisation there was the instant decision and almost supernatural foresightedness of a strategic genius which in another age might have conquered empires as debonairly as in this twentieth century it had conquered its own amazing empire among thieves. And Patricia Holm was a listener to whom very few explanations had to be made more than once.

Hoppy Uniatz was a less gifted audience. The primitive machinery of conditioned reflexes which served him for some of the simpler functions of a brain had never been designed for one-shot lubrication. Simon had to go over the same ground with him at least three times before the scowl of agony smoothed itself out of Mr Uniatz's rough-hewn façade, indicating that the torture of concentration was over and the idea had finally taken root inside his skull, where at least it could be relied upon to remain with the solidity of an amalgam filling in a well-excavated molar.

The evening papers arrived before they left, after the hectic preliminaries of organisation were completed, when the Saint was relaxing briefly over a parting glass of sherry, and Mr Uniatz was placidly sluicing his arid tonsils with a fresh bottle of Scotch. Patricia glanced through the *Evening Standard* and giggled.

'Your friend Hogsbotham is still in the news,' she said. 'He's leading a deputation from the National Society for the Preservation of Public Morals to demonstrate outside the London Casino this evening before the dinner-time show. So it looks as if the coast will be clear for you at Chertsey.'

'Probably he heard that Simon was thinking of paying him another call, and hustled himself out of the way like a sensible peace-loving citizen,' said Peter Quentin, who had arrived shortly before that. 'If I'd known what I was going to be dragged into before I answered the telephone, I'd have gone off and led a demonstration somewhere myself.'

The Saint grinned.

'We really must do something about Hogsbotham, one of these days,' he said.

It was curious that that adventure had begun with Mr Hogsbotham, and had just led back to Mr Hogsbotham; and yet he still did not dream how importantly Mr Hogsbotham was still to be concerned.

IX

The Hirondel's headlights played briefly over the swinging sign of the Three Horseshoes, in Laleham, and swung off to the left on a road that turned towards the river. In a few seconds they were lighting up the smooth grey water and striking dull reflections from a few cars parked close to the bank; and then they blinked out as Simon pulled the car close to the grass verge and set the handbrake.

'Get him out, darling,' he said over his shoulder.

He stepped briskly out from behind the wheel; and Hoppy Uniatz, who had been sitting beside him, slid into his place. The Saint waited a moment to assure himself that Angela Lindsay was having no trouble with the fourth member of the party; and then he leaned over the side and spoke close to Hoppy's ear.

'Well,' he said, 'do you remember it all?'

'Sure, I remember it,' said Mr Uniatz confidently. He paused to refresh himself from the bottle he was still carrying, and replaced the cork with an air of reluctance. 'It's in de bag,' he said, with the pride of knowing what he was talking about.

'Mind you don't miss the turning, like we did last night. And for God's sake try not to have any kind of noise. You'll have to manage without headlights, too—someone might notice them . . .' Once you've got the Beef Trust there, Pat'll take care of keeping them busy. I don't want you to pay any attention to anything except watching for the ungodly and passing the tip to her.'

'OK, boss.'

The Saint looked round again. Verdean was out of the car.

'On your way, then.'

He stepped back. The gears meshed, and the Hirondel swung round in a tight semicircle and streaked away towards the main road.

Angela Lindsay stared after it, and caught the Saint's sleeve with sudden uncertainty. Her eyes were wide in the gloom.

'What's that for? Where is he going?'

'To look after our alibi,' Simon answered truthfully. 'Anything may happen here tonight, and you don't know Teal's nasty suspicious mind as well as I do. I'm pretty sure we shook off our shadows in Walton, but there's no need to take any chances.'

She was looking about her uneasily. 'But this isn't Chertsey—'

'This is Laleham, on the opposite side of the river. We came this way to make it more confusing, and also because it'll make it a lot harder for our shadows if they're still anywhere behind. Unless my calculations are all wrong, Hogsbotham's sty ought to be right over there.' His arm pointed diagonally over the stream. 'Let's find out.'

His hand took Verdean's arm close up under the shoulder. The girl walked on the bank manager's other side. Verdean was easy to lead. He seemed to have no more will of his own. His head kept rolling idiotically from side to side, and his voice went on unceasingly with an incoherent and practically unintelligible mumbling. His legs tried to fold intermittently at the joints, as if they had turned into putty; but the Saint's powerful grip held him up.

They crossed a short stretch of grass to the water's edge. The Saint also went on talking, loudly and irrelevantly, punctuating himself with squeals of laughter at his own wit. If any of the necking parties in the parked cars had spared them any attention at all, the darkness would have hidden any details, and the sound effects would infallibly have combined to stamp them as nothing but a party of noisy drunks. It must have been successful, for the trip was completed without a hitch. They came down to the river margin in uneventful co-ordination; and any spectators who may have been there continued to sublimate their biological urges unconcerned.

There was an empty punt moored to the bank at exactly the point where they reached the water. Why it should have been there so fortunately was something that the girl had no time to stop and ask; but the Saint showed no surprise about it. He seemed to have been expecting it. He steered Verdean on board and lowered him on to the cushions, and cast off the mooring chain and settled himself in the stern as she followed.

His paddle dug into the water with long deep strokes, driving the punt out into the dark. The bank which they had just left fell away into blackness behind. For a short while there was nothing near them but the running stream bounded by nebulous masses of deep shadow on either side. Verdean's monotonous muttering went on, but it had become no more obtrusive than the murmur of traffic heard from a closed room in a city building.

She said, after a time: 'I wonder why this all seems so different?'

He asked: 'Why?'

She was practically invisible from where he sat. Her voice came out of a blurred emptiness.

'I've done all sorts of things before—with Judd,' she said. 'But doing this with you . . . You make it an adventure. I always wanted it to be an adventure, and yet it never was.'

'Adventure is the way you look at it,' he said, and did not feel that the reply was trite when he was making it.

For the second time since he had picked her up at the Stag and Hounds he was wondering whether a surprise might still be in store for him that night. All his planning was cut and dried, as far as any of it was under his control; but there could still be surprises. In all his life nothing had ever gone mechanically and unswervingly according to a rigid and inviolable schedule: adventure would soon have become boring if it had. And tonight he had a feeling of fine-drawn aliveness that was the reverse of boredom.

The feeling stayed with him the rest of the way across the water, and through the disembarkation on the other side. It stayed with him on the short walk up Greenleaf Road from the tow-path to the gates of Mr Hogsbotham's house. It was keener and more intense as they went up the drive, with Verdean keeping pace in his grasp with docile witlessness. It brought up all the undertones of the night in sharp relief—the stillness everywhere around, the silence of the garden, the whisper of leaves, the sensation of having stepped out of the inhabited world into a shrouded wilderness.

Some of that could have been due to the trees that shut them in, isolating them in a tenebrous closeness in which there was no sight or sound of other life, so that even Verdean's own house next door did not intrude on their awareness by so much as a glimmer of light or the silhouette of a roof, and the Saint could not tell whether a light would have been visible in it if there had been a light to see. Some of the feeling was still left unaccounted for even after that. The Saint stood on the porch and wondered if he was misunderstanding his own intuition, while Verdean fumbled with keys at the door, muttering fussily about his stolen fortune. And his mind was still divided when they went into the hall, where a single dim light was burning, and he saw the bank manager stagger drunkenly away and throw himself shakily up the stairs.

He felt the girl's fingers cling to his arm. And in spite of all he knew about her, her physical nearness was something that his senses could not ignore.

'He's going to get it,' she breathed.

The Saint nodded. That psychic electricity was still coursing through his nerves, only now he began to find its meaning. From force of habit, his right hand slid under the cuff of his left sleeve and touched the hilt of the razor-edged throwing knife in its sheath strapped to his forearm, the only weapon he had thought it worth while to bring with him, making sure that it would slip easily out if he needed it; but the action was purely automatic. His thoughts were a thousand miles away from such things as his instinct associated with that deadly slender blade. He smiled suddenly.

'We ought to be there to give him a cheer,' he said.

He took her up the stairs with him. From the upper landing he saw an open door and a lighted room from which came confused scurrying noises combined with Verdean's imbecile grunting and chattering. Simon went to the door. The room was unquestionably Mr Ebenezer Hogsbotham's bedroom. He would have known it even without being told. Nobody but an Ebenezer Hogsbotham could ever have slept voluntarily in such a dismally austere and mortifying chamber. And he saw Robert Verdean in the centre of the room. The bank manager had lugged a shabby suitcase out of some hiding-place, and he had it open on the bed; he was pawing and crooning crazily over the contents—ruffling the edges of packets of pound notes, crunching the bags of silver. Simon stood for a moment and watched him, and it was like looking at a scene from a play that he had seen before.

Then he stepped quietly in and laid his hand on Verdean's shoulder.

'Shall I help you take care of it?' he said gently.

He had not thought much about how Verdean would be likely to respond to the interruption, but he had certainly not quite expected the response he got.

For the first time since Hoppy had applied his remarkable treatment, the bank manager seemed to become aware of outside personalities in a flash of distorted recognition. He squinted upwards and sidelong at the Saint, and his face twisted.

'I won't give it to you!' he screamed. 'I'll kill you first!'

He flung himself at the Saint's throat, his fingers clawing, his eyes red and maniacal.

Simon had very little choice. He felt highly uncertain about the possible results of a third concussion on Verdean's already inflamed cerebral tissue, following so closely upon the two previous whacks which it had suffered in the last twenty-four hours; but on the other hand he felt that in Mr Verdean's present apparent state of mind, to be tied up and gagged and left to struggle impotently while he watched his loot being taken away from him would be hardly less likely to cause a fatal haemorrhage. He therefore adopted the less troublesome course, and put his trust in any guardian angels that Mr Verdean might have on his overburdened payroll. His fist travelled up about eight explosive inches, and Mr Verdean travelled down . . .

Simon picked him up and laid him on the bed.

'You know,' he remarked regretfully, 'if this goes on much longer, there is going to come a time when Comrade Verdean is going to wonder whether fifteen thousand quid is really worth it.'

Angela Lindsay did not answer.

He looked at her. She stood close by the bed, gazing without expression at Verdean's unconscious body and the suitcase full of money at his feet. Her face was tired.

Still without saying anything, she went to the window and stood there with her back to him.

She said, after a long silence: 'Well, you got what you wanted, as usual.'

'I do that sometimes,' he said.

'And what happens next?'

'You'll get the share you asked for,' he answered carefully. 'You can take it now, if you like.'

'And that's all.'

'Did we agree to anything else?'

She turned round; and he found that he did not want to look at her eyes.

'Are you sure you're never going to need any more help?' she said.

He did not need to hear any more. He had known more than she could have told him, before that. He understood all of the presentiment that had troubled him on the way there. For that moment he was without any common vanity, and very calm.

'I may often need it,' he said, and there was nothing but compassion in his voice. 'But I must take it where I'm lucky enough to find it . . . I know what you mean. But I never tried to make you fall in love with me. I wouldn't wish that kind of trouble on anyone.'

'I knew that,' she said, just as quietly. 'But I couldn't help wishing it.'

She came towards him, and he stood up to meet her. He knew that she was going to kiss him, and he did not try to stop her.

Her mouth was hot and hungry against his. His own lips could not be cold. That would have been hypocrisy. Perhaps because his understanding went so much deeper than the superficial smartness that any other man might have been feeling at that time, he was moved in a way that would only have been cheapened if he had tried to put words to it. He felt her lithe softness pressed against him, her arms encircling him, her hands moving over him, and did not try to hold her away.

Presently she drew back from him. Her hands were under his coat, under his arms, holding him. The expression in her eyes was curiously hopeless.

'You haven't got any gun,' she said.

He smiled faintly. He knew that her hands had been learning that even while she kissed him; and yet it made no difference.

'I didn't think I should need one,' he said.

It seemed as if she wanted to speak, and could not.

'That was your mistake,' said the harsh voice of Judd Kaskin. 'Get your hands up.'

The Saint turned, without haste. Kaskin stood just inside the door, with a heavy automatic in his hand. His florid face was savagely triumphant. Morris Dolf sidled into the room after him.

X

They were tying the Saint to a massive fake-antique wooden chair placed close to the bed. His ankles were corded to the legs, and Kaskin was knotting his wrists behind the back of it. Dolf kept him covered while it was being done. The gun in his thin hand was steady and impersonal: his weasel face and bright beady eyes held a cold-blooded sneer which made it plain that he would have welcomed an opportunity to demonstrate that he was not holding his finger off the trigger because he was afraid of the bang.

But the Saint was not watching him very intently. He was looking most of the time at Angela Lindsay. To either of the other two men his face would have seemed utterly impassive, his brow serene and amazingly unperturbed, the infinitesimal smile that lingered on his lips only adding to the enigma of his self-control. But that same inscrutable face talked to the girl as clearly as if it had used spoken words.

Her eyes stared at him in a blind stunned way that said: 'I

772

know. I know. You think I'm a heel. But what could I do? I didn't have long enough to think . . .'

And his own cool steady eyes, and that faintly lingering smile, all of his face so strangely free from hatred or contempt, answered in the same silent language: 'I know, kid. I understand. You couldn't help it. What the hell?'

She looked at him with an incredulity that ached to believe.

Kaskin tightened his last knot and came round from behind the chair.

'Well, smart guy,' he said gloatingly. 'You weren't so smart, after all.'

The Saint had no time to waste. Even with his wrists tied behind him, he could still reach the hilt of his knife with his fingertips. They hadn't thought of searching for a weapon like that, under his sleeve. He eased it out of its sheath until his fingers could close on the handle.

'You certainly did surprise me, Judd,' he admitted mildly.

'Thought you were making a big hit with the little lady, didn't you?' Kaskin jeered. 'Well, that's what you were meant to think. I never knew a smart guy yet that wasn't a sucker for a jane. We had it all figured out. She tipped us off as soon as she left your house this afternoon. We could have hunted out the dough and got away with it then, but that would have still left you running around. It was worth waiting a bit to get you as well. We knew you'd be here. We just watched the house until you got here, and came in after you. Then we only had to wait until Angela got close enough to you to grab your gun. Directly we heard her say you hadn't got one, we walked in.' His arm slid round the girl's waist. 'Cute . . . little actress, ain't she, Saint? I'll bet you thought you were in line for a big party.'

Simon had his knife in his hand. He had twisted the blade back to saw it across the cords on his wrists, and it was keen enough to lance through them like butter. He could feel them loosening strand by strand, and stopped cutting just before they would have fallen away altogether; but one strong jerk of his arms would have been enough to set him free. 'So what?' he inquired coolly.

'So you get what's coming to you,' Kaskin said.

He dug into a bulging coat pocket.

The Saint tensed himself momentarily. Death was still very near. His hands might be practically free, but his legs were still tied to the chair. And even though he could throw his knife faster than most men could pull a trigger, it could only be thrown once. But he had taken that risk from the beginning, with his eyes open. He could only die once, too; and all his life had been a gamble with death.

He saw Kaskin's hand come out. But it didn't come out with a gun. It came out with something that looked like an ordinary tin can with a length of smooth cord wound round it. Kaskin unwrapped the cord, and laid the can on the edge of the bed, where it was only a few inches both from the Saint's elbow and Verdean's middle. He stretched out the cord, which terminated at one end in a hole in the top of the can, struck a match, and put it to the loose end. The end began to sizzle slowly.

'It's a slow fuse,' he explained, with vindictive satisfaction. 'It'll take about fifteen minutes to burn. Time enough for us to get a long way off before it goes off, and time enough for you to do plenty of thinking before you go sky-high with Verdean. I'm going to enjoy thinking about you thinking.'

Only the Saint's extraordinarily sensitive ears would have caught the tiny mouse-like sound that came from somewhere in the depths of the house. And any other ears that had heard it might still have dismissed it as the creak of a dry board.

'The only thing that puzzles me,' he said equably, 'is what you think you're going to think with.'

Kaskin stepped up and hit him unemotionally in the face.

'That's for last night,' he said hoarsely, and turned to the others. 'Let's get started.'

Morris Dolf pocketed his automatic and went out, with a last cold stare over the scene.

Kaskin went to the bed, closed the bulging valise, and picked it up. He put his arm round the girl again and drew her to the door.

'Have a good time,' he said.

The Saint looked out on to an empty landing. But what he saw was the last desperate glance that the girl flung at him as Kaskin led her out.

He tensed his arms for an instant, and his wrists separated. The scraps of cord scuffed on the floor behind him. He took a better grip on his knife. But he still made no other movement. He sat where he was, watching the slowly smouldering fuse, waiting and listening for two sounds that all his immobility was tuned for. One of them he knew he would hear, unless some disastrous accident had happened to cheat his calculations; the other he was only hoping for, and yet it was the one that his ears were most wishfully strained to catch.

Then he saw Angela Lindsay's bag lying on a corner of the dresser, and all his doubts were supremely set at rest.

He heard her voice, down on the stairs, only a second after his eyes had told him that he must hear it.

And he heard Kaskin's growling answer.

'Well, hurry up, you fool . . . The car's out in front of the house opposite.'

The Saint felt queerly content.

Angela Lindsay stood in the doorway again, looking at him.

She did not speak. She picked up her bag and tucked it under her arm. Then she went quickly over to the bed and took hold of the trailing length of fuse. She wound it round her hand and tore it loose from the bomb, and threw it still smouldering into a far corner.

Then she bent over the Saint and kissed him, very swiftly.

He did not move for a moment. And then, even more swiftly, his free hands came from behind him and caught her wrists.

She tried to snatch herself back in sudden panic, but his grip was too strong. And he smiled at her.

'Don't go for a minute,' he said softly.

She stood frozen.

Down on the ground floor, all at once, there were many sounds.

The sounds of heavy feet, deep voices that were neither Dolf's nor Kaskin's, quick violent movements . . . Her eyes grew wide, afraid, uncomprehending, questioning. But those were the sounds that he had been sure of hearing. His face was unlined and unstartled. He still smiled. His head moved fractionally in answer to the question she had not found voice to ask.

'Yes,' he said evenly. 'It is the police. Do you still want to go?'

Her mouth moved.

'You knew they'd be here.'

'Of course,' he said. 'I arranged for it. I wanted them to catch Morrie and Judd with the goods on them. I knew you meant to double-cross me, all the time. So I pulled a double double-cross. That was before you kissed me—so you could find out where I kept my gun . . . Then I was only hoping you'd make some excuse to come back and do what you just did. You see, everything had to be in your own hands.'

Down below, a gun barked. The sound came up the stairs dulled and thickened. Other guns answered it. A man screamed shrilly, and was suddenly silent. The brief fusillade rattled back into throbbing stillness. Gradually the muffled voices droned in again.

The fear and bewilderment died out of the girl's face, and left a shadowy kind of peace.

'It's too late now,' she said. 'But I'm still glad I did it.'

'Like hell it's too late,' said the Saint.

He let go of her and put away his knife, and bent to untie his legs. His fingers worked like lightning. He did not need to give any more time to thought. Perhaps in those few seconds after his hands were free and the others had left the room, when he had sat without moving and only listened, wondering whether the girl would come back, his subconscious mind had raced on and worked out what his adaptation would be if she did come back. However it had come to him, the answer was clear in his mind now—as clearly as if he had known that it would be needed when he planned for the other events which had just come to pass.

And the aspect of it that was doing its best to dissolve his seriousness into a spasm of ecstatic daftness was that it would also do something towards taking care of Mr Ebenezer Hogsbotham. He had, he realised, been almost criminally neglectful about Mr Hogsbotham, having used him as an excuse to start the adventure, having just borrowed his house to bring it to a dénouement, and yet having allowed himself to be so led away by the intrusion of mere sordid mercenary objectives that he had had no spare time to devote towards consummating the lofty and purely idealistic mission that had taken him to Chertsey in the first place. Now he could see an atonement for his remissness that would invest the conclusion of that story with a rich completeness which would be something to remember.

'Listen,' he said, and the rapture of supreme inspiration was blazing in his eyes.

In the hall below, Chief Inspector Claud Eustace Teal straightened up from his business-like examination of the two still figures sprawled close together on the floor. A knot of uniformed local men, one of whom was twisting a handkerchief round a bleeding wrist, made way for him as he stepped back.

'All right,' Teal said grimly. 'One of you phone for an ambulance to take them away. Neither of them is going to need a doctor.'

He moved to the suitcase which had fallen from Judd Kaskin's hand when three bullets hit him, and opened it. He turned over some of the contents, and closed it again.

A broad-shouldered young officer with a sergeant's stripes on his sleeve shifted up from behind him and said: 'Shall I look after it, sir?'

Teal surrendered the bag.

'Put it in the safe at the station for tonight,' he said. 'I'll get somebody from the bank to check it over in the morning. It looks as if it was all there.'

'Yes, sir.'

The sergeant stepped back towards the door.

Chief Inspector Teal fumbled in an inner pocket, and drew out a small oblong package. From the package he extracted a thinner oblong of pink paper. From the paper he unwrapped a fresh crisp slice of spearmint. He slid the slice of spearmint into his mouth and champed purposefully on it. His salivary glands reacted exquisitely to succulent stimulus. He began to feel some of the deep spiritual contentment of a cow with a new cud.

Mr Teal, as we know, had had a trying day. But for once he seemed to have earned as satisfactory a reward for his tribulations as any reasonable man had a right to expect. It was true that he had been through one disastrously futile battle with the Saint. But to offset that, he had cleared up the case to which he had been assigned, with the criminals caught red-handed while still in possession of their booty and justifiably shot down after they had tried to shoot their way out, which would eliminate most of the tedious legal rigmaroles which so often formed a wearisome anticlimax to such dramatic victories; and he had recovered the booty itself apparently intact. All in all, he felt that this was one occasion when even his tyrannical superiors at Scotland Yard would be unable to withhold the commendation which was his due. There was something almost like human tolerance in his sleepy eyes as they glanced around and located Hoppy Uniatz leaning against the wall in the background.

'That was quick work,' he said, making the advance with some difficulty. 'We might have had a lot more trouble if you hadn't been with us.'

Mr Uniatz had a jack-knife of fearsome dimensions in one hand. He appeared to be carving some kind of marks on the butt of his gun. He waved the knife without looking up from his work.

'Aw, nuts,' he said modestly. 'All youse guys need is a little practice.'

Mr Teal swallowed.

Patricia Holm squeezed through between two burly constables and smiled at him.

'Well,' she said sweetly, 'don't you owe us all some thanks? I won't say anything about an apology.'

'I suppose I do,' Teal said grudgingly. It wasn't easy for him to say it, or even to convince himself that he meant it. The sadly acquired suspiciousness that had become an integral part of his souring nature had driven its roots too deep for him to feel really comfortable in any situation where there was even a hint of the involvement of any member of the Saint's entourage. But for once he was trying nobly to be just. He grumbled half heartedly: 'But you had us in the wrong house, all the same. If Uniatz hadn't happened to notice them coming in here—'

'But he did, didn't he?'

'It was a risk that none of you had any right to take,' Teal said starchily. 'Why didn't the Saint tell me what he knew this morning?'

'I've told you,' she said. 'He felt pretty hurt about the way you were trying to pin something on to him. Of course, since he knew he'd never been to Verdean's house, he figured out that the second two men the maid saw were just a couple of other crooks trying to hijack the job. He guessed that Kaskin and Dolf had scared them off and taken Verdean away to go on working him over in their own time—'

That hypersensitive congenital suspicion stabbed Mr Teal again like a needle prodded into a tender boil.

'You never told me he knew their names!' he barked. 'How did he know that?'

'Didn't I?' she said ingenuously. 'Well, of course he knew. Or at any rate he had a pretty good idea. He'd heard a rumour weeks ago that Kaskin and Dolf were planning a bank hold-up with an inside stooge. You know how these rumours get around; only I suppose Scotland Yard doesn't hear them. So naturally he thought of them. He knew their favourite hide-outs, so it wasn't hard to find them. And as soon as he knew they'd broken Verdean down, he had me get hold of you while he went on following them. He sent Hoppy to fetch us directly he knew they were coming here. Naturally he thought they'd be going to Verdean's house, but of course Verdean might always have hidden the money somewhere else close by, so that's why I had Hoppy watching outside. Simon just wanted to get even with you by handing you the whole thing on a platter; and you can't really blame him. After all, he was on the side of the law all the time. And it all worked out. Now, why don't you admit that he got the best of you and did you a good turn at the same time?'

Chief Inspector Teal scowled at the toes of his official boots. He had heard it all before, but it was hard for him to believe. And yet it indisputably fitted with the facts as he knew them . . . He hitched his gum stolidly across to the other side of his mouth.

'Well, I'll be glad to thank him,' he growled; and then a twinge of surprising alarm came suddenly into his face. 'Hey, where is he? If they caught him following them—'

'I was wondering when you'd begin to worry about me,' said the Saint's injured voice. Mr Teal looked up.

Simon Templar was coming down the stairs, lighting a cigarette, mocking and immaculate and quite obviously unharmed.

But it was not the sight of the Saint that petrified Mr Teal into tottering stillness and bulged his china-blue eyes half out of their sockets, exactly as the eyes of all the other men in the hall were also bulged as they looked upwards with him. It was the sight of the girl who was coming down the stairs after the Saint. It was Angela Lindsay.

The reader has already been made jerry to the fact that the clinging costumes which she ordinarily affected suggested that underneath them she possessed an assortment of curves and contours of exceptionally enticing pulchritude. This suggestion was now elevated to the realms of scientifically observable fact. There was no further doubt about it, for practically all of them were open to inspection. The sheer and diaphanous underwear which was now their only covering left nothing worth mentioning to the imagination. And she seemed completely unconcerned about the exposure, as if she knew that she had a right to expect a good deal of admiration for what she had to display. Mr Teal blinked groggily.

'Sorry to be so long,' Simon was saying casually, 'but our pals left a bomb upstairs, and I thought I'd better put it out of action. They left Verdean lying on top of it. But I'm afraid he didn't really need it. Somebody hit him once too often, and it looks as if he has kind of passed away . . . What's the matter, Claud? You look slightly boiled. The old tum-tum isn't going back on you again, is it?'

The detective found his voice.

'Who is that you've got with you?' he asked in a hushed and quivering voice.

Simon glanced behind him.

'Oh, Miss Lindsay,' he said airily. 'She was tied up with the bomb, too. You see, it appears that Verdean used to look after this house when the owner was away—it belongs to a guy named Hogsbotham—so he had a key, and when he was looking for a place to cache the boodle, he thought this would be as safe as anywhere. Well, Miss Lindsay was in the bedroom when the boys got here, so they tied her up along with Verdean. I just cut her loose—'

'You found 'er in 'Ogsbotham's bedroom?' repeated one of the local men hoarsely, with his traditional phlegm battered to limpness by the appalling thought.

The Saint raised his eyebrows.

'Why not?' he said innocently. 'I should call her an ornament to anyone's bedroom.'

'I should say so,' flared the girl stridently. 'I never had any complaints yet.'

The silence was numbing to the ears.

Simon looked over the upturned faces, the open mouths, the protruding eyeballs, and read there everything that he wanted to read. One of the constables finally gave it voice. Gazing upwards with the stalk-eyed stare of a man hypnotised by the sight of a miracle beyond human expectation, he distilled the inarticulate emotions of his comrades into one reverent and pregnant ejaculation.

'Gor-blimey!' he said.

The Saint filled his lungs with a breath of inenarrable peace. Such moments of immortal bliss, so ripe, so full, so perfect, so superb, so flawless and unalloyed and exquisite, were beyond the range of any feeble words. They flooded every corner of the soul and every fibre of the body, so that the heart was filled to overflowing with a nectar of cosmic content. The very tone in which that one word had been spoken was a benediction. It gave indubitable promise that within a few hours the eye-witness evidence of Ebenezer Hogsbotham's depravity would have spread all over Chertsey, within a few hours more it would have reached London, before the next sunset it would have circulated over all England; and all the denials and protestations that Hogsbotham might make would never restore his self-made pedestal again.

## XI

Simon Templar braked the Hirondel to a stop in the pool of blackness under an overhanging tree less than a hundred yards beyond the end of Greenleaf Road. He blinked his lights three times, and lighted a cigarette while he waited. Patricia Holm held his arm tightly. From the back of the car came the gurgling sucking sounds of Hoppy Uniatz renewing his acquaintance with the bottle of Vat 69 which he had been forced by circumstances to neglect for what Mr Uniatz regarded as an indecent length of time.

A shadow loomed out of the darkness beside the road, whistling very softly. The shadow carried a shabby valise in one hand. It climbed into the back seat beside Hoppy.

Simon Templar moved the gear lever, let in the clutch; and the Hirondel rolled decorously and almost noiselessly on its way.

At close quarters, the shadow which had been added to the passenger list could have been observed to be wearing a policeman's uniform with a sergeant's stripes on the sleeve, and a solid black moustache which obscured the shape of its mouth as much as the brim of its police helmet obscured the exact appearance of its eyes. As the car got under way, it was hastily stripping off these deceptive scenic effects and changing into a suit of ordinary clothes piled on the seat.

Simon spoke over his shoulder as the Hirondel gathered speed through the village of Chertsey.

'You really ought to have been a policeman, Peter,' he murmured. 'You look the part better than anyone I ever saw.'

Peter Quentin snorted.

'Why don't you try somebody else in the part?' he inquired acidly. 'My nerves won't stand it many more times. I still don't know how I got away with it this time.'

The Saint grinned in the dark, his eyes following the road.

'That was just your imagination,' he said complacently. 'There wasn't really much danger. I knew that Claud wouldn't have been allowed to bring his own team down from Scotland Yard. He was just assigned to take charge of the case. He might have brought an assistant of his own, but he had to use the local cops for the mob work. In the excitement, nobody was going to pay much attention to you. The local men just thought you came down from Scotland Yard with Teal, and Teal just took it for granted that you were one of the local men. It was in the bag—literally and figuratively.'

'Of course it was,' Peter said sceptically. 'And just what do you think is going to happen when Teal discovers that he hasn't got the bag?'

'Why, what on earth could happen?' Simon retorted blandly. 'We did our stuff. We produced the criminals, and Hoppy blew them off, and Teal got the boodle. He opened the bag and looked it over right there in the house. And Pat and Hoppy and I were in more or less full view all the time. If he goes and loses it again after we've done all that for him, can he blame us?'

Peter Quentin shrugged himself into a tweed sports jacket, and sighed helplessly. He felt sure that there was a flaw in the Saint's logic somewhere, but he knew that it was no use to argue. The Saint's conspiracies always seemed to work out, in defiance of reasonable argument. And this episode had not yet shown any signs of turning into an exception. It would probably work out just like all the rest. And there was unarguably a suitcase containing about fifteen thousand pounds in small change lying on the floor of the car at his feet to lend weight to the probability. The thought made Peter Quentin reach out for Mr Uniatz's bottle with a reckless feeling that he might as well make the best of the crazy life into which his association with the Saint had led him.

Patricia told him what had happened at the house after he faded away unnoticed with the bag.

'And you left her there?' he said, with a trace of wistfulness.

'One of the local cops offered to take her back to town,' Simon explained. 'I let him do it, because it'll give her a chance to build up the story ... I don't think we shall hear a lot more about Hogsbotham from now on.'

'So while I was sweating blood and risking about five hundred years in penal servitude,' Peter said bitterly, 'you were having a grand time helping her take her clothes off.'

'You have an unusually evil mind,' said the Saint, and drove on, one part of his brain working efficiently over the alibi that Peter was still going to need before morning, and all the rest of him singing.

# The Saint Club

*And so, my friends, dear bookworms, most noble fellow drinkers, frustrated burglars, affronted policemen, upright citizens with furled umbrellas and secret buccaneering dreams that seems to be very nearly all for now. It has been nice having you with us, and we hope you will come again, not once, but many times.*

*Only because of our great love for you, we would like to take this parting opportunity of mentioning one small matter which we have very much at heart ...*        Leslie Charteris, The First Saint Omnibus (1939)

Leslie Charteris founded The Saint Club in 1936 with the aim of providing a constructive fan base for Saint devotees. Before the War it donated profits to a London hospital where, for several years, a 'Saint' ward was maintained. With the nationalisation of hospitals profits were, for many years, donated to the Arbour Youth Centre in Stepney, London.

In the 21$^{st}$ Century we've carried on this tradition but have also donated to the Red Cross and a number of different children's charities.

The Club acts as a focal point for anyone interested in the adventures of Leslie Charteris and the work of Simon Templar and offers merchandise that includes DVDs of the old TV series and various Saint-related publications through to its own exclusive range of notepaper, pin badges and polo shirts. All profits are donated to charity.

The Club also maintains two popular web sites and supports many more Saint-related sites.

Since Leslie Charteris' death, the Club has recruited three new vice-presidents; Roger Moore, Ian Ogilvy and Simon Dutton have all pledged their support whilst Audrey and Patricia Charteris have been retained as Saints-in-Chief. But some things do not change for the back of the membership card still mischievously proclaims that ...

*'The bearer of this card is probably a person of hideous antecedents and low moral character, and upon apprehension for any cause should be immediately released in order to save other prisoners from contamination.'*

## To join ...

Membership costs £3.50 (or US$7) per year or £30 (US$60) for life membership.

Send a cheque, payable to **The Saint Club**, for the relevant amount to The Saint Club, PO Box 258, Romsey, Hants. SO51 6WY, England.

WATCH FOR THE SIGN OF THE SAINT.
HE WILL BE BACK IN VOLUME TWO!